KIPPS
The Story of a Simple Soul

◆

THE HISTORY OF MR POLLY

Kipps
The Story of a Simple Soul

◆

The History of Mr Polly

──── ◆ ────

H. G. WELLS

with an Introduction and Notes by
JONATHAN WILD
University of Edinburgh

WORDSWORTH CLASSICS

For my husband
ANTHONY JOHN RANSON
with love from your wife, the publisher.
Eternally grateful for your unconditional love.

Readers who are interested in other titles from
Wordsworth Editions are invited to visit our website at
www.wordsworth-editions.com

First published in 2017 by Wordsworth Editions Limited
8B East Street, Ware, Hertfordshire SG12 9HJ

ISBN 978 1 84022 743 7

Text © Wordsworth Editions Limited, 2017
Introduction and Notes © Jonathan Wild, 2017

Wordsworth® is a registered trademark of
Wordsworth Editions Limited

Wordsworth Editions
is the company founded in 1987 by
MICHAEL TRAYLER

Typeset in Great Britain by Antony Gray
Printed and bound by Clays Ltd, St Ives plc

Contents

Kipps: The Story of a Simple Soul

page 25

The History of Mr Polly

page 307

ENDNOTES TO *Kipps: The Story of a Simple Soul*

page 481

ENDNOTES TO *The History of Mr Polly*

page 483

GENERAL INTRODUCTION

Wordsworth Classics are inexpensive editions designed to appeal to the general reader and students. We commissioned teachers and specialists to write wide-ranging, jargon-free Introductions and to provide Notes that would assist the understanding of our readers rather than interpret the stories for them. In the same spirit, because the pleasures of reading are inseparable from the surprises, secrets and revelations that all narratives contain, we strongly advise you to enjoy this book before turning to the Introduction.

KEITH CARABINE
General Adviser
Rutherford College,
University of Kent at Canterbury

BIOGRAPHY OF THE AUTHOR

Herbert George Wells, known as 'Bertie' or 'H. G.', was born on 21 September 1866 in Atlas House, on the High Street of what was then the Kentish market town of Bromley. His father Joseph, a former gardener, kept a shop and played professional cricket; after his father broke his leg when Wells was ten, Wells's mother Sarah returned to domestic service at the country house Uppark, near Midhurst, in Sussex.

Wells's elder brothers had both been apprenticed to drapers, a trade that Sarah Wells considered to be highly respectable. Wells was apprenticed to drapers in Windsor and Southsea but was much keener to continue to be educated, and he persuaded his mother to let him become a pupil-teacher at Midhurst Grammar School. Wells's exam results at Midhurst were so strong that he won a scholarship aimed at increasing the number of science teachers in Britain at the Normal School (now Imperial College London), under 'Darwin's bulldog', the biologist T. H. Huxley. Wells drew extensively on his experiences as a student for his 1900 novel *Love and Mr Lewisham*. Ill-fed, poor and increasingly discontented by both the quality of the teaching he received and the social organisation of the world, Wells became more and more interested in politics and in imaginative literature, especially Plato, Blake and Carlyle. He also began writing, providing articles and a time-travel story, 'The Chronic Argonauts', for the college magazine the *Science Schools Journal*.

Wells failed his final exams and found work as a teacher in Wales. After being fouled in a rugby game, he suffered severe kidney damage, and for much of the 1890s Wells feared he would die prematurely. Returning to London and completing his degree, he worked as a correspondence tutor and in 1893 wrote his first books *Honours Physiography* and *A Textbook of Biology*. His writing branched out into literary journalism and popular scientific writing, and in 1895 alone Wells published four further books: *Select Conversations with an Uncle*, *The Wonderful Visit*, *The Stolen Bacillus and Other Incidents* and his masterpiece, *The Time Machine*. This first 'scientific romance' was swiftly followed by *The Island of Doctor Moreau* (1896), *The Invisible Man* (1897) and *The War of the Worlds* (1898). None has ever been out of print since; Wells was swiftly hailed as a man of genius by his contemporaries. Both sociable and irascible, Wells became friends, and fell out with, other writers such as George Gissing, Joseph Conrad, Stephen Crane, George Bernard Shaw, Arnold Bennett, Ford Madox Ford and Henry James, whom Wells would later cruelly lampoon in his 1915 novel *Boon*, the climax of a long disagreement between the two writers about the purpose and nature of the novel.

Wells never wanted to be limited to writing scientific romances, and during this period he also wrote realistic prose fiction set in a recognisable real world, whose disorganisation and unfairness these novels sought to diagnose: *The Wheels of Chance* (1896), *Kipps* (1905), *Tono-Bungay*, *Ann Veronica* (both 1909) and *The History of Mr Polly* (1910). Wells's early-twentieth-century science fiction, such as *The Food of the Gods* (1905) and *In the Days of the Comet* (1906), increasingly showed a vision of the world as Wells would want to order it. His political and utopian writing from *Anticipations of the Reactions of Mechanical and Scientific Progress upon Human Life and Thought* (1901) and *A Modern Utopia* (1905) also demonstrated Wells's commitment to creating a utopian government, a World State that would ensure that mankind would never go to war.

Following the First World War, Wells's passion for this project intensified, and he embarked on an ambitious collaborative project to write the first history of the world, hoping that if future generations were better educated, then rivalries between nations would be unnecessary, and world government would follow. *The Outline of History* (1919) was Wells's best-selling book in his own lifetime, selling millions of copies internationally, and was followed by the school version *A Short History of the World* (1922) and by equivalents for science, *The Science of Life* (1930), and social science, *The Work, Wealth and Happiness of Mankind* (1931). At its height, Wells's fame was as much as a thinker and public intellectual as a novelist. He met or corresponded with the greatest figures of the first half of the twentieth century: Winston Churchill, Lenin and Stalin, Theodore and Franklin Roosevelt, Albert Einstein and Sigmund Freud. His later novels from *The New Machiavelli* (1911) onward tend to be more overtly engaged with Wells's 'Open Conspiracy' to convert his readership to his own political point of view, often at a cost to these books' literary merit and subsequent afterlife.

Wells had married his cousin Isabel in 1891, but the couple proved incompatible and he left her for his pupil Amy Catherine Robbins whom he rechristened 'Jane'. In spite of Wells's many infidelities, which Jane seemed prepared to tolerate, the couple were happily married until Jane's death from cancer in 1928; and they had two sons, Gip and Frank. An affair with the writer Amber Reeves produced a daughter, Anna Jane, and Wells's long affair with novelist Rebecca West saw the birth of a further son, Anthony West. Wells also enjoyed liaisons with, amongst others, Dorothy Richardson, Elizabeth von Arnim, Margaret Sanger and, following Jane's death, Odette Keun and Moura Budberg.

Wells's writing was prophetic in both senses of the term: as exhorting humankind to mend its ways, and in foreseeing the future. His writing imagined before they existed the aeroplane, the tank, space travel, the atomic bomb and the internet. In later life, the emphasis of his political writing turned more towards the rights of the individual, and his 1940 book *The Rights of Man: Or, What Are We Fighting For?* is a key text in the history of human rights.

Wells often despaired of his warnings ever being sufficiently heeded, declaring that his epitaph should be: 'God *damn* you, you fools – I told you so.' None the less, the influence of his hundred and fifty books and pamphlets of science fiction, novels, politics, utopia, history, biography and autobiography has been enormous throughout the twentieth century and beyond.

SIMON J. JAMES

Professor of English Literature at Durham University
and author of *Maps of Utopia: H. G. Wells,
Modernity and the End of Culture*

INTRODUCTION

The novels included in this volume are every bit as revolutionary as Thomas Paine's *Rights of Man* (1791) or Karl Marx and Frederick Engels's *The Communist Manifesto* (1848). Like those landmark political texts, Wells's *Kipps* (1905) and *The History of Mr Polly* (1910) proposed nothing short of the radical reformation of present-day society. This restructuring, again like that anticipated in those earlier works, was designed to disrupt a current social order split between the privileged few and the disadvantaged majority. But Wells's approach in these texts spares his readers the hectoring tone of the political agitator, employing instead more humane and certainly more entertaining forms of persuasion. Like Jonathan Swift in the eighteenth century and Charles Dickens in the nineteenth, Wells makes skilful use of comedy to encourage his readers to look with fresh eyes on 'a meanly conceived' world in need of change (*Kipps*, p. 260). After sharing his perspective, Wells implicitly asks, which right-thinking individual would not want to bring about that change? Why, for example, should we tacitly endorse those arbitrary and ludicrous rules of etiquette which erect barriers between classes? Who would not wish to change a rotten public education system seemingly constructed to deaden the intellectual development and ambition of bright children from humble backgrounds? Which reasonable person would defend the enslavement of fourteen-year-olds in respectable but fruitless occupations? And what sort of rational social order would support the meaningless conventions governing sexual relationships and marriage? The imbalanced society in which these iniquitous institutions and conventions are evident is fixed in place, Wells argues, by individuals who have little practical understanding of the lives they govern.

Wells further intensifies the effect of his often satirical comedy by applying it to a very particular cohort of modern citizens: lower-middle-class young men. The title characters in these novels, Artie Kipps and Alfred Polly, two apparently unremarkable individuals, are perfectly judged to represent this class, one that was characteristically associated with drapers, clerks and small shopkeepers. The factual counterparts of Kipps and Polly had emerged in vast numbers in the wake of those Victorian Education Acts (beginning with the 1870 'Forster' Act) which were designed to secure education for all children in England and Wales irrespective of their circumstances. Although members of this generation were an increasingly recognisable phenomenon on the streets of late Victorian and Edwardian Britain, they had left relatively little mark on the period's literary culture. Wells, himself originally a member of this class cohort, wanted to remedy this by firmly establishing in print the nature, importance and humanity of the contemporary lower-middle class. But more than simply drawing the general reading public's attention to the lives and plight of this social class, Wells aimed to empower members of this generation with a sense of their own worth and potential. He wanted to convince them of the truth that slowly dawns upon the unhappy shopkeeper Mr Polly that 'if the world does not please you, *you can change it*' (p. 438). This liberating message was designed to cut through the sense of a circumscribed destiny which Wells believed was instilled into this class of young men. In addition, Wells wields humour in both *Kipps* and *Polly* to convince readers of the folly of blind obedience to one's 'betters', urging instead the need for all individuals, irrespective of background, to take control of their destiny. After all, as the narrator of *Polly* reminds readers, just because somebody is a draper who drops his 'aitches' doesn't mean that he lacks 'a capacity for joy and beauty at least as keen and subtle as yours or mine' (p. 409). This message of social equality offered a vital rejoinder to a social milieu that, as the experiences of Kipps and Polly make clear, was not designed with them in mind.

KIPPS

Wells was not the sort of author who agonised much over the writing of his novels. Unlike his friend and fellow novelist Henry James, Wells considered that the important thing was to get his ideas in front of the public as quickly and clearly as possible. This meant that he was almost entirely free of the impulse endlessly to revise the style and form of his work in search of an elusive perfection. But, as Harris Wilson notes, *Kipps* was exceptional among Wells novels in that its manuscript (currently held at the University of Illinois) consists of 'six thousand-odd sheets written intermittently over a period of seven years' (Wilson, p. 63). This epic version of Wells's 'Kipps' text (begun in 1898 as *The Wealth of Mr Waddy*) was abandoned, he later reflected, because he had 'planned his task upon too colossal a scale', and this approach had left him 'no way of publishing [that] held out any hope of fair payment for the work that remained' (Preface to Volume VIII of the Atlantic Edition, pp. xvii–xviii). Although this project was shelved, Wells took the character of Kipps out of the abandoned text and placed him at the centre of a new work that would conform 'to the dimensions of a practicable book' (ibid.). The aims of this volume are summarised in a note that Wells appended to the novel's first edition in 1905:

> *Kipps* is essentially a novel, and is designed to present a typical member of the English lower-middle class in all its limitations and feebleness. Beneath a treatment deliberately kindly and genial, the book provides a sustained and fairly exhaustive criticism of the ideals and ways of life of the great mass of middle-class English people.

For Wells this declaration of intent was a highly personal one, and his passionate investment in the novel's politics helps explain why *Kipps* was so important to him. Indeed, it is impossible properly to understand *Kipps* and the energy Wells invested into it without appreciating the autobiographical element buried in the opening phases of this novel.

Like Kipps, Wells was apprenticed to a draper when he was fourteen, and his memories of this existence are meticulously recaptured in often quite ghastly detail in Book One of the novel. Although the location of the drapery where Wells worked is transposed across the south coast of England (from Southsea in Hampshire to Folkestone in Kent), the account of daily drudgery and servitude owes much to its factual model. Wells's time at the Southsea Drapery Emporium remained with him in a way that mirrors Charles Dickens's childhood experience of working in a blacking factory. For both writers, the time they spent in these occupations left them with a keen sense of the effect of exploitative working conditions on young people. In Wells's own case, the knowledge that boys and girls barely in their teens might be contracted by their parents into 'respectable' drapery apprenticeships fuelled his campaigning zeal. In his own case he managed, after three years, to persuade his mother to allow his release from the drapery trade so that he might take the first steps towards a career in school teaching. The pathetic letters he sent to his mother from Southsea are testament to his feeling of entrapment at this time. Here, for example, a sixteen-year-old Wells begs his mother to release him early from his indentures:

> It is very painful for me each night to reflect on the one day more that has gone to add to the bulk that has already accumulated of time wasted. It is very painful to be here an inferior of those to whom I cannot but feel myself in some respects superior. I am wearing out good clothes wasting valuable time fretting away myself here and I ask you to grant me one more kindness – shorten my stay here at the Vile Sinful town & this Unhappy shop.   [Smith, p. 30]

But while Wells was successful in effecting his escape, initially to Midhurst Grammar School in Sussex as a pupil teacher, and later to study for a degree at the Normal School of Science in London, he remembered the fate of his fellow drapers when writing the novel that would finally appear as *Kipps* in 1905. By this time Wells was a highly successful author with a string of commercially and critically acclaimed works behind him, and this position gave him a platform from which to expose what he saw as the iniquitous world of 'respectable' employment. The form which this critique takes is economically conveyed in one of many moments in the text when the narrator directly addresses the reader. Here the narrator imagines Kipps lying awake in the dormitory of his drapery shop (unmarried staff were typically obliged to 'live in' during this period) while thinking 'dismally' of his 'outlook':

> Dimly he perceived the thing that had happened to him – how the great, stupid machine of retail trade had caught his life into its wheels, a vast, irresistible force which he had neither strength of will nor knowledge to escape. This was to be his life until his days should end. No adventures, no glory, no change, no freedom. [p. 62]

One of Kipps's fellow drapers memorably describes this experience as being 'in a blessed drainpipe', adding that 'we've got to crawl along it till we die' (p. 61). The bleak nature of the shopworker's life was, Wells felt, largely unknown to the general public, who would have little immediate sense of an exploited workforce when they encountered smartly-turned-out and well-mannered individuals behind shop counters. For this reason, Wells used the opening sections of *Kipps* to draw the attention of readers to what he considered a growing but little recognised blight on modern society.

Rather, however, than centring the entire book on the dismal lives and prospects of those employed in the drapery trade, Wells abruptly shifts his focus on to an entirely different sphere at the end of Book One. This occurs when Kipps, like Pip in Dickens's *Great Expectations*, finds himself, after a change in fortune, obliged almost overnight to adopt the manners and mores of a higher social class. For Wells, this plot manoeuvre allows him to apply the methods of a scientist (a profession for which he had trained) in effectively placing Kipps on a microscope slide. Once Kipps is under his lens, Wells observes his behaviour as he encounters a variety of those organisms populating his new environment. For members of this supposedly elevated society, Kipps is a vulgar simpleton whose good fortune alone has brought him into their orbit. But, as the rules of polite social engagement mean that he cannot simply be ignored, the established middle classes of Folkestone find ways of relating to him. These forms of engagement take two distinct paths: they either offer Kipps the benefit of their patronage and education; or alternatively make him a target for their financial exploitation. Kipps proves powerless to resist either of these overtures because his upbringing has conditioned him to an unshakeable belief in his own inferiority to those above him on the social scale. He was, according to the novel's narrator, 'by the nature of his training . . . indistinct in his speech, confused in his mind, and retreating in his manners' (p. 52). This social conditioning leaves Kipps ill-suited to join his 'betters' on a level of equality, placing him instead in an agony of indecision and embarrassment as he attempts to navigate the polite conventions that govern his new world. These rules are seemingly designed to expose class transgression and intended to keep individuals in their place. Wells dramatises this point brilliantly and perceptively in an episode in which Kipps stays at a grand London hotel. Aware that 'appropriate' actions and behaviour are expected of him at every moment of his stay, Kipps is left almost paralysed by equal measures of anguish and embarrassment. While on one level Wells seems to manipulate these scenes of Kipps's social awkwardness for our entertainment, on a more fundamental level they expose the emptiness of those social protocols to which Kipps attempts adherence: his slavish reading of 'Manners and Rules of Good Society, by a Member of the Aristocracy . . . TWENTY-FIRST EDITION' (p. 151) underlines the futility of his quest. The comedy in these scenes, far from being exploitative, places us firmly on Kipps's side as he struggles to do the right thing. His confusion in not knowing whom to tip or which piece of cutlery to use provides a dilemma to which many of Wells's readers would readily relate. Comedy is the active agent here that encourages us to take sides, the humour of these scenes forcing us to think about our own role in sustaining polite social mores.

Wells is also highly alert in this novel to the ways in which these strict rules of social engagement might distort the most fundamental instances of decision making. The choice of romantic partner, for example, should be a relatively straightforward matter (at least in the first stage) of intellectual compatibility and sexual attraction. But, as Wells dramatises in *Kipps*, the complex conventions governing class interactions in Kipps's day tended to complicate matters. Kipps's own decision to propose marriage to Helen is one based on an indistinct understanding of his own feelings and almost no practical experience of relationships with the opposite sex. His choice is dictated instead by a feeling of gratitude that a woman of good breeding would accept the proposal of an inferior being such as him. Marriage for many of Kipps's generation was entered into along similar lines, with both parties locked for life into an unequal and incompatible partnership with people they barely knew. While Wells presents mismatched relationships comically, he also demonstrates his frustration at the blind obedience to convention which dictated contemporary sexual and marital unions; he himself had made an ill-judged and short-lived marriage to his cousin Isabel in 1891. Wells's scientific background alongside his own personal experience encouraged him to advocate a greater freedom of choice among men and women in picking their partners. The dividends from this form of liberation would clearly be paid out in greater personal happiness, but in Wells's characteristically holistic vision, this ability to exercise free choice would also serve to strengthen the race at large; the progeny of physically compatible and intellectually well-matched individuals would, according to this argument, counter the deleterious effects of breeding via more socially acceptable unions. A widespread belief at this time in the increasingly degenerate nature of town-bred children – an impression given authority by the physical deficiencies evident in many of those young men who had volunteered for the Anglo-Boer War (1899–1902) – offered a new imperative for those like Wells who looked to find ways of improving the health of the nation's stock.

The trenchant criticisms of modern society that Wells offers on almost every page of *Kipps* are mediated through a distinctive narrative voice. There is perhaps a temptation to interpret this voice as that of Wells himself, an association encouraged by the common political ground shared between writer and narrator. But this way of reading the novel simplifies what is in fact a carefully conceived and subtly handled relationship at the heart of the book. This relationship features on one hand a wry, wise and kindly narrator, and on the other hand an un-remarkable and relatively inarticulate subject. To make this union effective, Wells's narrator has to make his audience care about the fate of someone who might appear on the surface of things a very ordinary and unappealing victim. Unlike those central characters of great Victorian novels, such as *David Copperfield* or *Jane Eyre*, Kipps is ill-equipped to master his circumstances by force of will or by exercising latent talent. He is instead one of those everyday people with an ordinary mind who had tended to occupy the margins rather than the centre of novels before this era. Wells therefore needed to craft a narrative voice capable of connecting us to Kipps, allowing readers to become invested in a character who seems powerless to resist the injustice and condescension to which he is daily subjected. The skilful way in which Wells manages this can be seen at the point of the story in which Kipps first encounters his future fiancée Helen. Beginning by telling us, in his characteristically companionable register, that 'it will be well if the reader gets the picture of her correctly in mind', the narrator goes on: 'I think she was as beautiful as most beautiful people, and to Kipps she was altogether beautiful' (p. 70). This is a deceptively slippery sentence, begging readers to consider the standards of judgement employed by various parties here. The narrator's qualification of his own initial declaration of Helen's beauty – she is only as beautiful 'as most beautiful people' – alerts us to the potential hollowness of this subjective marker of value. In spite of this qualification though, the narrator's 'I' places him in the frame as somebody who recognises the complexity of judgements based on subjective and emotional criteria. For this reason, he can be generous and empathetic with Kipps, and this warmth of interpretation encourages us as readers to share his perspective. There is an intimacy in this rendering of the scene which conditions our knowledge that Kipps found Helen 'altogether beautiful'. He is clearly being naïve, as the surrounding details confirm, but his is an intelligible naïvety, one that is entirely conditioned by his limited knowledge of the world. The genial narrator suggests that Kipps's inchoate stage of emotional and intellectual development is hardly his fault, being rather the product of a society which seems determined to keep him and his kind in a raw state. Far from offering an impatient and satirical interpretation of a simpleton then, the narrator's management of this scene gently guides our hand and eye. It is Kipps's untrained heart that governs his 'utmost admiration' (p. 70) of Helen (and the poor choices that will result from this admiration), and it would be an act of bad faith on the reader's part to interpret this in any other way. To patronise Kipps would place the reader in league with the wonderfully realised Chester Coote, a pretentious snob with whom few would wish to be allied.

The critical response to *Kipps* suggests much about its wider impact. The liberal politician C. F. G. Masterman who reviewed the novel in the *Daily News*, for example, argued that he knew 'of no recent novel which so completely convinces the reader of the transparent truthfulness of the author' (Parrinder, p. 123). Masterman, who as a highly regarded social critic in his day was well placed to assess the book's contemporary significance, further claimed that 'the draper's assistant, interpreted against a background of real experience, will become a figure of ultimate significance' (ibid.). For Wells, though, it was his friend Henry James's recognition of the novel's strengths that offered him particular encouragement. After calling Kipps a 'born gem', James went on to describe the novel more generally as displaying 'a brilliancy of *true* truth' (Parrinder, p. 126). For James, Wells in this novel had achieved 'two particular things for the first time of their doing among us': '(1) You have written the first closely and intimately, the first intelligently and consistently ironic or satiric novel; and (2) You have for the very first time treated the English "lower-middle" class, etc., without the picturesque, the grotesque, the fantastic and romantic interference of which Dickens . . . is so misleadingly . . . full' (ibid.). So in James's view *Kipps* held an important place in both cultural and political history. The contemporary opinions of James and Masterman in this way offer vital perspectives on what might otherwise appear simply an amusing portrait of small-town life in Edwardian England. Seen through James's and Masterman's eyes, we are able to understand *Kipps*'s key role in mapping out an emerging class at the start of the new century. But, as James suggests, Wells's foremost achievement here is in arguably managing this venture with an innovative use of comedy that grasps and holds the reader's attention. In understanding this we can return to Wells's designation of Artie Kipps in the novel's subtitle as a 'simple soul' with a clearer sense of the satirical irony embedded from its opening page.

THE HISTORY OF MR POLLY

Five years after the publication of *Kipps*, Wells returned in *The History of Mr Polly* to many of the issues that had governed that earlier novel. Once more he chose a lower-middle-class draper, this time Alfred Polly, as his central protagonist and once again focused the text around topics that had a central bearing on that individual's quality of life: education, work, marriage and class. But *Polly* is by no means a simple rehashing by Wells of familiar characters, scenes and concerns. While the novel clearly shares much common ground with *Kipps* (and therefore makes an ideal companion piece for this edition), it is also a singular delight, being arguably the most high spirited and best constructed of Wells's social comedies. Aside from the pleasures generated by its tone and shape, *Polly* is also an important political novel. The task that Wells began in *Kipps* of delineating and empowering a social class reaches its zenith in *Polly*. At points, indeed, *Polly* seems to function as a self-help guide for this class, with Wells rallying his lower-middle-class readers to take control of their lives after realising their true worth. The connection between this novel and those key works of political literature mentioned at the start of this Introduction is at its most evident during these passages of rhetorical persuasion. Just as Marx and Engels had prepared their proletariat readers for the coming revolution, Wells's narrator invites his own readers to understand that for them 'there was no inevitable any more'. Like Mr Polly, they too might break 'through the paper walls of everyday circumstance, those unsubstantial walls that hold so many of us securely prisoned from the cradle to the grave' (p. 438). Once liberated from any sense that the shape of their life was preordained, they were free to embrace an almost boundless horizon of possibility. And, as *Polly* confirms, while what lay beyond the 'paper walls' of circumstance might include high achievement (something that Wells's own biography exemplifies), it might equally incorporate more modest ends. Mr Polly's discovery of contentment while employed as a handyman at a rural Kentish inn suggests the importance and fitness of dictating one's own destiny rather than leaving it in the hands of others.

As in *Kipps*, but perhaps even more so, this serious message is conveyed in a novel that is written in an infectiously light-hearted register: Wells himself described *Polly* as a work which was 'warm with a pervading affection' (Preface to Volume XVII of the Atlantic Edition). For Wells this was his 'happiest book', and like the parent of a favourite child, he considered it 'the one he care[d] for most' (ibid.). This appears a surprising endorsement on Wells's part when we take into account the novel's dark subject matter: the apparently cheerless life of a suicidal draper. All the more surprising, given Wells's evident fondness for the book, is the knowledge that it was written under circumstances which were far from happy. At this time, in 1909, he had left his wife and children and moved to the Continent with his lover, Amber Reeves, to live in a rented chalet in Le Touquet. Here, as he later reflected, he 'looked isolation in the face', while contemplating the likely ruination of both his personal life and his professional life. Wells himself remained puzzled that he was able to create such successful work under such desolate circumstances: 'it is odd to recall that some of the best of [*Polly*] I wrote weeping bitterly like a frustrated child' (G. P. Wells, p. 81).

The febrile state in which the book was written probably explains the heightened emotions that emerge throughout the novel. Nowhere is this more clearly evinced than in its opening lines where the book's prevailing mood is economically established. Here we are introduced to a dyspeptic Mr Polly sitting on a country stile while contemplating the intolerable nature of his life and circumstances:

> 'Hole!' said Mr Polly, and then for a change, and with greatly increased emphasis: ' '*Ole!*' He paused, and then broke out with one of his private and peculiar idioms. 'Oh! *Beastly* Silly Wheeze of a hole!'   [p. 312]

Polly's loveless marriage and detested occupation ('he hated his shop' [p. 314]) delineated over the next few pages offer a context for this intemperate outburst. But before we encounter this detail, Polly's distinctive use of language has already animated him in dramatic fashion. His memorable description of his environment as a '*Beastly* Silly Wheeze of a hole' places him in linguistic control of his surroundings, ensuring that they remain in the background while he resolutely occupies the narrative's foreground. Language for Polly in this way operates as a means of exercising power, and while he often wields this power in uncertain ways, he instinctively understands its value. We can recognise this in the ways in which he 'plunged into' a world of words which for him held 'a terror and fascination' (p. 327). While his limited education, which had left him uncertain of 'spelling and pronunciation', had inspired the terrifying side of his relationship with language, he none the less remained dynamically 'attracted' to language. His coinages, often inspired by exaggerated mispronunciation of tricky words – including 'Sesquippledan verboojuice' (p. 327), Rapsodooce' (p. 327), 'Rabooloose' (p. 328) and 'catechunations' (p. 355) – evoke the sheer joy he takes in playfully engaging with words. Polly is indeed a kind of artist with words, a primitive artist admittedly, but none the less an artist.

Wells sets up Polly in this way to make a symbolic statement about the contemporary lower-middle class and their place in contemporary society. This issue is directly addressed in an intriguing passage in the novel supposedly voiced by a 'high-browed gentleman . . . wearing a golden *pince-nez*' (p. 344). This individual offers a satirical portrait of those Edwardian social critics who confidently interpreted the nation's 'collective intelligence' from the comfort of their London clubs: in this case the 'beautiful . . . library of the Reform Club' (p. 344). Although Wells had little time for such patrician figures, he uses this interlude in the novel to take stock of the contemporary status of the lower-middle class in Britain, and more particularly to examine the position of Polly's fellow small shopkeepers. This unit of society, the 'high-browed gentlemen' avers, does 'little or nothing for the community in return

for what they consume', living lives instead that are 'essentially . . .
failures':

> not the sharp and tragic failure of the labourer who gets out of work
> and starves, but a slow, chronic process of consecutive small losses
> which may end if the individual is exceptionally fortunate in an
> impoverished deathbed before actual bankruptcy or destitution
> supervenes.   [p. 408]

This is a deceptively complex passage to interpret because while the
figure who voices this perspective is satirised by Wells, his damning
criticism of this class is largely supported by what we witness in the text.

Polly's fellow shopkeepers, according to this novel, do live what the
American writer Henry David Thoreau claimed in a different context
were 'lives of quiet desperation', and this state of affairs should clearly
be an abomination for any reasonably organised society. Wells had
direct personal knowledge of what he was writing about here, his own
father Joseph having been an unsuccessful and impoverished small
shopkeeper, who lived out his pathetic life in later years relying on the
charity of his family. What was needed here, Wells considered, was the
kind of evolutionary shift that would allow this class of individuals to
break free from the fixed attitudes that confined them in ultimately
profitless occupations. In this respect Mr Polly provides an instructive
and in many ways a symbolic example. For Wells he represents an
intermediate stage for his social class, being caught between a first
generation of largely compliant citizens, and a subsequent generation
who would, he anticipated, move beyond those narrow channels of
life uncomplainingly accepted by their forebears. The late-Victorian
emergence of compulsory education for all children was a potentially
crucial element in this evolutionary movement. Although the weakness
of the education offered to children at this time – something wittily
described in Polly's case as representing merely 'the valley of the
shadow of education' (p. 319) – seemed in Wells's view to hinder rather
than propel this class's progression, at a rudimentary level teachers in
state-run schools might still ignite a spark of enlightenment in their
pupils. In Polly's case, his schooling (at equally hopeless state and
private schools) had at least managed to suggest to him 'the idea that
there was interest and happiness' in a world in which 'beauty' and
'delight' existed somewhere, 'magically inaccessible perhaps, but still
somewhere' (p. 319).

The fact that Polly was aware of these qualities represents for Wells
an important step in his evolutionary development, demonstrating his

potential to take a more active share in the world's 'interest and happiness'. But while Polly's potential is amply evident in his intense curiosity and sensibility, he, like many of his class, has little real sense of how to harness these qualities for his own permanent benefit. Polly, during the novel's first half, is securely fixed in his social cage, with happiness, beauty and delight seemingly attainable only for an elect that he was never destined to join. But one of the central aims of *Polly* is to convince a whole class of people that life-affirming pleasures such as these are in fact within reach of everyone. The history of Mr Polly is wholly designed by Wells to prove this truth, with Polly himself leading the way for his class. He is an unlikely trailblazer in this respect, but this improbability is very much at the heart of Wells's strategy. There would be little point in simply offering readers yet another *David Copperfield*-type narrative, featuring an evidently bright and able young man who eventually receives his worldly due after being socially displaced at the novel's outset. It was far more effective, given the political aims Wells had rehearsed in *Kipps*, to demonstrate the liberation of an ordinary man who lacked the spark of ambition commonly found in more conventional fiction. Mr Polly, the middle-aged dyspeptic shopkeeper, as initially witnessed on his country stile contemplating the ruins of his life, is probably the last person one would expect to escape his dire circumstances. Other than via the hackneyed device of the unexpected legacy, something Wells had already employed in *Kipps*, there would seem little hope for the benighted little man. But Polly does, admittedly after a somewhat bizarre sequence of events, break away from the 'inevitable' while taking control of his life. He proves, in the process, the viewpoint espoused by Wells's narrator that 'there are no circumstances in the world that determined action cannot alter, unless perhaps they are the walls of a prison cell, and even those will dissolve and change . . . for the man who can fast with resolution' (p. 438). If Wells's own determined action had allowed him to break free from a life behind the drapery counter, then why might not Polly, and by extension readers in similar circumstances, achieve the same form of liberation. The rewards for escapees were plain, as Polly himself reflects towards the end of the novel: 'he was really glad, for all that drawback of fear, that he had had the courage to set fire to his house, and fly, and come to the Potwell Inn' (p. 472). Courage, in Wells's summation, was the most important quality required for those who wanted to break free from their chains.

The effectiveness of this political message is greatly enhanced by the attention Wells devotes to the novel's structure. When he later drew comparisons between *Kipps* and *Polly* he recognised their 'many affinities' but also understood that the latter novel was 'done with a surer hand' (Preface to Volume XVII of the Atlantic Edition). Whereas *Kipps* offers a clear and organised presentation of its title character's life for much of the narrative, this tightness in construction falls away in Book Three which opens with a lengthy digression on the perils of house building; here Wells was able indulgently to reflect upon the frustrations he himself had experienced while building his own home at the beginning of the century. This loosening of narrative grip by Wells meant that much of the book's earlier energy was dissipated as it drew towards its conclusion. The 'surer hand' Wells invested in *Polly* suggests his understanding of the pitfalls of failing to maintain a reader's attention for the whole of a book intended as a work of political persuasion. The shorter length of *Polly* also implies Wells's recognition of the benefits of relative brevity while constructing an essentially political work. With a smaller canvas to work on Wells was better able to retain his readers' concentration, allowing them to keep all of the stages of Mr Polly's 'history' in mind without unnecessary distraction.

While *Polly* is undoubtedly an attractively persuasive and well-made text, it is difficult to quantify with any accuracy the extent to which it directly altered the thinking of its readers. Although numerous state-school children read *Polly* as a set text for examinations during the twentieth century, few have publically acknowledged it as a foundational text of their personal emancipation; it is perhaps revealing in this respect that out of more than three thousand 'castaways' interviewed for the popular and long-running BBC radio programme *Desert Island Discs*, only one, the horror-fiction writer James Herbert, has picked *Polly* as a book choice. But in a wider sense the sorts of empowerment and class liberation that Wells promoted in *Kipps* and *Polly* did, in significant ways, come to fruition during the early years of the twentieth century. Changing attitudes towards members of the lower-middle class by society in general, and changes in self-perception by members of that class themselves, indeed happened quite rapidly in the period after Wells's novels were published. These changes, like many of the social and political developments that occurred during the twentieth century, came about as a direct result of the Great War. We can reasonably speculate that among the legions of individuals who joined up in 1914, many would have felt kinship with Kipps and Polly. Like them, these volunteers were typically desperate to escape from the drudgery of work behind drapery counters and office desks, and the war seemed to offer them a once-in-a-lifetime opportunity to evade their fate. Although many of these individuals would become casualties of the war, others survived to become what were known at the period as 'temporary gentlemen'. This term refers to individuals commissioned for the duration of the war in an effort to plug gaps left by early casualties; this first wave of wartime officers had been drawn mainly from the public schools. The literate, numerate and articulate young men of the lower-middle class were typically well suited to these roles, and the army greatly benefited from their services. Had Polly or Kipps become 'temporary gentlemen' at a time beyond the immediate action of these novels, they would have enjoyed access to the officers' mess, been permitted to travel first class on railways, and gained membership of London clubs. It is difficult to imagine any former clerk, draper or small shopkeeper who had attained such a privileged wartime status returning after the end of the conflict to their pre-1914 acceptance of social subordination; would Kipps have been quite as deferential to the snobbish Chester Coote, we might ask, had he observed him cowering in a shell-hole? John Galsworthy, a close observer of social change at this time, has a character in his *Forsyte Saga* novel *The White Monkey* (1924) remark in relation to the lower-middle class that while the war 'took the linch-pins out of the cart', it also proved evidence of 'the grit there is about, when it comes to being up against it' (p. 277). Wells had proclaimed this fact well in advance of the war but would certainly not have willed such a cataclysmic event to hasten its wider acceptance. For Wells, however, this proved a positive by-product of an otherwise disastrous war. After 1914, the worlds of deference and servility depicted in *Kipps* and *Polly* were swept away, and as Philip Larkin writes in his poem 'MCMXIV', there would be 'Never such innocence again' (Larkin, p. 28). While Larkin is nostalgic here for an innocence destroyed by war, the sort of paralysing innocence envisaged by Wells in his Edwardian social comedies offers a very different perspective on this lost world.

JONATHAN WILD

WORK CITED

Galsworthy, John, *A Modern Comedy* (including *The White Monkey*), Heinemann, London, 1948

Larkin, Philip, *The Whitsun Weddings*, Faber, London, 1964

Parrinder, Patrick (ed.), *H. G. Wells, The Critical Heritage*, Routledge & Kegan Paul, London, 1972

Smith, David C. (ed.), *The Correspondence of H.,G. Wells, Volume 1, 1880–1903*, Pickering & Chatto, London, 1998

Wells, G. P. (ed.), *H. G. Wells in Love*, Faber and Faber, London, 1984

Wells, H. G., *Kipps* (Atlantic Edition of the Works of H. G. Wells), T. Fisher Unwin, London, 1924

Wells, H. G., *The History of Mr Polly* (Atlantic Edition of the Works of H. G. Wells), T. Fisher Unwin, London, 1924

Wilson, Harris, 'The Death of Masterman: A Repressed Episode in H. G. Wells's *Kipps*', *PMLA*, Vol. 86, No. 1, January 1971, pp. 63–9

Kipps
The Story of a Simple Soul

Kipps

The Story of a Simple Soul

◆

H. G. WELLS

Kipps was first published in Great Britain in 1905 by
Macmillan & Co in London, and in the United States by
Charles Scribner's Sons, New York

Contents

BOOK ONE

The Making of Kipps

Those individuals who have led secluded or isolated lives, or have hitherto moved in other spheres than those wherein well-bred people move, will gather all the information necessary from these pages to render them thoroughly conversant with the manners and amenities of society.

Manner and Rules of Good Society
BY A MEMBER OF THE ARISTOCRACY

CHAPTER ONE

The Little Shop at New Romney

UNTIL HE WAS NEARLY ARRIVED at adolescence it did not become clear to Kipps how it was that he was under the care of an aunt and uncle instead of having a father and mother like other boys. Yet he had vague memories of a somewhere else that was not New Romney – of a dim room, a window looking down on white buildings – and of a some one else who talked to forgotten people, and who was his mother. He could not recall her features very distinctly, but he remembered with extreme definition a white dress she wore, with a pattern of little sprigs of flowers and little bows of ribbon upon it, and a girdle of straight-ribbed white ribbon about the waist. Linked with this, he knew not how, were clouded half-obliterated recollections of scenes in which there was weeping, weeping in which he was inscrutably moved to join. Some terrible tall man with a loud voice played a part in these scenes, and either before or after them there were impressions of looking for interminable periods out of the windows of railway trains in the company of these two people –

He knew, though he could not remember that he had ever been told, that a certain faded, wistful face, that looked at him from a plush and gilt framed daguerreotype above the mantel of the 'sitting-room', was the face of his mother. But that knowledge did not touch his dim memories with any elucidation. In that photograph she was a girlish figure, leaning against a photographer's stile, and with all the self-conscious shrinking natural to that position. She had curly hair and a face far younger and prettier than any other mother in his experience. She swung a Dolly Varden hat[1] by the string, and looked with obedient respectful eyes on the photographer-gentleman who had commanded the pose. She was very slight and pretty. But the phantom mother that haunted his memory so elusively was not like that, though he could not remember how she differed. Perhaps she was older, or a little less shrinking, or, it may be, only dressed in a different way . . .

It is clear she handed him over to his aunt and uncle at New Romney with explicit directions and a certain endowment. One gathers she had something of that fine sense of social distinctions that subsequently played so large a part in Kipps's career. He was not to go to a 'common' school, she provided, but to a certain seminary in Hastings that was not only a 'middle-class academy', with mortar boards and every evidence of a higher social tone, but also remarkably cheap. She seems to have been animated by the desire to do her best for Kipps, even at a certain sacrifice of herself, as though Kipps were in some way a superior sort of person. She sent pocket-money to him from time to time for a year or more after Hastings had begun for him, but her face he never saw in the days of his lucid memory.

His aunt and uncle were already high on the hill of life when first he came to them. They had married for comfort in the evening or at any rate in the late afternoon of their days. They were at first no more than vague figures in the background of proximate realities, such realities as familiar chairs and tables, quiet to ride and drive, the newel of the staircase, kitchen furniture, pieces of firewood, the boiler tap, old news-papers, the cat, the High Street, the back yard and the flat fields that are always so near in that little town. He knew all the stones in the yard individually, the creeper in the corner, the dustbin and the mossy wall, better than many men know the faces of their wives. There was a corner under the ironing-board which by means of a shawl could, under propitious gods, be made a very decent cubby-house, a corner that served him for several years as the indisputable hub of the world; and the stringy places in the carpet, the knots upon the dresser, and the several corners of the rag hearthrug his uncle had made, became essential parts of his mental foundations. The shop he did not know so thoroughly – it was a forbidden region to him; yet somehow he managed to know it very well.

His aunt and uncle were, as it were, the immediate gods of this world; and, like the gods of the world of old, occasionally descended right into it, with arbitrary injunctions and disproportionate punishments. And, unhappily, one rose to their Olympian level at meals. Then one had to say one's 'grace', hold one's spoon and fork in mad, unnatural ways called 'properly', and refrain from eating even nice sweet things 'too fast'. If he 'gobbled' there was trouble, and at the slightest *abandon* with knife, fork and spoon, his aunt rapped his knuckles, albeit his uncle always finished up his gravy with his knife. Sometimes, moreover, his uncle would come, pipe in hand, out of a sedentary remoteness in the most disconcerting way, when a little boy was doing the most natural and attractive things, with 'Drat and drabbit that young rascal! What's he a-doing of now?' And his aunt would appear at door or window to interrupt interesting conversation with children who were upon unknown grounds considered 'low' and undesirable, and call him in.

The pleasantest little noises, however softly you did them – drumming on tea-trays, trumpeting your fists, whistling on keys, ringing chimes with a couple of pails, or playing tunes on the window-panes – brought down the gods in anger. Yet what noise is fainter than your finger on the window – gently done? Sometimes, however, these gods gave him broken toys out of the shop, and then one loved them better – for the shop they kept was, among other things, a toy shop. (The other things included books to read and books to give away and local photographs; it had some pretensions also to be a china shop, and the fascia spoke of glass; it was also a stationer's shop with a touch of haberdashery about it, and in the windows and odd corners were mats and terracotta dishes, and milking-stools for painting; and there was a hint of picture-frames, and fire-screens, and fishing tackle, and air-guns, and bathing suits, and tents: various things, indeed, but all cruelly attractive to a small boy's fingers.) Once his aunt gave him a trumpet if he would *promise* faithfully not to blow it, and afterwards took it away again. And his aunt made him say his catechism and something she certainly called the 'Colic for the Day'[2] every Sunday in the year.

As the two grew old while he grew up, and as his impression of them modified insensibly from year to year, it seemed to him at last that they had always been as they were when, in his adolescent days, his impression of things grew fixed. His aunt he thought of as always lean, rather worried-looking, and prone to a certain obliquity of cap, and his uncle massive, many-chinned and careless about his buttons. They neither visited nor received visitors. They were always very suspicious about their neighbours and other people generally; they feared the 'low' and they hated and despised the 'stuck-up', and so they 'kept themselves *to* themselves', according to the English ideal. Consequently little Kipps had no playmates, except through the sin of disobedience. By inherent nature he had a sociable disposition. When he was in the High Street he made a point of saying 'Hello!' to passing cyclists, and he would put his tongue out at the Quodling[3] children whenever their nursemaid was not looking. And he began a friendship with Sid Pornick, the son of the haberdasher next door, that, with wide intermissions, was destined to last his lifetime through.

Pornick, the haberdasher, I may say at once, was, according to old Kipps, a 'blaring jackass'; he was a teetotaller, a 'nyar, nyar, 'im-singing Methodis' ', and altogether distasteful and detrimental, he and his together, to true Kipps ideals, so far as little Kipps could gather them. This Pornick certainly possessed an enormous voice, and he annoyed old Kipps greatly by calling 'You – Arn' and 'Siddee' up and down his house. He annoyed old Kipps by private choral services on Sunday, all his family 'nyar, nyar-ing'; and by mushroom culture; by behaving as though the pilaster between the two shops was common property; by making a noise of hammering in the afternoon, when old Kipps wanted to be quiet after his midday meal; by going up and down uncarpeted stairs in his boots; by having a black beard; by attempting to be friendly; and by – all that sort of thing. In fact, he annoyed old Kipps. He annoyed him especially with his shop doormat. Old Kipps never beat his mat, preferring to let sleeping dust lie; and, seeking a motive for a foolish proceeding, he held that Pornick waited until there was a suitable wind in order that the dust disengaged in that operation might defile his neighbour's shop. These issues would frequently develop into loud and vehement quarrels, and on one occasion came so near to violence as to be subsequently described by Pornick (who read his newspaper) as a 'Disgraceful Frackass'. On that occasion he certainly went into his own shop with extreme celerity.

But it was through one of these quarrels that the friendship of little Kipps and Sid Pornick came about. The two small boys found themselves one day looking through the gate at the doctor's goats together; they exchanged a few contradictions about which goat could fight which, and then young Kipps was moved to remark that Sid's father was a 'blaring jackass'. Sid said he wasn't, and Kipps repeated that he was, and quoted his authority. Then Sid, flying off at a tangent rather alarmingly, said he could fight young Kipps with one hand, an assertion young Kipps with a secret want of confidence denied. There were some vain repetitions, and the incident might have ended there, but happily a sporting butcher boy chanced on the controversy at this stage, and insisted upon seeing fair play.

The two small boys under his pressing encouragement did at last button up their jackets, square and fight an edifying drawn battle, until it seemed good to the butcher boy to go on with Mrs Holyer's mutton. Then, according to his directions and under his experienced stage management, they shook hands and made it up. Subsequently, a little tear-stained perhaps, but flushed with the butcher boy's approval ('tough little kids'), and with cold stones down their necks as he advised, they sat side by side on the doctor's gate, projecting very much behind, staunching an honourable bloodshed, and expressing respect for one another. Each had a bloody nose and a black eye – three days later they matched to a shade – neither had given in, and, though this was tacit, neither wanted any more.

It was an excellent beginning. After this first encounter the attributes of their parents and their own relative value in battle never rose between them, and if anything was wanted to complete the warmth of their regard it was found in a joint dislike of the eldest Quodling. The eldest Quodling lisped, had a silly sort of straw hat and a large pink face (all covered over with self-satisfaction) and he went to the National School with a green-baize bag – a contemptible thing to do. They called him names and threw stones at him, and when he replied by threatenings ('Look 'ere, young Art Kipth, you better *thtoppit!*') they were moved to attack and put him to flight.

And after that they broke the head of Ann Pornick's doll, so that she went home weeping loudly – a wicked and endearing proceeding. Sid was whacked, but, as he explained, he wore a newspaper tactically adjusted during the transaction, and really it didn't hurt him at all . . . And Mrs Pornick put her head out of the shop door suddenly, and threatened Kipps as he passed.

2

'Cavendish Academy', the school that had won the limited choice of Kipps's vanished mother, was established in a battered private house in the part of Hastings remotest from the sea; it was called an Academy for Young Gentlemen, and many of the young gentlemen had parents in 'India', and other unverifiable places. Others were the sons of credulous widows, anxious, as Kipps's mother had been, to get something a little 'superior' to a board-school education as cheaply as possible; and others again were sent to demonstrate the dignity of their parents and guardians. And of course there were boys from France.

Its 'principal' was a lean, long creature of indifferent digestion and temper, who proclaimed himself on a gilt-lettered board in his front garden George Garden Woodrow, F.S.Sc., letters indicating that he had paid certain guineas for a bogus diploma. A bleak whitewashed outhouse constituted his schoolroom, and the scholastic quality of its carved and worn desks and forms was enhanced by a slippery blackboard and two large yellow out-of-date maps, one of Africa and the other of Wiltshire, that he had picked up cheap at a sale. There were other maps and globes in his study, where he interviewed enquiring parents, but these his pupils never saw. And in a glass cupboard in the passage were several-shillings-worth of test tubes and chemicals, a tripod, a glass retort and a damaged Bunsen burner, manifesting that the 'Scientific Laboratory' mentioned in the prospectus was no idle boast.

This prospectus, which was in dignified but incorrect English, laid particular stress on the sound preparation for a commercial career given at the Academy, but the army, navy and civil service were glanced at in an ambiguous sentence. There was something vague in the prospectus about 'examinational successes' – though Woodrow, of course, disapproved of 'cram' – and a declaration that the curriculum included 'art', 'modern foreign languages' and 'a sound technical and scientific training'. Then came insistence upon the 'moral well-being' of the pupils, and an emphatic boast of the excellence of the religious instruction, 'so often neglected nowadays even in schools of wide repute'. 'That's bound to fetch 'em,' Mr Woodrow had remarked when he drew up the prospectus. And in conjunction with the mortar boards it certainly did. Attention was directed to the 'motherly' care of Mrs Woodrow – in reality a small partially effaced woman with a plaintive face and a mind above cookery; and the prospectus concluded with a phrase intentionally vague, 'Fare unrestricted, and our own milk and produce.'

The memories Kipps carried from that school into afterlife were set in an atmosphere of stuffiness and mental muddle; and included countless pictures of sitting on creaking forms bored and idle, of blot licking and the taste of ink, of torn books with covers that set one's teeth on edge, of the slimy surface of the laboured slates, of furtive marble-playing, whispered storytelling, and of pinches, blows and a thousand such petty annoyances being perpetually 'passed on' according to the custom of the place; of standing up in class and being hit suddenly and unreasonably for imaginary misbehaviour; of Mr Woodrow's raving days, when a scarcely sane injustice prevailed; of the cold vacuity of the hour of preparation before the bread-and-butter breakfast; and of horrible headaches and queer, unprecedented, internal feelings resulting from Mrs Woodrow's motherly rather than intelligent cookery. There were dreary walks, when the boys marched two by two, all dressed in the mortar-board caps that so impressed the widowed mothers; there were dismal half-holidays when the weather was wet and the spirit of evil temper and evil imagination had the pent boys to work its will on; there were unfair, dishonourable fights and miserable defeats and victories, there was bullying and being bullied. A coward boy Kipps particularly afflicted, until at last he was goaded to revolt by incessant persecution and smote Kipps to tolerance with whirling fists. There were memories of sleeping three in a bed, of the dense leathery smell of the schoolroom when one returned thither after ten minutes' play, of a playground of mud and incidental sharp flints. And there was much furtive foul language.

'Our Sundays are our happiest days,' was one of Woodrow's formulae with the enquiring parent, but Kipps was not called in evidence. They were to him terrible gaps of inanity – no work, no play, a drear expanse of time with the mystery of church twice and plum duff once in the middle. The afternoon was given up to furtive relaxations, among which 'Torture Chamber' games with the less agreeable, weaker boys figured. It was from the difference between this day and common days that Kipps derived his first definite conceptions of the nature of God and Heaven. His instinct was to evade any closer acquaintance as long as he could.

The school work varied, according to the prevailing mood of Mr Woodrow. Sometimes that was a despondent lethargy; copybooks were distributed or sums were 'set', or the great mystery of book-keeping was declared in being, and beneath these superficial activities lengthy conversations and interminable guessing games with marbles went on while Mr Woodrow sat inanimate at his desk heedless of school affairs, staring in front of him at unseen things. At times his face was utterly inane; at times it had an expression of stagnant amaze-ment, as if he saw before his eyes with pitiless clearness the dishonour and mischief of his being . . .

At other times the F.S.Sc. roused himself to action, and would stand up a wavering class and teach it, goading it with bitter mockery and blows through a chapter of Ahn's *First French Course*, or *France and the French*,[4] or a dialogue about a traveller's washing or the parts of an opera-house. His own knowledge of French had been obtained years ago in another English private school, and he had refreshed it by occasional weeks of loafing and mean adventure in Dieppe. He would sometimes in their lessons hit upon some reminiscence of these brighter days, and then he would laugh inexplicably and repeat French phrases of an unfamiliar type.

Among the commoner exercises he prescribed the learning of long passages of poetry from a 'Potry Book', which he would delegate an elder boy to 'hear', and there was reading aloud from the Holy Bible, verse by verse – it was none of your 'godless' schools! – so that you counted the verses up to your turn and then gave yourself to con-versation; and sometimes one read from a cheap History of this land. They did, as Kipps reported, 'loads of catechism'. Also there was much learning of geographical names and lists, and sometimes Woodrow in an outbreak of energy would see these names were actually found on a map. And once, just once, there was a chemistry lesson – a lesson of indescribable excitement – glass things of the strangest shape, a smell like bad eggs, something bubbling in something, a smash and stench, and Mr Woodrow saying quite distinctly – they thrashed it out in the dormitory afterwards – 'Damn!' followed by the whole school being kept in, with extraordinary severities, for an hour . . .

But interspersed with the memories of this grey routine were certain patches of brilliant colour – the holidays, his holidays, which in spite of the feud between their seniors, he spent as much as possible with Sid Pornick, the son of the irascible black-bearded haberdasher next door. They seemed to be memories of a different world. There were glorious days of 'mucking about' along the beach, the siege of unresisting Martello towers, the incessant interest of the mystery and motion of windmills, the windy excursions with boarded feet over the yielding shingle to Dungeness lighthouse – Sid Pornick and he far adrift from reality, smugglers and armed men from the moment they left Great Stone behind them – wanderings in the hedgeless reedy marsh, long excursions reaching even to Hythe, where the machine-guns of the Empire are forever whirling and tapping, and to Rye and Winchelsea, perched like dream-cities on their little hills. The sky in these memories was the blazing hemisphere of the marsh heaven in summer, or its wintry tumult of sky and sea; and there were wrecks, real wrecks, in it (near Dymchurch pitched high and blackened and rotting were the ribs of a fishing smack flung aside like an empty basket when the sea had devoured its crew); and there was bathing all naked in the sea, bathing to one's armpits and even trying to swim in the warm sea-water (spite of his aunt's prohibition), and (with her indulgence) the rare eating of dinner from a paper parcel miles away from home. Cake and cold ground-rice puddin' with plums it used to be – there is no better food at all. And for the background, in the place of Woodrow's mean, fretting rule, were his aunt's spare but frequently quite amiable figure – for though she insisted on his repeating the English Church Catechism every Sunday, she had an easy way over dinners that one wanted to take abroad – and his uncle, corpulent and irascible, but sedentary and easily escaped. And freedom!

The holidays were indeed very different from school. They were free, they were spacious, and though he never knew it in these words – they had an element of beauty. In his memory of his boyhood they shone like strips of stained-glass window in a dreary waste of scholastic wall, they grew brighter and brighter as they grew remoter. There came a time at last and moods when he could look back to them with a feeling akin to tears.

The last of these windows was the brightest, and instead of the kaleidoscopic effects of its predecessors its glory was a single figure. For in the last of his holidays, before the Moloch of Retail Trade got hold of him, Kipps made his first tentative essays at the mysterious shrine of Love. Very tentative they were, for he had become a boy of subdued passions, and potential rather than actual affectionateness.

And the object of these first stirrings of the great desire was no other than Ann Pornick, the head of whose doll he and Sid had broken long ago, and rejoiced over long ago, in the days when he had yet to learn the meaning of a heart.

3

Negotiations were already on foot to make Kipps into a draper before he discovered the lights that lurked in Ann Pornick's eyes. School was over, absolutely over, and it was chiefly present to him that he was never to go to school again. It was high summer. The 'breaking up' of school had been hilarious; and the excellent maxim, 'Last Day's Pay Day', had been observed by him with a scrupulous attention to his honour. He had punched the heads of all his enemies, wrung wrists and kicked shins; he had distributed all his unfinished copybooks, all his schoolbooks, his collection of marbles and his mortar-board cap among such as loved him; and he had secretly written in obscure pages of their books, 'remember Art Kipps'. He had also split the anaemic Woodrow's cane, carved his own name deeply in several places about the premises, and broken the scullery window. He had told everybody so often that he was to learn to be a sea captain that he had come almost to believe the thing himself. And now he was home, and school was at an end for him for evermore.

He was up before six on the day of his return, and out in the hot sunlight of the yard. He set himself to whistle a peculiarly penetrating arrangement of three notes supposed by the boys of the Hastings Academy and himself and Sid Pornick, for no earthly reason whatever, to be the original Huron[5] war-cry. As he did this he feigned not to be doing it because of the hatred between his uncle and the Pornicks, but to be examining with respect and admiration a new wing of the dustbin recently erected by his uncle – a pretence that would not have deceived a nestling tomtit.

Presently there came a familiar echo from the Pornick hunting-ground. Then Kipps began to sing, 'Ar pars eight tra-la, in the lane be'ind the church.' To which an unseen person answered, 'Ar pars eight it is, in the lane be'ind the church.' The 'tra-la' was considered to render this sentence incomprehensible to the uninitiated. In order to conceal their operations still more securely, both parties to this duet then gave vent to a vocalisation of the Huron war-cry again, and after a lingering repetition of the last and shrillest note, dispersed severally, as became boys in the enjoyment of holidays, to light the house fires for the day.

Half-past eight found Kipps sitting on the sunlit gate at the top of the long lane that runs towards the sea, clashing his boots in a slow rhythm, and whistling with great violence all that he knew of an excruciatingly pathetic air. There appeared along by the churchyard wall a girl in a short frock, brown-haired, quick-coloured, and with dark-blue eyes. She had grown so that she was a little taller than Kipps, and her colour had improved. He scarcely remembered her, so changed was she since last holidays – if indeed he had seen her last holidays, a thing he could not clearly remember. Some vague emotion arose at the sight of her. He stopped whistling and regarded her, oddly tongue-tied.

'He can't come,' said Ann, advancing boldly. 'Not yet.'

'What – not Sid?'

'No. Father's made him dust all his boxes again.'

'What for?'

'I dunno. Father's in a stew 'smorning.'

'Oh!'

Pause. Kipps looked at her, and then was unable to look at her again. She regarded him with interest. 'You left school?' she remarked after a pause.

'Yes.'

'So's Sid.'

The conversation languished. Ann put her hands on the top of the gate, and began a stationary hopping, a sort of ineffectual gymnastic experiment.

'Can you run?' she said presently.

'Run you any day,' said Kipps.

'Gimme a start?'

'Where for?' said Kipps.

Ann considered, and indicated a tree. She walked towards it, and turned. 'Gimme to here?' she called.

Kipps, standing now and touching the gate, smiled to express conscious superiority. 'Farther!' he said.

'Here?'

'Bit more!' said Kipps, and then, repenting of his magnanimity, said

'Orf!' suddenly, and so recovered his lost concession.

They arrived abreast at the tree, flushed and out of breath.

'Tie!' said Ann, throwing her hair back from her face with her hand.

'I won,' panted Kipps.

They disputed firmly but quite politely.

'Run it again, then,' said Kipps. '*I* don't mind.'

They returned towards the gate.

'You don't run bad,' said Kipps, temperately expressing sincere admiration. 'I'm pretty good, you know.'

Ann sent her hair back by an expert toss of the head. 'You give me a start,' she allowed.

They became aware of Sid approaching them.

'You better look out, young Ann,' said Sid, with that irreverent want of sympathy usual in brothers. 'You been out nearly 'arf-hour. Nothing ain't been done upstairs. Father said he didn't know where you was, but when he did he'd warm y'r young ear.'

Ann prepared to go.

'How about that race?' asked Kipps.

'Lor!' cried Sid, quite shocked. 'You ain't been racing *her*!'

Ann swung herself round the end of the gate with her eyes on Kipps, and then turned away suddenly and ran off down the lane.

Kipps's eyes tried to go after her, and came back to Sid's.

'I give her a lot of start,' said Kipps apologetically. 'It wasn't a proper race.' And so the subject was dismissed. But Kipps was *distrait* for some seconds, perhaps, and the mischief had begun in him.

4

They proceeded to the question of how two accomplished Hurons might most satisfactorily spend the morning. Manifestly their line lay straight along the lane to the sea.

'There's a new wreck,' said Sid, 'and my! – don't it stink just!'

'Stink?'

'Fair make you sick. It's rotten wheat.'

They fell to talking of wrecks, and so came to ironclads and wars and suchlike manly matters.

Halfway to the wreck Kipps made a casual irrelevant remark. 'Your sister ain't a bad sort,' he said offhandedly.

'I clout her a lot,' said Sidney modestly, and after a pause the talk reverted to more suitable topics.

The new wreck was full of rotting grain, and smelt abominably, even as Sid had said. This was excellent. They had it all to themselves. They took possession of it in force, at Sid's suggestion, and had speedily to defend it against enormous numbers of imaginary 'natives', who were at last driven off by loud shouts of *bang*, *bang*, and vigorous thrusting and shoving of sticks. Then, also at Sid's direction, they sailed with it into the midst of a combined French, German and Russian fleet, demolishing the combination unassisted, and, having descended to the beach, clambered up the side and cut out their own vessel in brilliant style, they underwent a magnificent shipwreck (with vocalised thunder) and floated '*waterlogged*' – so Sid insisted – upon an exhausted sea.

These things drove Ann out of mind for a time. But at last, as they drifted without food or water upon a stagnant ocean, haggard-eyed, chins between their hands, looking in vain for a sail, she came to mind again abruptly.

'It's rather nice 'aving sisters,' remarked one perishing mariner.

Sid turned round and regarded him thoughtfully. 'Not it!' he said.

'No?'

'Not a bit of it.' He grinned confidentially. 'Know too much,' he said; and afterwards, 'Get out of things.'

He resumed his gloomy scrutiny of the hopeless horizon. Presently he fell to spitting jerkily between his teeth, as he had read was the way with such ripe manhood as chews its quid.

'Sisters,' he said, 'is rot. That's what sisters are. Girls if you like, but sisters – no!'

'But ain't sisters girls?'

'*N–eaow!*' said Sid, with unspeakable scorn.

And Kipps answered, 'Of course. I didn't mean – I wasn't thinking of that.'

'You got a girl?' asked Sid, spitting very cleverly again.

Kipps admitted his deficiency. He felt compunction.

'You don't know who *my* girl is, Art Kipps – I bet.'

'Who *is*, then?' asked Kipps, still chiefly occupied by his own poverty.

'Ah!'

Kipps let a moment elapse before he did his duty. 'Tell us!'

Sid eyed him and hesitated. 'Secret?' he said.

'Secret.'

'Dying solemn?'

'Dying solemn!' Kipps's self-concentration passed into curiosity.

Sid administered a terrible oath. Even after that precaution he adhered lovingly to his facts. 'It begins with a Nem,' he said, doling them out parsimoniously. 'M-A-U-D,' he spelt, with a stern eye on Kipps, 'C-H-A-R-T-E-R-I-S.'

Now, Maud Charteris was a young person of eighteen and the daughter of the vicar of St Bavon's – besides which she had a bicycle – so that as her name unfolded the face of Kipps lengthened with respect. 'Get out!' he gasped incredulously. 'She ain't your girl, Sid Pornick.'

'She is!' answered Sid, stoutly.

'What – truth?'

'*Truth*.'

Kipps scrutinised his face. 'Reely?'

Sid touched wood, whistled, and repeated a binding doggerel with great solemnity.

Kipps still struggled with the amazing new light on the world about him. 'D'you mean – she knows?'

Sid flushed deeply, and his aspect became stern and gloomy. He resumed his wistful scrutiny of the sunlit sea. 'I'd die for that girl, Art Kipps,' he said presently, and Kipps did not press a question he felt to be ill timed. 'I'd do anything she asked me to do,' said Sid – 'just anything. If she was to ask me to chuck myself into the sea,' he met Kipps's eye, 'I *would*,' he said.

They were pensive for a space, and then Sid began to discourse in fragments of Love, a theme upon which Kipps had already in a furtive way meditated a little, but which, apart from badinage, he had never yet heard talked about in the light of day. Of course many and various aspects of life had come to light in the muffled exchange of knowledge that went on under the shadow of Woodrow, but this of Sentimental Love was not among them. Sid, who was a boy with an imagination, having once broached this topic, opened his heart, or at any rate a new wing of his heart, to Kipps, and found no fault with Kipps for a lack of return. He produced a thumbed novelette that had played a part in his sentimental awakening; he proffered it to Kipps, and confessed there was a character in it, a baronet, singularly like himself. This baronet was a person of volcanic passions which he concealed beneath a demeanour of 'icy cynicism'. The utmost expression he permitted himself was to grit his teeth; and now his attention was called to it, Kipps remarked that Sid also had a habit of gritting his teeth – and indeed had had all the morning. They read for a time, and presently Sid talked again. The conception of love Sid made evident was compact of devotion and much spirited fighting and a touch of mystery; but through all that cloud of talk there floated before Kipps a face that was flushed and hair that was tossed aside.

So they budded, sitting on the blackening old wreck in which men had lived and died, looking out to sea, talking of that other sea upon which they must presently embark –

They ceased to talk, and Sid read; but Kipps falling behind with the reading and not wishing to admit that he read slowlier than Sid, whose education was of the inferior elementary school brand, lapsed into meditation.

'I *would* like to 'ave a girl,' said Kipps. 'I mean just to talk to and all that . . . '

A floating object distracted them at last from this obscure topic. They abandoned the wreck and followed the new interest a mile along the beach, bombarding it with stones until it came to land. They had inclined to a view that it would contain romantic mysteries, but it was simply an ill-preserved kitten – too much even for them. And at last they were drawn dinnerward and went home hungry and pensive side by side.

5

But Kipps's imagination had been warmed by that talk of love, and in the afternoon, when he saw Ann Pornick in the High Street and said 'Hello!' it was a different 'hello' from that of their previous intercourse. And when they had passed they both looked back and caught each other doing so. Yes, he *did* want a girl badly . . .

Afterwards he was distracted by a traction engine going through the town, and his aunt had got some sprats for supper. When he was in bed, however, sentiment came upon him again in a torrent quite abruptly and abundantly, and he put his head under the pillow and whispered very softly, 'I love Ann Pornick,' as a sort of supplementary devotion.

In his subsequent dreams he ran races with Ann, and they lived in a wreck together, and always her face was flushed and her hair about her face. They just lived in a wreck and ran races, and were very, very fond of one another. And their favourite food was rock-chocolate, dates, such as one buys off barrows, and sprats – fried sprats . . .

In the morning he could hear Ann singing in the scullery next door. He listened to her for some time, and it was clear to him that he must put things before her.

Towards dusk that evening they chanced on one another at the gate by the church; but though there was much in his mind, it stopped there with a resolute shyness until he and Ann were out of breath catching cockchafers, and were sitting on that gate of theirs again. Ann sat up upon the gate, dark against vast masses of flaming crimson and darkling purple, and her eyes looked at Kipps from a shadowed face. There came a stillness between them, and quite abruptly he was moved to tell his love.

'Ann,' he said, 'I *do* like you. I wish you was my girl . . . I say, Ann: will you *be* my girl?'

Ann made no pretence of astonishment. She weighed the proposal for a moment with her eyes on Kipps. 'If you like, Artie,' she said lightly. '*I* don't mind if I am.'

'All right,' said Kipps, breathless with excitement, 'then you are.'

'All right,' said Ann.

Something seemed to fall between them, and they no longer looked openly at one another. 'Lor'!' cried Ann suddenly, 'see that one!' and jumped down and darted after a cockchafer that had boomed within a yard of her face. And with that they were girl and boy again . . .

They avoided their new relationship painfully.

They did not recur to it for several days, though they met twice. Both felt that there remained something before this great experience was complete, but there was an infinite diffidence about the next step. Kipps talked in fragments of all sorts of matters, telling particularly of the great things that were being done to make a man and a draper of him; how he had two new pairs of trousers and a black coat and four new shirts. And all the while his imagination was urging him to that unknown next step, and when he was alone and in the dark he became even an enterprising wooer. It became evident to him that it would be nice to take Ann by the hand; even the decorous novelettes Sid affected egged him on to that greater nearness of intimacy.

Then a great idea came to him, in a paragraph called 'Lovers' Tokens' that he read in a torn fragment of *Tit-Bits*.[6] It fell into the measure of his courage – a divided sixpence! He secured his aunt's best scissors, fished a sixpence out of his jejune tin money-box, and jabbed his finger in a varied series of attempts to get it in half. When they met again the sixpence was still undivided. He had not intended to mention the matter to her at that stage, but it came up spontaneously. He endeavoured to explain the theory of broken sixpences and his unexpected failure to break one.

'But what you break it for?' said Ann. 'It's no good if it's broke.'

'It's a Token,' said Kipps.

'Like – ?'

'Oh, you keep half and I keep half, and when we're sep'rated you look at your half and I look at mine – see! Then we think of each other.'

'Oh!' said Ann, and appeared to assimilate this information.

'Only *I* can't get it in 'arf nohow,' said Kipps.

They discussed this difficulty for some time without illumination. Then Ann had a happy thought. 'Tell you what,' she said, starting away from him abruptly and laying a hand on his arm, 'you let *me* 'ave it, Artie. I know where father keeps his file.'

Kipps handed her the sixpence, and they came upon a pause.

'I'll easy do it,' said Ann.

In considering the sixpence side by side, his head had come near her cheek. Quite abruptly he was moved to take his next step into the unknown mysteries of love.

'Ann,' he said, and gulped at his temerity, 'I *do* love you. Straight. I'd do anything for you, Ann. Reely – I would.'

He paused for breath. She answered nothing, but she was no doubt enjoying herself. He came yet closer to her – his shoulder touched hers. 'Ann, I wish you'd – '

He stopped.

'What?' said Ann.

'Ann – lemme kiss you.'

Things seemed to hang for a space; his tone, the drop of his courage, made the thing incredible as he spoke. Kipps was not of that bold order of wooers who impose conditions.

Ann perceived that she was not prepared for kissing after all. Kissing, she said, was silly, and when Kipps would have displayed a belated enterprise, she flung away from him. He essayed argument. He stood afar off, as it were – the better part of a yard – and said she *might* let him kiss her, and then that he didn't see what good it was for her to be his girl if he couldn't kiss her.

She repeated that kissing was silly. A certain estrangement took them homeward. They arrived in the dusky High Street not exactly together, and not exactly apart, but struggling. They had not kissed, but all the guilt of kissing was between them. When Kipps saw the portly contours of his uncle standing dimly in the shop doorway, his footsteps faltered, and the space between our young couple increased. Above, the window over Pornick's shop was open, and Mrs Pornick was visible, taking the air. Kipps assumed an expression of extreme innocence. He found himself face to face with his uncle's advanced outposts of waistcoat buttons.

'Where ye bin, my boy?'

'Bin for a walk, uncle.'

'Not along of that brat of Pornick's?'

'Along of who?'

'That gell' – indicating Ann with his pipe.

'Oh, no, uncle!' – very faintly.

'Run in, my boy.'

Old Kipps stood aside, with an oblique glance upward, and his nephew brushed clumsily by him and vanished out of sight of the street into the vague obscurity of the little shop. The door closed behind old Kipps with a nervous jangle of its bell, and he set himself to light the single oil lamp that illuminated his shop at nights. It was an operation requiring care and watching, or else it flared and 'smelt'. Often it smelt after all. Kipps for some reason found the dusky living-room with his aunt in it too populous for his feelings, and went upstairs.

'That brat of Pornick's!' It seemed to him that a horrible catastrophe had occurred. He felt he had identified himself inextricably with his uncle, and cut himself off from her for ever by saying 'Oh, no!' At supper he was so visibly depressed that his aunt asked him if he wasn't feeling well. Under this imminent threat of medicine he assumed an unnatural cheerfulness . . .

He lay awake for nearly half an hour that night, groaning because things had all gone wrong – because Ann wouldn't let him kiss her, and because his uncle had called her a brat. It seemed to Kipps almost as though he himself had called her a brat –

There came an interval during which Ann was altogether inaccessible. One, two, three days passed, and he did not see her. Sid he met several times; they went fishing, and twice they bathed; but though Sid lent and received back two further love stories, they talked no more of love. They kept themselves in accord, however, agreeing that the most flagrantly sentimental story was 'proper'. Kipps was always wanting to speak of Ann, but never daring to do so. He saw her on Sunday evening going off to chapel. She was more beautiful than ever in her Sunday clothes, but she pretended not to see him because her mother was with her. But he thought she pretended not to see him because she had given him up for ever. Brat! – who could be expected ever to forgive that? He abandoned himself to despair, he ceased even to haunt the places where she might be found . . .

With paralysing unexpectedness came the end.

Mr Shalford, the draper at Folkestone to whom he was to be bound apprentice, had expressed a wish to 'shape the lad a bit' before the autumn sale. Kipps became aware that his box was being packed, and gathered the full truth of things on the evening before his departure. He became feverishly eager to see Ann just once more. He made silly and needless excuses to go out into the yard, he walked three times across the street without any excuse at all, to look up at the Pornick windows. Still she was hidden. He grew desperate. It was within half an hour of his departure that he came on Sid.

'Hello!' he said; 'I'm orf!'

'Business?'

'Yes.'

Pause.

'I say, Sid. You going 'ome?'

'Straight now.'

'D'you mind? Ask Ann about that.'

'About what?'

'She'll know.'

And Sid said he would. But even that, it seemed, failed to evoke Ann.

At last the Folkestone bus rumbled up, and he ascended. His aunt stood in the doorway to see him off. His uncle assisted with the box and portmanteau. Only furtively could he glance up at the Pornick windows, and still it seemed Ann hardened her heart against him. 'Get up!' said the driver, and the hoofs began to clatter. No – she would not come out even to see him off. The bus was in motion, and old Kipps was going back into his shop. Kipps stared in front of him, assuring himself that he did not care.

He heard a door slam, and instantly craned out his neck to look back. He knew that slam so well. Behold! out of the haberdasher's door a small, untidy figure in homely pink print had shot resolutely into the road and was sprinting in pursuit. In a dozen seconds she was abreast of the bus. At the sight of her Kipps's heart began to beat very quickly, but he made no immediate motion of recognition.

'Artie!' she cried breathlessly. 'Artie! Artie! You know! I got *that*!'

The bus was already quickening its pace, and leaving her behind again, when Kipps realised what 'that' meant. He became animated, he gasped, and, gathering his courage together, he mumbled an incoherent request to the driver to 'stop jest a jiff for sunthin' '. The driver grunted, as the disparity of their years demanded, and then the bus had pulled up, and Ann was below.

She leapt up upon the wheel. Kipps looked down into Ann's face, and it was foreshortened and resolute. He met her eyes just for one second as their hands touched. He was not a reader of eyes. Something passed quickly from hand to hand, something that the driver, alert at the corner of his eye, was not allowed to see. Kipps hadn't a word to say, and all she said was, 'I done it, 'smorning.' It was like a blank space in which something pregnant should have been written and wasn't. Then she dropped down, and the bus moved forward.

After the lapse of about ten seconds it occurred to him to stand and wave his new bowler hat at her over the corner of the bus top, and to shout hoarsely, 'Goo'bye, Ann! Don' forget me – while I'm away!'

She stood in the road looking after him, and presently she waved her hand.

He remained standing unstably, his bright, flushed face looking back at her, and his hair fluffing in the wind, and he waved his hat until at last the bend of the road hid her from his eyes. Then he turned about and sat down, and presently he began to put the half sixpence he held clenched in his hand into his trouser pocket. He looked sideways at the driver, to judge how much he had seen.

Then he fell a-thinking. He resolved that, come what might, when he came back to New Romney at Christmas, he would by hook or by crook kiss Ann.

Then everything would be perfect and right, and he would be perfectly happy.

The Emporium

When Kipps left New Romney, with a small yellow tin box, a still smaller portmanteau, a new umbrella and a keepsake half-sixpence, to become a draper, he was a youngster of fourteen, thin, with whimsical drakes' tails at the poll of his head, smallish features and eyes that were sometimes very light and sometimes very dark, gifts those of his birth; and by the nature of his training he was indistinct in his speech, confused in his mind and retreating in his manners. Inexorable fate had appointed him to serve his country in commerce, and the same national bias towards private enterprise and leaving bad alone, which entrusted his general education to Mr Woodrow, now indentured him firmly into the hands of Mr Shalford, of the Folkestone Drapery Bazaar. Apprenticeship is still the recognised English way to the distributing branch of the social service. If Mr Kipps had been so unfortunate as to have been born a German he might have been educated in an elaborate and costly special school ('over-educated – crammed up' – old Kipps) to fit him for his end – such being their pedagogic way. He might . . . But why make unpatriotic reflections in a novel? There was nothing pedagogic about Mr Shalford.

He was an irascible, energetic little man with hairy hands, for the most part under his coat-tails, a long, shiny, bald head, a pointed aquiline nose a little askew, and a neatly trimmed beard. He walked lightly and with a confident jerk, and he was given to humming. He had added to exceptional business 'push', bankruptcy under the old dispensation and judicious matrimony. His establishment was now one of the most considerable in Folkestone, and he insisted on every inch of frontage by alternate stripes of green and yellow down the houses over the shops. His shops were numbered 3, 5 and 7 on the street, and on his billheads '3 to 7'. He encountered the abashed and awestricken Kipps with the praises of his System and himself. He spread himself out behind his desk with a grip on the lapels of his coat and made Kipps a sort of speech. 'We expect y'r to work, y'r know, and we expect y'r to study our interests,' explained Mr Shalford in the regal and commercial plural. 'Our System here is the best system y'r could have. I made it, and I ought to know. I began at the very bottom of the ladder when I was fourteen, and there isn't a step in it I don't know. Not a step. Mr Booch in the desk will give y'r the card of rules and fines. Jest wait a minute.' He pretended to be busy with some dusty memoranda under a paperweight, while Kipps stood in a sort of paralysis of awe regarding his new master's oval baldness. 'Two thous'n' three forty-seven pounds,' whispered Mr Shalford audibly, feigning forgetfulness of Kipps. Clearly a place of great transactions!

Mr Shalford rose, and handing Kipps a blotting-pad and an inkpot to carry – mere symbols of servitude, for he made no use of them – emerged into a counting-house where three clerks had been feverishly busy ever since his door handle had turned. 'Booch,' said Mr Shalford, ' 'ave y'r copy of the rules?' and a downtrodden, shabby little old man, with a ruler in one hand and a quill pen in his mouth, silently held out a small book with green and yellow covers, mainly devoted, as Kipps presently discovered, to a voracious system of fines. He became acutely aware that his hands were full, and that everybody was staring at him. He hesitated a moment before putting the inkpot down to free a hand.

'Mustn't fumble like *that*,' said Mr Shalford as Kipps pocketed the rules. 'Won't do here. Come along, come along,' and he cocked his coat-tails high, as a lady might hold up her dress, and led the way into the shop.

A vast interminable place it seemed to Kipps, with unending shining counters and innumerable faultlessly dressed young men and presently houri-like young women staring at him. Here there was a long vista of gloves dangling from overhead rods, there ribbons and baby-linen. A short young lady in black mittens was making out the account of a customer, and was clearly confused in her addition by Shalford's eagle eye.

A thickset young man with a bald head and a round, very wise face, who was profoundly absorbed in adjusting all the empty chairs down the counter to absolutely equal distances, awoke out of his preoccupation and answered respectfully to a few Napoleonic and quite unnecessary remarks from his employer. Kipps was told that this young man's name was Mr Buggins, and that he was to do whatever Mr Buggins told him to do.

They came round a corner into a new smell, which was destined to be the smell of Kipps's life for many years, the vague, distinctive smell of Manchester goods.[7] A fat man with a large nose jumped – actually jumped – at their appearance, and began to fold a pattern of damask in front of him exactly like an automaton that is suddenly set going.

'Carshot, see to this boy tomorrow,' said the master. 'See he don't fumble. Smart'n 'im up.'

'Yussir,' said Carshot fatly, glanced at Kipps, and resumed his pattern-folding with extreme zeal.

'Whatever Mr Carshot says y'r to do, ye *do*,' said Mr Shalford, trotting onward; and Carshot blew out his face with an appearance of relief.

They crossed a large room full of the strangest things Kipps had ever seen. Ladylike figures, surmounted by black wooden knobs in the place of the refined heads one might have reasonably expected, stood about with a lifelike air of conscious fashion.

'Costume room,' said Shalford.

Two voices engaged in some sort of argument – 'I can assure you, Miss Mergle, you are entirely mistaken – entirely, in supposing I should do anything so unwomanly' – sank abruptly, and they discovered two young ladies, taller and fairer than any of the other young ladies, and with black trains to their dresses, who were engaged in writing at a little table. Whatever they told him to do, Kipps gathered he was to do. He was also, he understood, to do whatever Carshot and Booch told him to do. And there were also Buggins and Mr Shalford. And not to forget or fumble!

They descended into a cellar called 'The Warehouse', and Kipps had an optical illusion of errand boys fighting. Some aerial voice said, 'Teddy!' and the illusion passed. He looked again, and saw quite clearly that they were packing parcels and always would be, and that the last thing in the world that they would or could possibly do was to fight. Yet he gathered from the remarks Mr Shalford addressed to their busy backs that they had been fighting – no doubt at some past period of their lives.

Emerging in the shop again among a litter of toys and what are called 'fancy articles', Shalford withdrew a hand from beneath his coat-tails to indicate an overhead change-carrier. He entered into elaborate calculations to show how many minutes in one year were saved thereby, and lost himself among the figures. 'Seven tums eight seven nine – was it? Or seven eight nine? Now, *now*! Why, when I was a boy your age I c'd do a sum like that as soon as hear it. We'll soon get y'r into better shape than that. Make you Fishent. Well, y'r must take my word it comes to pounds and pounds saved in the year – pounds and pounds. System! System everywhere. Fishency.' He went on murmuring 'Fishency' and 'System' at intervals for some time.

They passed into a yard, and Mr Shalford waved his hand at his three delivery vans all striped green and yellow – 'uniform – green, yell'r – System.' All over the premises were pinned absurd little cards, 'This door locked after 7:30. By order, Edwin Shalford', and the like.

Mr Shalford always wrote 'By order', though it conveyed no earthly meaning to him. He was one of those people who collect technicalities upon them as the Reduvius bug collects dirt. He was the sort of man who is not only ignorant, but absolutely incapable of English. When he wanted to say he had a sixpenny-ha'penny longcloth to sell, he put it thus to startled customers: 'Can DO you one six half, if y' like.' He always omitted pronouns and articles and so forth; it seemed to him the very essence of the efficiently businesslike. His only preposition was 'as' or the compound 'as per'. He abbreviated every word he could; he would have considered himself the laughing-stock of Wood Street if he had chanced to spell *socks* in any way but 'sox'. But, on the other hand, if he saved words here, he wasted them there: he never acknowledged an order that was not an esteemed favour, nor sent a pattern without begging to submit it. He never stipulated for so many months' credit, but bought in November 'as Jan'. It was not only words he abbreviated in his London communications. In paying his wholesalers his 'System' admitted of a constant error in the discount of a penny or twopence, and it 'facilitated business', he alleged, to ignore odd pence in the cheques he wrote. His ledger clerk was so struck with the beauty of this part of the System, that he started a private one on his own account with the stamp box that never came to Shalford's knowledge.

This admirable British merchant would glow with a particular pride of intellect when writing his London orders.

'Ah! do y'r think *you'll* ever be able to write London orders?' he would say with honest pride to Kipps, waiting impatiently long after closing time to take these triumphs of commercial efficiency to post, and so end the interminable day.

Kipps shook his head, anxious for Mr Shalford to get on.

'Now, here, f'example, I've written – see? – "1 piece 1 in cott blk elas 1/ or". What do I mean by that *or*, eh? – d'ye know?'

Kipps promptly hadn't the faintest idea.

'And then, "2 ea silk net as per patts herewith"; *ea*, eh?'

'Dunno, sir.'

It was not Mr Shalford's way to explain things. 'Dear, dear! Pity you couldn't get some c'mercial education at your school. 'Stid of all this lit'ry stuff. Well, my boy, if y'r not a bit sharper y'll never write London orders, *that's* pretty plain. Jest stick stamps on all those letters, and mind y'r stick 'em right way up, and try and profit a little more by the opportunities your aunt and uncle have provided ye. Can't say *what*'ll happen t'ye if ye don't.'

And Kipps, tired, hungry and belated, set about stamping with vigour and despatch.

'Lick the *envelope*,' said Mr Shalford, 'lick the *envelope*,' as though he grudged the youngster the postage-stamp gum. 'It's the little things mount up,' he would say; and, indeed, that was his philosophy of life – to bustle and save, always to bustle and save. His political creed linked Reform, which meant nothing, with Efficiency, which meant a sweated service, and Economy, which meant a sweated expenditure, and his conception of a satisfactory municipal life was to 'keep down the rates'. Even his religion was to save his soul, and to preach a similar cheese-paring to the world.

2

The indentures that bound Kipps to Mr Shalford were antique and complex: they insisted on the latter gentleman's parental privileges; they forbade Kipps to dice and game; they made him over body and soul to Mr Shalford for seven long years, the crucial years of his life. In return there were vague stipulations about teaching the whole art and mystery of the trade to him; but as there was no penalty attached to negligence, Mr Shalford, being a sound, practical businessman, considered this a mere rhetorical flourish, and set himself assiduously to get as much out of Kipps and to put as little into him as he could in the seven years of their intercourse.

What he put into Kipps was chiefly bread and margarine, infusions of chicory and tea-dust, colonial meat by contract at threepence a pound, potatoes by the sack and watered beer. If, however, Kipps chose to buy any supplementary material for growth, Mr Shalford had the generosity to place his kitchen resources at his disposal free – if the fire chanced to be going. He was also allowed to share a bedroom with eight other young Englishmen, and to sleep in a bed which, except in very severe weather, could be made with the help of his overcoat and private under-linen, not to mention newspapers, quite sufficiently warm for any reasonable soul. In addition, Kipps was taught the list of fines; and how to tie up parcels; to know where goods were kept in Mr Shalford's systematised shop; to hold his hands extended upon the counter and to repeat such phrases as, 'What can I have the pleasure . . . ?' 'No trouble, I 'ssure you,' and the like; to block, fold and measure materials of all sorts; to lift his hat from his head when he passed Mr Shalford abroad, and to practise a servile obedience to a large number of people. But he was not, of course, taught the 'cost' mark of the goods he sold, nor anything of the method of buying such goods. Nor was his attention directed to the unfamiliar social habits and fashions to which his trade ministered. The use of half the goods he saw sold and was presently to assist in selling he did not understand: materials for hangings, cretonnes, chintzes, and the like; serviettes and all the bright, hard whitewear of a well-ordered house; pleasant dress materials, linings, stiffenings – they were to him from first to last no more than things heavy and difficult to handle in bulk, that one folded up, unfolded, cut in lengths and saw dwindle and pass away out into that mysterious happy world in which the Customer dwells. Kipps hurried from piling linen tablecloths, that were collectively as heavy as lead, to eat off oilcloth in a gas-lit dining-room underground; and he dreamt of combing endless blankets beneath his overcoat, spare undershirt and three newspapers. So he had at least the chance of learning the beginnings of philosophy.

In return for these benefits he worked so that he commonly went to bed exhausted and footsore. His round began at half-past six in the morning, when he would descend unwashed and shirtless, in old clothes and a scarf, and dust boxes and yawn, and take down wrappers and clean the windows until eight. Then in half an hour he would complete his toilet and take an austere breakfast of bread and margarine and what only an Imperial Englishman would admit to be coffee, after which refreshment he ascended to the shop for the labours of the day.

Commonly these began with a mighty running to and fro with planks and boxes and goods for Carshot, the window-dresser, who, whether he worked well or ill, nagged persistently by reason of a chronic in-digestion, until the window was done. Sometimes the costume window had to be dressed, and then Kipps staggered down the whole length of the shop from the costume room with one after another of those ladylike shapes grasped firmly, but shamefully, each about her single ankle of wood. Such days as there was no window-dressing, there was a mighty carrying and lifting of blocks and bales of goods into piles and stacks. After this there were terrible exercises, at first almost despairfully difficult: certain sorts of goods that came in folded had to be rolled upon rollers, and for the most part refused absolutely to be rolled, at any rate by Kipps; and certain other sorts of goods that came from the wholesalers rolled had to be measured and folded, which folding makes young apprentices wish they were dead. All of it, too, quite avoidable trouble, you know, that is not avoided because of the cheapness of the genteeler sorts of labour and the dearness of forethought in the world. And then consignments of new goods had to be marked off and packed into proper parcels; and Carshot packed like conjuring tricks, and Kipps packed like a boy with tastes in some other direction – not ascertained. And always Carshot nagged . . .

He had a curious formula of appeal to his visceral economy, had Carshot, that the refinement of the times and the earnest entreaties of my friends oblige me to render by an etiolated paraphrase.

'My Heart and Liver! I never see such a boy,' so I present Carshot's refrain; and even when he was within a foot or so of the customer's face the disciplined ear of Kipps would still at times develop a featureless, intercalary murmur into – well, 'My Heart and Liver!'

There came a blessed interval when Kipps was sent abroad 'matching'. This consisted chiefly in supplying unexpected defects in buttons, ribbon, lining, and so forth in the dressmaking department. He was given a written paper of orders with patterns pinned thereto, and discharged into the sunshine and interest of the street. Then, until he thought it wise to return and stand the racket of his delay, he was a free man, clear of all reproach.

He made remarkable discoveries in topography, as, for example, that the most convenient way from the establishment of Mr Adolphus Davis to the establishment of Messrs Plummer, Roddis & Tyrrel, two of his principal places of call, is not as is generally supposed down the Sandgate Road, but up the Sandgate Road, round by West Terrace and along the Leas to the lift, watch the lift up and down *twice*, but not longer, because that wouldn't do, back along the Leas, watch the harbour for a short time, and then round by the churchyard, and so (hurrying) into Church Street and Rendezvous Street. But on some exceptionally fine days the route lay through Radnor Park to the pond where the little boys sail ships and there are interesting swans.

He would return to find the shop settling down to the business of serving customers. And now he had to stand by to furnish any help that was necessary to the seniors who served, to carry parcels and bills about the shop, to clear away 'stuff' after each engagement, to hold up curtains until his arms ached, and, what was more difficult than all, to do nothing, and not stare disconcertingly at customers when there was nothing for him to do. He plumbed an abyss of boredom, or stood a mere carcase, with his mind far away fighting the enemies of the Empire, or steering a dream ship perilously into unknown seas. To be recalled sharply to our higher civilisation by some bustling senior's, 'Nar then, Kipps. *Look* alive! Ketch 'old. (My Heart and Liver!)'

At half-past seven o'clock – except on late nights – a feverish activity of 'straightening up' began, and when the last shutter was up outside,

Kipps with the speed of an arrow leaving a bow would start hanging wrappers over the fixtures and over the piles of wares upon the counters, preparatory to a vigorous scattering of wet sawdust and the sweeping out of the shop.

Sometimes people would stay long after the shop was closed – 'They don't mind a bit at Shalford's,' these ladies used to say – it is always ladies do this sort of thing – and while they loitered it was forbidden to touch a wrapper, or take any measures to conclude the day until the doors closed behind them.

Mr Kipps would watch these later customers from the shadow of a stack of goods, and death and disfigurement was the least he wished for them. Rarely much later than nine, a supper of bread and cheese and watered beer awaited him upstairs, and, that consumed, the rest of the day was entirely at his disposal for reading, recreation and the improvement of his mind . . .

The front door was locked at half-past ten, and the gas in the dormitory extinguished at eleven.

3

On Sundays he was obliged to go to church once, and commonly he went twice, for there was nothing else to do. He sat in the free seats at the back; he was too shy to sing, and not always clever enough to keep his place in the Prayer Book, and he rarely listened to the sermon. But he had developed a sort of idea that going to church had a tendency to alleviate life. His aunt wanted to have him confirmed, but he evaded this ceremony for some years.

In the intervals between services he walked about Folkestone with an air of looking for something. Folkestone was not so interesting on Sundays as on weekdays, because the shops were shut; but on the other hand there was a sort of confusing brilliance along the front of the Leas in the afternoon. Sometimes the apprentice next above him would condescend to go with him; but when the apprentice next but one above him condescended to go with the apprentice next above him, then Kipps, being habited as yet in ready-made clothes without tails, and unsuitable therefore to appear in such company, went alone.

Sometimes he would strike out into the country – still as if looking for something he missed – but the rope of meal-times haled him home again; and sometimes he would invest the major portion of the weekly allowance of a shilling that old Booch handed out to him in a sacred concert on the pier. He would sometimes walk up and down the Leas between twenty and thirty times after supper, desiring much the courage to speak to some other person in the multitude similarly employed. Almost invariably he ended his Sunday footsore.

He never read a book; there were none for him to read, and besides, in spite of Mr Woodrow's guidance through a cheap and cheaply annotated edition of *The Tempest* (English Literature), he had no taste that way; he never read any newspapers, except occasionally *Tit-Bits* or a ha'penny 'comic'. His chief intellectual stimulus was an occasional argy-bargy that sprang up between Carshot and Buggins at dinner. Kipps listened as if to unparalleled wisdom and wit, and treasured all the gems of repartee in his heart against the time when he, too, should be a Buggins and have the chance and courage for speech.

At times there came breaks in this routine – sale times, darkened by extra toil and work past midnight, but brightened by a sprat supper and some shillings in the way of 'premiums'. And every year – not now and then, but every year – Mr Shalford, with parenthetic admiration of his own generosity and glancing comparisons with the austerer days when *he* was apprenticed, conceded Kipps no less than ten days' holiday – ten whole days every year! Many a poor soul at Portland might well envy the fortunate Kipps. Insatiable heart of man! but how those days were grudged and counted as they snatched themselves away from him one after another!

Once a year came stocktaking and at intervals gusts of 'marking off' goods newly arrived. Then the splendours of Mr Shalford's being shone with oppressive brilliancy. 'System!' he would say, 'system. Come! *'ussel!'* and issue sharp, confusing, contradictory orders very quickly. Carshot trotted about, confused, perspiring, his big nose up in the air, his little eye on Mr Shalford, his forehead crinkled, his lips always going to the formula, 'Oh, my Heart and Liver!' The smart junior and the second apprentice vied with one another in obsequious alacrity. The smart junior aspired to Carshot's position, and that made him almost violently subservient to Shalford. They all snapped at Kipps. Kipps held the blotting-pad and the safety inkpot and a box of tickets, and ran and fetched things. If he put the ink down before he went to fetch things Mr Shalford usually knocked it over, and if he took it away Mr Shalford wanted it before he returned. 'You make my tooth ache, Kipps,' Mr Shalford would say. 'You gimme n'ralgia. You got no more System in you than a bad potato.' And at the times when Kipps carried off the inkpot, Mr Shalford would become purple in the face and jab round with his dry pen at imaginary inkpots and swear, and Carshot would stand and vociferate, and the smart junior would run to the corner of the department and vociferate, and the second apprentice would pursue Kipps, vociferating, 'Look Alive, Kipps! Look Alive! Ink, Man! Ink!'

A vague self-disgust, that shaped itself as an intense hate of Shalford and all his fellow creatures, filled the soul of Kipps during these periods of storm and stress. He felt that the whole business was unjust and idiotic, but the why and the wherefore were too much for his unfortunate brain. His mind was a welter. One desire, the desire to dodge some at least of a pelting storm of disagreeable comment, guided him through a fumbling performance of his duties. His disgust was infinite! It was not decreased by the inflamed ankles and sore feet that form a normal incident in the business of making an English draper; and the senior apprentice, Minton, a gaunt, sullen-faced youngster with close-cropped, wiry, black hair, a loose, ugly mouth, and a moustache like a smudge of ink, directed his attention to deeper aspects of the question and sealed his misery.

'When you get too old to work they chuck you away,' said Minton. 'Lor! you find old drapers everywhere – tramps, beggars, dock labourers, bus conductors – Quod. Anywhere but in a crib.'

'Don't they get shops of their own?'

'Lord! '*Ow* are they to get shops of their own? They 'aven't any capital! How's a draper's shopman to save up five hundred pounds even? I tell you it can't be done. You got to stick to cribs until it's over. I tell you we're in a blessed drainpipe, and we've got to crawl along it till we die.'

The idea that fermented perpetually in the mind of Minton was to 'hit the little beggar slap in the eye' – the little beggar being Mr Shalford – 'and see how his blessed System met that.'

The threat filled Kipps with splendid anticipations whenever Shalford went marking off in Minton's department. He would look at Minton and look at Shalford, and decide where he would best like Shalford hit . . . But for reasons known to himself Shalford never pished and tushed with Minton as he did at the harmless Carshot, and this interesting experiment upon the System was never attempted.

There were times when Kipps would lie awake, all others in the dormitory asleep and snoring, and think dismally of the outlook Minton pictured. Dimly he perceived the thing that had happened to him – how the great, stupid machine of retail trade had caught his life into its wheels, a vast, irresistible force which he had neither strength of will nor knowledge to escape. This was to be his life until his days should end. No adventures, no glory, no change, no freedom. Neither – though the force of that came home to him later – might he dream of effectual love and marriage. And there was a terrible something called the 'swap', or 'the key of the street', and 'crib hunting', of which the talk was scanty but sufficient. Night after night he would resolve to enlist, to run away to sea, to set fire to the warehouse, or drown himself; and morning after morning he rose up and hurried downstairs in fear of a sixpenny fine. He would compare his dismal round of servile drudgery with those windy, sunlit days at Littlestone, those windows of happiness shining ever brighter as they receded. The little figure of Ann seemed in all these windows now.

She, too, had happened on evil things. When Kipps went home for the first Christmas after he was bound, that great suspended resolve of his to kiss her flared up to hot determination, and he hurried out and whistled in the yard. There was a still silence, and then old Kipps appeared behind him.

'It's no good your whistling there, my boy,' said old Kipps in a loud, clear tone, designed to be audible over the wall. 'They've cleared out all you 'ad any truck with. *She*'s gone as help to Ashford, my boy. *Help!* Slavey is what we used to call 'em, but times are changed. Wonder they didn't say lady-'elp while they was about it. It 'ud be like 'em.'

And Sid? Sid had gone, too. 'Arrand boy or somethink,' said old Kipps. 'To one of these here brasted bicycle shops.'

'*Has* 'e!' said Kipps, with a feeling that he had been gripped about the chest, and he turned quickly and went indoors.

Old Kipps, still supposing him present, went on to further observations of an anti-Pornick tendency.

When Kipps got upstairs safe in his own bedroom, he sat down on the bed and stared at nothing. They were caught – they were all caught. All life took on the hue of one perpetual, dismal Monday morning. The Hurons were scattered, the wrecks and the beach had passed away from him, the sun of those warm evenings at Littlestone had set for evermore . . .

The only pleasure left for the brief remainder of his holiday after that was to think he was not in the shop. Even that was transient. Two more days – one more day – half a day. When he went back there were one or two very dismal nights indeed. He went so far as to write home some vague intimation of his feelings about business and his prospects, quoting Minton. But Mrs Kipps answered him, 'Did he want the Pornicks to say he wasn't good enough to be a draper?' This dreadful possibility was of course conclusive in the matter. No, he resolved they should not say he failed at that.

He derived much help from a 'manly' sermon delivered in an enormous voice by a large, fat, sun-red clergyman, just home from a colonial bishopric he had resigned on the plea of ill-health, exhorting him that whatever his hand found to do, he was to do with all his might; and the revision of his catechism preparatory to his confirmation reminded him that it behoved him to do his duty in that state of life into which it had pleased God to call him.

After a time the sorrows of Kipps grew less acute, and save for a miracle the brief tragedy of his life was over. He subdued himself to his position even as his Church required of him, seeing moreover no way out of it.

The earliest mitigation of his lot was that his soles and ankles became indurated to the perpetual standing. The next was an unexpected weekly whiff of freedom that came every Thursday. Mr Shalford, after a brave stand for what he called 'Innyvishal lib'ty' and the 'Idea of my System', a stand which he explained he made chiefly on patriotic grounds, was at last, under pressure of certain of his customers, compelled to fall in line with the rest of the local Early Closing Association,[8] and Mr Kipps could emerge in daylight and go where he listed for long, long hours. Moreover, Minton, the pessimist, reached the end of his appointed time and left – to enlist in a cavalry regiment and go about this planet leading an insubordinate but interesting life, that ended at last in an intimate, vivid and really, you know, by no means painful or tragic night grapple in the Terah Valley. In a little while Kipps cleaned windows no longer; he was serving customers (of the less important sort) and taking goods out on approval; and presently he was third apprentice, and his moustache was visible, and there were three apprentices whom he might legally snub and cuff. But one was (most dishonestly) too big to cuff in spite of his greener years . . .

There came still other distractions, the natural distractions of adolescence, to take his mind off the inevitable. His costume, for example, began to interest him more; he began to realise himself as a visible object, to find an interest in the costume-room mirrors and the eyes of the girl apprentices.

In this he was helped by counsel and example. Pierce, his immediate senior, was by way of being what was called a Masher,[9] and preached his cult. During slack times grave discussions about collars, ties, the cut of trouser legs and the proper shape of a boot-toe, were held in the Manchester department. In due course, Kipps went to a tailor, and his short jacket was replaced by a morning coat with tails. Stirred by this, he purchased at his own expense three stand-up collars to replace his former turndown ones. They were nearly three inches high, higher than those Pierce wore, and they made his neck quite sore and left a red mark under his ears . . . So equipped, he found himself fit company even for this fashionable apprentice, who had now succeeded Minton in his seniority.

Most potent help of all in the business of forgetting his cosmic disaster was this, that so soon as he was in tail coats the young ladies of the establishment began to discover that he was no longer a 'horrid little boy'. Hitherto they had tossed heads at him and kept him in his place. Now they discovered that he was a 'nice boy', which is next door at least to being a 'feller', and in some ways even preferable. It is painful to record that his fidelity to Ann failed at their first onset. I am fully sensible how entirely better this story would be from a sentimental point of view if he had remained true to that early love. Only then it would have been a different story altogether. And at least Kipps was thus far true, that with none of these later loves was there any of that particular quality that linked Ann's flushed face and warmth and the inner things of life so inseparably together. Though they were not without emotions of various sorts.

It was one of the young ladies in the costume-room who first showed by her manner that he was a visible object and capable of exciting interest. She talked to him, she encouraged him to talk to her, she lent him a book she possessed, and darned a sock for him, and said she would be his elder sister. She allowed him to escort her to church with a great air of having induced him to go. Then she investigated his eternal welfare, overcame a certain affectation of virile indifference to religion and extorted a promise that he would undergo 'confirmation'. This excited the other young lady in the costumes, her natural rival, and she set herself with great charm and subtlety to the capture of the ripening heart of Kipps. She took a more worldly line. She went for a walk with him to the pier on Sunday afternoon, and explained to him how a gentleman must always walk 'outside' a lady on a pavement, and how all gentlemen wore, or at least carried, gloves, and generally the broad beginnings of the British social ideal. Afterwards the ladies exchanged 'words', upon Sabbatical grounds. In this way was the *toga virilis* bestowed on Kipps, and he became recognised as a suitable object for that Platonic Eros whose blunted darts devastate even the very highest-class establishments. In this way, too, did that pervading ambition of the British young man to be if not a 'gentleman' at least mistakably like one take root in his heart.

He took to these new interests with quite natural and personal zest. He became initiated into the mysteries of 'flirting', and – at a slightly later stage, and with some leading hints from Pierce, who was of a communicative disposition in these matters – of the milder forms of 'spooning'. Very soon he was engaged. Before two years were out he had been engaged six times, and was beginning to be rather a desperate fellow, so far as he could make out. Desperate, but quite gentlemanly, be it understood, and without let or hindrance to the fact that he was, in four brief lessons, 'prepared' by a distant-mannered and gloomy young curate and 'confirmed' a member of the Established Church.

The engagements in drapery establishments do not necessarily involve a subsequent marriage. They are essentially more refined, less coarsely practical, and altogether less binding than the engagements of the vulgar rich. These young ladies do not like not to be engaged – it is so unnatural; and Mr Kipps was as easy to get engaged to as one could wish. There are, from the young lady's point of view, many conveniences in being engaged. You get an escort for church and walks and so forth. It is not quite the thing to walk abroad with a 'feller', much more to 'spoon' with him, when he is neither one's fiancé nor an adopted brother; it is considered either a little *fast*, or else as savouring of the 'walking-out' habits of the servant girls. Now, such is the sweetness of human charity, that the shop young lady in England has just the same horror of doing anything that savours of the servant girl as the lady journalist, let us say, has of anything savouring of the shop girl, or the really quite nice young lady has of anything savouring of any sort of girl who has gone down into the economic battlefield to earn herself a living . . . But the very deepest of these affairs was still among the shallow places of love; at best it was paddling where it is decreed that men must sink or swim. Of the deep and dangerous places, and of the huge buoyant lift of its waves, he tasted nothing. Affairs of clothes and vanities they were, jealousies about a thing said, flatteries and mutual boastings, climaxes in the answering grasp of hands, the temerarious use of Christian names, culminations in a walk, or a near confidence, or a little pressure more or less. Close-sitting on a seat after twilight, with some little fondling, was indeed the boldest of a lover's adventures, the utmost limit of his enterprises in the service of that stark Great Lady, who is daughter of Uranus and the sea. The 'young ladies' who reigned in his heart came and went like people in an omnibus: there was the vehicle, so to speak, upon the road, and they entered and left it without any cataclysm of emotion. For all that, this development of the sex interest was continuously very interesting to Kipps, and kept him going as much as anything through all these servile years . . .

6

For a tailpiece to this chapter one may vignette one of those little affairs.

It is a bright Sunday afternoon; the scene is a secluded little seat halfway down the front of the Leas, and Kipps is four years older than when he parted from Ann. There is a quite perceptible down upon his upper lip, and his costume is just as tremendous a 'mash' as lies within his means. His collar is so high that it scars his inaggressive jawbone, and his hat has a curly brim, his tie shows taste, his trousers are modestly brilliant, and his boots have light cloth uppers that button at the side. He jabs at the gravel before him with a cheap cane, and glances sideways at Flo Bates, the young lady from the cash desk. She is wearing a brilliant blouse and a gaily trimmed hat. There is an air of fashion about her that might disappear under the analysis of a woman of the world, but which is quite sufficient to make Kipps very proud to be distinguished as her particular 'feller', and to be allowed at temperate intervals to use her Christian name.

The conversation is light and gay in the modern style, and Flo keeps on smiling, good temper being her special charm.

'Ye see, you don' mean what *I* mean,' he is saying.

'Well, what do *you* mean?'

'Not what you mean!'

'Well, tell me.'

'*Ah!* That's another story.'

Pause. They look meaningly at one another.

'You *are* a one for being roundabout,' says the lady.

'Well, you're not so plain, you know.'

'Not plain?'

'No.'

'You don't mean to say I'm roundabout?'

'No. I mean to say . . . though – '

Pause.

'Well?'

'You're not a bit plain – you're' (his voice jumps up to a squeak) 'pretty. See?'

'Oh, get *out!*' her voice lifts also – with pleasure.

She strikes at him with her glove, then glances suddenly at a ring upon her finger. Her smile disappears momentarily. Another pause. Eyes meet and the smile returns.

'I wish I knew – ' says Kipps.

'Knew – ?'

'Where you got that ring.'

She lifts the hand with the ring until her eyes just show (very prettily) over it. 'You'd just *like* to know,' she says slowly, and smiles still more brightly with the sense of successful effect.

'I des say I could guess.'

'I des say you couldn't.'

'Couldn't I?'

'No!'

'Guess it in three.'

'Not the name.'

'Ah!'

'*Ah!*'

'Well, anyhow, lemme look at it.'

He looks at it.

Pause. Giggles, slight struggle, and a slap on Kipps's coat-sleeve. A passer-by appears down the path, and she hastily withdraws her hand.

She glances at the face of the approaching man. They maintain a bashful silence until he has passed . . .

CHAPTER THREE

The Wood-Carving Class

Though these services to Venus Epipontia, the seaside Venus, and these studies in the art of dress, did much to distract his thoughts and mitigate his earlier miseries, it would be mere optimism to present Kipps as altogether happy. A vague dissatisfaction with life drifted about him and every now and again enveloped him like a sea fog. During these periods it was greyly evident that there was something, something vital in life, lacking. For no earthly reason that Kipps could discover, he was haunted by a suspicion that life was going wrong or had already gone wrong in some irrevocable way. The ripening self-consciousness of adolescence developed this into a clearly felt insufficiency. It was all very well to carry gloves, open doors, never say 'Miss' to a girl, and walk 'outside', but were there not other things, conceivably even deeper things, before the complete thing was attained? For example, certain matters of knowledge. He perceived great bogs of ignorance about him, fumbling traps, where other people, it was alleged, *real* gentlemen and ladies, for example, and the clergy, had knowledge and assurance, bogs which it was sometimes difficult to elude. A girl arrived in the millinery department who could, she said, *speak* French and German. She snubbed certain advances, and a realisation of inferiority blistered Kipps. But he tried to pass the thing off as a joke by saying, 'Parlez-vous Francey,' whenever he met her, and inducing the junior apprentice to say the same.

He even made some dim half-secret experiments towards remedying the deficiencies he suspected. He spent five shillings on five serial numbers of a *Home Educator*,[10] and bought (and even thought of reading) a Shakespeare and a Bacon's *Advancement of Learning* and the poems of Herrick from a chap who was hard up. He battled with Shakespeare all one Sunday afternoon, and found the 'English Literature' with which Mr Woodrow had equipped him had vanished down some crack in his mind. He had no doubt it was very splendid stuff, but he couldn't quite make out what it was all about. There was an occult meaning, he knew, in literature, and he had forgotten it. Moreover, he discovered one day, while taunting the junior apprentice with ignorance, that his 'rivers of England' had also slipped his memory, and he laboriously restored that fabric of rote learning: 'Ty Wear Tees 'Umber . . . '

I suppose some such phase of discontent is a normal thing in every adolescence. The ripening mind seeks something upon which its will may crystallise, upon which its discursive emotions, growing more abundant with each year of life, may concentrate. For many, though not for all, it takes a religious direction, but in those particular years the mental atmosphere of Folkestone was exceptionally free from any revivalistic disturbance that might have reached Kipps's mental being. Sometimes they fall in love. I have known this uneasiness end in different cases in a vow to read one book (not a novel) every week, to read the Bible through in a year, to pass in the Honours division of the London Matriculation examination, to become an accomplished chemist, and never more to tell a lie. It led Kipps finally into Technical Education as we understand it in the south of England.

It was in the last year of his apprenticeship that he had pursued his researches after that missing qualification into the Folkestone Young Men's Association, where Mr Chester Coote prevailed. Mr Chester Coote was a young man of semi-independent means who inherited a share in a house agency, read Mrs Humphry Ward, and took an interest in social work. He was a whitish-faced young man with a prominent nose, pale blue eyes, and a quivering quality in his voice. He was very active upon committees; he was very prominent and useful on all social occasions, in evidence upon platforms and upon all those semi-public occasions when the Great descend. He lived with an only sister. To Kipps and his kind in the Young Men's Association he read a stimulating paper on 'Self-Help'.[11] He said it was the noblest of all our distinctive English characteristics, and he was very much down upon the 'over-educated' Germans. At the close a young German hairdresser made a few commendatory remarks which developed somehow into an oration on Hanoverian politics. As he became excited he became guttural and obscure; the meeting sniggered cheerfully at such ridiculous English, and Kipps was so much amused that he forgot a private project to ask this Chester Coote how he might set about a little self-help on his own private account in such narrow margins of time as the System of Mr Shalford spared him. But afterwards in the night-time it came to him again.

It was a few months later, and after his apprenticeship was over and Mr Shalford had with depreciatory observations taken him on as an improver at twenty pounds a year, that this question was revived by a casual article on Technical Education in a morning paper that a commercial traveller had left behind him. It played the role of the word in season. Something in the nature of conversion, a faint sort of concentration of purpose, really occurred in him then. The article was written with penetrating vehemence, and it stimulated him to the pitch of enquiring about the local Science and Art Classes, and after he had told everybody in the shop about it and taken the advice of all who supported his desperate resolution, he joined. At first he attended the class in Freehand, that being the subject taught on early-closing night; and he had already made some progress in that extraordinary routine of reproducing freehand 'copies' which for two generations had passed with English people for instruction in art, when the dates of the classes were changed. Thereby just as the March winds were blowing he was precipitated into the wood-carving class, and his mind diverted first to this useful and broadening pursuit, and then to its teacher.

2

The class in wood-carving was an extremely select class, conducted at that time by a young lady named Walshingham, and as this young lady was destined by fortune to teach Kipps a great deal more than wood carving, it will be well if the reader gets the picture of her correctly in mind. She was only a year or so older than he was; she had a pale, intellectual face, dark grey eyes and black hair, which she wore over her forehead in an original and striking way that she had adopted from a picture by Rossetti in the South Kensington Museum. She was slender, so that without ungainliness she had an effect of being tall, and her hands were shapely and white when they came into contrast with hands much exercised in rolling and blocking. She dressed in those loose and pleasant forms and those soft and tempered shades that arose in England in the socialistic-aesthetic epoch and remain to this day among us as the badge of those who read Turgenev's novels, scorn current fiction, and think on higher planes. I think she was as beautiful as most beautiful people, and to Kipps she was altogether beautiful. She had, Kipps learnt, matriculated at London University, an astounding feat to his imagination; and the masterly way in which she demonstrated how to prod and worry honest pieces of wood into useless and unedifying patterns in relief extorted his utmost admiration.

At first, when Kipps had learnt he was to be taught by a 'girl', he was inclined to resent it, the more so as Buggins had recently been very strong on the gross injustice of feminine employment.

'We have to keep wives,' said Buggins (though as a matter of fact he did not keep even one), 'and how are we to do it with a lot of girls coming in to take the work out of our mouths?'

Afterwards Kipps, in conjunction with Pierce, looked at it from another point of view, and thought it would be rather a 'lark'. Finally, when he saw her, and saw her teaching and coming nearer to him with an impressive deliberation, he was breathless with awe and the quality of her dark, slender femininity.

The class consisted of two girls and a maiden lady of riper years, friends of Miss Walshingham's, and anxious rather to support her in an interesting experiment than to become really expert wood-carvers; an oldish young man with spectacles and a black beard, who never spoke to anyone, and who was evidently too short-sighted to see his work as a whole; a small boy who was understood to have a 'gift' for wood-carving; and a lodging-house keeper who 'took classes' every winter, she told Mr Kipps, as though they were a tonic, and 'found they did her good'. And occasionally Mr Chester Coote – refined and gentlemanly – would come into the class, with or without papers, ostensibly on committee business, but in reality to talk to the less attractive one of the two girl students; and sometimes a brother of Miss Walshingham's, a slender, dark young man with a pale face, and fluctuating resemblances to the young Napoleon, would arrive just at the end of the class-time to see his sister home.

All these personages impressed Kipps with a sense of inferiority that in the case of Miss Walshingham became positively abysmal. The ideas and knowledge they appeared to have, their personal capacity and freedom, opened a new world to his imagination. These people came and went, with a sense of absolute assurance, against an overwhelming background of plaster casts, diagrams and tables, benches and a black-board – a background that seemed to him to be saturated with recondite knowledge and the occult and jealously guarded tips and secrets that constitute Art and the Higher Life. They went home, he imagined, to homes where the piano was played with distinction and freedom, and books littered the tables, and foreign languages were habitually used. They had complicated meals, no doubt – with serviettes. They 'knew etiquette', and how to avoid all the errors for which Kipps bought penny manuals, *What to Avoid*, *Common Errors in Speaking*, and the like. He knew nothing about it all – nothing whatever; he was a creature of the outer darkness blinking in an unsuspected light.

He heard them speak easily and freely to one another of examinations, of books and paintings, of 'last year's Academy' – a little contemptuously; and once, just at the end of the class-time, Mr Chester Coote and young Walshingham and the two girls argued about something or other called, he fancied, 'Vagner' or 'Vargner' – they seemed to say it both ways – which presently shaped itself more definitely as the name of a man who made up music. (Carshot and Buggins weren't in it with them.) Young Walshingham, it appeared, said something or other that was an 'epigram', and they all applauded him. Kipps, I say, felt himself a creature of outer darkness, an inexcusable intruder in an altitudinous world. When the epigram happened, he first of all smiled, to pretend he understood, and instantly suppressed the smile to show he did not listen. Then he became extremely hot and uncomfortable, though nobody had noticed either phase.

It was clear his only chance of concealing his bottomless baseness was to hold his tongue, and meanwhile he chipped with earnest care, and abased his soul before the very shadow of Miss Walshingham. She used to come and direct and advise him, with, he felt, an effort to conceal the scorn she had for him; and, indeed, it is true that at first she thought of him chiefly as the clumsy young man with the red ears.

And as soon as he emerged from the first effect of pure and awe-stricken humility – he was greatly helped to emerge from that condition to a perception of human equality by the need the lodging-house keeper was under to talk while she worked, and as she didn't like Miss Walshingham and her friends very much, and the young man with spectacles was deaf, she naturally talked to Kipps – he perceived that he was in a state of adoration for Miss Walshingham that it seemed almost a blasphemous familiarity to speak of as being in love.

This state, you must understand, had nothing to do with 'flirting' or 'spooning' and that superficial passion that flashes from eye to eye upon the leas and pier – absolutely nothing. That he knew from the first. Her rather pallid, intelligent young face, beneath those sombre clouds of hair, put her in a class apart; towards her the thought of 'attentions' paled and vanished. To approach such a being, to perform sacrifices and to perish obviously for her, seemed the limit he might aspire to, he or any man. For if his love was abasement, at any rate it had this much of manliness, that it covered all his sex. It had not yet come to Kipps to acknowledge any man as his better in his heart of hearts. When one does that the game is played and one grows old indeed.

The rest of his sentimental interests vanished altogether in this great illumination. He meditated about her when he was blocking cretonne; her image was before his eyes at teatime, and blotted out the more immediate faces, and made him silent and preoccupied, and so careless in his bearing that the junior apprentice, sitting beside him, mocked at and parodied his enormous bites of bread and butter unreproved. He became conspicuously less popular on the 'fancy' side, 'costumes' was chilly with him and 'millinery' cutting. But he did not care. An intermittent correspondence with Flo Bates, that had gone on since she left Mr Shalford's desk for a position at Tunbridge 'nearer home', and which had roused Kipps in its earlier stages to unparalleled heights of epistolatory effort, died out altogether by reason of his neglect. He heard with scarcely a pang that, as a consequence perhaps of his neglect, Flo was 'carrying on with a chap who managed a farm'.

Every Thursday he jabbed and gouged at his wood, jabbing and gouging intersecting circles and diamond traceries, and that laboured inane which our mad world calls ornament, and he watched Miss Walshingham furtively whenever she turned away. The circles in consequence were jabbed crooked, and his panels, losing their symmetry, became comparatively pleasing to the untrained eye – and once he jabbed his finger. He would cheerfully have jabbed all his fingers if he could have found some means of using the opening to express himself of the vague emotions that possessed him. But he shirked conversation just as earnestly as he desired it; he feared that profound general ignorance of his might appear.

3

There came a time when she could not open one of the classroom windows. The man with the black beard pored over his chipping heedlessly . . .

It did not take Kipps a moment to grasp his opportunity. He dropped his gouge and stepped forward. 'Lem *me*,' he said . . .

He could not open the window either!

'Oh, please don't trouble,' she said.

' 'Sno trouble,' he gasped.

Still the sash stuck. He felt his manhood was at stake. He gathered himself together for a tremendous effort, and the pane broke with a snap, and he thrust his hand into the void beyond.

'*There!*' said Miss Walshingham, and the glass fell ringing into the courtyard below.

Then Kipps made to bring his hand back, and felt the keen touch of the edge of the broken glass at his wrist. He turned dolefully. 'I'm tremendously sorry,' he said in answer to the accusation in Miss

Walshingham's eyes. 'I didn't think it would break like that' – as if he had expected it to break in some quite different and entirely more satisfactory manner. The boy with the gift for wood-carving, having stared at Kipps's face for a moment, became involved in a Laocoön struggle with a giggle.

'You've cut your wrist,' said one of the girl friends, standing up and pointing. She was a pleasant-faced, greatly freckled girl, with a helpful disposition, and she said, 'You've cut your wrist,' as brightly as if she had been a trained nurse.

Kipps looked down, and saw a swift line of scarlet rush down his hand. He perceived the other man student regarding this with magnified eyes. 'You *have* cut your wrist,' said Miss Walshingham, and Kipps regarded his damage with greater interest.

'He's cut his wrist,' said the maiden lady to the lodging-house keeper, and seemed in doubt what a lady should do. 'It's – ' she hesitated at the word 'bleeding', and nodded to the lodging-house keeper instead.

'Dreadfully,' said the maiden lady, and tried to look and tried not to look at the same time.

'Of *course* he's cut his wrist,' said the lodging-house keeper, momentarily quite annoyed at Kipps; and the other young lady, who thought Kipps rather common, went on quietly with her wood-cutting with an air of its being the proper thing to do – though nobody else seemed to know it.

'You must tie it up,' said Miss Walshingham.

'We must tie it up,' said the freckled girl.

'I 'adn't the slightest idea that window was going to break like that,' said Kipps, with candour. 'Nort the slightest.'

He glanced again at the blood on his wrist, and it seemed to him that it was on the very point of dropping on the floor of that cultured classroom. So he very neatly licked it off, feeling at the same time for his handkerchief. 'Oh, *don't!*' said Miss Walshingham as he did so, and the girl with the freckles made a movement of horror. The giggle got the better of the boy with the gift, and celebrated its triumph by unseemly noises; in spite of which it seemed to Kipps at the moment that the act that had made Miss Walshingham say, 'Oh, *don't!*' was rather a desperate and manly treatment of what was after all a creditable injury.

'It ought to be tied up,' said the lodging-house keeper, holding her chisel upright in her hand. 'It's a bad cut to bleed like that.'

'We must tie it up,' said the freckled girl, and hesitated in front of Kipps. 'Have you got a handkerchief?' she said.

'I dunno 'ow I managed *not* to bring one,' said Kipps. 'I – Not 'aving a cold I suppose some'ow I didn't think – '

He checked a further flow of blood.

The girl with the freckles caught Miss Walshingham's eye, and held it for a moment. Both glanced at Kipps's injury. The boy with the gift, who had reappeared with a chastened expression from some noisy pursuit beneath his desk, made the neglected motions of one who proffers shyly. Miss Walshingham under the spell of the freckled girl's eye produced a handkerchief. The voice of the maiden lady could be heard in the background. 'I've been through all the technical education ambulance classes twice, and I know you go *so* if it's a vein, and *so* if it's an artery – at least you go *so* for one and *so* for the other, whichever it may be; but . . . '

'If you will give me your hand,' said the freckled girl, and proceeded with Miss Walshingham's assistance to bandage Kipps in a most businesslike way. Yes, they actually bandaged Kipps. They pulled up his cuff – happily his cuffs were not a very frayed pair – and held his wrist, and wrapped the soft handkerchief round it, and tightened the knot together. And Miss Walshingham's face, the face of that almost divine Over-human,[12] came close to the face of Kipps.

'We're not hurting you, are we?' she said.

'Not a bit,' said Kipps, as he would have said if they had been sawing his arm off.

'We're not experts, you know,' said the freckled girl.

'I'm sure it's a dreadful cut,' said Miss Walshingham.

'It ain't much reely,' said Kipps; 'and you're taking a lot of trouble. I'm sorry I broke that window. I can't think what I could have been doing.'

'It isn't so much the cut at the time, it's the poisoning afterwards,' came the voice of the maiden lady.

'Of course I'm quite willing to pay for the window,' panted Kipps opulently.

'We must make it just as tight as possible, to stop the bleeding,' said the freckled girl.

'I don't think it's much reely,' said Kipps. 'I'm awful sorry I broke that window, though.'

'Put your finger on the knot, dear,' said the freckled girl.

'Eh?' said Kipps; 'I mean – '

Both the young ladies became very intent on the knot, and Mr Kipps was very red and very intent upon the two young ladies.

'Mortified, and had to be sawn off,' said the maiden lady.

'Sawn off?' said the lodging-house keeper.

'Sawn *right* off,' said the maiden lady, and jabbed at her mangled design.

'*There*,' said the freckled girl, 'I think that ought to do. You're sure it's not too tight?'

'Not a bit,' said Kipps.

He met Miss Walshingham's eye, and smiled to show how little he cared for wounds and pain. 'It's only a little cut,' he added.

The maiden lady appeared as an addition to their group. 'You should have washed the wound, dear,' she said. 'I was just telling Miss Collis.' She peered through her glasses at the bandage. 'That doesn't look *quite* right,' she remarked critically. 'You should have taken the ambulance classes. But I suppose it will have to do. Are you hurting?'

'Not a bit,' said Kipps, and he smiled at them all with the air of a brave soldier in hospital.

'I'm sure it *must* hurt,' said Miss Walshingham.

'Anyhow, you're a very good patient,' said the girl with the freckles.

Mr Kipps became quite pink. 'I'm only sorry I broke the window – that's all,' he said. 'But who would have thought it was going to break like that?'

Pause.

'I'm afraid you won't be able to go on carving tonight,' said Miss Walshingham.

'I'll try,' said Kipps. 'It reelly doesn't hurt – not anything to matter.'

Presently Miss Walshingham came to him as he carved heroically with his hand bandaged in her handkerchief. There was a touch of novel interest in her eyes. 'I'm afraid you're not getting on very fast,' she said.

The freckled girl looked up and regarded Miss Walshingham.

'I'm doing a little, anyhow,' said Kipps. 'I don't want to waste any time. A feller like me hasn't much time to spare.'

It struck the girls that there was a quality of modest disavowal about that 'feller like me'. It gave them a light into this obscure person, and Miss Walshingham ventured to commend his work as 'promising' and to ask whether he meant to follow it up. Kipps didn't 'altogether know' – 'things depended on so much', but if he was in Folkestone next winter he certainly should. It did not occur to Miss Walshingham at the time to ask why his progress in art depended upon his presence in Folkestone. There were some more questions and answers – they continued to talk to him for a little time, even when Mr Chester Coote had come into the room – and when at last the conversation had died out it dawned upon Kipps just how much his cut wrist had done for him –

He went to sleep that night revising that conversation for the twentieth time, treasuring this and expanding that, and inserting things he might have said to Miss Walshingham, things he might still say about himself – in relation, more or less explicit, to her. He wasn't quite sure if he wouldn't like his arm to mortify a bit, which would make him interesting, or to heal up absolutely, which would show the exceptional purity of his blood . . .

4

The affair of the broken window happened late in April, and the class came to an end in May. In that interval there were several small incidents and great developments of emotion. I have done Kipps no justice if I have made it seem that his face was unsightly. It was, as the freckled girl pointed out to Helen Walshingham, an 'interesting' face, and that aspect of him which presented chiefly erratic hair and glowing ears ceased to prevail.

They talked him over, and the freckled girl discovered there was something 'wistful' in his manner. They detected a 'natural delicacy', and the freckled girl set herself to draw him out from that time forth. The freckled girl was nineteen, and very wise and motherly and bene-volent, and really she greatly preferred drawing out Kipps to wood-carving. It was quite evident to her that Kipps was in love with Helen Walshingham, and it struck her as a queer and romantic and pathetic and extremely interesting phenomenon. And as at that time she regarded Helen as 'simply lovely', it seemed only right and proper that she should assist Kipps in his modest efforts to place himself in a state of absolute *abandon* upon her altar.

Under her sympathetic management the position of Kipps was presently defined quite clearly. He was unhappy in his position – mis-understood. He told her he 'didn't seem to get on like' with customers, and she translated this for him as his being 'too sensitive'. The dis-content with his fate in life, the dreadful feeling that education was slipping by him, troubles that time and usage were glazing over a little, revived to their old acuteness but not to their old hopelessness. As a basis for sympathy, indeed, they were even a source of pleasure.

And one day at dinner it happened that Carshot and Buggins fell to talking of 'these here writers', and how Dickens had been a labeller of blacking and Thackeray 'an artist who couldn't sell a drawing', and how Samuel Johnson had walked to London without any boots, having thrown away his only pair 'out of pride'.

'It's luck,' said Buggins, 'to a very large extent. They just happen to hit on something that catches on, and there you are!'

'Nice easy life they have of it, too,' said Miss Mergle. 'Write just an hour or so, and done for the day! Almost like gentlefolks.'

'There's more work in it than you'd think,' said Carshot, stooping to a mouthful.

'I wouldn't mind changing, for all that,' said Buggins. 'I'd like to see one of these here authors marking off with Jimmy.'

'I think they copy from each other a good deal,' said Miss Mergle.

'Even then (chup, chup, chup),' said Carshot, 'there's writing it out in their own hands.'

They proceeded to enlarge upon the literary life, on its ease and dignity, on the social recognition accorded to those who led it, and on the ample gratifications their vanity achieved. 'Pictures everywhere – never get a new suit without being photographed – almost like Royalty,' said Miss Mergle.

And all this talk impressed the imagination of Kipps very greatly. Here was a class that seemed to bridge the gulf. On the one hand essentially Low, but by factitious circumstances capable of entering upon those levels of social superiority to which all true Englishmen aspire, those levels from which one may tip a butler, scorn a tailor, and even commune with those who lead 'men' into battle. 'Almost like gentlefolks' – that was it! He brooded over these things in the afternoon, until they blossomed into daydreams. Suppose, for example, he had chanced to write a book, a well-known book, under an assumed name, and yet kept on being a draper all the time . . . Impossible, of course; but *suppose* – it made quite a long dream.

And at the next wood-carving class he let it be drawn from him that his real choice in life was to be a Nawther – 'only one doesn't get a chance'.

After that there were times when Kipps had that pleasant sense that comes of attracting interest. He was a mute, inglorious Dickens, or at any rate something of that sort, and they were all taking him at that. The discovery of this indefinable 'something' in him, the development of which was now painfully restricted and impossible, did much to bridge the gulf between himself and Miss Walshingham. He was unfortunate, he was futile, but he was not 'common'. Even now with help . . . ? The two girls, and the freckled girl in particular, tried to 'stir him up' to some effort to do his imputed potentialities justice. They were still young enough to believe that to nice and niceish members of the male sex – more especially when under the stimulus of feminine encouragement – nothing is finally impossible.

The freckled girl was, I say, the stage manager of this affair, but Miss Walshingham was the presiding divinity. A touch of proprietorship came into her eyes at times when she looked at him. He was hers – unconditionally – and she knew it.

To her directly Kipps scarcely ever made a speech. The enterprising things that he was continually devising to say to her, he usually did not say, or he said them in a suitably modified form to the girl with the freckles. And one day the girl with the freckles smote him to the heart. She said to him, with the faintest indication of her head across the classroom to where her friend reached a cast from the shelf, 'I do think Helen Walshingham is sometimes the most lovely person in the world. Look at her now!'

Kipps gasped for a moment. The moment lengthened, and she regarded him as an intelligent young surgeon might regard an operation without anaesthetics.

'You're right,' he said, and then looked at her with an entire abandonment of visage. She coloured under his glare of silent avowal, and he blushed brightly. 'I think so, too,' he said hoarsely, cleared his throat, and after a meditative moment proceeded sacramentally with his wood-carving.

'You *are* wonderful,' said the freckled girl to Miss Walshingham, apropos of nothing, as they went on their way home together. 'He simply adores you.'

'But, my dear, what have I done?' said Helen.

'That's just it,' said the freckled girl. 'What *have* you done?'

And then with a terrible swiftness came the last class of the course, to terminate this relationship altogether. Kipps was careless of dates, and the thing came upon him with an effect of abrupt surprise. Just as his petals were expanding so hopefully, 'Finis', and the thing was at an end. But Kipps did not fully appreciate that the end was indeed and really and truly the end, until he was back in the Emporium after the end was over.

The end began practically in the middle of the last class, when the freckled girl broached the topic of terminations. She developed the question of just how he was going on after the class ended. She hoped he would stick to certain resolutions of self-improvement he had breathed. She said quite honestly that he owed it to himself to develop his possibilities. He expressed firm resolve, but dwelt on difficulties.

He had no books. She instructed him how to get books from the public library. He was to get a form of application for a ticket signed by a ratepayer; and he said 'of course', when she said Mr Shalford would do that, though all the time he knew perfectly well it would 'never do' to ask Mr Shalford for anything of the sort. She explained that she was going to North Wales for the summer, information he received without immediate regret. At intervals he expressed his intention of going on with wood-carving when the summer was over, and once he added, 'if – '

She considered herself extremely delicate not to press for the completion of that 'if – '

After that talk there was an interval of languid wood-carving and watching Miss Walshingham.

Then presently there came a bustle of packing, a great ceremony of hand-shaking all round by Miss Collis and the maiden lady of ripe years, and then Kipps found himself outside the classroom, on the landing with his two friends. It seemed to him he had only just learnt that this was the last class of all. There came a little pause, and the freckled girl suddenly went back into the classroom, and left Kipps and Miss Walshingham alone together for the first time. Kipps was instantly breathless. She looked at his face with a glance that mingled sympathy and curiosity, and held out her white hand.

'Well, goodbye, Mr Kipps,' she said.

He took her hand and held it. 'I'd do anything,' said Kipps, and had not the temerity to add, 'for you.' He stopped awkwardly. He shook her hand and said, 'Goodbye.'

There was a little pause.

'I hope you will have a pleasant holiday,' she said.

'I shall come back to the class next year, anyhow,' said Kipps valiantly, and turned abruptly to the stairs.

'I hope you will,' said Miss Walshingham.

He turned back towards her. 'Reelly?' he said.

'I hope everybody will come back.'

'I will – anyhow,' said Kipps. 'You may count on that,' and he tried to make his tones significant.

They looked at one another through a little pause.

'Goodbye,' she said.

Kipps lifted his hat. She turned towards the classroom.

'Well?' said the freckled girl, coming back towards her.

'Nothing,' said Helen. 'At least – presently.' And she became very energetic about some scattered tools on a desk.

The freckled girl went out and stood for a moment at the head of the stairs. When she came back she looked very hard at her friend. The incident struck her as important – wonderfully important. It was unassimilable, of course, and absurd, but there it was, the thing that is so cardinal to a girl, the emotion, the subservience, the crowning triumph of her sex. She could not help feeling that Helen took it, on the whole, a little too hardly.

CHAPTER FOUR

Chitterlow

The hour of the class on the following Thursday found Kipps in a state of nearly incredible despondency. He was sitting with his eyes on the reading-room clock, his chin resting on his fists and his elbows on the accumulated comic papers that were comic, alas, in vain! He paid no heed to the little man in spectacles glaring opposite to him, famishing for *Fun*.[13] In this place it was he had sat night after night, each night more blissful than the last, waiting until it should be time to go to Her! And then – bliss! And now the hour had come and there was no class! There would be no class now until next October; it might be there would never be a class so far as he was concerned again.

It might be there would never be a class again, for Shalford, taking exception to a certain absent-mindedness that led to mistakes and more particularly to the ticketing of several articles in Kipps's Manchester window upside down, had been 'on to' him for the past few days in an exceedingly onerous manner.

He sighed profoundly, pushed the comic papers back – they were rent away from him instantly by the little man in spectacles – and tried the old engravings of Folkestone in the past that hung about the room. But these, too, failed to minister to his bruised heart. He wandered about the corridors for a time and watched the library indicator for awhile. Wonderful thing that! But it did not hold him for long. People came and laughed near him and that jarred with him dreadfully. He went out of the building and a beastly cheerful barrel-organ mocked him in the street. He was moved to a desperate resolve to go down to the beach. There it might be he would be alone. The sea might be rough – and attuned to him. It would certainly be dark.

'If I 'ad a penny I'm blest if I wouldn't go and chuck myself off the end of the pier . . . *She*'d never miss me . . . ' He followed a deepening vein of thought.

'Penny though! It's tuppence,' he said after a space.

He went down Dover Street in a state of profound melancholia – at the pace and mood, as it were, of his own funeral procession – and he crossed at the corner of Tontine Street heedless of all mundane things.

And there it was that Fortune came upon him, in disguise and with a loud shout, the shout of a person endowed with an unusually rich, full voice, followed immediately by a violent blow in the back.

His hat was over his eyes and an enormous weight rested on his shoulders and something kicked him in the back of his calf.

Then he was on all fours in some mud that Fortune, in conjunction with the Folkestone corporation and in the pursuit of equally mysterious ends, had heaped together even lavishly for his reception.

He remained in that position for some seconds awaiting further developments and believing almost anything broken before his heart. Gathering at last that this temporary violence of things in general was over, and being perhaps assisted by a clutching hand, he arose, and found himself confronting a figure holding a bicycle and thrusting forward a dark face in anxious scrutiny.

'You aren't hurt, matey?' gasped the figure.

'Was that *you* 'it me?' said Kipps.

'It's these handles, you know,' said the figure with an air of being a fellow sufferer. 'They're too *low*. And when I go to turn, if I don't remember, Bif! – and I'm *in*to something.'

'Well – you give me a oner in the back – anyhow,' said Kipps, taking stock of his damages.

'I was coming downhill, you know,' explained the bicyclist. 'These little Folkestone hills are a Fair Treat. It isn't as though I'd been on the level. I came rather a whop.'

'You did *that*,' said Kipps.

'I was back-pedalling for all I was worth anyhow,' said the bicyclist. 'Not that I *am* worth much back-pedalling.'

He glanced round and made a sudden movement almost as if to mount his machine. Then he turned as rapidly to Kipps again, who was now stooping down, pursuing the tale of his injuries.

'Here's the back of my trouser leg all tore down,' said Kipps, 'and I believe I'm bleeding. You reely ought to be more careful – '

The stranger investigated the damage with a rapid movement. 'Holy Smoke, so you are!' He laid a friendly hand on Kipps's arm. 'I say – look here! Come up to my diggings and sew it up. I'm – Of course I'm to blame, and I say – ' his voice sank to a confidential friendliness. 'Here's a slop. Don't let on I ran you down. Haven't a lamp, you know. Might be a bit awkward, for *me*.'

Kipps looked up towards the advancing policeman. The appeal to his generosity was not misplaced. He immediately took sides with his assailant. He stood up as the representative of the law drew nearer. He assumed an air which he considered highly suggestive of an accident not having happened.

'All right,' he said, 'go on!'

'Right you are,' said the cyclist promptly, and led the way, and then, apparently with some idea of deception, called over his shoulder, 'I'm tremendous glad to have met you, old chap.

'It really isn't a hundred yards,' he said after they had passed the policeman, 'it's just round the corner.'

'Of course,' said Kipps, limping slightly, 'I don't want to get a chap into trouble. Accidents *will* happen. Still – '

'Oh! *rather*! I believe you. Accidents *will* happen. Especially when you get *me* on a bicycle.' He laughed. 'You aren't the first I've run down, not by any manner of means! I don't think you can be hurt much either. It isn't as though I was scorching. You didn't see me coming. I was back-pedalling like anything. Only naturally it seems to you I must have been coming fast. And I did all I could to ease off the bump as I hit you. It was just the treadle I think came against your calf. But it was All Right of you about that policeman, you know. That was a Fair Bit of All Right. Under the Circs, if you'd told him I was riding it might have been forty bob! Forty bob! I'd have had to tell 'em Time is Money just now for Mr H. C.

'I shouldn't have blamed you either, you know. Most men after a bump like that might have been spiteful. The least I can do is to stand you a needle and thread. And a clothes brush. It isn't everyone who'd have taken it like you.

'Scorching! Why if I'd been scorching you'd have – coming as we did – you'd have been knocked silly.

'But I tell you, the way you caught on about that slop was something worth seeing. When I asked you, I didn't half expect it. Bif! Right off. Cool as a cucumber. Had your line at once. I tell you that there isn't many men would have acted as you have done, I *will* say that. You acted like a gentleman over that slop.'

Kipps's first sense of injury disappeared. He limped along a pace or so behind, making depreciatory noises in response to these flattering remarks and taking stock of the very appreciative person who uttered them.

As they passed the lamps he was visible as a figure with a slight anterior plumpness, progressing buoyantly on knickerbockered legs, with quite enormous calves, legs that, contrasting with Kipps's own narrow practice, were even exuberantly turned out at the knees and toes. A cycling cap was worn very much on one side, and from beneath it protruded carelessly straight wisps of dark red hair, and ever and again an ample nose came into momentary view round the corner. The muscular cheeks of this person and a certain generosity of chin he possessed were blue shaven and he had no moustache. His carriage was spacious and confident, his gestures up and down the narrow deserted back street they traversed were irresistibly suggestive of ownership; a succession of broadly gesticulating shadows were born squatting on his feet, and grew and took possession of the road, and reunited at last with the shadows of the infinite as lamp after lamp was passed. Kipps saw by the flickering light of one of them that they were in Little Fenchurch Street, and then they came round a corner sharply into a dark court and stopped at the door of a particularly ramshackle looking little house, held up between two larger ones, like a drunken man between policemen.

The cyclist propped his machine carefully against the window, produced a key and blew down it sharply. 'The lock's a bit tricky,' he said, and devoted himself for some moments to the task of opening the door. Some mechanical catastrophe ensued and the door was open.

'You'd better wait here a bit while I get the lamp,' he remarked to Kipps; 'very likely it isn't filled,' and vanished into the blackness of the passage. 'Thank God for matches!' he said, and Kipps had an impression of a passage in the transitory pink flare and the bicyclist disappearing into a farther room. Kipps was so much interested by these things that for the time he forgot his injuries altogether.

An interval and Kipps was dazzled by a pink shaded kerosene lamp. 'You go in,' said the red-haired man, 'and I'll bring in the bike,' and for a moment Kipps was alone in the lamp-lit room. He took in rather vaguely the shabby ensemble of the little apartment, the round table covered with a torn, red, glass-stained cover on which the lamp stood, a mottled looking-glass over the fireplace reflecting this, a disused gas bracket, an extinct fire, a number of dusty postcards and memoranda stuck round the glass, a dusty, crowded paper-rack on the mantel with a number of cabinet photographs, a table littered with papers and cigarette ash and a syphon of soda water. Then the cyclist reappeared and Kipps saw his blue-shaved, rather animated face and bright reddish-brown eyes for the first time. He was a man perhaps ten years older than Kipps, but his beardless face made them in a way contemporary.

'You behaved all right about that policeman – anyhow,' he repeated as he came forward.

'I don't see 'ow else I could 'ave done,' said Kipps quite modestly. The cyclist scanned his guest for the first time and decided upon hospitable details.

'We'd better let that mud dry a bit before we brush it. Whisky there is, good old Methusaleh, Canadian Rye, and there's some brandy that's all right. Which'll you have?'

'*I* dunno,' said Kipps, taken by surprise, and then seeing no other course but acceptance, 'well – whisky, then.'

'Right you are, old boy, and if you'll take my advice you'll take it neat. I may not be a particular judge of this sort of thing, but I do know old Methusaleh pretty well. Old Methusaleh – four stars. That's me! Good old Harry Chitterlow and good old Methusaleh. Leave 'em together. Bif! He's gone!'

He laughed loudly, looked about him, hesitated and retired, leaving Kipps in possession of the room and free to make a more precise examination of its contents.

2

He particularly remarked the photographs that adorned the apartment. They were chiefly photographs of ladies, in one case in tights, which Kipps thought a 'bit 'ot', but one represented the bicyclist in the costume of some remote epoch. It did not take Kipps long to infer that the others were probably actresses and that his host was an actor, and the presence of the half of a large, coloured playbill seemed to confirm this. A note framed in an Oxford frame that was a little too large for it he presently demeaned himself to read. 'Dear Mr Chitterlow,' it ran its brief course, 'if after all you will send the play you spoke of I will endeavour to read it,' followed by a stylish but absolutely illegible signature, and across this was written in pencil, 'What price, Harry, now?' And in the shadow by the window was a rough and rather able sketch of the bicyclist in chalk on brown paper, calling particular attention to the curvature of the forward lines of his hull and calves and the jaunty carriage of his nose, and labelled unmistakably 'Chitterlow'. Kipps thought it 'rather a take-off'. The papers on the table by the syphon were in manuscript, Kipps observed, manuscript of a particularly convulsive and blottesque sort and running obliquely across the page.

Presently he heard the metallic clamour as if of a series of irreparable breakages with which the lock of the front door discharged its function, and then Chitterlow reappeared, a little out of breath as if from running and with a starry labelled bottle in his large, freckled hand.

'Sit down, old chap,' he said, 'sit down. I had to go out for it after all. Wasn't a solitary bottle left. However, it's all right now we're here.

No, don't sit on that chair, there's sheets of my play on that. That's the one – with the broken arm. I think this glass is clean, but anyhow wash it out with a squizz of syphon and shy it in the fireplace. Here! I'll do it! Lend it here!'

As he spoke Mr Chitterlow produced a corkscrew from a table drawer, attached and overcame good old Methusaleh's cork in a style a bartender might envy, washed out two tumblers in his simple, effectual manner, and poured a couple of inches of the ancient fluid into each. Kipps took his tumbler, said 'Thanks' in an offhand way, and after a momentary hesitation whether he should say, 'Here's to you!' or not, put it to his lips without that ceremony. For a space fire in his throat occupied his attention to the exclusion of other matters, and then he discovered Mr Chitterlow with an intensely bulldog pipe alight, seated on the opposite side of the empty fireplace and pouring himself out a second dose of whisky.

'After all,' said Mr Chitterlow, with his eye on the bottle and a little smile wandering to hide amidst his larger features, 'this accident might have been worse. I wanted someone to talk to a bit, and I didn't want to go to a pub, leastways not a Folkestone pub, because as a matter of fact I'd promised Mrs Chitterlow, who's away, not to, for various reasons – though of course if I'd wanted to I'm just that sort that should have all the same – and here we are! It's curious how one runs up against people out bicycling!'

'Isn't it!' said Kipps, feeling that the time had come for him to say something.

'Here we are, sitting and talking like old friends, and half an hour ago we didn't know we existed. Leastways we didn't know each other existed. I might have passed you in the street perhaps and you might have passed me, and how was I to tell that, put to the test, you would have behaved as decently as you have behaved. Only it happened otherwise, that's all. You're not smoking!' he said. 'Have a cigarette?'

Kipps made a confused reply that took the form of not minding if he did, and drank another sip of old Methusaleh in his confusion. He was able to follow the subsequent course of that sip for quite a long way. It was as though the old gentleman was brandishing a burning torch through his vitals, lighting him here and lighting him there until at last his whole being was in a glow. Chitterlow produced a tobacco pouch and cigarette papers and, with an interesting parenthesis that was a little difficult to follow about some lady named Kitty something or other who had taught him the art when he was as yet only what you might call a nice boy, made Kipps a cigarette, and with a consideration that won

Kipps's gratitude suggested that after all he might find a little soda water an improvement with the whisky. 'Some people like it that way,' said Chitterlow, and then with voluminous emphasis, '*I don't.*'

Emboldened by the weakened state of his enemy, Kipps promptly swallowed the rest of him and had his glass at once hospitably replenished. He began to feel he was of a firmer consistency than he commonly believed, and turned his mind to what Chitterlow was saying with the resolve to play a larger part in the conversation than he had hitherto done. Also he smoked through his nose quite successfully, an art he had only very recently acquired.

Meanwhile Chitterlow explained that he was a playwright, and the tongue of Kipps was unloosened to respond that he knew a chap, or rather one of their fellows knew a chap, or at least to be perfectly correct this fellow's brother did, who had written a play. In response to Chitterlow's enquiries, he could not recall the title of the play, nor where it had appeared, nor the name of the manager who produced it, though he thought the title was something about 'Love's Ransom', or something like that.

'He made five 'undred pounds by it, though,' said Kipps. 'I know that.'

'That's nothing,' said Chitterlow, with an air of experience that was extremely convincing. 'Nothing. May seem a big sum to *you*, but *I* can assure you it's just what one gets any day. There's any amount of money, an-ny amount, in a good play.'

'I des say,' said Kipps, drinking.

'Any amount of money!'

Chitterlow began a series of illustrative instances. He was clearly a person of quite unequalled gift for monologue. It was as though some conversational dam had burst upon Kipps, and in a little while he was drifting along upon a copious rapid of talk about all sorts of theatrical things by one who knows all about them, and quite incapable of anticipating whither that rapid meant to carry him. Presently somehow they had got to anecdotes about well-known theatrical managers – little Teddy Bletherskite, artful old Chumps and the magnificent Behemoth, 'petted to death, you know, fair sickened, by all these society women'. Chitterlow described various personal encounters with these personages, always with modest self-depreciation, and gave Kipps a very amusing imitation of old Chumps in a state of intoxication. Then he took two more stiff doses of old Methusaleh in rapid succession.

Kipps reduced the hither end of his cigarette to a pulp as he sat 'des saying' and 'quite believing' Chitterlow in the sagest manner and admiring the easy way in which he was getting on with this very novel and entertaining personage. He had another cigarette made for him, and then Chitterlow, assuming by insensible degrees more and more of the manner of a rich and successful playwright being interviewed by a young admirer, set himself to answer questions which sometimes Kipps asked and sometimes Chitterlow, about the particulars and methods of his career. He undertook this self-imposed task with great earnestness and vigour, treating the matter indeed with such fullness that at times it seemed lost altogether under a thicket of parentheses, footnotes and episodes that branched and budded from its stem. But it always emerged again, usually by way of illustration to its own degressions. Practically it was a mass of material for the biography of a man who had been everywhere and done everything (including the Hon. Thomas Norgate, which was a record), and in particular had acted with great distinction and profit (he dated various anecdotes, 'when I was getting thirty, or forty, or fifty dollars a week') throughout America and the entire civilised world.

And as he talked on and on in that full, rich, satisfying voice he had, and as old Methusaleh, indisputably a most drunken old reprobate of a whisky, busied himself throughout Kipps, lighting lamp after lamp until the entire framework of the little draper was illuminated and glowing like some public building on a festival, behold Chitterlow and Kipps with him and the room in which they sat were transfigured! Chitterlow became in very truth that ripe, full man of infinite experience and humour and genius, fellow of Shakespeare and Ibsen and Maeterlinck (three names he placed together quite modestly far above his own), and no longer ambiguously dressed in a sort of yachting costume with cycling knickerbockers but elegantly if unconventionally attired, and the room ceased to be a small and shabby room in a Folkestone slum, and grew larger and more richly furnished, and the fly-blown photographs were curious old pictures, and the rubbish on the walls the most rare and costly bric-à-brac, and the indisputable paraffin lamp, a soft and splendid light. A certain youthful heat that to many minds might have weakened old Methusaleh's starry claim to a ripe antiquity vanished in that glamour, two burnt holes and a claimant darn in the tablecloth, moreover, became no more than the pleasing contradictions natural in the house of genius, and as for Kipps! – Kipps was a bright young man of promise, distinguished by recent quick, courageous proceedings not too definitely insisted upon, and he had been rewarded by admission to a sanctum and confidences for which the common prosperous, for which 'society women' even, were notoriously sighing in vain. 'Don't *want* them, my boy; they'd simply play old Harry with the work, you know!

Chaps outside, bank clerks and university fellows, think the life's all *that* sort of thing. Don't you believe 'em. Don't you believe 'em.'

And then – !

'Boom . . . Boom . . . Boom . . . Boom . . . ' right in the middle of a most entertaining digression on flats who join touring companies under the impression that they are actors, Kipps much amused at their flatness as exposed by Chitterlow.

'Lor'!' said Kipps like one who awakens, 'that's not eleven!'

'Must be,' said Chitterlow. 'It was nearly ten when I got that whisky. It's early yet – '

'All the same I must be going,' said Kipps, and stood up. 'Even now – maybe. Fact is – I 'ad *no* idea. The 'ouse door shuts at 'arf-past ten, you know. I ought to 'ave thought before.'

'Well, if you *must* go! I tell you what. I'll come, too . . . Why! There's your leg, old man! Clean forgot it! You can't go through the streets like that. I'll sew up the tear. And meanwhile have another whisky.'

'I ought to be getting on *now*,' protested Kipps feebly; and then Chitterlow was showing him how to kneel on a chair in order that the rent trouser leg should be attainable, and old Methusaleh on his third round was busy repairing the temporary eclipse of Kipps's arterial glow. Then suddenly Chitterlow was seized with laughter and had to leave off sewing to tell Kipps that the scene wouldn't make a bad bit of business in a farcical comedy, and then he began to sketch out the farcical comedy and that led him to a digression about another farcical comedy of which he had written a ripping opening scene which wouldn't take ten minutes to read. It had something in it that had never been done on the stage before, and was yet perfectly legitimate, namely, a man with a live beetle down the back of his neck trying to seem at his ease in a roomful of people –

'*They* won't lock you out,' he said, in a singularly reassuring tone, and began to read and act what he explained to be (not because he had written it, but simply because he knew it was so on account of his exceptional experience of the stage) and what Kipps also quite clearly saw to be, one of the best opening scenes that had ever been written.

When it was over Kipps, who rarely swore, was inspired to say the scene was 'damned fine' about six times over, whereupon, as if by way of recognition, Chitterlow took a simply enormous portion of the inspiring antediluvian, declaring at the same time that he had rarely met a '*finer*' intelligence than Kipps's (stronger there might be, *that* he couldn't say with certainty as yet, seeing how little after all they had seen of each other, but a finer *never*); that it was a shame such a gallant and discriminating intelligence should be nightly either locked up or locked out at ten – well, ten-thirty then – and that he had half a mind to recommend old somebody or other (apparently the editor of a London daily paper) to put on Kipps forthwith as a dramatic critic in the place of the current incapable.

'I don't think I've ever made up anything for print,' said Kipps; 'ever. I'd have a thundering good try, though, if ever I got a chance. I would that! I've written window tickets orfen enough. Made 'em up and every-thing. But that's different.'

'You'd come to it all the fresher for not having done it before. And the way you picked up every point in that scene, my boy, was a Fair Treat! I tell you, you'd knock William Archer[14] into fits. Not so literary, of course, you'd be, but I don't believe in literary critics any more than in literary playwrights. Plays *aren't* literature – that's just the point they miss. Plays are plays. No! That won't hamper you anyhow. You're wasted down here, I tell you. Just as I was, before I took to acting. I'm hanged if I wouldn't like your opinion on these first two acts of that tragedy I'm on to. I haven't told you about that. It wouldn't take me more than an hour to read . . . '

3

Then so far as he could subsequently remember, Kipps had 'another', and then it would seem that suddenly, regardless of the tragedy, he insisted that he 'reelly *must* be getting on', and from that point his memory became irregular. Certain things have remained quite clearly, and as it is a matter of common knowledge that intoxicated people forget what happens to them, it follows that he was not intoxicated. Chitterlow came with him partly to see him home and partly for a freshener before turning in. Kipps recalled afterwards very distinctly how in Little Fen-church Street he discovered that he could not walk straight and also that Chitterlow's needle and thread in his still unmended trouser leg was making an annoying little noise on the pavement behind him. He tried to pick up the needle suddenly by surprise, and somehow tripped and fell, and then Chitterlow, laughing uproariously, helped him up. 'It wasn't a bicycle this time, old boy,' said Chitterlow, and that appeared to them both at the time as being a quite extraordinarily good joke indeed. They punched each other about on the strength of it.

For a time after that Kipps certainly pretended to be quite desperately drunk and unable to walk and Chitterlow entered into the pretence and supported him. After that Kipps remembered being struck with the extremely laughable absurdity of going downhill to Tontine Street in order to go uphill again to the Emporium, and trying to get that idea into Chitterlow's head and being unable to do so on account of his own merriment or Chitterlow's evident intoxication, and his next memory after that was of the exterior of the Emporium, shut and darkened, and, as it were, frowning at him with all its stripes of yellow and green. The chilly way in which SHALFORD glittered in the moonlight printed itself with particular vividness on his mind. It appeared to Kipps that that establishment was closed to him for evermore. Those gilded letters, in spite of appearances, spelt FINIS for him and exile from Folkestone. He would never do wood-carving, never see Miss Walshingham again. Not that he had ever hoped to see her again. But this was the knife, this was final. He had stayed out, he had got drunk, there had been that row about the Manchester window-dressing only three days ago . . . In the retrospect he was quite sure that he was perfectly sober then and at bottom extremely unhappy, but he kept a brave face on the matter nevertheless, and declared stoutly he didn't care if he *was* locked out.

Whereupon Chitterlow slapped him on the back very hard and told him that was a 'Bit of All Right', and assured him that when he himself had been a clerk in Sheffield before he took to acting he had been locked out sometimes for six nights running.

'What's the result?' said Chitterlow. 'I could go back to that place now, and they'd be glad to have me . . . Glad to have me,' he repeated, and then added, 'that is to say, if they remember me – which isn't very likely.'

Kipps asked a little weakly, 'What am I to do?'

'Keep out,' said Chitterlow. 'You can't knock 'em up now – that would give you away *Right* away. You'd better try and sneak in in the morning with the cat. That'll do you. You'll probably get in all right in the morning if nobody gives you away.'

Then for a time – perhaps as the result of that slap in the back – Kipps felt decidedly queer, and acting on Chitterlow's advice went for a bit of a freshener upon the Leas. After a time he threw off the temporary queerness and found Chitterlow patting him on the shoulder and telling him that he'd be all right now in a minute and all the better for it – which he was. And the wind having dropped and the night being now a really very beautiful moonlight night indeed, and all before Kipps to spend as he liked and with only a very little tendency to spin round now and again to mar its splendour, they set out to walk the whole length of the Leas to the Sandgate lift and back, and as they walked Chitterlow spoke first of moonlight transfiguring the sea and then of moonlight transfiguring faces, and so at last he came to the topic of Love, and upon that he dwelt a great while, and with a wealth of experience and illustrative anecdote that seemed remarkably pungent and material to Kipps. He forgot his lost Miss Walshingham and his outraged employer again. He became as it were a desperado by reflection.

Chitterlow had had adventures, a quite astonishing variety of adventures in this direction; he was a man with a past, a really opulent past, and he certainly seemed to like to look back and see himself amidst its opulence.

He made no consecutive history, but he gave Kipps vivid, momentary pictures of relations and entanglements. One moment he was in flight – only too worthily in flight – before the husband of a Malay woman in Cape Town. At the next he was having passionate complications with the daughter of a clergyman in York. Then he passed to a remarkable grouping at Seaford.

'They say you can't love two women at once,' said Chitterlow. 'But I tell you – ' He gesticulated and raised his ample voice. 'It's *Rot!* *Rot!*'

'I know that,' said Kipps.

'Why, when I was in the smalls with Bessie Hopper's company there were three.' He laughed and decided to add, 'Not counting Bessie, that is.'

He set out to reveal Life as it is lived in touring companies, a quite amazing jungle of interwoven 'affairs' it appeared to be, a mere amorous winepress for the crushing of hearts.

'People say this sort of thing's a nuisance and interferes with Work. I tell you it isn't. The Work couldn't go on without it. They *must* do it. They haven't the Temperament if they don't. If they hadn't the Temperament they wouldn't want to act; if they have – Bif!'

'You're right,' said Kipps. 'I see that.'

Chitterlow proceeded to a close criticism of certain historical indiscretions of Mr Clement Scott[15] respecting the morals of the stage. Speaking in confidence and not as one who addresses the public, he admitted regretfully the general truth of these comments. He proceeded to examine various typical instances that had almost forced themselves upon him personally, and with especial regard to the contrast between his own character towards women and that of the Hon. Thomas Norgate, with whom it appeared he had once been on terms of great intimacy . . .

Kipps listened with emotion to these extraordinary recollections. They were wonderful to him, they were incredibly credible. The tumultuous, passionate, irregular course was the way life ran – except in high-class establishments! Such things happened in novels, in plays – only he had been fool enough not to understand they happened. His share in the conversation was now indeed no more than faint writing in the margin; Chitterlow was talking quite continuously. He expanded his magnificent voice into huge guffaws, he drew it together into a confidential intensity, it became drawlingly reminiscent, he was frank, frank with the effect of a revelation, reticent also with the effect of a revelation, a stupendously gesticulating moonlit black figure, wallowing in itself, preaching Adventure and the Flesh to Kipps. Yet withal shot with something of sentiment, with a sort of sentimental refinement very coarsely and egotistically done. The Times he had had! – even before he was as old as Kipps he had had innumerable Times.

Well, he said with a sudden transition, he had sown his wild oats – one had to somewhen – and now, he fancied he had mentioned it earlier in the evening, he was happily married. She was, he indicated, a 'born lady'. Her father was a prominent lawyer, a solicitor in Kentish Town, 'done a lot of public-house business'; her mother was second cousin to the wife of Abel Jones, the fashionable portrait painter – 'almost Society people in a way'. That didn't count with Chitterlow. He was no snob. What *did* count was that she possessed what, he ventured to assert without much fear of contradiction, was the very finest, completely untrained contralto voice in all the world. ('But to hear it properly,' said Chitterlow, 'you want a Big Hall.') He became rather vague and jerked his head about to indicate when and how he had entered matrimony. She was, it seemed, 'away with her people'. It was clear that Chitterlow did not get on with these people very well. It would seem they failed to appreciate his playwriting, regarding it as an unremunerative pursuit, whereas, as he and Kipps knew, wealth beyond the dreams of avarice would presently accrue. Only patience and persistence were needful.

He went off at a tangent to hospitality. Kipps must come down home with him. They couldn't wander about all night, with a bottle of the right sort pining at home for them. 'You can sleep on the sofa. You won't be worried by broken springs anyhow, for I took 'em all out myself two or three weeks ago. I don't see what they ever put 'em in for. It's a point I know about. I took particular notice of it when I was with Bessie Hopper. Three months we were and all over England, North Wales and the Isle of Man, and I never struck a sofa in diggings any-where that hadn't a broken spring. Not once – all the time.'

He added almost absently: 'It happens like that at times.'

They descended the slant road towards Harbour Street and went on past the Pavilion Hotel.

They came into the presence of old Methusaleh again, and that worthy under Chitterlow's direction at once resumed the illumination of Kipps's interior with the conscientious thoroughness that distinguished him. Chitterlow took a tall portion to himself with an air of asbestos, lit the bulldog pipe again, and lapsed for a space into meditation, from which Kipps roused him by remarking that he expected 'a nacter 'as a lot of ups and downs like, now and then'.

At which Chitterlow seemed to bestir himself. 'Ra-ther,' he said. 'And sometimes it's his own fault and sometimes it isn't. Usually it is. If it isn't one thing it's another. If it isn't the manager's wife it's bar-bragging. I tell you things happen at times. I'm a fatalist. The fact is Character has you. You can't get away from it. You may think you do, but you don't.'

He reflected for a moment. 'It's that what makes tragedy. Psychology really. It's the Greek irony – Ibsen and – all that. Up to date.'

He emitted this exhaustive summary of high-toned modern criticism as if he was repeating a lesson while thinking of something else, but it seemed to rouse him as it passed his lips by including the name of Ibsen.

He became interested in telling Kipps, who was indeed open to any information whatever about this quite novel name, exactly where he thought Ibsen fell short, points where it happened that Ibsen was defective just where it chanced that he, Chitterlow, was strong. Of course he had no desire to place himself in any way on an equality with Ibsen; still the fact remained that his own experience in England and America and the colonies was altogether more extensive than that of Ibsen. Ibsen had probably never seen 'one decent bar scrap' in his life. That, of course, was not Ibsen's fault or his own merit, but there the thing was. Genius, he knew, was supposed to be able to do anything or to do without anything; still he was now inclined to doubt that. He had a play in hand that might perhaps not please William Archer – whose opinion, after all, he did not value as he valued Kipps's opinion – but which he thought was at any rate as well constructed as anything Ibsen ever did.

So with infinite deviousness Chitterlow came at last to his play. He decided he would not read it to Kipps, but tell him about it. This was the simpler because much of it was still unwritten. He began to explain his plot. It was a complicated plot and all about a nobleman who had seen everything and done everything and knew practically all that

Chitterlow knew about women, that is to say 'all about women', and suchlike matters. It warmed and excited Chitterlow. Presently he stood up to act a situation which could not be explained. It was an extremely vivid situation.

Kipps applauded the situation vehemently. 'Tha's dam' fine,' said the new dramatic critic, quite familiar with his part now, striking the table with his fist and almost upsetting his third portion (in the second series) of old Methusaleh. 'Tha's dam' fine, Chit'low!'

'You see it?' said Chitterlow, with the last vestiges of that incidental gloom disappearing. 'Good, old boy! I thought you'd see it. But it's just the sort of thing the literary critic can't see. However, it's only a beginning – '

He replenished Kipps and proceeded with his exposition.

In a little while it was no longer necessary to give that over-advertised Ibsen the purely conventional precedence he had hitherto had. Kipps and Chitterlow were friends and they could speak frankly and openly of things not usually admitted. 'Any'ow,' said Kipps, a little irrelevantly and speaking over the brim of the replenishment, 'what you read jus' now was dam' fine. Nothing can't alter that.'

He perceived a sort of faint, buzzing vibration about things that was very nice and pleasant, and with a little care he had no difficulty whatever in putting his glass back on the table. Then he perceived Chitterlow was going on with the scenario, and then that old Methusaleh had almost entirely left his bottle. He was glad there was so little more Methusaleh to drink because that would prevent his getting drunk. He knew that he was not now drunk, but he knew that he had had enough. He was one of those who always know when they have had enough. He tried to interrupt Chitterlow to tell him this, but he could not get a suitable opening. He doubted whether Chitterlow might not be one of those people who did not know when they had had enough. He discovered that he disapproved of Chitterlow. Highly. It seemed to him that Chitterlow went on and on like a river. For a time he was inexplicably and quite unjustly cross with Chitterlow and wanted to say to him, 'you got the gift of the gab', but he only got so far as to say 'the gift', and then Chitterlow thanked him and said he was better than Archer any day. So he eyed Chitterlow with a baleful eye until it dawned upon him that a most extraordinary thing was taking place. Chitterlow kept mentioning someone named Kipps. This presently began to perplex Kipps very greatly. Dimly but decidedly he perceived this was wrong.

'Look 'ere,' he said suddenly, '*what* Kipps?'

'This chap Kipps I'm telling you about.'

'What chap Kipps you're telling which about?'

'I told you.'

Kipps struggled with a difficulty in silence for a space. Then he reiterated firmly, '*What* chap Kipps?'

'This chap in my play – man who kisses the girl.'

'Never kissed a girl,' said Kipps; 'leastwise – ' and subsided for a space. He could not remember whether he had kissed Ann or not – he knew he had meant to. Then suddenly in a tone of great sadness and addressing the hearth he said, '*My* name's Kipps.'

'Eh?' said Chitterlow.

'Kipps,' said Kipps, smiling a little cynically.

'What about him?'

'He's me.' He tapped his breastbone with his middle finger to indicate his essential self.

He leant forward very gravely towards Chitterlow. 'Look 'ere, Chit'low,' he said, 'you haven't no business putting my name into play. You mustn't do things like that. You'd lose me my crib, right away.' And they had a little argument – so far as Kipps could remember. Chitterlow entered upon a general explanation of how he got his names. These, he had for the most part got out of a newspaper that was still, he believed, 'lying about'. He even made to look for it, and while he was doing so Kipps went on with the argument, addressing himself more particularly to the photograph of the girl in tights. He said that at first her costume had not commended her to him, but now he perceived she had an extremely sensible face. He told her she would like Buggins if she met him; he could see she was just that sort. She would admit, all sensible people would admit, that using names in plays was wrong. You could, for example, have the law on him.

He became confidential. He explained that he was already in sufficient trouble for stopping out all night, without having his name put in plays. He was certain to be in the deuce of a row, the deuce of a row. Why had he done it? Why hadn't he gone at ten? Because one thing leads to another. One thing, he generalised, always does lead to another . . .

He was trying to tell her that he was utterly unworthy of Miss Walshingham, when Chitterlow gave up the search and suddenly accused him of being drunk and talking 'Rot – '

CHAPTER FIVE

'Swapped'[16]

He awoke on the thoroughly comfortable sofa that had had all its springs removed, and although he had certainly not been intoxicated, he awoke with what Chitterlow pronounced to be, quite indisputably, a Head and a Mouth. He had slept in his clothes and he felt stiff and uncomfortable all over, but the head and mouth insisted that he must not bother over little things like that. In the head was one large, angular idea that it was physically painful to have there. If he moved his head the angular idea shifted about in the most agonising way. This idea was that he had lost his situation and was utterly ruined and that it really mattered very little. Shalford was certain to hear of his escapade, and that, coupled with that row about the Manchester window – !

He raised himself into a sitting position under Chitterlow's urgent encouragement.

He submitted apathetically to his host's attentions. Chitterlow, who admitted being a 'bit off it' himself and in need of an egg-cupful of brandy, just an egg-cupful neat, dealt with that Head and Mouth as a mother might deal with the fall of an only child. He compared it with other Heads and Mouths that he had met, and in particular to certain experienced by the Hon. Thomas Norgate. 'Right up to the last,' said Chitterlow, 'he couldn't stand his liquor. It happens like that at times.' And after Chitterlow had pumped on the young beginner's head and given him some anchovy paste piping hot on buttered toast, which he preferred to all the other remedies he had encountered, Kipps resumed his crumpled collar, brushed his clothes, tacked up his trouser-leg and prepared to face Mr Shalford and the reckoning for this wild, un-precedented night – the first 'night out' that ever he had taken.

Acting on Chitterlow's advice to have a bit of a freshener before returning to the Emporium, Kipps walked some way along the Leas and back and then went down to a shop near the Harbour to get a cup of coffee. He found that extremely reinvigorating, and he went on up the High Street to face the inevitable terrors of the office, a faint touch of pride in his depravity tempering his extreme self-abasement. After all, it was not an unmanly headache; he had been out all night, and he had been drinking and his physical disorder was there to witness the fact. If it wasn't for the thought of Shalford he would have been even a proud man to discover himself at last in such a condition. But the thought of Shalford was very dreadful. He met two of the apprentices snatching a walk before shop began. At the sight of them he pulled his spirits together, put his hat back from his pallid brow, thrust his hands into his trouser pockets and adopted an altogether more dissipated carriage; he met their innocent faces with a wan smile. Just for a moment he was glad that the rent in his trousers was, after all, visible and that some at least of the mud on his clothes had refused to move at Chitterlow's brushing. What wouldn't they think he had been up to? He passed them without speaking. He could imagine how they regarded his back. Then he recollected Mr Shalford . . .

The deuce of a row certainly and perhaps – ! He tried to think of plausible versions of the affair. He could explain he had been run down by rather a wild sort of fellow who was riding a bicycle, almost stunned for the moment (even now he felt the effects of the concussion in his head) and had been given whisky to restore him, and 'the fact is, sir' – with an upward inflection of the voice, an upward inflection of the eyebrows and an air of its being the last thing one would have expected whisky to do, the manifestation indeed of a practically unique physiological weakness – 'it got into my *'ed*!' . . .

Put like that it didn't look so bad.

He got to the Emporium a little before eight and the housekeeper with whom he was something of a favourite ('There's no harm in Mr Kipps,' she used to say) seemed to like him if anything better for having broken the rules and gave him a piece of dry toast and a good hot cup of tea.

'I suppose the G. V. – ' began Kipps.

'He knows,' said the housekeeper.

He went down to the shop a little before time, and presently Booch summoned him to the presence.

He emerged from the private office after an interval of ten minutes.

The junior clerk scrutinised his visage. Buggins put the frank question. Kipps answered with one word.

'Swapped!' said Kipps.

Kipps leant against the fixtures with his hands in his pockets and talked to the two apprentices under him.

'I don't care if I *am* swapped,' said Kipps. 'I been sick of Teddy and his System some time. I was a good mind to chuck it when my time was up. Wish I 'ad now.'

Afterwards Pierce came round and Kipps repeated this.

'What's it for?' said Pierce. 'That row about the window tickets?'

'No fear!' said Kipps and sought to convey a perspective of splendid depravity. 'I wasn't in las' night,' he said and made even Pierce, 'man about town' Pierce, open his eyes.

'Why! where did you get to?' asked Pierce.

He conveyed that he had been 'fair round the town'. 'With a Nactor chap, I know.'

'One can't *always* be living like a curit,' he said.

'No fear,' said Pierce, trying to play up to him.

But Kipps had the top place in that conversation.

'My Lor'!' said Kipps, when Pierce had gone, 'but wasn't my mouth and 'ed bad this morning before I 'ad a pick-me-up!'

'Whad jer 'ave?'

'Anchovy on 'ot buttered toast. It's the very best pick-me-up there is. You trust me, Rodgers. I never take no other and I don't advise you to. See?'

And when pressed for further particulars, he said again he had been 'fair all *round* the town, with a Nactor chap' he knew. They asked curiously all he had done and he said, 'Well, what do *you* think?' And when they pressed for still further details he said there were things little boys ought not to know and laughed darkly and found them some huckaback to roll.

And in this manner for a space did Kipps fend off the contemplation of the 'key of the street' that Shalford had presented him.

3

This sort of thing was all very well when junior apprentices were about, but when Kipps was alone with himself it served him not at all. He was uncomfortable inside and his skin was uncomfortable, and the Head and Mouth, palliated perhaps but certainly not cured, were still with him. He felt, to tell the truth, nasty and dirty and extremely disgusted with himself. To work was dreadful and to stand still and think still more dreadful. His torn trouser-leg reproached him. These were the second best of his three pairs of trousers, and they had cost him thirteen and sixpence. Practically ruined they were. His dusting pair were unfit for shop and he would have to degrade his best. When he was under inspection he affected the slouch of a desperado, but directly he found himself alone, this passed insensibly into the droop.

The financial aspect of things grew large before him. His whole capital in the world was the sum of five pounds in the Post Office Savings Bank and four and sixpence cash. Besides there would be two months' screw. His little tin box upstairs was no longer big enough for his belongings; he would have to buy another, let alone that it was not calculated to make a good impression in a new 'crib'. Then there would be paper and stamps needed in some abundance for answering advertisements and railway fares when he went 'crib hunting'. He would have to write letters, and he never wrote letters. There was spelling, for example, to consider. Probably if nothing turned up before his month was up he would have to go home to his uncle and aunt.

How would they take it? . . .

For the present at any rate he resolved not to write to them.

Such disagreeable things as these they were that lurked below the fair surface of Kipps's assertion, 'I've been wanting a change. If 'e 'adn't swapped me, I should very likely 'ave swapped '*im*.'

In the perplexed privacies of his own mind he could not understand how everything had happened. He had been the Victim of Fate, or at least of one as inexorable – Chitterlow. He tried to recall the successive steps that had culminated so disastrously. They were difficult to recall . . .

Buggins that night abounded in counsel and reminiscence.

'Curious thing,' said Buggins, 'but every time I've had the swap I've never believed I should get another crib – never. But I have,' said Buggins. 'Always. So don't lose heart, whatever you do –

'Whatever you do,' said Buggins, 'keep hold of your collars and cuffs – shirts if you can, but collars anyhow. Spout them last. And anyhow, it's summer! – you won't want your coat . . . You got a good umbrella . . .

'You'll no more get a shop from New Romney, than – anything. Go straight up to London, get the cheapest room you can find – and hang out. Don't eat too much. Many a chap's put his prospects in his stomach. Get a cup o' coffee and a slice – egg if you like – but remember you got to turn up at the Warehouse tidy. The best places *now*, I believe, are the old cabmen's eating houses. Keep your watch and chain as long as you can . . .

'There's lots of shops going,' said Buggins. 'Lots!'

And added reflectively, 'But not this time of year perhaps.'

He began to recall his own researches. ' 'Stonishing lot of chaps you see,' he said. 'All sorts. Look like dukes some of 'em. High hat. Patent boots. Frock coat. All there. All right for a West End crib. Others – Lord! It's a caution, Kipps. Boots been inked in some reading rooms – *I* used to write in a Reading Room in Fleet Street, regular penny club – hat been wetted, collar frayed, tail coat buttoned up, black chest-plaster tie – spread out. Shirt, you know, gone – ' Buggins pointed upward with a pious expression.

'No shirt, I expect?'

'Ate it,' said Buggins.

Kipps meditated. 'I wonder where old Merton is,' he said at last. 'I often wondered about 'im.'

4

It was the morning following Kipps's snotice of dismissal that Miss Walshingham came into the shop. She came in with a dark, slender lady, rather faded, rather tightly dressed, whom Kipps was to know someday as her mother. He discovered them in the main shop at the counter of the ribbon department. He had come to the opposite glove counter with some goods enclosed in a parcel that he had unpacked in his own department. The two ladies were both bent over a box of black ribbon.

He had a moment of tumultuous hesitations. The etiquette of the situation was incomprehensible. He put down his goods very quietly and stood hands on counter, staring at these two ladies. Then, as Miss Walshingham sat back, the instinct of flight seized him . . .

He returned to his Manchester shop wildly agitated. Directly he was out of sight of her he wanted to see her. He fretted up and down the counter, and addressed some snappish remarks to the apprentice in the window. He fumbled for a moment with a parcel, untied it needlessly, began to tie it up again and then bolted back again into the main shop. He could hear his own heart beating.

The two ladies were standing in the manner of those who have completed their purchases and are waiting for their change. Mrs Walshingham regarded some remnants with impersonal interest; Helen's eyes searched the shop. They distinctly lit up when they discovered Kipps.

He dropped his hands to the counter by habit and stood for a moment regarding her awkwardly. What would she do? Would she cut him? She came across the shop to him.

'How are *you*, Mr Kipps?' she said, in her clear, distinct tones, and she held out her hand.

'Very well, thank you,' said Kipps; 'how are you?'

She said she had been buying some ribbon.

He became aware of Mrs Walshingham very much surprised. This checked something allusive about the class and he said instead that he supposed she was glad to be having her holidays now. She said she was, it gave her more time for reading and that sort of thing. He supposed that she would be going abroad and she thought that perhaps they *would* go to Knocke or Bruges for a time.

Then came a pause and Kipps's soul surged within him. He wanted to tell her he was leaving and would never see her again. He could find neither words nor voice to say it. The swift seconds passed. The girl in the ribbons was handing Mrs Walshingham her change. 'Well,' said Miss Walshingham, 'Goodbye,' and gave him her hand again.

Kipps bowed over her hand. His manners, his counter manners, were the easiest she had ever seen upon him. She turned to her mother. It was no good now, no good. Her mother! You couldn't say a thing like that before her mother! All was lost but politeness. Kipps rushed for the door. He stood at the door bowing with infinite gravity, and she smiled and nodded as she went out. She saw nothing of the struggle within him, nothing but a gratifying emotion. She smiled like a satisfied goddess as the incense ascends.

Mrs Walshingham bowed stiffly and a little awkwardly.

He remained holding the door open for some seconds after they had passed out, then rushed suddenly to the back of the 'costume' window to watch them go down the street. His hands tightened on the window rack as he stared. Her mother appeared to be asking discreet questions. Helen's bearing suggested the offhand replies of a person who found the world a satisfactory place to live in. 'Really, Mumsie, you cannot expect me to cut my own students dead,' she was in fact saying . . .

They vanished round Henderson's corner.

Gone! And he would never see her again – never!

It was as though someone had struck his heart with a whip. Never! Never! Never! And she didn't know! He turned back from the window and the department with its two apprentices was impossible. The whole glaring world was insupportable.

He hesitated and made a rush head down for the cellar that was his Manchester warehouse. Rodgers asked him a question that he pretended not to hear.

The Manchester warehouse was a small cellar apart from the general basement of the building and dimly lit by a small gas flare. He did not turn that up, but rushed for the darkest corner, where on the lowest shelf the sale window-tickets were stored. He drew out the box of these with trembling hands and upset them on the floor, and so having made himself a justifiable excuse for being on the ground with his head well in the dark, he could let his poor bursting little heart have its way with him for a space.

And there he remained until the cry of 'Kipps! Forward!' summoned him once more to face the world.

CHAPTER SIX

The Unexpected

Now in the slack of that same day, after the midday dinner and before the coming of the afternoon customers, this disastrous Chitterlow descended upon Kipps with the most amazing coincidence in the world. He did not call formally, entering and demanding Kipps, but privately, in a confidential and mysterious manner.

Kipps was first aware of him as a dark object bobbing about excitedly outside the hosiery window. He was stooping and craning and peering in the endeavour to see into the interior between and over the socks and stockings. Then he transferred his attention to the door, and after a hovering scrutiny, tried the baby-linen display. His movements and gestures suggested a suppressed excitement.

Seen by daylight, Chitterlow was not nearly such a magnificent figure as he had been by the subdued nocturnal lightings and beneath the glamour of his own interpretation. The lines were the same indeed, but the texture was different. There was a quality about the yachting cap, an indefinable finality of dustiness, a shiny finish on all the salient surfaces of the reefer coat. The red hair and the profile, though still forcible and fine, were less in the quality of Michelangelo and more in that of the merely picturesque. But it was a bright brown eye still that sought amidst the interstices of the baby-linen.

Kipps was by no means anxious to interview Chitterlow again. If he had felt sure that Chitterlow would not enter the shop he would have hid in the warehouse until the danger was past, but he had no idea of Chitterlow's limitations. He decided to keep up the shop in the shadows until Chitterlow reached the side window of the Manchester department and then to go outside as if to inspect the condition of the window and explain to him that things were unfavourable to immediate intercourse. He might tell him he had already lost his situation . . .

' 'Ello, Chit'low,' he said, emerging.

'Very man I want to see,' said Chitterlow, shaking with vigour. 'Very man I want to see.' He laid a hand on Kipps's arm. 'How *old* are you, Kipps?'

'One-and-twenty,' said Kipps. 'Why?'

'Talk about coincidences! And your name now? Wait a minute.' He held out a finger. '*Is* it Arthur?'

'Yes,' said Kipps.

'You're the man,' said Chitterlow.

'What man?'

'It's about the thickest coincidence I ever struck,' said Chitterlow, plunging his extensive hand into his breast coat pocket. 'Half a jiff and I'll tell you your mother's Christian name.' He laughed and struggled with his coat for a space, produced a washing book and two pencils, which he deposited in his side pocket; then in one capacious handful, a bent but by no means finally disabled cigar, the rubber proboscis of a bicycle pump, some twine and a lady's purse, and finally a small pocket book, and from this, after dropping and recovering several visiting cards, he extracted a carelessly torn piece of newspaper. 'Euphemia', he read and brought his face close to Kipps's. 'Eh?' He laughed noisily. 'It's about as fair a Bit of All Right as anyone *could* have – outside a coincidence play. Don't say her name wasn't Euphemia, Kipps, and spoil the whole blessed show.'

'Whose name – Euphemia?' asked Kipps.

'Your mother's.'

'Lemme see what it says on the paper.'

Chitterlow handed him the fragment and turned away. 'You may say what you like,' he said, addressing a vast, deep laugh to the street generally.

Kipps attempted to read. ' "Waddy or Kipps. If Arthur Waddy or Arthur Kipps, the son of Margaret Euphemia Kipps, who – " '

Chitterlow's finger swept over the print. 'I went down the column and every blessed name that seemed to fit my play I took. I don't believe in made-up names. As I told you. I'm all with Zola on that. Documents whenever you can. I like 'em hot and real. See? Who was Waddy?'

'Never heard his name.'

'Not Waddy?'

'No!'

Kipps tried to read again and abandoned the attempt. 'What does it mean?' he said. 'I don't understand.'

'It means,' said Chitterlow, with a momentary note of lucid exposition, 'so far as I can make out that you're going to strike it Rich. Never mind about the Waddy – that's a detail. What does it usually mean? You'll hear of something to your advantage – very well. I took that newspaper up to get my names by the merest chance. Directly I saw it again and read that – I knew it was you. I believe in coincidences. People say they don't happen. *I* say they do. Everything's a coincidence. Seen properly. Here you are. Here's one! Incredible? Not a bit of it! See? It's you! Kipps! Waddy be damned! It's a Mascot. There's luck in my play. Bif! You're there. *I'm* there. Fair *in* it! Snap!' And he discharged his fingers like a pistol. 'Never you mind about the "Waddy". '

'Eh?' said Kipps, with a nervous eye on Chitterlow's fingers.

'You're all right,' said Chitterlow; 'you may bet the seat of your only breeches on that! Don't you worry about the Waddy – that's as clear as day. You're about as right side up as a billiard ball – whatever you do. Don't stand there gaping, man! Read the paper if you don't believe me. Read it!'

He shook it under Kipps's nose.

Kipps became aware of the second apprentice watching them from the shop. His air of perplexity gave place to a more confident bearing.

' – "who was born at East Grinstead". I certainly was born there. I've 'eard my aunt say – '

'I knew it,' said Chitterlow, taking hold of one edge of the paper and bringing his face close alongside Kipps's.

' " – on September the first, eighteen hundred and seventy-eight" – '

'*That's* all right,' said Chitterlow. 'It's all, all right, and all you have to do is write to Watson and Bean and get it – '

'Get what?'

'Whatever it is.'

Kipps sought his moustache. 'You'd write?' he asked.

'Ra-ther.'

'But what d'you think it is?'

'That's the fun of it!' said Chitterlow, taking three steps in some as yet uninvented dance. 'That's where the joke comes in. It may be anything – it may be a million. If so! Where does little Harry come in? Eh?'

Kipps was trembling slightly. 'But – ' he said, and thought. 'If you was me – ' he began. 'About that Waddy – ?'

He glanced up and saw the second apprentice disappear with amazing swiftness from behind the goods in the window.

'*What?*' asked Chitterlow, but he never had an answer.

'Lor'! There's the guv'nor!' said Kipps, and made a prompt dive for the door.

He dashed in only to discover that Shalford, with the junior apprentice in attendance, had come to mark off remnants of Kipps's cotton dresses and was demanding him. 'Hello, Kipps,' he said, 'outside – ?'

'Seein' if the window was straight, sir,' said Kipps.

'Umph!' said Shalford.

For a space Kipps was too busily employed to think at all of Chitterlow or the crumpled bit of paper in his trouser pocket. He was, however, painfully aware of a suddenly disconnected excitement at large in the street. There came one awful moment when Chitterlow's nose loomed interrogatively over the ground glass of the department door, and his bright little red-brown eye sought for the reason for Kipps's disappearance, and then it became evident that he saw the high light of Shalford's baldness and grasped the situation and went away. And then Kipps (with that advertisement in his pocket) was able to come back to the business in hand.

He became aware that Shalford had asked a question. 'Yessir, nosir, rightsir. I'm sorting up zephyrs tomorrow, sir,' said Kipps.

Presently he had a moment to himself again, and, taking up a safe position behind a newly unpacked pile of summer lace curtains, he straightened out the piece of paper and reperused it. It was a little perplexing. That 'Arthur Waddy or Arthur Kipps' – did that imply two persons or one? He would ask Pierce or Buggins. Only –

It had always been impressed upon him that there was something demanding secrecy about his mother.

'Don't you answer no questions about your mother,' his aunt had been wont to say. 'Tell them you don't know, whatever it is they ask you.'

'Now this – ?'

Kipps's face became portentously careful and he tugged at his moustache, such as it was, hard.

He had always represented his father as being a 'gentleman farmer'. 'It didn't pay,' he used to say with a picture in his own mind of a penny-magazine aristocrat prematurely worn out by worry. 'I'm a Norfan, both sides,' he would explain, with the air of one who had seen trouble. He said he lived with his uncle and aunt, but he did not say that they kept a toy shop, and to tell anyone that his uncle had been a butler – *a servant!* – would have seemed the maddest of indiscretions. Almost all the assistants in the Emporium were equally reticent and vague, so great was their horror of 'Lowness' of any sort. To ask about this 'Waddy or Kipps' would upset all these little fictions. He was not, as a matter of fact, perfectly clear about his real status in the world (he was not, as a matter of fact, perfectly clear about anything), but he knew that there was a quality about his status that was – detrimental.

Under the circumstances – ?

It occurred to him that it would save a lot of trouble to destroy the advertisement there and then.

In which case he would have to explain to Chitterlow!

'Eng!' said Mr Kipps.

'Kipps,' cried Carshot, who was shopwalking; 'Kipps, Forward!'

He thrust back the crumpled paper into his pocket and sallied forth to the customer.

'I want,' said the customer, looking vaguely about her through glasses, 'a little bit of something to cover a little stool I have. Anything would do – a remnant or anything – '

The matter of the advertisement remained in abeyance for half an hour, and at the end the little stool was still a candidate for covering and Kipps had a thoroughly representative collection of the textile fabrics in his department to clear away. He was so angry about the little stool that the crumpled advertisement lay for a space in his pocket absolutely forgotten.

2

Kipps sat on his tin box under the gas bracket that evening, and looked up the name Euphemia and learnt what it meant in the *Enquire Within About Everything*[17] that constituted Buggins's reference library. He hoped Buggins, according to his habit, would ask him what he was looking for, but Buggins was busy turning out his week's washing. 'Two collars,' said Buggins, 'half pair socks, two dickeys. Shirt? . . . M'm. There ought to be another collar somewhere.'

'Euphemia,' said Kipps at last, unable altogether to keep to himself this suspicion of a high origin that floated so delightfully about him, 'Eu-phemia; it isn't a name *common* people would give to a girl, is it?'

'It isn't the name any decent people would give to a girl,' said Buggins, ' – common or not.'

'Lor'!' said Kipps. 'Why?'

'It's giving girls names like that,' said Buggins, 'that nine times out of ten makes 'em go wrong. It unsettles 'em. If ever I was to have a girl, if ever I was to have a dozen girls, I'd call 'em all Jane. Every one of 'em. You couldn't have a better name than that. Euphemia indeed! What next? . . . Good Lord! . . . That isn't one of my collars there, is it? under your bed?' . . .

Kipps got him the collar.

'I don't see no great 'arm in Euphemia,' he said as he did so.

After that he became restless. 'I'm a good mind to write that letter,' he said; and then, finding Buggins preoccupied wrapping his washing up in the 'half sox', added to himself, 'a thundering good mind.'

So he got his penny bottle of ink, borrowed the pen from Buggins and with no very serious difficulty in spelling or composition, did as he had resolved.

He came back into the bedroom about an hour afterwards a little out of breath and pale. 'Where you been?' said Buggins, who was now reading the *Daily World Manager*, which came to him in rotation from Carshot.

'Out to post some letters,' said Kipps, hanging up his hat.

'Crib hunting?'

'Mostly,' said Kipps. 'Rather,' he added, with a nervous laugh; 'what else?'

Buggins went on reading. Kipps sat on his bed and regarded the back of the *Daily World Manager* thoughtfully.

'Buggins,' he said at last.

Buggins lowered his paper and looked.

'I say, Buggins, what do these here advertisements mean that say so-and-so will hear of something greatly to his advantage?'

'Missin' people,' said Buggins, making to resume reading.

'How d'yer mean?' asked Kipps. 'Money left and that sort of thing?'

Buggins shook his head. 'Debts,' he said, 'more often than not.'

'But that ain't to his advantage.'

'They put that to get 'old of 'em,' said Buggins. 'Often it's wives.'

'What you mean?'

'Deserted wives, try and get their husbands back that way.'

'I suppose it *is* legacies sometimes, eh? Perhaps if someone was left a hundred pounds by someone – '

'Hardly ever,' said Buggins.

'Well, 'ow – ?' began Kipps and hesitated.

Buggins resumed reading. He was very much excited by a leader on Indian affairs. 'By Jove!' he said, 'it won't do to give these here Blacks votes.'

'No fear,' said Kipps.

'They're different altogether,' said Buggins. 'They 'aven't the sound sense of Englishmen, and they 'aven't the character. There's a sort of tricky dishonesty about 'em – false witness and all that – of which an Englishman has no idea. Outside their courts of law – it's a pos'tive fact, Kipps – there's witnesses waitin' to be 'ired. Reg'lar trade. Touch their 'ats as you go in. Englishmen 'ave no idea, I tell you – not ord'nary Englishmen. It's in their blood. They're too timid to be honest. Too slavish. They aren't used to being free like we are, and if you gave 'em freedom they wouldn't make a proper use of it. Now *we* – Oh, *damn*!'

For the gas had suddenly gone out and Buggins had the whole column of Society Club Chat still to read.

Buggins could talk of nothing after that but Shalford's meanness in turning off the gas, and after being extremely satirical indeed about their employer, undressed in the dark, hit his bare toe against a box and subsided after unseemly ejaculations into silent ill-temper.

Though Kipps tried to get to sleep before the affair of the letter he had just posted resumed possession of his mind he could not do so. He went over the whole thing again, quite exhaustively. Now that his first terror was abating he couldn't quite determine whether he was glad or sorry that he had posted that letter. If it *should* happen to be a hundred pounds!

It *must* be a hundred pounds!

If it was he could hold out for a year, for a couple of years even, before he got a Crib.

Even if it was fifty pounds – !

Buggins was already breathing regularly when Kipps spoke again. '*Bug*-gins,' he said.

Buggins pretended to be asleep, and thickened his regular breathing (a little too hastily) to a snore.

'I say Buggins,' said Kipps after an interval.

'*What's* up now?' said Buggins unamiably.

' 'Spose *you* saw an advertisement in a paper, with your name in it, see, asking you to come and see someone, like, so as to hear of something very much to your – '

'Hide,' said Buggins shortly.

'But – '

'I'd hide.'

'Er?'

'Goo'-night, o' man,' said Buggins, with convincing earnestness. Kipps lay still for a long time, then blew profoundly, turned over and stared at the other side of the dark.

He had been a fool to post that letter!

Lord! *Hadn't* he been a fool!

3

It was just five days and a half after the light had been turned out while Buggins was reading, that a young man with a white face and eyes bright and wide-open emerged from a side road upon the Leas front. He was dressed in his best clothes, and, although the weather was fine, he carried

his umbrella, just as if he had been to church. He hesitated and turned to
the right. He scanned each house narrowly as he passed it, and presently
came to an abrupt stop. 'Hughenden', said the gateposts in firm, black
letters, and the fanlight in gold repeated 'Hughenden'. It was a stucco
house fit to take your breath away, and its balcony was painted a beautiful
sea-green, enlivened with gilding. He stood looking up at it.

'Gollys!' he said at last in an awestricken whisper.

It had rich-looking crimson curtains to all the lower windows and
brass railed blinds above. There was a splendid tropical plant in a large,
artistic pot in the drawing-room window. There was a splendid bronzed
knocker (ring also) and two bells – one marked 'servants'.

'Gollys! *Servants*, eh?'

He walked past away from it, with his eyes regarding it, and then
turned and came back. He passed through a further indecision, and
finally drifted away to the seafront and sat down on a seat a little
way along the Leas and put his arm over the back and regarded
'Hughenden'. He whistled an air very softly to himself, put his head
first on one side and then on the other. Then for a space he scowled
fixedly at it.

A very stout old gentleman, with a very red face and very protuberant
eyes, sat down beside Kipps, removed a Panama hat of the most
abandoned desperado cut, and mopped his brow and blew. Then he
began mopping the inside of his hat. Kipps watched him for a space,
wondering how much he might have a year, and where he bought his
hat. Then 'Hughenden' reasserted itself.

An impulse overwhelmed him. 'I say,' he said, leaning forward to the
old gentleman.

The old gentleman started and stared.

'*Whad* d'you say?' he asked fiercely.

'You wouldn't think,' said Kipps, indicating with his forefinger, 'that
that 'ouse there belongs to me.'

The old gentleman twisted his neck round to look at 'Hughenden'.
Then he came back to Kipps, looked at his mean, little garments with
apoplectic intensity and blew at him by way of reply.

'It does,' said Kipps, a little less confidently.

'Don't be a Fool,' said the old gentleman, and put his hat on and wiped
out the corners of his eyes. 'It's hot enough,' panted the old gentleman
indignantly, 'without Fools.' Kipps looked from the old gentleman to
the house and back to the old gentleman. The old gentleman looked
at Kipps and snorted and looked out to sea, and again, snorting very
contemptuously, at Kipps.

'Mean to say it doesn't belong to me?' said Kipps.

The old gentleman just glanced over his shoulder at the house in dispute and then fell to pretending Kipps didn't exist. 'It's been lef' me this very morning,' said Kipps. 'It ain't the only one that's been lef' me, neither.'

'Aw!' said the old gentleman, like one who is sorely tried. He seemed to expect the passers-by presently to remove Kipps.

'It *'as,'* said Kipps. He made no further remark to the old gentleman for a space, but looked with a little less certitude at the house . . .

'I got – ' he said and stopped. 'It's no good telling you if you don't believe,' he said.

The old gentleman, after a struggle with himself, decided not to have a fit. 'Try that game on with me,' he panted. 'Give you in charge.'

'What game?'

'Wasn't born yesterday,' said the old gentleman, and blew. 'Besides,' he added, *'look* at you! I know you,' and the old gentleman coughed shortly and nodded to the horizon and coughed again.

Kipps looked dubiously from the house to the old gentleman and back to the house. Their conversation, he gathered, was over. Presently he got up and went slowly across the grass to its stucco portal again. He stood and his mouth shaped the precious word, 'Hughenden'. It was all *right*! He looked over his shoulder as if in appeal to the old gentleman, then turned and went his way. The old gentleman was so evidently past all reason!

He hung for a moment some distance along the parade, as though some invisible string was pulling him back. When he could no longer see the house from the pavement he went out into the road. Then with an effort he snapped the string.

He went on down a quiet side street, unbuttoned his coat furtively, took out three bank notes in an envelope, looked at them and replaced them. Then he fished up five new sovereigns from his trouser pocket and examined them. To such a confidence had his exact resemblance to his dead mother's portrait carried Messrs Watson and Bean.

It was right enough.

It really was *all* right.

He replaced the coins with grave precaution and went his way with a sudden briskness. It was all right – he had it now – he was a rich man at large. He went up a street and round a corner and along another street, and started towards the Pavilion and changed his mind and came round back, resolved to go straight to the Emporium and tell them all.

He was aware of someone crossing a road far off ahead of him, someone curiously relevant to his present extraordinary state of mind. It was Chitterlow. Of course it was Chitterlow who had told him first of the whole thing! The playwright was marching buoyantly along a cross street. His nose was in the air, the yachting cap was on the back of his head and the large freckled hand grasped two novels from the library, a morning newspaper, a new hat done up in paper and a lady's net bag full of onions and tomatoes –

He passed out of sight behind the wine merchant's at the corner, as Kipps decided to hurry forward and tell him of the amazing change in the Order of the Universe that had just occurred.

Kipps uttered a feeble shout, arrested as it began, and waved his umbrella. Then he set off at a smart pace in pursuit. He came round the corner and Chitterlow had gone; he hurried to the next and there was no Chitterlow; he turned back unavailingly and his eyes sought some other possible corner. His hand fluttered to his mouth and he stood for a space at the pavement edge, staring about him. No good!

But the sight of Chitterlow was a wholesome thing, it connected events together, joined him on again to the past at a new point, and that was what he so badly needed –

It was all right – all right.

He became suddenly very anxious to tell everybody at the Emporium, absolutely everybody, all about it. That was what wanted doing. He felt that telling was the thing to make this business real. He gripped his umbrella about the middle and walked very eagerly.

He entered the Emporium through the Manchester department. He flung open the door (over whose ground glass he had so recently, in infinite apprehension, watched the nose of Chitterlow) and discovered the second apprentice and Pierce in conversation. Pierce was prodding his hollow tooth with a pin and talking in fragments about the distinctive characteristics of Good Style.

Kipps came up in front of the counter.

'I say,' he said; 'what d'yer think?'

'What?' said Pierce over the pin.

'Guess.'

'You've slipped out because Teddy's in London.'

'Something more.'

'What?'

'Been left a fortune.'

'Garn!'

'I 'ave.'

'Get out!'

'Straight. I been lef' twelve 'undred pounds – twelve 'undred pounds a year!'

He moved towards the little door out of the department into the house, moving, as heralds say, *regardant passant*. Pierce stood with mouth wide open and pin poised in air. 'No!' he said at last.

'It's right,' said Kipps, 'and I'm going.'

And he fell over the doormat into the house.

4

It happened that Mr Shalford was in London buying summer sale goods – and no doubt also interviewing aspirants to succeed Kipps.

So that there was positively nothing to hinder a wild rush of rumour from end to end of the Emporium. All the masculine members began their report with the same formula: 'Heard about Kipps?'

The new girl in the cashdesk had had it from Pierce and had dashed out into the fancy shop to be the first with the news on the fancy side. Kipps had been left a thousand pounds a year, twelve thousand pounds a year. Kipps had been left twelve hundred thousand pounds. The figures were uncertain, but the essential facts they had correct. Kipps had gone upstairs. Kipps was packing his box. He said he wouldn't stop another day in the old Emporium, not for a thousand pounds! It was said that he was singing ribaldry about old Shalford.

He had come down! He was in the counting house. There was a general movement thither. Poor old Buggins had a customer and couldn't make out what the deuce it was all about! Completely out of it was Buggins.

There was a sound of running to and fro and voices saying this, that and the other thing about Kipps. Ring-a-dinger, ring-a-dinger went the dinner bell all unheeded. The whole of the Emporium was suddenly bright-eyed, excited, hungry to tell somebody, to find at any cost somebody who didn't know and be first to tell them, 'Kipps has been left thirty – forty – fifty thousand pounds!'

'*What!*' cried the senior porter. 'Him!' and ran up to the counting house as eagerly as though Kipps had broken his neck.

'One of our chaps just been left sixty thousand pounds,' said the first apprentice, returning after a great absence to his customer.

'Unexpectedly?' said the customer.

'Quite,' said the first apprentice . . .

'I'm sure if Anyone deserves it, it's Mr Kipps,' said Miss Mergle, and her train rustled as she hurried to the counting house.

There stood Kipps amidst a pelting shower of congratulations. His face was flushed and his hair disordered. He still clutched his hat and best umbrella in his left hand. His right hand was anyone's to shake rather than his own. (Ring-a-dinger, ring-a-dinger, ding, ding, ding, dang you! went the neglected dinner bell.)

'Good old Kipps,' said Pierce, shaking; 'Good old Kipps.'

Booch rubbed one anaemic hand upon the other. 'You're sure it's all right, Mr Kipps,' he said in the background.

'I'm sure we all congratulate him,' said Miss Mergle.

'Great Scott!' said the new young lady in the glove department. 'Twelve hundred a year! Great Scott! You aren't thinking of marrying anyone, are you, Mr Kipps?'

'Three pounds five and ninepence a day,' said Mr Booch, working in his head almost miraculously . . .

Everyone, it seemed, was saying how glad they were it was Kipps, except the junior apprentice, upon whom – he being the only son of a widow and used to having the best of everything as a right – an intolerable envy, a sense of unbearable wrong, had cast its gloomy shade. All the rest were quite honestly and simply glad – gladder perhaps at that time than Kipps because they were not so overpowered . . .

Kipps went downstairs to dinner, emitting fragmentary, disconnected statements. 'Never expected anything of the sort . . . When this here old Bean told me, you could have knocked me down with a feather . . . He says, "You b'en lef' money." Even then I didn't expect it'd be mor'n a hundred pounds perhaps. Something like that.'

With the sitting down to dinner and the handing of plates, the excitement assumed a more orderly quality. The housekeeper emitted congratulations as she carved and the maidservant became dangerous to clothes with the plates – she held them anyhow, one expected to see one upside down even – she found Kipps so fascinating to look at. Everyone was the brisker and hungrier for the news (except the junior apprentice) and the housekeeper carved with unusual liberality. It was High Old Times there under the gaslight, High Old Times. 'I'm sure if Anyone deserves it,' said Miss Mergle – 'pass the salt, please – it's Kipps.'

The babble died away a little as Carshot began barking across the table at Kipps. 'You'll be a bit of a Swell, Kipps,' he said. 'You won't hardly know yourself.'

'Quite the gentleman,' said Miss Mergle.

'Many real gentlemen's families,' said the housekeeper, 'have to do with less.'

'See you on the Leas,' said Carshot. 'My gu – !' He met the housekeeper's eye. She had spoken about that before. 'My eye!' he said tamely, lest words should mar the day.

'You'll go to London, I reckon,' said Pierce. 'You'll be a man about town. We shall see you mashing 'em, with violets in your button'ole, down the Burlington Arcade.

'One of these West End flats. That'd be *my* style,' said Pierce. 'And a first-class club.'

'Aren't these clubs a bit 'ard to get into?' asked Kipps, open-eyed, over a mouthful of potato.

'No fear. Not for Money,' said Pierce. And the girl in the laces who had acquired a cynical view of Modern Society from the fearless exposures of Miss Marie Corelli,[18] said, 'Money goes everywhere nowadays, Mr Kipps.'

But Carshot showed the true British strain.

'If I was Kipps,' he said, pausing momentarily for a knifeful of gravy, 'I should go to the Rockies and shoot bears.'

'I'd certainly 'ave a run over to Boulogne,' said Pierce, 'and look about a bit. I'm going to do that next Easter myself, anyhow – see if I don't.'

'Go to Oireland, Mr Kipps,' came the soft insistence of Biddy Murphy, who managed the big workroom, flushed and shining in the Irish way as she spoke. 'Go to Oireland. Ut's the loveliest country in the world. Outside Currrs. Fishin', shootin', huntin'. An' pretty gals! Eh! You should see the Lakes of Killarney, Mr Kipps!' And she expressed ecstasy by a facial pantomime and smacked her lips.

And presently they crowned the event.

It was Pierce who said, 'Kipps, you ought to stand Sham!'

And it was Carshot who found the more poetical word, 'Champagne.'

'Rather!' said Kipps hilariously, and the rest was a question of detail and willing emissaries. 'Here it comes!' they said as the apprentice came down the staircase. 'How about the shop?' said someone. 'Oh! *hang* the shop!' said Carshot and made gruntulous demands for a corkscrew with a thing to cut the wire. Pierce, the dog! had a wire-cutter in his pocket knife. How Shalford would have stared at the gold-tipped bottles if he had chanced to take an early train! Bang went the corks, and bang! Gluck, gluck, gluck, and sizzle!

When Kipps found them all standing about him under the gas flare, saying almost solemnly, 'Kipps!' with tumblers upheld – 'Have it in tumblers,' Carshot had said; 'have it in tumblers. It isn't a wine like you have in glasses. Not like port and sherry. It cheers you up, but you don't get drunk. It isn't hardly stronger than lemonade. They drink it at dinner, some of 'em, every day.'

'What! At three and six a bottle!' said the housekeeper incredulously.

'*They* don't stick at *that*,' said Carshot; 'not the champagne sort.'

The housekeeper pursed her lips and shook her head . . .

When Kipps, I say, found them all standing up to toast him in that manner, there came such a feeling in his throat and face that for the life of him he scarcely knew for a moment whether he was not going to cry. 'Kipps!' they all said, with kindly eyes. It was very good of them, it was very good of them, and hard there wasn't a stroke of luck for them all!

But the sight of upturned chins and glasses pulled him together again . . .

They did him honour. Unenviously and freely they did him honour.

For example, Carshot, being subsequently engaged in serving cretonne and desiring to push a number of rejected blocks up the counter in order to have space for measuring, swept them by a powerful and ill-calculated movement of the arm, with a noise like thunder, partly on to the floor and partly on to the foot of the still gloomily preoccupied junior apprentice. And Buggins, whose place it was to shopwalk while Carshot served, shopwalked with quite unparalleled dignity, dangling a new season's sunshade with a crooked handle on one finger. He arrested each customer who came down the shop with a grave and penetrating look. 'Showing very 'tractive line new sheason's shunshade,' he would remark, and, after a suitable pause, ' 'Markable thing, one our 'sistant leg'sy twelve 'undred a year. V'ry 'tractive. Nothing more today, mum? No!' And he would then go and hold the door open for them with perfect decorum and with the sunshade dangling elegantly from his left hand . . .

And the second apprentice, serving a customer with cheap ticking, and being asked suddenly if it was strong, answered remarkably, 'Oo! *no*, mum! Strong! Why it ain't 'ardly stronger than lemonade . . . '

The head porter, moreover, was filled with a virtuous resolve to break the record as a lightning packer and make up for lost time. Mr Swaffenham, of the Sandgate Riviera, for example, who was going out to dinner that night at seven, received at half-past six, instead of the urgently needed dress shirt he expected, a corset specially adapted to the needs of persons inclined to embonpoint. A parcel of summer underclothing selected by the elder Miss Waldershawe was somehow distributed in the form of gratis additions throughout a number of parcels of a less intimate nature, and a box of millinery on approval to Lady Pamshort (at Wampachs) was enriched by the addition of the junior porter's cap . . .

These little things, slight in themselves, witness perhaps none the less eloquently to the unselfish exhilaration felt throughout the Emporium at the extraordinary and unexpected enrichment of Mr Kipps.

5

The bus that plies between New Romney and Folkestone is painted a British red and inscribed on either side with the word 'Tip-top' in gold amidst voluptuous scrolls. It is a slow and portly bus; even as a young bus it must have been slow and portly. Below it swings a sort of hold, hung by chains between the wheels, and in the summertime the top has garden seats. The front over the two dauntless unhurrying horses rises in tiers like a theatre: there is first a seat for the driver and his company, and above that a seat, and above that, unless my memory plays me false, a seat. You sit in a sort of composition by some Italian painter – a celestial group of you. There are days when this bus goes and days when it doesn't go – you have to find out. And so you get to New Romney. So you will continue to get to New Romney for many years, for the light-railway concession along the coast is happily in the South Eastern Railway Company's keeping and the peace of the Marsh is kept inviolate except for the bicycle bells of such as Kipps and I.

This bus it was, this ruddy, venerable and immortal bus, that came down the Folkestone hill with unflinching deliberation, and trundled through Sandgate and Hythe, and out into the windy spaces of the Marsh, with Kipps and all his fortunes on its brow. You figure him there. He sat on the highest seat diametrically above the driver and his head was spinning and spinning with champagne and this stupendous Tomfoolery of Luck, and his heart was swelling, swelling indeed at times as though it would burst him, and his face towards the sunlight was transfigured. He said never a word, but ever and again as he thought of this or that, he laughed. He seemed full of chuckles for a time, detached and independent chuckles, chuckles that rose and burst in him like bubbles in a wine . . . He held a banjo sceptre-fashion and restless on his knee. He had always wanted a banjo, and now he had got one at Malchior's while he was waiting for the bus.

There sat beside him a young servant who was sucking peppermint and a little boy with a sniff, whose flitting eyes showed him curious to know why ever and again Kipps laughed, and beside the driver were two young men in gaiters talking about 'tegs'. And there sat Kipps, all unsuspected, twelve hundred a year, as it were, except for the protrusion of the banjo, disguised as a common young man. And the young man in gaiters to the left of the driver eyed Kipps and his banjo, and especially his banjo, ever and again as if he found it and him, with his rapt face, an insoluble enigma. And many a king has ridden into a conquered city with a lesser sense of splendour than Kipps.

Their shadows grew long behind them and their faces were transfigured in gold as they rumbled on towards the splendid West. The sun set before they had passed Dymchurch, and as they came lumbering into New Romney past the windmill the dusk had come.

The driver handed down the banjo and the portmanteau, and Kipps having paid him – 'That's aw right,' he said to the change, as a gentleman should – turned about and ran the portmanteau smartly into old Kipps, whom the sound of the stopping of the bus had brought to the door of the shop in an aggressive mood and with his mouth full of supper.

' 'Ello, uncle, didn't see you,' said Kipps.

'Blunderin' ninny,' said old Kipps. 'What's brought *you* here? Ain't early closing, is it? Not Toosday?'

'Got some news for you, uncle,' said Kipps, dropping the portmanteau.

'Ain't lost your situation, 'ave you? What's that you got there? I'm blowed if it ain't a banjo. Goo' Lord! Spendin' your money on banjoes! Don't put down your portmanty there – anyhow. Right in the way of everybody. I'm blowed if ever I saw such a boy as you've got lately. Here! Molly! And, look here! What you got a portmanty for? Why! Goo' Lord! You ain't *really* lost your place, 'ave you?'

'Somethin's happened,' said Kipps slightly dashed. 'It's all right, uncle. I'll tell you in a minute.'

Old Kipps took the banjo as his nephew picked up the portmanteau again.

The living-room door opened quickly, showing a table equipped with elaborate simplicity for supper, and Mrs Kipps appeared.

'If it ain't young Artie,' she said. 'Why! Whatever's brought *you* 'ome?'

' 'Ello aunt,' said Artie. 'I'm coming in. I got somethin' to tell you. I've 'ad a bit of Luck.'

He wouldn't tell them all at once. He staggered with the portmanteau round the corner of the counter, set a bundle of children's tin pails into clattering oscillation, and entered the little room. He deposited his luggage in the corner beside the tall clock, and turned to his aunt and uncle again. His aunt regarded him doubtfully; the yellow light from the little lamp on the table escaped above the shade and lit her forehead and the tip of her nose. It would be all right in a minute. He wouldn't tell them all at once. Old Kipps stood in the shop door with the banjo in his hand, breathing noisily. 'The fact is, aunt, I've 'ad a bit of Luck.'

'You ain't been backin' gordless 'orses, Artie?' she asked.

'No fear.'

'It's a draw he's been in,' said old Kipps, still panting from the impact of the portmanteau; 'it's a dratted draw. Jest look here, Molly. He's won this 'ere trashy banjer and throwed up his situation on the strength of it – that's what he's done. Goin' about singing. Dash and plunge! Jest the very fault poor Pheamy always 'ad. Blunder right in and no one mustn't stop 'er!'

'You ain't thrown up your place, Artie, 'ave you?' said Mrs Kipps.

Kipps perceived his opportunity. 'I 'ave,' he said; 'I've throwed it up.'

'What for?' said old Kipps.

'So's to learn the banjo!'

'Goo' *Lord*!' said old Kipps, in horror to find himself verified.

'I'm going about playing!' said Kipps with a giggle. 'Goin' to black my face, aunt, and sing on the beach. I'm going to 'ave a most tremenjous lark and earn any amount of money – you see. Twenty-six fousand pounds I'm going to earn just as easy as nothing!'

'Kipps,' said Mrs Kipps, 'he's been drinking!'

They regarded their nephew across the supper table with long faces. Kipps exploded with laughter and broke out again when his Aunt shook her head very sadly at him. Then suddenly he fell grave. He felt he could keep it up no longer. 'It's all right, aunt. Reely. I ain't mad and I ain't been drinking. I been lef' money. I been left twenty-six fousand pounds.'

Pause.

'And you thrown up your place?' said old Kipps.

'Yes,' said Kipps. 'Rather!'

'And bort this banjer, put on your best noo trousers and come right on 'ere?'

'Well,' said Mrs Kipps, '*I* never did.'

'These ain't my noo trousers, aunt,' said Kipps regretfully. 'My noo trousers wasn't done.'

'I shouldn't ha' thought that *even you* could ha' been such a fool as that,' said old Kipps.

Pause.

'It's *all* right,' said Kipps, a little disconcerted by their distrustful solemnity. 'It's all right – reely! Twenny-six fousan' pounds. And a 'ouse – '

Old Kipps pursed his lips and shook his head.

'A 'ouse on the Leas. I could have gone there. Only I didn't. I didn't care to. I didn't know what to say. I wanted to come and tell you.'

'How d'yer know the 'ouse – ?'

'They told me.'

'Well,' said old Kipps, and nodded his head portentously towards his nephew, with the corners of his mouth pulled down in a portentous, discouraging way. 'Well, you *are* a young Gaby.'

'I didn't *think* it of you, Artie!' said Mrs Kipps.

'Wadjer mean?' asked Kipps faintly, looking from one to the other with a withered face.

Old Kipps closed the shop door. 'They been 'avin' a lark with you,' said old Kipps in a mournful undertone. 'That's what I mean, my boy. They jest been seein' what a Gaby like you 'ud do.'

'I des say that young Quodling was in it,' said Mrs Kipps. ' 'E's jest that sort.'

(For Quodling of the green-baize bag had grown up to be a fearful dog, the terror of New Romney.)

'It's somebody after your place very likely,' said old Kipps.

Kipps looked from one sceptical, reproving face to the other, and round him at the familiar shabby little room, with his familiar cheap portmanteau on the mended chair, and that banjo amidst the supper things like some irrevocable deed. Could he be rich indeed? Could it be that these things had really happened? Or had some insane fancy whirled him hither?

Still – perhaps a hundred pounds –

'But,' he said. 'It's all right, reely, uncle. You don't think – ? I 'ad a letter.'

'Got up,' said old Kipps.

'But I answered it and went to a norfis.'

Old Kipps felt staggered for a moment, but he shook his head and chins sagely from side to side. As the memory of old Bean revived, the confidence of Kipps came back to him.

'I saw a nold gent, uncle – perfect gentleman. And 'e told me all about it. Mos' respectable 'e was. Said 'is name was Watson and Bean – leastways 'e was Bean. Said it was lef' me – ' Kipps suddenly dived into his breast pocket – 'by my grandfather – '

The old people started.

Old Kipps uttered an exclamation and wheeled round towards the mantelshelf above which the daguerreotype of his lost younger sister smiled its fading smile upon the world.

'Waddy 'is name was,' said Kipps, with his hand still deep in his pocket. 'It was *'is* son was my father – '

'Waddy!' said old Kipps.

'Waddy!' said Mrs Kipps.

'She'd never say,' said old Kipps.

There was a long silence.

Kipps fumbled with a letter, a crumpled advertisement and three bank notes. He hesitated between these items.

'Why! That young chap what was arsting questions – ' said old Kipps, and regarded his wife with an eye of amazement.

'Must 'ave been,' said Mrs Kipps.

'Must 'ave been,' said old Kipps.

'James,' said Mrs Kipps, in an awestricken voice, 'after all – perhaps – it's true!'

''*Ow* much did you say?' asked old Kipps. ' 'Ow much did you say 'e'd lef' you, me b'y?'

It was thrilling, though not quite in the way Kipps had expected. He answered almost meekly across the meagre supper things, with his documentary evidence in his hand: 'Twelve 'undred pounds. 'Proximately, he said. Twelve 'undred pounds a year. 'E made 'is will, jest before 'e died – not more'n a month ago. When 'e was dying, 'e seemed to change like, Mr Bean said. 'E'd never forgiven 'is son, never – not till then. 'Is son 'ad died in Australia, years and years ago, and *then* 'e 'adn't forgiven 'im. You know – 'is son what was my father. But jest when 'e was ill and dying 'e seemed to get worried like and longing for someone of 'is own. And 'e told Mr Bean it was 'im that had prevented them marrying. So 'e thought. That's 'ow it all come about . . . '

6

At last Kipps's flaring candle went up the narrow uncarpeted staircase to the little attic that had been his shelter and refuge during all the days of his childhood and youth. His head was whirling. He had been advised, he had been warned, he had been flattered and congratulated, he had been given whisky and hot water and lemon and sugar, and his health had been drunk in the same. He had also eaten two Welsh rarebits – an unusual supper. His uncle was chiefly for his going into Parliament, his aunt was consumed with a great anxiety. 'I'm afraid he'll go and marry beneath 'im.'

'Y'ought to 'ave a bit o' shootin' somewheer,' said old Kipps.

'It's your *duty* to marry into a county family, Artie. Remember that.'

'There's lots of young noblemen'll be glad to 'ang on to you,' said old Kipps. 'You mark my words. And borry your money. And then, good-day to ye.'

'I got to be precious Careful,' said Kipps. 'Mr Bean said that.'

'And you got to be precious careful of this old Bean,' said old Kipps. 'We may be out of the world in Noo Romney, but I've 'eard a bit about s'licitors, for all that. You keep your eye on old Bean, me b'y.

' 'Ow do we know what 'e's up to, with your money, even now?' said old Kipps, pursuing this uncomfortable topic.

' 'E *looked* very respectable,' said Kipps –

Kipps undressed with great deliberation, and with vast gaps of pensive margin. Twenty-six thousand pounds!

His aunt's solicitude had brought back certain matters into the fore-ground that his 'twelve 'undred a year!' had for a time driven away altogether. His thoughts went back to the wood-carving class. Twelve Hundred a Year. He sat on the edge of the bed in profound meditation and his boots fell 'whop' and 'whop' upon the floor, with a long interval between each 'whop'. Twenty-sixthousand pounds. 'By gum!' He dropped the remainder of his costume about him on the floor, got into bed, pulled the patchwork quilt over him and put his head on the pillow that had been first to hear of Ann Pornick's accession to his heart. But he did not think of Ann Pornick now.

It was about everything in the world except Ann Pornick that he seemed to be trying to think of – simultaneously. All the vivid happenings of the day came and went in his overtaxed brain: 'that old Bean' explaining and explaining, the fat man who wouldn't believe, an over-powering smell of peppermint, the banjo, Miss Mergle saying he deserved it, Chitterlow's vanishing round a corner, the wisdom and advice and warnings of his aunt and uncle. She was afraid he would marry beneath him, *was* she? She didn't know . . .

His brain made an excursion into the wood-carving class and presented Kipps with the picture of himself amazing that class by a modest yet clearly audible remark, 'I been left twenty-six thousand pounds.'

Then he told them all quietly but firmly that he had always loved Miss Walshingham, always, and so he had brought all his twenty-six thousand pounds with him to give to her there and then. He wanted nothing in return . . . Yes, he wanted nothing in return. He would give it to her all in an envelope and go. Of course he would keep the banjo – and a little present for his aunt and uncle – and a new suit perhaps – and one or two other things she would not miss. He went off at a tangent. He might buy a motor car, he might buy one of these here things that will play you a piano – that would make old Buggins sit up! He could pretend he had learnt to play – he might buy a bicycle and a cyclist suit . . .

A terrific multitude of plans of what he might do and in particular of what he might buy, came crowding into his brain, and he did not so much fall asleep as pass into a disorder of dreams in which he was driving a four-horse Tip-Top coach down Sandgate Hill ('I shall have to be precious careful'), wearing innumerable suits of clothes, and through some terrible accident wearing them all wrong. Consequently he was being laughed at. The coach vanished in the interest of the costume. He was wearing golfing suits and a silk hat. This passed into a nightmare that he was promenading on the Leas in a Highland costume, with a kilt that kept shrinking, and Shalford was following him with three policemen. 'He's my assistant,' Shalford kept repeating; 'he's escaped. He's an escaped Improver. Keep by him and in a minute you'll have to run him in. I know 'em. We say they wash, but they won't.' . . . He could feel the kilt creeping up his legs. He would have tugged at it to pull it down only his arms were paralysed. He had an impression of giddy crisis. He uttered a shriek of despair. '*Now!*' said Shalford. He woke in horror, his quilt had slipped off the bed.

He had a fancy he had just been called, that he had somehow overslept himself and missed going down for dusting. Then he perceived it was still night and light by reason of the moonlight, and that he was no longer in the Emporium. He wondered where he could be. He had a curious fancy that the world had been swept and rolled up like a carpet and that he was nowhere. It occurred to him that perhaps he was mad. 'Buggins!' he said. There was no answer, not even the defensive snore. No room, no Buggins, nothing!

Then he remembered better. He sat on the edge of his bed for some time. Could anyone have seen his face they would have seen it white and drawn with staring eyes. Then he groaned weakly. 'Twenty-six thousand pounds!' he whispered.

Just then it presented itself in an almost horribly overwhelming mass.

He remade his bed and returned to it. He was still dreadfully wakeful. It was suddenly clear to him that he need never trouble to get up punctually at seven again. That fact shone out upon him like a star through clouds. He was free to lie in bed as long as he liked, get up when he liked, go where he liked, have eggs every morning for breakfast or rashers or bloater paste or . . . Also he was going to astonish Miss Walshingham . . .

Astonish her and astonish her . . .

*   *   *

He was awakened by a thrush singing in the fresh dawn. The whole room was flooded with warm, golden sunshine. 'I say!' said the thrush. 'I say! I say! Twelve 'undred a year! Twelve 'Undred a Year! Twelve 'UNDRED a Year! I say! I say! I say!'

He sat up in bed and rubbed the sleep from his eyes with his knuckles. Then he jumped out of bed and began dressing very eagerly. He did not want to lose any time in beginning the new life.

BOOK TWO

Mr Coote, the Chaperon

CHAPTER ONE

The New Conditions

There comes a gentlemanly figure into these events who for a space takes a leading part therein; a Good Influence, a refined and amiable figure, Mr Chester Coote. You must figure him as about to enter our story, walking with a curious rectitude of bearing through the evening dusk towards the Public Library, erect, large-headed – he had a great, big head full of the suggestion of a powerful mind well under control – with a large, official-looking envelope in his white and knuckly hand. In the other he carries a gold-handled cane. He wears a silken grey jacket suit, buttoned up, and anon he coughs behind the official envelope. He has a prominent nose, slatey grey eyes and a certain heaviness about the mouth. His mouth hangs breathing open, with a slight protrusion of the lower jaw. His straw hat is pulled down a little in front, and he looks each person he passes in the eye, and directly his look is answered looks away.

Thus Mr Chester Coote, as he was on the evening when he came upon Kipps. He was a local house agent and a most active and gentlemanly person, a conscious gentleman, equally aware of society and the serious side of life. From amateur theatricals of a nice refined sort to science classes, few things were able to get along without him. He supplied a fine, full bass, a little flat and quavery perhaps, but very abundant, to the St Stylites' choir . . .

He passes on towards the Public Library, lifts the envelope in salutation to a passing curate, smiles and enters . . .

It was in the Public Library that he came upon Kipps.

By that time Kipps had been rich a week or more, and the change in his circumstances was visible upon his person. He was wearing a new suit of drab flannels, a Panama hat and a red tie for the first time, and he carried a silver-mounted stick with a tortoiseshell handle. He felt extraordinarily different, perhaps more different than he really was, from the meek Improver of a week ago. He felt as he felt dukes must feel, yet at bottom he was still modest. He was leaning on his stick and regarding the indicator with a respect that never palled. He faced round to meet Mr Coote's overflowing smile.

'What are you doang hea?' said Mr Chester Coote.

Kipps was momentarily abashed. 'Oh,' he said slowly, and then, 'Mooching round a bit.'

That Coote should address him with this easy familiarity was a fresh reminder of his enhanced social position. 'Jes' mooching round,' he said. 'I been back in Folkestone free days now. At my 'ouse, you know.'

'Ah!' said Mr Coote. 'I haven't yet had an opportunity of congratulating you on your good fortune.'

Kipps held out his hand. 'It was the cleanest surprise that ever was,' he said. 'When Mr Bean told me of it – you could have knocked me down with a feather.'

'It must mean a tremendous change for you.'

'O-o. Rather. Change? Why, I'm like the chap in the song they sing, I don't 'ardly know where I are. *You* know.'

'An extraordinary change,' said Mr Coote. 'I can quite believe it. Are you stopping in Folkestone?'

'For a bit. I got a 'ouse, you know. What my gran'father 'ad. I'm stopping there. His housekeeper was kep' on. Fancy – being in the same town and everything!'

'Precisely,' said Mr Coote. 'That's it!' and coughed like a sheep behind four straight fingers.

'Mr Bean got me to come back to see to things. Else I was out in New Romney, where my uncle and aunt live. But it's a Lark coming back. In a way . . .'

The conversation hung for a moment.

'Are you getting a book?' asked Coote.

'Well, I 'aven't got a ticket yet. But I shall get one all right, and have a go in at reading. I've often wanted to. Rather. I was just 'aving a look at this Indicator. First-class idea. Tells you all you want to know.'

'It's simple,' said Coote, and coughed again, keeping his eyes fixed on Kipps. For a moment they hung, evidently disinclined to part. Then Kipps jumped at an idea he had cherished for a day or more – not particularly in relation to Coote, but in relation to anyone.

'You doing anything?' he asked.

'Just called with a papah about the classes.'

'Because – Would you care to come up and look at my 'ouse and 'ave a smoke and a chat? Eh?' He made indicative back jerks of the head, and was smitten with a horrible doubt whether possibly this invitation might not be some hideous breach of etiquette. Was it, for example, the correct hour? 'I'd be awfully glad if you would,' he added.

Mr Coote begged for a moment while he handed the official-looking envelope to the librarian and then declared himself quite at Kipps's service. They muddled a moment over precedence at each door they went through and so emerged to the street.

'It feels awful rum to me at first, all this,' said Kipps ' 'Aving a 'ouse of my own and all that. It's strange, you know. 'Aving all day. Reely I don't 'ardly know what to do with my time.

'D'ju smoke?' he said suddenly, proffering a magnificent gold-decorated pigskin cigarette case, which he produced from nothing, almost as though it was some sort of trick. Coote hesitated and declined, and then, with great liberality, 'Don't let me hinder you . . . '

They walked a little way in silence, Kipps being chiefly concerned to affect ease in his new clothes and keeping a wary eye on Coote.

'It's rather a big windfall,' said Coote presently. 'It yields you an income – ?'

'Twelve 'undred a year,' said Kipps. 'Bit over – if anything.'

'Do you think of living in Folkestone?'

'Don't know 'ardly yet. I *may*. Then again, I may not. I got a furnished 'ouse, but I may let it.'

'Your plans are undecided?'

'That's jest it,' said Kipps.

'Very beautiful sunset it was tonight,' said Coote, and Kipps said, 'Wasn't it?' and they began to talk of the merits of sunsets. Did Kipps paint? Not since he was a boy. He didn't believe he could now. Coote said his sister was a painter and Kipps received this intimation with respect. Coote sometimes wished he could find time to paint himself – but one couldn't do everything, and Kipps said that was 'jest it'.

They came out presently upon the end of the Leas and looked down to where the squat dark masses of the harbour and harbour station, gemmed with pinpoint lights, crouched against the twilit grey of the sea. 'If one could do *that*,' said Coote, and Kipps was inspired to throw his head back, cock it on one side, regard the harbour with one eye shut and say that it would take some doing. Then Coote said something about 'Abend', which Kipps judged to be in a foreign language and got over by lighting another cigarette from his by no means completed first one. 'You're right, *puff, puff*.'

He felt that so far he had held up his end of the conversation in a very creditable manner, but that extreme discretion was advisable.

They turned away and Coote remarked that the sea was good for crossing, and asked Kipps if he had been over the water very much. Kipps said he hadn't been – 'much', but he thought very likely he'd have a run over to Boulogne soon, and Coote proceeded to talk of the charms of foreign travel, mentioning quite a number of unheard-of places by name. He had been to them! Kipps remained on the defensive, but behind his defences his heart sank. It was all very well to pretend, but presently it was bound to come out. *He* didn't know anything of all this . . .

So they drew near the house. At his own gate Kipps became extremely nervous. It was a fine, impressive door. He knocked neither a single knock nor a double, but about one and a half – an apologetic half. They were admitted by an irreproachable housemaid, with a steady eye, before which Kipps cringed dreadfully. He hung up his hat and fell about over hall chairs and things. 'There's a fire in the study, Mary?' he had the audacity to ask, though evidently he knew, and led the way upstairs panting. He tried to shut the door and discovered the housemaid behind him coming to light his lamp. This enfeebled him further. He said nothing until the door closed behind her. Meanwhile to show his *sang froid* he hummed and flitted towards the window, and here and there.

Coote went to the big hearthrug and turned and surveyed his host. His hand went to the back of his head and patted his occiput – a gesture frequent with him.

' 'Ere we are,' said Kipps, hands in his pockets and glancing round him.

It was a gaunt Victorian room with a heavy, dirty cornice, and the ceiling enriched by the radiant plaster ornament of an obliterated gas chandelier. It held two large glass-fronted bookcases, one of which was surmounted by a stuffed terrier encased in glass. There was a mirror over the mantel and hangings and curtains of magnificent crimson patternings. On the mantel were a huge black clock of classical design, vases in the Burslem Etruscan style, spills and toothpicks in large receptacles of carved rock, large lava ashtrays and an exceptionally big box of matches. The fender was very great and brassy. In a favourable position, under the window, was a spacious rosewood writing desk, and all the chairs and other furniture were of rosewood and well stuffed.

'This,' said Kipps, in something near an undertone, 'was the o' gentleman's study – my grandfather that was. 'E used to sit at that desk and write.'

'Books?'

'No. Letters to *The Times*, and things like that. 'E's got 'em all cut out – stuck in a book . . . Leastways, he 'ad. It's in that bookcase . . . Won't you sit down?'

Coote did, bowing very slightly, and Kipps secured his vacated position on the extensive black skin rug. He spread out his legs compass-fashion and tried to appear at his ease. The rug, the fender, the mantel and mirror conspired with great success to make him look a trivial and intrusive little creature amidst their commonplace hauteur, and his own shadow on the opposite wall seemed to think everything a great lark and mocked and made tremendous fun of him . . .

2

For a space Kipps played a defensive game and Coote drew the lines of the conversation. They kept away from the theme of Kipps's change of fortune, and Coote made remarks upon local and social affairs. 'You must take an interest in these things now,' was as much as he said in the way of personalities. But it speedily became evident that he was a person of wide and commanding social relationships. He spoke of 'society' being mixed in the neighbourhood and of the difficulty of getting people to work together, and 'do' things; they were cliquish. Incidentally he alluded quite familiarly to men with military titles, and once even to someone with a title, a Lady Punnet. Not snobbishly, you understand, nor deliberately, but quite in passing. He had, it appeared, talked to Lady Punnet about private theatricals! In connection with the Hospitals. She had been unreasonable and he had put her right, gently of course, but firmly. 'If you stand up to these people,' said Coote, 'they like you all the better.' It was also very evident he was at his ease with the clergy; 'My friend, Mr Densemore – a curate, you know, and rather curious, the Reverend *and* Honourable.' Coote grew visibly in Kipps's eyes as he said these things: he became not only the exponent of 'Vagner or Vargner', the man whose sister had painted a picture to be exhibited at the Royal Academy, the type of the hidden thing called culture, but a delegate, as it were, or at least an intermediary from that great world 'up there', where there were menservants, where there were titles, where people dressed for dinner, drank wine at meals, wine costing very often as much as three and sixpence the bottle, and followed through a maze of etiquette the most stupendous practices . . .

Coote sat back in the armchair smoking luxuriously and expanding pleasantly, with the delightful sense of Savoir Faire; Kipps sat forward, his elbows on his chair arm, alert, and his head a little on one side. You figure him as looking little and cheap and feeling smaller and cheaper amidst his new surroundings. But it was a most stimulating and interesting conversation. And soon it became less general and more serious and intimate. Coote spoke of people who had got on, and of people who hadn't, of people who seemed to be *in* everything and people who seemed to be *out* of everything, and then he came round to Kipps.

'You'll have a good time,' he said abruptly, with a smile that would have interested a dentist.

'I dunno,' said Kipps.

'There's mistakes, of course.'

'That's jest it.'

Coote lit a new cigarette. 'One can't help being interested in what you will do,' he remarked. 'Of course – for a young man of spirit, come suddenly into wealth – there's temptations.'

'I got to go careful,' said Kipps. 'O' Bean told me that at the very first.'

Coote went on to speak of pitfalls – of Betting, of Bad Companions.

'I know,' said Kipps, 'I know.'

'There's Doubt again,' said Coote. 'I know a young fellow – a solicitor – handsome, gifted. And yet, you know – utterly sceptical. Practically altogether a Sceptic.'

'Lor'!' said Kipps, 'not a Natheist?'

'I fear so,' said Coote. 'Really, you know, an awfully fine young fellow – Gifted! But full of this dreadful Modern Spirit – Cynical! All this Overman stuff. Nietzsche and all that . . . I wish I could do something for him.'

'Ah!' said Kipps and knocked the ash off his cigarette. 'I know a chap – one of our apprentices he was – once. Always scoffing . . . He lef'!' He paused. 'Never wrote for his refs,' he said, in the deep tone proper to a moral tragedy, and then, after a pause – 'Enlisted!'

'Ah!' said Coote.

'And often,' he said, after a pause, 'it's just the most spirited chaps, just the chaps one likes best, who Go Wrong.'

'It's temptation,' Kipps remarked.

He glanced at Coote, leant forward, knocked the ash from his cigarette into the mighty fender. 'That's jest it,' he said; 'you get tempted. Before you know where you are.'

'Modern life,' said Coote, 'is so – complex. It isn't everyone is Strong. Half the young fellows who go wrong, aren't really bad.'

'That's jest it,' said Kipps.

'One gets a tone from one's surroundings – '

'That's exactly it,' said Kipps.

He meditated. '*I* picked up with a chap,' he said. 'A Nacter. Leastways he writes plays. Clever fellow. But – '

He implied extensive moral obloquy by a movement of his head. 'Of course it's seeing life,' he added.

Coote pretended to understand the full implications of Kipps's remark. 'Is it *worth* it?' he asked.

'That's jest it,' said Kipps.

He decided to give some more. 'One gets talking,' he said. 'Then it's " 'ave a drink!" Old Methusaleh three stars – and where *are* you? *I* been drunk,' he said in a tone of profound humility, and added, 'lots of times.'

'Tut-tut,' said Coote.

'Dozens of times,' said Kipps, smiling sadly, and added, 'lately.'

His imagination became active and seductive. 'One thing leads to another. Cards, p'raps. Girls – '

'I know,' said Coote; 'I know.'

Kipps regarded the fire and flushed slightly. He borrowed a sentence that Chitterlow had recently used. 'One can't tell tales out of school,' he said.

'I can imagine it,' said Coote.

Kipps looked with a confidential expression into Coote's face. 'It was bad enough when money was limited,' he remarked. 'But now – ' he spoke with raised eyebrows, 'I got to steady down.'

'You *must*,' said Coote, protruding his lips into a sort of whistling concern for a moment.

'I must,' said Kipps, nodding his head slowly with raised eyebrows. He looked at his cigarette end and threw it into the fender. He was beginning to think he was holding his own in this conversation rather well, after all.

Kipps was never a good liar. He was the first to break silence. 'I don't mean to say I been reely bad or reely bad drunk. A 'eadache perhaps – three or four times, say. But there it is!'

'I have never tasted alcohol in my life,' said Coote, with an immense frankness, 'never!'

'No?'

'Never. I don't feel *I* should be likely to get drunk at all – it isn't that. And I don't go so far as to say even that in small quantities – at meals – it does one harm. But if I take it, someone else who doesn't know where to stop – you see?'

'That's jest it,' said Kipps, with admiring eyes.

'I smoke,' admitted Coote. 'One doesn't want to be a Pharisee.'

It struck Kipps what a tremendously Good chap this Coote was, not only tremendously clever and educated and a gentleman and one knowing Lady Punnet, but Good. He seemed to be giving all his time and thought to doing good things to other people. A great desire to confide certain things to him arose. At first Kipps hesitated whether he should confide an equal desire for Benevolent activities or for further Depravity – either was in his mind. He rather affected the pose of the Good Intentioned Dog. Then suddenly his impulses took quite a different turn, fell indeed into what was a far more serious rut in his mind. It seemed to him Coote might be able to do for him something he very much wanted done.

'Companionship accounts for so much,' said Coote.

'That's jest it,' said Kipps. 'Of course, you know, in my new position – That's just the difficulty.'

He plunged boldly at his most secret trouble. He knew that he wanted refinement – culture. It was all very well – but he knew. But how was one to get it? He knew no one, knew no people – He rested on the broken sentence. The shop chaps were all very well, very good chaps and all that, but not what one wanted. 'I feel be'ind,' said Kipps. 'I feel out of it. And consequently I feel it's no good. And then if temptation comes along . . . '

'Exactly,' said Coote.

Kipps spoke of his respect for Miss Walshingham and her freckled friend. He contrived not to look too self-conscious. 'You know, I'd like to talk to people like that, but I can't. A chap's afraid of giving himself away.'

'Of course,' said Coote, 'of course.'

'I went to a middle-class school, you know. You mustn't fancy I'm one of these here board-school chaps, but you know it reely wasn't a first-class affair. Leastways he didn't take pains with us. If you didn't want to learn you needn't – I don't believe it was *much* better than one of these here national schools. We wore mortar boards, o' course. But what's *that*?

'I'm a regular fish out of water with this money. When I got it – it's a week ago – reely I thought I'd got everything I wanted. But I dunno what to *do*.' His voice went up into a squeak. 'Practically,' he said, 'it's no good shuttin' my eyes to things – I'm a gentleman.'

Coote indicated a serious assent. 'And there's the responsibilities of a gentleman,' he remarked.

'That's jest it,' said Kipps.

'There's calling on people,' said Kipps. 'If you want to go on knowing Someone you knew before like. People that's refined.' He laughed nervously. 'I'm a regular fish out of water,' he said, with expectant eyes on Coote.

But Coote only nodded for him to go on.

'This actor chap,' he meditated, 'is a good sort of chap. But 'e isn't what *I* call a gentleman. I got to 'old myself in with 'im. 'E'd make me go it wild in no time. 'E's pretty near the on'y chap I know. Except the shop chaps. They've come round to 'ave supper once already and a bit of a sing-song afterwards. I sang. I got a banjo, you know, and I vamp a bit. Vamping – you know. Haven't got far in the book – *'Ow to Vamp* – but still I'm getting on. Jolly, of course, in a way, but what does it *lead* to? . . . Besides that, there's my aunt and uncle. *They*'re very good old people – very – jest a bit interfering p'r'aps and thinking one isn't grown up, but Right enough. Only – It isn't what I *want*. I feel I've got be'ind with everything. I want to make it up again. I want to get with educated people who know 'ow to do things – in the regular, proper way.'

His beautiful modesty awakened nothing but benevolence in the mind of Chester Coote.

'If I had someone like you,' said Kipps, 'that I knew regular like – '

From that point their course ran swift and easy. 'If I *could* be of any use to you,' said Coote . . .

'But you're so busy and all that.'

'Not *too* busy. You know, your case is a very interesting one. It was partly that made me speak to you and draw you out. Here you are with all this money and no experience, a spirited young chap – '

'That's jest it,' said Kipps.

'I thought I'd see what you were made of, and I must confess I've rarely talked to anyone that I've found quite so interesting as you have been – '

'I seem able to say things to you like, somehow,' said Kipps.

'I'm glad. I'm tremendously glad.'

'I want a Friend. That's it – straight.'

'My dear chap, if I – '

'Yes, but – '

'*I* want a Friend, too.'

'Reely?'

'Yes. You know, my dear Kipps – if I may call you that.'

'Go on,' said Kipps.

'I'm rather a lonely dog myself. *This* tonight – I've not had anyone I've spoken to so freely of my Work for months.'

'No?'

'Yes. And, my dear chap, if I can do anything to guide or help you – '
Coote displayed all his teeth in a kindly tremulous smile and his eyes were shiny.

'Shake 'ands,' said Kipps, deeply moved, and he and Coote rose and clasped with mutual emotion.

'It's reely too good of you,' said Kipps.

'Whatever I can do I will,' said Coote.

And so their compact was made. From that moment they were Friends, intimate, confidential, high-thinking, *sotto voce* friends. All the rest of their talk (and it inclined to be interminable) was an expansion of that. For that night Kipps wallowed in self-abandonment and Coote behaved as one who had received a great trust. That sinister passion for pedagogy to which the Good Intentioned are so fatally liable, that passion of infinite presumption that permits one weak human being to arrogate the direction of another weak human being's affairs, had Coote in its grip. He was to be a sort of lay confessor and director of Kipps, he was to help Kipps in a thousand ways, he was in fact to chaperon Kipps into the higher and better sort of English life. He was to tell him his faults, advise him about the right thing to do –

'It's all these things I don't know,' said Kipps. 'I don't know, for instance, what's the right sort of dress to wear – I don't even know if I'm dressed right now – '

'All these things' – Coote stuck out his lips and nodded rapidly to show he understood – 'Trust me for that,' he said, 'trust me.'

As the evening wore on Coote's manner changed, became more and more the manner of a proprietor. He began to take up his role, to survey Kipps with a new, with a critical affection. It was evident the thing fell in with his ideas. 'It will be awfully interesting,' he said. 'You know, Kipps, you're really good stuff.' (Every sentence now he said 'Kipps' or 'my dear Kipps' with a curiously authoritative intonation.)

'I know,' said Kipps, 'only there's such a lot of things I don't seem to be up to some'ow. That's where the trouble comes in.'

They talked and talked, and now Kipps was talking freely. They rambled over all sorts of things. Among others Kipps's character was dealt with at length. Kipps gave valuable lights on it. 'When I'm reely excited,' he said, 'I don't seem to care *what* I do. I'm like that.' And again, 'I don't like to do anything under'and. I *must* speak out . . . '

He picked a piece of cotton from his knee, the fire grimaced behind his back, and his shadow on the wall and ceiling was disrespectfully convulsed.

Kipps went to bed at last with an impression of important things settled, and he lay awake for quite a long time. He felt he was lucky. He had known – in fact Buggins and Carshot and Pierce had made it very clear indeed – that his status in life had changed and that stupendous adaptations had to be achieved, but the problem of their achievement had driven them into the realm of the incredible. Here in the simplest, easiest way was the adapter. The thing had become possible. Not of course easy, but possible.

There was much to learn through sheer intellectual toil – methods of address, bowing, an enormous complexity of laws. One broken, you are an outcast. How, for example, would one encounter Lady Punnet? It was quite possible some day he might really have to do that. Coote might introduce him. 'Lord!' he said aloud to the darkness between grinning and dismay. He figured himself going into the Emporium to buy a tie, for example, and there in the face of Buggins, Carshot, Pierce and the rest of them, meeting 'my friend, Lady Punnet!' It might not end with Lady Punnet! His imagination plunged and bolted with him, galloped, took wings and soared to romantic, to poetical altitudes . . .

Suppose some day one met Royalty. By accident, say! He soared to that! After all – twelve hundred a year is a lift, a tremendous lift. How did one address Royalty? 'Your Majesty's Goodness,' it would be, no doubt – something like that – and on the knees. He became impersonal. Over a thousand a year made him an Esquire, didn't it? He thought that was it. In which case, wouldn't he have to be presented at court? Velvet breeches like you wear cycling, and a sword! What a curious place a court must be! Kneeling and bowing, and what was it Miss Mergle used to talk about? Of course! – ladies with long trains walking about backwards. Everybody walked about backwards at court, he knew, when not actually on their knees. Perhaps, though, some people regular stood up to the King! Talked to him, just as one might talk to Buggins, say. Cheek, of course! Dukes, it might be, did that – by permission? Millionnaires? . . .

From such thoughts this free citizen of our Crowned Republic passed insensibly into dreams, turgid dreams of that vast ascent which constitutes the true-born Briton's social scheme, which terminates with retrogressive progression and a bending back.

The next morning he came down to breakfast looking grave – a man with much before him in the world.

Kipps made a very special thing of his breakfast. Daily once-hopeless dreams came true then. It had been customary in the Emporium to supplement Shalford's generous, indeed unlimited, supply of bread and butter-substitute by private purchases, and this had given Kipps very broad, artistic conceptions of what the meal might be. Now there would be a cutlet or so or a mutton chop – this splendour Buggins had reported from the great London clubs – haddock, kipper, whiting or fish-balls, eggs, boiled or scrambled, or eggs and bacon, kidney also frequently and sometimes liver. Amidst a garland of such themes, sausages, black and white puddings, bubble-and-squeak, fried cabbage and scallops came and went. Always as camp followers came potted meat in all varieties, cold bacon, German sausage, brawn, marmalade and two sorts of jam, and when he had finished these he would sit among his plates and smoke a cigarette and look at all these dishes crowded round him with a beatific approval. It was his principal meal. He was sitting with his cigarette regarding his apartment with that complacency begotten of a generous plan of feeding successfully realised, when newspapers and post arrived.

There were several things by the post, tradesmen's circulars and cards and two pathetic begging letters – his luck had got into the papers – and there was a letter from a literary man and a book to enforce his request for ten shillings to put down Socialism. The book made it very clear that prompt action on the part of property owners was becoming urgent, if property was to last out the year. Kipps dipped in it and was seriously perturbed. And there was a letter from old Kipps saying it was difficult to leave the shop and come over and see him again just yet, but that he had been to a sale at Lydd the previous day and bought a few good old books and things it would be difficult to find the equal of in Folkestone. 'They don't know the value of these things out here,' wrote old Kipps, 'but you may depend upon it they are valuable,' and a brief financial statement followed. 'There is an engraving someone might come along and offer you a lot of money for one of these days. Depend upon it, these old things are about the best investment you could make . . . '

Old Kipps had long been addicted to sales, and his nephew's good fortune had converted what had once been but a looking and a craving – he had rarely even bid for anything in the old days except the garden tools or the kitchen gallipots or things like that, things one gets for sixpence and finds a use for – into a very active pleasure. Sage and penetrating inspection, a certain mystery of bearing, tactical bids and Purchase! – Purchase! – the old man had had a good time.

While Kipps was rereading the begging letters and wishing he had the sound, clear common sense of Buggins to help him a little, the Parcels Post brought along the box from his uncle. It was a large, insecure-looking case, held together by a few still loyal nails, and by what the British War Office would have recognised at once as an Army Corps of string, rags and odds and ends tied together. Kipps unpacked it with a table knife, assisted at a critical point by the poker, and found a number of books and other objects of an antique type.

There were three bound volumes of early issues of *Chambers's Journal*, a copy of *Punch's Pocket Book* for 1875, Sturm's *Reflections*, an early version of Gill's *Geography* (slightly torn), an illustrated work on Spinal Curvature, an early edition of Kirke's *Human Physiology*, *The Scottish Chiefs*[19] and a little volume on *The Language of Flowers*. There was a fine steel engraving, oak-framed and with some rusty spots, done in the Colossal style and representing the Handwriting on the Wall. There were also a copper kettle, a pair of candle snuffers, a brass shoehorn, a tea caddy to lock, two decanters (one stoppered) and what was probably a portion of an eighteenth-century child's rattle.

Kipps examined these objects one by one and wished he knew more about them. Turning over the pages of the *Physiology* again he came upon a striking plate in which a youth of agreeable profile displayed his interior in an unstinted manner to the startled eye. It was a new view of humanity altogether for Kipps, and it arrested his mind.

'Chubes,' he whispered. 'Chubes.'

This anatomised figure made him forget for a space that he was 'practically a gentleman' altogether, and he was still surveying its extra-ordinary complications when another reminder of a world quite outside those spheres of ordered gentility into which his dreams had carried him overnight, arrived (following the servant) in the person of Chitterlow.

5

' 'El–*lo*!' said Kipps, rising.

'Not busy?' said Chitterlow, enveloping Kipps's hand for a moment in one of his own and tossing the yachting cap upon the monumental carved-oak sideboard.

'Only a bit of reading,' said Kipps.

'Reading, eh?' Chitterlow cocked the red eye at the books and other properties for a moment and then, 'I've been expecting you round again one night.'

'I been coming round,' said Kipps. 'On'y there's a chap 'ere – I was coming round last night on'y I met 'im.'

He walked to the hearthrug. Chitterlow drifted around the room for a time, glancing at things as he talked. 'I've altered that play tremendously since I saw you,' he said. 'Pulled it all to pieces.'

'What play's that, Chit'low?'

'The one we were talking about. You know. You said something – I don't know if you meant it – about buying half of it. Not the tragedy. I wouldn't sell my own twin brother a share in that. That's my investment. That's my Serious Work. No! I mean that new farce I've been on to. Thing with the business about a beetle.'

'Oo yes,' said Kipps. '*I* remember.'

'I thought you would. Said you'd take a fourth share for a hundred pounds. *You* know.'

'I seem to remember something – '

'Well, it's all different. Every bit of it. I'll tell you. You remember what you said about a butterfly? You got confused, you know – Old Meth. Kept calling the beetle a butterfly and that set me off. I've made it quite different. Quite different. Instead of Popplewaddle – thundering good farce name that, you know; for all that it came from a Visitors' List – instead of Popplewaddle getting a beetle down his neck and rushing about, I've made him a collector – collects butterflies, and this one you know's a rare one. Comes in at window, centre.' Chitterlow began to illustrate with appropriate gestures. 'Pop rushes about after it. Forgets he mustn't let on he's in the house. After that – Tells 'em. Rare butterfly, worth lots of money. Some are, you know. Everyone's on to it after that. Butterfly can't get out of room; every time it comes out to have a try, rush and scurry. Well, I've worked on that. Only – '

He came very close to Kipps. He held up one hand horizontally and tapped it in a striking and confidential manner with the fingers of the other. 'Something else,' he said. 'That's given me a Real Ibsenish Touch – like the *Wild Duck*. You know that woman – I've made her lighter – and she sees it. When they're chasing the butterfly the third time, she's on! She looks. "That's me!" she says. Bif! Pestered Butterfly. *She's* the Pestered Butterfly. It's legitimate. Much more legitimate than the *Wild Duck* – where there isn't a duck!

'Knock 'em! The very title ought to knock 'em. I've been working like a horse at it . . . You'll have a gold mine in that quarter share, Kipps . . . *I* don't mind. It's suited me to sell it, and suited you to buy. Bif!'

Chitterlow interrupted his discourse to ask, 'You haven't any brandy in the house, have you? Not to drink, you know. But I want just an eggcupful to pull me steady. My liver's a bit queer . . . It doesn't matter, if you haven't. Not a bit. I'm like that. Yes, whisky'll do. Better!'

Kipps hesitated for a moment, then turned and fumbled in the cupboard of his sideboard. Presently he disinterred a bottle of whisky and placed it on the table. Then he put out first one bottle of soda water and after the hesitation of a moment another. Chitterlow picked up the bottle and read the label. 'Good old Methusaleh,' he said. Kipps handed him the corkscrew and then his hand fluttered up to his mouth. 'I'll have to ring now,' he said, 'to get glasses.' He hesitated for a moment before doing so, leaning doubtfully as it were towards the bell.

When the housemaid appeared he was standing on the hearthrug with his legs wide apart, with the bearing of a desperate fellow. And after they had both had whiskies – 'You know a decent whisky,' Chitterlow remarked, and took another 'just to drink' – Kipps produced cigarettes and the conversation flowed again.

Chitterlow paced the room. He was, he explained, taking a day off; that was why he had come around to see Kipps. Whenever he thought of any extensive change in a play he was writing he always took a day off. In the end it saved time to do so. It prevented his starting rashly upon work that might have to be rewritten. There was no good in doing work when you might have to do it over again, none whatever.

Presently they were descending the steps by the Parade *en route* for The Warren, with Chitterlow doing the talking and going with a dancing drop from step to step . . .

They had a great walk, not a long one, but a great one. They went up by the Sanatorium and over the East Cliff and into that queer little wilderness of slippery and tumbling clay and rock under the chalk cliffs, a wilderness of thorn and bramble, wild rose and wayfaring tree, that adds so greatly to Folkestone's charm. They traversed its intricacies and clambered up to the crest of the cliffs at last by a precipitous path that Chitterlow endowed in some mysterious way with suggestions of Alpine adventure. Every now and then he would glance aside at sea and cliffs with a fresh boyishness of imagination that brought back New Romney and the stranded wrecks to Kipps's memory; but mostly he bored on with his great obsession of plays and playwriting, and that empty absurdity that is so serious to his kind, his Art. That was a thing that needed a monstrous lot of explaining. Along they went, sometimes abreast, sometimes in single file, up the little paths and down the little paths, and in among the bushes and out along the edge above the beach, and Kipps went along trying ever and again to get an insignificant word in edgeways, and the gestures of Chitterlow flew wide and far and his great voice rose and fell, and he said this and he said that and he biffed and banged into the circumambient Inane.

It was assumed that they were embarked upon no more trivial enterprise than the Reform of the British Stage, and Kipps found himself classed with many opulent and even royal and noble amateurs – the Honourable Thomas Norgate came in here – who had interested themselves in the practical realisation of high ideals about the Drama. Only he had a finer understanding of these things, and instead of being preyed upon by the common professional – 'and they *are* a lot,' said Chitterlow; 'I haven't toured for nothing' – he would have Chitterlow. Kipps gathered few details. It was clear he had bought the quarter of a farcical comedy – practically a gold mine – and it would appear it would be a good thing to buy the half. A suggestion, or the suggestion of a suggestion, floated out that he should buy the whole play and produce it forthwith. It seemed he was to produce the play upon a royalty system of a new sort, whatever a royalty system of any sort might be. Then there was some doubt, after all, whether that farcical comedy was in itself sufficient to revolutionise the present lamentable state of the British Drama. Better perhaps for such a purpose was that tragedy – as yet unfinished – which was to display all that Chitterlow knew about women, and which was to centre about a Russian nobleman embodying the fundamental Chitterlow personality. Then it became clearer that Kipps was to produce several plays. Kipps was to produce a great number of plays. Kipps was to found a National Theatre . . .

It is probable that Kipps would have expressed some sort of disavowal, if he had known how to express it. Occasionally his face assumed an expression of whistling meditation, but that was as far as he got towards protest.

In the clutch of Chitterlow and the Incalculable, Kipps came round to the house in Fenchurch Street and was there made to participate in the midday meal. He came to the house forgetting certain confidences, and was reminded of the existence of a Mrs Chitterlow (with the finest completely untrained contralto voice in England) by her appearance. She had an air of being older than Chitterlow, although probably she wasn't, and her hair was a reddish brown, streaked with gold. She was dressed in one of those complaisant garments that are dressing gowns or tea gowns or bathing wraps or rather original evening robes according to the exigencies of the moment – from the first Kipps was aware that she possessed a warm and rounded neck, and her well-moulded arms came and vanished from the sleeves – and she had large, expressive brown eyes that he discovered ever and again fixed in an enigmatical manner upon his own.

A simple but sufficient meal had been distributed with careless spontaneity over the little round table in the room with the photographs and looking glass; and when a plate had by Chitterlow's direction been taken from under the marmalade in the cupboard and the kitchen fork and a knife that was not loose in its handle had been found for Kipps, they began and made a tumultuous repast. Chitterlow ate with quiet enormity, but it did not interfere with the flow of his talk. He introduced Kipps to his wife very briefly; she had evidently heard of Kipps before, and he made it vaguely evident that the production of the comedy was the thing chiefly settled. His reach extended over the table, and he troubled nobody. When Mrs Chitterlow, who for a little while seemed socially self-conscious, reproved him for taking a potato with a jab of his fork, he answered, 'Well, you shouldn't have married a man of Genius,' and from a subsequent remark it was perfectly clear that Chitterlow's standing in this respect was made no secret of in his household.

They drank old Methusaleh and syphon soda, and there was no clearing away; they just sat among the plates and things, and Mrs Chitterlow took her husband's tobacco pouch and made a cigarette and smoked and blew smoke and looked at Kipps with her large brown eyes. Kipps had seen cigarettes smoked by ladies before, 'for fun', but this was real smoking. It frightened him rather. He felt he must not encourage this lady – at any rate in Chitterlow's presence.

They became very cheerful after the repast, and as there was now no waste to deplore, such as one experiences in the windy open air, Chitterlow gave his voice full vent. He fell to praising Kipps very highly and loudly. He said he had known Kipps was the right sort, he had seen it from the first, almost before he got up out of the mud on that memorable night. 'You can,' he said, 'sometimes. That was why – ' he stopped, but he seemed on the verge of explaining that it was his certainty of Kipps being the right sort had led him to confer this great Fortune upon him. He left that impression. He threw out a number of long sentences and material for sentences of a highly philosophical and incoherent character about Coincidences. It became evident he considered dramatic criticism in a perilously low condition . . .

About four Kipps found himself stranded, as it were, by a receding Chitterlow on a seat upon the Leas.

He was chiefly aware that Chitterlow was an overwhelming personality. He puffed his cheeks and blew.

No doubt this was seeing life, but had he particularly wanted to see life that day? In a way Chitterlow had interrupted him. The day he had designed for himself was altogether different from this. He had been going to read through a precious little volume called *Don't* that Coote had sent round for him, a book of invaluable hints, a summary of British deportment that had only the one defect of being at points a little out of date.

That reminded him he had intended to perform a difficult exercise called an Afternoon Call upon the Cootes, as a preliminary to doing it in deadly earnest upon the Walshinghams. It was no good today, anyhow, now.

He came back to Chitterlow. He would have to explain to Chitterlow he was taking too much for granted, he would have to do that. It was so difficult to do in Chitterlow's presence though; in his absence it was easy enough. This half share, and taking a theatre and all of it, was going too far.

The quarter share was right enough, he supposed, but even that – ! A hundred pounds! What wealth is there left in the world after one has paid out a hundred pounds from it?

He had to recall that in a sense Chitterlow had indeed brought him his fortune before he could face even that.

You must not think too hardly of him. To Kipps, you see, there was as yet no such thing as proportion in these matters. A hundred pounds went to his horizon. A hundred pounds seemed to him just exactly as big as any other large sum of money.

The Walshinghams

The Cootes live in a little house in Bouverie Square with a tangle of Virginia creeper up the verandah.

Kipps had been troubled in his mind about knocking double or single – it is these things show what a man is made of – but happily there was a bell.

A queer little maid with a big cap admitted Kipps and took him through a bead curtain and a door into a little drawing-room, with a black and gold piano, a glazed bookcase, a Moorish cosy corner and a draped looking-glass overmantel bright with Regent Street ornaments and photographs of various intellectual lights. A number of cards of invitation to meetings and the match list of a Band of Hope[20] cricket club were stuck into the looking-glass frame, with Coote's name as a vice-president. There was a bust of Beethoven over the bookcase and the walls were thick with conscientiously executed but carelessly selected 'views' in oil and watercolours in gilt frames. At the end of the room facing the light was a portrait that struck Kipps at first as being Coote in spectacles and feminine costume and that he afterwards decided must be Coote's mother. Then the original appeared and he discovered that it was Coote's elder and only sister who kept house for him. She wore her hair in a knob behind, and the sight of the knob suggested to Kipps an explanation for a frequent gesture of Coote's, a patting exploratory movement to the back of his head. And then it occurred to him that this was quite an absurd idea altogether.

She said, 'Mr Kipps, I believe,' and Kipps laughed pleasantly and said, 'That's it!' and then she told him that 'Chester' had gone down to the art school to see about sending off some drawings or other and that he would be back soon. Then she asked Kipps if he painted, and showed him the pictures on the wall. Kipps asked her where each one was 'of', and when she showed him some of the Leas slopes he said he never would have recognised them. He said it was funny how things looked in a picture very often. 'But they're awfully *good*,' he said. 'Did you do them?' He would look at them with his neck arched like a swan's, his head back and on one side, and then suddenly peer closely into them. 'They *are* good. I wish I could paint.'

'That's what Chester says,' she answered. 'I tell him he has better things to do.'

Kipps seemed to get on very well with her.

Then Coote came in and they left her and went upstairs together and had a good talk about reading and the Rules of Life. Or rather Coote talked, and the praises of thought and reading were in his mouth . . .

You must figure Coote's study, a little bedroom put to studious uses, and over the mantel an array of things he had been led to believe indicative of culture and refinement: an autotype of Rossetti's *Annunciation*, an autotype of Watts's *Minotaur*, a Swiss carved pipe with many joints and a photograph of Amiens Cathedral (these two the spoils of travel), a phrenological bust and some broken fossils from The Warren. A rotating bookshelf carried the *Encyclopaedia Britannica* (tenth edition), and on the top of it a large official-looking, age-grubby envelope bearing the mystic words 'On His Majesty's Service', a number or so of the *Bookman*[21] and a box of cigarettes were lying. A table under the window bore a little microscope, some dust in a saucer, some grimy glass slips and broken cover glasses; for Coote had 'gone in for' biology a bit. The longer side of the room was given over to bookshelves, neatly edged with pinked American cloth, and with an array of books – no worse an array of books than you find in any public library; an almost haphazard accumulation of obsolete classics, contemporary successes, the *Hundred Best Books* (including Samuel Warren's *Ten Thousand a Year*),[22] old school books, directories, *The Times Atlas*, Ruskin in bulk, Tennyson complete in one volume, Longfellow, Charles Kingsley, Smiles and Mrs Humphry Ward, a guide book or so, several medical pamphlets, odd magazine numbers, and much indescribable rubbish – in fact, a compendium of the contemporary British mind. And in front of this array stood Kipps, ill-taught and untrained, respectful, awestricken and, for a moment at any rate, willing to learn, while Coote, the exemplary Coote, talked to him like a bishop of reading and the virtue in books.

'Nothing enlarges the mind,' said Coote, 'like Travel and Books . . . And they're both so easy nowadays, and so cheap!'

'I've often wanted to 'ave a good go in at reading,' Kipps replied.

'You'd hardly believe,' Coote said, 'how much you can get out of books. Provided you avoid trashy reading, that is. You ought to make a rule, Kipps, and read one Serious Book a week. Of course, we can Learn even from Novels, Nace Novels that is, but it isn't the same thing as serious reading. I made a rule, One Serious Book and One

Novel – no more. There are some of the serious books I've been reading lately – on that table: *Sartor Resartus*,[23] Mrs Twaddletome's *Pond Life*, the *Scottish Chiefs*, *Life and Letters of Dean Farrar* . . . '

2

There came at last the sound of a gong and Kipps descended to tea in that state of nervous apprehension at the difficulties of eating and drinking that his aunt's knuckle rappings had implanted in him for ever. Over Coote's shoulder he became aware of a fourth person in the Moorish cosy corner, and he turned, leaving incomplete something incoherent he was saying to Miss Coote about his modest respect and desire for literature, to discover this fourth person was Miss Helen Walshingham, hatless and looking very much at home.

She rose at once with an extended hand to meet his hesitation.

'You're stopping in Folkestone, Mr Kipps?'

' 'Ere on a bit of business,' said Kipps. 'I thought you was away in Bruges.'

'That's later,' said Miss Walshingham. 'We're stopping until my brother's holiday begins and we're trying to let our house. Where are you staying in Folkestone?'

'I got a 'ouse of mine – on the Leas.'

'I've heard all about your good fortune – this afternoon.'

'Isn't it a Go!' said Kipps. 'I 'aven't nearly got to believe its reely 'appened yet. When that Mr Bean told me of it you could 'ave knocked me down with a feather . . . It's a tremenjous change for me.'

He discovered Miss Coote was asking him whether he took milk and sugar. '*I* don't mind,' said Kipps. 'Just as you like.'

Coote became active handing tea and bread and butter. It was thinly cut, and the bread was rather new, and half of the slice that Kipps took fell upon the floor. He had been holding it by the edge, for he was not used to this migratory method of taking tea without plates or table. This little incident ruled him out of the conversation for a time, and when he came to attend to it again they were talking about something or other prodigious – a performer of some sort – that was coming, called, it seemed, 'Padrooski'. So Kipps, who had quietly dropped into a chair, ate his bread and butter, said 'no, thenk you' to any more, and by this discreet restraint got more freedom with his cup and saucer.

Apart from the confusion natural to tea, he was in a state of tremulous excitement on account of the presence of Miss Walshingham. He glanced from Miss Coote to her brother and then at Helen. He regarded her over the top of his cup as he drank. Here she was, solid and real. It was wonderful. He remarked, as he had done at times before, the easy flow of the dark hair back from her brow over her ears, the shapeliness of the white hands that came out from her simple white cuffs, the delicate pencilling of her brow.

Presently she turned her face to him almost suddenly, and smiled with the easiest assurance of friendship.

'You will go, I suppose,' she said, and added, 'to the Recital.'

'If I'm in Folkestone I shall,' said Kipps, clearing away a little hoarseness. 'I don't *know* much about music, but what I do know I like.'

'I'm sure you'll like Paderewski,'[24] she said.

'If you do,' he said, 'I des say I shall.'

He found Coote very kindly taking his cup.

'Do you think of living in Folkestone?' asked Miss Coote, in a tone of proprietorship, from the hearthrug.

'No,' said Kipps, 'that's jest it – I hardly know.' He also said that he wanted to look around a bit before doing anything.

'There's so much to consider,' said Coote, smoothing the back of his head.

'I may go back to New Romney for a bit,' said Kipps. 'I got an uncle and aunt there. I reely don't know.'

Helen regarded him thoughtfully for a moment. 'You must come and see us,' she said, 'before we go to Bruges.'

'Oo, rather!' said Kipps. 'If I may.'

'Yes, do,' she said, and suddenly stood up before Kipps could formulate an enquiry when he should call.

'You're sure you can spare that drawing board?' she said to Miss Coote, and the conversation passed out of range.

And when he had said goodbye to Miss Walshingham and she had repeated her invitation to call, he went upstairs again with Coote to look out certain initiatory books they had had under discussion. And then Kipps, blowing very resolutely, went back to his own place, bearing under his arm (1) *Sesame and Lilies*,[25] (2) *Sir George Tressady*,[26] (3) an anonymous book on *Vitality* that Coote particularly esteemed. And, having got to his own sitting-room, he opened *Sesame and Lilies* and read it with ruthless determination for some time.

Presently he leant back and gave himself up to the business of trying to imagine just exactly what Miss Walshingham could have thought of him when she saw him. Doubts about the precise effect of the grey-flannel suit began to trouble him. He turned to the mirror over the mantel, and then got on to a chair to study the hang of the trousers. It looked all right. Luckily, she had not seen the Panama hat. He knew that he had the brim turned up wrong, but he could not find out which way the brim was right. However, that she had not seen. He might perhaps ask at the shop where he bought it.

He meditated for awhile on his reflected face – doubtful whether he liked it or not – and then got down again and flitted across to the sideboard where there lay two little books, one in a cheap magnificent cover of red and gold and the other in green canvas. The former was called, as its cover witnessed, *Manners and Rules of Good Society, by a Member of the Aristocracy*,[27] and after the cover had indulged in a band of gilded decoration, light-hearted but natural under the circumstances, it added 'TWENTY-FIRST EDITION'. The second was that admirable classic *The Art of Conversing*. Kipps returned with these to his seat, placed the two before him, opened the latter with a sigh and flattened it under his hand.

Then with knitted brows he began to read onward from a mark, his lips moving.

Having thus acquired possession of an idea, the little ship should not be abruptly launched into deep waters, but should be first permitted to glide gently and smoothly into the shallows, that is to say, the conversation should not be commenced by broadly and roundly stating a fact, or didactically expressing an opinion, as the subject would be thus virtually or summarily disposed of, or perhaps be met with a 'Really' or 'Indeed', or some equally brief monosyllabic reply. If an opposite opinion were held by the person to whom the remark were addressed, he might not, if a stranger, care to express it in the form of a direct contradiction, or actual dissent. To glide imperceptibly into conversation is the object to be attained.

At this point Mr Kipps rubbed his fingers through his hair with an expression of some perplexity and went back to the beginning.

When Kipps made his call on the Walshinghams, it all happened so differently from the *Manners and Rules* prescription ('Paying Calls') that he was quite lost from the very outset. Instead of the footman or maidservant proper in these cases, Miss Walshingham opened the door to him herself. 'I'm so glad you've come,' she said, with one of her rare smiles.

She stood aside for him to enter the rather narrow passage.

'I thought I'd call,' he said, retaining his hat and stick.

She closed the door and led the way to a little drawing-room, which impressed Kipps as being smaller and less emphatically coloured than that of the Cootes, and in which at first only a copper bowl of white poppies upon the brown tablecloth caught his particular attention.

'You won't think it unconventional to come in, Mr Kipps, will you?' she remarked. 'Mother is out.'

'I don't mind,' he said, smiling amiably, 'if you don't.'

She walked around the table and stood regarding him across it, with that same look between speculative curiosity and appreciation that he remembered from the last of the art-class meetings.

'I wondered whether you would call or whether you wouldn't before you left Folkestone.'

'I'm not leaving Folkestone for a bit, and any'ow, I should have called on you.'

'Mother will be sorry she was out. I've told her about you, and she wants, I know, to meet you.'

'I saw 'er – if that was 'er – in the shop,' said Kipps.

'Yes – you did, didn't you! . . . She has gone out to make some duty calls, and I didn't go. I had something to write. I write a little, you know.'

'Reely!' said Kipps.

'It's nothing much,' she said, 'and it comes to nothing.' She glanced at a little desk near the window, on which there lay some paper. 'One must do something.' She broke off abruptly. 'Have you seen our outlook?' she asked and walked to the window, and Kipps came and stood beside her. 'We look on the square. It might be worse, you know. That out-porter's truck there is horrid – and the railings, but it's better than staring one's social replica in the face, isn't it? It's pleasant in early spring – bright green, laid on with a dry brush – and it's pleasant in autumn.'

'I like it,' said Kipps. 'That laylock there is pretty, isn't it?'

'Children come and pick it at times,' she remarked.

'I dessay they do,' said Kipps.

He rested on his hat and stick and looked appreciatively out of the window, and she glanced at him for one swift moment. A suggestion that might have come from *The Art of Conversing* came into his head. 'Have you a garden?' he said.

She shrugged her shoulders. 'Only a little one,' she said, and then, 'Perhaps you would like to see it.'

'I like gardenin',' said Kipps, with memories of a pennyworth of nasturtiums he had once trained over his uncle's dustbin.

She led the way with a certain relief.

They emerged through a four-seasons coloured-glass door to a little iron verandah that led by iron steps to a minute walled garden. There was just room for a patch of turf and a flower-bed; one sturdy variegated euonymus grew in the corner. But the early June flowers – the big narcissus, snow-upon-the-mountains and a fine show of yellow wallflowers – shone gay.

'That's our garden,' said Helen. 'It's not a very big one, is it?'

'I like it,' said Kipps.

'It's small,' she said, 'but this is the day of small things.'

Kipps didn't follow that.

'If you were writing when I came,' he remarked, 'I'm interrupting you.'

She turned round with her back to the railing and rested, leaning on her hands. 'I had finished,' she said. 'I couldn't get on.'

'Were you making up something?' asked Kipps.

There was a little interval before she smiled. 'I try – quite vainly – to write stories,' she said. 'One must do something. I don't know whether I shall ever do any good – at that – anyhow. It seems so hopeless. And, of course, one must study the popular taste. But, now my brother has gone to London, I get a lot of leisure.'

'I seen your brother, 'aven't I?'

'He came to the class once or twice. Very probably you have. He's gone to London to pass his examinations and become a solicitor. And then, I suppose, he'll have a chance. Not much, perhaps, even then. But he's luckier than I am.'

'You got your classes and things.'

'They ought to satisfy me. But they don't. I suppose I'm ambitious. We both are. And we hadn't much of a springboard.' She glanced over his shoulder at the cramped little garden with an air of reference in her gesture.

'I should think you could do anything if you wanted to,' said Kipps.

'As a matter of fact I can't do anything I want to.'

'You done a good deal.'

'What?'

'Well, didn't you pass one of these here University things?'

'Oh! I matriculated!'

'I should think I was no end of a swell if *I* did, I know that.'

'Mr Kipps, do you know how many people matriculate into London University every year?'

'How many then?'

'Between two and three thousand.'

'Well, just think how many don't!'

Her smile came again, and broke into a laugh. 'Oh, *they* don't count,' she said, and then, realising that might penetrate Kipps if he was left with it, she hurried on to, 'The fact is, I'm a discontented person, Mr Kipps. Folkestone, you know, is a Sea Front, and it values people by sheer vulgar prosperity. We're not prosperous, and we live in a back street. We have to live here because this is our house. It's a mercy we haven't to "let". One feels one hasn't opportunities. If one had, I suppose one wouldn't use them. Still – '

Kipps felt he was being taken tremendously into her confidence. 'That's jest it,' he said, very sagely.

He leant forward on his stick and said, very earnestly, 'I believe you could do anything you wanted to, if you tried.'

She threw out her hands in disavowal.

'I know,' said he, very sagely and nodding his head. 'I watched you once or twice when you were teaching that wood-carving class.'

For some reason this made her laugh – a rather pleasant laugh, and that made Kipps feel a very witty and successful person. 'It's very evident,' she said, 'that you're one of those rare people who believe in me, Mr Kipps,' to which he answered, 'Oo, I *do*!' and then suddenly they became aware of Mrs Walshingham coming along the passage. In another moment she appeared through the four-seasons door, bonneted and ladylike, and a little faded, exactly as Kipps had seen her in the shop. Kipps felt a certain apprehension at her appearance, in spite of the reassurances he had had from Coote.

'Mr Kipps has called on us,' said Helen, and Mrs Walshingham said it was very kind of him, and added that new people didn't call on them very much nowadays. There was nothing of the scandalised surprise Kipps had seen in the shop; she had heard, perhaps, he was a gentleman now. In the shop he had thought her rather jaded and haughty, but he had scarcely taken her hand, which responded to his touch with a friendly pressure, before he knew how mistaken he had been. She then told her daughter that someone called Mrs Wace had been out, and turned to Kipps again to ask him if he had had tea. Kipps said he had not, and Helen moved towards some mysterious interior. 'But *I* say,' said Kipps; 'don't you on my account – !'

Helen vanished, and he found himself alone with Mrs Walshingham, which, of course, made him breathless and Boreas-looking for a moment.

'You were one of Helen's pupils in the wood-carving class?' asked Mrs Walshingham, regarding him with the quiet watchfulness proper to her position.

'Yes,' said Kipps, 'that's 'ow I 'ad the pleasure – '

'She took a great interest in her wood-carving class. She is so energetic, you know, and it gives her an Outlet.'

'I thought she taught something splendid.'

'Everyone says she did very well. Helen, I think, would do anything well that she undertook to do. She's so very clever. And she throws herself into things so.'

She untied her bonnet strings with a pleasant informality.

'She has told me all about her class. She used to be full of it. And about your cut hand.'

'Lor'!' said Kipps; 'fancy, telling that!'

'Oh, yes! And how brave you were.' (Though, indeed, Helen's chief detail had been his remarkable expedient for checking bloodshed.)

Kipps became bright pink.

'She said you didn't seem to feel it a bit.'

Kipps felt he would have to spend weeks over *The Art of Conversing*.

While he still hung fire Helen returned with the apparatus for afternoon tea upon a tray.

'Do you mind pulling out the table?' asked Mrs Walshingham.

That, again, was very homelike. Kipps put down his hat and stick in the corner and, amidst an iron thunder, pulled out a little rusty, green-painted table, and then in the easiest manner followed Helen in to get chairs.

So soon as he had got rid of his teacup – he refused all food, of course, and they were merciful – he became wonderfully at his ease. Presently he was talking. He talked quite modestly and simply about his changed condition and his difficulties and plans. He spread what indeed had an air of being all his simple little soul before their eyes. In a little while his clipped, defective accent had become less perceptible to their ears, and they began to realise, as the girl with the freckles had long since realised, that there were passable aspects of Kipps. He confided, he submitted; and for both of them he had the realest, the most seductively flattering undertone of awe and reverence.

He remained about two hours, having forgotten how terribly incorrect it is to stay at such a length. They did not mind at all.

CHAPTER THREE

Engaged

Within two months, within a matter of three and fifty days, Kipps had clambered to the battlements of Heart's Desire.

It all became possible by the Walshinghams – it would seem at Coote's instigation – deciding, after all, not to spend the holidays at Bruges. Instead, they remained in Folkestone, and this happy chance gave Kipps just all those opportunities of which he stood in need.

His crowning day was at Lympne, and long before the summer warmth began to break, while, indeed, August still flamed on high. They had organised – no one seemed to know who suggested it first – a water party on the still reaches of the old military canal at Hythe, the canal that was to have stopped Napoleon if the sea failed us, and they were to picnic by the brick bridge, and afterwards to clamber to Lympne Castle. The host of the gathering, it was understood very clearly, was Kipps.

They went, a merry party. The canal was weedy, with only a few inches of water at the shallows, and so they went in three Canadian canoes. Kipps had learned to paddle – it had been his first athletic accomplishment, and his second – with the last three or four of ten private lessons still to come – was to be cycling. But Kipps did not paddle at all badly; muscles hardened by lifting pieces of cretonne could cut a respectable figure by the side of Coote's executions, and the girl with the freckles, the girl who understood him, came in his canoe. They raced the Walshinghams, brother and sister; and Coote, in a liquefying state and blowing mightily, but still persistent and always quite polite and considerate, toiled behind with Mrs Walshingham. She could not be expected to paddle (though, of course, she 'offered') and she reclined upon specially adjusted cushions under a black and white sunshade and watched Kipps and her daughter, and feared at intervals that Coote was getting hot.

They were all more or less in holiday costume, the eyes of the girls looked out under the shade of wide-brimmed hats; even the freckled girl was unexpectedly pretty, and Helen, swinging sunlit to her paddle, gave Kipps, almost for the first time, the suggestion of a graceful body. Kipps was arrayed in the completest boating costume, and when his fashionable Panama was discarded and his hair blown into disorder he became, in his white flannels, as sightly as most young men. His complexion was a notable asset.

Things favoured him, the day favoured him, everyone favoured him. Young Walshingham, the girl with the freckles, Coote and Mrs Walshingham, were playing up to him in the most benevolent way, and between the landing place and Lympne, Fortune, to crown their efforts, had placed a small, convenient field entirely at the disposal of an adolescent bull. Not a big, real, resolute bull, but, on the other hand, no calf; a young bull, in the same stage of emotional development as Kipps, 'standing where the two rivers meet'. Detachedly our party drifted towards him.

When they landed, young Walshingham, with the simple directness of a brother, abandoned his sister to Kipps and secured the freckled girl, leaving Coote to carry Mrs Walshingham's light wool wrap. He started at once, in order to put an effectual distance between himself and his companions, on the one hand, and a certain pervasive chaperonage that went with Coote, on the other. Young Walshingham, I think I have said, was dark, with a Napoleonic profile, and it was natural for him, therefore, to be a bold thinker and an epigrammatic speaker, and he had long ago discovered great possibilities of appreciation in the freckled girl. He was in a very happy frame that day because he had just been entrusted with the management of Kipps's affairs (old Bean inexplicably dismissed), and that was not a bad beginning for a solicitor of only a few months' standing, and, moreover, he had been reading Nietzsche, and he thought that in all probability he was the Non-Moral Overman referred to by that writer. He wore fairly large-sized hats. He wanted to expand the theme of the Non-Moral Overman in the ear of the freckled girl, to say it over, so to speak, and in order to seclude his exposition they went aside from the direct path and trespassed through a coppice, avoiding the youthful bull. They escaped to these higher themes but narrowly, for Coote and Mrs Walshingham, subtle chaperones both, and each indisposed for excellent reasons to encumber Kipps and Helen, were hot upon their heels. These two kept direct route to the stile of the bull's field, and the sight of the animal at once awakened Coote's innate aversion to brutality in any shape or form. He said the stiles were too high, and that they could do better by going around by the hedge, and Mrs Walshingham, nothing loath, agreed.

This left the way clear for Kipps and Helen, and they encountered the bull. Helen did not observe the bull, but Kipps did; but, that afternoon at any rate, he was equal to facing a lion. And the bull really came at them. It was not an affair of the bullring exactly, no desperate rushes and gorings; but he came; he regarded them with a large, wicked, bluish eye, opened a mouth below his moistly glistening nose and booed, at any rate, if he did not exactly bellow, and he shook his head wickedly and showed that tossing was in his mind. Helen was frightened, without any loss of dignity, and Kipps went extremely white. But he was perfectly calm, and he seemed to her to have lost the last vestiges of his accent and his social shakiness. He directed her to walk quietly towards the stile, and made an oblique advance towards the bull.

'You be orf!' he said.

When Helen was well over the stile Kipps withdrew in good order. He got over the stile under cover of a feint, and the thing was done – a small thing, no doubt, but just enough to remove from Helen's mind an incorrect deduction that a man who was so terribly afraid of a teacup as Kipps must necessarily be abjectly afraid of everything else in the world. In her moment of reaction she went perhaps too far in the opposite direction. Hitherto Kipps had always had a certain flimsiness of effect for her. Now suddenly he was discovered solid. He was discovered possible in many new ways. Here, after all, was the sort of back a woman can get behind! . . .

As these heirs of the immemorial ages went past the turf-crowned mass of Portus Lemanus up the steep slopes towards the mediaeval castle on the crest, the thing was also manifest in her eyes.

2

Everyone who stays in Folkestone gets, sooner or later, to Lympne. The castle became a farmhouse long ago, and the farmhouse, itself now ripe and venerable, wears the walls of the castle as a little man wears a big man's coat. The kindliest of farm ladies entertains a perpetual stream of visitors and shows her vast mangle, and her big kitchen, and takes you out upon the sunniest little terrace garden in all the world, and you look down the sheep-dotted slopes to where, beside the canal and under the trees, the crumpled memories of Rome sleep for ever. For hither to this lonely spot the galleys once came, the legions, the emperors, masters of the world. The castle is but a thing of yesterday, King Stephen's time or thereabouts, in that retrospect. One climbs the keep, up a tortuous spiral of stone, worn now to the pitch of perforation, and there one is lifted to the centre of far more than a hemisphere of view. Away below one's feet, almost at the bottom of the hill, the Marsh begins, and spreads and spreads in a mighty crescent that sweeps about the sea, the Marsh dotted with the church towers of forgotten mediaeval towns and breaking at last into the low blue hills of Winchelsea and Hastings; east hangs France, between the sea and the sky, and round the north, bounding the wide prospectives of farms and houses and woods, the Downs, with their hangers and chalk pits, sustain the passing shadows of the sailing clouds.

And here it was, high out of the world of everyday, and in the presence of spacious beauty, that Kipps and Helen found themselves agreeably alone. All six, it had seemed, had been coming for the Keep, but Mrs Walshingham had hesitated at the horrid little stairs, and then suddenly felt faint, and so she and the freckled girl had remained below, walking up and down in the shadow of the house and Coote had remembered they were all out of cigarettes, and had taken off young Walshingham into the village. There had been shouting to explain between ground and parapet, and then Helen and Kipps turned again to the view, and commended it and fell silent.

Helen sat fearlessly in an embrasure, and Kipps stood beside her.

'I've always been fond of scenery,' Kipps repeated, after an interval.

Then he went off at a tangent. 'D'you reely think that was right what Coote was saying?'

She looked interrogation.

'About my name?'

'Being really C-U-Y-P-S? I have my doubts. I thought at first – What makes Mr Coote add an S to Cuyp?'

'*I* dunno,' said Kipps, foiled. 'I was jest thinking . . . '

She shot one wary glance at him and then turned her eyes to the sea.

Kipps was out for a space. He had intended to lead from this question to the general question of surnames and change of names; it had seemed a light and witty way of saying something he had in mind, and suddenly he perceived that this was an unutterably vulgar and silly project. The hitch about that S had saved him. He regarded her profile for a moment, framed in weather-beaten stone, and backed by the blue elements.

He dropped the question of his name out of existence and spoke again of the view. 'When I see scenery – and things that – that are beautiful, it makes me feel – '

She looked at him suddenly, and saw him fumbling for his words.

'Silly like,' he said.

She took him in with her glance, the old look of proprietorship it was, touched with a certain warmth. She spoke in a voice as unambiguous as her eyes. 'You needn't,' she said. 'You know, Mr Kipps, you hold yourself too cheap.'

Her eyes and words smote him with amazement. He stared at her like a man who awakens. She looked down.

'You mean – ' he said; and then, 'don't you hold me cheap?'

She glanced up again and shook her head.

'But – for instance – you don't think of me – as an equal like.'

'Why not?'

'Oo! But reely – '

His heart beat very fast.

'If I thought – ' he said; and then, 'You know so much.'

'That's nothing,' she said.

Then, for a long time, as it seemed to them, both kept silence, a silence that said and accomplished many things.

'I know what I am,' he said, at length . . . 'If I thought it was possible . . . If I thought *you* . . . I believe I could do anything – '

He stopped, and she sat downcast and strikingly still.

'Miss Walshingham,' he said, 'is it possible that you . . . could care for me enough to – to 'elp me? Miss Walshingham, do you care for me at all?'

It seemed she was never going to answer. She looked up at him. 'I think,' she said, 'you are the most generous – look at what you have done for my brother! – the most generous and the most modest of men. And this afternoon – I thought you were the bravest.'

She turned her head, glanced down, waved her hand to someone on the terrace below, and stood up.

'Mother is signalling,' she said. 'We must go down.'

Kipps became polite and deferential by habit, but his mind was a tumult that had nothing to do with that.

He moved before her towards the little door that opened on the winding stairs – 'always precede a lady down or up stairs' – and then on the second step he turned resolutely. 'But – ' he said, looking up out of the shadow, flannel-clad and singularly like a man.

She looked down on him, with her hand upon the stone lintel.

He held out his hand as if to help her. 'Can you tell me?' he said. 'You must know – '

'What?'

'If you care for me?'

She did not answer for a long time. It was as if everything in the world had drawn to the breaking point, and in a minute must certainly break.

'Yes,' she said, at last, 'I know.'

Abruptly, by some impalpable sign, he knew what the answer would be, and he remained still.

She bent down over him and softened to her wonderful smile.

'Promise me,' she insisted.

He promised with his still face.

'If *I* do not hold you cheap! you will never hold yourself cheap – '

'If you do not hold me cheap! You mean – ?'

She bent down quite close beside him. 'I hold you,' she said, and then whispered, '*dear*.'

'Me?'

She laughed aloud.

He was astonished beyond measure. He stipulated, lest there might be some misconception, 'You will marry me?'

She was laughing, inundated by the sense of bountiful power, of possession and success. He looked quite a nice little man to have. 'Yes,' she laughed. 'What else could I mean?' and, 'Yes.'

He felt as a praying hermit might have felt, snatched from the midst of his quiet devotions, his modest sackcloth and ashes, and hurled neck and crop over the glittering gates of Paradise, smack among the iridescent wings, the bright-eyed Cherubim. He felt like some lowly and righteous man dynamited into Bliss . . .

His hand tightened upon the rope that steadied one upon the stairs of stone. He was for kissing her hand and did not.

He said not a word more. He turned about, and with something very like a scared expression on his face led the way into the obscurity of their descent . . .

3

Everyone seemed to understand. Nothing was said, nothing was explained, the merest touch of the eyes sufficed. As they clustered in the castle gateway Coote, Kipps remembered afterwards, laid hold of his arm as if by chance and pressed it. It was quite evident he knew. His eyes, his nose, shone with benevolent congratulations, shone, too, with the sense of a good thing conducted to its climax. Mrs Walshingham, who had seemed a little fatigued by the hill, recovered, and was even obviously stirred by affection for her daughter. There was, in passing, a motherly caress. She asked Kipps to give her his arm in walking down the steep. Kipps in a sort of dream obeyed. He found himself trying to attend to her, and soon he was attending.

She and Kipps talked like sober, responsible people and went slowly, while the others drifted down the hill together, a loose little group of four. He wondered momentarily what they would talk about and then sank into his conversation with Mrs Walshingham. He conversed, as it were, out of his superficial personality, and his inner self lay stunned in unsuspected depths within. It had an air of being an interesting and friendly talk, almost their first long talk together. Hitherto he had had a sort of fear of Mrs Walshingham, as of a person possibly satirical, but she proved a soul of sense and sentiment, and Kipps, for all of his abstraction, got on with her unexpectedly well. They talked a little upon scenery and the inevitable melancholy attaching to the old ruins and the thought of vanished generations.

'Perhaps they jousted here,' said Mrs Walshingham.

'They was up to all sorts of things,' said Kipps, and then the two came round to Helen. She spoke of her daughter's literary ambitions. 'She will do something, I feel sure. You know, Mr Kipps, it's a great responsibility to a mother to feel her daughter is – exceptionally clever.'

'I dessay it is,' said Kipps. 'There's no mistake about that.'

She spoke, too, of her son – almost like Helen's twin – alike, yet different. She made Kipps feel quite fatherly. 'They are so quick, so artistic,' she said, 'so full of ideas. Almost they frighten me. One feels they need opportunities – as other people need air.'

She spoke of Helen's writing. 'Even when she was quite a little dot she wrote verse.'

(Kipps, sensation.)

'Her father had just the same tastes – ' Mrs Walshingham turned a little beam of half-pathetic reminiscence on the past. 'He was more artist than businessman. That was the trouble . . . He was misled by his partner, and when the crash came everyone blamed him . . . Well, it doesn't do to dwell on horrid things – especially today. There are bright days, Mr Kipps, and dark days. And mine have not always been bright.'

Kipps presented a face of Coote-like sympathy.

She diverged to talk of flowers, and Kipps's mind was filled with the picture of Helen bending down towards him in the Keep . . .

They spread the tea under the trees before the little inn, and at a certain moment Kipps became aware that everyone in the party was simultaneously and furtively glancing at him. There might have been a certain tension had it not been first of all for Coote and his tact, and afterwards for a number of wasps. Coote was resolved to make this memorable day pass off well, and displayed an almost boisterous sense of fun. Then young Walshingham began talking of the Roman remains below Lympne, intending to lead up to the Overman. 'These old Roman chaps – ' he said, and then the wasps arrived. They killed three in the jam alone.

Kipps killed wasps, as if it were in a dream, and handed things to the wrong people, and maintained a thin surface of ordinary intelligence with the utmost difficulty. At times he became aware, aware with an extraordinary vividness, of Helen. Helen was carefully not looking at him and behaving with amazing coolness and ease. But just for that one time there was the faintest suggestion of pink beneath the ivory of her cheeks . . .

Tacitly the others conceded to Kipps the right to paddle back with Helen; he helped her into the canoe and took his paddle, and, paddling slowly, dropped behind the others. And now his inner self stirred again. He said nothing to her. How could he ever say anything to her again? She spoke to him at rare intervals about reflections and the flowers and the trees, and he nodded in reply. But his mind moved very slowly forward now from the point at which it had fallen stunned in the Lympne Keep, moving forward to the beginnings of realisation. As yet he did not say even in the recesses of his heart that she was his. But he perceived that the goddess had come from her altar amazingly, and had taken him by the hand!

The sky was a vast splendour, and then close to them were the dark, protecting trees and the shining, smooth, still water. He was an erect, black outline to her; he plied his paddle with no unskilful gesture, the water broke to snaky silver and glittered far behind his strokes. Indeed, he did not seem so bad to her. Youth calls to youth the wide world through, and her soul rose in triumph over his subjection. And behind him was money and opportunity, freedom and London, a great background of seductively indistinct hopes. To him her face was a warm dimness. In truth, he could not see her eyes, but it seemed to his love-witched brain he did and that they shone out at him like dusky stars.

All the world that evening was no more than a shadowy frame of darkling sky and water and dipping bows about Helen. He seemed to see through things with an extraordinary clearness; she was revealed to him certainly, as the cause and essence of it all.

He was indeed at his Heart's Desire. It was one of those times when there seems to be no future, when Time has stopped and we are at an end. Kipps, that evening, could not have imagined a tomorrow; all that his imagination had pointed towards was attained. His mind stood still and took the moments as they came.

About nine that night Coote came around to Kipps's new apartment in the Upper Sandgate Road – the house on the Leas had been let furnished – and Kipps made an effort towards realisation. He was discovered sitting at the open window and without a lamp, quite still. Coote was deeply moved, and he pressed Kipps's palm and laid a knobby white hand on his shoulder and displayed the sort of tenderness becoming in a crisis. Kipps too was moved that night, and treated Coote like a very dear brother.

'She's splendid,' said Coote, coming to it abruptly.

'Isn't she?' said Kipps.

'I couldn't help noticing her face,' said Coote . . . 'You know, my dear Kipps, this is better than a legacy.'

'I don't deserve it,' said Kipps.

'You can't say that.'

'I don't. I can't 'ardly believe it. I can't believe it at all. No!'

There followed an expressive stillness.

'It's wonderful,' said Kipps. 'It takes me like that.'

Coote made a faint blowing noise, and so again they came for a time on silence.

'And it began – before your money?'

'When I was in 'er class,' said Kipps, solemnly.

Coote, speaking out of a darkness which he was illuminating strangely with efforts to strike a match, said that it was beautiful. He could not have *wished* Kipps a better fortune –

He lit a cigarette, and Kipps was moved to do the same, with a sacramental expression. Presently speech flowed more freely.

Coote began to praise Helen and her mother and brother. He talked of when 'it' might be; he presented the thing as concrete and credible. 'It's a county family, you know,' he said. 'She is connected, you know, with the Beauprés family – you know Lord Beauprés.'

'No!' said Kipps, 'reely!'

'Distantly, of course,' said Coote. 'Still – '

He smiled a smile that glimmered in the twilight.

'It's too much,' said Kipps, overcome. 'It's so all like that.'

Coote exhaled. For a time Kipps listened to Helen's praises and matured a point of view.

'I say, Coote,' he said. 'What ought I to do now?'

'What do you mean?' said Coote.

'I mean about calling on 'er and all that.'

He reflected. 'Naturally, I want to do it all right.'

'Of course,' said Coote.

'It would be awful to go and do something – now – all wrong.'

Coote's cigarette glowed as he meditated. 'You must call, of course,' he decided. 'You'll have to speak to Mrs Walshingham.'

' 'Ow?' said Kipps.

'Tell her you mean to marry her daughter.'

'I dessay she knows,' said Kipps, with defensive penetration.

Coote's head was visible, shaking itself judiciously.

'Then there's the ring,' said Kipps. 'What 'ave I to do about that?'

'What ring do you mean?'

' 'Ngagement Ring. There isn't anything at all about that in *Manners and Rules of Good Society* – not a word.'

'Of course you must get something – tasteful. Yes.'

'What sort of a ring?'

'Something nace. They'll show you in the shop.'

'Of course. I 'spose I got to take it to 'er, eh? Put it on her finger.'

'Oh, no! Send it. Much better.'

'Ah!' said Kipps, for the first time with a note of relief.

'Then, 'ow about this call – on Mrs Walshingham, I mean. 'Ow ought one to go?'

'Rather a ceremonial occasion,' reflected Coote.

'Wadyer mean? Frock coat?'

'I *think* so,' said Coote, with discrimination.

'Light trousers and all that?'

'Yes.'

'Rose?'

'I think it might run to a buttonhole.'

The curtain that hung over the future became less opaque to the eyes of Kipps. Tomorrow, and then other days, became perceptible at least as existing. Frock coat, silk hat and a rose! With a certain solemnity he contemplated himself in the process of slow transformation into an English gentleman, Arthur Cuyps, frock-coated on occasions of ceremony, the familiar acquaintance of Lady Punnet, the recognised wooer of a distant connection of the Earl of Beauprés.

Something like awe at the magnitude of his own fortune came upon him. He felt the world was opening out like a magic flower in a transformation scene at the touch of this wand of gold. And Helen, nestling beautiful in the red heart of the flower. Only ten weeks ago he had been no more than the shabbiest of improvers and shamefully dismissed for dissipation, the mere soil-buried seed, as it were, of these glories. He resolved the engagement ring should be of expressively excessive quality and appearance, in fact, the very best they had.

'Ought I to send 'er flowers?' he speculated.

'Not necessarily,' said Coote. 'Though, of course, it's an attention . . .'

Kipps meditated on flowers.

'When you see her,' said Coote, 'you'll have to ask her to name the day.'

Kipps started. 'That won't be just yet a bit, will it?'

'Don't know any reason for delay.'

'Oo, but – a year, say.'

'Rather a long taime,' said Coote.

'Is it?' said Kipps, turning his head sharply. 'But – '

There was quite a long pause.

'I say,' he said, at last, and in an altered voice, 'you'll 'ave to 'elp me about the wedding.'

'Only too happy,' said Coote.

'Of course,' said Kipps, 'I didn't think – ' He changed his line of thought. 'Coote,' he asked, 'wot's a "tate-eh-tate"?'

'A "tate-ah-tay"!' said Coote, improvingly, 'is a conversation alone together.'

'Lor'!' said Kipps, 'but I thought – It says *strictly* we oughtn't to enjoy a tater-tay, not sit together, walk together, ride together, or meet during any part of the day. That don't leave much time for meeting, does it?'

'The books says that?' asked Coote.

'I jest learnt it by 'eart before you came. I thought that was a bit rum, but I s'pose it's all right.'

'You won't find Miss Walshingham so strict as all that,' said Coote. 'I think that's a bit extreme. They'd only do that now in very strict old aristocratic families. Besides, the Walshinghams are so modern – advanced, you might say. I expect you'll get plenty of chances of talking together.'

'There's a tremendous lot to think about,' said Kipps, blowing a profound sigh. 'D'you mean – p'r'aps we might be married in a few months or so?'

'You'll *have* to be,' said Coote. 'Why not?' . . .

Midnight found Kipps alone, looking a little tired and turning over the leaves of the red-covered textbook with a studious expression. He paused for a moment on page 233, his eye caught by the words: 'FOR AN AUNT OR UNCLE BY MARRIAGE the period is six weeks black, with jet trimmings.'

'No,' said Kipps, after a vigorous mental effort. 'That's not it.' The pages rustled again. He stopped and flattened out the little book decisively at the beginning of the chapter on 'Weddings'.

He became pensive. He stared at the lamp-wick. 'I suppose I ought to go over and tell them,' he said, at last.

5

Kipps called on Mrs Walshingham attired in the proper costume for ceremonial Occasions in the Day. He carried a silk hat, and he wore a deep-skirted frock coat, his boots were patent leather and his trousers dark grey. He had generous white cuffs with gold links, and his grey gloves, one thumb of which had burst when he put them on, he held loosely in his hand. He carried a small umbrella rolled to an exquisite tightness. A sense of singular correctness pervaded his being and warred with the enormity of the occasion for possession of his soul. Anon he touched his silk cravat. The world smelt of his rosebud.

He seated himself on a new re-covered chintz armchair and stuck out the elbow of the arm that held his hat.

'I know,' said Mrs Walshingham, 'I know everything,' and helped him out most amazingly. She deepened the impression he had already received of her sense and refinement. She displayed an amount of tenderness that touched him.

'This is a great thing,' she said, 'to a mother,' and her hand rested for a moment on his impeccable coat sleeve.

'A daughter, Arthur,' she explained, 'is so much more than a son.'

Marriage, she said, was a lottery, and without love and toleration there was much unhappiness. Her life had not always been bright – there had been dark days and bright days. She smiled rather sweetly. 'This is a bright one,' she said.

She said very kind and flattering things to Kipps, and she thanked him for his goodness to her son. ('That wasn't anything,' said Kipps.) And then she expanded upon the theme of her two children. 'Both so accomplished,' she said, 'so clever. I call them my Twin Jewels.'

She was repeating a remark that she had made at Lympne, that she always said her children needed opportunities, as other people needed air, when she was abruptly arrested by the entry of Helen. They hung on a pause, Helen perhaps surprised by Kipps's weekday magnificence. Then she advanced with outstretched hand.

Both the young people were shy. 'I jest called round,' began Kipps, and became uncertain how to end.

'Won't you have some tea?' asked Helen.

She walked to the window, looked out at the familiar out-porter's barrow, turned, surveyed Kipps for a moment ambiguously, said 'I will get some tea,' and so departed again.

Mrs Walshingham and Kipps looked at one another and the lady smiled indulgently. 'You two young people mustn't be shy of each other,' said Mrs Walshingham, which damaged Kipps considerably.

She was explaining how sensitive Helen always had been, even about quite little things, when the servant appeared with the tea things, and then Helen followed, and taking up a secure position behind the little banboo tea table, broke the ice with officious tea-cup clattering. Then she introduced the topic of a forthcoming open-air performance of *As You Like It*, and steered past the worst of the awkwardness. They discussed stage illusion. 'I mus' say,' said Kipps, 'I don't quite like a play in a theayter. It seems sort of unreal, some'ow.'

'But most plays are written for the stage,' said Helen, looking at the sugar.

'I know,' admitted Kipps.

They finished tea. 'Well,' said Kipps, and rose.

'You mustn't go yet,' said Mrs Walshingham, rising and taking his hand. 'I'm sure you two must have heaps to say to each other,' and so she escaped towards the door.

6

Among other projects that seemed almost equally correct to Kipps at that exalted moment was one of embracing Helen with ardour as soon as the door closed behind her mother, and one of headlong flight through the open window. Then he remembered he ought to hold the door open for Mrs Walshingham, and turned from that duty to find Helen still standing, beautifully inaccessible, behind the tea things. He closed the door and advanced towards her with his arms akimbo and his hands upon his coat skirts. Then, feeling angular, he moved his right hand to his moustache. Anyhow, he was dressed all right. Somewhere at the back of his mind, dim and mingled with doubt and surprise, appeared the perception that he felt now quite differently towards her, that something between them had been blown from Lympne Keep to the four winds of heaven . . .

She regarded him with an eye of critical proprietorship.

'Mother has been making up to you,' she said, smiling slightly.

She added, 'It was nice of you to come around to see her.'

They stood through a brief pause, as though each had expected something different in the other and was a little perplexed at its not being there. Kipps found he was at the corner of the brown-covered table, and he picked up a little flexible book that lay upon it to occupy his mind.

'I bought you a ring today,' he said, bending the book and speaking for the sake of saying something, and then he was moved to genuine speech. 'You know,' he said, 'I can't 'ardly believe it.'

Her face relaxed slightly again. 'No?' she said, and may have breathed, 'Nor I.'

'No,' he went on. 'It's as though everything 'ad changed. More even than when I got my money. 'Ere we are going to marry. It's like being someone else. What I feel is – '

He turned a flushed and earnest face to her. He seemed to come alive to her with one natural gesture. 'I don't *know* things. I'm not good enough. I'm not refined. The more you'll see of me the more you'll find me out.'

'But I'm going to help you.'

'You'll 'ave to 'elp me a fearful lot.'

She walked to the window, glanced out of it, made up her mind, turned and came towards him, with her hands clasped behind her back.

'All these things that trouble you are very little things. If you don't mind – if you will let me tell you things – '

'I wish you would.'

'Then I will.'

'They're little things to you, but they aren't to me.'

'It all depends, if you don't mind being told.'

'By you?'

'I don't expect you to be told by strangers.'

'Oo!' said Kipps, expressing much.

'You know, there are just a few little things. For instance, you know, you are careless with your pronunciation . . . You don't mind my telling you?'

'I like it,' said Kipps.

'There are aitches.'

'I know,' said Kipps, and then, endorsingly, 'I been told. Fact is, I know a chap, a Nacter, *he*'s told me. He's told me, and he's going to give me a lesson or so.'

'I'm glad of that. It only requires a little care.'

'Of course. On the stage they got to look out. They take regular lessons.'

'Of course,' said Helen, a little absently.

'I dessay I shall soon get into it,' said Kipps.

'And then there's dress,' said Helen, taking up her thread again.

Kipps became pink, but he remained respectfully attentive.

'You don't mind?' she said.

'Oo, no.'

'You mustn't be too – too dressy. It's possible to be over-conventional, over-elaborate. It makes you look like a shop – like a common, well-off person. There's a sort of easiness that is better. A real gentleman looks right, without looking as though he had tried to be right.'

'Jest as though 'e'd put on what came first?' said the pupil, in a faded voice.

'Not exactly that, but a sort of ease.'

Kipps nodded his head intelligently. In his heart he was kicking his silk hat about the room in an ecstasy of disappointment.

'And you must accustom yourself to be more at your ease when you are with people,' said Helen. 'You've only got to forget yourself a little and not be anxious – '

'I'll try,' said Kipps, looking rather hard at the teapot. 'I'll do my best to try.'

'I know you will,' she said, and laid a hand for an instant upon his shoulder and withdrew it.

He did not perceive her caress. 'One has to learn,' he said. His attention was distracted by the strenuous efforts that were going on in the back of his head to translate, 'I say, didn't you ought to name the day?' into easy as well as elegant English, a struggle that was still undecided when the time came for them to part . . .

He sat for a long time at the open window of his sitting-room with an intent face, recapitulating that interview. His eyes rested at last almost reproachfully on the silk hat beside him. ' 'Ow *is* one to know?' he asked. His attention was caught by a rubbed place in the nap, and, still thoughtful, he rolled up his handkerchief skilfully into a soft ball and began to smooth this down.

His expression changed slowly.

' 'Ow the Juice is one to know?' he said, putting down the hat with some emphasis.

He rose up, went across the room to the sideboard, and, standing there, opened and began to read *Manners and Rules*.

CHAPTER FOUR

The Bicycle Manufacturer

So Kipps embarked upon his engagement, steeled himself to the high enterprise of marrying above his breeding. The next morning found him dressing with a certain quiet severity of movement, and it seemed to his landlady's housemaid that he was unusually dignified at breakfast. He meditated profoundly over his kipper and his kidney and bacon. He was going to New Romney to tell the old people what had happened and where he stood. And the love of Helen had also given him courage to do what Buggins had once suggested to him as a thing he would do were he in Kipps's place, and that was to hire a motor car for the afternoon. He had an early cold lunch, and then, with an air of quiet resolution, assumed a cap and coat he had purchased to this end, and thus equipped strolled around, blowing slightly, to the motor shop. The transaction was unexpectedly easy, and within the hour Kipps, spectacled and wrapped about, was tootling through Dymchurch.

They came to a stop smartly and neatly outside the little toy shop. 'Make that thing 'oot a bit, will you,' said Kipps. 'Yes, that's it.'

'Whup,' said the motor car. 'Whurrup!'

Both his aunt and uncle came out on the pavement. 'Why, it's Artie,' cried his aunt, and Kipps had a moment of triumph.

He descended to hand claspings, removed wraps and spectacles, and the motor driver retired to take 'an hour off'. Old Kipps surveyed the machinery and disconcerted Kipps for a moment by asking him in a knowing tone what they asked him for a thing like that. The two men stood inspecting the machine and impressing the neighbours for a time, and then they strolled through the shop into the little parlour for a drink.

'They ain't settled,' old Kipps had said to the neighbours. 'They ain't got no further than experiments. There's a bit of take-in about each. You take my advice and wait, me boy, even if it's a year or two, before you buy one for your own use.'

(Though Kipps had said nothing of doing anything of the sort.)

' 'Ow d'you like that whisky I sent?' asked Kipps, dodging the old familiar bunch of children's pails.

Old Kipps became tactful. 'It's a very good whisky, my boy,' said old

Kipps. 'I 'aven't the slightest doubt it's a very good whisky and cost you a tidy price. But – dashed if it soots me! They put this here Foozle Ile in it, my boy, and it ketches me jest 'ere.' He indicated his centre of figure. 'Gives me the heartburn,' he said, and shook his head rather sadly.

'It's a very good whisky,' said Kipps. 'It's what the actor manager chaps drink in London, I 'appen to know.'

'I des say they do, my boy,' said old Kipps, 'but then they've 'ad their livers burnt out, and I 'aven't. They ain't dellicat like me. My stummik always *'as* been extrey dellicat. Sometimes it's almost been as though nothing would lay on it. But that's in passing. I liked those segars. You can send me some more of them segars . . . '

You cannot lead a conversation straight from the gastric consequences of Foozle Ile to Love, and so Kipps, after a friendly inspection of a rare old engraving after Morland[28] (perfect except for a hole kicked through the centre) that his uncle had recently purchased by private haggle, came to the topic of the old people's removal.

At the outset of Kipps's great fortunes there had been much talk of some permanent provision for them. It had been conceded they were to be provided for comfortably, and the phrase 'retire from business' had been very much in the air. Kipps had pictured an ideal cottage, with a creeper always in exuberant flower about the door, where the sun shone for ever and the wind never blew and a perpetual welcome hovered in the doorway. It was an agreeable dream, but when it came to the point of deciding upon this particular cottage or that, and on this particular house or that, Kipps was surprised by an unexpected clinging to the little home, which he had always understood to be the worst of all possible houses.

'We don't want to move in a 'urry,' said Mrs Kipps.

'When we want to move, we want to move for life. I've had enough moving about in my time,' said old Kipps.

'We can do here a bit more, now we done here so long,' said Mrs Kipps.

'You lemme look about a bit *fust*,' said old Kipps.

And in looking about old Kipps found perhaps a finer joy than any mere possession could have given. He would shut his shop more or less effectually against the intrusion of customers, and toddle abroad seeking new matter for his dream; no house was too small and none too large for his knowing enquiries. Occupied houses took his fancy more than vacant ones, and he would remark, 'You won't be a-livin' 'ere for ever, even if you think you will,' when irate householders protested against the unsolicited examination of their more intimate premises –

Remarkable difficulties arose of a totally unexpected sort.

'If we 'ave a larger 'ouse,' said Mrs Kipps with sudden bitterness, 'we shall want a servant, and I don't want no gells in the place larfin' at me, sniggerin' and larfin' and prancin' and trapesin', lardy da! If we 'ave a smaller 'ouse, there won't be room to swing a cat.'

Room to swing a cat it seemed was absolutely essential. It was an infrequent but indispensable operation.

'When we *do* move,' said old Kipps, 'if we could get a bit of shootin' – I don't want to sell off all this here stock for nothin'. It's took years to 'cumulate. I put a ticket in the winder sayin' "sellin' orf", but it 'asn't brought nothing like a roosh. One of these 'ere dratted visitors pretendin' to want an airgun, was all we 'ad in yesterday. Jest an excuse for spyin' round and then go away and larf at you. No-thanky to everything, it didn't matter what . . . That's 'ow *I* look at it, Artie.'

They pursued meandering fancies about the topic of their future settlement for a space and Kipps became more and more hopeless of any proper conversational opening that would lead to his great announcement, and more and more uncertain how such an opening should be taken. Once, indeed, old Kipps, anxious to get away from this dangerous subject of removals, began: 'And what are you a-doin' of in Folkestone? I shall have to come over and see you one of these days,' but before Kipps could get in upon that, his uncle had passed into a general exposition of the proper treatment of landladies and their humbugging, cheating ways, and so the opportunity vanished. It seemed to Kipps the only thing to do was to go out into the town for a stroll, compose an effectual opening at leisure, and then come back and discharge it at them in its consecutive completeness. And even out of doors and alone he found his mind distracted by irrelevant thoughts.

2

His steps led him out of the High Street towards the church, and he leant for a time over the gate that had once been the winning-post of his race with Ann Pornick, and presently found himself in a sitting position on the top rail. He had to get things smooth again, he knew; his mind was like a mirror of water after a breeze. The image of Helen and his great future was broken and mingled into fragmentary reflections of remoter things, of the good name of Old Methusaleh Three Stars, of long dormant memories the High Street saw fit, by some trick of light and atmosphere, to arouse that afternoon . . .

Abruptly a fine, full voice from under his elbow shouted, 'What-o, Art!' and, behold, Sid Pornick was back in his world, leaning over the gate beside him, and holding out a friendly hand.

He was oddly changed and yet oddly like the Sid that Kipps had known. He had the old broad face and mouth, abundantly freckled, the same short nose and the same blunt chin, the same odd suggestion of his sister Ann without a touch of her beauty; but he had quite a new voice, loud and a little hard, and his upper lip carried a stiff and very fair moustache.

Kipps shook hands. 'I was jest thinking of *you*, Sid,' he said, 'jest this very moment and wondering if ever I should see you again, ever. And 'ere you are!'

'One likes a look round at times,' said Sid. 'How are *you*, old chap?'

'All right,' said Kipps. 'I just been lef' – '

'You aren't changed much,' interrupted Sid.

'Ent I?' said Kipps, foiled.

'I knew your back directly I came round the corner. Spite of that 'at you got on. Hang it, I said, that's Art Kipps or the devil. And so it was.'

Kipps made a movement of his neck as if he would look at his back and judge. Then he looked Sid in the face. 'You got a moustache, Sid,' he said.

'I s'pose you're having your holidays?' said Sid.

'Well, partly. But I just been lef' – '

'*I'm* taking a bit of a holiday,' Sid went on. 'But the fact is, I have to give *myself* holidays nowadays. I've set up for myself.'

'Not down here?'

'No fear! I'm not a turnip. I've started in Hammersmith, manufacturing.' Sid spoke offhand as though there was no such thing as pride.

'Not drapery?'

'No fear! Engineer. Manufacture bicycles.' He clapped his hand to his breast pocket and produced a number of pink handbills. He handed one to Kipps and prevented him reading it by explanations and explanatory dabs of a pointing finger. 'That's our make, my make to be exact, The Red Flag, see? – I got a transfer with my name – Pantocrat tyres, eight pounds – yes, *there* – Clinchers ten, Dunlop's eleven, Ladies' one pound more – that's the lady's. Best machine at a democratic price in London. No guineas and no discounts – honest trade. I build 'em – to order. I've built,' he reflected, looking away seaward – 'seventeen. Counting orders in 'and . . . Come down to look at the old place a bit. Mother likes it at times.'

'Thought you'd all gone away – '

'What! after my father's death? No! My mother's come back, and she's living at Muggett's cottages. The sea air suits 'er. She likes the old place better than Hammersmith . . . and I can afford it. Got an old crony or so here . . . Gossip . . . have tea . . . S'pose *you* ain't married, Kipps?'

Kipps shook his head, 'I – ' he began.

'*I* am,' said Sid. 'Married these two years and got a nipper. Proper little chap.'

Kipps got his word in at last. 'I got engaged day before yesterday,' he said.

'Ah!' said Sid airily. 'That's all right. Who's the fortunate lady?'

Kipps tried to speak in an offhand way. He stuck his hands in his pockets as he spoke. 'She's a solicitor's daughter,' he said, 'in Folkestone. Rather'r nice set. County family. Related to the Earl of Beauprés – '

'Steady on!' cried Sid.

'You see, I've 'ad a bit of luck, Sid. Been lef' money.'

Sid's eye travelled instinctively to mark Kipps's garments. 'How much?' he asked.

' 'Bout twelve 'undred a year,' said Kipps, more offhandedly than ever.

'Lord!' said Sid, with a note of positive dismay, and stepped back a pace or two.

'My granfaver it was,' said Kipps, trying hard to be calm and simple. ' 'Ardly knew I *'ad* a granfaver. And then – bang! When o' Bean, the solicitor, told me of it, you could 'ave knocked me down – '

''*Ow* much?' demanded Sid, with a sharp note in his voice.

'Twelve 'undred pound a year – 'proximately, that is . . . '

Sid's attempt at genial unenvious congratulation did not last a minute. He shook hands with an unreal heartiness and said he was jolly glad. 'It's a bloomin' stroke of Luck,' he said.

'It's a bloomin' stroke of Luck,' he repeated; 'that's what it is,' with the smile fading from his face. 'Of course, better you 'ave it than me, o' chap. So I don't envy you, anyhow. *I* couldn't keep it, if I did 'ave it.'

' 'Ow's that?' said Kipps, a little hipped by Sid's patent chagrin.

'I'm a Socialist, you see,' said Sid. 'I don't 'old with Wealth. What *is* Wealth? Labour robbed out of the poor. At most it's only yours in Trust. Leastways, that 'ow *I* should take it.' He reflected. 'The Present distribution of Wealth,' he said and stopped.

Then he let himself go, with unmasked bitterness. 'It's no sense at all. It's jest damn foolishness. Who's going to work and care in a muddle like this? Here first you do – something anyhow – of the world's work, and it pays you hardly anything, and then it invites you to do nothing, nothing whatever, and pays you twelve hundred pounds a year. Who's going to respect laws and customs when they come to damn silliness like that?' He repeated, 'Twelve hundred pounds a year!'

At the sight of Kipps's face he relented slightly.

'It's not you I'm thinking of, o' man; it's the system. Better you than most people. Still – '

He laid both hands on the gate and repeated to himself, 'Twelve 'undred a year . . . Gee-whizz, Kipps! You'll be a swell!'

'I shan't,' said Kipps with imperfect conviction. 'No fear.'

'You can't 'ave money like that and not swell out. You'll soon be too big to speak to – 'ow do they put it? – a mere mechanic like me.'

'No fear, Siddee,' said Kipps with conviction. 'I ain't that sort.'

'Ah!' said Sid, with a sort of unwilling scepticism, 'money'll be too much for you. Besides – you're caught by a swell already.'

' 'Ow d'you mean?'

'That girl you're going to marry. Masterman says – '

'Oo's Masterman?'

'Rare good chap I know – takes my first-floor front room. Masterson says it's always the wife pitches the key. Always. There's no social differences – till women come in.'

'Ah!' said Kipps profoundly. 'You don't know.'

Sid shook his head. 'Fancy!' he reflected, 'Art Kipps! . . . Twelve 'Undred a Year!'

Kipps tried to bridge that opening gulf. 'Remember the Hurons, Sid?'

'Rather,' said Sid.

'Remember that wreck?'

'I can smell it now – sort of sour smell.'

Kipps was silent for a moment with reminiscent eyes on Sid's still troubled face.

'I say, Sid, 'ow's Ann?'

'*She*'s all right,' said Sid.

'Where is she now?'

'In a place . . . Ashford.'

'Oh!'

Sid's face had become a shade sulkier than before.

'The fact is,' he said, 'we don't get on very well together. *I* don't hold with service. We're common people, I suppose, but I don't like it. I don't see why a sister of mine should wait at other people's tables. No. Not even if they got Twelve 'Undred a Year.'

Kipps tried to change the point of application. 'Remember 'ow you came out once when we were racing here? . . . She didn't run bad for a girl.'

And his own words raised an image brighter than he could have supposed, so bright it seemed to breathe before him and did not fade altogether even when he was back in Folkestone an hour or so later.

But Sid was not to be deflected from that other rankling theme by any reminiscences of Ann.

'I wonder what you will do with all that money,' he speculated. 'I wonder if you will do any good at all. I wonder what you *could* do. You should hear Masterman. He'd tell you things. Suppose it came to me, what should I do? It's no good giving it back to the state as things are. Start an Owenite profit-sharing factory[29] perhaps. Or a new Socialist paper. We want a new Socialist paper.'

He tried to drown his personal chagrin in elaborate exemplary suggestions . . .

3

'I must be gettin' on to my motor,' said Kipps at last, having to a large extent heard him out.

'What! Got a motor?'

'No!' said Kipps apologetically. 'Only jobbed for the day.'

' 'Ow much?'

'Five pounds.'

'Keep five families for a week! Good Lord!' That seemed to crown Sid's disgust.

Yet drawn by a sort of fascination he came with Kipps and assisted at the mounting of the motor. He was pleased to note it was not the most modern of motors, but that was the only grain of comfort. Kipps mounted at once, after one violent agitation of the little shop-door to set the bell a-jingle and warn his uncle and aunt. Sid assisted with the great fur-lined overcoat and examined the spectacles.

'Goodbye, o' chap!' said Kipps.

'Goodbye, o' chap!' said Sid.

The old people came out to say goodbye.

Old Kipps was radiant with triumph. ' 'Pon my Sammy, Artie! I'm a goo' mind to come with you,' he shouted, and then, 'I got something you might take with you!'

He dodged back into the shop and returned with the perforated engraving after Morland.

'You stick to this, my boy,' he said. 'You get it repaired by someone who knows. It's the most vallyble thing I got you so far, you take my word.'

'Warrup!' said the motor, and tuff, tuff, tuff, and backed and snorted while old Kipps danced about on the pavement as if foreseeing complex catastrophes, and told the driver, 'That's all right.'

He waved his stout stick to his receding nephew. Then he turned to Sid. 'Now, if you could make something like that, young Pornick, you *might* blow a bit!'

'I'll make a doocid sight better than *that* before I'm done,' said Sid, hands deep in his pockets.

'Not *you*,' said old Kipps.

The motor set up a prolonged sobbing moan and vanished around the corner. Sid stood motionless for a space, unheeding some further remark from old Kipps. The young mechanic had just discovered that to have manufactured seventeen bicycles, including orders in hand, is not so big a thing as he had supposed, and such discoveries try one's manhood –

'Oh well!' said Sid at last, and turned his face towards his mother's cottage.

She had got a hot teacake for him, and she was a little hurt that he was dark and preoccupied as he consumed it. He had always been such a boy for teacake, and then when one went out specially and got him one – !

He did not tell her – he did not tell anyone – he had seen young Kipps. He did not want to talk about Kipps for a bit to anyone at all.

CHAPTER FIVE

The Pupil Lover

When Kipps came to reflect upon his afternoon's work he had his first inkling of certain comprehensive incompatibilities lying about the course of true love in his particular case. He had felt without understanding the incongruity between the announcement he had failed to make and the circle of ideas of his aunt and uncle. It was this rather than the want of a specific intention that had silenced him, the perception that when he travelled from Folkestone to New Romney he travelled from an atmosphere where his engagement to Helen was sane and excellent to an atmosphere where it was only to be regarded with incredulous suspicion. Coupled and associated with this jar was his sense of the altered behaviour of Sid Pornick, the evident shock to that ancient alliance caused by the fact of his enrichment, the touch of hostility in his 'You'll soon be swelled too big to speak to a poor mechanic like me.' Kipps was unprepared for the unpleasant truth that the path of social advancement is and must be strewn with broken friendships. This first protrusion of that fact caused a painful confusion in his mind. It was speedily to protrude in a far more serious fashion in relation to the 'hands' from the Emporium, and Chitterlow.

From the day at Lympne Castle his relations with Helen had entered upon a new footing. He had prayed for Helen as good souls pray for Heaven, with as little understanding of what it was he prayed for. And now that period of standing humbly in the shadows before the shrine was over, and the goddess, her veil of mystery flung aside, had come down to him and taken hold of him, a good, strong, firm hold, and walked by his side . . . She liked him. What was singular was that very soon she had kissed him thrice, whimsically upon the brow, and he had never kissed her at all. He could not analyse his feelings, only he knew the world was wonderfully changed about them; but the truth was that, though he still worshipped and feared her, though his pride in his engagement was ridiculously vast, he loved her now no more. That subtle something. woven of the most delicate strands of self-love and tenderness and desire, had vanished imperceptibly and was gone now for ever. But that she did not suspect in him, nor as a matter of fact did he.

She took him in hand in perfect good faith. She told him things about his accent, she told him things about his bearing, about his costume and his way of looking at things. She thrust the blade of her intelligence into the tenderest corners of Kipps's secret vanity, she slashed his most intimate pride to bleeding tatters. He sought very diligently to anticipate some at least of these informing thrusts by making great use of Coote. But the unanticipated made a brave number –

She found his simple willingness a very lovable thing.

Indeed she liked him more and more. There was a touch of motherliness in her feelings towards him. But his upbringing and his associations had been, she diagnosed, 'awful'. At New Romney she glanced but little; that was remote. But in her inventory – she went over him as one might go over a newly taken house, with impartial thoroughness – she discovered more proximate influences: surprising intimations of nocturnal 'sing-songs' – she pictured it as almost shocking that Kipps should sing to the banjo – much low-grade wisdom treasured from a person called Buggins – 'Who *is* Buggins?' said Helen – vague figures of indisputable vulgarity, Pierce and Carshot – and more particularly, a very terrible social phenomenon, Chitterlow.

Chitterlow blazed upon them with unheralded oppressive brilliance the first time they were abroad together.

They were going along the front of the Leas to see a school play in Sandgate – at the last moment Mrs Walshingham had been unable to come with them – when Chitterlow loomed up into the new world. He was wearing the suit of striped flannel and the straw hat that had followed Kipps's payment in advance for his course in elocution, his hands were deep in his side pockets and animated the corners of his jacket, and his attentive gaze at the passing loungers, the faint smile under his boldly drawn nose, showed him engaged in studying character – no doubt for some forthcoming play.

'What-HO!' said he, at the sight of Kipps, and swept off the straw hat with so ample a clutch of his great, flat hand that it suggested to Helen's startled mind a conjurer about to palm a halfpenny.

' 'Ello, Chitt'low,' said Kipps a little awkwardly and not saluting.

Chitterlow hesitated. 'Half a mo', my boy,' he said, and arrested Kipps by extending a large hand over his chest. 'Excuse me, my dear,' he said, bowing like his Russian count by way of apology to Helen, and with a smile that would have killed at a hundred yards. He affected a semi-confidential grouping of himself and Kipps, while Helen stood in white amazement.

'About that play,' he said.

' 'Ow about it?' asked Kipps, acutely aware of Helen.

'It's all right,' said Chitterlow. 'There's a strong smell of syndicate in the air, I may tell you – Strong.'

'That's aw right,' said Kipps.

'You needn't tell everybody,' said Chitterlow, with a transitory confidential hand to his mouth which pointed the application of the 'everybody' just a trifle too strongly, 'but I think it's coming off. However – I mustn't detain you now. So long. You'll come round, eh?'

'Right you are,' said Kipps.

'Tonight?'

'At eight.'

And then, and more in the manner of a Russian prince than any common count, Chitterlow bowed and withdrew. Just for a moment he allowed a conquering eye to challenge Helen's, and noted her for a girl of quality.

There was a silence between our lovers for a space.

'That,' said Kipps with an allusive movement of the head, 'was Chitterlow.'

'Is he – a friend of yours?'

'In a way ... You see – I met 'im. Leastways 'e met me. Run into me with a bicycle, 'e did, and so we got talking together.'

He tried to appear at his ease.

The young lady scrutinised his profile. 'What is he?'

' 'E's a Nacter chap,' said Kipps. 'Leastways 'e writes plays.'

'And sells them?'

'Partly.'

'Whom to?'

'Different people. Shares he sells ... It's all right, reely – I meant to tell you about him before.'

Helen looked over her shoulder to catch a view of Chitterlow's retreating aspect. It did not compel her complete confidence.

She turned to her lover and said in a tone of quiet authority, 'You must tell me all about Chitterlow. Now.'

The explanation began ...

The school play came almost as a relief to Kipps. In the flusterment of going in he could almost forget for a time his Laocoön struggle to explain, and in the intervals he did his best to keep forgetting. But Helen, with a gentle insistence, resumed the explanation of Chitterlow as they returned towards Folkestone.

Chitterlow was confoundedly difficult to explain. You could hardly imagine!

There was an almost motherly anxiety in Helen's manner, blended with the resolution of a schoolmistress to get to the bottom of the affair. Kipps's ears were soon quite brightly red.

'Have you seen one of his plays?'

' 'E's tole me about one.'

'But on the stage.'

'No. He 'asn't 'ad any on the stage yet. That's all coming . . . '

'Promise me,' she said in conclusion, 'you won't do anything without consulting me.'

And, of course, Kipps promised. 'Oo – no!'

They went on their way in silence.

'One can't know everybody,' said Helen in general.

'Of course,' said Kipps; 'in a sort of way it was him that helped me to my money.' And he indicated in a confused manner the story of the advertisement. 'I don't like to drop 'im all at once,' he added.

Helen was silent for a space, and when she spoke she went off at a tangent. 'We shall live in London – soon,' she remarked. 'It's only while we are here.'

It was the first intimation she gave him of their post-nuptial prospects.

'We shall have a nice little flat somewhere, not too far west, and there we shall build up a circle of our own.'

2

All that declining summer Kipps was the pupil lover. He made an extraordinarily open secret of his desire for self-improvement; indeed Helen had to hint once or twice that his modest frankness was excessive, and all this new circle of friends did, each after his or her manner, everything that was possible to supplement Helen's efforts and help him to ease and skill in the more cultivated circles to which he had come. Coote was still the chief teacher, the tutor – there are so many little difficulties that a man may take to another man that he would not care to propound to the woman he loves – but they were all, so to speak, upon the staff. Even the freckled girl said to him once in a pleasant way, 'You mustn't say "contre temps", you must say "contraytom",' when he borrowed that expression from *Manners and Rules*, and she tried at his own suggestion to give him clear ideas upon the subject of 'as' and 'has'. A certain confusion between these words was becoming evident, the first fruits of a lesson from Chitterlow on the aspirate. Hitherto he had discarded that dangerous letter almost altogether, but now he would pull up at words beginning with 'h' and draw a sawing breath – rather like a startled kitten – and then aspirate with vigour.

Said Kipps one day, ' '*As* 'e? – I should say, ah – Has 'e? Ye know I got a lot of difficulty over them two words, which is which?'

'Well, "as" is a conjunction and "has" is a verb.'

'I know,' said Kipps, 'but when is "has" a conjunction and when is "as" a verb?'

'Well,' said the freckled girl, preparing to be very lucid. 'It's *has* when it means one has, meaning having, but if it isn't it's *as*. As for instance one says 'e – I mean *he* – He has. But one says "as he has".'

'I see,' said Kipps. 'So I ought to say "as 'e?" '

'No, if you are asking a question you say *has* 'e – I mean he – 'as he?' She blushed quite brightly, but still clung to her air of lucidity.

'I see,' said Kipps. He was about to say something further, but he desisted. 'I got it much clearer now. *Has* 'e? *Has* 'e as. Yes.'

'If you remember about having.'

'Oo, I will,' said Kipps . . .

Miss Coote specialised in Kipps's artistic development. She had early formed an opinion that he had considerable artistic sensibility, his remarks on her work had struck her as decidedly intelligent, and whenever he called around to see them she would show him some work of art – now an illustrated book, now perhaps a colour print of a Botticelli, now the *Hundred Best Paintings*, now 'Academy Pictures', now a German art handbook and now some magazine of furniture and design. 'I know you like these things,' she used to say, and Kipps said, 'Oo, I *do*.' He soon acquired a little armoury of appreciative sayings. When presently the Walshinghams took him up to the Arts and Crafts, his deportment was intelligent in the extreme. For a time he kept a wary silence until suddenly he pitched upon a colour print. 'That's rather nace,' he said to Mrs Walshingham. 'That lill' thing. There.' He always said things like that by preference to the mother rather than the daughter unless he was perfectly sure.

He quite took to Mrs Walshingham. He was impressed by her conspicuous tact and refinement; it seemed to him that the ladylike could go no further. She was always dressed with a delicate fussiness that was never disarranged and even a sort of faded quality about her hair and face and bearing and emotions contributed to her effect. Kipps was not a big man, and commonly he did not feel a big man, but with Mrs Walshingham he always felt enormous and distended, as though he was a navvy who had taken some disagreeable poison which puffed him up inside his skin as a preliminary to bursting. He felt, too, as though he had been rolled in clay and his hair dressed with gum. And he felt that his voice was strident and his accent like somebody swinging a crowded pig's pail in a free and careless manner. All this increased and enforced his respect for her. Her hand, which flitted often and again to his hand and arm, was singularly well shaped and cool. 'Arthur,' she called him from the very beginning.

She did not so much positively teach and tell him as tactfully guide and infect him. Her conversation was not so much didactic as exemplary. She would say, 'I *do* like people to do' so and so. She would tell him anecdotes of nice things done, of gentlemanly feats of graceful consideration; she would record her neat observations of people in trains and omnibuses; how, for example, a man had passed her change to the conductor, 'quite a common man he looked', but he had lifted his hat. She stamped Kipps so deeply with the hat-raising habit that he would uncover if he found himself in the same railway ticket-office with a lady and so had to stand ceremoniously until the difficulties of change drove him to an apologetic provisional oblique resumption of his headgear . . . And robbing these things of any air of personal application, she threw about them an abundant talk about her two children – she called them her Twin Jewels quite frequently – about their gifts, their temperaments, their ambition, their need of opportunity. They needed opportunity, she would say, as other people needed air . . .

In his conversations with her Kipps always assumed, and she seemed to assume, that she was to join that home in London Helen foreshadowed, but he was surprised one day to gather that this was not to be the case. 'It wouldn't do,' said Helen, with decision. 'We want to make a circle of our own.'

'But won't she be a bit lonely down here?' asked Kipps.

'There's the Waces, and Mrs Prebble, and Mrs Bindon Botting and – lots of people she knows.' And Helen dismissed this possibility . . .

Young Walshingham's share in the educational syndicate was smaller. But he shone out when they went to London on that Arts and Crafts expedition. Then this rising man of affairs showed Kipps how to buy the more theatrical weeklies for consumption in the train, how to buy and what to buy in the way of cigarettes with gold tips and shilling cigars, and how to order hock for lunch and sparkling Moselle for dinner, how to calculate the fare of a hansom cab – penny a minute while he goes – how to look intelligently at a hotel tape, and how to sit still in a train like a thoughtful man instead of talking like a fool and giving yourself away. And he, too, would glance at the good time coming when they were to be in London for good and all.

That prospect expanded and developed particulars. It presently took up a large part of Helen's conversation. Her conversations with Kipps were never of a grossly sentimental sort; there was a shyness of speech in that matter with both of them, but these new adumbrations were at least as interesting and not so directly disagreeable as the clear-cut intimations of personal defect that for a time had so greatly chastened Kipps's delight in her presence. The future presented itself with an almost perfect frankness as a joint campaign of Mrs Walshingham's Twin Jewels upon the Great World, with Kipps in the capacity of baggage and supply. They would still be dreadfully poor, of course – this amazed Kipps, but he said nothing – until 'Brudderkins' began to succeed, but if they were clever and lucky they might do a great deal.

When Helen spoke of London, a brooding look, as of one who contemplates a distant country, came into her eyes. Already it seemed they had the nucleus of a set. Brudderkins was a member of the Theatrical Judges, an excellent and influential little club of journalists and literary people, and he knew Shimer and Stargate and Whiffle, of the 'Red Dragon'; and besides these were the Revels. They knew the Revels quite well. Sidney Revel, before his rapid rise to prominence as a writer of epigrammatic essays that were quite above the ordinary public, had been an assistant master at one of the best Folkestone schools. Brudderkins had brought him home to tea several times, and it was he had first suggested Helen should try and write. 'It's perfectly easy,' Sidney had said. He had been writing occasional things for the evening papers and for the weekly reviews even at that time. Then he had gone up to London and had almost unavoidedly become a dramatic critic. Those brilliant essays had followed, and then *Red Hearts a-Beating*, the romance that had made him. It was a tale of spirited adventure, full of youth and beauty and naïve passion and generous devotion, bold, as the *Bookman* said, and frank in places, but never in the slightest degree morbid. He had met and married an American widow with quite a lot of money, and they had made a very distinct place for themselves, Kipps learnt, in the literary and artistic society of London. Helen seemed to dwell on the Revels a great deal; it was her exemplary story, and when she spoke of Sidney – she often called him Sidney – she would become thoughtful. She spoke most of him naturally because she had still to meet Mrs Revel . . . Certainly they would be in the world in no time, even if the distant connection with the Beauprés family came to nothing.

Kipps gathered that with his marriage and the movement to London they were to undergo that subtle change of name Coote had first adumbrated. They were to become 'Cuyps', Mr and Mrs Cuyps. Or, was it Cuyp?

'It'll be rum at first,' said Kipps. 'I dessay I shall soon get into it . . .'

So in their several ways they all contributed to enlarge and refine and exercise the intelligence of Kipps. And behind all these other influences, and, as it were, presiding over and correcting these influences, was Kipps's nearest friend, Coote, a sort of master of the ceremonies. You figure his face, blowing slightly with solicitude, his slate-coloured, projecting but not unkindly eye intent upon our hero. The thing, he thought, was going off admirably. He studied Kipps's character immensely. He would discuss him with his sister, with Mrs Walshingham, with the freckled girl, with anyone who would stand it. 'He is an interesting character,' he would say, 'likable – a sort of gentleman by instinct. He takes to all these things. He improves every day. He'll soon get *Sang Froid*. We took him up just in time. He wants now – well – Next year, perhaps, if there is a good Extension Literature course[30] he might go in for it. He wants to go in for something like that.'

'He's going in for his bicycle now,' said Mrs Walshingham.

'That's all right for summer,' said Coote, 'but he wants to go in for some serious, intellectual interest, something to take him out of himself a little more. *Savoir Faire* and self-forgetfulness are more than half the secret of *Sang Froid*.'

3

The world as Coote presented it was in part an endorsement, in part an amplification and in part a rectification of the world of Kipps, the world that derived from the old couple in New Romney and had been developed in the Emporium; the world, in fact, of common British life. There was the same subtle sense of social graduation that had moved Mrs Kipps to prohibit intercourse with labourers' children and the same dread of anything 'common' that had kept the personal quality of Mr Shalford's establishment so high. But now a certain disagreeable doubt about Kipps's own position was removed and he stood with Coote inside the sphere of gentlemen assured. Within the sphere of gentlemen there are distinctions of rank indeed, but none of class; there are the Big People and the modest, refined, gentlemanly little people like Coote, who may even dabble in the professions and counterless trades; there are lords and magnificences, and there are gentlefolk who have to manage; but they can all call on one another, they preserve a general equality of deportment throughout, they constitute that great state within the state, Society.

'But reely,' said the Pupil, 'not what you call being in Society?'

'Yes,' said Coote. 'Of course, down here one doesn't see much of it, but there's local society. It has the same rules.'

'Calling and all that?'

'Precisely,' said Coote.

Kipps thought, whistled a bar, and suddenly broached a question of conscience. 'I often wonder,' he said, 'whether I oughtn't to dress for dinner – when I'm alone 'ere.'

Coote protruded his lips and reflected. 'Not full dress,' he adjudicated; 'that would be a little excessive. But you should *change*, you know. Put on a mess jacket and that sort of thing – easy dress. That is what *I* should do, certainly, if I wasn't in harness – and poor.'

He coughed modestly and patted his hair behind.

And after that the washing bill of Kipps quadrupled, and he was to be seen at times by the bandstand with his light summer overcoat unbuttoned to give a glimpse of his nice white tie. He and Coote would be smoking the gold-tipped cigarettes young Walshingham had prescribed as *chic*, and appreciating the music highly. 'That's – puff – a very nice bit,' Kipps would say; or better, 'That's nace.' And at the first grunts of the loyal anthem up they stood with religiously uplifted hats. Whatever else you might call them, you could never call them disloyal.

The boundary of Society was admittedly very close to Coote and Kipps, and a leading solicitude of the true gentleman was to detect clearly those 'beneath' him, and to behave towards them in a proper spirit. 'It's jest there it's so 'ard for me,' said Kipps. He had to cultivate a certain 'distance', to acquire altogether the art of checking the presumption of bounders and old friends. It was difficult, Coote admitted.

'I got mixed up with this lot 'ere,' said Kipps. 'That's what, so harkward – I mean awkward.'

'You could give them a hint,' said Coote.

' 'Ow?'

'Oh! – the occasion will suggest something.'

The occasion came one early-closing night when Kipps was sitting in a canopy chair near the bandstand, with his summer overcoat fully open and a new Gibus pulled slightly forward over his brow, waiting for Coote. They were to hear the band for an hour and then go down to assist Miss Coote and the freckled girl in trying over some of Beethoven's duets, if they remembered them, that is, sufficiently well.

And as Kipps lounged back in his chair and occupied his mind with his favourite amusement on such evenings, which consisted chiefly in supposing that everyone about him was wondering who he was, there came a rude rap at the canvas back and the voice of Pierce.

'It's nice to be a gentleman,' said Pierce, and swung a penny chair into position while Buggins appeared smiling agreeably on the other side and leant upon his stick. *He was smoking a common briar pipe!*

Two real ladies, very fashionably dressed and sitting close at hand, glanced quickly at Pierce, and then away again, and it was evident *their* wonder was at an end.

'*He*'s all right,' said Buggins, removing his pipe and surveying Kipps.

' 'Ello, Buggins!' said Kipps, not too cordially. ' 'Ow goes it?'

'All right. Holiday's next week. If you don't look out, Kipps, I shall be on the Continong before you. Eh?'

'You going t' Boologne?'

'Ra-ther. Parley vous Francey. You bet.'

'*I* shall 'ave a bit of a run over there one of these days,' said Kipps.

There came a pause. Pierce applied the top of his stick to his mouth for a space and regarded Kipps. Then he glanced at the people about them.

'I say, Kipps,' he said in a distinct, loud voice, 'see 'er Ladyship lately?'

Kipps perceived the audience was to be impressed, but he responded half-heartedly, 'No, I 'aven't,' he said.

'She was along of Sir William the other night,' said Pierce, still loud and clear, 'and she asked to be remembered to you.'

It seemed to Kipps that one of the two ladies smiled faintly and said something to the other, and then certainly they glanced at Pierce. Kipps flushed scarlet. '*Did* she?' he answered.

Buggins laughed good-humouredly over his pipe.

'Sir William suffers a lot from his gout,' Pierce continued unabashed. (Buggins much amused with his pipe between his teeth.)

Kipps became aware of Coote at hand.

Coote nodded rather distantly to Pierce. 'Hope I haven't kept you waiting, Kipps,' he said.

'I kep' a chair for you,' said Kipps and removed a guardian foot.

'But you've got your friends,' said Coote.

'Oh! *we* don't mind,' said Pierce cordially, 'the more the merrier,' and, 'Why don't you get a chair, Buggins?' Buggins shook his head in a sort of aside to Pierce and Coote coughed behind his hand.

'Been kep' late at business?' asked Pierce.

Coote turned quite pale and pretended not to hear. His eyes sought in space for a time and with a convulsive movement he recognised a distant acquaintance and raised his hat.

Pierce had also become a little pale. He addressed himself to Kipps in an undertone.

'Mr Coote, isn't he?' he asked.

Coote addressed himself to Kipps directly and exclusively. His manner had the calm of extreme tension.

'I'm rather late,' he said. 'I think we ought almost to be going on *now*.'

Kipps stood up. 'That's all right,' he said.

'Which way are you going?' said Pierce, standing also, and brushing some crumbs of cigarette ash from his sleeve.

For a moment Coote was breathless. 'Thank you,' he said, and gasped. Then he delivered the necessary blow: 'I don't think we're in need of your society, you know,' and turned away.

Kipps found himself falling over chairs and things in the wake of Coote, and then they were clear of the crowd.

For a space Coote said nothing; then he remarked abruptly and quite angrily for him, 'I think that was *awful* Cheek!'

Kipps made no reply . . .

The whole thing was an interesting little object lesson in distance, and it stuck in the front of Kipps's mind for a long time. He had particularly vivid the face of Pierce, with an expression between astonishment and anger. He felt as though he had struck Pierce in the face under circumstances that gave Pierce no power to reply. He did not attend very much to the duets and even forgot at the end of one of them to say how perfectly lovely it was.

4

But you must not imagine that the national ideal of a gentleman, as Coote developed it, was all a matter of deportment and selectness, a mere isolation from debasing associations. There is a Serious Side, a deeper aspect of the True Gentleman. But it is not vocal. The True Gentleman does not wear his heart on his sleeve. He is a polished surface above deeps. For example, he is deeply religious, as Coote was, as Mrs Walshingham was, but outside the walls of a church it never appears, except perhaps now and then in a pause, in a profound look, in a sudden avoidance. In quite a little while Kipps also had learnt the pause, the profound look, the sudden avoidance, that final refinement of spirituality, impressionistic piety.

And the True Gentleman is patriotic also. When one saw Coote lifting his hat to the National Anthem, then perhaps one got a glimpse of what patriotic emotions, what worship, the polish of a gentleman may hide. Or singing out his deep notes against the Hosts of Midian, in the St Stylites choir; then indeed you plumbed his spiritual side.

> Christian, dost thou heed them,
> On the holy ground,
> How the hosts of Mid-i-an,
> Prowl and prowl around!
> Christian, up and smai–it them . . .

But these were but gleams. For the rest, Religion, Nationality, Passion, Money, Politics, much more so those cardinal issues, Birth and Death, the True Gentleman skirted about, and became facially rigid towards, and ceased to speak and panted and blew.

'One doesn't talk of that sort of thing,' Coote would say with a gesture of the knuckly hand.

'O' course,' Kipps would reply, with an equal significance.

Profundities. Deep, as it were, blowing too deep.

One does not talk, but on the other hand one is punctilious to do. Actions speak. Kipps – in spite of the fact that the Walshinghams were more than a little lax – Kipps, who had formerly flitted Sunday after Sunday from one Folkestone church to another, had now a sitting of his own, paid for duly at Saint Stylites. There he was to be seen, always at the surplice evening service, and sometimes of a morning, dressed with a sober precision, and with an eye on Coote in the chancel. No difficulties now about finding the place in his book. He became a communicant again – he had lapsed soon after his confirmation when the young lady in the costume-room, who was his adopted sister, left the Emporium – and he would sometimes go around to the vestry for Coote after the service. One evening he was introduced to the Hon. and Revd Densemore. He was much too confused to say anything, and the noble cleric had nothing to say, but indisputably they were introduced –

No! you must not imagine our national ideal of a gentleman is without its 'serious side', without even its stern and uncompromising side. The imagination no doubt refuses to see Coote displaying extraordinary refinements of courage upon the stricken field, but in the walks of peace there is sometimes sore need of sternness. Charitable as one may be, one must admit there are people who *do* things, impossible things; people who place themselves 'out of it' in countless ways; people, moreover, who are by a sort of predestination out of it from the beginning, and against these Society has invented a terrible protection for its Cootery, the Cut. The cut is no joke for anyone. It is excommunication. You may be cut by an individual, you may be cut by a set or you may be – and this is so tragic that beautiful romances have been written about it – 'Cut by the County'. One figures Coote discharging this last duty and cutting somebody – Coote, erect and pale, never speaking, going past with eyes of pitiless slate, lower jaw protruding a little, face pursed up and cold and stiff . . .

It never dawned upon Kipps that he would one day have to face this terrible front, to be to Coote not only as one dead, but as one gone more than a stage or so in decay, cut and passed, banned and outcast for ever. It never dawned upon either of them.

Yet so it was to be!

One cannot hide any longer that all this fine progress of Kipps is doomed to end in collapse. So far indeed you have seen him ascend. You have seen him becoming more refined and careful day by day, more carefully dressed, less clumsy in the uses of social life. You have seen the gulf widening between himself and his former low associates. I have brought you at last to the vision of him, faultlessly dressed and posed, in an atmosphere of candlelight and chanting, in his own sitting in one of the most fashionable churches in Folkestone . . . All the time I have refrained from the lightest touch upon the tragic note that must now creep into my tale. Yet the net of his low connections has been about his feet, and moreover there was something interwoven in his being . . .

CHAPTER SIX

Discords

One day Kipps set out upon his newly-mastered bicycle to New
Romney to break the news of his engagement to his uncle and aunt –
this time positively. He was now a finished cyclist, but as yet an
unseasoned one; the south-west wind, even in its summer guise, as one
meets it in the Marsh, is the equivalent of a reasonable hill, and ever
and again he got off and refreshed himself by a spell of walking. He
was walking just outside New Romney preparatory to his triumphal
entry (one hand off) when abruptly he came upon Ann Pornick.

It chanced he was thinking about her at the time. He had been
thinking curious things; whether, after all, the atmosphere of New
Romney and the Marsh had not some difference, some faint impalpable
quality that was missing in the great and fashionable world of Folkestone
behind there on the hill. Here there was a homeliness, a familiarity. He
had noted as he passed that old Mr Cliffordown's gate had been mended
with a fresh piece of string. In Folkestone he didn't take notice and he
didn't care if they built three hundred houses. Come to think of it, that
was odd. It was fine and grand to have twelve hundred a year; it was fine
to go about on trams and omnibuses and think not a person aboard was
as rich as oneself; it was fine to buy and order this and that and never
have any work to do and to be engaged to a girl distantly related to the
Earl of Beauprés, but yet there had been a zest in the old time out here,
a rare zest in the holidays, in sunlight, on the sea beach and in the High
Street, that failed from these new things. He thought of those bright
windows of holiday that had seemed so glorious to him in the retrospect
from his apprentice days. It was strange that now, amidst his present
splendours, they were glorious still!

All those things were over now – perhaps that was it! Something had
happened to the world and the old light had been turned out. He himself
was changed, and Sid was changed, terribly changed, and Ann no doubt
was changed.

He thought of her with the hair blown about her flushed cheeks as
they stood together after their race . . .

Certainly she must be changed, and all the magic she had been fraught
with to the very hem of her short petticoats gone no doubt for ever.

And as he thought that, or before and while he thought it, for he came to all these things in his own vague and stumbling way, he looked up and there was Ann!

She was seven years older and greatly altered; yet for the moment it seemed to him that she had not changed at all. 'Ann!' he said, and she, with a lifting note, 'It's Art Kipps!'

Then he became aware of changes – improvements. She was as pretty as she had promised to be, her blue eyes as dark as his memory of them, and with a quick, high colour, but now Kipps by several inches was the taller again. She was dressed in a simple grey dress that showed her very clearly as a straight and healthy little woman, and her hat was Sundayfied with pink flowers. She looked soft and warm and welcoming. Her face was alight to Kipps with her artless gladness at their encounter.

'It's Art Kipps!' she said.

'Rather,' said Kipps.

'You got your holidays?'

It flashed upon Kipps that Sid had not told her of his great fortune. Much regretful meditation upon Sid's behaviour had convinced him that he himself was to blame for exasperating boastfulness in that affair, and this time he took care not to err in that direction. He erred in the other.

'I'm taking a bit of a 'oliday,' he said.

'So'm I,' said Ann.

'You been for a walk?' asked Kipps.

Ann showed him a bunch of wayside flowers.

'It's a long time since I seen you, Ann. Why, 'ow long must it be? Seven – eight years nearly.'

'It don't do to count,' said Ann.

'It don't look like it,' said Kipps, with the slightest emphasis.

'You got a moustache,' said Ann, smelling her flowers and looking at him over them, not without admiration.

Kipps blushed . . . Presently they came to the bifurcation of the roads.

'I'm going down this way to mother's cottage,' said Ann.

'I'll come a bit your way if I may.'

In New Romney social distinctions that are primary realities in Folkestone are absolutely non-existent, and it seemed quite permissible for him to walk with Ann, for all that she was no more than a servant. They talked with remarkable ease to one another; they slipped into a vein of intimate reminiscence in the easiest manner.

In a little while Kipps was amazed to find Ann and himself at this: 'You r'ember that half sixpence? What you cut for me?'

'Yes.'

'I got it still.'

She hesitated. 'Funny, wasn't it?' she said; and then, 'You got yours, Artie?'

'Rather,' said Kipps. 'What do *you* think?' and wondered in his heart of hearts why he had never looked at that sixpence for so long.

Ann smiled at him frankly.

'I didn't expect you'd keep it,' she said. 'I thought often – it was silly to keep mine. Besides,' she reflected, 'it didn't mean anything really.'

She glanced at him as she spoke and met his eye.

'Oh, didn't it!' said Kipps, a little late with his response, and realising his infidelity to Helen even as he spoke.

'It didn't mean much anyhow,' said Ann. 'You still in the drapery?'

'I'm living at Folkestone,' began Kipps and decided that that sufficed. 'Didn't Sid tell you he met me?'

'No! Here?'

'Yes. The other day. 'Bout a week or more ago.'

'That was before I came.'

'Ah! that was it,' said Kipps.

' 'E's got on,' said Ann. 'Got 'is own shop now, Artie.'

' 'E tole me.'

They found themselves outside Muggett's cottages. 'You going in?' said Kipps.

'I s'pose so,' said Ann.

They both hung upon the pause. Ann took a plunge.

'D'you often come to New Romney?' she said.

'I ride over a bit at times,' said Kipps.

Another pause. Ann held out her hand.

'I'm glad I seen you,' she said.

Extraordinary impulses arose in neglected parts of Kipps's being. 'Ann – ' he said and stopped.

'Yes,' said she, and was bright to him.

They looked at one another.

All and more than all of those first emotions of his adolescence had come back to him. Her presence banished a multitude of countervaling considerations. It was Ann more than ever. She stood breathing close to him, with her soft-looking lips a little apart and gladness in her eyes.

'I'm awful glad to see you again,' he said; 'it brings back old times.'

'Doesn't it?'

Another pause. He would have liked to have had a long talk to her, to have gone for a walk with her or something, to have drawn nearer to her in any conceivable way, and, above all, to have had some more of the appreciation that shone in her eyes, but a vestige of Folkestone still clinging to him told him it 'wouldn't do'.

'Well,' he said, 'I must be getting on,' and turned away reluctantly, with a will under compulsion . . .

When he looked back from the corner she was still at the gate. She was perhaps a little disconcerted by his retreat. He felt that. He hesitated for a moment, half turned, stood and suddenly did great things with his hat. That hat! The wonderful hat of our civilisation! . . .

In another minute he was engaged in a singularly absent-minded conversation with his uncle about the usual topics.

His uncle was very anxious to buy him a few upright clocks as an investment for subsequent sale. And there were also some very nice globes, one terrestrial and the other celestial, in a shop at Lydd, that would look well in a drawing-room and inevitably increase in value . . . Kipps either did or did not agree to this purchase; he was unable to recollect.

The south-west wind perhaps helped him back; at any rate he found himself through Dymchurch without having noticed the place. There came an odd effect as he drew near Hythe. The hills on the left and the trees on the right seemed to draw together and close in upon him until his way was straight and narrow. He could not turn around on that treacherous, half-tamed machine, but he knew that behind him, he knew so well, spread the wide, vast flatness of the Marsh shining under the afternoon sky. In some way this was material to his thoughts. And as he rode through Hythe he came upon the idea that there was a considerable amount of incompatibility between the existence of one who was practically a gentleman and of Ann.

In the neighbourhood of Seabrook he began to think he had, in some subtle way, lowered himself by walking along by the side of Ann . . . After all, she was only a servant.

Ann!

She called out all the least gentlemanly instincts of his nature. There had been a moment in their conversation when he had quite distinctly thought it would really be an extremely nice thing for someone to kiss her lips . . . There was something warming about Ann – at least for Kipps. She impressed him as having somewhen during their vast interval of separation contrived to make herself in some distinctive way his.

Fancy keeping that half sixpence all this time!

It was the most flattering thing that had ever happened to Kipps.

He found himself presently sitting over *The Art of Conversing*, lost in the strangest musings. He got up, walked about, became stagnant at the window for a space, roused himself and by way of something lighter tried *Sesame and Lilies*. From that, too, his attention wandered. He sat back. Anon he smiled, anon sighed. He arose, pulled his keys from his pocket, looked at them, decided and went upstairs. He opened the little yellow box that had been the nucleus of all his possessions in the world and took out a small 'escritoire', the very humblest sort of present, and opened it – kneeling. And there, in the corner, was a little packet of paper, sealed as a last defence against any prying invader with red sealing wax. It had gone untouched for years. He held this little packet between finger and thumb for a moment, regarding it, and then put down the escritoire and broke the seal . . .

As he was getting into bed that night he remembered something for the first time! 'Dash it!' he said. 'Dashed if I told 'em *this* time . . . *Well!* I shall 'ave to go over to New Romney again!'

He got into bed and remained sitting pensively on the pillow for a space. 'It's a rum world,' he reflected after a vast interval.

Then he recalled that she had noticed his moustache and embarked upon a sea of egotistical musings.

He imagined himself telling Ann how rich he was. What a surprise that would be for her!

Finally he sighed profoundly, blew out his candle and snuggled down, and in a little while he was asleep.

But the next morning and at intervals afterwards he found himself thinking of Ann – Ann, the bright, the desirable, the welcoming, and with an extraordinary streakiness he wanted quite badly to go and then as badly not to go over to New Romney again.

Sitting on the Leas in the afternoon, he had an idea. 'I ought to 'ave told 'er, I suppose, about my being engaged.

'Ann!'

All sorts of dreams and impressions that had gone clean out of his mental existence came back to him, changed and brought up to date to fit her altered presence. He thought of how he had gone back to New Romney for his Christmas holidays, determined to kiss her, and of the awful blankness of the discovery that she had gone away.

It seemed incredible now, and yet not wholly incredible, that he had cried real tears for her – how many years was it ago?

Daily I should thank my Maker that He did not appoint me Censor of the world of men. I should temper a fierce injustice with a spasmodic indecision that would prolong rather than mitigate the bitterness of the Day. For human dignity, for all conscious human superiority, I should lack the beginnings of charity; for bishops, prosperous schoolmasters, judges and all large respect-pampered souls. And more especially bishops, towards whom I bear an atavistic Viking grudge, dreaming not infrequently and with invariable zest of galleys and landings and well-known living ornaments of the episcopal bench sprinting inland on twinkling gaiters before my thirsty blade – all these people, I say, I should treat below their deserts; but, on the other hand, for such as Kipps – There the exasperating indecisions would come in. The Judgement would be arrested at Kipps. Everyone and everything would wait. *You* would wait. The balance would sway and sway, and whenever it heeled towards an adverse decision, my finger would set it swaying again. Kings, warriors, statesmen, brilliant women of our first families, 'personalities' panting with indignation, headline humanity in general, would stand undamned, unheeded, or be damned in the most casual manner for their importunity, while my eye went about for anything possible that could be said on behalf of Kipps . . . Albeit I fear nothing can save him from condemnation upon this present score, that within two days he was talking to Ann again.

One seeks excuses. Overnight there had been an encounter of Chitterlow and young Walshingham in his presence that had certainly warped his standards. They had called within a few minutes of each other, and the two, swayed by virile attentions to Old Methuselah Three Stars, had talked against each other, over and at the hospitable presence of Kipps. Walshingham had seemed to win at the beginning, but finally Chitterlow had made a magnificent display of vociferation and swept him out of existence. At the beginning Chitterlow had opened upon the great profits of playwrights and young Walshingham had capped him at once with a cynical, but impressive, display of knowledge of High Finance. If Chitterlow boasted his thousands, young Walshingham boasted his hundreds of thousands, and was for a space left in sole possession of the stage, juggling with the wealth of nations. He was going on by way of Financial Politics to the Overman, before Chitterlow recovered from his first check and came back to victory. 'Talking of Women,' said Chitterlow, coming in abruptly upon some things not generally known beyond Walshingham's more immediate circle about a recently departed Empire-builder; 'Talking of Women and the way they Get at a man – '

(Though as a matter of fact they had been talking of the Corruption of Society by Speculation.)

Upon this new topic Chitterlow was soon manifestly invincible. He knew so much, he had known so many. Young Walshingham did his best with epigrams and reservations, but even to Kipps it was evident that this was a book-learned depravity. One felt Walshingham had never known the inner realities of passion. But Chitterlow convinced and amazed. He had run away with girls, he had been run away with by girls, he had been in love with several at a time – 'not counting Bessie' – he had loved and lost, he had loved and refrained, and he had loved and failed. He threw remarkable lights upon the moral state of America – in which country he had toured with great success. He set his talk to the tune of one of Mr Kipling's best-known songs.[31] He told an incident of simple romantic passion, a delirious dream of love and beauty in a Saturday-to-Monday steamboat trip up the Hudson, and tagged his end with, 'I learnt about women from 'er!' After that he adopted the refrain, and then lapsed into the praises of Kipling. 'Little Kipling,' said Chitterlow, with the familiarity of affection, '*he* knows,' and broke into quotation:

> "I've taken my fun where I've found it;
>   I've rogued and I've ranged in my time;
> I've 'ad my picking of sweet'earts,
>   An' four of the lot was Prime." '

(These things, I say, affect the moral standards of the best of us.)

'*I'd* have liked to have written that,' said Chitterlow. 'That's Life, that is! But go and put it on the Stage, put even a bit of the Realities of Life on the Stage, and see what they'll do to you! Only Kipling could venture on a job like that. That Poem KNOCKED me! I don't say Kipling hasn't knocked me before and since, but that was a Fair Knock Out.

'And yet – you know – there's one thing in it . . . this:

> "I've taken my fun where I've found it,
>   And now I must pay for my fun,
> For the more you 'ave known o' the others,
>   The less will you settle to one – "

Well. In my case anyhow – I don't know how much that proves, seeing I'm exceptional in so many things and there's no good denying it – but so far as I'm concerned – I tell you two, but of course you needn't let it go any further – I've been perfectly faithful to Muriel ever since I married her – ever since . . . Not once. Not even by accident have I ever said or done anything in the slightest – ' His little brown eye became pensive after this flattering intimacy and the gorgeous draperies of his abundant voice fell into graver folds. '*I learnt about women from 'er,*' he said impressively.

'Yes,' said Walshingham, getting into the hinder spaces of that splendid pause, 'a man must know about women. And the only sound way of learning is the experimental method.'

'If you want to know about the experimental method, my boy,' said Chitterlow, resuming . . .

So they talked. *Ex pede Herculem,* as Coote, that cultivated polyglot, would have put it. And in the small hours Kipps went to bed, with his brain whirling with words and whisky, and sat for an unconscionable time upon his bed edge, musing sadly upon the unmanly monogamy that had cast its shadow upon his career, musing with his thoughts pointing around more and more certainly to the possibility of at least duplicity with Ann.

4

For a whole day he had refrained with some insistence from going off to New Romney again . . .

I do not know if this may count in palliation of his misconduct. Men, real Strong-Souled, Healthy Men, should be, I suppose, impervious to conversational atmospheres, but I have never claimed for Kipps a place at these high levels. The unquenchable fact remains that the next day he spent the afternoon with Ann and found no scruple in displaying himself a budding lover.

He had met her in the High Street, had stopped her, and almost on the spur of the moment had boldly proposed a walk, 'for the sake of old times'.

'*I* don't mind,' said Ann.

Her consent almost frightened Kipps. His imagination had not carried him to that. 'It would be a lark,' said Kipps, and looked up the street and down. 'Now?' he said.

'I don't mind a bit, Artie. I was just going for a walk along towards St Mary's.'

'Let's go that way be'ind the church,' said Kipps, and presently they found themselves drifting seaward in a mood of pleasant common-place. For a while they talked of Sid. It went clean out of Kipps's head at that early stage even that Ann was a 'girl' according to the exposition of Chitterlow, and for a time he remembered only that she was Ann. But afterwards, with the reek of that talk in his head, he lapsed a little from that personal relation. They came out upon the beach and sat down in a tumbled pebbly place, where a meagre grass and patches of sea poppy were growing, and Kipps reclined on his elbow and tossed pebbles in his hand, and Ann sat up, sunlit, regarding him. They talked in fragments. They exhausted Sid, they exhausted Ann, and Kipps was chary of his riches.

He declined to a faint lovemaking. 'I got that 'arf sixpence still,' he said.

'Reely?'

That changed the key. 'I always kept mine, some'ow,' said Ann, and there was a pause.

They spoke of how often they had thought of each other during those intervening years. Kipps may have been untruthful, but Ann perhaps was not. 'I met people here and there,' said Ann; 'but I never met anyone quite like you, Artie.'

'It's jolly our meeting again, anyhow,' said Kipps. 'Look at that ship out there. She's pretty close in . . . '

He had a dull period, became indeed almost pensive, and then he was enterprising for a while. He tossed up his pebbles so that as if by accident they fell on Ann's hand. Then, very penitently, he stroked the place. That would have led to all sorts of coquetries on the part of Flo Banks, for example, but it disconcerted and checked Kipps to find Ann made no objection, smiled pleasantly down on him, with eyes half shut because of the sun. She was taking things very much for granted.

He began to talk, and Chitterlow standards resuming possession of him he said he had never forgotten her.

'I never forgotten you either, Artie,' she said. 'Funny, isn't it?'

It impressed Kipps also as funny.

He became reminiscent, and suddenly a warm summer's evening came back to him. 'Remember them cockchafers, Ann?' he said. But the reality of the evening he recalled was not the chase of cockchafers. The great reality that had suddenly arisen between them was that he had never kissed Ann in his life. He looked up and there were her lips.

He had wanted to very badly, and his memory leaped and annihilated an interval. That old resolution came back to him and all sorts of new resolutions passed out of mind. And he had learnt something since those boyish days. This time he did not ask. He went on talking, his nerves began very faintly to quiver and his mind grew bright.

Presently, having satisfied himself that there was no one to see, he sat up beside her and remarked upon the clearness of the air, and how close Dungeness seemed to them. Then they came upon a pause again.

'Ann,' he whispered, and put an arm that quivered about her.

She was mute and unresisting, and, as he was to remember, solemn.

He turned her face towards him, and kissed her lips, and she kissed him back again – kisses frank and tender as a child's.

5

It was curious that in the retrospect he did not find nearly the satisfaction in this infidelity he had imagined was there. It was no doubt desperately doggish, doggish to an almost Chitterlowesque degree, to recline on the beach at Littlestone with a 'girl', to make love to her and to achieve the triumph of kissing her, when he was engaged to another 'girl' at Folkestone, but somehow these two people were not 'girls', they were Ann and Helen. Particularly Helen declined to be considered as a 'girl'. And there was something in Ann's quietly friendly eyes, in her frank smile, in the naïve pressure of her hand, there was something undefended and welcoming that imparted a flavour to the business upon which he had not counted. He had learnt about women from her. That refrain ran through his mind and deflected his thoughts, but as a matter of fact he had learnt about nothing but himself.

He wanted very much to see Ann some more and explain. He did not clearly know what it was he wanted to explain.

He did not clearly know anything. It is the last achievement of the intelligence to get all of one's life into one coherent scheme, and Kipps was only in a measure more aware of himself as a whole than is a tree. His existence was an affair of dissolving and recurring moods. When he thought of Helen or Ann or any of his friends, he thought sometimes of this aspect and sometimes of that – and often one aspect was finally incongruous with another. He loved Helen, he revered Helen. He was also beginning to hate her with some intensity. When he thought of that expedition to Lympne, profound, vague, beautiful emotions flooded his being; when he thought of paying calls with her perforce, or of her latest comment on his bearing, he found himself rebelliously composing fierce and pungent insults, couched in the vernacular. But Ann, whom he had seen so much less of, was a simpler memory. She was pretty, she was almost softly feminine, and she was possible to his imagination just exactly where Helen was impossible. More than anything else, she carried the charm of respect for him, the slightest glance of her eyes was balm for his perpetually wounded self-conceit.

Chance suggestions it was set the tune of his thoughts, and his state of health and repletion gave the colour. Yet somehow he had this at least almost clear in his mind, that to have gone to see Ann a second time, to have implied that she had been in possession of his thoughts through all this interval, and, above all, to have kissed her, was shabby and wrong. Only unhappily this much of lucidity had come now just a few hours after it was needed.

6

Four days after this it was that Kipps got up so late. He got up late, cut his chin while shaving, kicked a slipper into his sponge bath and said, 'Desh!'

Perhaps you know those intolerable mornings, dear Reader, when you seem to have neither the heart nor the strength to rise, and your nervous adjustments are all wrong, and your fingers thumbs, and you hate the very birds for singing. You feel inadequate to any demand whatever. Often such awakenings follow a poor night's rest, and commonly they mean indiscriminate eating, or those subtle mental influences old Kipps ascribed to 'Foozle Ile' in the system, or worry. And with Kipps – albeit Chitterlow had again been his guest overnight – assuredly worry had played a leading role. Troubles had been gathering upon him for days, there had been a sort of concentration of these hosts of Midian overnight, and in the grey small hours Kipps had held his review.

The predominating trouble marched under this banner:

Mr Kipps
Mrs Bindon Botting
At Home
Thursday, September 16th
Anagrams, 4 to 6:30   *R. S. V. P.*

a banner that was the facsimile of a card upon his looking glass in the room below. And in relation to this terribly significant document, things had come to a pass with Helen that he could only describe in his own expressive idiom as 'words'.

It had long been a smouldering issue between them that Kipps was not availing himself with any energy or freedom of the opportunities he had of social exercises, much less was he seeking additional opportunities. He had, it was evident, a peculiar dread of that universal afternoon enjoyment, the Call, and Helen made it unambiguously evident that this dread was 'silly' and had to be overcome. His first display of this unmanly weakness occurred at the Cootes' on the day before he kissed Ann. They were all there, chatting very pleasantly, when the little servant with the big cap announced the younger Miss Wace.

Whereupon Kipps manifested a lively horror and rose partially from his chair. 'O Gum!' he protested. 'Carn't I go upstairs?'

Then he sank back, for it was too late. Very probably the younger Miss Wace had heard him as she came in.

Helen said nothing of that, though her manner may have shown her surprise, but afterwards she told Kipps he must get used to seeing people, and suggested that he should pay a series of calls with Mrs Walshingham and herself. Kipps gave a reluctant assent at the time and afterwards displayed a talent for evasion that she had not suspected in him. At last she did succeed in securing him for a call upon Miss Punchafer, of Radnor Park – a particularly easy call because Miss Punchafer being so deaf one could say practically what one liked – and then outside the gate he shirked again. 'I can't go in,' he said in a faded voice.

'You *must*,' said Helen, beautiful as ever, but even more than a little hard and forbidding.

'I can't.'

He produced his handkerchief hastily, thrust it to his face, and regarded her over it with rounded, hostile eyes.

' 'Possible,' he said in a hoarse, strange voice out of the handkerchief. 'Nozzez bleedin' . . . '

But that was the end of his power of resistance, and when the rally for the Anagram Tea occurred she bore down his feeble protests altogether. She insisted. She said frankly, 'I am going to give you a good talking to about this,' and she did . . .

From Coote he gathered something of the nature of Anagrams and Anagram parties. An anagram, Coote explained, was a word spelt the same way as another, only differently arranged, as, for instance, TOCOE would be an anagram for his own name, Coote.

'TOCOE,' repeated Kipps very carefully.

'Or TOCOE,' said Coote.

'Or TOCOE,' said Kipps, assisting his poor head by nodding it at each letter.

'Toe Company like,' he said in his efforts to comprehend.

When Kipps was clear what an anagram meant, Coote came to the second heading – the Tea. Kipps gathered there might be from thirty to sixty people present, and that each one would have an anagram pinned on. 'They give you a card to put your guesses on, rather like a dance programme, and then, you know, you go around and guess,' said Coote. 'It's rather good fun.'

'Oo rather!' said Kipps, with simulated gusto.

'It shakes everybody up together,' said Coote.

Kipps smiled and nodded . . .

In the small hours all his painful meditations were threaded by the vision of that Anagram Tea; it kept marching to and fro and in and out of all his other troubles; from thirty to sixty people, mostly ladies and callers, and a great number of the letters of the alphabet, and more particularly PIKPS and TOCOE, and he was trying to make one word out of the whole interminable procession . . .

This word, as he finally gave it with some emphasis to the silence of the night, was, '*Demn!*'

Then, wreathed as it were in this lettered procession, was the figure of Helen as she had appeared at the moment of 'words'; her face a little hard, a little irritated, a little disappointed. He imagined himself going around and guessing under her eye . . .

He tried to think of other things, without lapsing upon a still deeper uneasiness that was wreathed with yellow sea poppies; and the figures of Buggins, Pierce and Carshot, three murdered Friendships, rose reproachfully in the stillness and changed horrible apprehensions into unspeakable remorse. Last night had been their customary night for the banjo, and Kipps, with a certain tremulous uncertainty, had put old Methuselah amidst a retinue of glasses on the table and opened a box of choice cigars. In vain. They were in no need, it seemed, of *his* society. But instead Chitterlow had come, anxious to know if it was all right about that syndicate plan. He had declined anything but a very weak whisky and soda, 'just to drink', at least until business was settled, and had then opened the whole affair with an effect of great orderliness to Kipps. Soon he was taking another whisky by sheer inadvertency, and the complex fabric of his conversation was running more easily from the broad loom of his mind. Into that pattern had been inter-woven a narrative of extensive alterations in The Pestered Butterfly' –

the neck and beetle business was to be restored – the story of a grave difference of opinion with Mrs Chitterlow, where and how to live after the play had succeeded, the reasons why the Hon. Thomas Norgate had never financed a syndicate, and much matter also about the syndicate now under discussion. But if the current of their conversation had been vortical and crowded, the outcome was perfectly clear. Kipps was to be the chief participator in the syndicate, and his contribution was to be two thousand pounds. Kipps groaned and rolled over and found Helen, as it were, on the other side. 'Promise me,' she had said, 'you won't do anything without consulting me.'

Kipps at once rolled back to his former position, and for a space lay quite still. He felt like a very young rabbit in a trap.

Then suddenly, with extraordinary distinctness, his heart cried out for Ann, and he saw her as he had seen her at New Romney, sitting amidst the yellow sea poppies with the sunlight on her face. His heart called out for her in the darkness as one calls for rescue. He knew, as though he had known it always, that he loved Helen no more. He wanted Ann, he wanted to hold her and be held by her, to kiss her again and again, to turn his back for ever on all these other things . . .

He rose late, but this terrible discovery was still there, undispelled by cockcrow or the day. He rose in a shattered condition, and he cut himself while shaving, but at last he got into his dining-room and could pull the bell for the hot constituents of his multifarious breakfast. And then he turned to his letters. There were two real letters in addition to the customary electric-belt advertisement, continental lottery circular and betting tout's card. One was in a slight mourning envelope and addressed in an unfamiliar hand. This he opened first and discovered a note:

> *Mrs Raymond Wace*
> *requests the pleasure of*
> *Mr Kipps's*
> *Company at Dinner*
> *on Tuesday, September 21st, at 8 o'clock*
>
> *RSVP*

With a hasty movement Kipps turned his mind to the second letter. It was an unusually long one from his uncle, and ran as follows:

MY DEAR NEPHEW – We are considerably startled by your letter, though expecting something of the sort and disposed to hope for the best. If the young lady is a relation to the Earl of Beaupres well and good but take care you are not being imposed upon for there are many who will be glad enough to snap you up now your circumstances are altered – I waited on the old Earl once while in service and he was remarkably close with his tips and suffered from corns. A hasty old gent and hard to please – I dare say he has forgotten me altogether – and anyhow there is no need to rake up bygones. Tomorrow is bus day and as you say the young lady is living near by we shall shut up shop for there is really nothing doing now what with all the visitors bringing everything with them down to their very children's pails and say how de do to her and give her a bit of a kiss and encouragement if we think her suitable – she will be pleased to see your old uncle – We wish we could have had a look at her first but still there is not much mischief done and hoping that all will turn out well yet I am

    Your affectionate Uncle

EDWARD GEORGE KIPPS

My heartburn still very bad. I shall bring over a few bits of rhubub I picked up, a sort you won't get in Folkestone, and if possible a good bunch of flowers for the young lady.

'Comin' over today,' said Kipps, standing helplessly with the letter in his hand.

' 'Ow, the Juice – ?

'I carn't.

'Kiss 'er!'

A terrible anticipation of that gathering framed itself in his mind – a hideous, impossible disaster.

'I carn't even face 'er – !' His voice went up to a note of despair. 'And it's too late to telegrarf and stop 'em!'

7

About twenty minutes after this, an out-porter in Castle Hill Avenue was accosted by a young man with a pale, desperate face, an exquisitely rolled umbrella and a heavy Gladstone bag.

'Carry this to the station, will you?' said the young man. 'I want to ketch the nex' train to London . . . You'll 'ave to look sharp – I 'aven't very much time.'

CHAPTER SEVEN

London

London was Kipps's third world. There were no doubt other worlds, but Kipps knew only these three: first, New Romney and the Emporium, constituting his primary world, his world of origin, which also contained Ann; secondly, the world of culture and refinement, the world of which Coote was chaperon and into which Kipps was presently to marry, a world it was fast becoming evident absolutely incompatible with the first; and, thirdly, a world still to a large extent unexplored, London. London presented itself as a place of great grey spaces and incredible multitudes of people, centring about Charing Cross Station and the Royal Grand Hotel, and containing at unexpected arbitrary points shops of the most amazing sort, statuary, squares, restaurants – where it was possible for clever people like Walshingham to order a lunch item by item, to the waiters' evident respect and sympathy – exhibitions of incredible things – the Walshinghams had taken him to the Arts and Crafts and to a picture gallery – and theatres. London, moreover, is rendered habitable by hansom cabs. Young Walshingham was a natural cab-taker; he was an all-round large-minded young man, and he had in the course of their two days' stay taken Kipps into no less than nine, so that Kipps was singularly not afraid of these vehicles. He knew that wherever you were, so soon as you were thoroughly lost you said, 'Hi!' to a cab, and then, 'Royal Grand Hotel.' Day and night these trusty conveyances are returning the strayed Londoner back to his point of departure, and were it not for their activity, in a little while the whole population, so vast and incomprehensible is the intricate complexity of this great city, would be hopelessly lost for ever. At any rate, that is how the thing presented itself to Kipps, and I have heard much the same from visitors from America.

His train was composed of corridor carriages, and he forgot his trouble for a time in the wonders of this modern substitute for railway compartments. He went from the non-smoking to the smoking carriage and smoked a cigarette, and strayed from his second-class carriage to a first and back. But presently Black Care got aboard the train and came and sat beside him. The exhilaration of escape had evaporated now, and he was presented with a terrible picture of his aunt and uncle arriving at his lodgings and finding him fled. He had left a hasty message that he was called away suddenly on business, 'ver' important business', and they were to be sumptuously entertained. His immediate motive had been his passionate dread of an encounter between these excellent but unrefined old people and the Walshinghams, but now that end was secured, he could see how thwarted and exasperated they would be.

How to explain to them?

He ought never to have written to tell them!

He ought to have got married and told them afterwards.

He ought to have consulted Helen.

'Promise me,' she had said.

'Oh, *desh*!' said Kipps, and got up and walked back into the smoking car and began to consume cigarettes.

Suppose, after all, they found out the Walshinghams' address and went there!

At Charing Cross, however, there were distractions again. He took a cab in an entirely Walshingham manner, and was pleased to note the enhanced respect of the cabman when he mentioned the Royal Grand. He followed Walshingham's routine on their previous visit with perfect success. They were very nice in the office, and gave him an excellent room at fourteen shillings the night.

He went up and spent a considerable time in examining the furniture of his room, scrutinising himself in its various mirrors and sitting on the edge of the bed whistling. It was a vast and splendid apartment, and cheap at fourteen shillings. But, finding the figure of Ann inclined to resume possession of his mind, he roused himself and descended by the staircase, after a momentary hesitation before the lift. He had thought of lunch, but he drifted into the great drawing-room and read a guide to the Hotels of Europe for a space, until a doubt whether he was entitled to use this palatial apartment without extra charge arose in his mind. He would have liked something to eat very much now, but his inbred terror of the table was very strong. He did at last get by a porter in uniform towards the dining-room, but at the sight of a number of waiters and tables, with remarkable complications of knives and glasses, terror seized him, and he backed out again, with a mumbled remark to the waiter in the doorway about this not being the way.

He hovered in the hall and lounge until he thought the presiding porter regarded him with suspicion, and then went up to his room again by the staircase, got his hat and umbrella and struck boldly across the courtyard. He would go to a restaurant instead.

He had a moment of elation in the gateway. He felt all the Strand must notice him as he emerged through the great gate of the Hotel. 'One of these here rich swells,' they would say. 'Don't they do it just!' A cabman touched his hat. 'No fear,' said Kipps, pleasantly . . .

Then he remembered he was hungry.

Yet he decided he was in no great hurry for lunch, in spite of an internal protest, and turned eastward along the Strand in a leisurely manner. He would find a place to suit him soon enough. He tried to remember the sort of dihes Walshingham had ordered. Before all things he didn't want to go into a place and look like a fool. Some of these places rook you dreadful, besides making fun of you. There was a place near Essex Street where there was a window brightly full of chops, tomatoes and lettuce. He stopped at this and reflected for a time, and then it occurred to him that you were expected to buy these things raw and cook them at home. Anyhow, there was sufficient doubt in the matter to stop him. He drifted on to a neat window with champagne bottles, a dish of asparagus and a framed menu for a two-shilling lunch. He was about to enter, when fortunately he perceived two waiters looking at him over the back screen of the window with a most ironical expression, and he sheered off at once. There was a wonderful smell of hot food halfway down Fleet Street and a nice-looking tavern with several doors, but he could not decide which door. His nerve was going under the strain.

He hesitated at Farringdon Street and drifted up to St Paul's and round the churchyard, full chiefly of dead bargains in the shop windows, to Cheapside. But now Kipps was getting demoralised, and each house of refreshment seemed to promise still more complicated obstacles to food. He didn't know how you went in and what was the correct thing to do with your hat; he didn't know what you said to the waiter or what you called the different things; he was convinced absolutely he would 'fumble', as Shalford would have said, and look like a fool. Somebody might laugh at him! The hungrier he got the more unendurable was the thought that anyone should laugh at him. For a time he considered an extraordinary expedient to account for his ignorance. He would go in and pretend to be a foreigner and not know English. Then they might understand . . . Presently he had drifted into a part of London where there did not seem to be any refreshment places at all.

'Oh, *desh*!' said Kipps, in a sort of agony of indecisiveness. 'The very nex' place I see, in I go.'

The next place was a fried fish shop in a little side street, where there were also sausages on a gas-lit grill.

He would have gone in, but suddenly a new scruple came to him, that he was too well dressed for the company he could see dimly through the steam sitting at the counter and eating with a sort of nonchalant speed.

2

He was half minded to resort to a hansom and brave the terrors of the dining-room of the Royal Grand – they wouldn't know why he had gone out really – when the only person he knew in London appeared (as the only person one does know will do in London) and slapped him on the shoulder. Kipps was hovering at a window at a few yards from the fish shop, pretending to examine some really strikingly cheap pink baby linen, and trying to settle finally about those sausages.

'Hello, Kipps!' cried Sid; 'spending the millions?'

Kipps turned, and was glad to perceive no lingering vestige of the chagrin that had been so painful at New Romney. Sid looked grave and important, and he wore a quite new silk hat that gave a commercial touch to a generally socialistic costume. For a moment the sight of Sid uplifted Kipps wonderfully. He saw him as a friend and helper, and only presently did it come clearly into his mind that this was the brother of Ann.

He made amiable noises.

'I've just been up this way,' Sid explained, 'buying a second-hand 'namelling stove . . . I'm going to 'namel myself.'

'Lor'!' said Kipps.

'Yes. Do me a lot of good. Let the customer choose his colour. See? What brings *you* up?'

Kipps had a momentary vision of his foiled uncle and aunt. 'Jest a bit of a change,' he said.

Sid came to a swift decision. 'Come down to my little show. I got someone I'd like to see talking to you.'

Even then Kipps did not think of Ann in this connection.

'Well,' he said, trying to invent an excuse on the spur of the moment. 'Fact is,' he explained, 'I was jest looking round to get a bit of lunch.'

'Dinner, we call it,' said Sid. 'But that's all right. You can't get anything to eat hereabout. If you're not too haughty to do a bit of slumming, there's some mutton spoiling for me now – '

The word 'mutton' affected Kipps greatly.

'It won't take us 'arf an hour,' said Sid, and Kipps was carried.

He discovered another means of London locomotion in the Underground Railway, and recovered his self-possession in that interest. 'You

don't mind going third?' asked Sid, and Kipps said, 'Nort a *bit* of it.'
They were silent in the train for a time, on account of strangers in the
carriage, and then Sid began to explain who it was that he wanted Kipps
to meet. 'It's a chap named Masterman – do you no end of good.

'He occupies our first-floor front room, you know. It isn't so much
for gain I let as company. We don't *want* the whole 'ouse, that's one
thing ,and another is, I knew the man before. Met him at our Socio-
logical, and after a bit he said he wasn't comfortable where he was.
That's how it came about. He's a first-class chap – first-class. Science!
You should see his books!

'Properly he's a sort of journalist. He's written a lot of things, but he's
been too ill lately to do very much. Poetry he's written, all sorts. He
writes for the *Commonweal*[32] sometimes, and sometimes he reviews
books. 'E's got 'eaps of books – 'eaps. Besides selling a lot.

'He knows a regular lot of people, and all sorts of things. He's been a
dentist, and he's a qualified chemist, an' I seen him often reading
German and French. Taught 'imself. He was here – '

Sid indicated South Kensington, which had come opportunely outside
the carriage windows, with a nod of his head, ' – three years. Studying
science. But you'll see 'im. When he really gets to talking – he *pours* it
out.'

'Ah!' said Kipps, nodding sympathetically, with his two hands on his
umbrella knob.

'He'll do big things some day,' said Sid. 'He's written a book on
science already. *Physiography*, it's called. *Elementary Physiography*! Some
day he'll write an Advanced – when he gets time.'

He let this soak into Kipps.

'I can't introduce you to lords and swells,' he went on, 'but I *can*
show you a Famous Man, that's going to be. I *can* do that. Leastways –
unless – '

Sid hesitated.

'He's got a frightful cough,' he said.

'He won't care to talk with me,' weighed Kipps.

'That's all right; *he* won't mind. He's fond of talking. He'd talk to
anyone,' said Sid, reassuringly, and added a perplexing bit of Londonised
Latin. 'He doesn't *pute* anything, *non alienum*. You know.'

'*I* know,' said Kipps, intelligently, over his umbrella knob, though of
course that was altogether untrue.

Kipps found Sid's shop a practical-looking establishment, stocked with the most remarkable collection of bicycles and pieces of bicycle that he had ever beheld. 'My hiring stock,' said Sid, with a wave to this ironmongery, 'and there's the best machine at a democratic price in London, The Red-Flag, built by *me*. See?' He indicated a graceful, grey-brown framework in the window. 'And there's my stock of accessories – store prices.

'Go in for motors a bit,' added Sid.

'Mutton?' said Kipps, not hearing him distinctly.

'Motors, I *said* . . . 'Owever, Mutton Department 'ere,' and he opened a door that had a curtain-guarded window in its upper panel, to reveal a little room with red walls and green furniture and a white-clothed table and the generous promise of a meal. 'Fanny!' he shouted. 'Here's Art Kipps.'

A bright-eyed young woman of five- or six-and-twenty in a pink print appeared, a little flushed from cooking, and wiped a hand on an apron and shook hands and smiled, and said it would all be ready in a minute. She went on to say she had heard of Kipps and his luck, and meanwhile Sid vanished to draw the beer, and returned with two glasses for himself and Kipps.

'Drink that,' said Sid, and Kipps felt all the better for it.

'I give Mr Masterman *'is* upstairs a hour ago,' said Mrs Sid. 'I didn't think 'e ought to wait.'

A rapid succession of brisk movements on the part of everyone, and they were all four at dinner – the fourth person being Master Walt Whitman Pornick, a cheerful young gentleman of one and a half, who was given a spoon to hammer on the table with to keep him quiet, and who got 'Kipps' right at the first effort and kept it all through the meal, combining it first with this previous acquisition and then that. 'Peacock Kipps,' said Master Walt, at which there was great laughter, and also, 'More Mutton, Kipps.'

'He's a regular oner,' said Mrs Sid, 'for catching up words. You can't say a word but what 'e's on to it.'

There were no serviettes and less ceremony, and Kipps thought he had never enjoyed a meal so much. Everyone was a little excited by the meeting and chatting, and disposed to laugh, and things went off easily from the very beginning. If there was a pause Master Walt filled it in. Mrs Sid, who tempered her enormous admiration for Sid's intellect and his socialism and his severe business methods by a motherly sense of her sex and seniority, spoke of them both as 'you boys', and dilated – when she was not urging Kipps to have some more of this or that – on the disparity between herself and her husband.

'Shouldn't ha' thought there was a year between you,' said Kipps; 'you seem jest a match.'

'I'm *his* match, anyhow,' said Mrs Sid, and no epigram of young Walshingham's was ever better received.

'Match,' said young Walt, coming in on the trail of the joke and getting a round for himself.

Any sense of superior fortune had long vanished from Kipps's mind, and he found himself looking at host and hostess with enormous respect. Really, old Sid was a wonderful chap, here in his own house at two and twenty, carving his own mutton and lording it over wife and child. No legacies needed by him! And Mrs Sid, so kind and bright and hearty! And the child, old Sid's child! Old Sid had jumped round a bit. It needed the sense of his fortune at the back of his mind to keep Kipps from feeling abject. He resolved he'd buy young Walt something tremendous in toys at the first opportunity.

'Drop more beer, Art?'

'Right you are, old man.'

'Cut Mr Kipps a bit more bread, Sid.'

'Can't I pass *you* a bit?' . . .

Sid was all right, Sid was, and there was no mistake about that. It was growing up in his mind that Sid was the brother of Ann, but he said nothing about her for excellent reasons. After all, Sid's irritation at her name when they had met in New Romney seemed to show a certain separation. They didn't tell each other much . . . He didn't know how things might be between Ann and Sid, either.

Still, for all that, Sid was Ann's brother.

The furniture of the room did not assert itself very much above the cheerful business at the table, but Kipps was impressed with the idea that it was pretty. There was a dresser at the end with a number of gay plates and a mug or so, a Labour Day poster, by Walter Crane,[33] on the wall, and through the glass and over the blind of the shop door one had a glimpse of the bright-coloured advertisement cards of bicycle dealers, and a shelf full of boxes labelled, The Paragon Bell, The Scarum Bell, and The Patent Omi! Horn . . .

It seemed incredible that he had been in Folkestone that morning, and even now his aunt and uncle – !

B-r-r-r. It didn't do to think of his aunt and uncle.

When Sid repeated his invitation to come and see Masterman, Kipps, now flushed with beer and Irish stew, said he didn't mind if he did, and after a preliminary shout from Sid that was answered by a voice and a cough, the two went upstairs.

'Masterman's a rare one,' said Sid over his arm and in an undertone. 'You should hear him speak at a meeting . . . If he's in form, that is.'

He rapped and went into a large, untidy room.

'This is Kipps,' he said. 'You know. The chap I told you of. With twelve 'undred a year.'

Masterman sat gnawing at an empty pipe and as close to the fire as though it was alight and the season midwinter. Kipps concentrated upon him for a space, and only later took in something of the frowsy furniture, the little bed half behind – and evidently supposed to be wholly behind – a careless screen, the spittoon by the fender, the remains of a dinner on the chest of drawers and the scattered books and papers. Masterman's face showed him a man of forty or more, with curious hollows at the sides of his forehead and about his eyes. His eyes were very bright; there was a spot of red in each cheek, and the wiry black moustache under his short red nose had been trimmed with scissors into a sort of brush along his upper lip. His teeth were darkened ruins. His jacket collar was turned up about a knitted white neck wrap, and his sleeves betrayed no cuffs. He did not rise to greet Kipps, but held out a thin-wristed hand and pointed with the other to a bedroom armchair.

'Glad to see you,' he said. 'Sit down and make yourself at home. Will you smoke?'

Kipps said he would, and produced his store. He was about to take one, and then, with a civil afterthought, handed the packet first to Masterman and Sid. Masterman pretended surprise to find his pipe out before he took one. There was an interlude of matches. Sid pushed the end of the screen out of his way, sat down on the bed thus frankly admitted, and prepared, with a certain quiet satisfaction of manner, to witness Masterman's treatment of Kipps.

'And how does it feel to have twelve hundred a year?' asked Masterman, holding his cigarette to his nose tip in a curious manner.

'It's rum,' confided Kipps, after a reflective interval. 'It feels juiced rum.'

'I've never felt it,' said Masterman.

'It takes a bit of getting into,' said Kipps. 'I can tell you that.'

Masterman smoked and regarded Kipps with curious eyes.

'I expect it does,' he said presently.

'And has it made you perfectly happy?' he asked, abruptly.

'I couldn't 'ardly say *that*,' said Kipps.

Masterman smiled. 'No,' he said. 'Has it made you much happier?'

'It did at first.'

'Yes. But you got used to it. How long, for example, did the real delirious excitement last?'

'Oo, *that*! Perhaps a week,' said Kipps.

Masterman nodded his head. 'That's what discourages *me* from amassing wealth,' he said to Sid. 'You adjust yourself. It doesn't last. I've always had an inkling of that, and it's interesting to get it confirmed. I shall go on sponging for a bit longer on *you*, I think.'

'You don't,' said Sid. 'No fear.'

'Twenty-six thousand pounds,' said Masterman, and blew a cloud of smoke. 'Lord! Doesn't it worry you?'

'It is a bit worrying at times . . . Things 'appen.'

'Going to marry?'

'Yes.'

'H'm. Lady, I guess, of a superior social position?'

'Rather,' said Kipps. 'Cousin to the Earl of Beauprés.'

Masterman readjusted his long body with an air of having accumulated all the facts he needed. He snuggled his shoulder-blades down into the chair and raised his angular knees. 'I doubt,' he said, flicking cigarette ash into the atmosphere, 'if any great gain or loss of money does – as things are at present – make more than the slightest difference in one's happiness. It ought to – if money was what it ought to be, the token for given service; one ought to get an increase in power and happiness for every pound one got. But the plain fact is the times are out of joint, and money – money, like everything else, is a deception and a disappointment.'

He turned his face to Kipps and enforced his next words with the index finger of his lean, lank hand. 'If I thought otherwise,' he said, 'I should exert myself to get some. But, if one sees things clearly, one is so discouraged. So confoundedly discouraged . . . When you first got your money, you thought that it meant you might buy just anything you fancied?'

'I was a bit that way,' said Kipps.

'And you found that you couldn't. You found that for all sorts of things it was a question of where to buy and how to buy, and what you didn't know how to buy with your money, straight away this world planted something else upon you – '

'I got rather done over a banjo first day,' said Kipps. 'Leastways, my uncle says so.'

'Exactly,' said Masterman.

Sid began to speak from the bed. 'That's all very well, Masterman,' he said, 'but, after all, money *is* Power, you know. You can do all sorts of things – '

'I'm talking of happiness,' said Masterman. 'You can do all sorts of things with a loaded gun in the Hammersmith Broadway, but nothing – practically – that will make you or anyone else very happy. Nothing. Power's a different matter altogether. As for happiness, you want a world in order before money or property or any of those things have any real value; and this world, I tell you, is hopelessly out of joint. Man is a social animal with a mind nowadays that goes around the globe, and a community cannot be happy in one part and unhappy in another. It's all or nothing, no patching any more for ever. It is the standing mistake of the world not to understand that. Consequently people think there is a class or order somewhere, just above them or just below them, or a country or place somewhere, that is really safe and happy. The fact is, Society is one body, and it is either well or ill. That's the law. This society we live in is ill. It's a fractious, feverish invalid, gouty, greedy and ill-nourished. You can't have a happy left leg with neuralgia, or a happy throat with a broken leg. That's my position, and that's the knowledge you'll come to. I'm so satisfied of it that I sit here and wait for my end quite calmly, sure that I can't better things by bothering – in my time, and so far as I am concerned, that is. I'm not even greedy any more – my egotism's at the bottom of a pond, with a philosophical brick around its neck. The world is ill, my time is short and my strength is small. I'm as happy here as anywhere.'

He coughed and was silent for a moment, then brought the index finger around to Kipps again. 'You've had the opportunity of sampling two grades of society, and you don't find the new people you're among much better or any happier than the old?'

'No,' said Kipps, reflectively. 'No. I 'aven't seen it quite like that before, but – no. They're not.'

'And you might go all up the scale and down the scale and find the same thing. Man's a gregarious beast, a gregarious beast, and no money will buy you out of your own time – any more than out of your own skin. All the way up and all the way down the scale there's the same discontent. No one is quite sure where they stand, and everyone's fretting. The herd's uneasy and feverish. All the old tradition goes or has gone, and there's no one to make a new tradition. Where are your nobles now? Where are your gentlemen? They vanished directly the peasant found out he wasn't happy and ceased to be a peasant. There's big men and little men mixed up together, that's all. None of us know where we are. Your cads in a bank-holiday train and your cads in a two-thousand-pound motor – except for a difference in scale, there's not a pin to choose between them. Your smart society is as low and vulgar and uncomfortable for a balanced soul as a gin palace, no more and no less; there's no place or level of honour or fine living left in the world; so what's the good of climbing?'

' 'Ear, 'ear!' said Sid.

'It's true,' said Kipps.

'*I* don't climb,' said Masterman, and accepted Kipps's silent offer of another cigarette.

'No,' he said. 'This world is out of joint. It's broken up, and I doubt if it will heal. I doubt very much if it'll heal. We're in the beginning of the Sickness of the World.'

He rolled his cigarette in his lean fingers and repeated with satisfaction: 'The Sickness of the World.'

'It's we've got to make it better,' said Sid, and looked at Kipps.

'Ah, Sid's an optimist,' said Masterman.

'So are you, most times,' said Sid.

Kipps lit another cigarette with an air of intelligent participation.

'Frankly,' said Masterman, recrossing his legs and expelling a jet of smoke luxuriously, 'frankly, I think this civilisation of ours is on the topple.'

'There's Socialism,' said Sid.

'There's no imagination to make use of it.'

'We've got to *make* one,' said Sid.

'In a couple of centuries perhaps,' said Masterman. 'But meanwhile we're going to have a pretty acute attack of confusion. Universal confusion. Like one of those crushes when men are killed and maimed for no reason at all, going into a meeting or crowding for a train. Commercial and Industrial Stresses. Political Exploitation. Tariff Wars. Revolutions. All the bloodshed that will come of some fools calling half the white world yellow. These things alter the attitude of everybody to everybody. Everybody's going to feel 'em. Every fool in the world panting and shoving. We're all going to be as happy and comfortable as a household during a removal. What else can we expect?'

Kipps was moved to speak, but not in answer to Masterman's enquiry.

'I've never rightly got the 'eng of this Socialism,' he said. 'What's it going to do, like?'

They had been imagining that he had some elementary idea in the matter, but as soon as he had made it clear that he hadn't, Sid plunged at exposition, and in a little while Masterman, abandoning his pose of the detached man ready to die, joined in. At first he joined in only to correct Sid's version, but afterwards he took control. His manner changed. He sat up and rested his elbow on his knees, and his cheek flushed a little. He expanded his case against Property and the property class with such vigour that Kipps was completely carried away, and never thought of asking for a clear vision of the thing that would fill the void this abolition might create. For a time he quite forgot his own private opulence. And it was as if something had been lit in Masterman. His languor passed. He enforced his words by gestures of his long thin hands. And as he passed swiftly from point to point of his argument it was evident he grew angry.

'Today,' he said, 'the world is ruled by rich men; they may do almost anything they like with the world. And what are they doing? Laying it waste!'

'Hear, hear!' said Sid, very sternly.

Masterman stood up, gaunt and long, thrust his hands in his pockets and turned his back to the fireplace.

'Collectively, the rich today have neither heart nor imagination. No! They own machinery, they have knowledge and instruments and powers beyond all previous dreaming, and what are they doing with them? Think what they are doing with them, Kipps, and think what they might do. God gives them a power like the motor car, and all they can do with it is to go careering about the roads in goggled masks killing children and making machinery hateful to the soul of man! ['True,' said Sid, 'true.'] God gives them means of communication, power unparalleled of every sort, time and absolute liberty! They waste it all in folly! Here under their feet [and Kipps's eyes followed the direction of a lean index finger to the hearthrug], under their accursed wheels, the great mass of men festers and breeds in darkness, darkness those others make by standing in the light. The darkness breeds and breeds. It knows no better . . . Unless you can crawl or pander or rob you must stay in the stew you are born in. And those rich beasts above claw and clutch as though they had nothing! They grudge us our schools, they grudge us a gleam of light and air, they cheat us and then seek to forget us . . . There is no rule, no guidance, only accidents and happy flukes . . . Our multitudes of poverty increase, and this crew of rulers makes no provision, foresees nothing, anticipates nothing . . . '

He paused and made a step, and stood over Kipps in a white heat of anger. Kipps nodded in a non-committal manner and looked hard and rather gloomily at his host's slipper as he talked.

'It isn't as though they had something to show for the waste they make of us, Kipps. They haven't. They are ugly and cowardly and mean. Look at their women! Painted, dyed and drugged, hiding their ugly shapes under a load of dress! There isn't a woman in the swim of society at the present time wouldn't sell herself, body and soul, who wouldn't lick the boots of a Jew or marry a nigger, rather than live decently on a hundred a year! On what would be wealth for you and me! They know it. They know we know it . . . No one believes in them. No one believes in nobility any more. Nobody believes in kingship any more. Nobody believes there is justice in the law . . . But people have habits, people go on in the old grooves, as long as there's work, as long as there's weekly money . . . It won't last, Kipps.'

He coughed and paused. 'Wait for the lean years,' he cried. 'Wait for the lean years.' And suddenly he fell into a struggle with his cough and spat a gout of blood. 'It's nothing,' he said to Kipps's note of startled horror.

He went on talking, and the protests of his cough interlaced with his words, and Sid beamed in an ecstasy of painful admiration.

'Look at the fraud they have let life become, the miserable mockery of the hope of one's youth. What have *I* had? I found myself at thirteen being forced into a factory like a rabbit into a chloroformed box. Thirteen! – when *their* children are babies. But even a child of that age could see what it meant, that hell of a factory! Monotony and toil and contempt and dishonour! And then death. So I fought – at thirteen!'

Minton's 'crawling up a drainpipe until you die' echoed in Kipps's mind, but Masterman, instead of Minton's growl, spoke in a high, indignant tenor.

'I got out at last – somehow,' he said, quietly, suddenly plumping back in his chair. He went on after a pause. 'For a bit. Some of us get out by luck, some by cunning, and crawl on to the grass, exhausted and crippled, to die. That's a poor man's success, Kipps. Most of us don't get out at all. I worked all day and studied half the night, and here I am with the common consequences. Beaten! And never once have I had a fair chance, never once!' His lean, clenched fist flew out in a gust of tremulous anger. 'These Skunks shut up all the university scholarships at nineteen for fear of men like me. And then – do *nothing* . . . We're wasted for nothing. By the time I'd learnt something the doors were locked. I thought knowledge would do it – I did think that! I've fought for knowledge as other men fight for bread. I've starved for knowledge. I've turned my back on women; I've done even that. I've burst my accursed lung . . . ' His voice rose with impotent anger. 'I'm a better man than any ten princes alive! And I'm beaten and wasted. I've been crushed, trampled and defiled by a drove of hogs. I'm no use to myself or the world. I've thrown my life away to make myself too good for use in this huckster's scramble. If I had gone in for business, if I had gone in for plotting to cheat my fellow men – ah, well! It's too late. It's too late for that, anyhow. It's too late for anything now! And I couldn't have done it . . . And over in New York now there's a pet of society making a corner in wheat!

'By God!' he cried hoarsely, with a clutch of the lean hand. 'By God! If I had his throat! Even now I might do something for the world.'

He glared at Kipps, his face flushed deep, his sunken eyes glowing with passion, and then suddenly he changed altogether.

There was a sound of tea things rattling upon a tray outside the door, and Sid rose to open it.

'All of which amounts to this,' said Masterman, suddenly quiet and again talking against time. 'The world is out of joint, and there isn't a soul alive who isn't half waste or more. You'll find it the same with you in the end, wherever your luck may take you . . . I suppose you won't mind my having another cigarette?'

He took Kipps's cigarette with a hand that trembled so violently it almost missed its object, and stood up, with something of guilt in his manner, as Mrs Sid came into the room.

Her eye met his and marked the flush upon his face.

'Been talking Socialism?' said Mrs Sid, a little severely.

5

Six o'clock that day found Kipps drifting eastward along the southward margin of Rotten Row. You figure him a small, respectably attired figure going slowly through a sometimes immensely difficult and always immense world. At times he becomes pensive and whistles softly. At times he looks about him. There are a few riders in the Row, a carriage flashes by every now and then along the roadway, and among the great rhododendrons and laurels and upon the greensward there are a few groups and isolated people dressed in the style Kipps adopted to call upon the Walshinghams when first he was engaged. Amid the complicated confusion of Kipps's mind was a regret that he had not worn his other things . . .

Presently he perceived that he would like to sit down; a green chair tempted him. He hesitated at it, took possession of it, and leant back and crossed one leg over the other.

He rubbed his underlip with his umbrella handle and reflected upon Masterman and his denunciation of the world.

'Bit orf 'is 'ead, poor chap,' said Kipps; and added: 'I wonder –'

He thought intently for a space.

'I wonder what he meant by the lean years?'

The world seemed a very solid and prosperous concern just here, and well out of reach of Masterman's dying clutch. And yet –

It was curious he should have been reminded of Minton.

His mind turned to a far more important matter. Just at the end Sid had said to him, 'Seen Ann?' and as he was about to answer, 'You'll see a bit more of her now. She's got a place in Folkestone.'

It had brought him back from any concern about the world being out of joint or anything of that sort.

Ann!

One might run against her any day.

He tugged at his little moustache.

He would like to run against Ann very much . . .

'And it would be juiced awkward if I did!'

In Folkestone! It was a jolly sight too close . . .

Then, at the thought that he might run against Ann in his beautiful evening dress on the way to the band, he fluttered into a momentary dream that jumped abruptly into a nightmare.

Suppose he met her when he was out with Helen! 'Oh, Lor'!' said Kipps. Life had developed a new complication that would go on and go on. For some time he wished with the utmost fervour that he had not kissed Ann, that he had not gone to New Romney the second time. He marvelled at his amazing forgetfulness of Helen on that occasion. Helen took possession of his mind. He would have to write to Helen, an easy, offhand letter, to say that he had come to London for a day or so. He tried to imagine her reading it. He would write just such another letter to the old people, and say he had had to come up on business. That might do for *them* all right, but Helen was different. She would insist on explanations.

He wished he could never go back to Folkestone again. That would settle the whole affair.

A passing group attracted his attention, two faultlessly dressed gentle-men and a radiantly expensive lady. They were talking, no doubt, very brilliantly. His eyes followed them. The lady tapped the arm of the left-hand gentleman with a daintily tinted glove. Swells! No end . . .

His soul looked out upon life in general as a very small nestling might peep out of its nest. What an extraordinary thing life was, to be sure, and what a remarkable variety of people there were in it!

He lit a cigarette and speculated upon that receding group of three, and blew smoke and watched them. They seemed to do it all right. Probably they all had incomes of very much over twelve hundred a year. Perhaps not. Probably none of them suspected, as they went past, that he, too, was a gentleman of independent means, dressed, as he was, without distinction. Of course things were easier for them. They were brought up always to dress well and do the right thing from their very earliest years; they started clear of all his perplexities; they had never got mixed up with all sorts of different people who didn't go together. If, for example, that lady there got engaged to that gentleman, she would be quite safe from any encounter with a corpulent, osculatory uncle, or Chitterlow, or the dangerously significant eye of Pierce.

His thoughts came round to Helen.

When they were married and Cuyps – or Cuyp, Coote had failed to justify his 's' – and in that West End flat and shaken free of all these low-class associations, would he and she parade here of an afternoon dressed like that? It would be rather fine to do so. If one's dress was all right.

Helen!

She was difficult to understand at times.

He blew extensive clouds of cigarette smoke.

There would be teas, there would be dinners, there would be calls. Of course he would get into the way of it.

But Anagrams were a bit stiff to begin with!

It was beastly confusing at first to know when to use your fork at dinner, and all that. Still –

He felt an extraordinary doubt whether he would get into the way of it. He was interested for a space by a girl and groom on horseback, and then he came back to his personal preoccupations.

He would have to write to Helen. What could he say to explain his absence from the Anagram Tea? She had been pretty clear she wanted him to come. He recalled her resolute face without any great tenderness. He *knew* he would look like a silly ass at that confounded tea! Suppose he shirked it and went back in time for the dinner! Dinners were beastly difficult, too, but not as bad as Anagrams. The very first thing that might happen when he got back to Folkestone would be to run against Ann. Suppose, after all, he did meet Ann when he was with Helen!

What queer encounters were possible in the world!

Thank goodness, they were going to live in London!

But that brought him around to Chitterlow. The Chitterlows were coming to London, too. If they didn't get money they'd come after it; they weren't the sort of people to be choked off easily; and if they did they'd come to London to produce their play. He tried to imagine some seemly social occasion invaded by Chitterlow and his rhetoric, by his torrential thunder of self-assertion, the whole company flattened thereunder like wheat under a hurricane.

Confound and hang Chitterlow! Yet, somehow, somewhen, one would have to settle accounts with him! And there was Sid! Sid was Ann's brother. He realised with sudden horror the social indiscretion of accepting Sid's invitation to dinner.

Sid wasn't the sort of chap one could snub or cut, and besides – Ann's brother! He didn't want to cut him. It would be worse than cutting Buggins and Pierce – a sight worse. And after that lunch!

It would be the next thing to cutting Ann herself. And even as to Ann –

Suppose he was with Helen or Coote! . . .

'Oh, Blow!' he said, at last, and then, viciously, '*Blow!*' and so rose and flung away his cigarette end and pursued his reluctant, dubitating way towards the really quite uncongenial splendours of the Royal Grand –

And it is vulgarly imagined that to have money is to have no troubles at all!

6

Kipps endured splendour at the Royal Grand Hotel for three nights and days, and then he retreated in disorder. The Royal Grand defeated and overcame and routed Kipps, not of intention, but by sheer royal grandeur, grandeur combined with an organisation for his comfort carried to excess. On his return he came upon a difficulty: he had lost his circular piece of cardboard with the number of his room, and he drifted about the hall and passages in a state of perplexity for some time, until he thought all the porters and officials in gold-lace caps must be watching him and jesting to one another about him. Finally, in a quiet corner, down below the hairdresser's shop, he found a kindly-looking personage in bottle green, to whom he broached his difficulty. 'I say,' he said, with a pleasant smile, 'I can't find my room nohow.' The personage in bottle green, instead of laughing in a nasty way, as he might well have done, became extremely helpful, showed Kipps what to do, got his key, and conducted him by lift and passage to his chamber. Kipps tipped him half a crown.

Safe in his room, Kipps pulled himself together for dinner. He had learnt enough from young Walshingham to bring his dress clothes, and now he began to assume them. Unfortunately, in the excitement of his flight from his aunt and uncle, he had forgotten to put in his other boots, and he was some time deciding between his purple cloth slippers, with a golden marigold, and the prospect of cleaning the boots he was wearing with the towel, but finally, being a little footsore, he took the slippers.

Afterwards, when he saw the porters and waiters and the other guests catch a sight of the slippers, he was sorry he had not chosen the boots. However, to make up for any want of style at that end, he had his crush hat under his arm.

He found the dining-room without excessive trouble. It was a vast and splendidly decorated place, and a number of people, evidently quite *au fait*, were dining there at little tables lit with electric red-shaded candles, gentlemen in evening dress and ladies with dazzling, astonishing necks. Kipps had never seen evening dress in full vigour before, and he doubted his eyes. And there were also people not in evening dress, who no doubt wondered what noble family Kipps represented. There was a band in a decorated recess, and the band looked collectively at the purple slippers, and so lost any chance they may have had of a donation so far as Kipps was concerned. The chief drawback to this magnificent place was the excessive space of floor that had to be crossed before you got your purple slippers hidden under a table.

He selected a little table – not the one where a rather impudent looking waiter held a chair, but another – sat down, and finding his gibus in his hand, decided after a moment of thought to rise slightly and sit on it. (It was discovered in his abandoned chair at a late hour by a supper party, and restored to him next day.)

He put the napkin carefully on one side, selected his soup without difficulty, 'Clear, please,' but he was rather floored by the presentation of a quite splendidly bound wine card. He turned it over, discovered a section devoted to whisky, and had a bright idea.

' 'Ere,' he said to the waiter, with an encouraging movement of his head, and then in a confidential manner, 'you haven't any Old Methuselah Three Stars, 'ave you?'

The waiter went away to enquire, and Kipps went on with his soup with an enhanced self-respect. Finally, Old Methuselah being unobtainable, he ordered a claret from about the middle of the list. 'Let's 'ave some of this,' he said. He knew claret was a good sort of wine.

'A half-bottle?' said the waiter.

'Right you are,' said Kipps.

He felt he was getting on. He leant back after his soup, a man of the world, and then slowly brought his eyes around to the ladies in evening dress on his right . . .

He couldn't have thought it!

They were scorchers. Jest a bit of black velvet over the shoulders!

He looked again. One of them was laughing, with a glass of wine half raised – wicked-looking woman she was – the other, the black velvet one, was eating bits of bread with nervous quickness and talking fast.

He wished old Buggins could see them.

He found a waiter regarding him and blushed deeply. He did not look again for some time, and became confused about his knife and fork over the fish. Presently he remarked a lady in pink to the left of him eating the fish with an entirely different implement.

It was over the *vol-au-vent* that he began to go to pieces. He took a knife to it; then saw the lady in pink was using a fork only, and hastily put down his knife, with a considerable amount of rich creaminess on the blade, upon the cloth. Then he found that a fork in his inexperienced hand was an instrument of chase rather than capture. His ears became violently red, and then he looked up to discover the lady in pink glancing at him and then smiling as she spoke to the man beside her.

He hated the lady in pink very much.

He stabbed a large piece of the *vol-au-vent* at last, and was too glad of his luck not to make a mouthful of it. But it was an extensive fragment, and pieces escaped him. Shirt front! 'Desh it!' he said, and had resort to his spoon. His waiter went and spoke to two other waiters, no doubt jeering at him. He became very fierce suddenly. ' 'Ere!' he said, gesticulating, and then, 'clear this away!'

The entire dinner party on his right, the party of the ladies in advanced evening dress, looked at him . . . He felt that everyone was watching him and making fun of him, and the injustice of this angered him. After all, they had every advantage he hadn't. And then, when they got him there doing his best, what must they do but glance and sneer and nudge one another. He tried to catch them at it, and then took refuge in a second glass of wine.

Suddenly and extraordinarily he found himself a Socialist. He did not care how close it was to the lean years when all these things would end.

Lamb came with peas. He arrested the hand of the waiter. 'No peas,' he said. He knew something of the difficulty and danger of eating peas. Then, when the peas went away he was embittered again . . . Echoes of Masterman's burning rhetoric began to reverberate in his mind. Nice lot of people these were to laugh at anyone! Women half undressed! It was that made him so beastly uncomfortable. How could one eat one's dinner with people about him like that? Nice lot they were. He was glad he wasn't one of them, anyhow. Yes, they might look. He resolved if they looked at him again he would ask one of the men who he was staring at. His perturbed and angry face would have concerned anyone. The band by an unfortunate accident was playing truculent military music. The mental change Kipps underwent was, in its way, what psychologists call a conversion. In a few moments all Kipps's ideals were changed. He who had been 'practically a gentle-man', the sedulous pupil of Coote, the punctilious raiser of hats, was instantly a rebel, an outcast, the hater of everything 'stuck up', the foe of Society and the social order of today. Here they were among the profits of their robbery, these people who might do anything with the world . . .

'No, thenks,' he said to a dish.

He addressed a scornful eye at the shoulders of the lady to his left.

Presently he was refusing another dish. He didn't like it – fussed up food! Probably cooked by some foreigner. He finished up his wine and his bread . . .

'No, thenks.'

'No, thenks . . . '

He discovered the eye of a diner fixed curiously upon his flushed face. He responded with a glare. Couldn't he go without things if he liked?

'What's this?' said Kipps to a great green cone.

'Ice,' said the waiter.

'I'll 'ave some,' said Kipps.

He seized a fork and spoon and assailed the bombe. It cut rather stiffly. 'Come up!' said Kipps, with concentrated bitterness, and the truncated summit of the bombe flew off suddenly, travelling eastward with remarkable velocity. Flop, it went upon the floor a yard away, and for a while time seemed empty.

At the adjacent table they were laughing together.

Shy the rest of the bombe at them?

Flight?

At any rate a dignified withdrawal.

'No!' said Kipps, 'no more,' arresting the polite attempt of the waiter to serve him with another piece. He had a vague idea he might carry off the affair as though he had meant the ice to go on the floor – not liking ice, for example, and being annoyed at the badness of his dinner. He put both hands on the table, thrust back his chair, disengaged a purple slipper from his napkin, and rose. He stepped carefully over the prostrate ice, kicked the napkin under the table, thrust his hands deep into his pockets, and marched out – shaking the dust of the place, as it were, from his feet. He left behind him a melting fragment of ice upon the floor, his gibus hat, warm and compressed in his chair, and, in addition, every social ambition he had ever entertained in the world.

7

Kipps went back to Folkestone in time for the Anagram Tea. But you must not imagine that the change of heart that came to him in the dining-room of the Royal Grand Hotel involved any change of attitude towards this promised social and intellectual treat. He went back because the Royal Grand was too much for him.

Outwardly calm, or at most a little flushed and ruffled, inwardly Kipps was a horrible, tormented battleground of scruples, doubts, shames and self-assertions during that three days of silent, desperate grappling with the big hotel. He did not intend the monstrosity should beat him without a struggle, but at last he had sullenly to admit himself overcome. The odds were terrific. On the one hand himself – with, among other things, only one pair of boots; on the other a vast wilderness of rooms, covering several acres, and with over a thousand people, staff and visitors, all chiefly occupied in looking queerly at Kipps, in laughing at him behind his back, in watching for difficult corners at which to confront and perplex him and inflict humiliations upon him. For example, the hotel scored over its electric light. After the dinner the chambermaid, a hard, unsympathetic young woman with a superior manner, was summoned by a bell Kipps had rung under the impression the button was the electric light switch. 'Look 'ere,' said Kipps, rubbing a shin that had suffered during his search in the dark, 'why aren't there any candles or matches?' The hotel explained and scored heavily.

'It isn't everyone is up to these things,' said Kipps.

'No, it isn't,' said the chambermaid, with ill-concealed scorn, and slammed the door at him.

'S'pose I ought to have tipped her,' said Kipps.

After that Kipps cleaned his boots with a pocket-handkerchief and went for a long walk and got home in a hansom, but the hotel scored again by his not putting out his boots and so having to clean them again in the morning. The hotel also snubbed him by bringing him hot water when he was fully dressed and looking surprised at his collar, but he got a breakfast, I must admit, with scarcely any difficulty.

After that the hotel scored heavily by the fact that there are twenty-four hours in the day and Kipps had nothing to do in any of them. He was a little footsore from his previous day's pedestrianism, and he could make up his mind for no long excursions. He flitted in and out of the hotel several times, and it was the polite porter who touched his hat every time that first set Kipps tipping.

'What 'e wants is a tip,' said Kipps.

So at the next opportunity he gave the man an unexpected shilling, and having once put his hand in his pocket, there was no reason why he should not go on. He bought a newspaper at the bookstall and tipped the boy the rest of the shilling, and then went up by the lift and tipped the man a sixpence, leaving his newspaper inadvertently in the lift. He met his chambermaid in the passage and gave her half a crown. He resolved to demonstrate his position to the entire establishment in this way. He didn't like the place; he disapproved of it politically, socially, morally, but he resolved no taint of meanness should disfigure his sojourn in its luxurious halls. He went down by the lift (tipping again), and, being accosted by a waiter with his gibus, tipped the finder half a crown. He had a vague sense that he was making a flank movement upon the hotel and buying over its staff. They would regard him as a character. They would get to like him. He found his stock of small silver diminishing, and replenished it at a desk in the hall. He tipped a man in bottle green who looked like the man who had shown him his room the day before, and then he saw a visitor eyeing him, and doubted whether he was in this instance doing right. Finally he went out and took chance buses to their destinations, and wandered a little in remote, wonderful suburbs and returned. He lunched at a chop house in Islington, and found himself back in the Royal Grand, now un-mistakably footsore and London weary, about three. He was attracted to the drawing-room by a neat placard about afternoon tea.

It occurred to him that the campaign of tipping upon which he had embarked was perhaps after all a mistake. He was confirmed in this by observing that the hotel officials were watching him, not respectfully, but with a sort of amused wonder, as if to see whom he would tip next. However, if he backed out now, they would think him an awful fool. Everyone wasn't so rich as he was. It was his way to tip. Still –

He grew more certain the hotel had scored again.

He pretended to be lost in thought and so drifted by, and having put hat and umbrella in the cloakroom went into the drawing-room for afternoon tea.

There he did get what for a time he held to be a point in his favour. The room was large and quiet at first, and he sat back restfully until it occurred to him that his attitude brought his extremely dusty boots too prominently into the light, so instead he sat up, and then people of the upper and upper-middle classes began to come and group themselves about him and have tea likewise, and so revive the class animosities of the previous day.

Presently a fluffy, fair-haired lady came into prominent existence a few yards away. She was talking to a respectful, low-voiced clergyman, whom she was possibly entertaining at tea. 'No,' she said, 'dear Lady Jane wouldn't like that!'

'Mumble, mumble, mumble,' from the clergyman.

'Poor dear Lady Jane was always so sensitive,' the voice of the lady sang out clear and emphatic.

A fat, hairless, important-looking man joined this group, took a chair and planted it firmly with its back in the face of Kipps, a thing that offended Kipps mightily. 'Are you telling him,' gurgled the fat, hairless man, 'about dear Lady Jane's affliction?' A young couple, lady brilliantly attired and the man in a magnificently-cut frock coat, arranged themselves to the right, also with an air of exclusion towards Kipps. 'I've told him,' said the gentleman in a flat, abundant voice. 'My!' said the young lady, with an American smile. No doubt they all thought Kipps was out of it. A great desire to assert himself in some way surged up in his heart. He felt he would like to cut in on the conversation in some dramatic way. A monologue something in the manner of Masterman? At any rate, abandoning that as impossible, he would like to appear self-centred and at ease. His eyes, wandering over the black surfaces of a noble architectural mass close by, discovered a slot and an enamelled plaque of directions.

It was some sort of musical box! As a matter of fact, it was the very best sort of harmonicon and specially made to the scale of the hotel.

He scrutinised the plaque with his head at various angles and glanced about him at his neighbours.

It occurred to Kipps that he would like some music, that to inaugurate some would show him a man of taste and at his ease at the same time. He rose, read over a list of tunes, selected one haphazard, pressed his sixpence – it was sixpence! – home, and prepared for a confidential, refined little melody.

Considering the high social tone of the Royal Grand, it was really a very loud instrument indeed. It gave vent to three deafening brays and so burst the dam of silence that had long pent it in. It seemed to be chiefly full of the great-uncles of trumpets, megalo-trombones and railway brakes. It made sounds like shunting trains. It did not so much begin as blow up your counter-scarp and rush forward to storm under cover of melodious shrapnel. It had not so much an air as a ricochet. The music had, in short, the inimitable quality of Sousa. It swept down upon the friend of Lady Jane and carried away something socially striking into the eternal night of the unheard; the American girl to the left of it was borne shrieking into the inaudible. 'HIGH cockalorum Tootletootle tootle loo. HIGH cockalorum tootle lootle loo. BUMP, bump, bump – BUMP.' Joyous, exorbitant music it was from the gigantic nursery of the Future, bearing the hearer along upon its torrential succession of sounds, as if he was in a cask on Niagara. Whiroo! Yah and have at you! The strenuous Life! Yaha! Stop! A Reprieve! A Reprieve! No! Bang! Bump!

Everybody looked around, conversation ceased and gave place to gestures.

The friend of Lady Jane became terribly agitated.

'Can't it be stopped?' she vociferated, pointing a gloved finger and saying something to the waiter about 'that dreadful young man'.

'Ought not to be working,' said the clerical friend of Lady Jane.

The waiter shook his head at the fat, hairless gentleman. People began to move away. Kipps leant back luxurious, and then tipped with a half-crown to pay. He paid, tipped like a gentleman, rose with an easy gesture and strolled towards the door. His retreat evidently completed the indignation of the friend of Lady Jane, and from the door he could still discern her gestures as asking, 'Can't it be stopped?' The music followed him into the passage and pursued him to the lift and only died away completely in the quiet of his own room, and afterwards from his window he saw the friend of Lady Jane and her party having their tea carried out to a little table in the court. Certainly that was a point to him. But it was his only score; all the rest of the game lay in the hands of the upper classes and the big hotel. And presently he was doubting whether even this was really a point. It seemed a trifle vulgar, come to think it over, to interrupt people when they were talking.

He saw a clerk peering at him from the office, and suddenly it occurred to him that the place might get back at him tremendously over the bill.

They would probably take it out on him by charging pounds and pounds.

Suppose they charged more than he had!

The clerk had a particularly nasty face, just the face to take advantage of a vacillating Kipps.

He became aware of a man in a cap touching it, and produced his shilling automatically, but the strain was beginning to tell. It was a deuce and all of an expense – this tipping.

If the hotel chose to stick it on to the bill something tremendous what was Kipps to do? Refuse to pay? Make a row?

If he did he couldn't fight all these men in bottle green.

He went out about seven and walked for a long time and dined at last upon a chop in the Euston Road; then he walked along to the Edgeware Road and sat and rested in the Metropolitan Music Hall for a time until a trapeze performance unnerved him and finally he came back to bed. He tipped the lift-man sixpence and wished him good-night. In the silent watches of the night he reviewed the tale of the day's tipping, went over the horrors of the previous night's dinner, and heard again the triumphant bray of the harmonicon devil released from its long imprisonment. Everyone would be told about him tomorrow. He couldn't go on! He admitted his defeat. Never in their whole lives had any of these people seen such a Fool as he! Ugh . . . !

His method of announcing his withdrawal to the clerk was touched with bitterness.

'I'm going to get out of this,' said Kipps, blowing windily. 'Let's see what you got on my bill.'

'One breakfast?' asked the clerk.

'Do I *look* as if I'd ate two?' . . .

At his departure Kipps, with a hot face, convulsive gestures and an embittered heart, tipped everyone who did not promptly and actively resist, including an absent-minded South African diamond merchant, who was waiting in the hall for his wife and succumbed to old habit. He paid his cabman a four-shilling piece at Charing Cross, having no smaller change, and wished he could burn him alive. Then, in a sudden reaction of economy, he refused the proffered help of a porter and carried his bag quite violently to the train.

CHAPTER EIGHT

Kipps Enters Society

Submission to Inexorable Fate took Kipps to the Anagram Tea.

At any rate he would meet Helen there in the presence of other people and be able to carry off the worst of the difficulty of explaining his little jaunt to London. He had not seen her since his last portentous visit to New Romney. He was engaged to her, he would have to marry her, and the sooner he faced her again the better. Before wild plans of turning socialist, defying the world and repudiating all calling for ever, his heart on second thoughts sank. He felt Helen would never permit anything of the sort. As for the Anagrams, he could do no more than his best, and that he was resolved to do. What had happened at the Royal Grand, what had happened at New Romney, he must bury in his memory and begin again at the reconstruction of his social position. Ann, Buggins, Chitterlow, all these, seen in the matter-of-fact light of the Folkestone train, stood just as they stood before; people of an inferior social position who had to be eliminated from his world. It was a bother about Ann, a bother and a pity. His mind rested so for a space on Ann until the memory of these Anagrams drew him away. If he could see Coote that evening he might, he thought, be able to arrange some sort of connivance about the Anagrams, and his mind was chiefly busy sketching proposals for such an arrangement. It would not, of course, be ungentlemanly cheating, but only a little mystification. Coote very probably might drop him a hint of the solution of one or two of the things, not enough to win a prize, but enough to cover his shame. Or failing that he might take a humorous, quizzical line and pretend he was pretending to be very stupid. There were plenty of ways out of it if one kept a sharp lookout . . .

The costume Kipps wore to the Anagram Tea was designed as a compromise between the strict letter of high fashion and seaside laxity, a sort of easy, semi-state for afternoon. Helen's first reproof had always lingered in his mind. He wore a frock coat, but mitigated it by a Panama hat of romantic shape with a black band, grey gloves, but for relaxation brown button boots. The only other man besides the clergy present, a new doctor with an attractive wife, was in full afternoon dress. Coote was not there.

Kipps was a little pale, but quite self-possessed, as he approached Mrs Bindon Botting's door. He took a turn while some people went in and then faced it manfully. The door opened and revealed – Ann!

In the background through a draped doorway, behind a big fern in a great art pot, the elder Miss Botting was visible talking to two guests; the auditory background was a froth of feminine voices . . .

Our two young people were much too amazed to give one another any formula of greeting, though they had parted warmly enough. Each was already in a state of extreme tension to meet the demands of this great and unprecedented occasion, an Anagram Tea. 'Lor'!' said Ann, her sole remark, and then the sense of Miss Botting's eye ruled her straight again. She became very pale, but she took his hat mechanically, and he was already removing his gloves. 'Ann,' he said in a low tone, and then, 'Fency!' The elder Miss Botting knew Kipps was the sort of guest who requires nursing, and she came forward vocalising charm. She said it was 'awfully jolly of him to come, awfully jolly. It was awfully difficult to get any good men!'

She handed Kipps forward, mumbling and in a dazed condition, to the drawing-room, and there he encountered Helen looking unfamiliar in an unfamiliar hat. It was as if he had not met her for years.

She astonished him. She didn't seem to mind in the least his going to London. She held out a shapely hand, and smiled encouragingly. 'You've faced the anagrams?' she said.

The second Miss Botting accosted them, a number of oblong pieces of paper in her hand, mysteriously inscribed. 'Take an anagram,' she said; 'take an anagram,' and boldly pinned one of these brief documents to Kipps's lapel. The letters were 'Cypshi', and Kipps from the very beginning suspected this was an anagram for Cuyps. She also left a thing like a long dance programme, from which dangled a little pencil, in his hand. He found himself being introduced to people, and then he was in a corner with the short lady in a big bonnet, who was pelting him with gritty little bits of small talk that were gone before you could take hold of them and reply.

'Very hot,' said this lady. 'Very hot, indeed – hot all the summer – remarkable year – all the years remarkable now – don't know what we're coming to – don't you think so, Mr Kipps?'

'Oo, rather,' said Kipps, and wondered if Ann was still in the hall. Ann!

He ought not to have stared at her like a stuck fish and pretended not to know her. That couldn't be right. But what *was* right?

The lady in the big bonnet proceeded to a second discharge. 'Hope you're fond of anagrams, Mr Kipps – difficult exercise – still one must do something to bring people together – better than Ludo anyhow. Don't you think so, Mr Kipps?'

Ann fluttered past the open door. Her eyes met his in amazed enquiry. Something had got dislocated in the world for both of them . . .

He ought to have told her he was engaged. He ought to have explained things to her. Perhaps even now he might be able to drop her a hint.

'Don't you think so, Mr Kipps?'

'Oo, rather,' said Kipps for the third time.

A lady with a tired smile, who was labelled conspicuously 'Wogdelenk', drifted towards Kipps's interlocutor and the two fell into conversation. Kipps found himself socially aground. He looked about him. Helen was talking to a curate and laughing. Kipps was overcome by a vague desire to speak to Ann. He was for sidling doorward.

'What are *you*, please?' said an extraordinarily bold, tall girl, and arrested him while she took down 'Cypshi'.

'I'm sure I don't know what it means,' she explained. 'I'm Sir Bubh. Don't you think anagrams are something chronic?'

Kipps made stockish noises, and the young lady suddenly became the nucleus of a party of excited friends who were forming a syndicate to guess and barred his escape. She took no further notice of him. He found himself jammed against an occasional table and listening to the conversation of Mrs 'Wogdelenk' and his lady with the big bonnet.

'She packed her two beauties off together,' said the lady in the big bonnet. 'Time enough, too. Don't think much of this girl she's got as housemaid now. Pretty, of course, but there's no occasion for a house-maid to be pretty – none whatever. And she doesn't look particularly up to her work either. Kind of 'mazed expression.'

'You never can tell,' said the lady labelled 'Wogdelenk'; 'you never can tell. My wretches are big enough, heaven knows, and do they work? Not a bit of it!' . . .

Kipps felt dreadfully out of it with regard to all these people, and dreadfully in it with Ann.

He scanned the back of the big bonnet and concluded it was an extremely ugly bonnet indeed. It went jerking forward as each short dry sentence was snapped off at the end; and a plume of osprey on it jerked excessively. 'She hasn't guessed even one!' followed by a shriek of girlish merriment, came from the group about the tall, bold girl. They'd shriek at him presently, perhaps. Beyond thinking his own anagram might be Cuyps, he hadn't a notion. What a chatter they were all making! It was just like a summer sale! Just the sort of people who'd give a lot of trouble and swap you! And suddenly the smouldering fires of rebellion leapt to flame again. These were a rotten lot of people, and the anagrams were rotten nonsense, and he, Kipps, had been a rotten fool to come. There was Helen away there, still laughing, with her curate. Pity she couldn't marry a curate and leave him (Kipps) alone! Then he'd know what to do. He disliked the whole gathering collectively and in detail. Why were they all trying to make him one of themselves? He perceived unexpected ugliness everywhere about him. There were two great pins jabbed through the tall girl's hat, and the swirls of her hair below the brim with the minutest piece of tape tie-up showing did not repay close examination. Mrs 'Wogdelenk' wore a sort of mumps bandage of lace, and there was another lady perfectly dazzling with beads and jewels and bits of trimming. They were all flaps and angles and flounces – these women. Not one of them looked as neat and decent a shape as Ann's clean, trim little figure. Echoes of Masterman woke up in him again. Ladies indeed! Here were all these chattering people, with money, with leisure, with every chance in the world, and all they could do was to crowd like this into a couple of rooms and jabber nonsense about anagrams.

'Could Cypshi really mean Cuyps?' floated like a dissolving wreath of mist across his mind.

Abruptly resolution stood armed in his heart. He was going to get out of this!

' 'Scuse me,' he said, and began to wade neck deep through the bubbling tea party.

He was going to get out of it all!

He found himself close by Helen. 'I'm orf,' he said, but she gave him the briefest glance. She did not appear to hear him. 'Still, Mr Spratlingdown, you *must* admit there's a limit even to conformity,' she was saying . . .

He was in a curtained archway, and Ann was before him carrying a tray supporting several small sugar bowls.

He was moved to speech. '*What* a Lot!' he said, and then mysteriously, 'I'm engaged to *her*.' He indicated Helen's new hat, and became aware of a skirt he had stepped upon.

Ann stared at him helplessly, borne past in the grip of incomprehensible imperatives.

Why shouldn't they talk together?

He was in a small room, and then at the foot of the staircase in the hall. He heard the rustle of a dress, and what was conceivably his hostess was upon him.

'But you're not going, Mr Kipps?' she said.

'I must,' he said; 'I got to.'

'But, Mr Kipps!'

'I must,' he said. 'I'm not well.'

'But before the guessing! Without any tea!'

Ann appeared and hovered behind him.

'I got to go,' said Kipps.

If he parleyed with her Helen might awake to his desperate attempt.

'Of course if you *must* go.'

'It's something I've forgotten,' said Kipps, beginning to feel regrets. 'Reely I must.'

Mrs Botting turned with a certain offended dignity, and Ann in a state of flushed calm that evidently concealed much came forward to open the door.

'I'm very sorry,' he said; 'I'm very sorry,' half to his hostess and half to her, and was swept past her by superior social forces – like a drowning man in a millrace – and into the Upper Sandgate Road. He half turned upon the step, and then slam went the door ...

He retreated along the Leas, a thing of shame and perplexity – Mrs Botting's aggrieved astonishment uppermost in his mind.

Something – reinforced by the glances of the people he was passing – pressed its way to his attention through the tumultuous disorder of his mind.

He became aware that he was still wearing his little placard with the letters 'Cypshi'.

'Desh it!' he said, clutching off this abomination. In another moment its several letters, their task accomplished, were scattering gleefully before the breeze down the front of the Leas.

2

Kipps was dressed for Mrs Wace's dinner half an hour before it was time to start, and he sat waiting until Coote should come to take him round. *Manners and Rules of Good Society* lay before him neglected. He had read the polished prose of the Member of the Aristocracy on page 96, as far as

the acceptance of an invitation is, in the eyes of diners out, a binding obligation which only ill-health, family bereavement or some other all-important reason justifies being set on one side or otherwise evaded . . .

and then he had lapsed into gloomy thoughts.

That afternoon he had had a serious talk with Helen.

He had tried to express something of the change of heart that had happened to him. But to broach the real state of the matter had been altogether too terrible for him. He had sought a minor issue. 'I don't like all this Society,' he had said.

'But you must *see* people,' said Helen.

'Yes, but – it's the sort of people you see.' He nerved himself. 'I didn't think much of that lot at the Enegram Tea.'

'You have to see all sorts of people if you want to see the world,' said Helen.

Kipps was silent for a space and a little short of breath.

'My dear Arthur,' she began, almost kindly, 'I shouldn't ask you to go to these affairs if I didn't think it good for you, should I?'

Kipps acquiesced in silence.

'You will find the benefit of it all when we get to London. You learn to swim in a tank before you go out into the sea. These people here are good enough to learn upon. They're stiff and rather silly and dreadfully narrow and not an idea in a dozen of them, but it really doesn't matter at all. You'll soon get *Savoir Faire*.'

He made to speak again, and found his powers of verbal expression lacking. Instead he blew a sigh.

'You'll get used to it all very soon,' said Helen helpfully –

As he sat meditating over that interview and over the vistas of London that opened before him, on the little flat, and teas and occasions and the constant presence of Brudderkins and all the bright prospect of his new and better life, and how he would never see Ann any more, the housemaid entered with a little package, a small square envelope to 'Arthur Kipps, Esquire'.

'A young woman left this, sir,' said the housemaid, a little severely.

'Eh?' said Kipps; 'what young woman?' and then suddenly began to understand.

'She looked an ordinary young woman,' said the housemaid coldly.

'Ah!' said Kipps. '*That*'s orlright.'

He waited till the door had closed behind the girl, staring at the envelope in his hand, and then, with a curious feeling of increasing tension, tore it open. As he did so, some quicker sense than sight or touch told him its contents. It was Ann's half-sixpence. And, besides, not a word!

Then she must have heard him – !

She had kept the half-sixpence all these years!

He was standing with the envelope in his hand, trying to get on from that last inference, when Coote became audible without.

Coote appeared in evening dress, a clean and radiant Coote, with large greenish-white gloves and a particularly large white tie, edged with black. 'For a third cousin,' he presently explained. 'Nace, isn't it?' He could see Kipps was pale and disturbed and put this down to the approaching social trial. 'You keep your nerve up, Kipps, my dear chap, and you'll be all right,' said Coote, with a big, brotherly glove on Kipps's sleeve.

3

The dinner came to a crisis, so far as Kipps's emotions were concerned, with Mrs Bindon Botting's talk about servants, but before that there had been several things of greater or smaller magnitude to perturb and disarrange his social front. One little matter that was mildly insurgent throughout the entire meal was, if I may be permitted to mention so intimate a matter, the behaviour of his left brace. The webbing – which was of a cheerful scarlet silk – had slipped away from its buckle, fastened no doubt in agitation, and had developed a strong tendency to place itself obliquely, in the manner rather of an official decoration, athwart his spotless front. It first asserted itself before they went in to dinner. He replaced this ornament by a dexterous thrust when no one was looking, and thereafter the suppression of his novel innovation upon the stereotyped sombreness of evening dress became a standing pre-occupation. On the whole, he was inclined to think his first horror excessive; at any rate no one remarked upon it. However, you imagine him constantly throughout the evening with one eye and one hand, whatever the rest of him might be doing, predominantly concerned with the weak corner.

But this, I say, was a little matter. What exercised him much more was to discover Helen quite terribly in evening dress.

The young lady had let her imagination rove Londonward, and this costume was perhaps an anticipation of that clever little flat not too far west which was to become the centre of so delightful a literary and artistic set. It was, of all the feminine costumes present, most distinctly an evening dress. One was advised Miss Walshingham had arms and shoulders of a type by no means despicable, one was advised Miss

Walshingham was capable not only of dignity but charm, even a certain glow of charm. It was, you know, her first evening dress, a tribute paid by Walshingham finance to her brightening future. Had she wanted keeping in countenance, she would have had to have fallen back upon her hostess, who was resplendent in black and steel. The other ladies had to a certain extent compromised. Mrs Walshingham had dressed with just a refined little V, and Mrs Bindon Botting, except for her dear mottled arms, confided scarcely more of her plump charm to the world. The elder Miss Botting stopped short of shoulders, and so did Miss Wace. But Helen didn't. She was – had Kipps had eyes to see it – a quite beautiful human figure; she knew it and she met him with a radiant smile that had forgotten all the little difference of the afternoon. But to Kipps her appearance was the last release. With that, she had become as remote, as foreign, as incredible as a wife and mate, as though the Cnidian Venus herself, in all her simple elegance, was before witnesses, declared to be his. If, indeed, she had ever been credible as a wife and mate.

She ascribed his confusion to modest reverence, and having blazed smiling upon him for a moment turned a shapely shoulder towards him and exchanged a remark with Mrs Bindon Botting. Ann's poor little half-sixpence came against Kipps's fingers in his pocket and he clutched at it suddenly as though it was a talisman. Then he abandoned it to suppress his Order of the Brace. He was affected by a cough. 'Miss Wace tells me Mr Revel is coming,' Mrs Botting was saying.

'Isn't it delightful?' said Helen. 'We saw him last night. He's stopped on his way to Paris. He's going to meet his wife there.'

Kipps's eyes rested for a moment on Helen's dazzling deltoid, and then went enquiringly, accusingly almost, to Coote's face. Where, in the presence of this terrible emergence, was the gospel of suppression now – that Furtive treatment of Religion and Politics and Birth and Death and Bathing and Babies and 'all those things' which constitutes your True Gentleman? He had been too modest even to discuss this question with his Mentor, but surely, surely this quintessence of all that is good and nice could regard these unsolicited confidences only in one way. With something between relief and the confirmation of his worst fears he perceived, by a sort of twitching of the exceptionally abundant muscles about Coote's lower jaw, in a certain deliberate avoidance of one particular direction by those pale, but resolute, grey eyes, by the almost convulsive grip of the ample, greenish-white gloves behind him, a grip broken at times for controlling pats at the black-bordered tie and the back of that spacious head, and by a slight but increasing disposition to cough, that *Coote did not approve*!

To Kipps Helen had once supplied a delicately beautiful dream, a thing of romance and unsubstantial mystery. But this was her final materialisation, and the last thin wreath of glamour about her was dispelled. In some way (he had forgotten how and it was perfectly incomprehensible) he was bound to this dark, solid and determined young person whose shadow and suggestion he had once loved. He had to go through with the thing as a gentleman should. Still –

And when he was sacrificing Ann!

He wouldn't stand this sort of thing, whatever else he stood . . . Should he say something about her dress to her – tomorrow?

He could put his foot down firmly. He could say, 'Look 'ere. I don't care. I ain't going to stand it. See?'

She'd say something unexpected, of course. She always did say something unexpected.

Suppose for once he overrode what she said? Simply repeated his point?

He found these thoughts battling with certain conversational aggressions from Mrs Wace, and then Revel arrived and took the centre of the stage.

The author of that brilliant romance *Red Hearts a-Beating* was a less imposing man than Kipps had anticipated, but he speedily effaced that disappointment by his predominating manners. Although he lived habitually in the vivid world of London, his collar and tie were in no way remarkable, and he was neither brilliantly handsome nor curly nor long-haired. His personal appearance suggested armchairs, rather than the equestrian exercises and amorous toyings and passionate intensities of his masterpiece; he was inclined to be fat, with whitish flesh and muddy-coloured straight hair, he had a rather shapeless and truncated nose and his chin was asymmetrical. One eye was more inclined to stare than the other. He might have been esteemed a little undistinguished-looking were it not for his beeswaxed moustache, which came amidst his features with a pleasing note of incongruity, and the whimsical wrinkles above and about his greater eye. His regard sought and found Helen's as he entered the room and they shook hands presently with an air of intimacy Kipps, for no clear reason, found objectionable. He saw them clasp hands, heard Coote's characteristic cough – a sound rather more like a very, very old sheep, a quarter of a mile away, being blown to pieces by a small charge of gunpowder than anything else in the world – did some confused beginnings of a thought, and then they were all going in to dinner and Helen's shining bare arm lay along his sleeve.

Kipps was in no state for conversation. She glanced at him, and, though he did not know it, very slightly pressed his elbow. He struggled with strange respiratory dislocations. Before them went Coote, discoursing in amiable reverberations to Mrs Walshingham, and at the head of the procession was Mrs Bindon Botting talking fast and brightly beside the erect military figure of little Mr Wace. (He was not a soldier really, but he had caught a martinet bearing by living so close to Shorncliffe.) Revel came last, in charge of Mrs Wace's queenly black and steel, politely admiring in a flutelike cultivated voice the mellow wallpaper of the staircase. Kipps marvelled at everybody's self-possession.

From the earliest spoonful of soup it became evident that Revel considered himself responsible for the table talk. And before the soup was over it was almost as manifest that Mrs Bindon Botting inclined to consider his sense of responsibility excessive. In her circle Mrs Bindon Botting was esteemed an agreeable rattle, her manner and appearance were conspicuously vivacious for one so plump, and she had an almost Irish facility for humorous description. She would keep people amused all through an afternoon call with the story of how her jobbing gardener had got himself married and what his home was like, or how her favourite butt, Mr Stigson Warder, had had all his unfortunate children taught almost every conceivable instrument because they had the phrenological bump of music abnormally large. 'They got to trombones, my dear!' she would say, with her voice coming to a climax. Usually her friends conspired to draw her out, but on this occasion they neglected to do so, a thing that militated against her keen desire to shine in Revel's eyes. After a time she perceived that the only thing for her to do was to cut in on the talk on her own account, and this she began to do. She made several ineffectual snatches at the general attention and then Revel drifted towards a topic she regarded as particularly her own, the ordering of households.

They came to the thing through talk about localities. 'We are leaving our house in The Boltons,' said Revel, 'and taking a little place at Wimbledon, and I think of having rooms in Dane's Inn. It will be more convenient in many ways. My wife is furiously addicted to golf and exercise of all sorts, and I like to sit about in clubs – I haven't the strength necessary for these hygienic proceedings – and the old arrangement suited neither of us. And, besides, no one could imagine the demoralisation the domestics of West London have undergone during the last three years.'

'It's the same everywhere,' said Mrs Bindon Botting.

'Very possibly it is. A friend of mine calls it the servile tradition in decay and regards it all as a most hopeful phenomenon – '

'He ought to have had my last two criminals,' said Mrs Bindon Botting.

She turned to Mrs Wace while Revel came again a little too late with a 'Possibly – '

'And I haven't told you, my dear,' she said, speaking with voluble rapidity, 'I'm in trouble again.'

'The last girl?'

'The last girl. Before I can get a cook, my hard-won housemaid' – she paused – 'chucks it.'

'Panic?' asked young Walshingham.

'Mysterious grief! Everything merry as a marriage bell until my Anagram Tea! Then in the evening a portentous rigour of bearing, a word or so from my aunt, and immediately – Floods of Tears and Notice!' For a moment her eye rested thoughtfully on Kipps, as she said: 'Is there anything heartrending about Anagrams?'

'I find them so,' said Revel. 'I – '

But Mrs Bindon Botting got away again. 'For a time it made me quite uneasy – '

Kipps jabbed his lip with his fork rather painfully, and was recalled from a fascinated glare at Mrs Botting to the immediate facts of dinner.

' – whether anagrams might not have offended the good domestic's Moral Code – you never can tell. We made enquiries. No. No. No. She *must* go and that's all!'

'One perceives,' said Revel, 'in these disorders, dimly and distantly, the last dying glow of the age of Romance. Let us suppose, Mrs Botting, let us at least try to suppose – it is Love.'

Kipps clattered with his knife and fork.

'It's love,' said Mrs Botting; 'what else can it be? Beneath the orderly humdrum of our lives these romances are going on, until at last they bust up and give Notice and upset our humdrum altogether. Some fatal, wonderful soldier – '

'The passions of the common or house domestic,' said Revel, and recovered possession of the table.

Upon the troubled disorder of Kipps's table manners there had supervened a quietness, an unusual calm. For once in his life he had distinctly made up his mind on his own account. He listened no more to Revel. He put down his knife and fork and refused anything that followed. Coote regarded him with tactful concern and Helen flushed a little.

About half-past nine that night came a violent pull at the bell of Mrs Bindon Botting, and a young man in a dress suit, a gibus and other marks of exalted social position stood without. Athwart his white expanse of breast lay a ruddy bar of patterned silk that gave him a singular distinction and minimised the glow of a few small stains of burgundy. His gibus was thrust back and exposed a disorder of hair that suggested a reckless desperation. He had, in fact, burnt his boats and refused to join the ladies. Coote, in the subsequent conversation, had protested quietly, 'You're going on all right, you know,' to which Kipps had answered he didn't care a 'Eng' about that, and so, after a brief tussle with Walshingham's detaining arm, had got away. 'I got something to do,' he said. ' 'Ome.' And here he was – panting an extraordinary resolve. The door opened, revealing the pleasantly furnished hall of Mrs Bindon Botting, lit by rose-tinted lights, and in the centre of the picture, neat and pretty in black and white, stood Ann. At the sight of Kipps her colour vanished.

'Ann,' said Kipps, 'I want to speak to you. I got something to say to you right away. See? I'm – '

'This ain't the door to speak to me at,' said Ann.

'But, Ann! It's something special.'

'You spoke enough,' said Ann.

'Ann!'

'Besides. That's my door, down there. Basement. If I was caught talking at *this* door – !'

'But, Ann, *I'm* – '

'Basement after nine. Them's my hours. I'm a servant and likely to keep one. If you're calling here, what name, please? But you got your friends and I got mine, and you mustn't go talking to *me*.'

'But, Ann, I want to ask you – '

Someone appeared in the hall behind Ann.

'Not here,' said Ann. 'Don't know anyone of that name,' and incontinently slammed the door in his face.

'What was that, Ann?' said Mrs Bindon Botting's invalid aunt.

'Ge'm a little intoxicated, ma'am – asking for the wrong name, ma'am.'

'What name did he want?' asked the lady, doubtfully.

'No name that *we* know, ma'am,' said Ann, hustling along the hall towards the kitchen stairs.

'I hope you weren't too short with him, Ann.'

'No shorter than he deserved, considering 'ow he be'aved,' said Ann, with her bosom heaving.

And Mrs Bindon Botting's invalid aunt, perceiving suddenly that this call had some relation to Ann's private and sentimental trouble, turned, after one moment of hesitating scrutiny, away.

She was an extremely sympathetic lady, was Mrs Bindon Botting's invalid aunt; she took an interest in the servants, imposed piety, extorted confessions and followed human nature, blushing and lying defensively, to its reluctantly revealed recesses; but Ann's sense of privacy was strong and her manner, under drawing out and encouragement, sometimes even alarming . . .

So the poor old lady went upstairs again.

5

The basement door opened and Kipps came into the kitchen. He was flushed and panting.

He struggled for speech.

' 'Ere,' he said, and held out two half-sixpences.

Ann stood behind the kitchen table – face pale and eyes round, and now – and it simplified Kipps very much – he could see she had indeed been crying.

'Well?' she said.

'Don't you see?'

Ann moved her head slightly.

'I kep' it all these years.'

'You kep' it too long.'

His mouth closed and his flush died away. He looked at her. The amulet, it seemed, had failed to work.

'Ann!' he said.

'Well?'

'Ann.'

The conversation still hung fire.

'Ann,' he said, made a movement with his hands that suggested appeal, and advanced a step.

Ann shook her head more defiantly, and became defensive.

'Look here, Ann,' said Kipps. 'I been a fool.'

They stared into each other's miserable eyes.

'Ann,' he said. 'I want to marry you.'

Ann clutched the table edge. 'You can't,' she said faintly.

He made as if to approach her around the table, and she took a step that restored their distance.

'I must,' he said.

'You can't.'

'I must. You *got* to marry me, Ann.'

'You can't go marrying everybody. You got to marry 'er.'

'I shan't.'

Ann shook her head. 'You're engaged to that girl. Lady, rather. You can't be engaged to me.'

'I don't want to be engaged to you. I *been* engaged. I want to be married to you. See? Rightaway.'

Ann turned a shade paler. 'But what d'you mean?' she asked.

'Come right off to London and marry me. Now.'

'What d'you mean?'

Kipps became extremely lucid and earnest.

'I mean come right off and marry me now before anyone else can. *See?*'

'In London?'

'In London.'

They stared at one another again. They took things for granted in the most amazing way.

'I couldn't,' said Ann. 'For one thing, my month's not up for mor'n free weeks yet.'

They hung before that for a moment as though it was insurmountable.

'Look 'ere, Ann! Arst to go. Arst to go!'

'*She* wouldn't,' said Ann.

'Then come without arsting,' said Kipps.

'She'll keep my box – '

'She won't.'

'She will.'

'She won't.'

'You don't know 'er.'

'Well, desh 'er – let 'er! LET 'ER! Who cares? I'll buy you a 'undred boxes if you'll come.'

'It wouldn't be right towards Her.'

'It isn't Her you got to think about, Ann. It's me.'

'And you 'aven't treated me properly,' she said. 'You 'aven't treated me properly, Artie. You didn't ought to 'ave – '

'I didn't say I '*ad*,' he interrupted, 'did I? Ann,' he appealed, 'I didn't come to arguefy. I'm all wrong. I never said I wasn't. It's yes or no. Me or not . . . I been a fool. There! See? I been a fool. Ain't that enough?

I got myself all tied up with everyone and made a fool of myself all round . . . '

He pleaded, 'It isn't as if we didn't care for one another, Ann.'

She seemed impassive and he resumed his discourse.

'I thought I wasn't likely ever to see you again, Ann. I reely did. It isn't as though I was seein' you all the time. I didn't know what I wanted, and I went and be'aved like a fool – jest as anyone might. I know what I want and I know what I don't want now.

'Ann!'

'Well?'

'Will you come? . . . Will you come? . . . '

Silence.

'If you don't answer me, Ann – I'm desprit – if you don't answer me now, if you don't say you'll come, I'll go right out now – '

He turned doorward passionately as he spoke, with his threat incomplete.

'I'll go,' he said; 'I 'aven't a friend in the world! I been and throwed everything away. I don't know why I done things and why I 'aven't. All I know is I can't stand nothing in the world any more.' He choked. 'The pier – ' he said.

He fumbled with the door latch, grumbling some inarticulate self-pity, as if he sought a handle, and then he had it open.

Clearly he was going.

'Artie!' said Ann, sharply.

He turned about and the two hung, white and tense.

'I'll do it,' said Ann.

His face began to work; he shut the door and came a step back to her, staring; his face became pitiful and then suddenly they moved together. 'Artie!' she cried, 'don't go!' and held out her arms, weeping.

They clung close to one another . . .

'Oh! I *been* so mis'bel,' cried Kipps, clinging to this lifebuoy; and suddenly his emotion, having no further serious work in hand, burst its way to a loud *boohoo*! His fashionable and expensive gibus flopped off and fell and rolled and lay neglected on the floor.

'I been so mis'bel,' said Kipps, giving himself vent. 'Oh! I *been* so mis'bel, Ann.'

'Be quiet,' said Ann, holding his poor, blubbering head tightly to her heaving shoulder, and herself all a-quiver; 'be quiet. She's there! Listenin'. She'll 'ear you, Artie, on the stairs . . . '

6

Ann's last words when, an hour later, they parted, Mrs and Miss Bindon Botting having returned very audibly upstairs, deserve a section to themselves.

'I wouldn't do this for everyone, mind you,' whispered Ann.

CHAPTER NINE

The Labyrinthodon [34]

You imagine them fleeing through our complex and difficult social system as it were for life, first on foot and severally to the Folkestone Central Station, then in a first-class carriage, with Kipps's bag as sole chaperone, to Charing Cross, and then in a four-wheeler, a long, rumbling, palpitating, slow flight through the multitudinous swarming London streets to Sid. Kipps kept peeping out of the window. 'It's the next corner after this, I believe,' he would say. For he had a sort of feeling that at Sid's he would be immune from the hottest pursuit. He paid the cabman in a manner adequate to the occasion and turned to his prospective brother-in-law. 'Me and Ann,' he said, 'we're going to marry.'

'But I thought – ' began Sid.

Kipps motioned him towards explanations in the shop –

'It's no good, my arguing with you,' said Sid, smiling delightedly as the case unfolded. 'You done it now.' And Masterman, being apprised of the nature of the affair, descended slowly in a state of flushed congratulation.

'I thought you might find the Higher Life a bit difficult,' said Masterman, projecting a bony hand. 'But I never thought you'd have the originality to clear out . . . Won't the young lady of the superior classes swear! Never mind – it doesn't matter anyhow.

'You were starting a climb,' he said at dinner, 'that doesn't lead anywhere. You would have clambered from one refinement of vulgarity to another and never got to any satisfactory top. There isn't a top. It's a squirrel's cage. Things are out of joint, and the only top there is is a lot of blazing card-playing women and betting men, seasoned with archbishops and officials and all that sort of glossy, pandering Tosh . . . You'd have hung on, a disconsolate, dismal little figure somewhere up the ladder, far below even the motor-car class, while your wife larked about – or fretted because she wasn't a bit higher than she was . . . I found it all out long ago. I've seen women of that sort. And I don't climb any more.'

'I often thought about what you said last time I saw you,' said Kipps.

'I wonder what I said,' said Masterman in parenthesis. 'Anyhow, you're doing the right and sane thing, and that's a rare spectacle. You're going to marry your equal, and you're going to take your own line, quite independently of what people up there, or people down there, think you ought or ought not to do. That's about the only course one can take nowadays with everything getting more muddled and upside down every day. Make your own little world and your own house first of all, keep that right side up whatever you do, and marry your mate . . . That, I suppose, is what *I* should do – if *I* had a mate . . . But people of my sort, luckily for the world, don't get made in pairs. No!

'Besides – ! However – ' And abruptly, taking advantage of an interruption by Master Walt, he lapsed into thought.

Presently he came out of his musings.

'After all,' he said, 'there's hope.'

'What about?' said Sid.

'Everything,' said Masterman.

'Where there's life there's hope,' said Mrs Sid. 'But none of you aren't eating anything like you ought to.'

Masterman lifted his glass.

'Here's to Hope!' he said. 'The Light of the World!'

Sid beamed at Kipps as who should say, 'You don't meet a character like *this* every dinner time.'

'Here's to Hope,' repeated Masterman. 'The best thing one can have. Hope of life – yes.'

He imposed his moment of magnificent self-pity on them all. Even young Walt was impressed.

2

They spent the days before their marriage in a number of agreeable excursions together. One day they went to Kew by steamboat, and admired the house full of paintings of flowers extremely; and one day they went early to have a good long day at the Crystal Palace, and enjoyed themselves very much indeed. They got there so early that nothing was open inside, all the stalls were wrappered up and all the minor exhibitions locked and barred; they seemed the minutest creatures even to themselves in that enormous empty aisle and their echoing footsteps indecently loud. They contemplated realistic groups of plaster savages, and Ann thought they'd be queer people to have about. She was glad there were none in this country. They meditated upon replicas of classical statuary without excessive comment. Kipps said, at large, it must have been a queer world then, but Ann very properly doubted if they really went about like that. But the place at that early hour was really lonely. One began to fancy things. So they went out into the October sunshine of the mighty terraces, and wandered amidst miles of stucco tanks and about those quiet Gargantuan grounds. A great, grey emptiness it was, and it seemed marvellous to them, but not nearly so marvellous as it might have seemed. 'I never see a finer place, never,' said Kipps, turning to survey the entirety of the enormous glass front with Paxton's vast image in the centre.

'What it must 'ave cost to build!' said Ann, and left her sentence eloquently incomplete.

Presently they came to a region of caves and waterways, and amidst these waterways strange reminders of the possibilities of the Creator. They passed under an arch made of a whale's jaws, and discovered amidst herbage, as if they were browsing or standing unoccupied and staring as if amazed at themselves, huge effigies of iguanodons[35] and deinotheria and mastodons[36] and suchlike cattle, gloriously done in green and gold.

'They got everything,' said Kipps. 'Earl's Court isn't a patch on it.'

His mind was very greatly exercised by these monsters, and he hovered about them and returned to them. 'You'd wonder 'ow they ever got enough to eat,' he said several times.

3

It was later in the day, and upon a seat in the presence of the green-and-gold Labyrinthodon that looms so splendidly above the lake, that the Kippses fell into talk about their future. They had made a sufficient lunch in the palace, they had seen pictures and no end of remarkable things, and that and the amber sunlight made a mood for them, quiet and philosophical, a haven mood. Kipps broke a contemplative silence with an abrupt allusion to one principal preoccupation. 'I shall offer an 'pology and I shall offer 'er brother damages. If she likes to bring an action for Breach after that, well – I done all I can . . . They can't get much out of reading my letters in court, because I didn't write none. I dessay a thousan' or two'll settle all that, anyhow. I ain't much worried about that. That don't worry me very much, Ann – No.'

And then, 'It's a lark, our marrying. It's curious 'ow things come about. If I 'adn't run against you, where should I 'ave been now? Eh? . . . Even after we met, I didn't seem to see it like – not marrying you, I mean – until that night I came. I didn't – reely.'

'I didn't neither,' said Ann, with thoughtful eyes on the water.

For a time Kipps's mind was occupied by the prettiness of her thinking face. A faint, tremulous network of lights, reflected from the ripples of a passing duck, played subtly over her cheek and faded away.

Ann reflected. 'I s'pose things 'ad to be,' she said.

Kipps mused. 'It's curious 'ow ever I got on to be engaged to 'er.'

'She wasn't suited to you,' said Ann.

'Suited. No fear! That's jest it. 'Ow did it come about?'

'I expect she led you on,' said Ann.

Kipps was half-minded to assent. Then he had a twinge of conscience. 'It wasn't that, Ann,' he said. 'It's curious. I don't know what it was, but it wasn't that. I don't recollect . . . No . . . Life's jolly rum; that's one thing any'ow. And I suppose I'm a rum sort of feller. I get excited sometimes, and then I don't seem to care *what* I do. That's about what it was reely. Still – '

They meditated, Kipps with his arms folded and pulling at his scanty moustache. Presently a faint smile came over his face.

'We'll get a nice little 'ouse out 'Ythe way.'

'It's 'omelier than Folkestone,' said Ann.

'Jest a nice little 'ouse,' said Kipps. 'There's Hughenden, of course. But that's let. Besides being miles too big. And I wouldn't live in Folkestone again some'ow – not for anything.'

'I'd like to 'ave a 'ouse of my own,' said Ann. 'I've often thought, being in service, 'ow much I'd like to manage a 'ouse of my own.'

'You'd know all about what the servants was up to, anyhow,' said Kipps, amused.

'Servants! We don't want no servants,' said Ann, startled.

'You'll 'ave to 'ave a servant,' said Kipps. 'If it's only to do the 'eavy work of the 'ouse.'

'What! and not be able 'ardly to go into my own kitchen?' said Ann.

'You ought to 'ave a servant,' said Kipps.

'One could easy 'ave a woman in for anything that's 'eavy,' said Ann. 'Besides – If I 'ad one of the girls one sees about nowadays, I should want to be taking the broom out of 'er 'and and doing it all over myself. I'd manage better without 'er.'

'We ought to 'ave one servant anyhow,' said Kipps, 'else 'ow should we manage if we wanted to go out together or anything like that?'

'I might get a *young* girl,' said Ann, 'and bring 'er up in my own way.'

Kipps left the matter at that and came back to the house.

'There's little 'ouses going into Hythe, just the sort we want, not too big and not too small. We'll 'ave a kitching and a dining-room and a little room to sit in of a night.'

'It mustn't be a 'ouse with a basement,' said Ann.

'What's a basement?'

'It's a downstairs, where there's not arf enough light and everything got to be carried – up and down, up and down, all day – coals and everything. And it's got to 'ave a water-tap and sink and things upstairs. You'd 'ardly believe, Artie, if you 'adn't been in service, 'ow cruel and silly some 'ouses are built – you'd think they 'ad a spite against servants the way the stairs are made.'

'We won't 'ave one of that sort,' said Kipps . . . 'We'll 'ave a quiet little life. Now go out a bit – now come 'ome again. Read a book perhaps if we got nothing else to do. 'Ave old Buggins in for an evening at times. 'Ave Sid down. There's bicycles – '

'I don't fancy myself on a bicycle,' said Ann.

' 'Ave a trailer,' said Kipps, 'and sit like a lady. I'd take you out to New Romney easy as anything, jest to see the old people.'

'I wouldn't mind that,' said Ann.

'We'll jest 'ave a sensible little 'ouse, and sensible things. No art or anything of that sort, nothing stuck-up or anything, but jest sensible. We'll be as right as anything, Ann.'

'No Socialism,' said Ann, starting a lurking doubt.

'No Socialism,' said Kipps; 'just sensible, that's all.'

'I dessay it's all right for them that understand it, Artie, but I don't agree with this Socialism.'

'I don't neither, reely,' said Kipps. 'I can't argue about it, but it don't seem real like to me. All the same, Masterman's a clever fellow, Ann.'

'I didn't like 'im at first, Artie, but I do now – in a way. You don't understand 'im all at once.'

' 'E's so clever,' said Kipps. 'Arf the time I can't make out what 'e's up to. 'E's the cleverest chap I ever met. I never 'eard such talking. 'E ought to write a book . . . It's a rum world, Ann, when a chap like that isn't 'ardly able to earn a living.'

'It's 'is 'ealth,' said Ann.

'I expect it is,' said Kipps, and ceased to talk for a little while.

Then he spoke with deliberation, 'Sea air might be the saving of 'im, Ann.'

He glanced doubtfully at Ann, and she was looking at him even fondly.

'You think of other people a lot,' said Ann. 'I been looking at you sittin' there and thinking.'

'I suppose I do. I suppose when one's 'appy one does.'

'*You* do,' said Ann.

'We shall be 'appy in that little 'ouse, Ann. Don't y' think?'

She met his eyes and nodded.

'I seem to see it,' said Kipps, 'sort of cosy like. 'Bout tea time and muffins, kettle on the 'ob, cat on the 'earthrug – we must get a cat, Ann – and *you* there. Eh?'

They regarded each other with appreciative eyes and Kipps became irrelevant.

'I don't believe, Ann,' he said, 'I 'aven't kissed you not for 'arf an hour. Leastways not since we was in those caves.'

For kissing had already ceased to be a matter of thrilling adventure for them.

Ann shook her head. 'You be sensible and go on talking about Mr Masterman,' she said.

But Kipps had wandered to something else. 'I like the way your 'air turns back just there,' he said, with an indicative finger. 'It was like that, I remember, when you was a girl. Sort of wavy. I've often thought of it . . . 'Member when we raced that time – out be'ind the church?'

Then for a time they sat idly, each following out agreeable meditations.

'It's rum,' said Kipps.

'What's rum?'

' 'Ow everything's 'appened,' said Kipps. 'Who'd 'ave thought of our being 'ere like this six weeks ago? . . . Who'd 'ave thought of my ever 'aving any money?'

His eyes went to the big Labyrinthodon. He looked first carelessly and then suddenly with a growing interest in its vast face.

'I'm deshed,' he murmured. Ann became interested. He laid a hand on her arm and pointed. Ann scrutinised the Labyrinthodon and then came around to Kipps's face in mute interrogation.

'Don't you see it?' said Kipps.

'See what?'

' 'E's *jest* like old Coote.'

'It's extinct,' said Ann, not clearly apprehending.

'I dessay 'e is. But 'e's jest like old Coote all the same for that.'

Kipps meditated on the monstrous shapes in sight. 'I wonder 'ow all these old antediluvium animals *got* extinct,' he asked. 'No one couldn't possibly 'ave killed 'em.'

'Why! *I* know that,' said Ann. 'They was overtook by the Flood . . . '

Kipps meditated for a while. 'But I thought they had to take two of everything there was – '

'Within reason they 'ad,' said Ann . . .

The Kippses left it at that.

The great green-and-gold Labyrinthodon took no notice of their conversation. It gazed with its wonderful eyes over their heads into the infinite – inflexibly calm. It might indeed have been Coote himself there, Coote, the unassuming, cutting them dead.

4

And in due course these two simple souls married, and Venus Urania, the Goddess of Wedded Love, the Goddess of Tolerant Kindliness or Meeting Halfway, to whom all young couples should pray and offer sacrifices of self, who is indeed a very great and noble and kindly goddess, was in some manner propitiated and bent down and blessed them in their union.

BOOK THREE

Kippses

CHAPTER ONE

The Housing Problem

Honeymoons and all things come to an end, and you see at last Mr and Mrs Arthur Kipps descending upon the Hythe platform – coming to Hythe to find that nice *little* house – to realise that bright dream of a home they had first talked about in the grounds of the Crystal Palace. They are a valiant couple, you perceive, but small; and the world is a large incongruous system of complex and difficult things. Kipps wears a grey suit, with a wing-poke collar and a neat, smart tie. Mrs Kipps is the same bright and healthy little girl-woman you saw in the Marsh; not an inch has been added to her stature in all my voluminous narrative. Only now she wears a hat.

It is a hat very unlike the hats she used to wear on her Sundays out, a flourishing hat with feathers and buckle and bows and things. The price of that hat would take many people's breath away – it cost two guineas! Kipps chose it. Kipps paid for it. They left the shop with flushed cheeks and smarting eyes, glad to be out of range of the condescending saleswoman.

'Artie,' said Ann, 'you didn't ought to 'ave – '

That was all. And you know, the hat didn't suit Ann a bit. Her clothes did not suit her at all. The simple, cheap, clean brightness of her former style had given place not only to this hat, but to several other things in the same key. And out from among these things looked her pretty face, the face of a wise little child – an artless wonder struggling through a preposterous dignity.

They had bought that hat one day when they had gone to see the shops in Bond Street. Kipps had looked at the passers-by and it had suddenly occurred to him that Ann was dowdy. He had noted the hat of a very proud-looking lady passing in an electric brougham and had resolved to get Ann the nearest thing to that.

The railway porters perceived some subtle incongruity in Ann, the knot of cabmen in the station doorway, the two golfers and the lady with daughters, who had also got out of the train. And Kipps, a little pale, blowing a little, not in complete possession of himself, knew that they noticed her and him. And Ann – It is hard to say just what Ann observed of these things.

' 'Ere!' said Kipps to a cabman, and regretted too late a vanished 'H'.
'I got a trunk up there,' he said to a ticket inspector, 'marked A. K.'
'Ask a porter,' said the inspector, turning his back.
'Demn!' said Kipps, not altogether inaudibly.

2

It is all very well to sit in the sunshine and talk of the house you will have, and another altogether to achieve it. We English – all the world indeed today – live in a strange atmosphere of neglected great issues, of insistent, triumphant petty things; we are given up to the fine littlenesses of intercourse; table manners and small correctitudes are the substance of our lives. You do not escape these things for long even by so catastrophic a proceeding as flying to London with a young lady of no wealth and inferior social position. The mists of noble emotion swirl and pass and there you are divorced from all your deities and grazing in the meadows under the Argus eyes of the social system, the innumerable mean judgements you feel raining upon you, upon your clothes and bearing, upon your pretensions and movements.

Our world today is a meanly conceived one – it is only an added meanness to conceal that fact. For one consequence, it has very few nice little houses, such things do not come for the asking, they are not to be bought with money during ignoble times. Its houses are built on the ground of monstrously rich, shabbily extortionate landowners, by poor, parsimonious, greedy people in a mood of elbowing competition. What can you expect from such ridiculous conditions? To go house-hunting is to spy out the nakedness of this pretentious world, to see what our civilisation amounts to when you take away curtains and flounces and carpets and all the fluster and distraction of people and fittings. It is to see mean plans meanly executed for mean ends, the conventions torn aside, the secrets stripped, the substance underlying all such Chester Cootery soiled and worn and left.

So you see our poor dear Kippses going to and fro, in Hythe, in Sandgate, in Ashford and Canterbury and Deal and Dover – at last even in Folkestone, with 'orders to view', pink and green and white and yellow orders to view, and labelled keys in Kipps's hand and frowns and perplexity upon their faces . . . They did not clearly know what they wanted, but whatever it was they saw, they knew they did not want that. Always they found a confusing multitude of houses they could not take, and none they could. Their dreams began to turn mainly on empty, abandoned-looking rooms, with unfaded patches of paper to mark the place of vanished pictures and doors that had lost their keys. They saw rooms floored with boards that yawned apart and were splintered, skirtings eloquent of the industrious mouse, kitchens with a dead black-beetle in the empty cupboard and a hideous variety of coal-holes and dark cupboards under the stairs. They stuck their little heads through roof trap-doors and gazed at disorganised ball taps, at the bleak filthiness of unstopped roofs. There were occasions when it seemed to them that they must be the victims of an elaborate conspiracy of house agents, so bleak and cheerless is a second-hand empty house in comparison with the humblest of inhabited dwellings.

Commonly the houses were too big. They had huge windows that demanded vast curtains in mitigation, countless bedrooms, acreage of stone steps to be cleaned, kitchens that made Ann protest. She had come so far towards a proper conception of Kipps's social position as to admit the prospect of one servant – 'but lor'!' she would say, 'you'd want a manservant in this 'ouse.' When the houses were not too big, then they were almost invariably the product of speculative building, of that multitudinous hasty building for the extravagant multitude of new births that was the essential disaster of the nineteenth century. The new houses Ann refused as damp, and even the youngest of these that had been in use showed remarkable signs of a sickly constitution, the plaster flaked away, the floors gaped, the paper mouldered and peeled, the doors dropped, the bricks scaled and the railings rusted. Nature in the form of spiders, earwigs, cockroaches, mice, rats, fungi and remarkable smells, was already fighting her way back . . .

And the plan was invariably inconvenient, invariably. All the houses they saw had a common quality for which she could find no word, but for which the proper word is incivility. 'They build these 'ouses,' she said, 'as though girls wasn't 'uman beings.' Sid's social democracy had got into her blood perhaps, and anyhow they went about discovering the most remarkable inconsiderateness in the contemporary house. 'There's kitching stairs to go up, Artie!' Ann would say. 'Some poor girl's got to go up and down, up and down, and be tired out, jest because they haven't the sense to leave enough space to give their steps a proper rise – and no water upstairs anywhere – every drop got to be carried! It's 'ouses like this wear girls out.

'It's 'aving 'ouses built by men, I believe, makes all the work and trouble,' said Ann . . .

The Kippses, you see, thought they were looking for a reasonably simple little contemporary house, but they were in fact looking either for dreamland or 1975 AD or thereabouts, and it hadn't come.

But it was a foolish thing of Kipps to begin building a house.

He did that out of an extraordinary animosity for house agents he had conceived.

Everybody hates house agents just as everybody loves sailors. It is no doubt a very wicked and unjust hatred, but the business of a novelist is not ethical principle but facts. Everybody hates house agents because they have everybody at a disadvantage. All other callings have a certain amount of give and take; the house agent simply takes. All other callings want you: your solicitor is afraid you may change him, your doctor cannot go too far, your novelist – if only you knew it – is mutely abject towards your unspoken wishes, and as for your tradespeople, milkmen will fight outside your front door for you and greengrocers call in tears if you discard them suddenly; but who ever heard of a house agent struggling to serve anyone? You want to get a house; you go to him, you dishevelled and angry from travel, anxious, enquiring; he calm, clean, inactive, reticent, quietly doing nothing. You beg him to reduce rents, whitewash ceilings, produce other houses, combine the summer-house of No. 6 with the conservatory of No. 4 – much he cares! You want to dispose of a house; then he is just the same, serene, indifferent – on one occasion I remember he was picking his teeth all the time he answered me. Competition is a mockery among house agents, they are all alike; you cannot wound them by going to the opposite office, you cannot dismiss them, you can at most dismiss yourself. They are invulnerably placed behind mahogany and brass, too far usually even for a sudden swift lunge with an umbrella, and to throw away the keys they lend you instead of returning them is larceny and punishable as such.

It was a house agent in Dover who finally decided Kipps to build. Kipps, with a certain faltering in his voice, had delivered his ultimatum, no basement, not more than eight rooms, hot and cold water upstairs, coal cellar in the house but with intervening doors to keep dust from the scullery and so forth. He stood blowing. 'You'll have to build a house,' said the house agent, sighing wearily, 'if you want all that.' It was rather for the sake of effective answer than with any intention at the time that Kipps mumbled, 'That's about what I shall do if this goes on.'

Whereupon the house agent smiled. He smiled!

When Kipps came to turn the thing over in his mind he was surprised to find quite a considerable intention had germinated and was growing up in him. After all, lots of people *have* built houses. How could there be so many if they hadn't? Suppose he 'reely' did! Then he would go to the house agent and say, ' 'Ere, while you been getting me a sootable 'ouse, blowed if I 'aven't built one!' Go round to all of them; all the house agents in Folkestone, in Dover, Ashford, Canterbury, Margate, Ramsgate, saying that! Perhaps then they might be sorry. It was in the small hours that he awoke to a realisation that he had made up his mind in the matter.

'Ann,' he said, 'Ann,' and also used the sharp of his elbow.

Ann was at last awakened to the pitch of an indistinct enquiry what was the matter.

'I'm going to build a house, Ann.'

'Eh?' said Ann, suddenly, as if awake.

'Build a house.'

Ann said something incoherent about he'd better wait until the morning before he did anything of the sort, and immediately with a fine trustfulness went fast asleep again.

But Kipps lay awake for a long while building his house, and in the morning at breakfast he made his meaning clear. He had smarted under the indignities of house agents long enough, and this seemed to promise revenge – a fine revenge. 'And, you know, we might reely make rather a nice little 'ouse out of it – like we want.'

So resolved, it became possible for them to take a house for a year, with a basement, no service lift, black-leading to do everywhere, no water upstairs, no bathroom, vast sash windows to be cleaned from the sill, stone steps with a twist and open to the rain into the coal cellar, insufficient cupboards, unpaved path to the dustbin, no fireplace in the servant's bedroom, no end of splintery wood to scrub – in fact, a very typical English middle-class house. And having added to this house some furniture, and a languid young person with unauthentic golden hair named Gwendolen, who was engaged to a sergeant-major and had formerly been in a hotel, having 'moved in' and spent some sleepless nights varied by nocturnal explorations in search of burglars, because of the strangeness of being in a house for which they were personally responsible, Kipps settled down for a time and turned himself with considerable resolution to the project of building a home.

At first Kipps had gathered advice, finding an initial difficulty in how to begin. He went into a builder's shop at Seabrook one day, and told the lady in charge that he wanted a house built; he was breathless but quite determined, and he was prepared to give his order there and then, but she temporised with him and said her husband was out, and he left without giving his name. Also he went and talked to a man in a cart who was pointed out to him by a workman as the builder of a new house near Saltwood, but he found him first sceptical and then overpoweringly sarcastic. 'I suppose you build a 'ouse every 'oliday,' he said, and turned from Kipps with every symptom of contempt.

Afterwards Carshot told alarming stories about builders, and shook Kipps's expressed resolution a good deal, and then Pierce raised the question whether one ought to go in the first instance to a builder at all and not rather to an architect. Pierce knew a man at Ashford whose brother was an architect and, as it is always better in these matters to get someone you know, the Kippses decided, before Pierce had gone and Carshot's warnings had resumed their sway, to apply to him. They did so – rather dubiously.

The architect who was brother of Pierce's friend appeared as a small, alert individual with a black bag and a cylindrical silk hat, and he sat at the dining-room table, with his hat and his bag exactly equidistant right and left of him, and maintained a demeanour of impressive woodenness, while Kipps on the hearthrug, with a quaking sense of gigantic enterprise, vacillated answers to his enquiries. Ann held a watching brief for herself, in a position she had chosen as suitable to the occasion beside the corner of the carved oak sideboard. They felt, in a sense, at bay.

The architect began by asking for the site, and seemed a little discomposed to discover this had still to be found. 'I thought of building just anywhere,' said Kipps. 'I 'aven't made up my mind about that yet.' The architect remarked that he would have preferred to see the site in order to know where to put what he called his 'ugly side', but it was quite possible of course to plan a house 'in the air', on the level, 'simply with back and front assumed' – if they would like to do that. Kipps flushed slightly, and secretly hoping it would make no great difference in the fees, said a little doubtfully that he thought that would be all right.

The architect then marked off, as it were, the first section of his subject with a single dry cough, opened his bag, took out a spring tape measure, some hard biscuits, a metal flask, a new pair of dogskin gloves, a clockwork motor car partially wrapped in paper, a bunch of violets, a paper of small brass screws and, finally, a large distended notebook; he replaced the other objects carefully, opened his notebook, put a pencil to his lips and said: 'And what accommodation will you require?' To which Ann, who had followed his every movement with the closest attention and a deepening dread, replied with the violent suddenness of one who has long lain in wait, 'Cubbuds!

'Anyhow,' she added, catching her husband's eye.

The architect wrote it down.

'And how many rooms?' he said, coming to secondary matters.

The young people regarded one another. It was dreadfully like giving an order.

'How many bedrooms, for example?' asked the architect.

'One?' suggested Kipps, inclined now to minimise at any cost.

'There's Gwendolen,' said Ann.

'Visitors perhaps,' said the architect, and temperately, 'You never know.'

'Two, p'r'aps?' said Kipps. 'We don't want no more than a *little* 'ouse, you know.'

'But the merest shooting-box – ' said the architect . . .

They got to six; he beat them steadily from bedroom to bedroom; the word 'nursery' played across their imaginative skies – he mentioned it as the remotest possibility – and then six being reluctantly conceded, Ann came forward to the table, sat down and delivered herself of one of her prepared conditions: ' 'Ot and cold water,' she said, 'laid on to each room – any'ow.'

It was an idea long since acquired from Sid.

'Yes,' said Kipps, on the hearthrug, ' 'Ot and cold water laid on to each bedroom – we've settled on that.'

It was the first intimation to the architect that he had to deal with a couple of exceptional originality, and as he had spent the previous afternoon in finding three large houses in the *Builder*, which he intended to combine into an original and copyright design of his own, he naturally struggled against these novel requirements. He enlarged on the extreme expensiveness of plumbing, on the extreme expensiveness of everything not already arranged for in his scheme, and only when Ann declared she'd as soon not have the house as not have her requirements, and Kipps, blenching the while, had said he didn't mind what a thing cost him so long as he got what he wanted, did he allow a kindred originality of his own to appear beneath the acquired professionalism of his methods. He dismissed their previous talk with his paragraphic cough. 'Of course,' he said, 'if you don't mind being unconventional – '

He explained that he had been thinking of a Queen Anne style of architecture (Ann directly she heard her name shook her head at Kipps in an aside) so far as the exterior went. For his own part, he said, he liked to have the exterior of a house in a style, not priggishly in a style, but mixed, with one style uppermost; and the gables and dormers and casements of the Queen Anne style, with a little roughcast and sham timbering here and there and perhaps a bit of an overhang, diversified a house and made it interesting. The advantage of what he called a Queen Anne style was that it had such a variety of features . . . Still, if they were prepared to be unconventional it could be done. A number of houses were now built in the unconventional style and were often very pretty. In the unconventional style one frequently had what perhaps he might call Internal Features – for example, an Old English oak staircase and gallery. White roughcast and green paint were a good deal favoured in houses of this type.

He indicated that this excursus on style was finished by a momentary use of his cough, and reopened his notebook, which he had closed to wave about in a moment of descriptive enthusiasm while expatiating on the unbridled wealth of External Features associated with Queen Anne. 'Six bedrooms,' he said, moistening his pencil. 'One with barred windows suitable for a nursery if required.'

Kipps endorsed this huskily and reluctantly.

There followed a most interesting discussion upon house building, in which Kipps played a minor part. They passed from bedrooms to the kitchen and scullery, and there Ann displayed an intelligent exactingness that won the expressed admiration of the architect. They were particularly novel upon the position of the coal cellar, which Ann held to be altogether too low in the ordinary house, necessitating much heavy carrying. They dismissed as impracticable the idea of having coal cellar and kitchen at the top of the house, because that would involve carrying all the coal through the house, and therewith much subsequent cleaning, and for a time they dealt with a conception of a coal cellar on the ground floor with a light staircase running up outside to an exterior shoot. 'It might be made a Feature,' said the architect, a little doubtfully, jotting down a note of it. 'It would be apt to get black, you know.'

Thence they passed to the alternative of service lifts, and then by an inspiration of the architect to the possibilities of gas heating. Kipps did a complicated verbal fugue on the theme 'gas heating heats the air', with variable aspirates; he became very red and was lost to the discussion altogether for a time, though his lips kept silently moving.

Subsequently the architect wrote to say that he found in his note-book very full and explicit directions for bow windows to all rooms, for bedrooms, for water supply, lift, height of stairs and absence of twists therein, for a well-ventilated kitchen twenty feet square, with two dressers and a large box-window seat, for scullery and outhouses and offices, but nothing whatever about drawing-room, dining-room, library or study, or approximate cost, and he awaited further instruc-tions. He presumed there would be a breakfast-room, dining-room, drawing-room, and study for Mr Kipps, at least that was his con-ception, and the young couple discussed this matter long and ardently.

Ann was distinctly restrictive in this direction. 'I don't see what you want a drawin'-room and a dinin' *and* a kitchen for. If we was going to let in summer – well and good. But we're not going to let. Consequently we don't want so many rooms. Then there's a 'all. What use is a 'all? It only makes work. And a study!'

Kipps had been humming and stroking his moustache since he had read the architect's letter. 'I think I'd like a little bit of a study – not a big one, of course, but one with a desk and bookshelves, like there was in Hughenden. I'd like that.'

It was only after they had talked to the architect again and seen how scandalised he was at the idea of not having a drawing-room that they consented to that Internal Feature. They consented to please him. 'But we shan't never use it,' said Ann.

Kipps had his way about a study. 'When I get that study,' said Kipps, 'I shall do a bit of reading I've long wanted to do. I shall make a habit of going in there and reading something an hour every day. There's Shake-speare and a lot of things a man like me ought to read. Besides, we got to 'ave *somewhere* to put the *Encyclopaedia*. I've always thought a study was about what I've wanted all along. You can't 'elp reading if you got a study. If you 'aven't, there's nothing for it, so far's *I* can see, but treshy novels.'

He looked down at Ann and was surprised to see a joyless thought-fulness upon her face.

'Fency, Ann!' he said, not too buoyantly, ' 'aving a little 'ouse of our own!'

'It won't be a little 'ouse,' said Ann, 'not with all them rooms.'

Any lingering doubt in that matter was dispelled when it came to plans.

The architect drew three sets of plans on a transparent bluish sort of paper that smelt abominably. He painted them very nicely; brick-red and ginger, and arsenic green and a leaden sort of blue, and brought them over to show our young people. The first set were very simple, with practically no External Features – 'a plain style', he said it was – but it looked a big sort of house nevertheless; the second had such extras as a conservatory, bay windows of various sorts, one roughcast gable and one half-timbered ditto in plaster, and a sort of overhung veranda, and was much more imposing; and the third was quite fungoid with External Features, and honeycombed with Internal ones; it was, he said, 'practically a mansion', and altogether a very noble fruit of the creative mind of man. It was, he admitted, perhaps almost too good for Hythe; his art had run away with him and produced a modern mansion in the 'best Folkestone style'; it had a central hall with a staircase, a Moorish gallery and Tudor stained-glass window, crenelated battlements to the leading over the portico, an octagonal bulge with octagonal bay windows, surmounted by an oriental dome of metal, lines of yellow bricks to break up the red and many other richnesses and attractions. It was the sort of house, ornate and in its dignified way voluptuous, that a city magnate might build, but it seemed excessive to the Kippses. The first plan had seven bedrooms, the second eight, the third eleven; they had, the architect explained, 'worked in' as if they were pebbles in a mountaineer's boot.

'They're big 'ouses,' said Ann directly the elevations were unrolled.

Kipps listened to the architect with round eyes and an exuberant caution in his manner, anxious not to commit himself further than he had done to the enterprise, and the architect pointed out the Features and other objects of interest with the scalpel belonging to a pocket manicure set that he carried. Ann watched Kipps's face and communicated with him furtively over the architect's head. '*Not so big,*' said Ann's lips.

'It's a bit big for what I meant,' said Kipps, with a reassuring eye on Ann.

'You won't think it big when you see it up,' said the architect; 'you take my word for that.'

'We don't want no more than six bedrooms,' said Kipps.

'Make this one a boxroom, then,' said the architect.

A feeling of impotence silenced Kipps for a time.

'Now which,' said the architect, spreading them out, 'is it to be?'

He flattened down the plans of the most ornate mansion to show it to better effect.

Kipps wanted to know how much each would cost 'at the outside', which led to much alarmed signalling from Ann. But the architect could estimate only in the most general way.

They were not really committed to anything when the architect went away; Kipps had promised to think it over, that was all.

'We can't 'ave that 'ouse,' said Ann.

'They're miles too big – all of them,' agreed Kipps.

'You'd want – Four servants wouldn't be 'ardly enough,' said Ann.

Kipps went to the hearthrug and spread himself. His tone was almost offhand. 'Nex' time 'e comes,' said Kipps, 'I'll 'splain to him. It isn't at all the sort of thing we want. It's – it's a misunderstanding. You got no occasion to be anxious 'bout it, Ann.'

'I don't see much good reely in building an 'ouse at all,' said Ann.

'Oo, we *got* to build a 'ouse now we begun,' said Kipps. 'But now supposin' we 'ad – '

He spread out the most modest of the three plans and scratched his cheek.

6

It was unfortunate that old Kipps came over the next day.

Old Kipps always produced peculiar states of mind in his nephew, a rash assertiveness, a disposition towards display unlike his usual self. There had been great difficulty in reconciling both the old people to the Pornick *mésalliance*, and at times the controversy echoed in old Kipps's expressed thoughts. This perhaps it was, and no ignoble vanity, that set the note of florid successfulness going in Kipps's conversation whenever his uncle appeared. Mrs Kipps was, as a matter of fact, not reconciled at all; she had declined all invitations to come over on the bus, and was a taciturn hostess on the one occasion when the young people called at the toy shop *en route* for Mrs Pornick. She displayed a tendency to sniff that was clearly due to pride rather than catarrh, and except for telling Ann she hoped she would not feel too 'stuck up' about her marriage, confined her conversation to her nephew or the infinite. The call was a brief one and made up chiefly of pauses, no refreshment was offered or asked for, and Ann departed with a singularly high colour. For some reason she would not call at the toy shop when they found themselves again in New Romney.

But old Kipps, having adventured over and tried the table of the new *ménage* and found it to his taste, showed many signs of softening towards Ann. He came again and then again. He would come over by the bus, and, except when his mouth was absolutely full, he would give his nephew one solid and continuous mass of advice of the most subtle and disturbing description, until it was time to toddle back to the High Street for the afternoon bus. He would walk with him to the sea front, and commence *pourparlers* with boatmen for the purchase of one of their boats – 'You ought to keep a boat of your own,' he said, though Kipps was a singularly poor sailor – or he would pursue a plan that was forming in his mind in which he should own and manage what he called 'weekly' property in the less conspicuous streets of Hythe. The cream of that was to be a weekly collection of rents in person, the nearest approach to feudal splendour left in this democratised country. He gave no hint of the source of the capital he designed for this investment and at times it would appear he intended it as an occupation for his nephew rather than himself.

But there remained something in his manner towards Ann, in the glances of scrutiny he gave her unawares, that kept Kipps alertly expansive whenever he was about. And in all sorts of ways. It was on account of old Kipps, for example, that our Kipps plunged one day, a golden plunge, and brought home a box of cummerbundy ninepenny cigars and substituted blue-label Old Methusaleh Four Stars for the common and generally satisfactory white brand.

'Some of this is whisky, my boy,' said old Kipps when he tasted it, smacking critical lips.

'Saw a lot of young officery fellers coming along,' said old Kipps. 'You ought to join the volunteers, my boy, and get to know a few.'

'I dessay I shall,' said Kipps. 'Later.'

'They'd make you an officer, you know, 'n no time. They want officers,' said old Kipps. 'It isn't everyone can afford it. They'd be regular glad to 'ave you . . . Ain't bort a dog yet?'

'Not yet, uncle. 'Ave a segar?'

'Not a moty car?'

'Not yet, uncle.'

'There's no 'urry 'bout that. And don't get one of these 'ere trashy cheap ones when you do get it, my boy. Get one as'll last a lifetime . . . I'm surprised you don't 'ire a bit more.'

'Ann don't seem to fency a moty car,' said Kipps.

'Ah!' said old Kipps, 'I expect not,' and glanced a comment at the door. 'She ain't used to going out,' he said. 'More at 'ome indoors.'

'Fact is,' said Kipps, hastily, 'we're thinking of building a 'ouse.'

'I wouldn't do that, my boy,' began old Kipps, but his nephew was rooting in the cheffonier drawer amidst the plans. He got them in time to check some further comment on Ann. 'Um,' said the old gentleman, a little impressed by the extraordinary odour and the unusual transparency of the tracing paper Kipps put into his hands. 'Thinking of building a 'ouse, are you?'

Kipps began with the most modest of the three projects.

Old Kipps read slowly through his silver-rimmed spectacles: 'Plan of a 'ouse for Arthur Kipps Esquire – Um.'

He didn't warm to the project all at once, and Ann drifted into the room to find him still scrutinising the architect's proposals a little doubtfully.

'We couldn't find a decent 'ouse anywhere,' said Kipps, leaning against the table and assuming an offhand note. 'I didn't see why we shouldn't run up one for ourselves.'

Old Kipps could not help liking the tone of that.

'We thought we might see – ' said Ann.

'It's a spekerlation, of course,' said old Kipps, and held the plan at a distance of two feet or more from his glasses and frowned. 'This isn't exactly the 'ouse I should expect you to 'ave thought of, though,' he said. 'Practically it's a villa. It's the sort of 'ouse a bank clerk might 'ave. 'Tisn't what I should call a gentleman's 'ouse, Artie.'

'It's plain, of course,' said Kipps, standing beside his uncle and looking down at this plan, which certainly did seem a little less magnificent now than it had at the first encounter.

'You mustn't 'ave it too plain,' said old Kipps.

'If it's comfortable – ' Ann hazarded.

Old Kipps glanced at her over his spectacles. 'You ain't comfortable, my gal, in this world, not if you don't live up to your position,' so putting compactly into contemporary English that fine old phrase *noblesse oblige*. 'A 'ouse of this sort is what a retired tradesman might 'ave, or some little whippersnapper of a s'liciter. But *you* – '

'Course that isn't the o'ny plan,' said Kipps, and tried the middle one.

But it was the third one which won over old Kipps. 'Now that's a *'ouse*, my boy,' he said at the sight of it.

Ann came and stood just behind her husband's shoulder while old Kipps expanded upon the desirability of the largest scheme. 'You ought to 'ave a billiard-room,' he said; 'I don't see that, but all the rest's all right. A lot of these 'ere officers 'ere 'ud be glad of a game of billiards . . .

'What's all these dots?' said old Kipps.

'S'rubbery,' said Kipps. 'Flow'ing s'rubs.'

'There's eleven bedrooms in that 'ouse,' said Ann. 'It's a bit of a lot, ain't it, uncle?'

'You'll want 'em, my girl. As you get on, you'll be 'aving visitors. Friends of your 'usband, p'r'aps, from the School of Musketry, what you want 'im to get on with. You can't never tell.'

'If we 'ave a great s'rubbery,' Ann ventured, 'we shall 'ave to keep a gardener.'

'If you don't 'ave a s'rubbery,' said old Kipps, with a note of patient reasoning, ' 'ow are you to prevent every jackanapes that goes by starin' into your drorin'-room winder – p'r'aps when you get someone a bit special to entertain?'

'We ain't *used* to a s'rubbery,' said Ann, mulishly; 'we get on very well 'ere.'

'It isn't what you're used to,' said old Kipps, 'it's what you ought to 'ave *now*.' And with that Ann dropped out of the discussion.

'Study and lib'ry,' old Kipps read. 'That's right. I see a tantalus the other day over Brookland, the very thing for a gentleman's study. I'll try and get over and bid for it . . . '

By bus time old Kipps was quite enthusiastic about the house building, and it seemed to be definitely settled that the largest plan was the one decided upon. But Ann had said nothing further in the matter.

7

When Kipps returned from seeing his uncle into the bus – there always seemed a certain doubt whether that portly figure would go into the little red 'Tip-Top' box – he found Ann still standing by the table, looking with an expression of comprehensive disapproval at the three plans.

'There don't seem much the matter with uncle,' said Kipps, assuming the hearthrug, 'spite of 'is 'eartburn. 'E 'opped up them steps like a bird.'

Ann remained staring at the plans.

'You don't like them plans?' hazarded Kipps.

'No, I don't, Artie.'

'We got to build somethin' now.'

'But – it's a gentleman's 'ouse, Artie!'

'It's – it's a decent size, o' course.'

Kipps took a flirting look at the drawing and went to the window.

'Look at the cleanin'. Free servants'll be lost in that 'ouse, Artie.'

'We must 'ave servants,' said Kipps.

Ann looked despondently at her future residence.

'We got to keep up our position, any'ow,' said Kipps, turning towards her. 'It stands to reason, Ann, we got a position. Very well! I can't 'ave you scrubbin' floors. You got to 'ave a servant and you got to manage a 'ouse. You wouldn't 'ave me ashamed – '

Ann opened her lips and did not speak.

'What?' asked Kipps.

'Nothing,' said Ann, 'only I did want it to be a *little* 'ouse, Artie. I wanted it to be a 'andy little 'ouse, jest for us.'

Kipps's face was suddenly flushed and mulish. He took up the curiously smelling tracings again. 'I'm not a-going to be looked down upon,' he said. 'It's not only uncle I'm thinking of!'

Ann stared at him.

Kipps went on. 'I won't 'ave that young Walshingham f'r instance, sneering and sniffling at me. Making out as if we was all wrong. I see 'im yesterday . . . Nor Coote neether. I'm as good – we're as good – whatever's 'appened.'

Silence and the rustle of plans.

He looked up and saw Ann's eyes bright with tears. For a moment the two stared at one another.

'We'll 'ave the big 'ouse,' said Ann, with a gulp. 'I didn't think of that, Artie.'

Her aspect was fierce and resolute, and she struggled with emotion. 'We'll 'ave the big 'ouse,' she repeated. 'They shan't say I dragged you down wiv' me – none of them shan't say that. I've thought – I've always been afraid of that.'

Kipps looked again at the plan, and suddenly the grand house had become very grand indeed. He blew.

'No, Artie, none of them shan't say that,' and with something blind in her motions, Ann tried to turn the plan round to her . . .

After all, Kipps thought, there might be something to say for the milder project . . . But he had gone so far that now he did not know how to say it.

And so the plans went out to the builders, and in a little while Kipps was committed to two thousand five hundred pounds' worth of building. But then, you know, he had an income of twelve hundred a year.

It is extraordinary what minor difficulties cluster about house building.

'I say, Ann,' remarked Kipps one day, 'we shall 'ave to call this little 'ouse by a name. I was thinking of 'Ome Cottage. But I dunno whether 'Ome Cottage is quite the thing like. All these little fishermen's places are called Cottages.'

'I like "Cottage",' said Ann.

'It's got eleven bedrooms, y'see,' said Kipps. 'I don't see 'ow you can call it a cottage with more bedrooms than four. Prop'ly speaking, it's a Large Villa. Prop'ly, it's almost a Big 'Ouse. Leastways a 'Ouse.'

'Well,' said Ann, 'if you must call it Villa – Home Villa . . . I wish it wasn't.'

Kipps meditated.

' 'Ow about Eureka Villa?' he said, raising his voice.

'What's Eureka?'

'It's a name,' he said. 'There used to be Eureka Dress Fasteners. There's lots of names, come to think of it, to be got out of a shop. There's Pyjama Villa. I remember that in the hosiery. No, come to think, that wouldn't do. But Maraposa – sort of oatmeal cloth, that was . . . No! Eureka's better.'

Ann meditated. 'It seems silly like to 'ave a name that don't mean much.'

'Perhaps it does,' said Kipps. 'Though it's what people 'ave to do.'

He became meditative. 'I got it!' he cried.

'Not Oreeka!' said Ann.

'No! There used to be a 'ouse at Hastings opposite our school – quite a big 'ouse it was – St Ann's. Now *that* – '

'No,' said Mrs Kipps with decision. 'Thanking you kindly, but I won't have no butcher boys making game of me . . .'

They consulted Carshot, who suggested, after some days of reflection, Waddycombe, as a graceful reminder of Kipps's grandfather; old Kipps, who was for 'Upton Manor House', where he had once been second footman; Buggins, who favoured either a stern simple number, 'Number One' – if there were no other houses there – or something patriotic, as 'Empire Villa'; and Pierce, who inclined to 'Sandringham'; but in spite of all this help they were still undecided when, amidst violent perturbations of the soul, and after the most complex and difficult hagglings, wranglings, fears, muddles and goings to and fro, Kipps became the joyless owner of a freehold plot of three-eighths of an acre, and saw the turf being wheeled away from the site that should one day be his home.

CHAPTER TWO

The Callers

The Kippses sat at their midday dinner-table amidst the vestiges of rhubarb pie and discussed two postcards the one o'clock post had brought. It was a rare bright moment of sunshine in a wet and windy day in the March that followed their marriage. Kipps was attired in a suit of brown, with a tie of fashionable green, while Ann wore one of those picturesque loose robes that are usually associated with sandals and advanced ideas. But there weren't any sandals on Ann or any advanced ideas, and the robe had come quite recently through the counsels of Mrs Sid Pornick. 'It's Art-like,' said Kipps, but giving way. 'It's more comfortable,' said Ann. The room looked out by French windows upon a little patch of green and the Hythe parade. The parade was all shiny wet with rain, and the green-grey sea tumbled and tumbled between parade and sky.

The Kippses's furniture, except for certain chromo-lithographs[37] of Kipps's incidental choice that struck a quiet note amidst the wallpaper, had been tactfully forced by an expert salesman, and it was in a style of mediocre elegance. There was a sideboard of carved oak that had only one fault, it reminded Kipps at times of wood-carving, and its panel of bevelled glass now reflected the back of his head. On its shelf were two books from Parsons' Library, each with a 'place' marked by a slip of paper; neither of the Kippses could have told you the title of either book they read, much less the author's name. There was an ebonised over-mantel set with phials and pots of brilliant colour, each duplicated by looking-glass, and bearing also a pair of Chinese jars made in Birmingham, a wedding present from Mr and Mrs Sidney Pornick, and several sumptuous Japanese fans. And there was a Turkey carpet of great richness. In addition to these modern exploits of Messrs Bunt and Bubble, there were two inactive tall clocks, whose extreme dilapidation appealed to the connoisseur; a terrestrial and a celestial globe, the latter deeply indented; a number of good old iron-moulded and dusty books; and a stuffed owl wanting one (easily replaceable) glass eye, obtained by the exertions of Uncle Kipps. The table equipage was as much as possible like Mrs Bindon Botting's, only more costly, and in addition there were green and crimson wine glasses – though the Kippses never drank wine.

Kipps turned to the more legible of his two postcards again.

' "Unavoidably prevented from seein' me today", 'e says. I like 'is cheek. After I give 'im 'is start and everything.'

He blew.

' 'E certainly treats you a bit orf 'and,' said Ann.

Kipps gave vent to his dislike of young Walshingham. 'He's getting too big for 'is britches,' he said. 'I'm beginning to wish she *ad* brought an action for breach. Ever since *e* said she wouldn't, 'e's seemed to think I've got no right to spend my own money.'

' 'E's never liked your building the 'ouse,' said Ann.

Kipps displayed wrath. 'What the goodness 'as it got to do wiv' 'im? Overman indeed!' he added. 'Overmantel! . . . 'E tries that on with me, I'll tell 'im something 'e won't like.'

He took up the second card. 'Dashed if I can read a word of it. I can jest make out Chit'low at the end and that's all.'

He scrutinised it. 'It's like someone in a fit writing. This here might be W-H-A-T – *what*. P-R-I-C-E – *I* got it! What price Harry now? It was a sort of saying of 'is. I expect 'e's either done something or not done something towards starting that play, Ann.'

'I expect that's about it,' said Ann.

Kipps grunted with effort. 'I can't read the rest,' he said at last, 'nohow.'

A thoroughly annoying post. He pitched the card on the table, stood up and went to the window, where Ann, after a momentary reconnaissance at Chitterlow's hieroglyphics, came to join him.

'Wonder what I shall do this afternoon,' said Kipps, with his hands deep in his pockets.

He produced and lit a cigarette.

'Go for a walk, I s'pose,' said Ann.

'I *been* for a walk this morning . . . S'pose I must go for another,' he added, after an interval.

They regarded the windy waste of sea for a space.

'Wonder why it is 'e won't see me,' said Kipps, returning to the problem of young Walshingham. 'It's all lies about 'is being too busy.'

Ann offered no solution.

'Rain again!' said Kipps, as the lash of the little drops stung the window.

'Oo, bother!' said Kipps, 'you got to do something. Look 'ere, Ann! I'll go orf for a reg'lar tramp through the rain, up by Saltwood, round by Newington, over the camp, and so round and back, and see 'ow they're getting on about the 'ouse. See? And look 'ere! You get Gwendolen to go out a bit before I come back. If it's still rainy, she can easy go round and see 'er sister. Then we'll 'ave a bit of tea, with teacake – all buttery, see? Toce it ourselves, p'r'aps. Eh?'

'I dessay I can find something to do in the 'ouse,' said Ann, considering. 'You'll take your mackintosh and leggin's, I s'pose. You'll get wet without your mackintosh over those roads.'

'Righ-o,' said Kipps, and went to ask Gwendolen for his brown leggings and his other pair of boots.

2

Things conspired to demoralise Kipps that afternoon.

When he got outside the house everything looked so wet under the drive of the south-wester that he abandoned the prospect of the clay lanes towards Newington altogether, and turned east to Folkestone along the Seabrook digue. His mackintosh flapped about him, the rain stung his cheek; for a time he felt a hardy man. And then as abruptly the rain ceased and the wind fell, and before he was through Sandgate High Street it was a bright spring day. And there was Kipps in his mackintosh and squeaky leggings, looking like a fool!

Inertia carried him another mile to the Leas, and there the whole world was pretending there had never been such a thing as rain – ever. There wasn't a cloud in the sky; except for an occasional puddle the asphalt paths looked as dry as a bone. A smartly dressed man in one of those overcoats that look like ordinary cloth and are really most deceitfully and unfairly waterproof, passed him and glanced at the stiff folds of his mackintosh. 'Demn!' said Kipps. His mackintosh swished against his leggings, his leggings piped and whistled over his boot-tops.

'Why do I never get anything right?' Kipps asked of a bright implacable universe.

Nice old ladies passed him, refined people with tidy umbrellas, bright, beautiful, supercilious-looking children. Of course! the right thing for such a day as this was a light overcoat and an umbrella. A child might have known that. He had them at home, but how could one explain that? He decided to turn down by the Harvey monument and escape through Clifton Gardens towards the hills. And thereby he came upon Coote.

He already felt the most abject and propitiatory of social outcasts when he came upon Coote, and Coote finished him. He passed within a yard of Coote. Coote was coming along towards the Leas, and when

Kipps saw him his legs hesitated about their office and he seemed to himself to stagger about all over the footpath. At the sight of him Coote started visibly. Then a sort of *rigor vitae* passed through his frame, his jaw protruded and errant bubbles of air seemed to escape and run about beneath his loose skin. (Seemed, I say – I am perfectly well aware that there is really connective tissue in Coote as in all of us to prevent anything of the sort.) His eyes fixed themselves on the horizon and glazed. As he went by Kipps could hear his even, resolute breathing. He went by, and Kipps staggered on into a universe of dead cats and dust heaps, rind and ashes – *cut!*

It was part of the inexorable decrees of Providence that almost immediately afterwards the residuum of Kipps had to pass a very, very long and observant-looking girls' school.

Kipps recovered consciousness again on the road between Shorncliffe Station and Cheriton, though he cannot remember, indeed to this day he has never attempted to remember, how he got there. And he was back at certain thoughts suggested by his last night's novel reading that linked up directly with the pariah-like emotions of these last encounters. The novel lay at home upon the chiffonier; it was one of society and politics – there is no need whatever to give the title or name the author – written with a heavy-handed thoroughness that. overrode any possibility of resistance on the part of the Kipps mind. It had crushed all his poor little edifice of ideals, his dreams of a sensible, unassuming existence, of snugness, of not caring what people said and all the rest of it, to dust; it had reinstated, squarely and strongly again, the only proper conception of English social life. There was a character in the book who trifled with Art, who was addicted to reading French novels, who dressed in a loose, careless way, who was a sorrow to his dignified, silvery-haired, politico-religious mother, and met the admonitions of bishops with a front of brass. He treated a 'nice girl', to whom they had got him engaged, badly; he married beneath him – some low thing or other. And sank –

Kipps could not escape the application of the case. He was enabled to see how this sort of thing looked to decent people; he was enabled to gauge the measure of the penalties due. His mind went from that to the frozen marble of Coote's visage.

He deserved it!

That day of remorse! Later it found him coming upon the site of his building operations and surveying the disorder of preparation in a mood near to despair, his mackintosh over his arm.

Hardly anyone was at work that day – no doubt the builders were having him in some obscure manner – and the whole place seemed a dismal and depressing litter. The builder's shed, black-lettered WILKINS, BUILDER, HYTHE, looked like a stranded thing amidst a cast-up disorder of wheelbarrows and wheeling planks, and earth and sand and bricks. The foundations of the walls were trenches full of damp concrete, drying in patches; the rooms – it was incredible they could ever be rooms – were shaped out as squares and oblongs of coarse wet grass and sorrel. They looked absurdly small – dishonestly small. What could you expect? Of course the builders were having him, building too small, building all wrong, using bad materials! Old Kipps had told him a wrinkle or two. The builders were having him, young Walshingham was having him, everybody was having him! They were having him and laughing at him because they didn't respect him. They didn't respect him because he couldn't do things right. Who could respect him . . . ?

He was an outcast, he had no place in the society of mankind. He had had his chance in the world and turned his back on it. He had 'behaved badly' – that was the phrase . . .

Here a great house was presently to arise, a house to be paid for, a house neither he nor Ann could manage – with eleven bedrooms, and four disrespectful servants having them all the time!

How had it all happened exactly?

This was the end of his great fortune! What a chance he had had! If he had really carried out his first intentions and stuck to things, how much better everything might have been! If he had got a tutor – that had been in his mind originally – a special sort of tutor to show him everything right; a tutor for gentlemen of neglected education. If he had read more and attended better to what Coote had said!

Coote, who had just cut him!

Eleven bedrooms! What had possessed him? No one would ever come to see them, no one would ever have anything to do with them. Even his aunt cut him! His uncle treated him with a half-contemptuous sufferance. He had not a friend worth counting in the world! Buggins, Carshot, Pierce – shop assistants! The Pornicks – a low socialist lot! He stood among his foundations like a lonely figure among ruins; he stood among the ruins of his future, and owned himself a foolish and mistaken man. He saw himself and Ann living out their shameful lives in this great crazy place – as it would be – with everybody laughing secretly at them and their eleven bedrooms, and nobody approaching them – nobody nice and right that is, for ever. And Ann!

What was the matter with Ann? She'd given up going for walks lately, got touchy and tearful, been fitful with her food. Just when she didn't ought to. It was all a part of the judgement upon wrongdoing, it was all part of the social penalties that Juggernaut of a novel had brought home to his mind.

3

He let himself in with his latchkey. He went moodily into the dining-room and got out the plans to look at them. He had a vague hope that there would prove to be only ten bedrooms. But he found there were still eleven. He became aware of Ann standing over him. 'Look 'ere, Artie!' said Ann.

He looked up and found her holding a number of white oblongs. His eyebrows rose.

'It's Callers,' said Ann.

He put his plans aside slowly and took and read the cards in silence, with a sort of solemnity. Callers! Then perhaps he wasn't to be left out of the world after all. Mrs G. Porrett Smith, Miss Porrett Smith, Miss Mabel Porrett Smith, and two smaller cards of the Revd G. Porrett Smith. 'Lor'!' he said. '*Clergy!*'

'There was a lady,' said Ann, 'and two growed-up gals – all dressed up!'

'And 'im?'

'There wasn't no *'im*.'

'Not – ?' He held out the little cards.

'No; there was a lady and two young ladies.'

'But – these cards! Wad they go and leave these two little cards with the Revd G. Smith on for? Not if 'e wasn't with 'em.'

' 'E wasn't with 'em.'

'Not a little chap – dodgin' about be'ind the others? And didn't come in?'

'I didn't see no gentleman with them at all,' said Ann.

'Rum!' said Kipps. A half-forgotten experience came back to him. '*I* know,' he said, waving the reverend gentleman's card; ' 'e give 'em the slip, that's what he'd done. Gone off while they was rapping before you let 'em in. It's a fair call, any'ow.' He felt a momentary base satisfaction at his absence. 'What did they talk about, Ann?'

There was a pause. 'I didn't let 'em in,' said Ann.

He looked up suddenly and perceived that something unusual was the matter with Ann. Her face was flushed, her eyes were red and hard.

'Didn't let 'em in?'

'No! They didn't come in at all.'

He was too astonished for words.

'I answered the door,' said Ann; 'I'd been upstairs 'namelling the floor. 'Ow was I to think about Callers, Artie? We ain't never 'ad Callers all the time we been 'ere. I'd sent Gwendolen out for a bref of fresh air, and there I was upstairs 'namelling that floor she done so bad, so's to get it done before she came back. I thought I'd 'namel that floor and then get tea and 'ave it quiet with you, toce and all, before she came back. 'Ow was I to think about Callers?'

She paused. 'Well,' said Kipps, 'what then?'

'They came and rapped. 'Ow was I to know? I thought it was a tradesman or something. Never took my apron off, never wiped the 'namel off my 'ands – nothing. There they was!'

She paused again. She was getting to the disagreeable part.

'Wad they say?' said Kipps.

'She says, "Is Mrs Kipps at home?" See? To me.'

'Yes.'

'And me all painty and no cap on and nothing, neither missis nor servant like. There, Artie, I could 'a sunk through the floor with shame, I really could. I could 'ardly get my voice. I couldn't think of nothing to say but just, "Not at 'Ome," and out of 'abit like I 'eld the tray. And they give me the cards and went, and 'ow I shall ever look that lady in the face again I don't know . . . And that's all about it, Artie! They looked me up and down, they did, and then I shut the door on 'em.'

'Goo!' said Kipps.

Ann went and poked the fire needlessly with a passion-quivering hand.

'I wouldn't 'ave 'ad that 'appen for five pounds,' said Kipps. 'A clergy-man and all!'

Ann dropped the poker into the fender with some *éclat* and stood up and looked at her hot face in the glass. Kipps's disappointment grew. 'You did ought to 'ave known better than that, Ann! You reely did.'

He sat forward, cards in hand, with a deepening sense of social disaster. The plates were laid upon the table, toast sheltered under a cover at mid-fender, the teapot warmed beside it, and the kettle, just lifted from the hob, sang amidst the coals. Ann glanced at him for a moment, then stooped with the kettle-holder to wet the tea.

'Tcha!' said Kipps, with his mental state developing.

'I don't see it's any use getting in a state about it now,' said Ann.

'Don't you? I do. See? 'Ere's these people, good people, want to 'sociate with us, and 'ere you go and slap 'em in the face!'

'I didn't slap 'em in the face.'

'You do – practically. You slams the door in their face, and that's all we see of 'em ever. I wouldn't 'ave 'ad this 'appen not for a ten-pound note.'

He rounded his regrets with a grunt. For a while there was silence, save for the little stir of Ann's movements preparing the tea.

'Tea, Artie,' said Ann, handing him a cup.

Kipps took it.

'I put sugar *once*,' said Ann.

'Oo, dash it! Oo cares?' said Kipps, taking an extraordinarily large additional lump with fury-quivering fingers, and putting his cup with a slight excess of force on the recess cupboard. 'Oo cares?

'I wouldn't 'ave 'ad that 'appen,' he said, bidding steadily against accomplished things, 'for twenty pounds.'

He gloomed in silence through a long minute or so. Then Ann said the fatal thing that exploded him. 'Artie!' she said.

'What?'

'There's Buttud Toce down there! By your foot!' There was a pause, husband and wife regarded one another.

'Buttud Toce!' he said. 'You go and mess up them callers and then you try and stuff me up with Buttud Toce! Buttud Toce indeed! 'Ere's our first chance of knowing anyone that's at all fit to 'sociate with – Look 'ere, Ann! Tell you what it is – you got to return that call.'

'Return that call!'

'Yes, you got to return that call. That's what you got to do! I know – ' He waved his arm vaguely towards the miscellany of books in the recess. 'It's in *Manners and Rools of Good S'ity*. You got to find jest 'ow many cards to leave and you got to go and leave 'em. See?'

Ann's face expressed terror. 'But, Artie, 'ow *can* I?'

' 'Ow *can* you? 'Ow *could* you? You got to do it, any'ow. They won't know you – not in your Bond Street 'at! If they do, they won't say nothing.'

His voice assumed a note of entreaty. 'You mus', Ann.'

'I can't.'

'You mus'.'

'I can't and I won't. Anything in reason I'll do, but face those people again I can't – after what 'as 'appened.'

'You won't?'

'No!'

'So there they go – orf! And we never see them again! And so it goes on! So it goes on! We don't know nobody and we *shan't* know anybody!

And you won't put yourself out not a little bit, or take the trouble to find out anything 'ow it ought to be done.'

Terrible pause.

'I never ought to 'ave merried you, Artie, that's the troof.'

'Oh! *don't* go into that.'

'I never ought to 'ave merried you, Artie. I'm not equal to the position. If you 'adn't said you'd drown yourself – ' She choked.

'I don' see why you shouldn't *try*, Ann. *I've* improved. Why don't you? 'Stead of which you go sending out the servant and 'namelling floors, and then when visitors come – '

' 'Ow was *I* to know about y'r old visitors?' cried Ann in a wail, and suddenly got up and fled from amidst their ruined tea, the tea of which 'toce, all buttery' was to be the crown and glory.

Kipps watched her with a momentary consternation. Then he hardened his heart. 'Ought to 'ave known better,' he said, 'goin' on like that!' He remained for a space rubbing his knees and muttering. He emitted scornfully: 'I carn't an' I won't.' He saw her as the source of all his shames.

Presently, quite mechanically, he stooped down and lifted the flowery china cover. 'Ter dash 'er Buttud Toce!' he shouted at the sight of it, and clapped the cover down again hard –

When Gwendolen came back she perceived things were in a slightly unusual poise. Kipps sat by the fire in a rigid attitude reading a casually selected volume of the *Encyclopaedia Britannica*, and Ann was upstairs and inaccessible – to reappear at a later stage with reddened eyes. Before the fire and still in a perfectly assimilable condition was what was evidently an untouched supply of richly buttered toast under a cracked cover.

'They've 'ad a bit of a tiff,' said Gwendolen, attending to her duties in the kitchen, with her outdoor hat still on and her mouth full. 'They're rummuns – if ever! My eye!'

And she took another piece of Ann's generously buttered toast.

4

The Kippses spoke no more that day to one another.

The squabble about cards and buttered toast was as serious to them as the most rational of differences. It was all rational to them. Their sense of wrong burnt within them; their sense of what was owing to themselves, the duty of implacability, the obstinacy of pride. In the small hours Kipps lay awake at the nadir of unhappiness and came near groaning. He saw life as an extraordinarily desolating muddle: his futile house, his social discredit, his bad behaviour to Helen, his low marriage to Ann . . .

He became aware of something irregular in Ann's breathing –

He listened. She was awake and quietly and privately sobbing!

He hardened his heart; resolutely he hardened his heart.

And presently Ann lay still.

5

The stupid little tragedies of these clipped and limited lives!

What is the good of keeping up the idyllic sham and pretending that ill-educated, misdirected people 'get along very well', and that all this is harmlessly funny and nothing more? You think I'm going to write fat, silly, grinning novels about half-educated, under-trained people and keep it up all the time, that the whole thing's nothing but funny!

As I think of them lying unhappily there in the darkness, my vision pierces the night. See what I can see! Above them, brooding over them, I tell you, there is a monster, a lumpish monster, like some great, clumsy griffin thing, like the Crystal Palace labyrinthodon, like Coote, like the leaden goddess of *The Dunciad*,[38] like some fat, proud flunkey, like pride, like indolence, like all that is darkening and heavy and obstructive in life. It is matter and darkness, it is the anti-soul, it is the ruling power of this land, Stupidity. My Kippses live in its shadow. Shalford and his apprenticeship system, the Hastings Academy, the ideas of Coote, the ideas of the old Kippses, all the ideas that have made Kipps what he is, all these are a part of its shadow. But for that monster they might not be groping among false ideas and hurt one another so sorely; but for that, the glowing promise of childhood and youth might have had a happier fruition, thought might have awakened in them to meet the thought of the world, the quickening sunshine of literature pierced to the substance of their souls, their lives might not have been divorced, as now they are divorced, from the apprehension of beauty that we favoured ones are given – the vision of the Grail that makes life fine for ever. I have laughed, and I laugh at these two people; I have sought to make you laugh . . .

But I see through the darkness the souls of my Kippses as they are, as little pink strips of quivering living stuff, as things like the bodies of little, ill-nourished, ailing, ignorant children, children who feel pain, who are naughty and muddled and suffer and do not understand why. And the claw of this Beast rests upon them!

CHAPTER THREE

Terminations

Next morning came a remarkable telegram from Folkestone. 'Please come at once, urgent, Walshingham,' said the telegram, and Kipps, after an agitated but still ample breakfast, departed . . .

When he returned his face was very white and his countenance disordered. He let himself in with his latchkey and came into the dining-room where Ann sat, affecting to work at a little thing she called a bib. She heard his hat fall in the hall before he entered, as though he had missed the peg. 'I got something to tell you, Ann,' he said, disregarding their overnight quarrel, and went to the hearthrug and took hold of the mantel, and stared at Ann as though the sight of her was novel.

'Well?' said Ann, not looking up and working a little faster.

' 'E's gone!'

Ann looked up sharply and her hands stopped. '*Who's* gone?'

For the first time she perceived Kipps's pallor.

'Young Walshingham – I saw 'er and she tole me.'

'Gone? What d'you mean?'

'Cleared out! Gone off for good!'

'What for?'

'For 'is 'ealth,' said Kipps, with sudden bitterness. ' 'E's been specky-lating. He's speckylated our money and 'e's speckylated their money, and now 'e's took 'is 'ook. That's all about it, Ann.'

'You mean – ?'

'I mean 'e's orf and our twenty-four thousand's orf too! And 'ere we are! Smashed up! That's all about it, Ann.' He panted.

Ann had no vocabulary for such an occasion. 'Oh, Lor'!' she said, and sat still.

Kipps came about and stuck his hands deeply in his trouser pockets. 'Speckylated every penny – lorst it all – and gorn.'

Even his lips were white.

'You mean we ain't got nothin' left, Artie?'

'Not a penny! Not a bloomin' penny, Ann. No!'

A gust of passion whirled across the soul of Kipps. He flung out a knuckly fist. 'If I 'ad 'im 'ere,' he said, 'I'd – I'd – I'd wring 'is neck for 'im. I'd – I'd – ' His voice rose to a shout. He thought of Gwendolen in the kitchen and fell to, 'Ugh!'

'But, Artie,' said Ann, trying to grasp it, 'd'you mean to say he's took our money?'

'Speckylated it!' said Kipps, with an illustrative flourish of the arm that failed to illustrate. 'Bort things dear and sold 'em cheap, and played the 'anky-panky jackass with everything we got. That's what I mean 'e's done, Ann.' He repeated this last sentence with the addition of violent adverbs.

'D'you mean to say our money's *gone*, Artie?'

'Ter dash it, *Yes*, Ann!' swore Kipps, exploding in a shout. 'Ain't I tellin' you?'

He was immediately sorry. 'I didn't mean to 'oller at you, Ann,' he said, 'but I'm all shook up. I don't 'ardly know what I'm sayin'. Ev'ry penny.' . . .

'But, Artie – '

Kipps grunted. He went to the window and stared for a moment at a sunlit sea. 'Gord!' he swore.

'I mean,' he said, coming back to Ann and with an air of exasperation, 'that he's 'bezzled and 'ooked it. That's what I mean, Ann.'

Ann put down the bib. 'But wot are we going to *do*, Artie?'

Kipps indicated ignorance, wrath and despair with one comprehensive gesture of his hands. He caught an ornament from the mantel and replaced it. 'I'm going to bang about,' he said, 'if I ain't precious careful.'

'You saw '*er*, you say?'

'Yes.'

'What did she say 'xactly?' said Ann.

'Told me to see a s'licitor – tole me to get someone to 'elp me at once. She was there in black – like she used to be – and speaking cool and careful-like. 'Elen! . . . She's precious 'ard, is 'Elen. She looked at me straight. "It's my fault," she said, "I ought to 'ave warned you . . . Only under the circumstances it was a little difficult." Straight as anything. I didn't 'ardly say anything to 'er. I didn't seem to begin to take it in until she was showing me out. I 'adn't anything to say. Jest as well, perhaps. She talked – like a Call a'most. She said – what *was* it she said about her mother? "My mother's overcome with grief," she said, "so naturally everything comes on me." '

'And she told you to get someone to 'elp you?'

'Yes. I been to old Bean.'

'O' Bean?'

'Yes. What I took my business away from!'

'What did he say?'

'He was a bit off'and at first, but then 'e come round. He couldn't tell me anything till 'e knew the facts. What I know of young Walshingham, there won't be much 'elp in the facts. No!'

He reflected for a space. 'It's a smash-up, Ann. More likely than not, Ann, 'e's left us over'ead in debt. We got to get out of it just 'ow we can . . .

'We got to begin again,' he went on. ''Ow, I don't know. All the way 'ome my 'ead's been going. We got to get a living some'ow or other. 'Aving time to ourselves, and a bit of money to spend, and no hurry and worry, it's all over for ever, Ann. We was fools, Ann. We didn't know our benefits. We been caught. Gord! . . . Gord!'

He was on the verge of 'banging about' again.

They heard a jingle in the passage, the large soft impact of a servant's indoor boots. As if she were a part, a mitigatory part, of Fate, came Gwendolen to lay the midday meal. Kipps displayed self-control forthwith. Ann picked up the bib again and bent over it, and the Kippses bore themselves gloomily perhaps, but not despairfully, while their dependant was in the room. She spread the cloth and put out the cutlery with a slow inaccuracy, and Kipps, after a whisper to himself, went again to the window. Ann got up and put away her work methodically in the chiffonier.

'When I think,' said Kipps, as soon as the door closed again behind Gwendolen, 'when I think of the ole people and 'aving to tell 'em of it all – I want to smesh my 'ead against the nearest wall. Smesh my silly brains out! And Buggins – Buggins what I'd 'arf promised to start in a lill' outfitting shop in Rendezvous Street.' . . .

Gwendolen returned and restored dignity.

The midday meal spread itself slowly before them. Gwendolen, after her custom, left the door open and Kipps closed it carefully before sitting down.

He stood for a moment, regarding the meal doubtfully.

'I don't feel as if I could swaller a mouffül,' he said.

'You got to eat,' said Ann . . .

For a time they said little, and once swallowing was achieved, ate on with a sort of melancholy appetite. Each was now busy thinking.

'After all,' said Kipps, presently, 'whatever 'appens, they can't turn us out or sell us up before nex' quarter-day. I'm pretty sure about that.'

'Sell us up!' said Ann.

'I dessey we're bankrup',' said Kipps, trying to say it easily and helping himself with a trembling hand to unnecessary potatoes.

Then a long silence. Ann ceased to eat, and there were silent tears.

'More potatoes, Artie?' choked Ann.

'I couldn't,' said Kipps. 'No.'

He pushed back his plate, which was indeed replete with potatoes, got up and walked about the room. Even the dinner-table looked distraught and unusual.

'What to do, I *don't* know,' he said.

'Oh, *Lord*!' he ejaculated, and picked up and slapped down a book.

Then his eye fell upon another postcard that had come from Chitterlow by the morning's post, and which now lay by him on the mantelshelf. He took it up, glanced at its imperfectly legible message, and put it down.

'Delayed!' he said, scornfully. 'Not prodooced in the smalls. Or is it smells 'e says? 'Ow can one understand that? Any'ow 'e's 'umbugging again . . . Somefing about the Strand. No! Well, 'e's 'ad all the money 'e'll ever get out of me! . . . I'm done.'

He seemed to find a momentary relief in the dramatic effect of his announcement. He came near to a swagger of despair upon the hearthrug, and then suddenly came and sat down next to Ann and rested his chin on the knuckles of his two clenched hands.

'I been a fool, Ann,' he said in a gloomy monotone. 'I been a brasted fool. But it's 'ard on us, all the same. It's 'ard.'

' 'Ow was you to know?' said Ann.

'I ought to 'ave known. I did in a sort of way know. And 'ere we are! I wouldn't care so much if it was myself, but it's *you*, Ann! 'Ere we are! Regular smashed up! And you – ' He checked at an unspeakable aggravation of their disaster. 'I knew 'e wasn't to be depended upon and there I left it! And you got to pay . . . What's to 'appen to us all, I don't know.'

He thrust out his chin and glared at fate.

' 'Ow do you know 'e's speckylated everything?' said Ann, after a silent survey of him.

' 'E 'as,' said Kipps, irritably, holding firm to disaster.

'She say so?'

'She don't know, of course, but you depend upon it that's it. She told me she knew something was on, and when she found 'im gone and a note lef' for her she knew it was up with 'im. 'E went by the night boat. She wrote that telegrarf off to me straight away.'

Ann surveyed his features with tender, perplexed eyes; she had never seen him so white and drawn before, and her hand rested an inch or so away from his arm. The actual loss was still, as it were, afar from her. The immediate thing was his enormous distress.

' 'Ow do you know – ?' she said and stopped. It would irritate him too much.

Kipps's imagination was going headlong.

'Sold up!' he emitted presently, and Ann flinched. 'Going back to work, day after day – I can't stand it, Ann, I can't. And you – '

'It don't do to think of it,' said Ann.

Presently he came upon a resolve. 'I keep on thinking of it, and thinking of it, and what's to be done and what's to be done. I shan't be any good 'ome s'arfernoon. It keeps on going round and round in my 'ead, and round and round . I better go for a walk or something. I'd be no comfort to you, Ann. I should want to 'owl and 'ammer things if I 'ung about 'ome. My fingers 'r all atwitch. I shall keep on thinking 'ow I might 'ave stopped it and callin' myself a fool . . . '

He looked at her between pleading and shame. It seemed like deserting her.

Ann regarded him with tear-dimmed eyes.

'You'd better do what's good for you, Artie,' she said . . . '*I'll* be best cleaning. It's no use sending off Gwendolen before her month, and the top room wants turning out.' She added with a sort of grim humour: 'May as well turn it out now while I got it.'

'I *better* go for a walk,' said Kipps . . .

And presently our poor exploded Kipps was marching out to bear his sudden misery. Habit turned him up the road towards his growing house, and then suddenly he perceived his direction – 'Oh, Lor'!' – and turned aside and went up the steep way to the hill crest and the Sandling Road, and over the line by that tree-embowered Junction, and athwart the wide fields towards Postling – a little, black, marching figure – and so up the Downs and over the hills, whither he had never gone before . . .

2

He came back long after dark, and Ann met him in the passage.

'Where you been, Artie?' she asked, with a strained note in her voice.

'I been walking and walking – trying to tire myself out. All the time I been thinking what shall I do? Trying to fix something up all out of nothing.'

'I didn't know you meant to be out all this time.'

Kipps was gripped by compunction . . .

'I can't think what we ought to do,' he said, presently.

'You can't do anything much, Artie, not till you hear from Mr Bean.'

'No; I can't do anything much. That's jest it. And all this time I keep feelin' if I don't do something the top of my 'ead'll bust . . . Been trying to make up advertisements 'arf the time I been out – 'bout finding a place; good salesman and stock-keeper, and good Manchester dresses, window-dressing – Lor'! Fancy that all beginning again! . . . If you went to stay with Sid a bit – if I sent every penny I got to you – I dunno! I dunno!'

When they had gone to bed there was an elaborate attempt to get to sleep . . . In one of their great waking pauses Kipps remarked in a muffled tone: 'I didn't mean to frighten you, Ann, being out so late. I kep' on walking and walking, and some'ow it seemed to do me good. I went out to the 'illtop ever so far beyond Stanford, and sat there ever so long, and it seemed to make me better. Just looking over the Marsh like, and seeing the sun set . . .'

'Very likely,' said Ann, after a long interval, 'it isn't so bad as you think it is, Artie.'

'It's bad,' said Kipps.

'Very likely, after all, it isn't quite so bad. If there's only a little – '

There came another long silence.

'Ann,' said Kipps in the quiet darkness.

'Yes,' said Ann.

'Ann,' said Kipps, and stopped as though he had hastily shut a door upon speech.

'I kep' thinking,' he said, trying again, 'I kep' thinking – after all – I been cross with you and a fool about things – about them cards, Ann; but' – his voice shook to pieces – 'we 'ave been 'appy, Ann . . . some'ow . . . togever.'

And with that he and then she fell into a passion of weeping. They clung very tightly together – closer than they had been since ever the first brightness of their married days turned to the grey of common life again.

All the disaster in the world could not prevent their going to sleep at last with their poor little troubled heads close together on one pillow. There was nothing more to be done, there was nothing more to be thought. Time might go on with his mischiefs, but for a little while at least they still had one another.

Kipps returned from his second interview with Mr Bean in a state of strange excitement. He let himself in with his latchkey and slammed the door.

'Ann!' he shouted, in an unusual note; 'Ann!'

Ann replied distantly.

'Something to tell you,' said Kipps; 'something noo!'

Ann appeared apprehensive from the kitchen.

'Ann,' he said, going before her into the little dining-room, for his news was too dignified for the passage, 'very likely, Ann, o' Bean says, we shall 'ave – ' He decided to prolong the suspense. 'Guess!'

'I can't, Artie.'

'Think of a lot of money!'

'A 'undred pounds p'r'aps?'

He spoke with immense deliberation. '*Over a fousand pounds!*'

Ann stared and said nothing, only went a shade whiter.

'Over, he said. A'most certainly over.'

He shut the dining-room door and came forward hastily, for Ann, it was clear, meant to take this mitigation of their disaster with a complete abandonment of her self-control. She came near flopping; she fell into his arms.

'Artie,' she got to at last and began to weep, clinging tightly to him.

'Pretty near certain,' said Kipps, holding her. 'A fousand pounds!'

'I *said*, Artie,' she wailed on his shoulder with the note of accumulated wrongs, 'very likely it wasn't so bad . . . '

'There's things,' he said, when presently he came to particulars, ' 'e couldn't touch. The noo place! It's freehold and paid for, and with the bit of building on it, there's five or six 'undred pound p'r'aps – say worf free 'undred, for safety. We can't be sold up to finish it, like we thought. O' Bean says we can very likely sell it and get money. 'E says you often get a chance to sell a 'ouse lessen 'arf done, specially free'old. *Very* likely, 'e say. Then there's Hughenden. Hughenden 'asn't been mortgaged not for more than 'arf its value. There's a 'undred or so to be got on that, and the furniture and the rent for the summer still coming in. 'E says there's very likely other things. A fousand pounds, that's what 'e said. 'E said it might even be more . . . '

They were sitting now at the table.

'It alters everything,' said Ann.

'I been thinking that, Ann, all the way 'ome. I came in the motor car.

First ride I've 'ad since the smash. We needn't send off Gwendolen, leastways not till *after*. You know. We needn't turn out of 'ere – not for a long time. What we been doing for the o' people we can go on doing a'most as much. And your mother! . . . I wanted to 'oller, coming along. I pretty near run coming down the road by the hotel.'

'Oh, I *am* glad we can stop 'ere and be comfortable a bit,' said Ann. 'I *am* glad for that.'

'I pretty near told the driver on the motor – only 'e was the sort won't talk . . . You see, Ann, we'll be able to start a shop, we'll be able to get *into* something like. All about our 'aving to go back to places and that; all that doesn't matter any more.'

For a while they abandoned themselves to ejaculating transports. Then they fell talking to shape an idea to themselves of the new prospect that opened before them.

'We must start a sort of shop,' said Kipps, whose imagination had been working. 'It'll 'ave to be a shop.'

'Drapery?' said Ann.

'You want such a lot of capital for the drapery; mor'n a thousand pounds you want by a long way – to start it anything like proper.'

'Well, outfitting. Like Buggins was going to do.'

Kipps glanced at that for a moment, because the idea had not occurred to him. Then he came back to his prepossession.

'Well, I thought of something else, Ann,' he said. 'You see, I've always thought a little bookshop – It isn't like the drapery – 'aving to be learnt. I thought – even before this smash-up – 'ow I'd like to 'ave something to do, instead of always 'aving 'olidays always like we 'ave been 'aving.'

She reflected.

'You don't know *much* about books, do you, Artie?'

'You don't want to.' He illustrated. 'I noticed when we used to go to that lib'ry at Folkestone, ladies weren't anything like what they was in a draper's – if you 'aven't got *just* what they want it's "Oh, no!" and out they go. But in a bookshop it's different. One book's very like another – after all, what is it? Something to read and be done with. It's not a thing that matters like print dresses or serviettes – where you either like 'em or don't, and people judge you by. They take what you give 'em in bookshops and lib'ries, and glad to be told *what* to take. See 'ow we was – up at that lib'ry . . . '

He paused. 'You see, Ann –

'Well, I read 'n 'dvertisement the other day – I been asking Mr Bean. It said – five 'undred pounds.'

'What did?'

'Branches,' said Kipps.

Ann failed to understand. 'It's a sort of thing that gets up bookshops all over the country,' said Kipps. 'I didn't tell you, but I arst about it a bit. On'y I dropped it again. Before this smash, I mean. I'd thought I'd like to keep a shop for a lark, on'y then I thought it silly. Besides it 'ud 'ave been beneath me.'

He blushed vividly. 'It was a sort of projek of mine, Ann.

'On'y it wouldn't 'ave done,' he added.

It was a tortuous journey when the Kippses set out to explain anything to each other. But through a maze of fragmentary elucidations and questions, their minds did presently begin to approximate to a picture of a compact, bright, little shop as a framework for themselves.

'I thought of it one day when I was in Folkestone. I thought of it one day when I was looking in at a window. I see a chap dressin' a window and he was whistlin' reg'lar light-'arted . . . I thought then I'd like to keep a bookshop, any'ow, jest for something to do. And when people weren't about, then you could sit and read the books. See? It wouldn't be 'arf bad . . . '

They mused, each with elbows on table and knuckles to lips, looking with speculative eyes at each other.

'Very likely we'll be 'appier than we should 'ave been with more money,' said Kipps presently.

'We wasn't 'ardly suited – ' reflected Ann, and left her sentence incomplete.

'Fish out of water like,' said Kipps . . .

'You won't 'ave to return that call now,' said Kipps, opening a new branch of the question. 'That's one good thing.'

'Lor'!' said Ann, visibly brightening, 'no more I shan't!'

'I don't s'pose they'd want you to, even if you did – with things as they are.'

A certain added brightness came into Ann's face. 'Nobody won't be able to come leaving cards on us, Artie, now, any more. We are out of *that*!'

'There isn't no necessity for us to be stuck up,' said Kipps, 'any more for ever! 'Ere we are, Ann, common people, with jest no position at all, as you might say, to keep up. No se'v'nts, not if you don't like. No dressin' better than other people. If it wasn't we been robbed – dashed if I'd care a rap about losing that money. I b'lieve' – his face shone with the rare pleasure of paradox – 'I reely b'lieve, Ann, it'll prove a savin' in the end.'

The remarkable advertisement which had fired Kipps's imagination with this dream of a bookshop opened out in the most alluring way. It was one little facet in a comprehensive scheme of transatlantic origin, which was to make our old-world methods of bookselling 'sit up', and it displayed an imaginative briskness, a lucidity and promise, that aroused the profoundest scepticism in the mind of Mr Bean. To Kipps's renewed investigations it presented itself in an expository illustrated pamphlet (far too well printed, Mr Bean thought, for a reputable undertaking) of the most convincing sort. Mr Bean would not let him sink his capital in shares in its projected company that was to make all things new in the world of books, but he could not prevent Kipps becoming one of their associated booksellers. And so when presently it became apparent that an epoch was not to be made, and the 'Associated Booksellers' Trading Union (Limited)' receded and dissolved and liquidated (a few drops) and vanished and went away to talk about something else, Kipps remained floating undamaged in this interestingly uncertain universe as an independent bookseller.

Except that it failed, the Associated Booksellers' Trading Union had all the stigmata of success. Its fault, perhaps, was that it had them all instead of only one or two. It was to buy wholesale for all its members and associates and exchange stock, having a common books-in-stock list and a common lending library, and it was to provide a uniform registered shopfront to signify all these things to the intelligent passer-by. Except that it was controlled by buoyant young Overmen with a touch of genius in their arithmetic, it was, I say, a most plausible and hopeful project. Kipps went several times to London and an agent came to Hythe; Mr Bean made some timely interventions, and then behind a veil of planks and an announcement in the High Street, the uniform registered shopfront came rapidly into being. 'Associated Booksellers' Trading Union' said this shopfront, in a refined, artistic lettering that bookbuyers were going to value as wise men over forty value the proper label for Berncasteler Doctor, and then, 'Arthur Kipps'.

Next to starting a haberdasher's shop, I doubt if Kipps could have been more truly happy than during those weeks of preparation.

There is, of course, nothing on earth, and I doubt at times if there is a joy in heaven, like starting a small haberdasher's shop. Imagine, for example, having a drawerful of tapes (one whole piece most exquisitely blocked of every possible width of tape), or, again, an army of neat, large packages, each displaying one sample of hooks and eyes. Think of your cottons, your drawer of coloured silks, the little, less, least of the compartments and thin packets of your needle drawer! Poor princes and wretched gentlefolk mysteriously above retail trade, may taste only the faint unsatisfactory shadow of these delights with trays of stamps or butterflies. I write, of course, for those to whom these things appeal; there are clods alive who see nothing, or next to nothing, in spools of mercerised cotton and endless bands of paper-set pins. I write for the wise, and as I write I wonder that Kipps resisted haberdashery. He did. Yet even starting a bookshop is at least twenty times as interesting as building your own house to your own design in unlimited space and time, or any possible thing people with indisputable social position and sound securities can possibly find to do. Upon that I rest.

You figure Kipps 'going to have a look to see how the little shop is getting on', the shop that is not to be a loss and a spending of money, but a gain. He does not walk too fast towards it; as he comes into view of it his paces slacken and his head goes to one side. He crosses to the pavement opposite in order to inspect the fascia better; already his name is adumbrated in faint white lines; stops in the middle of the road and scrutinises imaginary details for the benefit of his future next-door neighbour, the curiosity-shop man, and so at last, in . . . A smell of paint and of the shavings of imperfectly seasoned pinewood! The shop is already glazed and a carpenter is busy over the fittings for adjustable shelves in the side windows. A painter is busy on the fixtures round about (shelving above and drawers below), which are to accommodate most of the stock, and the counter – the counter and desk are done. Kipps goes inside the desk, the desk which is to be the strategic centre of the shop, brushes away some sawdust, and draws out the marvellous till: here gold is to be, here silver, here copper – notes locked up in a cashbox in the well below. Then he leans his elbows on the desk, rests his chin on his fist and fills the shelves with imaginary stock; books beyond reading. Every day a man who cares to wash his hands and read uncut pages artfully may have his cake and eat it, among that stock. Under the counter to the right, paper and string are to lurk, ready to leap up and embrace goods sold; on the table to the left, art publications, whatever they may prove to be! He maps it out, serves an imaginary customer, receives a dream seven and six-pence, packs, bows out. He wonders how it was he ever came to fancy a shop a disagreeable place.

'It's different,' he says at last, after musing on that difficulty, 'being your own.'

It *is* different –

Or, again, you figure Kipps with something of the air of a young sacristan, handling his brightly virginal account-books, and looking, and looking again, and then still looking, at an unparalleled specimen of copperplate engraving, ruled money below and above bearing the words 'In Account with **ARTHUR KIPPS**' (loud flourishes), 'The Booksellers' Trading Union' (temperate decoration). You figure Ann sitting and stitching at one point of the circumference of the light of the lamp, stitching queer little garments for some unknown stranger, and over against her sits Kipps. Before him is one of those engraved memorandum forms, a moist pad, wet with some thick and greasy greenish-purple ink that is also spreading quietly but steadily over his fingers, a cross-nibbed pen for first-aid surgical assistance to the patient in his hand, a dating rubber stamp. At intervals he brings down this latter with great care and emphasis upon the paper, and when he lifts it there appears a beautiful oval design of which 'Paid, Arthur Kipps, The Associated Booksellers' Trading Union' and a date are the essential ingredients, stamped in purple ink.

Anon he turns his attention to a box of small, round, yellow labels, declaring, 'This book was bought from the Associated Booksellers' Trading Union.' He licks one with deliberate care, sticks it on the paper before him and defaces it with great solemnity. 'I can do it, Ann,' he says, looking up brightly. For the Associated Booksellers' Trading Union, among other brilliant notions and inspirations, devised an ingenious system of taking back its books again in part payment for new ones within a specified period. When it failed, all sorts of people were left with these unredeemed pledges in hand.

5

Amidst all this bustle and interest, all this going to and fro before they 'moved in' to the High Street, came the great crisis that hung over the Kippses, and one morning in the small hours Ann's child was born . . .

Kipps was coming to manhood swiftly now. The once rabbit-like soul that had been so amazed by the discovery of 'chubes' in the human interior and so shocked by the sight of a woman's shoulder-blades, that had found shame and anguish in a mislaid Gibus and terror in an Anagram Tea, was at last facing the greater realities. He came suddenly upon the master thing in life, birth. He passed through hours of listening, hours of impotent fear in the night and in the dawn, and then there was put into his arms something most wonderful, a weak and wailing creature, incredibly, heart-stirringly soft and pitiful, with minute appealing hands that it wrung his heart to see. He held this miracle in his arms and touched its tender cheek as if he feared his lips might injure it. And this marvel was his Son!

And there was Ann, with a greater strangeness and a greater familiarity in her quality than he had ever found before. There were little beads of perspiration on her temples and her lips, and her face was flushed, not pale as he had feared to see it. She had the look of one who emerges from some strenuous and invigorating act. He bent down and kissed her, and he had no words to say. She wasn't to speak much yet, but she stroked his arm with her hand and had to tell him one thing: 'He's over nine pounds, Artie,' she whispered. 'Bessie's – Bessie's wasn't no more than eight.'

To have given Kipps a pound of triumph over Sid seemed to her almost to justify Nunc Dimittis. She watched his face for a moment, then closed her eyes in a kind of blissful exhaustion as the nurse, with something motherly in her manner, pushed Kipps out of the room.

6

Kipps was far too much preoccupied with his own life to worry about the further exploits of Chitterlow. The man had got his two thousand; on the whole Kipps was glad he had had it rather than young Walshingham, and there was an end to the matter. As for the complicated transactions he achieved and proclaimed by mainly illegible and always incomprehensible postcards, they were like passing voices heard in the street as one goes about one's urgent concerns. Kipps put them aside and they got in between the pages of the stock and were lost for ever and sold in with the goods to customers who puzzled over them mightily.

Then one morning as our bookseller was dusting round before breakfast, Chitterlow returned, appeared suddenly in the shop doorway.

Kipps was overcome with amazement.

It was the most unexpected thing in the world. The man was in evening dress, evening dress in that singularly crumpled state it assumes after the hour of dawn, and above his dishevelled red hair, a smallish gibus had tilted rather forward. He opened the door and stood, tall and spread, with one vast white glove flung out as if to display how burst a glove might be, his eyes bright, such wrinkling of brow and mouth as only an experienced actor can produce, and a singular radiance of emotion upon his whole being; an altogether astonishing spectacle.

It was amazing beyond the powers of Kipps. The bell jangled for a bit and then gave it up and was silent. For a long second everything was quietly attentive. Kipps was amazed to his uttermost; had he had ten times the capacity he would still have been fully amazed. 'It's Chit'low!' he said at last, standing duster in hand.

But he doubted whether it was not a dream.

'Tzit!' gasped that most excitable and extraordinary person, still in an incredibly expanded attitude, and then with a slight forward jerk of the starry split glove, 'Bif!'

He could say no more. The tremendous speech he had had ready vanished from his mind. Kipps stared at his extraordinary facial changes, vaguely conscious of the truth of the teachings of Nisbet[39] and Lombroso[40] concerning men of genius.

Then suddenly Chitterlow's features were convulsed, the histrionic fell from him like a garment, and he was weeping. He said something indistinct about 'Old Kipps! *Good* old Kipps! Oh, old Kipps!' and somehow he managed to mix a chuckle and a sob in the most remarkable way. He emerged from somewhere near the middle of his original attitude, a merely life-size creature. 'My play, boo-hoo!' he sobbed, clutching at his friend's arm. 'My play, Kipps (sob)! You know?'

'Well?' cried Kipps, with his heart sinking in sympathy. 'It ain't – '

'No,' howled Chitterlow; 'no. It's a Success! My dear chap! my dear boy! Oh! It's a – bu – boo-hoo! – a Big Success!' He turned away and wiped streaming tears with the back of his hand. He walked a pace or so and turned. He sat down on one of the specially designed artistic chairs of the Associated Booksellers' Trading Union and produced an exiguous lady's handkerchief, extraordinarily belaced. He choked, '*My* play,' and covered his face here and there.

He made an unsuccessful effort to control himself, and shrank for a space to the dimensions of a small and pathetic creature. His great nose suddenly came through a careless place in the handkerchief.

'I'm knocked,' he said in a muffled voice, and so remained for a space – wonderful – veiled.

He made a gallant effort to wipe his tears away. 'I had to tell you,' he said, gulping. 'Be all right in a minute,' he added. 'Calm!' and sat still –

Kipps stared in commiseration of such success. Then he heard footsteps and went quickly to the house doorway. 'Jest a minute,' he said. 'Don't go in the shop, Ann, for a minute. It's Chitterlow. He's a bit essited. But he'll be better in a minute. It's knocked him over a bit. You see' – his voice sank to a hushed note as one who announces death – ' 'e's made a success with his play.'

He pushed her back lest she should see the scandal of another male's tears . . .

Soon Chitterlow felt better, but for a little while his manner was even alarmingly subdued. 'I *had* to come and tell you,' he said. 'I *had* to astonish someone. Muriel – she'll be first-rate, of course. But she's over at Dymchurch.' He blew his nose with enormous noise, and emerged instantly a merely garrulous optimist.

'I expect she'll be precious glad.'

'She doesn't know yet, my dear boy. She's at Dymchurch – with a friend. She's seen some of my first nights before . . . Better out of it . . . I'm going to her now. I've been up all night – talking to the boys and all that. I'm a bit off it just for a bit. But – it Knocked 'em. It Knocked everybody.'

He stared at the floor and went on in a monotone. 'They laughed a bit at the beginning – but nothing like a settled laugh – not until the second act – you know – the chap with the beetle down his neck. Little Chisholme did that bit to rights. Then they began – *to* rights.' His voice warmed and increased. 'Laughing! It made *me* laugh! We jumped 'em into the third act before they had time to cool. Everybody was on it. I never saw a first night go so fast. Laugh, laugh, laugh, LAUGH, LAUGH, LAUGH' (he howled the last repetition with stupendous violence). 'Everything they laughed at. They laughed at things that we hadn't meant to be funny – not for one moment. Bif! Bizz! Curtain. A Fair Knock-Out! . . . I went on – but I didn't say a word. Chisholme did the patter. Shouting! It was like walking under Niagara – going across that stage. It was like never having seen an audience before . . .

'Then afterwards – the Boys!'

His emotion held him for a space. 'Dear old Boys!' he murmured.

His words multiplied, his importance increased. In a little while he was restored to something of his old self. He was enormously excited. He seemed unable to sit down anywhere. He came into the breakfast-room so soon as Kipps was sure of him, shook hands with Mrs Kipps parenthetically, sat down and immediately got up again. He went to the bassinette in the corner and looked absent-mindedly at Kipps junior, and said he was glad if only for the youngster's sake. He immediately resumed the thread of his discourse . . . He drank a cup of coffee noisily and walked up and down the room talking, while they attempted break-fast amidst the gale of his excitement. The infant slept marvellously through it all.

'You won't mind my sitting down, Mrs Kipps. I couldn't sit down for anyone, or I'd do it for you. It's you I'm thinking of more than anyone, you and Muriel, and all Old Pals and Good Friends. It means wealth, it means money – hundreds and thousands . . . If you'd heard 'em, *you'd know*.'

He was silent through a portentous moment while topics battled for him and finally he burst and talked of them all together. It was like the rush of water when a dam bursts and washes out a fair-sized provincial town; all sorts of things floated along on the swirl. For example, he was discussing his future behaviour. 'I'm glad it's come now. Not before. I've had my lesson. I shall be very discreet now, trust me. We've learnt the value of money.' He discussed the possibility of a country house, of taking a Martello tower as a swimming-box (as one might say a shooting-box), of living in Venice because of its artistic associations and scenic possibilities, of a flat in Westminster or a house in the West End. He also raised the question of giving up smoking and drinking, and what classes of drink were especially noxious to a man of his constitution. But discourses on all this did not prevent a parenthetical computation of the probable profits on the supposition of a thousand nights here and in America, nor did it ignore the share Kipps was to have, nor the gladness with which Chitterlow would pay that share, nor the surprise and regret with which he had learnt, through an indirect source which awakened many associations, of the turpitude of young Walshingham, nor the distaste Chitterlow had always felt for young Walshingham and men of his type. An excursus upon Napoleon had got into the torrent somehow and kept bobbing up and down. The whole thing was thrown into the form of a single complex sentence, with parenthetical and subordinate clauses fitting one into the other like Chinese boxes, and from first to last it never even had an air of approaching anything in the remotest degree partaking of the nature of a full stop.

Into this deluge came the *Daily News*,[41] like the gleam of light in Watts's picture,[42] the waters were assuaged while its sheet was opened, and it had a column, a whole column, of praise. Chitterlow held the paper and Kipps read over his left hand, and Ann under his right. It made the affair more real to Kipps; it seemed even to confirm Chitterlow against lurking doubts he had been concealing. But it took him away. He departed in a whirl, to secure a copy of every morning paper, every blessed rag there was, and take them all to Dymchurch and Muriel forthwith. It had been the send-off the Boys had given him that had prevented his doing as much at Charing Cross – let alone that he only caught it by the skin of his teeth . . . Besides which the bookstall wasn't open. His white face, lit by a vast excitement, bid them a tremendous farewell, and he departed through the sunlight, with his buoyant walk buoyant almost to the tottering pitch. His hair, as one got it sunlit in the street, seemed to have grown in the night.

They saw him stop a newsboy.

'Every blessed rag' floated to them on the notes of that gorgeous voice.

The newsboy, too, had happened on luck. Something like a faint cheer from the newsboy came down the air to terminate that transaction.

Chitterlow went on his way swinging a great budget of papers, a figure of merited success. The newsboy recovered from his emotion with a jerk, examined something in his hand again, transferred it to his pocket, watched Chitterlow for a space, and then in a sort of hushed silence resumed his daily routine . . .

Ann and Kipps watched that receding happiness in silence, until he vanished round the bend of the road.

'I *am* glad,' said Ann at last, speaking with a little sigh.

'So'm I,' said Kipps, with emphasis. 'For if ever a feller 'as worked and waited – it's 'im.' . . .

They went back through the shop rather thoughtfully, and after a peep at the sleeping baby, resumed their interrupted breakfast. 'If ever a feller 'as worked and waited, it's 'im,' said Kipps, cutting bread.

'Very likely it's true,' said Ann, a little wistfully.

'What's true?'

'About all that money coming.'

Kipps meditated. 'I don't see why it shouldn't be,' he decided, and handed Ann a piece of bread on the tip of his knife.

'But we'll keep on the shop,' he said after an interval for further reflection, 'all the same . . . I 'aven't much trust in money after the things we've seen.'

7

That was two years ago, and as the whole world knows, the *Pestered Butterfly* is running still. It *was* true. It has made the fortune of a once declining little theatre in the Strand, night after night the great beetle scene draws happy tears from a house packed to repletion, and Kipps – for all that Chitterlow is not what one might call a businessman – is almost as rich as he was in the beginning. People in Australia, people in

Lancashire, Scotland, Ireland, in New Orleans, in Jamaica, in New York and Montreal, have crowded through doorways to Kipps's enrichment, lured by the hitherto unsuspected humours of the entomological drama. Wealth rises like an exhalation all over our little planet, and condenses, or at least some of it does, in the pockets of Kipps.

'It's rum,' said Kipps.

He sat in the little kitchen out behind the bookshop and philosophised and smiled, while Ann gave Arthur Waddy Kipps his evening tub before the fire. Kipps was always present at this ceremony unless customers prevented; there was something in the mixture of the odours of tobacco, soap and domesticity that charmed him unspeakably.

'Chuckerdee, o' man,' he said, affably, wagging his pipe at his son, and thought incidentally, after the manner of all parents, that very few children could have so straight and clean a body.

'Dadda's got a cheque,' said Arthur Waddy Kipps, emerging for a moment from the towel.

' E gets 'old of everything,' said Ann. 'You can't say a word – '

'Dadda got a cheque,' this marvellous child repeated.

'Yes, o' man, I got a cheque. And it's got to go into a bank for you, against when you got to go to school. See? So's you'll grow up knowing your way about a bit.'

'Dadda's got a cheque,' said the wonder son, and then gave his mind to making mighty splashes with his foot. Every time he splashed, laughter overcame him, and he had to be held up for fear he should tumble out of the tub in his merriment. Finally he was towelled to his toe-tips, wrapped up in warm flannel, and kissed, and carried off to bed by Ann's cousin and lady help, Emma. And then after Ann had carried away the bath into the scullery, she returned to find her husband with his pipe extinct and the cheque still in his hand.

'Two fousand pounds,' he said. 'It's dashed rum. Wot 'ave *I* done to get two fousand pounds, Ann?'

'What 'aven't you – not to?' said Ann.

He reflected upon this view of the case.

'I shan't never give up this shop,' he said at last.

'We're very 'appy 'ere,' said Ann.

'Not if I 'ad *fifty* fousand pounds.'

'No fear,' said Ann.

'You got a shop,' said Kipps, 'and you come along in a year's time and there it is. But money – look 'ow it come and goes! There's no sense in money. You may kill yourself trying to get it, and then it comes when you aren't looking. There's my 'riginal money! Where is it now? Gone!

And it's took young Walshingham with it, and 'e's gone, too. It's like playing skittles. 'Long comes the ball, right and left you fly, and there it is rolling away and not changed a bit. No sense in it! 'E's gone, and she's gone – gone off with that chap Revel, that sat with me at dinner. Married man! And Chit'low rich! Lor'! – what a fine place that Gerrik Club is, to be sure, where I 'ad lunch wiv' 'im! Better'n *any* 'otel. Footmen in powder they got – not waiters, Ann – footmen! 'E's rich and me rich – in a sort of way . . . Don't seem much sense in it, Ann, 'owever you look at it.' He shook his head.

'I know one thing,' said Kipps.

'What?'

'I'm going to put it in jest as many different banks as I can. See? Fifty 'ere, fifty there. 'Posit. I'm not going to 'nvest it – no fear.'

'It's only frowing money away,' said Ann.

'I'm 'arf a mind to bury some of it under the shop. Only I expect one 'ud always be coming down at nights to make sure it was there . . . I don't seem to trust anyone – not with money.' He put the cheque on the table corner and smiled and tapped his pipe on the grate, with his eyes on that wonderful document.

'S'pose old Bean started orf,' he reflected . . . 'One thing, 'e *is* a bit lame.'

' 'E wouldn't,' said Ann; 'not 'im.'

'I was only joking like.'

He stood up, put his pipe among the candlesticks on the mantel, took up the cheque and began folding it carefully to put it back in his pocketbook.

A little bell jangled.

'Shop!' said Kipps. 'That's right. Keep a shop and the shop'll keep you. That's 'ow I look at it, Ann.'

He drove his pocketbook securely into his breast pocket before he opened the living-room door . . .

But whether indeed it is the bookshop that keeps Kipps or whether it is Kipps who keeps the bookshop is just one of those commercial mysteries people of my unarithmetical temperament are never able to solve. They do very well, the dears, anyhow, thank heaven!

The bookshop of Kipps is on the left-hand side of the Hythe High Street coming from Folkestone, between the yard of the livery stable and the shop-window full of old silver and suchlike things – it is quite easy to find – and there you may see him for yourself and speak to him and buy this book of him if you like. He has it in stock, I know. Very delicately I've seen to that. His name is not Kipps, of course, you must understand that, but everything else is exactly as I have told you. You can talk to him about books, about politics, about going to Boulogne, about life, and the ups and downs of life. Perhaps he will quote you Buggins – from whom, by the by, one can now buy everything a gentleman's wardrobe should contain at the little shop in Rendezvous Street, Folkestone. If you are fortunate to find Kipps in a good mood he may even let you know how he inherited a fortune 'once'. 'Run froo it,' he'll say with a not unhappy smile. 'Got another afterwards – speckylating in plays. Needn't keep this shop if I didn't like. But it's something to do . . . '

Or he may be even more intimate. 'I seen some things,' he said to me once. 'Raver! Life! Why! once I – I *'loped*! I did – reely!'

(Of course you will not tell Kipps that he *is* 'Kipps', or that I have put him in this book. He has not the remotest suspicion of that. And you know, you never can tell how people are going to take that sort of thing. I am an old and trusted customer now, and for many amiable reasons I should prefer that things remained exactly on their present footing.)

8

One early-closing evening in July they left the baby to the servant cousin, and Kipps took Ann for a row on the Hythe canal. It was a glorious evening, and the sun set in a mighty blaze and left a world warm, and very still. The twilight came. And there was the water, shining bright, and the sky a deepening blue, and the great trees that dipped their boughs towards the water, exactly as it had been when he paddled home with Helen, when her eyes had seemed to him like dusky stars. He had ceased from rowing and rested on his oars, and suddenly he was touched by the wonder of life; the strangeness that is a presence stood again by his side.

Out of the darknesses beneath the shallow, weedy stream of his being rose a question, a question that looked up dimly and never reached the surface. It was the question of the wonder of the beauty, the purposeless, inconsecutive beauty, that falls so strangely among the happenings and memories of life. It never reached the surface of his mind, it never took to itself substance or form; it looked up merely as the phantom of a face might look, out of deep waters, and sank again to nothingness.

'Artie,' said Ann.

He woke up and pulled a stroke. 'What?' he said.

'Penny for your thoughts, Artie.'

He considered.

'I reely don't think I was thinking of anything,' he said at last with a smile. 'No.'

He still rested on his oars.

'I expect,' he said, 'I was thinking jest what a Rum Go everything is. I expect it was something like that.'

'Queer old Artie!'

'Ain't I? I don't suppose there ever was a chap quite like me before.'

He reflected for just another minute.

'Oo! I dunno,' he said, and roused himself to pull.

The History of Mr Polly

The History of Mr Polly

◆

H. G. WELLS

The History of Mr Polly was first published in Great Britain
in 1910 by Thomas Nelson & Sons, London,
and in the United States in 1909 by
Grosset & Dunlap, New York

Contents

CHAPTER ONE

Beginnings, and the Bazaar

'HOLE!' SAID MR POLLY, and then for a change, and with greatly increased emphasis: ''*Ole!*' He paused, and then broke out with one of his private and peculiar idioms. 'Oh! *Beastly* Silly Wheeze of a Hole!'

He was sitting on a stile between two threadbare-looking fields, and suffering acutely from indigestion.

He suffered from indigestion now nearly every afternoon of his life, but as he lacked introspection he projected the associated discomfort upon the world. Every afternoon he discovered afresh that life as a whole and every aspect of life that presented itself was 'beastly'. And this afternoon, lured by the delusive blueness of a sky that was blue because the wind was in the east, he had come out in the hope of snatching something of the joyousness of spring. The mysterious alchemy of mind and body refused, however, to permit any joyousness whatever in the spring.

He had had a little difficulty in finding his cap before he came out. He wanted his cap – the new golf cap – and Mrs Polly must needs fish out his old soft brown felt hat. ''*Ere*'s your 'at,' she said in a tone of insincere encouragement.

He had been routing among the piled newspapers under the kitchen dresser, and had turned quite hopefully and taken the thing. He put it on. But it didn't feel right. Nothing felt right. He put a trembling hand upon the crown of the thing and pressed it on his head, and tried it askew to the right and then askew to the left.

Then the full sense of the indignity offered him came home to him. The hat masked the upper sinister quarter of his face, and he spoke with a wrathful eye regarding his wife from under the brim. In a voice thick with fury he said: 'I s'pose you'd like me to wear that silly Mud Pie for ever, eh? I tell you I won't. I'm sick of it. I'm pretty near sick of everything, comes to that . . . Hat!'

He clutched it with quivering fingers. 'Hat!' he repeated. Then he flung it to the ground and kicked it with extraordinary fury across the kitchen. It flew up against the door and dropped to the ground with its ribbon-band half off.

'Shan't go out!' he said, and sticking his hands into his jacket pockets discovered the missing cap in the right one.

There was nothing for it but to go straight upstairs without a word, and out, slamming the shop door hard.

'Beauty!' said Mrs Polly at last to a tremendous silence, picking up and dusting the rejected headdress. 'Tantrums,' she added. 'I 'aven't patience.' And moving with the slow reluctance of a deeply offended woman, she began to pile together the simple apparatus of their recent meal, for transportation to the scullery sink.

The repast she had prepared for him did not seem to her to justify his ingratitude. There had been the cold pork from Sunday and some nice cold potatoes, and Rashdall's Mixed Pickles, of which he was inordinately fond. He had eaten three gherkins, two onions, a small cauliflower head and several capers with every appearance of appetite, and indeed with avidity; and then there had been cold suet pudding to follow, with treacle, and then a nice bit of cheese. It was the pale, hard sort of cheese he liked; red cheese he declared was indigestible. He had also had three big slices of greyish baker's bread, and had drunk the best part of the jugful of beer . . . But there seems to be no pleasing some people.

'Tantrums!' said Mrs Polly at the sink, struggling with the mustard on his plate and expressing the only solution of the problem that occurred to her.

And Mr Polly sat on the stile and hated the whole scheme of life – which was at once excessive and inadequate as a solution. He hated Foxbourne, he hated Foxbourne High Street, he hated his shop and his wife and his neighbours – every blessed neighbour – and with indescribable bitterness he hated himself.

'Why did I ever get in this silly Hole?' he said. 'Why did I ever?'

He sat on the stile, and looked with eyes that seemed blurred with impalpable flaws at a world in which even the spring buds were wilted, the sunlight metallic and the shadows mixed with blue-black ink.

To the moralist I know he might have served as a figure of sinful discontent, but that is because it is the habit of moralists to ignore material circumstances – if indeed one may speak of a recent meal as a circumstance rendering Mr Polly circum. Drink, indeed, our teachers will criticise nowadays both as regards quantity and quality, but neither church nor state nor school will raise a warning finger between a man and his hunger and his wife's catering. So on nearly every day in his life Mr Polly fell into a violent rage and hatred against the outer world in the afternoon, and never suspected that it was this inner world to which

I am with such masterly delicacy alluding that was thus reflecting its sinister disorder upon the things without. It is a pity that some human beings are not more transparent. If Mr Polly, for example, had been transparent or even passably translucent, then perhaps he might have realised from the Laocoön struggle[43] he would have glimpsed that indeed he was not so much a human being as a civil war.

Wonderful things must have been going on inside Mr Polly. Oh! wonderful things. It must have been like a badly managed industrial city during a period of depression: agitators, acts of violence, strikes, the forces of law and order doing their best, rushings to and fro, upheavals, the *Marseillaise*, tumbrils, the rumble and the thunder of the tumbrils –

I do not know why the east wind aggravates life to unhealthy people. It made Mr Polly's teeth seem loose in his head, and his skin feel like a misfit, and his hair a dry, stringy exasperation –

Why cannot doctors give us an antidote to the east wind?

'Never have the sense to get your hair cut till it's too long,' said Mr Polly, catching sight of his shadow, 'you blighted, degenerated Paint-brush! Ugh!' and he flattened down the projecting tails with an urgent hand.

2

Mr Polly's age was exactly thirty-five years and a half. He was a short, compact figure, and a little inclined to a localised *embonpoint*. His face was not unpleasing; the features fine, but a trifle too pointed about the nose to be classically perfect. The corners of his sensitive mouth were depressed. His eyes were ruddy brown and troubled, and the left one was round with more of wonder in it than its fellow. His complexion was dull and yellowish – that, as I have explained, on account of those civil disturbances. He was, in the technical sense of the word, clean shaved, with a small sallow patch under the right ear and a cut on the chin. His brow had the little puckerings of a thoroughly discontented man, little wrinklings and lumps, particularly over his right eye, and he sat with his hands in his pockets, a little askew on the stile, and swung one leg. 'Hole!' he repeated presently.

He broke into a quavering song. 'Ro–o–o–tten Be–e–astly Silly Hole!'

His voice thickened with rage, and the rest of his discourse was marred by an unfortunate choice of epithets.

He was dressed in a shabby black morning coat and waistcoat; the braid that bound these garments was a little loose in places; his collar was chosen from stock and had projecting corners; it was what was called in those days a 'wing-poke'; that and his tie, which was new and loose and rich in colouring, had been selected to encourage and stimulate customers – for he dealt in gentlemen's outfitting. His golf cap, which was also from stock and aslant over his eye, gave his misery a desperate touch. He wore brown leather boots – because he hated the smell of blacking.

Perhaps after all it was not simply indigestion that troubled him.

Behind the superficialities of Mr Polly's being, moved a larger and vaguer distress. The elementary education he had acquired had left him with the impression that arithmetic was a fluky science and best avoided in practical affairs, but even the absence of bookkeeping and a total inability to distinguish between capital and interest could not blind him for ever to the fact that the little shop in the High Street was not paying. An absence of returns, a constriction of credit, a depleted till, the most valiant resolves to keep smiling, could not prevail for ever against these insistent phenomena. One might bustle about in the morning before dinner and in the afternoon after tea and forget that huge dark cloud of insolvency that gathered and spread in the background, but it was part of the desolation of these afternoon periods, these grey spaces of time after meals, when all one's courage had descended to the unseen battles of the pit, that life seemed stripped to the bone and one saw with a hopeless clearness.

Let me tell the history of Mr Polly from the cradle to these present difficulties. 'First the infant, mewling and puking in its nurse's arms.'

There had been a time when two people had thought Mr Polly the most wonderful and adorable thing in the world, had kissed his toenails, saying 'myum, myum,' and marvelled at the exquisite softness and delicacy of his hair, had called to one another to remark the peculiar distinction with which he bubbled, had disputed whether the sound he had made was *just da da*, or truly and intentionally dadda, had washed him in the utmost detail, and wrapped him up in soft, warm blankets, and smothered him with kisses. A regal time that was, and four and thirty years ago; and a merciful forgetfulness barred Mr Polly from ever bringing its careless luxury, its autocratic demands and instant obedience, into contrast with his present condition of life. These two people had worshipped him from the crown of his head to the soles of his exquisite feet. And also they had fed him rather unwisely, for no one had ever troubled to teach his mother anything about the mysteries of a child's upbringing – though of course the monthly nurse and her charwoman gave some valuable hints – and by his fifth birthday the perfect rhythms of his nice new interior were already darkened with perplexity . . .

His mother died when he was seven.

He began only to have distinctive memories of himself in the time when his education had already begun.

I remember seeing a picture of Education – in some place. I think it was Education, but quite conceivably it represented the Empire teaching her Sons, and I have a strong impression that it was a wall painting upon some public building in Manchester or Birmingham or Glasgow, but very possibly I am mistaken about that. It represented a glorious woman with a wise and fearless face stooping over her children and pointing them to far horizons. The sky displayed the pearly warmth of a summer dawn, and all the painting was marvellously bright as if with the youth and hope of the delicately beautiful children in the foreground. She was telling them, one felt, of the great prospect of life that opened before them, of the spectacle of the world, the splendours of sea and mountain they might travel and see, the joys of skill they might acquire, of effort and the pride of effort and the devotions and nobilities it was theirs to achieve. Perhaps even she whispered of the warm triumphant mystery of love that comes at last to those who have patience and unblemished hearts . . . She was reminding them of their great heritage as English children, rulers of more than one-fifth of mankind, of the obligation to do and be the best that such a pride of empire entails, of their essential nobility and knighthood and the restraints and the charities and the disciplined strength that is becoming in knights and rulers . . .

The education of Mr Polly did not follow this picture very closely. He went for some time to a National School, which was run on severely economical lines to keep down the rates by a largely untrained staff, he was set sums to do that he did not understand, and that no one made him understand, he was made to read the catechism and Bible with the utmost industry and an entire disregard of punctuation or significance, and caused to imitate writing copies and drawing copies, and given object lessons upon sealing wax and silkworms and potato bugs and ginger and iron and suchlike things, and taught various other subjects his mind refused to entertain, and afterwards, when he was about twelve, he was jerked by his parent to 'finish off' in a private school of dingy aspect and still dingier pretensions, where there were no object lessons, and the studies of bookkeeping and French were pursued (but never effectually overtaken) under the guidance of an elderly gentleman who wore a nondescript gown and took snuff, wrote copperplate, explained nothing and used a cane with remarkable dexterity and gusto.

Mr Polly went into the National School at six and he left the private school at fourteen, and by that time his mind was in much the same state that you would be in, dear reader, if you were operated upon for appendicitis by a well-meaning, boldly enterprising, but rather over-worked and underpaid butcher boy, who was superseded towards the climax of the operation by a left-handed clerk of high principles but intemperate habits – that is to say, it was in a thorough mess. The nice little curiosities and willingnesses of a child were in a jumbled and thwarted condition, hacked and cut about – the operators had left, so to speak, all their sponges and ligatures in the mangled confusion – and Mr Polly had lost much of his natural confidence, so far as figures and sciences and languages and the possibilities of learning things were concerned. He thought of the present world no longer as a wonderland of experiences, but as geography and history, as the repeating of names that were hard to pronounce and lists of products and populations and heights and lengths, and as lists and dates – oh! and boredom indescribable. He thought of religion as the recital of more or less incomprehensible words that were hard to remember, and of the Divinity as of a limitless Being having the nature of a schoolmaster and making infinite rules, known and unknown rules, that were always ruthlessly enforced, and with an infinite capacity for punishment and, most horrible of all to think of! limitless powers of espial. (So to the best of his ability he did not think of that unrelenting eye.) He was uncertain about the spelling and pronunciation of most of the words in our beautiful but abundant and perplexing tongue – that especially was a pity because words attracted him, and under happier conditions he might have used them well – he was always doubtful whether it was eight sevens or nine eights that were sixty-three (he knew no method for settling the difficulty) and he thought the merit of a drawing consisted in the care with which it was 'lined in'. 'Lining in' bored him beyond measure.

But the indigestions of mind and body that were to play so large a part in his subsequent career were still only beginning. His liver and his gastric juice, his wonder and imagination kept up a fight against the things that threatened to overwhelm soul and body together. Outside the regions devastated by the school curriculum he was still intensely curious. He had cheerful phases of enterprise, and at about thirteen he suddenly discovered reading and its joys. He began to read stories voraciously, and books of travel, provided they were also adventurous. He got these chiefly from the local institute, and he also 'took in', irregularly but thoroughly, one of those inspiring weeklies that dull people used to call 'penny dreadfuls',[44] admirable weeklies crammed with imagination that the cheap boys' 'comics' of today have replaced. At fourteen, when he emerged from the valley of the shadow of education, there survived something, indeed it survived still, obscured and thwarted, at five and thirty, that pointed – not with a visible and prevailing finger like the finger of that beautiful woman in the picture, but pointed nevertheless – to the idea that there was interest and happiness in the world. Deep in the being of Mr Polly, deep in that darkness, like a creature which has been beaten about the head and left for dead but still lives, crawled a persuasion that over and above the things that were jolly and 'bits of all right', there was beauty, there was delight, that somewhere – magically inaccessible perhaps, but still somewhere – were pure and easy and joyous states of body and mind.

He would sneak out on moonless winter nights and stare up at the stars, and afterwards find it difficult to tell his father where he had been.

He would read tales about hunters and explorers, and imagine himself riding mustangs as fleet as the wind across the prairies of Western America, or coming as a conquering and adored white man into the swarming villages of Central Africa. He shot bears with a revolver – a cigarette in the other hand – and made a necklace of their teeth and claws for the chief's beautiful young daughter. Also he killed a lion with a pointed stake, stabbing through the beast's heart as it stood over him.

He thought it would be splendid to be a diver and go down into the dark green mysteries of the sea.

He led stormers against well-nigh impregnable forts, and died on the ramparts at the moment of victory. (His grave was watered by a nation's tears.)

He rammed and torpedoed ships, one against ten.

He was beloved by queens in barbaric lands, and reconciled whole nations to the Christian faith.

He was martyred, and took it very calmly and beautifully – but only once or twice after the Revivalist week. It did not become a habit with him.

He explored the Amazon, and found, newly exposed by the fall of a great tree, a rock of gold.

Engaged in these pursuits he would neglect the work immediately in hand, sitting somewhat slackly on the form and projecting himself in a manner tempting to a schoolmaster with a cane . . . And twice he had books confiscated.

Recalled to the realities of life, he would rub himself or sigh deeply as the occasion required, and resume his attempts to write as good as copperplate. He hated writing; the ink always crept up his fingers and the smell of ink offended him. And he was filled with unexpressed doubts. *Why* should writing slope down from right to left? *Why* should down strokes be thick and up strokes thin? *Why* should the handle of one's pen point over one's right shoulder?

His copy books towards the end foreshadowed his destiny and took the form of commercial documents. '*Dear Sir,*' they ran, '*Referring to your esteemed order of the 26th ult., we beg to inform you,*' and so on.

The compression of Mr Polly's mind and soul in the educational institutions of his time was terminated abruptly by his father between his fourteenth and fifteenth birthdays. His father – who had long since forgotten the time when his son's little limbs seemed to have come straight from God's hand, and when he had kissed five minute toenails in a rapture of loving tenderness – remarked: 'It's time that dratted boy did something for a living.'

And a month or so later Mr Polly began that career in business that led him at last to the sole proprietorship of a bankrupt outfitter's shop – and to the stile on which he was sitting.

3

Mr Polly was not naturally interested in hosiery and gentlemen's out-fitting. At times, indeed, he urged himself to a spurious curiosity about that trade, but presently something more congenial came along and checked the effort. He was apprenticed in one of those large, rather low-class establishments which sell everything from pianos and furniture to books and millinery, a department store in fact – the Port Burdock Drapery Bazaar at Port Burdock, one of the three townships that are grouped around the Port Burdock naval dockyards. There he remained six years. He spent most of the time inattentive to business, in a sort of uncomfortable happiness, increasing his indigestion.

On the whole he preferred business to school; the hours were longer but the tension was not nearly so great. The place was better aired, you were not kept in for no reason at all, and the cane was not employed. You watched the growth of your moustache with interest and impatience, and mastered the beginnings of social intercourse. You talked, and found there were things amusing to say. Also you had regular pocket money, and a voice in the purchase of your clothes, and presently a small salary. And there were girls. And friendship! In the retrospect Port Burdock sparkled with the facets of quite a cluster of remembered jolly times.

('Didn't save much money though,' said Mr Polly.)

The first-apprentices' dormitory was a long bleak room with six beds, six chests of drawers and looking glasses and a number of boxes of wood or tin; it opened into a still longer and bleaker room of eight beds, and this into a third apartment with yellow-grained paper and American-cloth tables, which was the dining-room by day and the men's sitting- and smoking-room after nine. Here Mr Polly, who had been an only child, first tasted the joys of social intercourse. At first there were attempts to bully him on account of his refusal to consider face-washing a diurnal duty, but two fights with the apprentices next above him established a useful reputation for choler, and the presence of girl apprentices in the shop somehow raised his standard of cleanliness to a more acceptable level. He didn't, of course, have very much to do with the feminine staff in his department, but he spoke to them casually as he traversed foreign parts of the Bazaar, or got out of their way politely, or helped them to lift down heavy boxes, and on such occasions he felt their scrutiny. Except in the course of business or at meal times the men and women of the establishment had very little opportunity of meeting; the men were in their rooms and the girls in theirs. Yet these feminine creatures, at once so near and so remote, affected him profoundly. He would watch them going to and fro, and marvel secretly at the beauty of their hair or the roundness of their necks or the warm softness of their cheeks or the delicacy of their hands. He would fall into passions for them at dinner time, and try and show devotion by his manner of passing the bread and margarine at tea. There was a very fair-haired, fair-skinned apprentice in the adjacent haberdashery to whom he said 'good-morning' every morning, and for a period it seemed to him the most significant event in his day. When she said, 'I *do* hope it will be fine tomorrow,' he felt it marked an epoch. He had had no sisters, and was innately disposed to worship womankind. But he did not betray as much to Platt and Parsons.

To Platt and Parsons he affected an attitude of seasoned depravity towards womankind. Platt and Parsons were his contemporary apprentices in departments of the drapery shop, and the three were drawn together into a close friendship by the fact that all their names began with P. They decided they were the Three Ps, and went about together of an evening with the bearing of desperate dogs. Sometimes, when they had money, they went into public houses and had drinks. Then they would become more desperate than ever, and walk along the pavement under the gas lamps arm in arm singing. Platt had a good tenor voice and had been in a church choir, and so he led the singing;

Parsons had a serviceable bellow, which roared and faded and roared again very wonderfully; Mr Polly's share was an extraordinary lowing noise, a sort of flat recitative which he called 'singing seconds'. They would have sung catches if they had known how to do it, but as it was they sang melancholy music-hall songs about dying soldiers and the old folks far away.

They would sometimes go into the quieter residential quarters of Port Burdock, where policemen and other obstacles were infrequent, and really let their voices soar like hawks and feel very happy. The dogs of the district would be stirred to hopeless emulation, and would keep it up for long after the Three Ps had been swallowed up by the night. One jealous brute of an Irish terrier made a gallant attempt to bite Parsons, but was beaten by numbers and solidarity.

The Three Ps took the utmost interest in each other and found no other company so good. They talked about everything in the world, and would go on talking in their dormitory after the gas was out until the other men were reduced to throwing boots; they skulked from their departments in the slack hours of the afternoon to gossip in the packing-room of the warehouse; on Sundays and Bank Holidays they went for long walks together, talking.

Platt was white-faced and dark, and disposed to undertones and mystery and a curiosity about society and the *demi-monde*. He kept himself *au courant* by reading a penny paper of infinite suggestion called *Modern Society*. Parsons was of an ampler build, already promising fatness, with curly hair and a lot of rolling, rollicking, curly features, and a large blob-shaped nose. He had a great memory and a real interest in literature. He knew great portions of Shakespeare and Milton by heart, and would recite them at the slightest provocation. He read everything he could get hold of, and if he liked it he read it aloud. It did not matter who else liked it. At first Mr Polly was disposed to be suspicious of this literature, but was carried away by Parsons's enthusiasm. The Three Ps went to a performance of *Romeo and Juliet* at the Port Burdock Theatre Royal, and hung over the gallery fascinated. After that they made a sort of password of: 'Do you bite your thumbs at us, sir?' To which the countersign was: 'We bite our thumbs.'

For weeks the glory of Shakespeare's Verona lit Mr Polly's life. He walked as though he carried a sword at his side, and swung a mantle from his shoulders. He went through the grimy streets of Port Burdock with his eye on the first-floor windows – looking for balconies. A ladder in the yard flooded his mind with romantic ideas. Then Parsons discovered an Italian writer, whose name Mr Polly rendered as 'Bocashieu',[45] and after some excursions into that author's remains the talk of Parsons became infested with the word '*amours*', and Mr Polly would stand in front of his hosiery fixtures trifling with paper and string and thinking of perennial picnics under dark olive trees in the everlasting sunshine of Italy.

And about that time it was that all three Ps adopted turndown collars and large, loose, artistic silk ties, which they tied very much on one side and wore with an air of defiance. And a certain swashbuckling carriage.

And then came the glorious revelation of that great Frenchman whom Mr Polly called 'Rabooloose'.[46] The Three Ps thought the birth feast of Gargantua the most glorious piece of writing in the world, and I am not certain they were wrong, and on wet Sunday evenings when there was danger of hymn singing they would get Parsons to read it aloud.

Towards the several members of the YMCA who shared the dormitory, the Three Ps always maintained a sarcastic and defiant attitude.

'We got a perfect right to do what we like in our corner,' Platt maintained. 'You do what you like in yours.'

'But the language!' objected Morrison, the white-faced, earnest-eyed improver, who was leading a profoundly religious life under great difficulties.

'*Language*, man!' roared Parsons, 'why, it's *Literature*!'

'Sunday isn't the time for Literature.'

'It's the only time we've got. And besides – '

The horrors of religious controversy would begin . . .

Mr Polly stuck loyally to the Three Ps, but in the secret places of his heart he was torn. A fire of conviction burnt in Morrison's eyes and spoke in his urgent persuasive voice; he lived the better life manifestly, chaste in word and deed, industrious, studiously kindly. When the junior apprentice had sore feet and homesickness Morrison washed the feet and comforted the heart, and he helped other men to get through with their work when he might have gone early, a superhuman thing to do. Polly was secretly a little afraid to be left alone with this man and the power of the spirit that was in him. He felt watched.

Platt, also struggling with things his mind could not contrive to reconcile, said 'that confounded hypocrite'.

'He's no hypocrite,' said Parsons, 'he's no hypocrite, o' man. But he's got no blessed *Joy de Vive*; that's what's wrong with him. Let's go down to the Harbour Arms and see some of those blessed old captains getting drunk.'

'Short of sugar, o' man,' said Mr Polly, slapping his trouser pocket.

'Oh, *carm* on,' said Parsons. 'Always do it on tuppence for a bitter.'

'Lemme get my pipe on,' said Platt, who had recently taken to smoking with great ferocity. 'Then I'm with you.'

Pause and struggle.

'Don't ram it down, o' man,' said Parsons, watching with knitted brows. 'Don't ram it down. Give it Air. Seen my stick, o' man? Right-o.'

And leaning on his cane he composed himself in an attitude of sympathetic patience towards Platt's incendiary efforts.

4

Jolly days of companionship they were for the incipient bankrupt on the stile to look back upon.

The interminable working hours of the Bazaar had long since faded from his memory – except for one or two conspicuous rows and one or two larks – but the rare Sundays and holidays shone out like diamonds among pebbles. They shone with the mellow splendour of evening skies reflected in calm water, and athwart them all went old Parsons bellowing an interpretation of life, gesticulating, appreciating and making appreciate, expounding books, talking of that mystery of his, the 'Joy de Vive'.

There were some particularly splendid walks on Bank Holidays. The Three Ps would start on Sunday morning early and find a room in some modest inn and talk themselves asleep, and return singing through the night, or having an 'argy bargy' about the stars, on Monday evening. They would come over the hills out of the pleasant English countryside in which they had wandered, and see Port Burdock spread out below, a network of interlacing street lamps and shifting tram lights against the black, beacon-gemmed immensity of the harbour waters.

'Back to the collar, o' man,' Parsons would say. There is no satisfactory plural to o' man, so he always used it in the singular.

'Don't mention it,' said Platt.

And once they got a boat for the whole summer day, and rowed up past the moored ironclads[47] and the black old hulks and the various shipping of the harbour, past a white troopship and past the trim front and the ships and interesting vistas of the dockyard to the shallow channels and rocky weedy wildernesses of the upper harbour. And Parsons and Mr Polly had a great dispute and quarrel that day as to how far a big gun could shoot.

The country over the hills behind Port Burdock is all that an old-fashioned, scarcely disturbed English countryside should be. In those days the bicycle was still rare and costly and the motor car had yet to come and stir up rural serenities. The Three Ps would take footpaths haphazard across fields, and plunge into unknown winding lanes between high hedges of honeysuckle and dog rose. Greatly daring, they would follow green bridle paths through primrose-studded undergrowths, or wander waist deep in the bracken of beech woods. About twenty miles from Port Burdock there came a region of hop gardens and hoast-crowned farms, and farther on, to be reached only by cheap tickets at Bank Holiday times, was a sterile ridge of very clean roads and red sand pits and pines and gorse and heather. The Three Ps could not afford to buy bicycles and they found boots the greatest item of their skimpy expenditure. They threw appearances to the winds at last and got ready-made workingmen's hobnails. There was much discussion and strong feeling over this step in the dormitory.

There is no countryside like the English countryside for those who have learnt to love it. Its firm yet gentle lines of hill and dale, its ordered confusion of features, its deer parks and downland, its castles and stately houses, its hamlets and old churches, its farms and ricks and great barns and ancient trees, its pools and ponds and shining threads of rivers; its flower-starred hedgerows, its orchards and woodland patches, its village greens and kindly inns. Other countrysides have their pleasant aspects, but none such variety, none that shine so steadfastly throughout the year. Picardy is pink and white and pleasant in the blossom time; Burgundy goes on with its sunshine and wide hillsides and cramped vineyards, a beautiful tune repeated and repeated; Italy gives salitas and wayside chapels and chestnuts and olive orchards; the Ardennes has its woods and gorges; Touraine and the Rhineland, the wide Campagna with its distant Apennines, and the neat prosperities and mountain backgrounds of South Germany, all clamour their especial merits at one's memory. And there are the hills and fields of Virginia, like an England grown very big and slovenly, the woods and big river sweeps of Pennsylvania, the trim New England landscape, a little bleak and rather fine like the New England mind, and the wide rough country roads and hills and woodland of New York State. But none of these change scene and character in three miles of walking, nor have so mellow a sunlight nor so diversified a cloudland, nor confess the per-petual refreshment of the strong soft winds that blow from off the sea, as our Mother England does.

It was good for the Three Ps to walk through such a land and forget for a time that indeed they had no footing in it all, that they were doomed to toil behind counters in such places as Port Burdock for the better part of their lives. They would forget the customers and shopwalkers and department buyers and everything and become just happy wanderers in a world of pleasant breezes and songbirds and shady trees.

The arrival at the inn was a great affair. No one, they were convinced, would take them for drapers, and there might be a pretty serving girl or a jolly old lady, or what Parsons called a 'bit of character' drinking in the bar.

There would always be weighty enquiries as to what they could have, and it would work out always at cold beef and pickles, or fried ham and eggs and shandygaff, two pints of beer and two bottles of ginger beer foaming in a huge round-bellied jug.

The glorious moment of standing lordly in the inn doorway, and staring out at the world, the swinging sign, the geese upon the green, the duck-pond, a waiting waggon, the church tower, a sleepy cat, the blue heavens, with the sizzle of the frying audible behind one! The keen smell of the bacon! The trotting of feet bearing the repast; the click and clatter as the tableware is finally arranged! A clean white cloth!

'Ready, sir!' or 'Ready, gentlemen.' Better hearing that than 'Forward Polly! look sharp!'

The going in! The sitting down! The falling to!

'Bread, o' man?'

'Right-o! Don't bag all the crust, o' man.'

Once a simple-mannered girl in a pink print dress stayed and talked with them as they ate; led by the gallant Parsons they professed to be all desperately in love with her, and courted her to say which she preferred of them, it was so manifest she did prefer one and so impossible to say which it was held her there, until a distant maternal voice called her away. Afterwards as they left the inn she waylaid them at the orchard corner and gave them, a little shyly, three keen yellow-green apples – and wished them to come again some day, and vanished, and reappeared looking after them as they turned the corner – waving a white hand-kerchief. All the rest of that day they disputed over the signs of her favour, and the next Sunday they went there again.

But she had vanished, and a mother of forbidding aspect afforded no explanations.

If Platt and Parsons and Mr Polly live to be a hundred, they will none of them forget that girl as she stood with a pink flush upon her, faintly smiling and yet earnest, parting the branches of the hedgerows and reaching down apple in hand.

And once they went along the coast, following it as closely as possible, and so came at last to Foxbourne, that easternmost suburb of Brayling and Hampsted-on-the-Sea.

Foxbourne seemed a very jolly little place to Mr Polly that afternoon. It has a clean sandy beach instead of the mud and pebbles and coaly defilements of Port Burdock, a row of six bathing-machines, and a shelter on the parade in which the Three Ps sat after a satisfying but rather expensive lunch that had included celery. Rows of verandahed villas proffered apartments; they had feasted in a hotel with a porch painted white and gay with geraniums above: and the High Street, with the old church at the head, had been full of an agreeable afternoon stillness.

'Nice little place for business,' said Platt sagely from behind his big pipe.

It stuck in Mr Polly's memory.

5

Mr Polly was not so picturesque a youth as Parsons. He lacked richness in his voice, and went about in those days with his hands in his pockets looking quietly speculative.

He specialised in slang and the misuse of English, and he played the role of an appreciative stimulant to Parsons. Words attracted him curiously, words rich in suggestion, and he loved a novel and striking phrase. His school training had given him little or no mastery of the mysterious pronunciation of English and no confidence in himself. His schoolmaster indeed had been both unsound and variable. New words had terror and fascination for him; he did not acquire them, he could not avoid them, and so he plunged into them. His only rule was not to be misled by the spelling. That was no guide anyhow. He avoided every recognised phrase in the language and mispronounced everything in order that he should be suspected of whim rather than ignorance

'Sesquippledan,' he would say. 'Sesquippledan verboojuice.'

'Eh?' said Platt.

'Eloquent Rapsodooce.'

'Where?' asked Platt.

'In the warehouse, o' man. All among the tablecloths and blankets. Carlyle. He's reading aloud. Doing the High Froth. Spuming! Wind-milling! Waw, waw! It's a sight worth seeing. He'll bark his blessed knuckles one of these days on the fixtures, o' man.'

He held an imaginary book in one hand and waved an eloquent

gesture. 'So too shall every Hero inasmuch as notwithstanding for evermore come back to Reality,' he parodied the enthusiastic Parsons, 'so that in fashion and thereby, upon things and not *under* things articulariously He stands.'

'I should laugh if the Governor dropped on him,' said Platt. 'He'd never hear him coming.'

'The o' man's drunk with it – fair drunk,' said Polly. 'I never did. It's worse than when he got on to Rabooloose.'

CHAPTER TWO

The Dismissal of Parsons

Suddenly Parsons got himself dismissed.

He got himself dismissed under circumstances of peculiar violence that left a deep impression on Mr Polly's mind. He wondered about it for years afterwards, trying to get the rights of the case.

Parsons's apprenticeship was over; he had reached the status of an Improver, and he dressed the window of the Manchester department.[48] By all the standards available he dressed it very well. By his own standards he dressed it wonderfully. 'Well, o' man,' he used to say, 'there's one thing about my position here – I *can* dress a window.'

And when trouble was under discussion he would hold that 'little Fluffums' – which was the apprentices' name for Mr Garvace, the senior partner and managing director of the Bazaar – would think twice before he got rid of the only man in the place who could make a windowful of Manchester goods *tell*.

Then like many a fellow artist he fell a prey to theories.

'The art of window-dressing is in its Infancy, o' man – in its blooming Infancy. All balance and stiffness like a blessed Egyptian picture. No Joy in it, no blooming Joy! Conventional. A shop window ought to get hold of people, *grip* 'em as they go along. It stands to reason. Grip!'

His voice would sink to a kind of quiet bellow. '*Do* they grip?'

Then after a pause, a savage roar: '*Naw!*'

'He's got a Heavy on,' said Mr Polly. 'Go it, o' man; let's have some more of it.'

'Look at old Morrison's dress-stuff windows! Tidy, tasteful, correct, I grant you, but Bleak!' He let out the word reinforced to a shout: 'Bleak!'

'Bleak!' echoed Mr Polly.

'Just pieces of stuff in rows, rows of tidy little puffs, perhaps one bit just unrolled, quiet tickets.'

'Might as well be in church, o' man,' said Mr Polly.

'A window ought to be exciting,' said Parsons; 'it ought to make you say: " 'El-*lo*!" when you see it.'

He paused, and Platt watched him over a snorting pipe.

'Rockcockyo,'[49] said Mr Polly.

'We want a new school of window-dressing,' said Parsons, regardless of the comment. 'A New School! The Port Burdock School. Day after tomorrow I change the Fitzallan Street stuff. This time, it's going to be a change. I mean to have a crowd or bust!'

And as a matter of fact he did both.

His voice dropped to a note of self-reproach. 'I've been timid, o' man. I've been holding myself in. I haven't done myself Justice. I've kept down the simmering, seething, teeming ideas . . . All that's over now.'

'Over,' gulped Polly.

'Over for good and all, o' man.'

2

Platt came to Polly, who was sorting up collar boxes. 'o' man's doing his Blooming Window.'

'What window?'

'What he said.'

Polly remembered.

He went on with his collar boxes with his eye on his senior, Mansfield. Mansfield was presently called away to the counting house, and instantly Polly shot out by the street door, and made a rapid transit along the street front past the Manchester window, and so into the silk-room door. He could not linger long, but he gathered joy, a swift and fearful joy, from his brief inspection of Parsons's unconscious back. Parsons had his tail coat off and was working with vigour; his habit of pulling his waistcoat straps to the utmost brought out all the agreeable promise of corpulence in his youthful frame. He was blowing excitedly and running his fingers through his hair, and then moving with all the swift eagerness of a man inspired. All about his feet and knees were scarlet blankets, not folded, not formally unfolded, but – the only phrase is – shied about. And a great bar sinister of roller towelling stretched across the front of the window on which was a ticket, and the ticket said in bold black letters: 'LOOK!'

So soon as Mr Polly got into the silk department and met Platt he knew he had not lingered nearly long enough outside. 'Did you see the boards at the back?' said Platt.

He hadn't. 'The High Egrugious is fairly On,' he said, and dived down to return by devious subterranean routes to the outfitting department.

Presently the street door opened and Platt, with an air of intense devotion to business assumed to cover his adoption of that unusual route, came in and made for the staircase down to the warehouse. He rolled up his eyes at Polly. 'Oh, *Lor*!' he said and vanished.

Irresistible curiosity seized Polly. Should he go through the shop to the Manchester department, or risk a second transit outside?

He was impelled to make a dive at the street door.

'Where are you going?' asked Mansfield.

'Li'le dog,' said Polly with an air of lucid explanation, and left him to get any meaning he could from it.

Parsons was worth the subsequent trouble. Parsons really was extremely rich. This time Polly stopped to take it in.

Parsons had made a huge asymmetrical pile of thick white and red blankets twisted and rolled to accentuate their woolly richness, heaped up in a warm disorder, with large window tickets inscribed in blazing red letters: 'Cosy Comfort at Cut Prices', and 'Curl up and Cuddle below Cost'. Regardless of the daylight he had turned up the electric light on that side of the window to reflect a warm glow upon the heap, and behind, in pursuit of contrasted bleakness, he was now hanging long strips of grey silesia and chilly-coloured linen dusterings.

It was wonderful, but –

Mr Polly decided that it was time he went in. He found Platt in the silk department, apparently on the verge of another plunge into the exterior world. 'Cosy Comfort at Cut Prices,' said Polly. 'Allittritions Artful Aid.'

He did not dare go into the street for the third time, and he was hovering feverishly near the window when he saw the governor, Mr Garvace, that is to say, the managing director of the Bazaar, walking along the pavement after his manner to assure himself all was well with the establishment he guided.

Mr Garvace was a short stout man, with that air of modest pride that so often goes with corpulence, choleric and decisive in manner, and with hands that looked like bunches of fingers. He was red-haired and ruddy, and after the custom of such complexions, hairs sprang from the tip of his nose. When he wished to bring the power of the human eye to bear upon an assistant, he projected his chest, knitted one brow and partially closed the left eyelid.

An expression of speculative wonder overspread the countenance of Mr Polly. He felt he must *see*. Yes, whatever happened, he must *see*. 'Want to speak to Parsons, sir,' he said to Mr Mansfield, and deserted his post hastily, dashed through the intervening departments and was in position behind a pile of Bolton sheeting as the governor came in out of the street.

'What on earth do you think you are doing with that window, Parsons?' began Mr Garvace.

Only the legs of Parsons and the lower part of his waistcoat and an intervening inch of shirt were visible. He was standing inside the window on the steps, hanging up the last strip of his background from the brass rail along the ceiling. Within, the Manchester shop window was cut off by a partition rather like the partition of an old-fashioned church pew from the general space of the shop. There was a panelled barrier, that is to say, with a little door like a pew door in it. Parsons's face appeared, staring with round eyes at his employer.

Mr Garvace had to repeat his question.

'Dressing it, sir – on new lines.'

'Come out of it,' said Mr Garvace.

Parsons stared, and Mr Garvace had to repeat his command.

Parsons, with a dazed expression, began to descend the steps slowly.

Mr Garvace turned about. 'Where's Morrison? Morrison!'

Morrison appeared.

'Take this window over,' said Mr Garvace, pointing his bunch of fingers at Parsons. 'Take all this muddle out and dress it properly.'

Morrison advanced and hesitated.

'I beg your pardon, sir,' said Parsons with an immense politeness, 'but this is *my* window.'

'Take it all out,' said Mr Garvace, turning away.

Morrison advanced. Parsons shut the door with a click that arrested Mr Garvace.

'Come out of that window,' he said. 'You can't dress it. If you want to play the fool with a window – '

'This window's All Right,' said the genius in window-dressing, and there was a little pause.

'Open the door and go right in,' said Mr Garvace to Morrison.

'You leave that door alone, Morrison,' said Parsons.

Polly was no longer even trying to hide behind the stack of Bolton sheeting. He realised he was in the presence of forces too stupendous to heed him.

'Get him out,' said Mr Garvace.

Morrison seemed to be thinking out the ethics of his position. The idea of loyalty to his employer prevailed with him. He laid his hand on the door to open it; Parsons tried to disengage his hand. Mr Garvace joined his effort to Morrison's. Then the heart of Polly leapt and the world blazed up to wonder and splendour. Parsons disappeared behind the partition for a moment and reappeared instantly, gripping a thin cylinder of rolled huckaback. With this he smote at Morrison's head. Morrison's head ducked under the resounding impact, but he clung on and so did Mr Garvace. The door came open, and then Mr Garvace was staggering back, hand to head; his autocratic, his sacred baldness, smitten. Parsons was beyond all control – a strangeness, a marvel. Heaven knows how the artistic struggle had strained that richly endowed temperament. 'Say I can't dress a window, you thundering old Humbug,' he said, and hurled the huckaback at his master. He followed this up by hurling first a blanket, then an armful of silesia, then a window support out of the window into the shop. It leapt into Polly's mind that Parsons hated his own effort and was glad to demolish it. For a crowded second Polly's mind was concentrated upon Parsons, infuriated, active, like a figure of earthquake with its coat off, shying things headlong.

Then he perceived the back of Mr Garvace and heard his gubernatorial voice crying to no one in particular and everybody in general: 'Get him out of the window. He's mad. He's dangerous. Get him out of the window.'

Then a crimson blanket was for a moment over the head of Mr Garvace, and his voice, muffled for an instant, broke out into unwonted expletive.

Then people had arrived from all parts of the Bazaar. Luck, the ledger clerk, blundered against Polly and said, 'Help him!' Somerville from the silks vaulted the counter, and seized a chair by the back. Polly lost his head. He clawed at the Bolton sheeting before him, and if he could have detached a piece he would certainly have hit somebody with it. As it was he simply upset the pile. It fell away from Polly, and he had an impression of somebody squeaking as it went down. It was the sort of impression one disregards. The collapse of the pile of goods just sufficed to end his subconscious efforts to get something to hit somebody with, and his whole attention focused itself upon the struggle in the window. For a splendid instant Parsons towered up over the active backs that clustered about the shop-window door, an active whirl of gesture, tearing things down and throwing them, and then he went under. There was an instant's furious struggle, a crash, a second crash and the crack of broken plate glass. Then a stillness and heavy breathing.

Parsons was overpowered . . .

Polly, stepping over scattered pieces of Bolton sheeting, saw his transfigured friend with a dark cut, that was not at present bleeding, on the forehead, one arm held by Somerville and the other by Morrison.

'You – you – you – you annoyed me,' said Parsons, sobbing for breath.

There are events that detach themselves from the general stream of occurrences and seem to partake of the nature of revelations. Such was this Parsons affair. It began by seeming grotesque; it ended disconcertingly. The fabric of Mr Polly's daily life was torn, and beneath it he discovered depths and terrors.

Life was not altogether a lark.

The calling in of a policeman seemed at the moment a pantomime touch. But when it became manifest that Mr Garvace was in a fury of vindictiveness, the affair took on a different complexion. The way in which the policeman made a note of everything and aspirated nothing impressed the sensitive mind of Polly profoundly. Polly presently found himself straightening up ties to the refrain of, ' 'E then 'it you on the 'ed – 'ard.'

In the dormitory that night Parsons had become heroic. He sat on the edge of the bed with his head bandaged, packing very slowly and insisting over and over again: 'He ought to have left my window alone, o' man. He didn't ought to have touched my window.'

Polly was to go to the police court in the morning as a witness. The terror of that ordeal almost overshadowed the tragic fact that Parsons was not only summoned for assault, but 'swapped' and packing his box. Polly knew himself well enough to know he would make a bad witness. He felt sure of one fact only, namely, that ' 'E then 'it 'im on the 'ed – 'ard. All the rest danced about in his mind now, and how it would dance about on the morrow heaven only knew. Would there be a cross-examination? Is it perjoocery to make a slip? People did sometimes perjuice themselves. Serious offence.

Platt was doing his best to help Parsons, and inciting public opinion against Morrison. But Parsons would not hear of anything against Morrison. 'He was all right, o' man – according to his lights,' said Parsons. 'It isn't him I complain of.'

He speculated on the morrow. 'I shall *'ave* to pay a fine,' he said. 'No good trying to get out of it. It's true I hit him. I hit him' – he paused and seemed to be seeking an exquisite accuracy; his voice sank to a confidential note – 'on the head – about here.'

He answered the suggestion of a bright junior apprentice in a corner of the dormitory. 'What's the good of a cross summons?' he replied; 'with old Corks, the chemist, and Mottishead, the house agent, and all that lot on the Bench? Humble Pie, that's my meal tomorrow, o' man. Humble Pie.'

Packing went on for a time.

'But Lord! what a Life it is!' said Parsons, giving his deep notes scope. 'Ten-thirty-five a man trying to do his Duty, mistaken perhaps, but trying his best; ten-forty – Ruined! Ruined!' He lifted his voice to a shout. 'Ruined!' and dropped it to, 'Like an earthquake.'

'Heated altaclation,' said Polly.

'Like a blooming earthquake!' said Parsons, with the notes of a rising wind.

He meditated gloomily upon his future and a colder chill invaded Polly's mind. 'Likely to get another crib, ain't I? – with assaulted the guv'nor on my reference. I suppose, though, he won't give me refs. Hard enough to get a crib at the best of times,' said Parsons.

'You ought to go round with a show, o' man,' said Mr Polly.

Things were not so dreadful in the police court as Mr Polly had expected. He was given a seat with other witnesses against the wall of the court, and after an interesting larceny case Parsons appeared and stood not in the dock but at the table. By that time Mr Polly's legs, which had been tucked up at first under his chair out of respect to the court, were extended straight before him and his hands were in his trouser pockets. He was inventing names for the four magistrates on the bench, and had got to 'the Grave and Reverend Signor with the palatial Boko', when his thoughts were recalled to gravity by the sound of his name. He rose with alacrity and was fielded by an expert police-man from a brisk attempt to get into the vacant dock. The clerk to the Justices repeated the oath with incredible rapidity.

'Right-o,' said Mr Polly, but quite respectfully, and kissed the book.

His evidence was simple and quite audible after one warning from the superintendent of police to 'speak up'. He tried to put in a good word for Parsons by saying he was 'naturally of a choleraic disposition', but the start and the slow grin of enjoyment upon the face of the grave and Reverend Signor with the palatial Boko suggested that the word was not so good as he had thought it. The rest of the bench was frankly puzzled and there were hasty consultations.

'You mean 'e 'as a 'ot temper,' said the presiding magistrate.

'I mean 'e 'as a 'ot temper,' replied Polly, magically incapable of aspirates for the moment.

'You don't mean 'e ketches cholera.'

'I mean – he's easily put out.'

'Then why can't you say so?' said the presiding magistrate.

Parsons was bound over.

He came for his luggage while everyone was in the shop, and Garvace would not let him invade the business to say goodbye. When Mr Polly went upstairs for margarine and bread and tea, he slipped on into the dormitory at once to see what was happening further in the Parsons case. But Parsons had vanished. There was no Parsons, no trace of Parsons. His cubicle was swept and garnished. For the first time in his life Polly had a sense of irreparable loss.

A minute or so after Platt dashed in.

'Ugh!' he said, and then discovered Polly. Polly was leaning out of the window and did not look around. Platt went up to him.

'He's gone already,' said Platt. 'Might have stopped to say goodbye to a chap.'

There was a little pause before Polly replied. He thrust his finger into his mouth and gulped.

'Bit on that beastly tooth of mine,' he said, still not looking at Platt. 'It's made my eyes water, something chronic. Anyone might think I'd been doing a blooming Pipe, by the look of me.'

CHAPTER THREE

Cribs

Port Burdock was never the same place for Mr Polly after Parsons had left it. There were no chest notes in his occasional letters, and little of the 'Joy de Vive' got through by them. Parsons had gone, he said, to London, and found a place as warehouseman in a cheap outfitting shop near St Paul's Churchyard, where references were not required. It became apparent as time passed that new interests were absorbing him. He wrote of Socialism and the rights of man, things that had no appeal for Mr Polly. He felt strangers had got hold of his Parsons, were at work upon him, making him into someone else, something less picturesque . . . Port Burdock became a dreariness, full of faded memories of Parsons, and work a bore. Platt revealed himself alone as a tiresome companion, obsessed by romantic ideas about intrigues and vices and 'society women'.

Mr Polly's depression manifested itself in a general slackness. A certain impatience in the manner of Mr Garvace presently got upon his nerves. Relations were becoming strained. He asked for a rise of salary to test his position, and gave notice to leave when it was refused.

It took him two months to place himself in another situation, and during that time he had quite a disagreeable amount of loneliness, disappointment, anxiety and humiliation.

He went at first to stay with a married cousin who had a house at Easewood. His widowed father had recently given up the music and bicycle shop (with the post of organist at the parish church) that had sustained his home, and was living upon a small annuity as a guest with this cousin, and growing a little tiresome on account of some mysterious internal discomfort that the local practitioner diagnosed as imagination. He had aged with mysterious rapidity and become excessively irritable, but the cousin's wife was a born manager, and contrived to get along with him. Our Mr Polly's status was that of a guest pure and simple, but after a fortnight of congested hospitality in which he wrote nearly a hundred letters beginning:

SIR – Refferring to your advt. in the *Christian World* for an Improver in Gents' outfitting, I beg to submit myself for the situation. Have had six years' experience . . .

and upset a penny bottle of ink over a toilet cover and the bedroom carpet, his cousin took him for a walk and pointed out the superior advantages of apartments in London from which to swoop upon the briefly yawning vacancy.

'Helpful,' said Mr Polly; 'very helpful, o' man, indeed. I might have gone on here for weeks,' and packed.

He got a room in an institution that was partly a benevolent hostel for men in his circumstances and partly a high-minded but forbidding coffee house and a centre for pleasant Sunday afternoons. Mr Polly spent a critical but pleasant Sunday afternoon in a back seat, inventing such phrases as: 'Soulful Owner of the Exorbiant Largenial Development' – an Adam's Apple being in question; 'Earnest Joy'; 'Exultant, Urgent Loogoobuosity'.

A manly young curate, marking and misunderstanding his pre-occupied face and moving lips, came and sat by him and entered into conversation with the idea of making him feel more at home. The conversation was awkward and disconnected for a minute or so, and then suddenly a memory of the Port Burdock Bazaar occurred to Mr Polly, and with a baffling whisper of 'Li'le dog', and a reassuring nod, he rose up and escaped, to wander out relieved and observant into the varied London streets.

He found the collection of men he met waiting about in wholesale establishments in Wood Street and St Paul's Churchyard (where they interview the buyers who have come up from the country) interesting and stimulating, but far too strongly charged with the suggestion of his own fate to be really joyful. There were men in all degrees between confidence and distress, and in every stage between extravagant smart-ness and the last stages of decay. There were sunny young men full of an abounding and elbowing energy, before whom the soul of Polly sank in hate and dismay. 'Smart Juniors,' said Polly to himself, 'full of Smart Juniosity. The Shoveacious Cult.' There were hungry-looking individuals of thirty-five or so that he decided must be 'Proletele-rians' – he had often wanted to find someone who fitted that attractive word. Middle-aged men, 'too old at forty', discoursed in the waiting-rooms on the outlook in the trade; it had never been so bad, they said, while Mr Polly wondered if 'Dejuiced' was a permissible epithet. There were men with an overweening sense of their importance, manifestly annoyed and angry to find themselves still disengaged, and inclined to suspect a plot, and men so faint-hearted one was terrified to imagine their behaviour when it came to an interview. There was a fresh-faced young man with an unintelligent face who seemed to think himself equipped against the world beyond all misadventure by a collar of exceptional height, and another who introduced a note of gaiety by wearing a flannel shirt and a check suit of remarkable virulence. Every day Mr Polly looked round to mark how many of the familiar faces had gone, and the deepening anxiety (reflecting his own) on the faces that remained, and every day some new type joined the drifting shoal. He realised how small a chance his poor letter from Easewood ran against this hungry cluster of competitors at the fountain head.

At the back of Mr Polly's mind while he made his observations was a disagreeable flavour of dentist's parlour. At any moment his name might be shouted, and he might have to haul himself into the presence of some fresh specimen of employer, and to repeat once more his passionate protestation of interest in the business, his possession of a capacity for zeal – zeal on behalf of anyone who would pay him a yearly salary of twenty-six pounds a year.

The prospective employer would unfold his ideals of the employee. 'I want a smart, willing young man, thoroughly willing – who won't object to take trouble. I don't want a slacker, the sort of fellow who has to be pushed up to his work and held there. I've got no use for him.'

At the back of Mr Polly's mind, and quite beyond his control, the insubordinate phrasemaker would be proffering such combinations as 'Chubby Chops', or 'Chubby Charmer', as suitable for the gentleman, very much as a hat salesman proffers hats.

'I don't think you'd find much slackness about *me*, sir,' said Mr Polly brightly, trying to disregard his deeper self.

'I want a young man who means getting on.'

'Exactly, sir. Excelsior.'

'I beg your pardon?'

'I said excelsior, sir. It's a sort of motto of mine. From Longfellow.[50] Would you want me to serve through?'

The chubby gentleman explained and reverted to his ideals, with a faint air of suspicion. 'Do *you* mean getting on?' he asked.

'I hope so, sir,' said Mr Polly.

'Get on or get out, eh?'

Mr Polly made a rapturous noise, nodded appreciation, and said indistinctly, '*Quite* my style.'

'Some of my people have been with me twenty years,' said the employer. 'My Manchester buyer came to me as a boy of twelve. You're a Christian?'

'Church of England,' said Mr Polly.

'H'm,' said the employer a little checked. 'For good all-round business work I should have preferred a Baptist. Still – '

He studied Mr Polly's tie, which was severely neat and businesslike, as became an aspiring outfitter. Mr Polly's conception of his own pose and expression was rendered by that uncontrollable phrasemonger at the back as 'Obsequies Deference'.

'I am inclined,' said the prospective employer in a conclusive manner, 'to look up your reference.'

Mr Polly stood up abruptly.

'Thank you,' said the employer and dismissed him.

'Chump chops! How about chump chops?' said the phrasemonger with an air of inspiration.

'I hope then to hear from you, sir,' said Mr Polly in his best salesman manner.

'If everything is satisfactory,' said the prospective employer.

2

A man whose brain devotes its hinterland to making odd phrases and nicknames out of ill-conceived words, whose conception of life is a lump of auriferous rock to which all the value is given by rare veins of unbusinesslike joy, who reads Boccaccio and Rabelais and Shakespeare with gusto, and uses 'Stertoraneous Shover' and 'Smart Junior' as terms of bitterest opprobrium, is not likely to make a great success under modern business conditions. Mr Polly dreamt always of picturesque and mellow things, and had an instinctive hatred of the strenuous life. He would have resisted the spell of ex-President Roosevelt, or General Baden Powell, or Mr Peter Keary, or the late Dr Samuel Smiles, quite easily; and he loved Falstaff and Hudibras and coarse laughter, and the old England of Washington Irving and the memory of Charles the Second's courtly days. His progress was necessarily slow. He did not get rises; he lost situations; there was something in his eye employers did not like; he would have lost his places oftener if he had not been at times an exceptionally brilliant salesman, rather carefully neat, and a slow but very fair window-dresser.

He went from situation to situation, he invented a great wealth of nicknames, he conceived enmities and made friends – but none so richly satisfying as Parsons. He was frequently but mildly and discursively in love, and sometimes he thought of that girl who had given him a yellow-green apple. He had an idea, amounting to a flattering certainty, whose

youthful freshness it was had stirred her to self-forgetfulness. And sometimes he thought of Foxbourne sleeping prosperously in the sun. And
he began to have moods of discomfort and lassitude and ill-temper due
to the beginnings of indigestion.

Various forces and suggestions came into his life and swayed him for
longer and shorter periods.

He went to Canterbury and came under the influence of Gothic
architecture. There was a blood affinity between Mr Polly and the
Gothic; in the Middle Ages he would no doubt have sat upon a
scaffolding and carved out penetrating and none too flattering portraits
of church dignitaries upon the capitals, and when he strolled, with his
hands behind his back, along the cloisters behind the cathedral, and
looked at the rich grass plot in the centre, he had the strangest sense of
being at home – far more than he had ever been at home before. 'Portly
capons,' he used to murmur to himself, under the impression that he
was naming a characteristic type of medieval churchman.

He liked to sit in the nave during the service, and look through the
great gates at the candles and choristers, and listen to the organ-
sustained voices, but the transepts he never penetrated because of the
charge for admission. The music and the long vista of the fretted roof
filled him with a vague and mystical happiness that he had no words,
even mispronounceable words, to express. But some of the smug
monuments in the aisles got a wreath of epithets: 'Metrorious urnfuls',
'funererial claims', 'dejected angelosity', for example. He wandered
about the precincts and speculated about the people who lived in the
ripe and cosy houses of grey stone that cluster there so comfortably.
Through green doors in high stone walls he caught glimpses of level
lawns and blazing flower beds; mullioned windows revealed shaded
reading-lamps and disciplined shelves of brown-bound books. Now
and then a dignitary in gaiters would pass him, 'Portly capon', or a
drift of white-robed choir boys cross a distant arcade and vanish in a
doorway, or the pink and cream of some girlish dress flit like a butterfly
across the cool still spaces of the place. Particularly he responded to the
ruined arches of the Benedictines' Infirmary and the view of Bell Harry
Tower from the school buildings. He was stirred to read the *Canterbury
Tales*, but he could not get on with Chaucer's old-fashioned English; it
fatigued his attention, and he would have given all the storytelling
very readily for a few adventures on the road. He wanted these nice
people to live more and yarn less. He liked the Wife of Bath very
much. He would have liked to have known that woman.

At Canterbury, too, he first to his knowledge saw Americans.

His shop did a good-class trade in Westgate Street, and he would see them go by on the way to stare at Chaucer's Chequers and then turn down Mercery Lane to Prior Goldstone's gate. It impressed him that they were always in a kind of quiet hurry, and very determined and methodical people – much more so than any English he knew.

'Cultured Rapacicity,' he tried.

'Vorocious Return to the Heritage.'

He would expound them incidentally to his attendant apprentices. He had overheard a little lady putting her view to a friend near the Christchurch gate. The accent and intonation had hung in his memory, and he would reproduce them more or less accurately. 'Now does this Marlowe monument really and truly *matter*?' he had heard the little lady enquire. 'We've no time for side shows and second-rate stunts, Mamie. We want just the Big Simple Things of the place, just the Broad Elemental Canterbury praposition. What is it saying to us? I want to get right hold of that, and then have tea in the very room that Chaucer did, and hustle to get that four-eighteen train back to London . . . '

He would go over these precious phrases, finding them full of an indescribable flavour. 'Just the Broad Elemental Canterbury praposition,' he would repeat . . .

He would try to imagine Parsons confronted with Americans. For his own part he knew himself to be altogether inadequate . . .

Canterbury was the most congenial situation Mr Polly ever found during these wander years, albeit a very desert so far as companionship went.

3

It was after Canterbury that the universe became really disagreeable to Mr Polly. It was brought home to him, not so much vividly as with a harsh and ungainly insistence, that he was a failure in his trade. It was not the trade he ought to have chosen, though what trade he ought to have chosen was by no means clear.

He made great but irregular efforts and produced a forced smartness that, like a cheap dye, refused to stand sunshine. He acquired a sort of parsimony also, in which acquisition he was helped by one or two phases of absolute impecuniosity. But he was hopeless in competition against the naturally gifted, the born hustlers, the young men who meant to get on.

He left the Canterbury place very regretfully. He and another commercial gentleman took a boat one Sunday afternoon at Sturry-on-the-Stour, when the wind was in the west, and sailed it very happily eastward for an hour. They had never sailed a boat before and it seemed simple and wonderful. When they turned they found the river too narrow for tacking and the tide running out like a sluice. They battled back to Sturry in the course of six hours (at a shilling the first hour and sixpence for each hour afterwards) rowing a mile in an hour and a half or so, until the turn of the tide came to help them, and then they had a night walk to Canterbury, and found themselves remorselessly locked out.

The Canterbury employer was an amiable, religious-spirited man and he would probably not have dismissed Mr Polly if that unfortunate tendency to phrase things had not shocked him. 'A Tide's a Tide, sir,' said Mr Polly, feeling that things were not so bad. 'I've no lune-attic power to alter *that*.'

It proved impossible to explain to the Canterbury employer that this was not a highly disrespectful and blasphemous remark.

'And besides, what good are you to me this morning, do you think?' said the Canterbury employer, 'with your arms pulled out of their sockets?'

So Mr Polly resumed his observations in the Wood Street warehouses once more, and had some dismal times. The shoal of fish waiting for the crumbs of employment seemed larger than ever.

He took counsel with himself. Should he 'chuck' the outfitting? It wasn't any good for him now, and presently when he was older and his youthful smartness had passed into the dullness of middle age it would be worse. What else could he do?

He could think of nothing. He went one night to a music hall and developed a vague idea of a comic performance; the comic men seemed violent rowdies and not at all funny; but when he thought of the great pit of the audience yawning before him he realised that his was an altogether too delicate talent for such a use. He was impressed by the charm of selling vegetables by auction in one of those open shops near London Bridge, but admitted upon reflection his general want of technical knowledge. He made some enquiries about emigration, but none of the colonies were in want of shop assistants without capital. He kept up his attendance in Wood Street.

He subdued his ideal of salary by the sum of five pounds a year, and was taken at that into a driving establishment in Clapham, which dealt chiefly in ready-made suits, fed its assistants in an underground dining-room and kept them until twelve on Saturdays. He found it hard to be cheerful there. His fits of indigestion became worse, and he began to lie awake at night and think. Sunshine and laughter seemed things lost for ever; picnics and shouting in the moonlight.

The chief shopwalker took a dislike to him and nagged him. 'Nar then, Polly!' 'Look alive, Polly!' became the burthen of his days. 'As smart a chap as you could have,' said the chief shopwalker, 'but no *Zest*. No *Zest*! No *Vim*! What's the matter with you?'

During his night vigils Mr Polly had a feeling – A young rabbit must have very much the feeling when, after a youth of gambolling in sunny woods and furtive jolly raids upon the growing wheat and exciting triumphant bolts before ineffectual casual dogs, it finds itself at last for a long night of floundering effort and perplexity in a net – for the rest of its life.

He could not grasp what was wrong with him. He made enormous efforts to diagnose his case. Was he really just a 'lazy slacker' who ought to 'buck up'? He couldn't find it in him to believe it. He blamed his father a good deal – it is what fathers are for – for putting him to a trade he wasn't happy to follow, but he found it impossible to say what he ought to have followed. He felt there had been something stupid about his school, but just where that came in he couldn't say. He made some perfectly sincere efforts to 'buck up' and 'shove' ruthlessly. But that was infernal – impossible. He had to admit himself miserable, with all the misery of a social misfit and with no clear prospect of more than the most incidental happiness ahead of him. And for all his attempts at self-reproach or self-discipline he felt at bottom that he wasn't at fault.

As a matter of fact all the elements of his troubles had been adequately diagnosed by a certain high-browed, spectacled gentleman living at Highbury, wearing a gold *pince-nez* and writing for the most part in the beautiful library of the Reform Club. This gentleman did not know Mr Polly personally, but he had dealt with him generally as 'one of those ill-adjusted units that abound in a society that has failed to develop a collective intelligence and a collective will for order, commensurate with its complexities'.

But phrases of that sort had no appeal for Mr Polly.

CHAPTER FOUR

Mr Polly an Orphan

Then a great change was brought about in the life of Mr Polly by the death of his father. His father had died suddenly – the local practitioner still clung to his theory that it was imagination he suffered from, but compromised in the certificate with the appendicitis that was then so fashionable – and Mr Polly found himself heir to a debateable number of pieces of furniture in the house of his cousin near Easewood Junction, a family Bible, an engraved portrait of Garibaldi and a bust of Mr Gladstone, an invalid gold watch, a gold locket formerly belonging to his mother, some minor jewellery and bric-à-brac, a quantity of nearly valueless old clothes and an insurance policy and money in the bank amounting altogether to the sum of three hundred and ninety-five pounds.

Mr Polly had always regarded his father as an immortal, as an eternal fact, and his father being of a reserved nature in his declining years had said nothing about the insurance policy. Both wealth and bereavement therefore took Mr Polly by surprise and found him a little inadequate. His mother's death had been a childish grief and long forgotten, and the strongest affection in his life had been for Parsons. An only child of sociable tendencies necessarily turns his back a good deal upon home, and the aunt who had succeeded his mother was an economist and furniture polisher, a knuckle rapper and sharp silencer, no friend for a slovenly little boy. He had loved other little boys and girls transitorily, none had been frequent and familiar enough to strike deep roots in his heart, and he had grown up with a tattered and dissipated affectionateness that was becoming wildly shy. His father had always been a stranger, an irritable stranger with exceptional powers of intervention and comment, and an air of being disappointed about his offspring. It was shocking to lose him; it was like an un-expected hole in the universe, the writing of 'Death' upon the sky, but it did not tear Mr Polly's heartstrings at first so much as rouse him to a pitch of vivid attention.

He came down to the cottage at Easewood in response to an urgent telegram, and found his father already dead. His cousin Johnson received him with much solemnity and ushered him upstairs, to look at a stiff, straight, shrouded form, with a face unwontedly quiet and, as it seemed by reason of its pinched nostrils, scornful.

'Looks peaceful,' said Mr Polly, disregarding the scorn to the best of his ability.

'It was a merciful relief,' said Mr Johnson.

There was a pause.

'Second – second Departed I've ever seen. Not counting mummies,' said Mr Polly, feeling it necessary to say something.

'We did all we could.'

'No doubt of it, o' man,' said Mr Polly.

A second long pause followed, and then, much to Mr Polly's great relief, Johnson moved towards the door.

Afterwards Mr Polly went for a solitary walk in the evening light, and as he walked, suddenly his dead father became real to him. He thought of things far away down the perspective of memory, of jolly moments when his father had skylarked with a wildly excited little boy; of a certain annual visit to the Crystal Palace pantomime, full of trivial glittering incidents and wonders; of his father's dread back while customers were in the old, minutely known shop. It is curious that the memory which seemed to link him nearest to the dead man was the memory of a fit of passion. His father had wanted to get a small sofa up the narrow winding staircase from the little room behind the shop to the bedroom above, and it had jammed. For a time his father had coaxed, and then groaned like a soul in torment and given way to blind fury; had sworn, kicked and struck at the offending piece of furniture and finally wrenched it upstairs, with considerable incidental damage to lath and plaster and one of the castors. That moment when self-control was altogether torn aside, the shocked discovery of his father's perfect humanity, had left a singular impression on Mr Polly's queer mind. It was as if something extravagantly vital had come out of his father and laid a warmly passionate hand upon his heart. He remembered that now very vividly, and it became a clue to endless other memories that had else been dispersed and confusing.

A weakly wilful being struggling to get obdurate things round impossible corners – in that symbol Mr Polly could recognise himself and all the trouble of humanity.

He hadn't had a particularly good time, poor old chap, and now it was all over. Finished . . .

Johnson was the sort of man who derives great satisfaction from a funeral; a melancholy, serious, practical-minded man of five and thirty, with great powers of advice. He was the up-line ticket clerk at Easewood

Junction, and felt the responsibilities of his position. He was naturally thoughtful and reserved, and greatly sustained in that by an innate rectitude of body and an overhanging and forward inclination of the upper part of his face and head. He was pale but freckled, and his dark grey eyes were deeply set. His lightest interest was cricket, but he did not take that lightly. His chief holiday was to go to a cricket match, which he did as if he was going to church, and he watched critically, applauded sparingly, and was darkly offended by any unorthodox play. His convictions upon all subjects were taciturnly inflexible. He was an obstinate player of draughts and chess, and an earnest and persistent reader of the *British Weekly*.[51] His wife was a pink, short, wilfully smiling, managing, ingratiating, talkative woman, who was determined to be pleasant and to take a bright hopeful view of everything, even when it was not really bright and hopeful. She had large blue expressive eyes and a round face, and she always spoke of her husband as Harold. She addressed sympathetic and considerate remarks about the deceased to Mr Polly in notes of brisk encouragement. 'He was really quite cheerful at the end,' she said several times, with congratulatory gusto, 'quite cheerful.'

She made dying seem almost agreeable.

Both these people were resolved to treat Mr Polly very well, and to help his exceptional incompetence in every possible way, and after a simple supper of ham and bread and cheese and pickles and cold apple tart and small beer had been cleared away, they put him into the arm-chair almost as though he was an invalid, and sat on chairs that made them look down on him, and opened a directive discussion of the arrangements for the funeral. After all a funeral is a distinct social opportunity, and rare when you have no family and few relations, and they did not want to see it spoilt and wasted.

'You'll have a hearse, of course,' said Mrs Johnson. 'Not one of them combinations with the driver sitting on the coffin. Disrespectful I think they are. I can't fancy how people can bring themselves to be buried in combinations.' She flattened her voice in a manner she used to intimate aesthetic feeling. 'I *do* like them glass hearses,' she said. 'So refined and nice they are.'

'Podger's hearse you'll have,' said Johnson conclusively. 'It's the best in Easewood.'

'Everything that's right and proper,' said Mr Polly.

'Podger's ready to come and measure at any time,' said Johnson.

'Then you'll want a mourners' carriage or two, according as to whom you're going to invite,' said Mr Johnson.

'Didn't think of inviting anyone,' said Mr Polly.

'Oh! you'll *have* to ask a few friends,' said Mrs Johnson. 'You can't let your father go to his grave without asking a few friends.'

'Funerial baked meats like,' said Mr Polly.

'Not baked, but of course you'll have to give them something. Ham and chicken's very suitable. You don't want a lot of cooking with the ceremony coming into the middle of it. I wonder who Alfred ought to invite, Harold. Just the immediate relations; one doesn't want a Great Crowd of People and one doesn't want not to show respect.'

'But he hated our relations – most of them.'

'He's not hating them *now*,' said Mr Johnson, 'you may be sure of that. It's just because of that I think they ought to come – all of them – even your Aunt Mildred.'

'Bit vulturial, isn't it?' said Mr Polly unheeded.

'Wouldn't be more than twelve or thirteen people if they *all* came,' said Mr Johnson.

'We could have everything put out ready in the back room and the gloves and whisky in the front room, and while we were all at the ceremony, Bessie could bring it all into the front room on a tray and put it out nice and proper. There'd have to be whisky and sherry or port for the ladies . . . '

'Where'll you get your mourning?' asked Johnson abruptly.

Mr Polly had not yet considered this by-product of sorrow. 'Haven't thought of it yet, o' man.'

A disagreeable feeling spread over his body as though he was blackening as he sat. He hated black garments.

'I suppose I must have mourning,' he said.

'Well!' said Johnson with a solemn smile.

'Got to see it through,' said Mr Polly indistinctly.

'If I were you,' said Johnson, 'I should get ready-made trousers. That's all you really want. And a black satin tie and a top hat with a deep mourning band. And gloves.'

'Jet cuff links he ought to have – as chief mourner,' said Mrs Johnson.

'Not obligatory,' said Johnson.

'It shows respect,' said Mrs Johnson.

'It shows respect of course,' said Johnson.

And then Mrs Johnson went on with the utmost gusto to the details of the 'casket', while Mr Polly sat more and more deeply and droopingly into the armchair, assenting with a note of protest to all they said. After he had retired for the night he remained for a long time perched on the edge of the sofa which was his bed, staring at the prospect before him. 'Chasing the o' man about to the last,' he said.

He hated the thought and elaboration of death as a healthy animal must hate it. His mind struggled with unwonted social problems.

'Got to put 'em away somehow, I suppose,' said Mr Polly. 'Wish I'd looked him up a bit more while he was alive.'

2

Bereavement came to Mr Polly before the realisation of opulence and its anxieties and responsibilities. That only dawned upon him on the morrow – which chanced to be Sunday – as he walked with Johnson before church time about the tangle of struggling building enterprise that constituted the rising urban district of Easewood. Johnson was off duty that morning, and devoted the time very generously to the admonitory discussion of Mr Polly's worldly outlook.

'Don't seem to get the hang of the business somehow,' said Mr Polly. 'Too much blooming humbug in it for my way of thinking.'

'If I were you,' said Mr Johnson, 'I should push for a first-class place in London – take almost nothing and live on my reserves. That's what I should do.'

'Come the Heavy,' said Mr Polly.

'Get a better-class reference.'

There was a pause. 'Think of investing your money?' asked Johnson.

'Hardly got used to the idea of having it yet, o' man.'

'You'll have to do something with it. Give you nearly twenty pounds a year if you invest it properly.'

'Haven't seen it yet in that light,' said Mr Polly defensively.

'There's no end of things you could put it into.'

'It's getting it out again I shouldn't feel sure of. I'm no sort of Fiancianier. Sooner back horses.'

'I wouldn't do that if I were you.'

'Not my style, o' man.'

'It's a nest egg,' said Johnson.

Mr Polly made an indeterminate noise.

'There's building societies,' Johnson threw out in a speculative tone. Mr Polly, with detached brevity, admitted there were.

'You might lend it on mortgage,' said Johnson. 'Very safe form of investment.'

'Shan't think anything about it – not till the o' man's underground,' said Mr Polly with an inspiration.

They turned a corner that led towards the junction.

'Might do worse,' said Johnson, 'than put it into a small shop.'

At the moment this remark made very little appeal to Mr Polly. But afterwards it developed. It fell into his mind like some small obscure seed, and germinated.

'These shops aren't in a bad position,' said Johnson.

The row he referred to gaped in the late painful stage in building before the healing touch of the plasterer assuages the roughness of the brickwork. The space for the shop yawned an oblong gap below, framed above by an iron girder: 'Windows and fittings to suit tenant' a board at the end of the row promised; and behind was the door space and a glimpse of stairs going up to the living-rooms above. 'Not a bad position,' said Johnson, and led the way into the establishment. 'Room for fixtures there,' he said, pointing to the blank wall. The two men went upstairs to the little sitting-room (or best bedroom it would have to be) above the shop. Then they descended to the kitchen below.

'Rooms in a new house always look a bit small,' said Johnson.

They came out of the house again by the prospective back door, and picked their way through builders' litter across the yard space to the road again. They drew nearer the junction where a pavement and shops already open and active formed the commercial centre of Easewood. On the opposite side of the way the side door of a flourishing little establishment opened, and a man and his wife and a little boy in a sailor suit came into the street. The wife was a pretty woman in brown with a floriferous straw hat, and the group was altogether very Sundayfied and shiny and spick and span. The shop itself had a large plate-glass window whose contents were now veiled by a buff blind on which was inscribed in scrolly letters: 'Rymer, Pork Butcher and Provision Merchant', and then with voluptuous elaboration: 'The World-Famed Easewood Sausage'.

Greetings were exchanged between Mr Johnson and this distinguished comestible.

'Off to church already?' said Johnson.

'Walking across the fields to Little Dorington,' said Mr Rymer.

'Very pleasant walk,' said Johnson.

'Very,' said Mr Rymer.

'Hope you'll enjoy it,' said Mr Johnson.

'That chap's done well,' said Johnson *sotto voce* as they went on. 'Came here with nothing – practically, four years ago. And as thin as a lath. Look at him now!

'He's worked hard of course,' added Johnson, improving the occasion. Thought fell between the cousins for a space.

'Some men can do one thing,' said Johnson, 'and some another . . . For a man who sticks to it there's a lot to be done in a shop.'

3

All the preparations for the funeral ran easily and happily under Mrs Johnson's skilful hands. On the eve of the sad event she produced a reserve of black sateen, the kitchen steps and a box of tin-tacks, and decorated the house with festoons and bows of black in the best possible taste. She tied up the knocker with black crape, and put a large bow over the corner of the steel engraving of Garibaldi, and swathed the bust of Mr Gladstone that had belonged to the deceased with inky swathings. She turned the two vases that had views of Tivoli and the Bay of Naples round, so that these rather brilliant landscapes were hidden and only the plain blue enamel showed, and she anticipated the long-contemplated purchase of a tablecloth for the front room, and substituted a violet purple cover for the now very worn and faded raptures and roses in plushette that had hitherto done duty there. Everything that loving consideration could do to impart a dignified solemnity to her little home was done.

She had released Mr Polly from the irksome duty of issuing invitations, and as the moments of assembly drew near she sent him and Mr Johnson out into the narrow long strip of garden at the back of the house, to be free to put a finishing touch or so to her preparations. She sent them out together because she had a queer little persuasion at the back of her mind that Mr Polly wanted to bolt from his sacred duties, and there was no way out of the garden except through the house.

Mr Johnson was a steady, successful gardener, and particularly good with celery and peas. He walked slowly along the narrow path down the centre pointing out to Mr Polly a number of interesting points in the management of peas, wrinkles neatly applied and difficulties wisely overcome, and all that he did for the comfort and propitiation of that fitful but rewarding vegetable. Presently a sound of nervous laughter and raised voices from the house proclaimed the arrival of the earlier guests, and the worst of that anticipatory tension was over.

When Mr Polly re-entered the house he found three entirely strange young women with pink faces, demonstrative manners and emphatic mourning engaged in an incoherent conversation with Mrs Johnson. All three kissed him with great gusto after the ancient English fashion. 'These are your cousins Larkins,' said Mrs Johnson; 'that's Annie (unexpected hug and smack), that's Miriam (resolute hug and smack), and that's Minnie (prolonged hug and smack).'

'Right-o,' said Mr Polly, emerging a little crumpled and breathless from this hearty introduction. 'I see.'

'Here's Aunt Larkins,' said Mrs Johnson, as an elderly and stouter edition of the three young women appeared in the doorway.

Mr Polly backed rather faint-heartedly, but Aunt Larkins was not to be denied. Having hugged and kissed her nephew resoundingly, she gripped him by the wrists and scanned his features. She had a round, sentimental, freckled face. 'I should 'ave known 'im anywhere,' she said with fervour.

'Hark at mother!' said the cousin called Annie. 'Why, she's never set eyes on him before!'

'I should 'ave known 'im anywhere,' said Mrs Larkins, 'for Lizzie's child. You've got her eyes! It's a Resemblance! And as for *never seeing 'im* – I've *dandled* him, Miss Imperence. I've dandled him.'

'You couldn't dandle him now, ma!' Miss Annie remarked with a shriek of laughter.

All the sisters laughed at that. 'The things you say, Annie!' said Miriam, and for a time the room was full of mirth.

Mr Polly felt it incumbent upon him to say something. '*My* dandling days are over,' he said.

The reception of this remark would have convinced a far more modest character than Mr Polly that it was extremely witty.

Mr Polly followed it up by another one almost equally good. 'My turn to dandle,' he said, with a sly look at his aunt, and convulsed everyone.

'Not me,' said Mrs Larkins, taking his point, '*thank* you,' and achieved a climax.

It was queer, but they seemed to be easy people to get on with anyhow. They were still picking little ripples and giggles of mirth from the idea of Mr Polly dandling Aunt Larkins when Mr Johnson, who had answered the door, ushered in a stooping figure, who was at once hailed by Mrs Johnson as 'Why! Uncle Pentstemon!' Uncle Pentstemon was rather a shock. His was an aged rather than venerable figure; Time had removed the hair from the top of his head and distributed a small dividend of the plunder in little bunches carelessly and impartially over the rest of his features; he was dressed in a very big old frock coat and a long cylindrical top hat, which he had kept on; he was very much bent, and he carried a rush basket from which protruded coy intimations of the lettuces and onions he had brought to grace the occasion. He hobbled into the room, resisting the efforts of Johnson to divest him of his various encumbrances, halted and surveyed the company with an expression of profound hostility, breathing hard. Recognition quickened in his eyes.

'*You* here,' he said to Aunt Larkins and then; 'You *would* be . . . These your gals?'

'They are,' said Aunt Larkins, 'and better gals – '

'That Annie?' asked Uncle Pentstemon, pointing a horny thumbnail. 'Fancy your remembering her name!'

'She mucked up my mushroom bed, the baggage!' said Uncle Pentstemon ungenially, 'and I give it to her to rights. Trounced her I did – fairly. I remember her. Here's some green stuff for you, Grace. Fresh it is and wholesome. I shall be wanting the basket back and mind you let me have it . . . Have you nailed him down yet? You always was a bit in front of what was needful.'

His attention was drawn inward by a troublesome tooth, and he sucked at it spitefully. There was something potent about this old man that silenced everyone for a moment or so. He seemed a fragment from the ruder agricultural past of our race, like a lump of soil among things of paper. He put his basket of vegetables very deliberately on the new violet tablecloth, removed his hat carefully and dabbled his brow, and wiped out his hat brim with an abundant crimson and yellow pocket handkerchief.

'I'm glad you were able to come, uncle,' said Mrs Johnson.

'Oh, I *came*' said Uncle Pentstemon. 'I *came*.'

He turned on Mrs Larkins. 'Gals in service?' he asked.

'They aren't and they won't be,' said Mrs Larkins.

'No,' he said with infinite meaning, and turned his eye on Mr Polly. 'You Lizzie's boy?' he said.

Mr Polly was spared much self-exposition by the tumult occasioned by further arrivals.

'Ah! here's May Punt!' said Mrs Johnson, and a small woman dressed in the borrowed mourning of a large woman and leading a very small long-haired observant little boy – it was his first funeral – appeared, closely followed by several friends of Mrs Johnson who had come to swell the display of respect and made only vague, confused impressions upon Mr Polly's mind. (Aunt Mildred, who was an unexplained family scandal, had declined Mrs Johnson's hospitality.)

Everybody was in profound mourning, of course, mourning in the modern English style, with the dyer's handiwork only too apparent, and hats and jackets of the current cut. There was very little crape, and the costumes had none of the goodness and specialisation and genuine enjoyment of mourning for mourning's sake that a similar Continental gathering would have displayed. Still that congestion of strangers in black sufficed to stun and confuse Mr Polly's impressionable mind. It seemed to him much more extraordinary than anything he had expected.

'Now, gals,' said Mrs Larkins, 'see if you can help,' and the three daughters became confusingly active between the front room and the back.

'I hope everyone'll take a glass of sherry and a biscuit,' said Mrs Johnson. 'We don't stand on ceremony,' and a decanter appeared in the place of Uncle Pentstemon's vegetables.

Uncle Pentstemon had refused to be relieved of his hat; he sat stiffly down on a chair against the wall with that venerable headdress between his feet, watching the approach of anyone jealously. 'Don't you go squashing my hat,' he said. Conversation became confused and general. Uncle Pentstemon addressed himself to Mr Polly. 'You're a little chap,' he said, 'a puny little chap. I never did agree to Lizzie marrying him, but I suppose bygones must be bygones now. I suppose they made you a clerk or something.'

'Outfitter,' said Mr Polly.

'I remember. Them girls pretend to be dressmakers.'

'They *are* dressmakers,' said Mrs Larkins across the room.

'I *will* take a glass of sherry. They 'old to it, you see.'

He took the glass Mrs Johnson handed him, and poised it critically between a horny finger and thumb. 'You'll be paying for this,' he said to Mr Polly. 'Here's *to* you . . . Don't you go treading on my hat, young woman. You brush your skirts against it and you take a shillin' off its value. It ain't the sort of 'at you see nowadays.'

He drank noisily.

The sherry presently loosened everybody's tongue, and the early coldness passed.

'There ought to have been a post-mortem,' Polly heard Mrs Punt remarking to one of Mrs Johnson's friends, and Miriam and another were lost in admiration of Mrs Johnson's decorations. 'So very nice and refined,' they were both repeating at intervals.

The sherry and biscuits were still being discussed when Mr Podger the undertaker arrived, a broad, cheerfully sorrowful, clean-shaven little man, accompanied by a melancholy-faced assistant. He conversed for a time with Johnson in the passage outside; the sense of his business stilled the rising waves of chatter and carried off everyone's attention in the wake of his heavy footsteps to the room above.

4

Things crowded upon Mr Polly. Everyone, he noticed, took sherry with a solemn avidity, and a small portion even was administered sacramentally to the Punt boy. There followed a distribution of black kid gloves, and much trying on and humouring of fingers. '*Good* gloves,' said one of Mrs Johnson's friends. 'There's a little pair there for Willie,' said Mrs Johnson triumphantly. Everyone seemed gravely content with the amazing procedure of the occasion. Presently Mr Podger was picking Mr Polly out as Chief Mourner to go with Mrs Johnson, Mrs Larkins and Annie in the first mourning carriage.

'Right-o,' said Mr Polly, and repented instantly of the alacrity of the phrase.

'There'll have to be a walking party,' said Mrs Johnson cheerfully. 'There's only two coaches. I dare say we can put in six in each, but that leaves three over.'

There was a generous struggle to be pedestrian, and the two other Larkins girls, confessing coyly to tight new boots and displaying a certain eagerness, were added to the contents of the first carriage.

'It'll be a squeeze,' said Annie.

'*I* don't mind a squeeze,' said Mr Polly.

He decided privately that the proper phrase for the result of that remark was 'hysterial catechunations'.

Mr Podger re-entered the room from a momentary supervision of the bumping business that was now proceeding down the staircase.

'Bearing up,' he said cheerfully, rubbing his hands together. 'Bearing up!'

That stuck very vividly in Mr Polly's mind, and so did the close-wedged drive to the churchyard, bunched in between two young women in confused dull and shiny black, and the fact that the wind was bleak and that the officiating clergyman had a cold and sniffed between his sentences. The wonder of life! The wonder of everything! What had he expected that this should all be so astoundingly different?

He found his attention converging more and more upon the Larkins cousins. The interest was reciprocal. They watched him with a kind of suppressed excitement and became risible with his every word and gesture. He was more and more aware of their personal quality. Annie had blue eyes and a red, attractive mouth, a harsh voice and a habit of extreme liveliness that even this occasion could not suppress; Minnie was fond, extremely free about the touching of hands and suchlike endearments; Miriam was dark and quieter than her sisters and regarded him earnestly. Mrs Larkins was very happy in her daughters, and they had the naïve affectionateness of those who see few people and find a strange cousin a wonderful outlet. Mr Polly had never been very much kissed, and it made his mind swim. He did not know for the life of him whether he liked or disliked all or any of the Larkins cousins. It was rather attractive to make them laugh; they laughed at anything.

There they were tugging at his mind, and the funeral tugging at his mind, too, and the sense of himself as Chief Mourner in a brand new silk hat with a broad mourning band. He watched the ceremony and missed his responses, and strange feelings twisted at his heartstrings.

5

Mr Polly walked back to the house because he wanted to be alone. Miriam and Minnie would have accompanied him, but finding Uncle Pentstemon beside the Chief Mourner they went on in front.

'You're wise,' said Uncle Pentstemon.

'Glad you think so,' said Mr Polly, rousing himself to talk.

'I likes a bit of walking before a meal,' said Uncle Pentstemon, and made a kind of large hiccup. 'That sherry rises,' he remarked. 'Grocer's stuff, I expect.'

He went on to ask how much the funeral might be costing, and seemed pleased to find Mr Polly didn't know.

'In that case,' he said impressively, 'it's pretty certain to cost more'n you expect, my boy.'

He meditated for a time. 'I've seen a mort of undertakers,' he declared; 'a mort of undertakers.'

The Larkins girls attracted his attention.

'Let's lodgin's and chars,' he commented. 'Leastways she goes out to cook dinners. And look at 'em! Dressed up to the nines. If it ain't borryd clothes, that is. And they goes out to work at a factory!'

'Did you know my father much, Uncle Pentstemon?' asked Mr Polly.

'Couldn't stand Lizzie throwin' herself away like that,' said Uncle Pentstemon, and repeated his hiccup on a larger scale.

'That *weren*'t good sherry,' said Uncle Pentstemon with the first note of pathos Mr Polly had detected in his quavering voice.

The funeral in the rather cold wind had proved wonderfully appetising, and every eye brightened at the sight of the cold collation that was now spread in the front room. Mrs Johnson was very brisk, and Mr Polly, when he re-entered the house found everybody sitting down. 'Come along, Alfred,' cried the hostess cheerfully. 'We can't very well begin without you. Have you got the bottled beer ready to open, Bessie? Uncle, you'll have a drop of whisky, I expect.'

'Put it where I can mix for myself,' said Uncle Pentstemon, placing his hat very carefully out of harm's way on the bookcase.

There were two cold boiled chickens, which Johnson carved with great care and justice, and a nice piece of ham, some brawn and a steak-and-kidney pie, a large bowl of salad and several sorts of pickles, and afterwards came cold apple tart, jam roll and a good piece of Stilton cheese, lots of bottled beer, some lemonade for the ladies and milk for Master Punt; a very bright and satisfying meal. Mr Polly found himself seated between Mrs Punt, who was much preoccupied with Master Punt's table manners, and one of Mrs Johnson's school friends, who was exchanging reminiscences of school days and news of how various common friends had changed and married with Mrs Johnson. Opposite him was Miriam and another of the Johnson circle, and also he had brawn to carve and there was hardly room for the helpful Bessie to pass behind his chair, so that altogether his mind would have been amply distracted from any mortuary broodings, even if a wordy warfare about the education of the modern young woman had not sprung up between Uncle Pentstemon and Mrs Larkins and threatened for a time, in spite of a word or so in season from Johnson, to wreck all the harmony of the sad occasion.

The general effect was after this fashion: First an impression of Mrs Punt on the right speaking in a refined undertone: 'You didn't, I suppose, Mr Polly, think to 'ave your poor dear father post-mortemed – '

Lady on the left side breaking in: 'I was just reminding Grace of the dear dead days beyond recall – '

Attempted reply to Mrs Punt: 'Didn't think of it for a moment. Can't give you a piece of this brawn, can I?'

Fragment from the left: 'Grace and Beauty they used to call us and we used to sit at the same desk – '

Mrs Punt, breaking out suddenly: 'Don't *swaller* your fork, Willy. You see, Mr Polly, I used to 'ave a young gentleman, a medical student, lodging with me – '

Voice from down the table: ' 'Am, Alfred? I didn't give you very much.'

Bessie became evident at the back of Mr Polly's chair, struggling wildly to get past. Mr Polly did his best to be helpful. 'Can you get past? Lemme sit forward a bit. Urr–oo! Right-o.'

Lady to the left going on valiantly and speaking to everyone who cares to listen, while Mrs Johnson beams beside her: 'There she used to sit as bold as brass, and the fun she used to make of things no one *could* believe – knowing her now. She used to make faces at the mistress through the – '

Mrs Punt keeping steadily on: 'The contents of the stummik at any rate *ought* to be examined.'

Voice of Mr Johnson. 'Elfrid, pass the mustid down.'

Miriam leaning across the table: 'Elfrid!'

'Once she got us all kept in. The whole school!'

Miriam, more insistently: 'Elfrid!'

Uncle Pentstemon, raising his voice defiantly: 'Trounce 'er again I would if she did as much now. That I would! Dratted mischief!'

Miriam, catching Mr Polly's eye: 'Elfrid! This lady knows Canterbury. I been telling her you been there.'

Mr Polly: 'Glad you know it.'

The lady shouting: 'I like it.'

Mrs Larkins, raising her voice: 'I won't 'ave my girls spoken of, not by nobody, old or young.'

Pop! imperfectly located.

Mr Johnson at large: '*Ain't* the beer up! It's the 'eated room.'

Bessie: ' 'Scuse me, sir, passing so soon again, but – ' Rest inaudible. Mr Polly, accommodating himself: 'Urr–oo! Right? Right-o.'

The knives and forks, probably by some secret common agreement, clash and clatter together and drown every other sound.

'Nobody 'ad the least idea 'ow 'e died – nobody . . . Willie, don't *golp* so. You ain't in a 'urry, are you? You don't want to ketch a train or anything – golping like that!'

'D'you remember, Grace, 'ow one day we 'ad writing lesson . . . '

'Nicer girls no one ever 'ad – though I say it who shouldn't.'

Mrs Johnson in a shrill clear hospitable voice: 'Harold, won't Mrs Larkins 'ave a teeny bit more fowl?'

Mr Polly rising to the situation. 'Or some brawn, Mrs Larkins?' Catching Uncle Pentstemon's eye: 'Can't send *you* some brawn, sir?'

'Elfrid!'

Loud hiccup from Uncle Pentstemon, momentary consternation followed by giggle from Annie.

The narration at Mr Polly's elbow pursued a quiet but relentless course. 'Directly the new doctor came in he said: "Everything must be took out and put in spirits – everything." '

Willie – audible ingurgitation.

The narration on the left was flourishing up to a climax. ' "Ladies," she sez, "dip their pens *in* their ink and keep their noses out of it!" '

'Elfrid!' – persuasively.

'Certain people may cast snacks at other people's daughters, never having had any of their own, though two poor souls of wives dead and buried through their goings on – '

Johnson ruling the storm: 'We don't want old scores dug up on such a day as this – '

'Old scores you may call them, but worth a dozen of them that put them to their rest, poor dears.'

'Elfrid!' – with a note of remonstrance.

'If you choke yourself, my lord, not another mouthful do you 'ave. No nice puddin'! Nothing!'

'And kept us in, she did, every afternoon for a week!'

It seemed to be the end, and Mr Polly replied with an air of being profoundly impressed: 'Really!'

'Elfrid!' – a little disheartened.

'And then they 'ad it! They found he'd swallowed the very key to unlock the drawer – '

'Then don't let people go casting snacks!'

'*Who's* casting snacks!'

'Elfrid! This lady wants to know, 'ave the Prossers left Canterbury?'

'No wish to make myself disagreeable, not to God's 'umblest worm – '

'Alf, you aren't very busy with that brawn up there!'

And so on for the hour.

The general effect upon Mr Polly at the time was at once confusing and exhilarating; but it led him to eat copiously and carelessly, and long before the end, when after an hour and a quarter a movement took the party and it pushed away its cheese plates and rose sighing and stretching from the remains of the repast, little streaks and bands of dyspeptic irritation and melancholy were darkening the serenity of his mind.

He stood between the mantel shelf and the window – the blinds were up now – and the Larkins sisters clustered about him. He battled with the oncoming depression and forced himself to be extremely facetious about two noticeable rings on Annie's hand. 'They ain't real,' said Annie coquettishly. 'Got 'em out of a prize packet.'

'Prize packet in trousers, I expect,' said Mr Polly, and awakened inextinguishable laughter.

'Oh! the Things you say!' said Minnie, slapping his shoulder.

Suddenly something he had quite extraordinarily forgotten came into his head.

'Bless my heart!' he cried, suddenly serious.

'What's the matter?' asked Johnson.

'Ought to have gone back to the shop – three days ago. They'll make no end of a row!'

'Lor, you *are* a Treat!' said cousin Annie, and screamed with laughter at a delicious idea. 'You'll get the Chuck,' she said.

Mr Polly made a convulsing grimace at her.

'I'll die!' she said. 'I don't believe you care a bit!'

Feeling a little disorganised by her hilarity and a shocked expression that had come to the face of cousin Miriam, he made some indistinct excuse and went out through the back room and scullery into the little garden. The cool air and a very slight drizzle of rain was a relief – anyhow. But the black mood of the replete dyspeptic had come upon him. His soul darkened hopelessly. He walked with his hands in his pockets down the path between the rows of exceptionally cultured peas, and unreasonably, overwhelmingly, he was smitten by sorrow for his father. The heady noise and muddle and confused excitement of the feast passed from him like a curtain drawn away. He thought of that hot and angry and struggling creature who had tugged and sworn so foolishly at the sofa upon the twisted staircase, and who was now lying still and hidden, at the bottom of a wall-sided oblong pit beside the heaped gravel that would presently cover him. The stillness of it! the wonder of it! the infinite reproach! Hatred for all these people – all of them – possessed Mr Polly's soul.

'Hen-witted gigglers,' said Mr Polly.

He went down to the fence, and stood with his hands on it staring away at nothing. He stayed there for what seemed a long time. From the house came a sound of raised voices that subsided, and then Mrs Johnson calling for Bessie.

'Gowlish gusto,' said Mr Polly. 'Jumping it in. Funererial Games. Don't hurt *him* of course. Doesn't matter to *him* . . .'

Nobody missed Mr Polly for a long time.

When at last he reappeared among them his eye was almost grim, but nobody noticed his eye. They were looking at watches, and Johnson was being omniscient about trains. They seemed to discover Mr Polly afresh just at the moment of parting, and said a number of more or less appropriate things. But Uncle Pentstemon was far too worried about his rush basket, which had been carelessly mislaid, he seemed to think with larcenous intentions, to remember Mr Polly at all. Mrs Johnson had tried to fob him off with a similar but inferior basket – his own had one handle mended with string according to a method of peculiar virtue and inimitable distinction known only to himself – and the old gentleman had taken her attempt as the gravest reflection upon his years and intelligence. Mr Polly was left very largely to the Larkins trio. Cousin Minnie became shameless and kept kissing him goodbye – and then finding out it wasn't time to go. Cousin Miriam seemed to think her silly, and caught Mr Polly's eye sympathetically. Cousin Annie ceased to giggle and lapsed into a nearly sentimental state. She said with real feeling that she had enjoyed the funeral more than words could tell.

CHAPTER FIVE

Mr Polly Takes a Vacation

Mr Polly returned to Clapham from the funeral celebration prepared for trouble, and took his dismissal in a manly spirit.

'You've merely antiseparated me by a hair,' he said politely.

And he told them in the dormitory that he meant to take a little holiday before his next crib, though a certain inherited reticence suppressed the fact of the legacy.

'You'll do that all right,' said Ascough, the head of the boot shop. 'It's quite the fashion just at present. Six Weeks in Wonderful Wood Street. They're running excursions . . . '

'A little holiday'; that was the form his sense of wealth took first, that it made a little holiday possible. Holidays were his life, and the rest merely adulterated living. And now he might take a little holiday and have money for railway fares and money for meals and money for inns. But – he wanted someone to take the holiday with.

For a time he cherished a design of hunting up Parsons, getting him to throw up his situation, and going with him to Stratford-on-Avon and Shrewsbury and the Welsh mountains and the Wye and a lot of places like that, for a really gorgeous, careless, illimitable old holiday of a month. But alas! Parsons had gone from the St Paul's Churchyard outfitter's long ago, and left no address.

Mr Polly tried to think he would be almost as happy wandering alone, but he knew better. He had dreamt of casual encounters with delightfully interesting people by the wayside – even romantic encounters. Such things happened in Chaucer and 'Bocashiew'; they happened with extreme facility in Mr Richard Le Gallienne's very detrimental book *The Quest of the Golden Girl*,[52] which he had read at Canterbury, but he had no confidence they would happen in England – to him.

When, a month later, he came out of the Clapham side door at last into the bright sunshine of a fine London day, with a dazzling sense of limitless freedom upon him, he did nothing more adventurous than order the cabman to drive to Waterloo and there take a ticket for Easewood.

He wanted – what *did* he want most in life? I think his distinctive craving is best expressed as fun – fun in companionship. He had already spent a pound or two upon three select feasts to his fellow assistants, sprat suppers they were, and there had been a great and very successful Sunday pilgrimage to Richmond, by Wandsworth and Wimbledon's open common, a trailing garrulous company walking about a solemnly happy host, to wonderful cold meat and salad at the Roebuck, a bowl of punch, punch! and a bill to correspond; but now it was a weekday, and he went down to Easewood with his bag and portmanteau in a solitary compartment, and looked out of the window upon a world in which every possible congenial soul seemed either toiling in a situation or else looking for one with a gnawing and hopelessly preoccupying anxiety. He stared out of the window at the exploitation roads of suburbs, and rows of houses all very much alike, either emphatically and impatiently To Let or full of rather busy unsocial people. Near Wimbledon he had a glimpse of golf links, and saw two elderly gentlemen who, had they chosen, might have been gentlemen of grace and leisure, addressing themselves to smite little hunted white balls great distances with the utmost bitterness and dexterity. Mr Polly could not understand them.

Every road he remarked, as freshly as though he had never observed it before, was bordered by inflexible palings or iron fences or severely disciplined hedges. He wondered if perhaps abroad there might be beautifully careless, unenclosed high roads. Perhaps after all the best way of taking a holiday is to go abroad.

He was haunted by the memory of what was either a half-forgotten picture or a dream: a carriage was drawn up by the wayside and four beautiful people, two men and two women graciously dressed, were dancing a formal ceremonious dance, full of bows and curtseys, to the music of a wandering fiddler they had encountered. They had been driving one way and he walking another – a happy encounter with this obvious result. They might have come straight out of happy Theleme, whose motto is: 'Do what thou wilt.' The driver had taken his two sleek horses out; they grazed unchallenged; and he sat on a stone clapping time with his hands while the fiddler played. The shade of the trees did not altogether shut out the sunshine, the grass in the wood was lush and full of still daffodils, the turf they danced on was starred with daisies.

Mr Polly, dear heart! firmly believed that things like that could and did happen – somewhere. Only it puzzled him that morning that he never saw them happening. Perhaps they happened south of Guildford. Perhaps they happened in Italy. Perhaps they ceased to happen a hundred years ago. Perhaps they happened just round the corner – on weekdays when all good Mr Pollys are safely shut up in shops. And so dreaming of delightful impossibilities until his heart ached for them, he was rattled along in the suburban train to Johnson's discreet home and the briskly stimulating welcome of Mrs Johnson.

2

Mr Polly translated his restless craving for joy and leisure into Harold Johnsonese by saying that he meant to look about him for a bit before going into another situation. It was a decision Johnson very warmly approved. It was arranged that Mr Polly should occupy his former room and board with the Johnsons in consideration of a weekly payment of eighteen shillings. And the next morning Mr Polly went out early and reappeared with a purchase, a safety bicycle,[53] which he proposed to study and master in the sandy lane below the Johnsons' house. But over the struggles that preceded his mastery it is humane to draw a veil.

And also Mr Polly bought a number of books: Rabelais for his own, and *The Arabian Nights*, the works of Sterne, a pile of *Tales from Blackwood*, cheap in a second-hand bookshop, the plays of William Shakespeare, a second-hand copy of Belloc's *Path to Rome*,[54] an odd volume of *Purchas his Pilgrimes*[55] and *The Life and Death of Jason*.[56]

'Better get yourself a good book on bookkeeping,' said Johnson, turning over perplexing pages.

A belated spring was now advancing with great strides to make up for lost time. Sunshine and a stirring wind were poured out over the land, fleets of towering clouds sailed upon urgent tremendous missions across the blue seas of heaven, and presently Mr Polly was riding a little unstably along unfamiliar Surrey roads, wondering always what was round the next corner, and marking the blackthorn and looking out for the first white flower-buds of the may. He was perplexed and distressed, as indeed are all right-thinking souls, that there is no may in early May.

He did not ride at the even pace sensible people use who have marked out a journey from one place to another, and settled what time it will take them. He rode at variable speeds, and always as though he was looking for something that, missing, left life attractive still, but a little wanting in significance. And sometimes he was so unreasonably happy he had to whistle and sing, and sometimes he was incredibly, but not at all painfully, sad. His indigestion vanished with air and exercise, and it was quite pleasant in the evening to stroll about the garden with Johnson and discuss plans for the future. Johnson was full of ideas. Moreover, Mr Polly had marked the road that led to Stamton, that rising populous suburb; and as his bicycle legs grew strong his wheel with a sort of inevitableness carried him towards the row of houses in a back street in which his Larkins cousins made their home together.

He was received with great enthusiasm.

The street was a dingy little street, a cul-de-sac of very small houses in a row, each with an almost flattened bow window and a blistered brown door with a black knocker. He poised his bright new bicycle against the window and knocked and stood waiting; he felt himself in his straw hat and black serge suit a very pleasant and prosperous-looking figure. The door was opened by cousin Miriam. She was wearing a bluish print dress that brought out a kind of sallow warmth in her skin, and although it was nearly four o'clock in the afternoon, her sleeves were tucked up, as if for some domestic work, above the elbows, showing her rather slender but very shapely yellowish arms. The loosely pinned bodice confessed a delicately rounded neck.

For a moment she regarded him with suspicion and a faint hostility, and then recognition dawned in her eyes.

'Why!' she said, 'it's cousin Elfrid!'

'Thought I'd look you up,' he said.

'Fancy you coming to see us like this!' she answered.

They stood confronting one another for a moment, while Miriam collected herself for the unexpected emergency.

'Exploratious menanderings,' said Mr Polly, indicating the bicycle.

Miriam's face betrayed no appreciation of the remark.

'Wait a moment,' she said, coming to a rapid decision, 'and I'll tell ma.'

She closed the door on him abruptly, leaving him a little surprised in the street. 'Ma!' he heard her calling, and swift speech followed, the import of which he didn't catch. Then she reappeared. It seemed but an instant, but she was changed; the arms had vanished into sleeves, the apron had gone, a certain pleasing disorder of the hair had been at least reproved.

'I didn't mean to shut you out,' she said, coming out upon the step. 'I just told ma. How are you, Elfrid? You *are* looking well. I didn't know you rode a bicycle. Is it a new one?'

She leaned upon his bicycle. 'Bright it is!' she said. 'What a trouble you must have to keep it clean!'

Mr Polly was aware of a rustling transit along the passage, and of the house suddenly full of hushed but strenuous movement.

'It's plated mostly,' said Mr Polly.

'What do you carry in that little bag thing?' she asked, and then branched off to: 'We're all in a mess today, you know. It's my cleaning up day today. I'm not a bit tidy I know, but I *do* like to 'ave a go in at things now and then. You got to take us as you find us, Elfrid. Mercy we wasn't all out.' She paused. She was talking against time. 'I *am* glad to see you again,' she repeated.

'Couldn't keep away,' said Mr Polly gallantly. 'Had to come over and see my pretty cousins again.'

Miriam did not answer for a moment. She coloured deeply. 'You *do say* things!' she said.

She stared at Mr Polly, and his unfortunate sense of fitness made him nod his head towards her, regard her firmly with a round brown eye, and add impressively: 'I don't say *which* of them.'

Her answering expression made him realise in an instant the terrible dangers he trifled with. Avidity flared up in her eyes. Minnie's voice came happily to dissolve the situation.

' 'Ello, Elfrid!' she said from the doorstep.

Her hair was just passably tidy, and she was a little effaced by a red blouse, but there was no mistaking the genuine brightness of her welcome.

He was to come in to tea, and Mrs Larkins, exuberantly genial in a floriferous but dingy flannel dressing gown, appeared to confirm that. He brought in his bicycle and put it in the narrow, empty passage, and everyone crowded into a small untidy kitchen, whose table had been hastily cleared of the debris of the midday repast.

'You must come in 'ere,' said Mrs Larkins, 'for Miriam's turning out the front room. I never did see such a girl for cleanin' up. Miriam's 'oliday's a scrub. You've caught us on the 'Op, as the sayin' is, but Welcome all the same. Pity Annie's at work today; she won't be 'ome till seven.'

Miriam put chairs and attended to the fire; Minnie edged up to Mr Polly and said: 'I *am* glad to see you again, Elfrid,' with a warm contiguous intimacy that betrayed a broken tooth. Mrs Larkins got out tea things, and descanted on the noble simplicity of their lives, and how he 'mustn't mind our simple ways'. They enveloped Mr Polly with a geniality that intoxicated his amiable nature; he insisted upon helping lay the things, and created enormous laughter by pretending not to know where plates and knives and cups ought to go. 'Who'm I going to sit next?' he said, and developed voluminous amusement by attempts to arrange the plates so that he could rub elbows with all three. Mrs Larkins had to sit down in the windsor chair by the grandfather clock (which was dark with dirt and not going) to laugh at her ease at his well-acted perplexity.

They got seated at last, and Mr Polly struck a vein of humour in telling them how he learnt to ride the bicycle. He found the mere repetition of the word 'wobble' sufficient to produce almost inextinguishable mirth.

'No foreseeing little accidentulous misadventures,' he said, 'none whatever.'

(Giggle from Minnie.)

'Stout elderly gentleman – shirt sleeves – large straw waste-paper-basket sort of hat – starts to cross the road – going to the oil shop – prodic refreshment of oil can – '

'Don't say you run 'im down,' said Mrs Larkins, gasping. 'Don't say you run 'im down, Elfrid!'

'Run 'im down! Not me, madam. I never run anything down. Wobble. Ring the bell. Wobble, wobble – '

(Laughter and tears.)

'No one's going to run him down. Hears the bell! Wobble. Gust of wind. Off comes the hat smack into the wheel. Wobble. *Lord! what's* going to happen? Hat across the road, old gentleman after it, bell, shriek. He ran into me. Didn't ring his bell, hadn't *got* a bell – just ran into me. Over I went clinging to his venerable head. Down he went with me clinging to him. Oil can blump, blump into the road.'

(Interlude while Minnie is attended to for crumb in the windpipe.)

'Well, what happened to the old man with the oil can?' said Mrs Larkins.

'We sat about among the debreece and had a bit of an argument. I told him he oughtn't to come out wearing such a dangerous hat – flying at things. Said if he couldn't control his hat he ought to leave it at home. High old jawbacious argument we had, I tell you. "I tell you, sir – " "I tell *you*, sir." Waw-waw-waw. Infuriacious. But that's the sort of thing that's constantly happening, you know – on a bicycle. People run into you, hens and cats and dogs and things. Everything seems to have its mark on you; everything.'

'*You* never run into anything.'

'Never. Swelpme,' said Mr Polly very solemnly.

'Never, 'e say!' squealed Minnie. 'Hark at 'im!' and relapsed into a condition that urgently demanded back thumping.

'Don't be so silly,' said Miriam, thumping hard.

Mr Polly had never been such a social success before. They hung upon his every word – and laughed. What a family they were for laughter! And he loved laughter. The background he apprehended dimly; it was very much the sort of background his life had always had. There was a threadbare tablecloth on the table, and the slop basin and teapot did not go with the cups and saucers, the plates were different again, the knives worn down, the butter lived in a greenish glass dish of its own. Behind was a dresser hung with spare and miscellaneous crockery, with a workbox and an untidy workbasket; there was an ailing musk plant in the window, and the tattered and blotched wallpaper was covered by bright-coloured grocers' almanacs. Feminine wrappings hung from pegs upon the door, and the floor was covered with a varied collection of fragments of oilcloth. The Windsor chair he sat in was unstable – which presently afforded material for humour. 'Steady, old nag,' he said; 'whoa, my friskiacious palfry!'

'The things he says! You never know what he won't say next!'

3

'You ain't talkin' of goin'!' cried Mrs Larkins.

'Supper at eight.'

'Stay to supper with *us*, now you 'ave come over,' said Mrs Larkins, with corroborating cries from Minnie. ' 'Ave a bit of a walk with the gals, and then come back to supper. You might all go and meet Annie while I straighten up and lay things out.'

'You're not to go touching the front room mind,' said Miriam.

'*Who's* going to touch yer front room?' said Mrs Larkins, apparently forgetful for a moment of Mr Polly.

Both girls dressed with some care while Mrs Larkins sketched the better side of their characters, and then the three young people went out to see something of Stamton. In the streets their risible mood gave way to a self-conscious propriety that was particularly evident in Miriam's bearing. They took Mr Polly to the Stamton Wreckeryation ground – that at least was what they called it – with its handsome custodian's cottage, its asphalt paths, its Jubilee drinking fountain, its clumps of wallflowers and daffodils, its charmingly artistic noticeboards with green borders and 'art' lettering, and so to the new cemetery and a distant view of the Surrey hills, and round by the gasworks to the canal and to the factory that presently disgorged a surprised and radiant Annie.

'El-*lo*,' said Annie.

It is very pleasant to every properly constituted mind to be a centre of amiable interest for one's fellow creatures; and when one is a young man conscious of becoming mourning and a certain wit, and the fellow creatures are three young and ardent and sufficiently expressive young women who dispute for the honour of walking by one's side, one may be excused a secret exaltation. They did dispute.

'I'm going to 'ave 'im now,' said Annie. 'You two've been 'aving 'im all the afternoon. Besides, I've got something to say to him.'

She had something to say to him. It came presently.

'I say,' she said abruptly. 'I *did* get them rings out of a prize packet.'

'What rings?' asked Mr Polly.

'What you saw at your poor father's funeral. You made out they meant something. They didn't – straight.'

'Then some people have been very remiss about their chances,' said Mr Polly, understanding.

'They haven't had any chances,' said Annie. 'I don't believe in making oneself too free with people.'

'Nor me,' said Mr Polly.

'I may be a bit larky and cheerful in my manner,' Annie admitted. 'But it don't *mean* anything. I ain't that sort.'

'Right-o,' said Mr Polly.

4

It was past ten when Mr Polly found himself riding back towards Easewood in a broad moonlight with a little Japanese lantern dangling from his handlebar and making a fiery circle of pinkish light on and round about his front wheel. He was mightily pleased with himself and the day. There had been four-ale to drink at supper mixed with ginger beer, very free and jolly in a jug. No shadow fell upon the agreeable excitement of his mind until he faced the anxious and reproachful face of Johnson, who had been sitting up for him, smoking and trying to read the odd volume of *Purchas his Pilgrimes* – about the monk who went into Sarmatia and saw the Tartar carts.

'Not had an accident, Elfrid?' said Johnson.

The weakness of Mr Polly's character came out in his reply. 'Not much,' he said. 'Pedal got a bit loose in Stamton, o' man. Couldn't ride it. So I looked up the cousins while I waited.'

'Not the Larkins lot?'

'Yes.'

Johnson yawned hugely and asked for and was given friendly particulars. 'Well,' he said, 'better get to bed. I have been reading that book of yours – rum stuff. Can't make it out quite. Quite out of date I should say if you asked me.'

'That's all right, o' man,' said Mr Polly.

'Not a bit of use for anything I can see.'

'Not a bit.'

'See any shops in Stamton?'

'Nothing to speak of,' said Mr Polly. 'Good-night, o' man.'

Before and after this brief conversation his mind ran on his cousins very warmly and prettily in the vein of high spring. Mr Polly had been drinking at the poisoned fountains of English literature, fountains so unsuited to the needs of a decent clerk or shopman, fountains charged with the dangerous suggestion that it becomes a man of gaiety and spirit to make love, gallantly and rather carelessly. It seemed to him that evening to be handsome and humorous and practicable to make love to all his cousins. It wasn't that he liked any of them particularly, but he liked something about them. He liked their youth and femininity, their resolute high spirits and their interest in him.

They laughed at nothing and knew nothing, and Minnie had lost a tooth and Annie screamed and shouted, but they were interesting, intensely interesting.

And Miriam wasn't so bad as the others. He had kissed them all and had been kissed in addition several times by Minnie – 'oscoolatory exercises'.

He buried his nose in his pillow and went to sleep – to dream of anything rather than getting on in the world, as a sensible young man in his position ought to have done.

5

And now Mr Polly began to lead a divided life. With the Johnsons he professed to be inclined, but not so conclusively inclined as to be inconvenient, to get a shop for himself – to be, to use the phrase he preferred, 'looking for an opening'. He would ride off in the afternoon upon that research, remarking that he was going to 'cast a strategetical eye' on Chertsey or Weybridge. But if not all roads still a great majority of them led by however devious ways to Stamton, and to laughter and increasing familiarity. Relations developed with Annie and Minnie and Miriam. Their various characters were increasingly interesting. The laughter became perceptibly less abundant, something of the fizz had gone from the first opening, still these visits remained wonderfully friendly and upholding. Then back he would come to grave but evasive discussions with Johnson.

Johnson was really anxious to get Mr Polly 'into something'. His was a reserved, honest character, and he would really have preferred to see his lodger doing things for himself than receive his money for housekeeping. He hated waste, anybody's waste, much more than he desired profit. But Mrs Johnson was all for Mr Polly's loitering. She seemed much the more human and likeable of the two to Mr Polly.

He tried at times to work up enthusiasm for the various avenues to wellbeing his discussion with Johnson opened. But they remained disheartening prospects. He imagined himself wonderfully smartened up, acquiring style and value in a London shop, but the picture was stiff and unconvincing. He tried to rouse himself to enthusiasm by the idea of his property increasing by leaps and bounds, by twenty pounds a year or so, let us say, each year, in a well-placed little shop, the corner shop Johnson favoured. There was a certain picturesque interest in imagining cut-throat economies, but his heart told him there would be little in practising them.

And then it happened to Mr Polly that real Romance came out of dreamland into life, and intoxicated and gladdened him with sweetly beautiful suggestions – and left him. She came and left him as that dear lady leaves so many of us, alas! not sparing him one jot or one tittle of the hollowness of her retreating aspect.

It was all the more to Mr Polly's taste that the thing should happen as things happen in books.

In a resolute attempt not to get to Stamton that day, he had turned due southward from Easewood towards a country where the abundance of bracken jungles, lady's smock, stitchwort, bluebells and grassy stretches by the wayside under shady trees does much to compensate the lighter type of mind for the absence of promising 'openings'. He turned aside from the road and wheeled his machine along a faintly marked attractive trail through bracken until he came to a heap of logs against a high old stone wall with damaged coping and wallflower plants already gone to seed. He sat down, balanced the straw hat on a convenient lump of wood, lit a cigarette, and abandoned himself to agreeable musings and the friendly observation of a cheerful little brown and grey bird his stillness presently encouraged to approach him. 'This is All Right,' said Mr Polly softly to the little brown and grey bird. 'Business – later.'

He reflected that he might go on this way for four or five years, and then be scarcely worse off than he had been in his father's lifetime.

'Vile Business,' said Mr Polly.

Then Romance appeared. Or, to be exact, Romance became audible.

Romance began as a series of small but increasingly vigorous movements on the other side of the wall, then as a voice murmuring, then as a falling of little fragments on the hither side and as ten pink fingertips, scarcely apprehended before Romance became startling and emphatically a leg, remained for a time a fine, slender, actively struggling limb, brown stockinged and wearing a brown toe-worn shoe, and then – A handsome red-haired girl wearing a short dress of blue linen was sitting astride the wall, panting, considerably disarranged by her climbing, and as yet unaware of Mr Polly . . .

His fine instincts made him turn his head away and assume an attitude of negligent contemplation, with his ears and mind alive to every sound behind him.

'Goodness!' said a voice with a sharp note of surprise.

Mr Polly was on his feet in an instant. 'Dear me! Can I be of any assistance?' he said with deferential gallantry.

'I don't know,' said the young lady, and regarded him calmly with clear blue eyes. 'I didn't know there was anyone here,' she added.

'Sorry,' said Mr Polly, 'if I am intrudaceous. I didn't know you didn't want me to be here.'

She reflected for a moment on the word. 'It isn't that,' she said, surveying him.

'I oughtn't to get over the wall,' she explained. 'It's out of bounds. At least in term time. But this being holidays – '

Her manner placed the matter before him.

'Holidays is different,' said Mr Polly.

'I don't want to actually *break* the rules,' she said.

'Leave them behind you,' said Mr Polly with a catch of the breath, 'where they are safe;' and marvelling at his own wit and daring, and indeed trembling within himself, he held out a hand for her.

She brought another brown leg from the unknown, and arranged her skirt with a dexterity altogether feminine. 'I think I'll stay on the wall,' she decided. 'So long as some of me's in bounds – '

She continued to regard him with eyes that presently danced in an irresistible smile of satisfaction. Mr Polly smiled in return.

'You bicycle?' she said.

Mr Polly admitted the fact, and she said she did too.

'All my people are in India,' she explained. 'It's beastly rot – I mean it's frightfully dull being left here alone.'

'All *my* people,' said Mr Polly, 'are in heaven!'

'I say!'

'Fact!' said Mr Polly. 'Got nobody.'

'And that's why – ' she checked her artless comment on his mourning. 'I say,' she said in a sympathetic voice, 'I *am* sorry. I really am. Was it a fire or a ship – or something?'

Her sympathy was very delightful. He shook his head. 'The ordinary tables of mortality,' he said. 'First one and then another.'

Behind his outward melancholy, delight was dancing wildly.

'Are *you* lonely?' asked the girl.

Mr Polly nodded.

'I was just sitting there in melancholy rectrospectatiousness,' he said, indicating the logs; and again a swift thoughtfulness swept across her face.

'There's no harm in our talking,' she reflected.

'It's a kindness. Won't you get down?'

She reflected, and surveyed the turf below and the scene around and him.

'I'll stay on the wall,' she said. 'If only for bounds' sake.'

She certainly looked quite adorable on the wall. She had a fine neck and pointed chin that was particularly admirable from below, and pretty eyes and fine eyebrows are never so pretty as when they look down upon one. But no calculation of that sort, thank heaven, was going on beneath her ruddy shock of hair.

6

'Let's talk,' she said, and for a time they were both tongue-tied.

Mr Polly's literary proclivities had taught him that under such circumstances a strain of gallantry was demanded. And something in his blood repeated that lesson.

'You make me feel like one of those old knights,' he said, 'who rode about the country looking for dragons and beautiful maidens and chivalresque adventures.'

'Oh!' she said. 'Why?'

'Beautiful maiden,' he said.

She flushed under her freckles with the quick bright flush those pretty red-haired people have. 'Nonsense!' she said.

'You are. I'm not the first to tell you that. A beautiful maiden imprisoned in an enchanted school.'

'*You* wouldn't think it enchanted!'

'And here am I – clad in steel. Well, not exactly, but my fiery war horse is anyhow. Ready to absquatulate all the dragons and rescue you.'

She laughed, a jolly laugh that showed delightfully gleaming teeth. 'I wish you could *see* the dragons,' she said with great enjoyment. Mr Polly felt they were a sun's distance from the world of everyday.

'Fly with me!' he dared.

She stared for a moment, and then went off into peals of laughter. 'You *are* funny!' she said. 'Why, I haven't known you five minutes.'

'One doesn't – in this medevial world. My mind is made up, anyhow.'

He was proud and pleased with his joke, and quick to change his key neatly. 'I wish one could,' he said.

'I wonder if people ever did!'

'If there were people like you.'

'We don't even know each other's names,' she remarked, with a descent to matters of fact.

'Yours is the prettiest name in the world.'

'How do you know?'

'It must be – anyhow.'

'It *is* rather pretty you know – it's Christabel.'

'What did I tell you?'

'And yours?'

'Poorer than I deserve. It's Alfred.'

'*I* can't call you Alfred.'

'Well, Polly.'

'It's a girl's name!'

For a moment he was out of tune. 'I wish it was!' he said, and could have bitten out his tongue at the Larkins sound of it.

'I shan't forget it,' she remarked consolingly.

'I say,' she said in the pause that followed. 'Why are you riding about the country on a bicycle?'

'I'm doing it because I like it.'

She sought to estimate his social status on her limited basis of experience. He stood leaning with one hand against the wall, looking up at her and tingling with daring thoughts. He was a littleish man, you must remember, but neither mean-looking nor unhandsome in those days, sunburnt by his holiday and now warmly flushed. He had an inspiration to simple speech that no practised trifler with love could have bettered. 'There *is* love at first sight,' he said, and said it sincerely.

She stared at him with eyes round and big with excitement.

'I think,' she said slowly, and without any signs of fear or retreat, 'I ought to get back over the wall.'

'It needn't matter to you,' he said. 'I'm just a nobody. But I know you are the best and most beautiful thing I've ever spoken to.' His breath caught against something. 'No harm in telling you that,' he said.

'I should have to go back if I thought you were serious,' she said after a pause, and they both smiled together.

After that they talked in a fragmentary way for some time. The blue eyes surveyed Mr Polly with kindly curiosity from under a broad, finely modelled brow, much as an exceptionally intelligent cat might survey a new sort of dog. She meant to find out all about him. She asked questions that riddled the honest knight in armour below, and probed ever nearer to the hateful secret of the shop and his normal servitude. And when he made a flourish and mispronounced a word a thoughtful shade passed like the shadow of a cloud across her face.

'Boom!' came the sound of a gong.

'Lordy!' cried the girl and flashed a pair of brown legs at him and was gone.

Then her pink fingertips reappeared, and the top of her red hair. 'Knight!' she cried from the other side of the wall. 'Knight there!'

'Lady!' he answered.

'Come again tomorrow!'

'At your command. But – '

'Yes?'

'Just one finger.'

'What do you mean?'

'To kiss.'

The rustle of retreating footsteps and silence . . .

But after he had waited next day for twenty minutes she reappeared, a little out of breath with the effort to surmount the wall – and head first this time. And it seemed to him she was lighter and more daring and altogether prettier than the dreams and enchanted memories that had filled the interval.

7

From first to last their acquaintance lasted ten days, but into that time Mr Polly packed ten years of dreams.

'He don't seem,' said Johnson, 'to take a serious interest in anything. That shop at the corner's bound to be snapped up if he don't look out.'

The girl and Mr Polly did not meet on every one of those ten days; one was Sunday and she could not come, and on the eighth the school reassembled and she made vague excuses. All their meetings amounted to this, that she sat on the wall, more or less in bounds as she expressed it, and let Mr Polly fall in love with her and try to express it below. She sat in a state of irresponsible exaltation, watching him and at intervals prodding a vivisecting point of encouragement into him – with that strange passive cruelty which is natural to her sex and age.

And Mr Polly fell in love, as though the world had given way beneath him and he had dropped through into another, into a world of luminous clouds and of a desolate hopeless wilderness of desiring and of wild valleys of unreasonable ecstasies, a world whose infinite miseries were finer and in some inexplicable way sweeter than the purest gold of the daily life, whose joys – they were indeed but the merest remote glimpses of joy – were brighter than a dying martyr's vision of heaven. Her smiling face looked down upon him out of heaven, her careless pose was the living body of life. It was senseless, it was utterly foolish, but all that was best and richest in Mr Polly's nature broke like a wave and foamed up at that girl's feet, and died, and never touched her. And she sat on the wall and marvelled at him and was amused, and once, suddenly moved and wrung by his pleading, she bent down rather shamefacedly and gave him a freckled, tennis-blistered little paw to kiss. And she looked into his eyes and suddenly felt a perplexity, a curious swimming of the mind that made her recoil and stiffen, and wonder afterwards and dream . . .

And then, with some dim instinct of self-protection, she went and told her three best friends, great students of character all, of this remarkable phenomenon she had discovered on the other side of the wall.

'Look here,' said Mr Polly, 'I'm wild for the love of you! I can't keep up this gesticulatious game any more! I'm not a Knight. Treat me as a human man. You may sit up there smiling, but I'd die in torments to have you mine for an hour. I'm nobody and nothing. But look here! Will you wait for me for five years? You're just a girl yet, and it wouldn't be hard.'

'Shut up!' said Christabel, in an aside he did not hear, and something he did not see touched her hand.

'I've always been just dilletentytating about till now, but I could work. I've just woke up. Wait till I've got a chance with the money I've got.'

'But you haven't got much money!'

'I've got enough to take a chance with, some sort of a chance. I'd find a chance. I'll do that anyhow. I'll go away. I mean what I say – I'll stop trifling and shirking. If I don't come back it won't matter. If I do – '

Her expression had become uneasy. Suddenly she bent down towards him.

'Don't!' she said in an undertone.

'Don't – what?'

'Don't go on like this! You're different! Go on being the knight who wants to kiss my hand as his – what did you call it?' The ghost of a smile curved her face. 'Gurdrum!'

'But – !'

Then through a pause they both stared at each other, listening.

A muffled tumult on the other side of the wall asserted itself.

'Shut *up*, Rosie!' said a voice.

'I tell you I will see! I can't half hear. Give me a leg up!'

'You Idiot! He'll see you. You're spoiling everything.'

The bottom dropped out of Mr Polly's world. He felt as people must feel who are going to faint.

'You've got someone – ' he said aghast.

She found life inexpressible to Mr Polly. She addressed some unseen hearers. 'You filthy little Beasts!' she cried with a sharp note of agony in her voice, and swung herself back over the wall and vanished. There was a squeal of pain and fear, and a swift, fierce altercation.

For a couple of seconds he stood agape.

Then a wild resolve to confirm his worst sense of what was on the other side of the wall made him seize a log, put it against the stones, clutch the parapet with insecure fingers, and lug himself to a momentary balance on the wall.

Romance and his goddess had vanished.

A red-haired girl with a pigtail was wringing the wrist of a school-fellow who shrieked with pain and cried: 'Mercy! mercy! Ooo! Christabel!'

'You idiot!' cried Christabel. 'You giggling Idiot!'

Two other young ladies made off through the beech trees from this outburst of savagery.

Then the grip of Mr Polly's fingers gave, and he hit his chin against the stones and slipped clumsily to the ground again, scraping his cheek against the wall and hurting his shin against the log by which he had reached the top. Just for a moment he crouched against the wall.

He swore, staggered to the pile of logs and sat down.

He remained very still for some time, with his lips pressed together.

'Fool,' he said at last; 'you Blithering Fool!' and began to rub his shin as though he had just discovered its bruises.

Afterwards he found his face was wet with blood – which was none the less red stuff from the heart because it came from slight abrasions.

CHAPTER SIX

Miriam

It is an illogical consequence of one human being's ill-treatment that we should fly immediately to another, but that is the way with us. It seemed to Mr Polly that only a human touch could assuage the smart of his humiliation. Moreover it had for some undefined reason to be a feminine touch, and the number of women in his world was limited.

He thought of the Larkins family – the Larkins whom he had not been near now for ten long days. Healing people they seemed to him now – healing, simple people. They had good hearts, and he had neglected them for a mirage. If he rode over to them he would be able to talk nonsense and laugh and forget the whirl of memories and thoughts that was spinning round and round so unendurably in his brain.

'Law!' said Mrs Larkins, 'come in! You're quite a stranger, Elfrid!'

'Been seeing to business,' said the unveracious Polly.

'None of 'em ain't at 'ome, but Miriam's just out to do a bit of shopping. Won't let me shop, she won't, because I'm so keerless. She's a wonderful manager, that girl. Minnie's got some work at the carpet place. 'Ope it won't make 'er ill again. She's a loving delikit sort, is Minnie . . . Come into the front parlour. It's a bit untidy, but you got to take us as you find us. Wot you been doing to your face?'

'Bit of a scrase with the bicycle,' said Mr Polly.

' 'Ow?'

'Trying to pass a carriage on the wrong side, and he drew up and ran me against a wall.'

Mrs Larkins scrutinised it. 'You ought to 'ave someone look after your scrases,' she said. 'That's all red and rough. It ought to be cold-creamed. Bring your bicycle into the passage and come in.'

She 'straightened up a bit', that is to say she increased the dislocation of a number of scattered articles, put a workbasket on the top of several books, swept two or three dog-eared numbers of the *Lady's Own Novelist* from the table into the broken armchair, and proceeded to sketch together the tea-things with various such interpolations as: 'Law, if I ain't forgot the butter!' All the while she talked of Annie's good spirits and cleverness with her millinery, and of Minnie's affection and Miriam's relative love of order and management. Mr Polly stood by the window uneasily and thought how good and sincere was the Larkins tone. It was well to be back again.

'You're a long time finding that shop of yours,' said Mrs Larkins.

'Don't do to be precipitous,' said Mr Polly.

'No,' said Mrs Larkins, 'once you got it you got it. Like choosing a 'usband. You better see you got it good. I kept Larkins 'esitating two years I did, until I felt sure of him. A 'ansom man 'e was as you can see by the looks of the girls, but 'ansom is as 'ansom does. You'd like a bit of jam to your tea, I expect? I 'ope they'll keep *their* men waiting when the time comes. I tell them if they think of marrying it only shows they don't know when they're well off. Here's Miriam!'

Miriam entered with several parcels in a net, and a peevish expression. 'Mother,' she said, 'you might 'ave prevented my going out with the net with the broken handle. I've been cutting my fingers with the string all the way 'ome.' Then she discovered Mr Polly and her face brightened.

' 'Ello, Elfrid!' she said. 'Where you been all this time?'

'Looking round,' said Mr Polly.

'Found a shop?'

'One or two likely ones. But it takes time.'

'You've got the wrong cups, mother.'

She went into the kitchen, disposed of her purchases, and returned with the right cups. 'What you done to your face, Elfrid?' she asked, and came and scrutinised his scratches. 'All rough it is.'

He repeated his story of the accident, and she was sympathetic in a pleasant homely way.

'You *are* quiet today,' she said as they sat down to tea.

'Meditatious,' said Mr Polly.

Quite by accident he touched her hand on the table, and she answered his touch.

'Why not?' thought Mr Polly, and looking up, caught Mrs Larkins's eye and flushed guiltily. But Mrs Larkins, with unusual restraint, said nothing. She merely made a grimace, enigmatical but in its essence friendly.

Presently Minnie came in with some vague grievance against the manager of the carpet-making place about his method of estimating piecework. Her account was redundant, defective and highly technical, but redeemed by a certain earnestness. 'I'm never within sixpence of what I reckon to be,' she said. 'It's a bit too 'ot.' Then Mr Polly, feeling that he was being conspicuously dull, launched into a description of the shop he was looking for and the shops he had seen. His mind warmed up as he talked.

'Found your tongue again,' said Mrs Larkins.

He had. He began to embroider the subject and work upon it. For the first time it assumed picturesque and desirable qualities in his mind. It stimulated him to see how readily and willingly they accepted his sketches. Bright ideas appeared in his mind from nowhere. He was suddenly enthusiastic.

'When I get this shop of mine I shall have a cat. Must make a home for a cat, you know.'

'What, to catch the mice?' said Mrs Larkins.

'No – sleep in the window. A venerable signor of a cat. Tabby. Cat's no good if it isn't tabby. Cat I'm going to have, and a canary! Didn't think of that before, but a cat and a canary seem to go, you know. Summer weather I shall sit at breakfast in the little room behind the shop, sun streaming in the window to rights, cat on a chair, canary singing and – Mrs Polly . . . '

' 'Ello!' said Mrs Larkins.

'Mrs Polly frying an extra bit of bacon. Bacon singing, cat singing, canary singing. Kettle singing. Mrs Polly – '

'But who's Mrs Polly going to be?' said Mrs Larkins.

'Figment of the imagination, ma'am,' said Mr Polly. 'Put in to fill up picture. No face to figure as yet. Still, that's how it will be, I can assure you. I think I must have a bit of garden. Johnson's the man for a garden of course,' he said, going off at a tangent, 'but I don't mean a fierce sort of garden. Earnest industry. Anxious moments. Fervous digging. Shan't go in for that sort of garden, ma'am. No! Too much backache for me. My garden will be just a patch of 'sturtiums and sweet pea. Red-brick yard, clothes-line. Trellis put up in odd time. Humorous wind vane. Creeper up the back of the house.'

'Virginia creeper?' asked Miriam.

'Canary creeper,' said Mr Polly.

'You *will* 'ave it nice,' said Miriam, desirously.

'Rather,' said Mr Polly. 'Ting-a-ling-a-ling. *Shop!*'

He straightened himself up and then they all laughed.

'Smart little shop,' he said. 'Counter. Desk. All complete. Umbrella stand. Carpet on the floor. Cat asleep on the counter. Ties and hose on a rail over the counter. All right.'

'I wonder you don't set about it right off,' said Miriam.

'Mean to get it exactly right, ma'am,' said Mr Polly.

'Have to have a tomcat,' said Mr Polly, and paused for an expectant moment. 'Wouldn't do to open shop one morning, you know, and find the window full of kittens. Can't sell kittens . . . '

When tea was over he was left alone with Minnie for a few minutes, and an odd intimation of an incident occurred that left Mr Polly rather scared and shaken. A silence fell between them – an uneasy silence. He sat with his elbows on the table looking at her. All the way from Easewood to Stamton his erratic imagination had been running upon neat ways of proposing marriage. I don't know why it should have done, but it had. It was a kind of secret exercise that had not had any definite aim at the time, but which now recurred to him with extra-ordinary force. He couldn't think of anything in the world that wasn't the gambit to a proposal. It was almost irresistibly fascinating to think how immensely a few words from him would excite and revolutionise Minnie. She was sitting at the table with a workbasket among the tea things, mending a glove in order to avoid her share of clearing away.

'I like cats,' said Minnie after a thoughtful pause. 'I'm always saying to mother, "I wish we 'ad a cat." But we couldn't 'ave a cat 'ere – not with no yard.'

'Never had a cat myself,' said Mr Polly. 'No!'

'I'm fond of them,' said Minnie.

'I like the look of them,' said Mr Polly. 'Can't exactly call myself fond.'

'I expect I shall get one someday. When about you get your shop.'

'I shall have my shop all right before long,' said Mr Polly. 'Trust me. Canary bird and all.'

She shook her head. 'I shall get a cat first,' she said. 'You never mean anything you say.'

'Might get 'em together,' said Mr Polly, with his sense of a neat thing outrunning his discretion.

'Why! 'ow d'you mean?' said Minnie, suddenly alert.

'Shop and cat thrown in,' said Mr Polly in spite of himself, and his head swam and he broke out into a cold sweat as he said it.

He found her eyes fixed on him with an eager expression. 'Mean to say – ' she began as if for verification.

He sprang to his feet, and turned to the window. 'Little dog!' he said, and moved doorward hastily. 'Eating my bicycle tyre, I believe,' he explained. And so escaped.

He saw his bicycle in the hall and cut it dead.

He heard Mrs Larkins in the passage behind him as he opened the front door.

He turned to her. 'Thought my bicycle was on fire,' he said. 'Outside. Funny fancy! All right, reely. Little dog outside . . . Miriam ready?'

'What for?'

'To go and meet Annie.'

Mrs Larkins stared at him. 'You're stopping for a bit of supper?'

'If I may,' said Mr Polly.

'You're a rum un,' said Mrs Larkins, and called: 'Miriam!'

Minnie appeared at the door of the room looking infinitely perplexed. 'There ain't a little dog anywhere, Elfrid,' she said.

Mr Polly passed his hand over his brow. 'I had a most curious sensation. Felt exactly as though something was up somewhere. That's why I said Little Dog. All right now.'

He bent down and pinched his bicycle tyre.

'You was saying something about a cat, Elfrid,' said Minnie.

'Give you one,' he answered without looking up. 'The very day my shop is opened.'

He straightened himself up and smiled reassuringly. 'Trust me,' he said.

2

When, after imperceptible manoeuvres by Mrs Larkins, he found himself starting circuitously through the inevitable recreation ground with Miriam to meet Annie, he found himself quite unable to avoid the topic of the shop that had now taken such a grip upon him. A sense of danger only increased the attraction. Minnie's persistent disposition to accompany them had been crushed by a novel and violent and urgently expressed desire on the part of Mrs Larkins to see her do something in the house sometimes –

'You really think you'll open a shop?' asked Miriam.

'I hate cribs,' said Mr Polly, adopting a moderate tone. 'In a shop there's this drawback and that, but one is one's own master.'

'That wasn't all talk?'

'Not a bit of it.

'After all,' he went on, 'a little shop needn't be so bad.'

'It's a 'ome,' said Miriam.

'It's a home.'

Pause.

'There's no need to keep accounts and that sort of thing if there's no assistant. I dare say I could run a shop all right if I wasn't interfered with.'

'I should like to see you in your shop,' said Miriam. 'I expect you'd keep everything tremendously neat.'

The conversation flagged.

'Let's sit down on one of those seats over there,' said Miriam. 'Where we can see those blue flowers.'

They did as she suggested, and sat down in a corner where a triangular bed of stock and delphinium brightened the asphalted traceries of the recreation ground.

'I wonder what they call those flowers,' she said. 'I always like them. They're handsome.'

'Delphicums and larkspurs,' said Mr Polly. 'They used to be in the park at Port Burdock.

'Floriferous corner,' he added approvingly.

He put an arm over the back of the seat, and assumed a more comfortable attitude. He glanced at Miriam, who was sitting in a lax, thoughtful pose with her eyes on the flowers. She was wearing her old dress – she had not had time to change - and the blue tones of her old dress brought out a certain warmth in her skin, and her pose exaggerated whatever was feminine in her rather lean and insufficient body, and rounded her flat chest delusively. A little line of light lay along her profile. The afternoon was full of transfiguring sunshine; children were playing noisily in the adjacent sandpit, some Judas trees were brightly a-bloom in the villa gardens that bordered the recreation ground, and all the place was bright with touches of young summer colour. It all merged with the effect of Miriam in Mr Polly's mind.

Her thoughts found speech. 'One did ought to be happy in a shop,' she said with a note of unusual softness in her voice.

It seemed to him that she was right. One did ought to be happy in a shop. Folly not to banish dreams that made one ache, dreams of townless woods and bracken tangles and red-haired linen-clad figures sitting in dappled sunshine upon grey and crumbling walls and looking queenly down on one with clear blue eyes. Cruel and foolish dreams they were, that ended in one's being laughed at and made a mock of. There was no mockery here.

'A shop's such a respectable thing to be,' said Miriam thoughtfully.

'*I* could be happy in a shop,' he said.

His sense of effect made him pause.

'If I had the right company,' he added.

She became very still.

Mr Polly swerved a little from the conversational ice-run upon which he had embarked.

'I'm not such a blooming Geezer,' he said, 'as not to be able to sell goods a bit. One has to be nosy over one's buying of course. But I shall do all right.'

He stopped, and felt falling, falling through the aching silence that followed.

'If you get the right company,' said Miriam.

'I shall get that all right.'

'You don't mean you've got someone – '

He found himself plunging.

'I've got someone in my eye, this minute,' he said.

'Elfrid!' she said, turning on him. 'You don't mean – '

Well, *did* he mean? 'I do!' he said.

'Not reely!' She clenched her hands to keep still.

He took the conclusive step.

'Well, you and me, Miriam, in a little shop – with a cat and a canary – ' He tried too late to get back to a hypothetical note. 'Just suppose it!'

'You mean,' said Miriam, 'you're in love with me, Elfrid?'

What possible answer can a man give to such a question but 'Yes!'

Regardless of the public park, the children in the sandpit and everyone, she bent forward and seized his shoulder and kissed him on the lips. Something lit up in Mr Polly at the touch. He put an arm about her and kissed her back, and felt an irrevocable act was sealed. He had a curious feeling that it would be very satisfying to marry and have a wife – only somehow he wished it wasn't Miriam. Her lips were very pleasant to him, and the feel of her in his arm.

They recoiled a little from each other and sat for a moment, flushed and awkwardly silent. His mind was altogether incapable of controlling its confusion.

'I didn't dream,' said Miriam, 'you cared – Sometimes I thought it was Annie, sometimes Minnie – '

'Always liked you better than them,' said Mr Polly.

'I loved you, Elfrid,' said Miriam, 'since ever we met at your poor father's funeral. Leastways I *would* have done, if I had thought – You didn't seem to mean anything you said.

'I *can't* believe it!' she added.

'Nor I,' said Mr Polly.

'You mean to marry me and start that little shop – '

'Soon as ever I find it,' said Mr Polly.

'I had no more idea when I came out with you – '

'Nor me!'

'It's like a dream.'

They said no more for a little while.

'I got to pinch myself to think it's real,' said Miriam. 'What they'll do without me at 'ome I can't imagine. When I tell them – '

For the life of him Mr Polly could not tell whether he was fullest of tender anticipations or regretful panic.

'Mother's no good at managing – not a bit. Annie don't care for 'ousework and Minnie's got no 'ed for it. What they'll do without me I can't imagine.'

'They'll have to do without you,' said Mr Polly, sticking to his guns.

A clock in the town began striking.

'Lor'!' said Miriam, 'we shall miss Annie – sitting 'ere and lovemaking!'

She rose and made as if to take Mr Polly's arm. But Mr Polly felt that their condition must be nakedly exposed to the ridicule of the world by such a linking, and evaded her movement.

Annie was already in sight before a flood of hesitation and terrors assailed Mr Polly.

'Don't tell anyone yet a bit,' he said.

'Only mother,' said Miriam firmly.

3

Figures are the most shocking things in the world. The prettiest little squiggles of black looked at in the right light, and yet consider the blow they can give you upon the heart. You return from a little careless holiday abroad, and turn over the page of a newspaper, and against the name of that distant, vague-conceived railway in mortgages upon which you have embarked the bulk of your capital you see instead of the familiar, persistent 95-6 (varying at most to 93 *ex. div.*) this slightly richer arrangement of marks: $76^{1}/_{2} – 78^{1}/_{2}$.

It is like the opening of a pit just under your feet!

So, too, Mr Polly's happy sense of limitless resources was obliterated suddenly by a vision of this tracery:

'298'

instead of the

'350'

he had come to regard as the fixed symbol of his affluence.

It gave him a disagreeable feeling about the diaphragm, akin in a remote degree to the sensation he had when the perfidy of the red-haired schoolgirl became plain to him. It made his brow moist.

'Going down a vortex!' he whispered.

By a characteristic feat of subtraction he decided that he must have spent sixty-two pounds.

'Funererial baked meats,' he said, recalling possible items.

The happy dream in which he had been living, of long warm days, of open roads, of limitless unchecked hours, of infinite time to look about him, vanished like a thing enchanted. He was suddenly back in the hard old economic world, that exacts work, that limits range, that discourages phrasing and dispels laughter. He saw Wood Street and its fearful suspenses yawning beneath his feet.

And also he had promised to marry Miriam, and on the whole rather wanted to.

He was distraught at supper. Afterwards, when Mrs Johnson had gone to bed with a slight headache, he opened a conversation with Johnson.

'It's about time, o' man, I saw about doing something,' he said. 'Riding about and looking at shops, all very debonnairious, o' man, but it's time I took one for keeps.'

'What did I tell you?' said Johnson.

'How do you think that corner shop of yours will figure out?' Mr Polly asked.

'You're really meaning it?'

'If it's a practable proposition, o' man. Assuming it's practable, what's your idea of the figures?'

Johnson went to the chiffonier, got out a letter and tore off the back sheet. 'Let's figure it out,' he said with solemn satisfaction. 'Let's see the lowest you could do it on.'

He squared himself to the task, and Mr Polly sat beside him like a pupil, watching the evolution of the grey, distasteful figures that were to dispose of his little hoard.

'What running expenses have we got to provide for?' said Johnson, wetting his pencil. 'Let's have them first. Rent? . . . '

At the end of an hour of hideous speculations, Johnson decided: 'It's close. But you'll have a chance.'

'M'm,' said Mr Polly. 'What more does a brave man want?'

'One thing you can do quite easily. I've asked about it.'

'What's that, o' man?' said Mr Polly.

'Take the shop without the house above it.'

'I suppose I might put my head in to mind it,' said Mr Polly, 'and get a job with my body.'

'Not exactly that. But I thought you'd save a lot if you stayed on here – being all alone as you are.'

'Never thought of that, o' man,' said Mr Polly, and reflected silently upon the needlessness of Miriam.

'We were talking of eighty pounds for stock,' said Johnson. 'Of course seventy-five is five pounds less, isn't it? Not much else we can cut.'

'No,' said Mr Polly.

'It's very interesting, all this,' said Johnson, folding up the half-sheet of paper and unfolding it. 'I wish sometimes I had a business of my own instead of a fixed salary. You'll have to keep books of course.'

'One wants to know where one is.'

'I should do it all by double entry,' said Johnson. 'A little troublesome at first, but far the best in the end.'

'Lemme see that paper,' said Mr Polly, and took it with the feeling of a man who takes a nauseating medicine, and scrutinised his cousin's neat figures with listless eyes.

'Well,' said Johnson, rising and stretching. 'Bed! Better sleep on it, o' man.'

'Right-o,' said Mr Polly, without moving; but indeed he could as well have slept upon a bed of thorns.

He had a dreadful night. It was like the end of the annual holiday, only infinitely worse. It was like a newly arrived prisoner's backward glance at the trees and heather through the prison gates. He had to go back to harness, and he was as fitted to go in harness as the ordinary domestic cat. All night, Fate, with the quiet complacency, and indeed at times the very face and gestures, of Johnson, guided him towards that undesired establishment at the corner near the station. 'O Lord!' he cried, 'I'd rather go back to cribs. I should keep my money anyhow.' Fate never winced.

'Run away to sea,' whispered Mr Polly, but he knew he wasn't man enough.

'Cut my blooming throat.'

Some braver strain urged him to think of Miriam, and for a little while he lay still . . .

'Well, o' man?' said Johnson, when Mr Polly came down to breakfast, and Mrs Johnson looked up brightly. Mr Polly had never felt breakfast so unattractive before.

'Just a day or so more, o' man – to turn it over in my mind,' he said.

'You'll get the place snapped up,' said Johnson.

There were times in those last few days of coyness with his destiny when his engagement seemed the most negligible of circumstances, and times – and these happened for the most part at nights after Mrs Johnson had indulged everybody in a Welsh rarebit – when it assumed so sinister and portentous an appearance as to make him think of suicide. And there were times too when he very distinctly desired to be married, now that the idea had got into his head, at any cost. Also he tried to recall all the circumstances of his proposal, time after time, and never quite succeeded in recalling what had brought the thing off. He went over to Stamton with a becoming frequency, and kissed all his cousins, and Miriam especially, a great deal, and found it very stirring and refreshing. They all appeared to know; and Minnie was tearful, but resigned. Mrs Larkins met him, and indeed enveloped him, with unwonted warmth, and there was a big pot of household jam for tea. But he could not make up his mind to sign his name to anything about the shop, though it crawled nearer and nearer to him, though the project had materialised now to the extent of a draft agreement with the place for his signature indicated in pencil.

One morning, just after Mr Johnson had gone to the station, Mr Polly wheeled his bicycle out into the road, went up to his bedroom, packed his long white nightshirt, a comb and a toothbrush in a manner that was as offhand as he could make it, informed Mrs Johnson, who was manifestly curious, that he was 'off for a day or two to clear his head', and fled forthright into the road; mounting, he turned his wheel towards the tropics and the equator and the south coast of England, and indeed more particularly to where the little village of Fishbourne slumbers and sleeps.

When he returned four days later, he astonished Johnson beyond measure by remarking so soon as the shop project was reopened: 'I've took a little contraption at Fishbourne, o' man, that I fancy suits me better.'

He paused, and then added in a manner, if possible, even more offhand: 'Oh! and I'm going to have a bit of a nuptial over at Stamton with one of the Larkins cousins.'

'Nuptial!' said Johnson.

'Wedding bells, o' man. Benedictine collapse.'

On the whole Johnson showed great self-control. 'It's your own affair, o' man,' he said, when things had been more clearly explained, 'and I hope you won't feel sorry when it's too late.'

But Mrs Johnson was first of all angrily silent, and then reproachful. 'I don't see what we've done to be made fools of like this,' she said. 'After all the trouble we've 'ad to make you comfortable and see after you. Out late and sitting up and everything. And then you go off as sly as sly without a word, and get a shop behind our backs as though you thought we meant to steal your money. I 'aven't patience with such deceitfulness, and I didn't think it of you, Elfrid. And now the letting season's 'arf gone by, and what I shall do with that room of yours I've no idea. Frank is frank, and fair play fair play; so *I* was told any'ow when I was a girl. Just as long as it suits you to stay 'ere you stay 'ere, and then it's off and no thank you whether we like it or not. Johnson's too easy with you. 'E sits there and doesn't say a word, and night after night 'e's been addin' and thinkin' for you, instead of seeing to his own affairs – '

She paused for breath.

'Unfortunate amoor,' said Mr Polly, apologetically and indistinctly. 'Didn't expect it myself.'

4

Mr Polly's marriage followed with a certain inevitableness.

He tried to assure himself that he was acting upon his own forceful initiative, but at the back of his mind was the completest realisation of his powerlessness to resist the gigantic social forces he had set in motion. He had got to marry under the will of society, even as in times past it has been appointed for other sunny souls under the will of society that they should be led out by serious and unavoidable fellow-creatures and ceremoniously drowned or burnt or hanged. He would have preferred infinitely a more observant and less conspicuous role, but the choice was no longer open to him. He did his best to play his part, and he procured some particularly neat check trousers to do it in. The rest of his costume, except for some bright-yellow gloves, a grey-and-blue-mixture tie and that the broad crape hat-band was changed for a livelier piece of silk, were the things he had worn at the funeral of his father. So nearly akin are human joy and sorrow.

The Larkins sisters had done wonders with grey sateen. The idea of orange blossom and white veils had been abandoned reluctantly on account of the expense of cabs. A novelette in which the heroine had stood at the altar in 'a modest going-away dress' had materially assisted this decision. Miriam was frankly tearful, and so indeed was Annie, but with laughter as well to carry it off. Mr Polly heard Annie say something vague, about never getting a chance because of Miriam always sticking about at home like a cat at a mouse-hole, that became, as people say, food for thought. Mrs Larkins was from the first flushed, garrulous, and wet and smeared by copious weeping; an incredibly soaked and crumpled and used-up pocket handkerchief never left the clutch of her plump red hand. 'Goo' girls, all of them,' she kept on saying in a tremulous voice; 'such-goo-goo-goo-girls!' She wetted Mr Polly dread-fully when she kissed him. Her emotion affected the buttons down the back of her bodice, and almost the last filial duty Miriam did before entering on her new life was to close that gaping orifice for the eleventh time. Her bonnet was small and ill-balanced, black adorned with red roses, and first it got over her right eye until Annie told her of it, and then she pushed it over her left eye and looked ferocious for a space, and after that baptismal kissing of Mr Polly the delicate millinery took fright and climbed right up to the back part of her head and hung on there by a pin, and flapped piteously at all the larger waves of emotion that filled the gathering. Mr Polly became more and more aware of that bonnet as time went on, until he felt for it like a thing alive. Towards the end it had yawning fits.

The company did not include Mrs Johnson, but Johnson came with a manifest surreptitiousness and backed against walls and watched Mr Polly with doubt and speculation in his large grey eyes and whistled noiselessly and doubtful on the edge of things. He was, so to speak, to be best man *sotto voce*. A sprinkling of girls in gay hats from Miriam's place of business appeared in church, great nudgers all of them, but only two came on afterwards to the house. Mrs Punt brought her son with his ever-widening mind – it was his first wedding – and a Larkins uncle, a Mr Voules, a licensed victualler, very kindly drove over in a gig from Sommershill with a plump, well-dressed wife to give the bride away. One or two total strangers drifted into the church and sat down observantly far away.

This sprinkling of people seemed only to enhance the cool brown emptiness of the church, the rows and rows of empty pews, disengaged prayer-books and abandoned hassocks. It had the effect of a preposterous misfit. Johnson consulted with a thin-legged, short-skirted verger about the disposition of the party. The officiating clergy appeared distantly in the doorway of the vestry, putting on his surplice, and relapsed into a contemplative cheek-scratching that was manifestly habitual. Before the bride arrived Mr Polly's sense of the church found an outlet in whispered criticisms of ecclesiastical architecture with Johnson. 'Early Norman arches, eh?' he said, 'or Perpendicular.'

'Can't say,' said Johnson.

'Telessated pavements, all right.'

'It's well laid anyhow.'

'Can't say I admire the altar. Scrappy rather with those flowers.'

He coughed behind his hand and cleared his throat. At the back of his mind he was speculating whether flight at this eleventh hour would be criminal or merely reprehensible bad taste. A murmur from the nudgers announced the arrival of the bridal party.

The little procession from a remote door became one of the enduring memories of Mr Polly's life. The verger had bustled to meet it, and arrange it according to tradition and morality. In spite of Mrs Larkins's 'Don't take her from me yet!' he made Miriam go first with Mr Voules and the bridesmaids followed – as did he himself, hopelessly unable to disentangle himself from the whispering maternal anguish of Mrs Larkins. Mrs Voules, a compact, rounded woman with a square, expressionless face, imperturbable dignity, and a dress of considerable fashion, completed the procession.

Mr Polly's eye fell first upon the bride; the sight of her filled him with a curious stir of emotion. Alarm, desire, affection, respect – and a queer element of reluctant dislike all played their part in that complex eddy. The grey dress made her a stranger to him, made her stiff and common-place; she was not even the rather drooping form that had caught his facile sense of beauty when he had proposed to her in the recreation ground. There was something too that did not please him in the angle of her hat; it was indeed an ill-conceived hat with large aimless rosettes of pink and grey. Then his mind passed to Mrs Larkins and the bonnet that was to gain such a hold upon him – it seemed to be flag-signalling as she advanced – and to the two eager, unrefined sisters he was acquiring.

A freak of fancy set him wondering where and when in the future a beautiful girl with red hair might march along some splendid aisle. Never mind! He became aware of Mr Voules.

He became aware of Mr Voules as a watchful, blue eye of intense forcefulness. It was the eye of a man who has got hold of a situation. He was a fat, short, red-faced man clad in a tight-fitting tail coat of black and white check with a coquettish bow tie under the lowest of a number of crisp little red chins. He held the bride under his arm with an air of invincible championship, and his free arm flourished a grey top hat of an equestrian type. Mr Polly instantly learnt from the eye that Mr Voules knew all about his longing for flight. Its azure pupil glowed with disciplined resolution. It said: 'I've come to give this girl away, and give her away I will. I'm here now and things have to go on all right. So don't think of it any more' – and Mr Polly didn't. A faint phantom of a certain 'li'le dog' that had hovered just beneath the threshold of consciousness vanished into black impossibility. Until the conclusive moment of the service was attained the eye of Mr Voules watched Mr Polly relentlessly, and then instantly he relieved guard, and blew his nose into a voluminous and richly patterned handkerchief, and sighed and looked round for the approval and sympathy of Mrs Voules, and nodded to her brightly like one who has always foretold a successful issue to things. Mr Polly felt then like a marionette that has just dropped off its wire. But it was long before that release arrived.

He became aware of Miriam breathing close to him.

'Hello!' he said, and feeling that was clumsy and would meet the eye's disapproval: 'Grey dress – suits you no end.'

Miriam's eyes shone under her hat-brim.

'Not reely!' she whispered.

'You're all right,' he said, with the feeling of the eye's observation and criticism stiffening his lips. He cleared his throat.

The verger's hand pushed at him from behind. Someone was driving Miriam towards the altar rail and the clergyman. 'We're in for it,' said Mr Polly to her sympathetically. 'Where? Here? Right-o.'

He was interested for a moment or so in something indescribably habitual in the clergyman's pose. What a lot of weddings he must have seen! Sick he must be of them!

'Don't let your attention wander,' said the eye.

'Got the ring?' whispered Johnson.

'Pawned it yesterday,' answered Mr Polly, and then had a dreadful moment under that pitiless scrutiny while he felt in the wrong waistcoat pocket . . .

The officiating clergy sighed deeply, began, and married them wearily and without any hitch.

'D' b'loved, we gath'd 'gether sight o' Gard 'n face this con'gation join 'gether Man Wom' Holy Mat'mony which is a 'bl state 'stooted by Gard in times man's innocency . . .'

Mr Polly's thoughts wandered wide and far, and once again something like a cold hand touched his heart, and he saw a sweet face in sunshine under the shadow of trees.

Someone was nudging him. It was Johnson's finger diverted his eyes to the crucial place in the Prayer Book to which they had come.

'Wiltou lover, cumfer, oner, keeper sickness and health . . .'

'Say, "I will." '

Mr Polly moistened his lips. 'I will,' he said hoarsely.

Miriam, nearly inaudible, answered some similar demand.

Then the clergyman said: 'Who gi's wom mar'd t' this man?'

'Well, *I'm* doing that,' said Mr Voules in a refreshingly full voice and looking round the church. 'You see, me and Martha Larkins being cousins – '

He was silenced by the clergyman's rapid grip directing the exchange of hands.

'Pete arf me,' said the clergyman to Mr Polly. 'Take thee Mirum wed' wife – '

'Take thee Mirum wed' wife,' said Mr Polly.

'Have hold this day ford.'

'Have hold this day ford.'

'Betworse, richpoo' – '

'Betworse, richpoo' . . . '

Then came Miriam's turn.

'Lego hands,' said the clergyman; 'got the ring? No! On the book. So! Here! Pete arf me, "Wi'is ring Ivy wed." '

'Wi'is ring Ivy wed – '

So it went on, blurred and hurried, like the momentary vision of an utterly beautiful thing seen through the smoke of a passing train –

'Now, my boy,' said Mr Voules at last, gripping Mr Polly's elbow tightly, 'you've got to sign the registry, and there you are! Done!'

Before him stood Miriam, a little stiffly, the hat with a slight rake across her forehead, and a kind of questioning hesitation in her face. Mr Voules urged him past her.

It was astounding. She was his wife!

And for some reason Miriam and Mrs Larkins were sobbing, and Annie was looking grave. Hadn't they after all wanted him to marry her? Because if that was the case – !

He became aware for the first time of the presence of Uncle Pentstemon, in the background but approaching, wearing a tie of a light mineral-blue colour, and grinning and sucking enigmatically and judiciously round his principal tooth.

5

It was in the vestry that the force of Mr Voules's personality began to show at its true value. He seemed to open out, like the fisherman's Ginn from the pot, and spread over things directly the restraints of the ceremony were at an end.

'Everything,' he said to the clergyman, 'excellent.' He also shook hands with Mrs Larkins, who clung to him for a space, and kissed Miriam on the cheek. 'First kiss for me,' he said, 'anyhow.'

He led Mr Polly to the register by the arm, and then got chairs for Mrs Larkins and his wife. He then turned on Miriam. 'Now, young people,' he said. 'One! or *I* shall again.

'That's right!' said Mr Voules. 'Same again, miss.'

Mr Polly was overcome with modest confusion, and turning, found a refuge from this publicity in the arms of Mrs Larkins. Then in a state of profuse moisture he was assaulted and kissed by Annie and Minnie, who were immediately kissed upon some indistinctly stated grounds by Mr Voules, who then kissed the entirely impassive Mrs Voules and smacked his lips and remarked: 'Home again safe and sound!' Then with a strange harrowing cry Mrs Larkins seized upon and bedewed Miriam with kisses, Annie and Minnie kissed each other, and Johnson went abruptly to the door of the vestry and stared into the church – no doubt with ideas of sanctuary in his mind. 'Like a bit of a kiss round sometimes,' said Mr Voules, and made a kind of hissing noise with his teeth, and suddenly smacked his hands together with great *éclat* several times. Meanwhile the clergyman scratched his cheek with one hand and fiddled the pen with the other and the verger coughed protestingly.

'The dog cart's just outside,' said Mr Voules. 'No walking home today for the bride, ma'am.'

'Not going to drive us?' cried Annie.

'The happy pair, miss. *Your* turn soon.'

'Get out!' said Annie. 'I shan't marry – ever.'

'You won't be able to help it. You'll have to do it – just to disperse the crowd.' Mr Voules laid his hand on Mr Polly's shoulder. 'The bridegroom gives his arm to the bride. Hands across and down the middle. Prump, Prump, Perump-pump-pump-pump-perump.'

Mr Polly found himself and the bride leading the way towards the western door.

Mrs Larkins passed close to Uncle Pentstemon, sobbing too earnestly to be aware of him. 'Such a goo-goo-goo-girl!' she sobbed.

'Didn't think *I'd* come, did you?' said Uncle Pentstemon, but she swept past him, too busy with the expression of her feelings to observe him.

'She didn't think I'd come, I lay,' said Uncle Pentstemon, a little foiled, but effecting an auditory lodgement upon Johnson.

'I don't know,' said Johnson uncomfortably. 'I suppose you were asked. How are you getting on?'

'I was *arst*,' said Uncle Pentstemon, and brooded for a moment.

'I goes about seeing wonders,' he added, and then in a sort of enhanced undertone: 'One of 'er girls gettin' married. That's what I mean by wonders. Lord's goodness! Wow!'

'Nothing the matter?' asked Johnson.

'Got it in the back for a moment. Going to be a change of weather, I suppose,' said Uncle Pentstemon. 'I brought 'er a nice present, too, what I got in this passel. Vallyble old tea caddy that uset' be my mother's. What I kep' my baccy in for years and years – till the hinge at the back got broke. It ain't been no use to me particular since, so thinks I, drat it! I may as well give it 'er as not . . . '

Mr Polly found himself emerging from the western door.

Outside, a crowd of half a dozen adults and about fifty children had collected, and hailed the approach of the newly wedded couple with a faint, indeterminate cheer. All the children were holding something in little bags, and his attention was caught by the expression of vindictive concentration upon the face of a small big-eared boy in the foreground. He didn't for the moment realise what these things might import. Then he received a stinging handful of rice in the ear, and a great light shone.

'Not yet, you young fool!' he heard Mr Voules saying behind him, and then a second handful spoke against his hat.

'Not yet,' said Mr Voules with increasing emphasis, and Mr Polly became aware that he and Miriam were the focus of two crescents of small boys, each with the light of massacre in his eyes and a grubby fist clutching into a paper bag for rice; and that Mr Voules was warding off probable discharges with a large red hand.

The dog cart was in charge of a loafer, and the horse and the whip were adorned with white favours, and the back seat was confused, but not untenable, with hampers. 'Up we go,' said Mr Voules, 'old birds in front and young ones behind.' An ominous group of ill-restrained rice-throwers followed them up as they mounted.

'Get your handkerchief for your face,' said Mr Polly to his bride, and taking the place next the pavement with considerable heroism, held on, gripped his hat, shut his eyes and prepared for the worst. 'Off!' said Mr Voules, and a concentrated fire came stinging Mr Polly's face.

The horse shied, and when the bridegroom could look at the world again it was manifest the dog cart had just missed an electric tram by a hair's breadth, and far away outside the church railings the verger and Johnson were battling with an active crowd of small boys for the life of the rest of the Larkins family. Mrs Punt and her son had escaped across the road, the son trailing and stumbling at the end of a remorseless arm, but Uncle Pentstemon, encumbered by the tea-caddy, was the centre of a little circle of his own, and appeared to be dratting them all very heartily. Remoter, a policeman approached with an air of tranquil unconsciousness.

'Steady, you idiot. Stead-y!' cried Mr Voules, and then over his shoulder: 'I brought that rice! I like old customs! Whoa! Stead-y.'

The dog cart swerved violently, and then, evoking a shout of ground-less alarm from a cyclist, took a corner, and the rest of the wedding party was hidden from Mr Polly's eyes.

'We'll get the stuff into the house before the old gal comes along,' said Mr Voules, 'if you'll hold the hoss.'

'How about the key?' asked Mr Polly.

'I got the key, coming.'

And while Mr Polly held the sweating horse and dodged the foam that dripped from its bit, the house absorbed Miriam and Mr Voules altogether. Mr Voules carried in the various hampers he had brought with him, and finally closed the door behind him.

For some time Mr Polly remained alone with his charge in the little blind alley outside the Larkins's house, while the neighbours scrutinised him from behind their blinds. He reflected that he was a married man, that he must look very like a fool, that the head of a horse is a silly shape and its eye a bulger; he wondered what the horse thought of him, and whether it really liked being held and patted on the neck or whether it only submitted out of contempt. Did it know he was married? Then he wondered if the clergyman had thought him much of an ass, and then whether the individual lurking behind the lace curtains of the front room next door was a man or a woman. A door opened over the way, and an elderly gentleman in a kind of embroidered fez appeared smoking a pipe with a quiet satisfied expression. He regarded Mr Polly for some time with mild but sustained curiosity. Finally he called: 'Hi!'

'Hello!' said Mr Polly.

'You needn't 'old that 'orse,' said the old gentleman.

'Spirited beast,' said Mr Polly. 'And' – with some faint analogy to ginger beer in his mind – 'he's up today.'

' 'E won't turn 'isself round,' said the old gentleman, 'any'ow. And there ain't no way through for 'im to go.'

'*Verbum sap*,' said Mr Polly, and abandoned the horse and turned to the door. It opened to him just as Mrs Larkins on the arm of Johnson, followed by Annie, Minnie, two friends, Mrs Punt and her son and at a slight distance Uncle Pentstemon, appeared round the corner.

'They're coming,' he said to Miriam, and put an arm about her and gave her a kiss.

She was kissing him back when they were startled violently by the shying of two empty hampers into the passage. Then Mr Voules appeared holding a third.

'Here! you'll 'ave plenty of time for that presently,' he said, 'get these hampers away before the old girl comes. I got a cold collation here to make her sit up. My eye!'

Miriam took the hampers, and Mr Polly under compulsion from Mr Voules went into the little front room. A profuse pie and a large ham had been added to the modest provision of Mrs Larkins, and a number of select-looking bottles shouldered the bottle of sherry and the bottle of port she had got to grace the feast. They certainly went better with the iced wedding cake in the middle. Mrs Voules, still impassive, stood by the window regarding these things with a faint approval.

'Makes it look a bit thicker, eh?' said Mr Voules, and blew out both his cheeks and smacked his hands together violently several times. 'Surprise the old girl no end.'

He stood back and smiled and bowed with arms extended as the others came clustering at the door.

'Why, *Un-cle* Voules!' cried Annie, with a rising note.

It was his reward.

And then came a great wedging and squeezing and crowding into the little room. Nearly everyone was hungry, and eyes brightened at the sight of the pie and the ham and the convivial array of bottles. 'Sit down everyone,' cried Mr Voules. 'Leaning against anything counts as sitting, and makes it easier to shake down the grub!'

The two friends from Miriam's place of business came into the room among the first, and then wedged themselves so hopelessly against Johnson in an attempt to get out again and take off their things upstairs that they abandoned the attempt. Amid the struggle Mr Polly saw Uncle Pentstemon relieve himself of his parcel by giving it to the bride. 'Here!' he said and handed it to her. 'Weddin' present,' he explained, and added with a confidential chuckle, '*I* never thought I'd 'ave to give you one – ever.'

'Who says steak-and-kidney pie?' bawled Mr Voules. 'Who says steak-and-kidney pie? You 'ave a drop of old Tommy, Martha. That's what you want to steady you . . . Sit down everyone and don't all speak at once. Who says steak-and-kidney pie? . . . '

'Vocificeratious,' whispered Mr Polly. 'Convivial vociferations.'

'Bit of 'am with it?' shouted Mr Voules, poising a slice of ham on his knife. 'Anyone 'ave a bit of 'am with it? Won't that little man of yours, Mrs Punt – won't 'e 'ave a bit of 'am . . . ?

'And now, ladies and gentlemen,' said Mr Voules, still standing and dominating the crammed roomful, 'now you got your plates filled and something I can warrant you good in your glasses, wot about drinking the 'ealth of the bride?'

'Eat a bit fust,' said Uncle Pentstemon, speaking with his mouth full, amidst murmurs of applause. 'Eat a bit fust.'

So they did, and the plates clattered and the glasses chinked.

Mr Polly stood shoulder to shoulder with Johnson for a moment.

'In for it,' said Mr Polly cheeringly. 'Cheer up, o' man, and peck a bit. No reason why *you* shouldn't eat, you know.'

The Punt boy stood on Mr Polly's boots for a minute, struggling violently against the compunction of Mrs Punt's grip.

'Pie,' said the Punt boy, 'Pie!'

'You sit 'ere and 'ave 'am, my lord!' said Mrs Punt, prevailing. 'Pie you can't 'ave and you won't.'

'Lor' bless my heart, Mrs Punt!' protested Mr Voules, 'let the boy 'ave a bit if he wants it – wedding and all!'

'You 'aven't 'ad 'im sick on your 'ands, Uncle Voules,' said Mrs Punt. 'Else you wouldn't want to humour his fancies as you do . . .'

'I can't help feeling it's a mistake, o' man,' said Johnson, in a confidential undertone. 'I can't help feeling you've been Rash. Let's hope for the best.'

'Always glad of good wishes, o' man,' said Mr Polly. 'You'd better have a drink of something. Anyhow, sit down to it.'

Johnson subsided gloomily, and Mr Polly secured some ham and carried it off and sat himself down on the sewing machine on the floor in the corner to devour it. He was hungry, and a little cut off from the rest of the company by Mrs Voules's hat and back, and he occupied himself for a time with ham and his own thoughts. He became aware of a series of jangling concussions on the table. He craned his neck and discovered that Mr Voules was standing up and leaning forward over the table in the manner distinctive of after-dinner speeches, tapping upon the table with a black bottle. 'Ladies and gentlemen,' said Mr Voules, raising his glass solemnly in the empty desert of sound he had made, and paused for a second or so. 'Ladies and gentlemen – the Bride.' He searched his mind for some suitable wreath of speech, and brightened at last with discovery. 'Here's luck to her!' he said at last.

'Here's luck!' said Johnson hopelessly but resolutely, and raised his glass. Everybody murmured: 'Here's luck.'

'Luck!' said Mr Polly, unseen in his corner, lifting a forkful of ham.

'That's all right,' said Mr Voules with a sigh of relief at having brought off a difficult operation. 'And now, who's for a bit more pie?'

For a time conversation was fragmentary again. But presently Mr Voules rose from his chair again; he had subsided with a contented smile after his first oratorical effort, and produced a silence by renewed hammering. 'Ladies and gents,' he said, 'fill up for the second toast – the happy Bridegroom!' He stood for half a minute searching his mind for the apt phrase that came at last in a rush. 'Here's (hic) luck to *him*,' said Mr Voules.

'Luck to him!' said everyone, and Mr Polly, standing up behind Mrs Voules, bowed amiably, amidst enthusiasm.

'He may say what he likes,' said Mrs Larkins, 'he's *got* luck. That girl's a treasure of treasures, and always has been ever since she tried to nurse her own little sister, being but three at the time, and fell the full flight of stairs from top to bottom; no hurt that any outward eye 'as even seen, but always ready and helpful, always tidying and busy. A treasure, I must say, and a treasure I will say, giving no more than her due . . . '

She was silenced altogether by a rapping sound that would not be denied. Mr Voules had been struck by a fresh idea and was standing up and hammering with the bottle again.

'The third toast, ladies and gentlemen,' he said; 'fill up, please. The Mother of the Bride. I – er . . . Uoo . . . Ere! . . . Ladies and gents, 'ere's luck to 'er! . . . '

7

The dingy little room was stuffy and crowded to its utmost limit, and Mr Polly's skies were dark with the sense of irreparable acts. Everybody seemed noisy and greedy and doing foolish things. Miriam, still in that unbecoming hat – for presently they had to start off to the station together – sat just beyond Mrs Punt and her son, doing her share in the hospitalities, and ever and again glancing at him with a deliberately encouraging smile. Once she leant over the back of the chair to him and whispered cheeringly: 'Soon be together now.' Next to her sat Johnson, profoundly silent, and then Annie, talking vigorously to a friend. Uncle Pentstemon was eating voraciously opposite, but with a kindling eye for Annie. Mrs Larkins sat next to Mr Voules. She was unable to eat a mouthful, she declared, it would choke her, but ever and again Mr Voules wooed her to swallow a little drop of liquid refreshment.

There seemed a lot of rice upon everybody, in their hats and hair and the folds of their garments.

Presently Mr Voules was hammering the table for the fourth time in the interests of the Best Man . . .

All feasts come to an end at last, and the break-up of things was precipitated by alarming symptoms on the part of Master Punt. He was taken out hastily after a whispered consultation, and since he had got into the corner between the fireplace and the cupboard, that meant everyone moving to make way for him. Johnson took the opportunity to say, 'Well – so long,' to anyone who might be listening, and disappear. Mr Polly found himself smoking a cigarette and walking up and down outside in the company of Uncle Pentstemon, while Mr Voules replaced bottles in hampers and prepared for departure, and the womenkind of the party crowded upstairs with the bride. Mr Polly felt taciturn, but the events of the day had stirred the mind of Uncle Pentstemon to speech. And so he spoke, discursively and disconnectedly, a little heedless of his listener as wise old men will.

'They do say,' said Uncle Pentstemon, 'one funeral makes many. This time it's a wedding. But it's all very much of a muchness . . .

' 'Am *do* get in my teeth nowadays,' said Uncle Pentstemon, 'I can't understand it. 'Tisn't like there was nubblicks or strings or such in 'am. It's a plain food, sure-ly.

'You *got* to get married,' said Uncle Pentstemon, resuming his discourse. 'That's the way of it. Some has. Some hain't. I done it long before I was your age. It hain't for me to blame you. You can't 'elp being the marrying sort any more than me. It's nat'ral – like poaching or drinking or wind on the stummik. You can't 'elp it and there you are! As for the good of it, there ain't no particular good in it as I can see. It's a toss up. The hotter come, the sooner cold; but they all gets tired of it sooner or later . . . I hain't no grounds to complain. Two I've 'ad and berried, and might 'ave 'ad a third, and never no worrit with kids – never . . .

'You done well not to 'ave the big gal. I will say that for ye. She's a gadabout grinny, she is, if ever was. A gadabout grinny. Mucked up my mushroom bed to rights, she did, and I 'aven't forgot it. Got the feet of a centipede, she 'as – all over everything and neither with your leave nor by your leave. Like a stray 'en in a pea patch. Cluck! cluck! Trying to laugh it off. *I* laughed 'er off, I did. Dratted lumpin baggage! . . . '

For a while he mused malevolently upon Annie, and routed out a reluctant crumb from some coy sitting-out place in his tooth.

'Wimmin's a toss up,' said Uncle Pentstemon. 'Prize packets they are, and you can't tell what's in 'em till you took 'em 'ome and undone 'em. Never was a bachelor married yet that didn't buy a pig in a poke. Never. Marriage seems to change the very natures in 'em through and through. You can't tell what they won't turn into – nohow.

'I seen the nicest girls go wrong,' said Uncle Pentstemon, and added with unusual thoughtfulness, 'Not that I mean *you* got one of that sort.'

He sent another crumb on to its long home with a sucking, encouraging noise.

'The *wust* sort's the grizzler,' Uncle Pentstemon resumed. 'If ever I'd 'ad a grizzler I'd up and 'it 'er on the 'ed with sumpthin' pretty quick. I don't think I could abide a grizzler,' said Uncle Pentstemon. 'I'd liefer 'ave a lump-about like that other gal. I would indeed. I lay I'd make 'er stop laughing after a bit for all 'er airs. And mind where her clumsy great feet went . . .

'A man's got to tackle 'em, whatever they be,' said Uncle Pentstemon, summing up the shrewd observation of an old-world lifetime. 'Good or bad,' said Uncle Pentstemon, raising his voice fearlessly, 'a man's got to tackle 'em.'

8

At last it was time for the two young people to catch the train for Waterloo *en route* for Fishbourne. They had to hurry, and as a concluding glory of matrimony they travelled second-class, and were seen off by all the rest of the party except the Punts, Master Punt being now beyond any question unwell.

'Off!' The train moved out of the station.

Mr Polly remained waving his hat and Mrs Polly her handkerchief until they were hidden under the bridge. The dominating figure to the last was Mr Voules. He had followed them along the platform waving the equestrian grey hat and kissing his hand to the bride.

They subsided into their seats.

'Got a compartment to ourselves anyhow,' said Mrs Polly after a pause.

Silence for a moment.

'The rice 'e must 'ave bought. Pounds and pounds!'

Mr Polly felt round his collar at the thought.

'Ain't you going to kiss me, Elfrid, now we're alone together?'

He roused himself to sit forward, hands on knees, cocked his hat over one eye, and assumed an expression of avidity becoming to the occasion.

'Never!' he said. 'Ever!' and feigned to be selecting a place to kiss with great discrimination.

'Come here,' he said, and drew her to him.

'Be careful of my 'at,' said Mrs Polly, yielding awkwardly.

CHAPTER SEVEN

The Little Shop at Fishbourne

For fifteen years Mr Polly was a respectable shopkeeper in Fishbourne.

Years they were in which every day was tedious, and when they were gone it was as if they had gone in a flash. But now Mr Polly had good looks no more, he was as I have described him in the beginning of this story, thirty-seven and fattish in a not very healthy way, dull and yellowish about the complexion, and with discontented wrinklings round his eyes. He sat on the stile above Fishbourne and cried to the heavens above him: 'Oh! Ro-o-o-tten Be-e-astly Silly Hole!' And he wore a rather shabby black morning coat and waistcoat, and his tie was richly splendid, being from stock, and his golf cap aslant over one eye.

Fifteen years ago, and it might have seemed to you that the queer little flower of Mr Polly's imagination must be altogether withered and dead, and with no living seed left in any part of him. But indeed it still lived as an insatiable hunger for bright and delightful experiences, for the gracious aspects of things, for beauty. He still read books when he had a chance, books that told of glorious places abroad and glorious times, that wrung a rich humour from life and contained the delight of words freshly and expressively grouped. But alas! there are not many such books, and for the newspapers and the cheap fiction that abounded more and more in the world Mr Polly had little taste. There was no epithet in them. And there was no one to talk to, as he loved to talk. And he had to mind his shop.

It was a reluctant little shop from the beginning.

He had taken it to escape the doom of Johnson's choice and because Fishbourne had a hold upon his imagination. He had disregarded the ill-built cramped rooms behind it in which he would have to lurk and live, the relentless limitations of its dimensions, the inconvenience of an underground kitchen that must necessarily be the living-room in winter, the narrow yard behind giving upon the yard of the Royal Fishbourne Hotel, the tiresome sitting and waiting for custom, the restricted prospects of trade. He had visualised himself and Miriam first as at breakfast on a clear bright winter morning amidst a tremendous smell of bacon, and then as having muffins for tea. He had also thought of sitting on the beach on Sunday afternoons and of going for a walk in the country behind the town and picking marguerites and poppies. But, in fact, Miriam and he were extremely cross at breakfast, and it didn't run to muffins at tea. And she didn't think it looked well, she said, to go trapesing about the country on Sundays.

It was unfortunate that Miriam never took to the house from the first. She did not like it when she saw it, and liked it less as she explored it. 'There's too many stairs,' she said, 'and the coal being indoors will make a lot of work.'

'Didn't think of that,' said Mr Polly, following her round.

'It'll be a hard house to keep clean,' said Miriam.

'White paint's all very well in its way,' said Miriam, 'but it shows the dirt something fearful. Better 'ave 'ad it nicely grained.'

'There's a kind of place here,' said Mr Polly, 'where we might have some flowers in pots.'

'Not me,' said Miriam. 'I've 'ad trouble enough with Minnie and 'er musk . . . '

They stayed for a week in a cheap boarding house before they moved in. They had bought some furniture in Stamton, mostly second-hand, but with new cheap cutlery and china and linen, and they had supplemented this from the Fishbourne shops. Miriam, relieved from the hilarious associations of home, developed a meagre and serious quality of her own, and went about with knitted brows pursuing some ideal of ' 'aving everything right'. Mr Polly gave himself to the arrangement of the shop with a certain zest, and whistled a good deal until Miriam appeared and said that it went through her head. So soon as he had taken the shop he had filled the window with aggressive posters announcing in no measured terms that he was going to open, and now he was getting his stuff put out he was resolved to show Fishbourne what window-dressing could do. He meant to give them boater straws, imitation panamas, bathing dresses with novelties in stripes, light flannel shirts, summer ties, and ready-made flannel trousers for men, youths and boys. Incidentally he watched the small fishmonger over the way, and had a glimpse of the china dealer next door, and wondered if a friendly nod would be out of place. And on the first Sunday in this new life he and Miriam arrayed themselves with great care, he in his wedding-funeral hat and coat and she in her going-away dress, and went processionally to church – a more respectable-looking couple you could hardly imagine – and looked about them.

Things began to settle down next week into their places. A few customers came, chiefly for bathing suits and hat guards, and on Saturday night the cheapest straw hats and ties, and Mr Polly found himself more and more drawn towards the shop door and the social charm of the street. He found the china dealer unpacking a crate at the edge of the pavement, and remarked that it was a fine day. The china dealer gave a reluctant assent, and plunged into the crate in a manner that presented no encouragement to a loquacious neighbour.

'Zealacious commerciality,' whispered Mr Polly to that unfriendly back view . . .

2

Miriam combined earnestness of spirit with great practical incapacity. The house was never clean nor tidy, but always being frightfully disarranged for cleaning or tidying up, and she cooked because food had to be cooked and with a sound moralist's entire disregard of the quality of the consequences. The food came from her hands done rather than improved, and looking as uncomfortable as savages clothed under duress by a missionary with a stock of outsizes. Such food is too apt to behave resentfully, rebel and work Obi.[57] She ceased to listen to her husband's talk from the day she married him, and ceased to unwrinkle the kink in her brow at his presence, giving herself up to mental states that had a quality of secret preoccupation. And she developed an idea, for which perhaps there was legitimate excuse, that he was lazy. He seemed to stand about in the shop a great deal, to read – an indolent habit – and presently to seek company for talking. He began to attend the bar parlour of the God's Providence Inn with some frequency, and would have done so regularly in the evening if cards, which bored him to death, had not arrested conversation. But the perpetual foolish variation of the permutations and combinations of two and fifty cards taken five at a time, and the meagre surprises and excitements that ensue, had no charms for Mr Polly's mind, which was at once too vivid in its impressions and too easily fatigued.

It was soon manifest the shop paid only in the least exacting sense, and Miriam did not conceal her opinion that he ought to bestir himself and 'do things', though what he was to do was hard to say. You see, when you have once sunk your capital in a shop you do not very easily get it out again. If customers will not come to you cheerfully and freely, the law sets limits upon the compulsion you may exercise. You cannot pursue people about the streets of a watering place, compelling them either by threats or importunity to buy flannel trousers. Additional sources of income for a tradesman are not always easy to find.

Wintershed, at the bicycle and gramophone shop to the right, played the organ in the church, and Clamp of the toy shop was pew opener and so forth; Gambell, the greengrocer, waited at table and his wife cooked, and Carter, the watchmaker, left things to his wife while he went about the world winding clocks; but Mr Polly had none of these arts, and wouldn't, in spite of Miriam's quietly persistent protests, get any other. And on summer evenings he would ride his bicycle about the country, and if he discovered a sale where there were books he would as often as not waste half the next day in going again to acquire a job lot of them haphazard, and bring them home tied about with a string, and hide them from Miriam under the counter in the shop. That is a heart-breaking thing for any wife with a serious investigatory turn of mind to discover. She was always thinking of burning these finds, but her natural turn for economy prevailed with her.

The books he read during those fifteen years! He read everything he got except theology, and as he read his little unsuccessful circumstances vanished and the wonder of life returned to him, the routine of reluctant getting up, opening shop, pretending to dust it with zest, breakfasting with a shop egg underdone or overdone or a herring raw or charred, and coffee made Miriam's way and full of little particles, the return to the shop, the morning paper, the standing, standing at the door saying, 'How do!' to passers-by, or getting a bit of gossip, or watching unusual visitors, all these things vanished as the auditorium of a theatre vanishes when the stage is lit. He acquired hundreds of books at last, old dusty books, books with torn covers and broken covers, fat books whose backs were naked string and glue – an inimical litter to Miriam.

There was, for example, *The Voyage of La Perouse*,[58] with many careful, explicit woodcuts and the frankest revelations of the ways of the eight-eenth-century sailorman, homely, adventurous, drunken, incontinent and delightful, until he floated, smooth and slow, with all sails set and mirrored in the glassy water, until his head was full of the thought of shining, kindly, brown-skinned women, who smiled at him and wreathed his head with unfamiliar flowers. He had, too, a piece of a book about the lost palaces of Yucatan, those vast terraces buried in primordial forest, of whose makers there is now no human memory. With La Perouse he linked *The Island Nights' Entertainments*,[59] and it never palled upon him that in the dusky stabbing of the 'Island of Voices' something poured over the stabber's hands 'like warm tea'. Queer incommunicable joy it is, the joy of the vivid phrase that turns the statement of the horridest fact to beauty!

And another book which had no beginning for him was the second

volume of the travels of the Abbés Huc and Gabet.[60] He followed
those two sweet souls from their lessons in Tibetan under Sandura the
Bearded (who called them donkeys, to their infinite benefit, and stole
their store of butter) through a hundred misadventures to the very
heart of Lhassa; and it was a thirst in him that was never quenched to
find the other volume, and whence they came, and who in fact they
were. He read Fenimore Cooper[61] and *Tom Cringle's Log*[62] side by side
with Joseph Conrad, and dreamt of the many-hued humanity of the
East and West Indies until his heart ached to see those sun-soaked
lands before he died. Conrad's prose had a pleasure for him that he was
never able to define, a peculiar deep-coloured effect. He found too one
day among a pile of soiled sixpenny books at Port Burdock, to which
place he sometimes rode on his ageing bicycle, Bart Kennedy's *A Sailor
Tramp*,[63] all written in livid jerks, and had for ever after a kindlier and
more understanding eye for every burly rough who slouched through
Fishbourne High Street. Sterne he read with a wavering appreciation
and some perplexity, but, except for the *Pickwick Papers*, for some reason
that I do not understand he never took at all kindly to Dickens. Yet he
liked Lever, and Thackeray's *Catherine*, and all Dumas until he got to
The Vicomte de Bragelonne.[64] I am puzzled by his insensibility to Dickens,
and I record it as a good historian should, with an admission of my
perplexity. It is much more understandable that he had no love for
Scott. And I suppose it was because of his ignorance of the proper
pronunciation of words that he infinitely preferred any prose to any
metrical writing.

A book he browsed over with a recurrent pleasure was Waterton's
Wanderings in South America.[65] He would even amuse himself by inventing descriptions of other birds in the Watertonian manner, new
birds that he invented, birds with peculiarities that made him chuckle
when they occurred to him. He tried to make Rusper, the ironmonger,
share this joy with him. He read Bates,[66] too, about the Amazon, but
when he discovered that you could not see one bank from the other, he
lost, through some mysterious action of the soul that again I cannot
understand, at least a tithe of the pleasure he had taken in that river. But
he read all sorts of things; a book of old Celtic stories collected by Joyce
charmed him and Mitford's *Tales of Old Japan*,[67] and a number of paper-
covered volumes, *Tales from Blackwood*, he had acquired at Easewood
remained a stand-by. He developed a quite considerable acquaintance
with the plays of William Shakespeare, and in his dreams he wore cinque
cento or Elizabethan clothes, and walked about a stormy, ruffling,
taverning, teeming world. Great land of sublimated things, thou World

of Books, happy asylum, refreshment and refuge from the world of everyday . . . !

The essential thing of those fifteen long years of shopkeeping is Mr Polly, well athwart the counter of his rather ill-lit shop, lost in a book or rousing himself with a sigh to attend to business.

Meanwhile he got little exercise; indigestion grew with him until it ruled all his moods; he fattened and deteriorated physically, great moods of distress invaded and darkened his skies, little things irritated him more and more, and casual laughter ceased in him. His hair began to come off until he had a large bald space at the back of his head. Suddenly one day it came to him – forgetful of those books and all he had lived and seen through them – that he had been in his shop for exactly fifteen years, that he would soon be forty, and that his life during that time had not been worth living, that it had been in apathetic and feebly hostile and critical company, ugly in detail and mean in scope – and that it had brought him at last to an outlook utterly hopeless and grey.

3

I have already had occasion to mention, indeed I have quoted, a certain high-browed gentleman living at Highbury, wearing a golden *pince-nez* and writing for the most part in that beautiful room, the library of the Reform Club. There he wrestles with what he calls 'social problems' in a bloodless but at times, I think one must admit, an extremely illuminating manner. He has a fixed idea that something called a 'collective intelligence' is wanted in the world, which means in practice that you and I and everyone have to think about things frightfully hard and pool the results, and oblige ourselves to be shamelessly and per- sistently clear and truthful and support and respect (I suppose) a perfect horde of professors and writers and artists and ill-groomed difficult people, instead of using our brains in a moderate, sensible manner to play golf and bridge (pretending a sense of humour prevents our doing anything else with them) and generally taking life in a nice, easy, gentle- manly way, confound him! Well, this dome-headed monster of intellect alleges that Mr Polly was unhappy entirely through that.

A rapidly complicating society [he writes], which as a whole declines to contemplate its future or face the intricate problems of its organis- ation, is in exactly the position of a man who takes no thought of dietary or regimen, who abstains from baths and exercise and gives his appetites free play. It accumulates useless and aimless lives as a man accumulates fat and morbid products in his blood, it declines in its collective efficiency and vigour and secretes discomfort and misery. Every phase of its evolution is accompanied by a maximum of avoidable distress and inconvenience and human waste . . .

Nothing can better demonstrate the collective dullness of our community, the crying need for a strenuous intellectual renewal, than the consideration of that vast mass of useless, uncomfortable, under-educated, under-trained and altogether pitiable people we contemplate when we use that inaccurate and misleading term, the Lower-Middle Class. A great proportion of the lower-middle class should properly be assigned to the unemployed and the unemployable. They are only not that because the possession of some small hoard of money, savings during a period of wage earning, an insurance policy or suchlike capital, prevents a direct appeal to the rates. But they are doing little or nothing for the community in return for what they consume; they have no understanding of any relation of service to the community, they have never been trained nor their imaginations touched to any social purpose. A great proportion of small shop-keepers, for example, are people who have, through the inefficiency that comes from inadequate training and sheer aimlessness, or improvements in machinery or the drift of trade, been thrown out of employment, and who set up in needless shops as a method of eking out the savings upon which they count. They contrive to make sixty or seventy per cent of their expenditure, the rest is drawn from the shrinking capital. Essentially their lives are failures, not the sharp and tragic failure of the labourer who gets out of work and starves, but a slow, chronic process of consecutive small losses which may end if the individual is exceptionally fortunate in an impoverished deathbed before actual bankruptcy or destitution supervenes. Their chances of ascendant means are less in their shops than in any lottery that was ever planned. The secular development of transit and communications has made the organisation of distributing businesses upon large and economical lines inevitable; except in the chaotic confusions of newly opened countries, the day when a man might earn an independent living by unskilled or practically unskilled retailing has gone for ever. Yet every year sees the melancholy procession towards petty bankruptcy and imprisonment for debt go on, and there is no statesmanship in us to avert it. Every issue of every trade journal has its four or five columns of abridged bankruptcy proceedings, nearly every item in which means the final collapse of another struggling family upon the resources of the community, and continually a fresh supply of superfluous artisans and shop assistants, coming out of employment with savings or 'help' from relations, of widows with a husband's insurance money, of the ill-trained sons of parsimonious fathers, replaces the fallen in the ill-equipped, jerry-built shops that everywhere abound . . .

I quote these fragments from a gifted, if unpleasant, contemporary for what they are worth. I feel this has come in here as the broad aspect of this *History*. I come back to Mr Polly sitting upon his gate and swearing in the east wind, and I so returning have a sense of floating across unbridged abysses between the General and the Particular. There, on the one hand, is the man of understanding, seeing clearly – I suppose he sees clearly – the big process that dooms millions of lives to thwarting and discomfort and unhappy circumstances, and giving us no help, no hint, by which we may get that better 'collective will and intelligence' which would dam the stream of human failure, and, on the other hand, Mr Polly sitting on his gate, untrained, unwarned, confused, distressed, angry, seeing nothing except that he is, as it were, netted in greyness and discomfort – with life dancing all about him; Mr Polly with a capacity for joy and beauty at least as keen and subtle as yours or mine.

4

I have hinted that our Mother England had equipped Mr Polly for the management of his internal concerns no whit better than she had for the direction of his external affairs. With a careless generosity she affords her children a variety of foods unparalleled in the world's history, including many condiments and preserved preparations novel to the human economy. And Miriam did the cooking. Mr Polly's system, like a confused and ill-governed democracy, had been brought to a state of perpetual clamour and disorder, demanding now evil and unsuitable internal satisfactions, such as pickles and vinegar and the crackling on pork, and now vindictive external expression, war and bloodshed throughout the world. So that Mr Polly had been led into hatred and a series of disagreeable quarrels with his landlord, his wholesalers, and most of his neighbours.

Rumbold, the china dealer next door, seemed hostile from the first for no apparent reason, and always unpacked his crates with a full back to his new neighbour, and from the first Mr Polly resented and hated that uncivil breadth of expressionless humanity, wanted to prod it, kick it, satirise it. But you cannot satirise a hack, if you have no friend to nudge while you do it.

At last Mr Polly could stand it no longer. He approached and prodded Rumbold.

' 'Ello!' said Rumbold, suddenly erect and turned about.

'Can't we have some other point of view?' said Mr Polly. 'I'm tired of the end elevation.'

'Eh?' said Mr Rumbold, frankly puzzled.

'Of all the vertebracious animals man alone raises his face to the sky, o' man. Well, why invert it?'

Rumbold shook his head with a helpless expression.

'Don't like so much Arreary Pensy.'

Rumbold distressed in utter obscurity.

'In fact, I'm sick of your turning your back on me, see?'

A great light shone on Rumbold. '*That*'s what you're talking about!' he said.

'That's it,' said Polly.

Rumbold scratched his ear with the three strawy jampots he held in his hand. 'Way the wind blows, I expect,' he said. 'But what's the fuss?'

'No fuss!' said Mr Polly. 'Passing Remark. I don't like it, o' man, that's all.'

'Can't help it, if the wind blows my stror,' said Mr Rumbold, still far from clear about it.

'It isn't ordinary civility,' said Mr Polly.

'Got to unpack 'ow it suits me. Can't unpack with the stror blowing into one's eyes.'

'Needn't unpack like a pig rooting for truffles, need you?'

'Truffles?'

'Needn't unpack like a pig.'

Mr Rumbold apprehended something.

'Pig!' he said, impressed. 'You calling me a pig?'

'It's the side I seem to get of you.'

' 'Ere,' said Mr Rumbold, suddenly fierce and shouting and marking his point with gesticulated jampots, 'you go indoors. I don't want no row with you, and I don't want you to row with me. I don't know what you're after, but I'm a peaceable man – teetotaller, too, and a good thing if *you* was. See? You go indoors!'

'You mean to say – I'm asking you civilly to stop unpacking with your back to me.'

'Pig ain't civil, and you ain't sober. You go indoors and lemme go on unpacking. You – you're excited.'

'D'you mean – !' Mr Polly was foiled.

He perceived an immense solidity about Rumbold.

'Get back to your shop and lemme get on with my business,' said Mr Rumbold. 'Stop calling me pigs. See? Sweep your pavemint.'

'I came here to make a civil request.'

'You came 'ere to make a row. I don't want no truck with you. See? I don't like the looks of you. See? And I can't stand 'ere all day arguing. See?'

Pause of mutual inspection.

It occurred to Mr Polly that probably he was to some extent in the wrong.

Mr Rumbold, blowing heavily, walked past him, deposited the jam-pots in his shop with an immense affectation that there was no Mr Polly in the world, returned, turned a scornful back on Mr Polly and dived to the interior of the crate. Mr Polly stood baffled. Should he kick this solid mass before him? Should he administer a resounding kick?

No!

He plunged his hands deeply into his trouser pockets, began to whistle and returned to his own doorstep with an air of profound unconcern. There for a time, to the tune of 'Men of Harlech', he contemplated the receding possibility of kicking Mr Rumbold hard. It would be splendid – and for the moment satisfying. But he decided not to do it. For indefinable reasons he could not do it. He went indoors and straightened up his dress ties very slowly and thoughtfully. Presently he went to the window and regarded Mr Rumbold obliquely. Mr Rumbold was still unpacking . . .

Mr Polly had no human intercourse thereafter with Rumbold for fifteen years. He kept up a Hate.

There was a time when it seemed as if Rumbold might go, but he had a meeting of his creditors and then went on unpacking as obtusely as ever.

5

Hinks, the saddler, two shops farther down the street, was a different case. Hinks was the aggressor – practically.

Hinks was a sporting man in his way, with that taste for checks in costume and tight trousers which is, under Providence, so mysteriously and invariably associated with equestrian proclivities. At first Mr Polly took to him as a character, became frequent in the God's Providence Inn under his guidance, stood and was stood drinks and concealed a great ignorance of horses until Hinks became urgent for him to play billiards or bet.

Then Mr Polly took to evading him, and Hinks ceased to conceal his opinion that Mr Polly was in reality a softish sort of flat.

He did not, however, discontinue conversation with Mr Polly; he would come along to him whenever he appeared at his door, and converse about sport and women and fisticuffs and the pride of life with an air of extreme initiation, until Mr Polly felt himself the faintest underdeveloped intimation of a man that had ever hovered on the verge of non-existence.

So he invented phrases for Hinks's clothes and took Rusper, the iron-monger, into his confidence upon the weaknesses of Hinks. He called him the 'chequered Careerist', and spoke of his patterned legs as 'shivery shakys'. Good things of this sort are apt to get round to people.

He was standing at his door one day, feeling bored, when Hinks appeared down the street, stood still and regarded him with a strange malignant expression for a space.

Mr Polly waved a hand in a rather belated salutation.

Mr Hinks spat on the pavement and appeared to reflect. Then he came towards Mr Polly portentously and paused, and spoke between his teeth in an earnest confidential tone.

'You been flapping your mouth about me, I'm told,' he said.

Mr Polly felt suddenly spiritless. 'Not that I know of,' he answered.

'Not that you know of, be blowed! You been flapping your mouth.'

'Don't see it,' said Mr Polly.

'Don't see it, be blowed! You go flapping your silly mouth about me and I'll give you a poke in the eye. See?'

Mr Hinks regarded the effect of this coldly but firmly, and spat again.

'Understand me?' he enquired.

'Don't recollect – ' began Mr Polly.

'Don't recollect, be blowed! You flap your mouth a damn sight too much. This place gets more of your mouth than it wants . . . Seen this?'

And Mr Hinks, having displayed a freckled fist of extraordinary size and pugginess in an ostentatiously familiar manner to Mr Polly's close inspection by sight and smell, turned it about this way and that and shaken it gently for a moment or so, replaced it carefully in his pocket as if for future use, receded slowly and watchfully for a pace, and then turned away as if to other matters, and ceased to be, even in outward seeming, a friend . . .

Mr Polly's intercourse with all his fellow tradesmen was tarnished sooner or later by some such adverse incident, until not a friend remained to him, and loneliness made even the shop door terrible. Shops bankrupted all about him and fresh people came and new acquaintances sprang up, but sooner or later a discord was inevitable; the tension under which these badly fed, poorly housed, bored and bothered neighbours lived made it inevitable. The mere fact that Mr Polly had to see them every day, that there was no getting away from them, was in itself sufficient to make them almost unendurable to his frettingly active mind.

Among other shopkeepers in the High Street there was Chuffles, the grocer, a small, hairy, silently intent polygamist, who was given rough music by the youth of the neighbourhood because of a scandal about his wife's sister, but who was nevertheless totally uninteresting, and Tonks, the second grocer, an old man with an older, very enfeebled wife, both submerged by piety. Tonks went bankrupt, and was succeeded by a branch of the National Provision Company, with a young manager exactly like a fox, except that he barked. The toy and sweetstuff shop was kept by an old woman of repellent manners, and so was the little fish shop at the end of the street. The Berlin wool shop, having gone bankrupt, became a newspaper shop, then fell to a haberdasher in consumption, and finally to a stationer; the three shops at the end of the street wallowed in and out of insolvency in the hands of a bicycle repairer and dealer, a gramophone dealer, a tobacconist, a sixpenny-halfpenny bazaar-keeper, a shoemaker, a greengrocer, and the exploiter of a cinematograph peep-show – but none of them supplied friendship to Mr Polly.

These adventurers in commerce were all more or less distraught souls, driving without intelligible comment before the gale of fate. The two milkmen of Fishbourne were brothers who had quarrelled about their father's will, and started up in opposition to each other; one was stone deaf and no use to Mr Polly, and the other was a sporting man with a natural dread of epithet who sided with Hinks. So it was all about him; on every hand it seemed were uncongenial people, uninteresting people or people who conceived the deepest distrust and hostility towards him, a magic circle of suspicious, preoccupied and dehumanised humanity. So the poison in his system poisoned the world without.

(But Boomer, the wine merchant, and Tashingford, the chemist, be it

noted, were fraught with pride and held themselves to be a cut above
Mr Polly. They never quarrelled with him, preferring to bear themselves from the outset as though they had already done so.)

As his internal malady grew upon Mr Polly and he became more and
more a battleground of fermenting foods and warring juices, he came to
hate the very sight, as people say, of every one of these neighbours.
There they were, every day and all the days, just the same, echoing his
own stagnation. They pained him all round the top and back of his
head; they made his legs and arms weary and spiritless. The air was
tasteless by reason of them. He lost his human kindliness.

In the afternoons he would hover in the shop, bored to death with his
business and his home and Miriam, and yet afraid to go out because of
his inflamed and magnified dislike and dread of these neighbours. He
could not bring himself to go out and run the gauntlet of the observant
windows and the cold estranged eyes.

One of his last friendships was with Rusper, the ironmonger. Rusper
took over Worthington's shop about three years after Mr Polly opened.
He was a tall, lean, nervous, convulsive man, with an upturned, back-
thrown, oval head, who read newspapers and the *Review of Reviews*[68]
assiduously, had belonged to a Literary Society somewhere once, and
had some defect of the palate that at first gave his lightest word a charm
and interest for Mr Polly. It caused a peculiar clicking sound, as though
he had something between a giggle and a gas-meter at work in his neck.

His literary admirations were not precisely Mr Polly's literary admirations; he thought books were written to enshrine Great Thoughts,
and that art was pedagogy in fancy dress, he had no sense of phrase or
epithet or richness of texture, but still he knew there were books. He
did know there were books and he was full of large windy ideas of the
sort he called 'Modern (kik) Thought', and seemed needlessly and
helplessly concerned about '(kik) the Welfare of the Race'.

Mr Polly would dream about that (kik) at nights.

It seemed to that undesirable mind of his that Rusper's head was the
most egg-shaped head he had ever seen; the similarity weighed upon
him, and when he found an argument growing warm with Rusper he
would say: 'Boil it some more, o' man; boil it harder!' or, 'Six minutes at
least,' allusions Rusper could never make head or tail of, and got at last
to disregard as a part of Mr Polly's general eccentricity. For a long time
that little tendency threw no shadow over their intercourse, but it
contained within it the seeds of an ultimate disruption.

Often during the days of this friendship Mr Polly would leave his shop
and walk over to Mr Rusper's establishment, and stand in his doorway

and enquire: 'Well, o' man, how's the Mind of the Age working?' and get quite an hour of it, and sometimes Mr Rusper would come into the outfitter's shop with, 'Heard the (kik) latest?' and spend the rest of the morning.

Then Mr Rusper married, and he married very inconsiderately a woman who was totally uninteresting to Mr Polly. A coolness grew between them from the first intimation of her advent. Mr Polly couldn't help thinking when he saw her that she drew her hair back from her forehead a great deal too tightly, and that her elbows were angular. His desire not to mention these things in the apt terms that welled up so richly in his mind made him awkward in her presence, and that gave her an impression that he was hiding some guilty secret from her. She decided he must have a bad influence upon her husband, and she made it a point to appear whenever she heard him talking to Rusper.

One day they became a little heated about the German peril.[69]

'I lay (kik) they'll invade us,' said Rusper.

'Not a bit of it. William's not the Xerxiacious sort.'

'You'll see, o' man.'

'Just what I shan't do.'

'Before (kik) five years are out.'

'Not it.'

'Yes.'

'No.'

'Yes.'

'Oh! Boil it hard!' said Mr Polly.

Then he looked up and saw Mrs Rusper standing behind the counter half hidden by a trophy of spades and garden shears and a knife-cleaning machine, and by her expression he knew instantly that she understood.

The conversation paled and presently Mr Polly withdrew.

After that, estrangement increased steadily.

Mr Rusper ceased altogether to come over to the outfitter's, and Mr Polly called upon the ironmonger only with the completest air of casuality. And everything they said to each other led now to flat contradiction and raised voices. Rusper had been warned in vague and alarming terms that Mr Polly insulted and made game of him; he couldn't discover exactly where; and so it appeared to him now that every word of Mr Polly's might be an insult meriting his resentment, meriting it none the less because it was masked and cloaked.

Soon Mr Polly's calls upon Mr Rusper ceased also, and then Mr Rusper, pursuing incomprehensible lines of thought, became afflicted with a specialised short-sightedness that applied only to Mr Polly. He would look in other directions when Mr Polly appeared, and his large oval face assumed an expression of conscious serenity and deliberate happy unawareness that would have maddened a far less irritable person than Mr Polly. It evoked a strong desire to mock and ape, and produced in his throat a cough of singular scornfulness, more particularly when Mr Rusper also assisted, with an assumed unconsciousness that was all his own.

Then one day Mr Polly had a bicycle accident.

His bicycle was now very old, and it is one of the concomitants of a bicycle's senility that its free wheel should one day obstinately cease to be free. It corresponds to that epoch in human decay when an old gentleman loses an incisor tooth. It happened just as Mr Polly was approaching Mr Rusper's shop, and the untoward chance of a motor car trying to pass a waggon on the wrong side gave Mr Polly no choice but to get on to the pavement and dismount. He was always accustomed to take his time and step off his left pedal at its lowest point, but the jamming of the free wheel gear made that lowest moment a transitory one, and the pedal was lifting his foot for another revolution before he realised what had happened. Before he could dismount according to his habit the pedal had to make a revolution, and before it could make a revolution Mr Polly found himself among the various sonorous things with which Mr Rusper adorned the front of his shop – zinc dustbins, household pails, lawn mowers, rakes, spades and all manner of clattering things. Before he got among them he had one of those agonising moments of helpless wrath and suspense that seem to last ages, in which one seems to perceive everything and think of nothing but words that are better forgotten. He sent a column of pails thundering across the doorway and dismounted with one foot in a sanitary dustbin amidst an enormous uproar of falling ironmongery.

'Put all over the place!' he cried, and found Mr Rusper emerging from his shop with the large tranquillities of his countenance puckered to anger, like the frowns in the brow of a reefing sail. He gesticulated speechlessly for a moment.

'(kik) Jer doing?' he said at last.

'Tin mantraps!' said Mr Polly.

'Jer (kik) doing?'

'Dressing all over the pavement as though the blessed town belonged to you! Ugh!'

And Mr Polly in attempting a dignified movement realised his entanglement with the dustbin for the first time. With a low embittering expression, he kicked his foot about in it for a moment very noisily, and finally sent it thundering to the kerb. On its way it struck a pail or so. Then Mr Polly picked up his bicycle and proposed to resume his homeward way. But the hand of Mr Rusper arrested him.

'Put it (kik) all (kik kik) back (kik).'

'Put it (kik) back yourself.'

'You got (kik) t'put it back.'

'Get out of the (kik) way.'

Mr Rusper laid one hand on the bicycle handle, and the other gripped Mr Polly's collar urgently. Whereupon Mr Polly said: 'Leggo!' and again, 'D'you *hear*! Leggo!' and then drove his elbow with considerable force into the region of Mr Rusper's midriff. Whereupon Mr Rusper, with a loud impassioned cry, resembling 'Woo (kik)' more than any other combination of letters, released the bicycle handle, seized Mr Polly by the cap and hair, and bore his head and shoulders downward. Thereat Mr Polly, emitting such words as everyone knows and nobody prints, butted his utmost into the concavity of Mr Rusper, entwined a leg about him and, after terrific moments of swaying instability, fell headlong beneath him amidst the bicycle and pails. There on the pavement these inexpert children of a pacific age, untrained in arms and uninured to violence, abandoned themselves to amateurish and absurd efforts to hurt and injure one another – of which the most palpable consequences were dusty backs, ruffled hair and torn and twisted collars. Mr Polly, by accident, got his finger into Mr Rusper's mouth, and strove earnestly for some time to prolong that aperture in the direction of Mr Rusper's ear before it occurred to Mr Rusper to bite him (and even then he didn't bite very hard), while Mr Rusper concentrated his mind almost entirely on an effort to rub Mr Polly's face on the pavement. (And their positions bristled with chances of the deadliest sort!) They didn't, from first to last, draw blood.

Then it seemed to each of them that the other had become endowed with many hands and several voices and great accessions of strength. They submitted to fate and ceased to struggle. They found themselves torn apart and held up by outwardly scandalised and inwardly delighted neighbours, and invited to explain what it was all about.

'Got to (kik) puttem all back!' panted Mr Rusper, in the expert grasp of Hinks. 'Merely asked him to (kik) puttem all back.'

Mr Polly was under restraint of little Clamp, of the toy shop, who was holding his hands in a complex and uncomfortable manner that he afterwards explained to Wintershed was a combination of something romantic called 'Ju-jitsu' and something else still more romantic called the 'Police Grip'.

'Pails,' explained Mr Polly in breathless fragments. 'All over the road. Pails. Bungs up the street with his pails. Look at them!'

'Deliber(kik)lib(kik)liberately rode into my goods (kik). Constantly (kik) annoying me (kik)!' said Mr Rusper.

They were both tremendously earnest and reasonable in their manner. They wished everyone to regard them as responsible and intellectual men acting for the love of right and the enduring good of the world. They felt they must treat this business as a profound and publicly significant affair. They wanted to explain and orate and show the entire necessity of everything they had done. Mr Polly was convinced he had never been so absolutely correct in all his life as when he planted his foot in the sanitary dustbin, and Mr Rusper considered his clutch at Mr Polly's hair as the one faultless impulse in an otherwise undistinguished career. But it was clear in their minds they might easily become ridiculous if they were not careful, if for a second they stepped over the edge of the high spirit and pitiless dignity they had hitherto maintained. At any cost they perceived they must not become ridiculous.

Mr Chuffles, the scandalous grocer, joined the throng about the principal combatants, mutely as became an outcast, and with a sad, distressed, helpful expression picked up Mr Polly's bicycle. Gambell's summer errand boy, moved by example, restored the dustbin and pails to their self-respect.

' '*E* ought – '*e* ought (kik) t'pick them up,' protested Mr Rusper.

'What's it all about?' said Mr Hinks for the third time, shaking Mr Rusper gently. 'As 'e been calling you names?'

'Simply ran into his pails – as anyone might,' said Mr Polly, 'and out he comes and scrags me!'

'(kik) Assault!' said Mr Rusper.

'He assaulted *me*,' said Mr Polly.

'Jumped (kik) into my dus'bin!' said Mr Rusper. 'That assault? Or isn't it?'

'You better drop it,' said Mr Hinks.

'Great pity they can't be'ave better, both of 'em,' said Mr Chuffles, glad for once to find himself morally unassailable.

'Anyone see it begin?' said Mr Wintershed.

'*I* was in the shop,' said Mrs Rusper suddenly from the doorstep, piercing the little group of men and boys with the sharp horror of an unexpected woman's voice. 'If a witness is wanted, I suppose I've got a tongue. I suppose I got a voice in seeing my own 'usband injured. My husband went out and spoke to Mr Polly, who was jumping off his bicycle all among our pails and things, and immediately 'e butted him in the stomach – immediately – most savagely – butted him. Just after his dinner too, and him far from strong. I could have screamed. But Rusper caught hold of him right away, I will say that for Rusper . . . '

'I'm going,' said Mr Polly suddenly, releasing himself from the Anglo-Japanese grip and holding out his hands for his bicycle.

'Teach you (kik) to leave things alone,' said Mr Rusper, with an air of one who has given a lesson.

The testimony of Mrs Rusper continued relentlessly in the background.

'You'll hear of me through a summons,' said Mr Polly, preparing to wheel his bicycle.

'(kik) Me too,' said Mr Rusper.

Someone handed Mr Polly a collar. 'This yours?'

Mr Polly investigated his neck. 'I suppose it is. Anyone seen a tie?'

A small boy produced a grimy strip of spotted blue silk.

'Human life isn't safe with you,' said Mr Polly as a parting shot.

'(kik) Yours isn't,' said Mr Rusper.

And they got small satisfaction out of the Bench, which refused altogether to perceive the relentless correctitude of the behaviour of either party, and reproved the eagerness of Mrs Rusper – speaking to her gently, firmly but exasperatingly as 'My Good Woman' and telling her to 'Answer the Question! Answer the Question!'

'Seems a Pity,' said the chairman, when binding them over to keep the peace, 'you can't behave like Respectable Tradesmen. Seems a Great Pity. Bad Example to the Young and all that. Don't do any Good to the town, don't do any Good to yourselves, don't do any manner of Good to have all the Tradesmen in the Place scrapping about the Pavement of an Afternoon. Think we're letting you off very easily this time, and hope it will be a Warning to you. Don't expect Men of your Position to come up before us. Very Regrettable Affair. Eh?'

He addressed the latter enquiry to his two colleagues.

'Exactly, exactly,' said the colleague to the right.

'Er – (kik),' said Mr Rusper.

7

But the disgust that overshadowed Mr Polly's being as he sat upon the stile had other and profounder justification than his quarrel with Rusper and the indignity of appearing before the county bench. He was for the first time in his business career short with his rent for the approaching quarter day, and, so far as he could trust his own handling of figures, he was sixty or seventy pounds on the wrong side of solvency. And that was the outcome of fifteen years of passive endurance of dullness throughout the best years of his life! What would Miriam say when she learnt this, and was invited to face the prospect of exile – heaven knows what sort of exile! – from their present home? She would grumble and scold and become limply unhelpful, he knew, and none the less so because he could not help things. She would say he ought to have worked harder, and a hundred such exasperating pointless things. Such thoughts as these require no aid from undigested cold pork and cold potatoes and pickles to darken the soul, and with these aids his soul was black indeed.

'May as well have a bit of a walk,' said Mr Polly at last, after nearly intolerable meditations, and sat round and put a leg over the stile.

He remained still for some time before he brought over the other leg.

'Kill myself,' he murmured at last.

It was an idea that came back to his mind nowadays with a continually increasing attractiveness – more particularly after meals. Life he felt had no further happiness to offer him. He hated Miriam, and there was no getting away from her whatever might betide. And for the rest there was toil and struggle, toil and struggle with a failing heart and dwindling courage, to sustain that dreary duologue. 'Life's insured,' said Mr Polly; 'place is insured. I don't see it does any harm to her or anyone.'

He stuck his hands in his pockets. 'Needn't hurt much,' he said. He began to elaborate a plan.

He found it quite interesting elaborating his plan. His countenance became less miserable and his pace quickened.

There is nothing so good in all the world for melancholia as walking, and the exercise of the imagination in planning something presently to be done, and soon the wrathful wretchedness had vanished from Mr Polly's face. He would have to do the thing secretly and elaborately, because otherwise there might be difficulties about the life insurance. He began to scheme how he could circumvent that difficulty . . .

He took a long walk, for after all what is the good of hurrying back to shop when you are not only insolvent but very soon to die? His dinner and the east wind lost their sinister hold upon his soul, and when at last he came back along the Fishbourne High Street, his face was unusually bright and the craving hunger of the dyspeptic was returning. So he went into the grocer's and bought a ruddily decorated tin of a brightly pink fishlike substance known as 'Deep Sea Salmon'. This he was resolved to consume, regardless of cost, with vinegar and salt and pepper as a relish to his supper.

He did, and since he and Miriam rarely talked, and Miriam thought honour and his recent behaviour demanded a hostile silence, he ate fast and copiously and soon gloomily. He ate alone, for she refrained, to mark her sense of his extravagance. Then he prowled into the High Street for a time, thought it an infernal place, tried his pipe and found it foul and bitter, and retired wearily to bed.

He slept for an hour or so and then woke up to the contemplation of Miriam's hunched back and the riddle of life – and this bright attractive idea of ending for ever and ever and ever all the things that were locking him in, this bright idea that shone like a baleful star above all the reek and darkness of his misery . . .

CHAPTER EIGHT

Making an End to Things

Mr Polly designed his suicide with considerable care, and a quite remarkable altruism. His passionate hatred for Miriam vanished directly the idea of getting away from her for ever became clear in his mind. He found himself full of solicitude then for her welfare. He did not want to buy his release at her expense. He had not the remotest intention of leaving her unprotected with a painfully dead husband and a bankrupt shop on her hands. It seemed to him that he could contrive to secure for her the full benefit of both his life insurance and his fire insurance if he managed things in a tactful manner. He felt happier than he had done for years scheming out this undertaking, albeit it was perhaps a larger and somberer kind of happiness than had fallen to his lot before. It amazed him to think he had endured his monotony of misery and failure for so long.

But there were some queer doubts and questions in the dim, half-lit background of his mind that he had very resolutely to ignore. 'Sick of it,' he had to repeat to himself aloud, to keep his determination clear and firm. His life was a failure, there was nothing more to hope for but unhappiness. Why shouldn't he?

His project was to begin the fire with the stairs that led from the ground floor to the underground kitchen and scullery. These he would soak with paraffin, and assist with firewood and paper and a brisk fire in the coal cellar underneath. He would smash a hole or so in the stairs to ventilate the blaze, and have a good pile of boxes and paper, and a convenient chair or so, in the shop above. He would have the paraffin can upset and the shop lamp, as if awaiting refilling, at a convenient distance in the scullery ready to catch. Then he would smash the house lamp on the staircase – a fall with that in his hand was to be the ostensible cause of the blaze – and then he would cut his throat at the top of the kitchen stairs, which would then become his funeral pyre. He would do all this on Sunday evening while Miriam was at church, and it would appear that he had fallen downstairs with the lamp and been burnt to death. There was really no flaw whatever that he could see in the scheme. He was quite sure he knew how to cut his throat, deep at the side and not to saw at the windpipe, and he was reasonably sure it wouldn't hurt him very much. And then everything would be at an end.

There was no particular hurry to get the thing done, of course, and meanwhile he occupied his mind with possible variations of the scheme . . .

It needed a particularly dry and dusty east wind, a Sunday dinner of exceptional virulence, a conclusive letter from Konk, Maybrick, Ghool and Gabbitas, his principal and most urgent creditors, and a conversation with Miriam arising out of arrears of rent and leading on to mutual character sketching, before Mr Polly could be brought to the necessary pitch of despair to carry out his plans. He went for an embittering walk, and came back to find Miriam in a bad temper over the tea things, with the brewings of three-quarters of an hour in the pot, and hot buttered muffin gone leathery. He sat eating in silence with his resolution made.

'Coming to church?' said Miriam after she had cleared away.

'Rather. I got a lot to be grateful for,' said Mr Polly.

'You got what you deserve,' said Miriam.

'Suppose I have,' said Mr Polly, and went and stared out of the back window at a despondent horse in the hotel yard.

He was still standing there when Miriam came downstairs dressed for church. Something in his immobility struck home to her. 'You'd better come to church than mope,' she said.

'I shan't mope,' he answered.

She remained still for a moment. Her presence irritated him. He felt that in another moment he should say something absurd to her, make some last appeal for that understanding she had never been able to give.

'Oh! *go* to church!' he said.

In another moment the outer door slammed upon her. 'Good riddance!' said Mr Polly.

He turned about. 'I've had my whack,' he said.

He reflected. 'I don't see she'll have any cause to holler,' he said. 'Beastly Home! Beastly Life!'

For a space he remained thoughtful. 'Here goes!' he said at last.

2

For twenty minutes Mr Polly busied himself about the house, making his preparations very neatly and methodically.

He opened the attic windows in order to make sure of a good draught through the house, and drew down the blinds at the back and shut the kitchen door to conceal his arrangements from casual observation. At the end he would open the door on the yard and so make a clean clear draught right through the house. He hacked at, and wedged off, the tread of a stair. He cleared out the coals from under the staircase, and built a neat fire of firewood and paper there, he splashed about paraffin and arranged the lamps and can even as he had designed, and made a fine inflammable pile of things in the little parlour behind the shop. 'Looks pretty arsonical,' he said as he surveyed it all. 'Wouldn't do to have a caller now. Now for the stairs!'

'Plenty of time,' he assured himself, and took the lamp which was to explain the whole affair and went to the head of the staircase between the scullery and the parlour. He sat down in the twilight with the unlit lamp beside him and surveyed things. He must light the fire in the coal cellar under the stairs, open the back door, then come up them very quickly and light the paraffin puddles on each step, then sit down here again and cut his throat.

He drew his razor from his pocket and felt the edge. It wouldn't hurt much, and in ten minutes he would be indistinguishable ashes in the blaze.

And this was the end of life for him!

The end! And it seemed to him now that life had never begun for him, never! It was as if his soul had been cramped and his eyes bandaged from the hour of his birth. Why had he lived such a life? Why had he submitted to things, blundered into things? Why had he never insisted on the things he thought beautiful and the things he desired, never sought them, fought for them, taken any risk for them, died rather than abandon them? They were the things that mattered. Safety did not matter. A living did not matter unless there were things to live for . . .

He had been a fool, a coward and a fool; he had been fooled, too, for no one had ever warned him to take a firm hold upon life, no one had ever told him of the littleness of fear, or pain, or death; but what was the good of going through it now again? It was over and done with.

The clock in the back parlour pinged the half hour.

'Time!' said Mr Polly, and stood up.

For an instant he battled with an impulse to put it all back, hastily, guiltily, and abandon this desperate plan of suicide for ever.

But Miriam would smell the paraffin!

'No way out this time, o' man,' said Mr Polly; and he went slowly downstairs, matchbox in hand.

He paused for five seconds, perhaps, to listen to noises in the yard of the Royal Fishbourne Hotel before he struck his match. It trembled a little in his hand. The paper blackened, and an edge of blue flame ran outward and spread. The fire burnt up readily, and in an instant the wood was crackling cheerfully.

Someone might hear. He must hurry.

He lit a pool of paraffin on the scullery floor, and instantly a nest of snaky, wavering blue flame became agog for prey. He went up the stairs three steps at a time with one eager blue flicker in pursuit of him. He seized the lamp at the top. 'Now!' he said and flung it smashing. The chimney broke, but the glass receiver stood the shock and rolled to the bottom, a potential bomb. Old Rumbold would hear that and wonder what it was! . . . He'd know soon enough!

Then Mr Polly stood hesitating, razor in hand, and then sat down. He was trembling violently, but quite unafraid.

He drew the blade lightly under one ear. 'Lord!' but it stung like a nettle!

Then he perceived a little blue thread of flame running up his leg. It arrested his attention, and for a moment he sat, razor in hand, staring at it. It must be paraffin on his trousers that had caught fire on the stairs. Of course his legs were wet with paraffin! He smacked the flicker with his hand to put it out, and felt his leg burn as he did so. But his trousers still charred and glowed. It seemed to him necessary that he must put this out before he cut his throat. He put down the razor beside him to smack with both hands very eagerly. And as he did so a thin tall red flame came up through the hole in the stairs he had made and stood still, quite still as it seemed, and looked at him. It was a strange-looking flame, a flattish salmon colour, redly streaked. It was so queer and quiet-mannered that the sight of it held Mr Polly agape.

'Whuff!' went the can of paraffin below, and boiled over with stinking white fire. At the outbreak the salmon-coloured flames shivered and ducked and then doubled and vanished, and instantly all the staircase was noisily ablaze.

Mr Polly sprang up and backwards, as though the uprushing tongues of fire were a pack of eager wolves.

'Good Lord!' he cried like a man who wakes up from a dream.

He swore sharply and slapped again at a recrudescent flame upon his leg.

'What the deuce shall I do? I'm soaked with the confounded stuff!'

He had nerved himself for throat-cutting, but this was fire!

He wanted to delay things, to put them off for a moment while he did his business. The idea of arresting all this hurry with water occurred to him.

There was no water in the little parlour and none in the shop. He hesitated for a moment whether he should not run upstairs to the bedrooms and get a ewer of water to throw on the flames. At this rate Rumbold's would be ablaze in five minutes! Things were going all too fast for Mr Polly. He ran towards the staircase door, and its hot breath pulled him up sharply. Then he dashed out through his shop. The catch of the front door was sometimes obstinate; it was now, and instantly he became frantic. He rattled and stormed and felt the parlour already ablaze behind him. In another moment he was in the High Street with the door wide open.

The staircase behind him was crackling now like horsewhips and pistol shots.

He had a vague sense that he wasn't doing as he had proposed, but the chief thing was his sense of that uncontrolled fire within. What was he going to do? There was the fire brigade station next door but one.

The Fishbourne High Street had never seemed so empty.

Far off at the corner by the God's Providence Inn a group of three stiff hobbledehoys in their black, best clothes, conversed intermittently with Taplow, the policeman.

'Hi!' bawled Mr Polly to them. 'Fire! Fire!' and struck by a horrible thought, the thought of Rumbold's deaf mother-in-law upstairs, began to bang and kick and rattle with the utmost fury at Rumbold's shop door.

'Hi!' he repeated. 'Fire!'

3

That was the beginning of the great Fishbourne fire, which burnt its way sideways into Mr Rusper's piles of crates and straw, and backwards to the petrol and stabling of the Royal Fishbourne Hotel, and spread from that basis until it seemed half Fishbourne would be ablaze. The east wind, which had been gathering in strength all that day, fanned the flames; everything was dry and ready, and the little shed beyond Rumbold's in which the local fire brigade kept its manual was alight before the Fishbourne fire hose could be saved from disaster. In marvellously little time a great column of black smoke, shot with red streamers, rose out of the middle of the High Street, and all Fishbourne was alive with excitement.

Much of the more respectable elements of Fishbourne society was in church or chapel; many, however, had been tempted by the blue sky and the hard freshness of spring to take walks inland, and there had been the usual disappearance of loungers and conversationalists from the beach and the back streets when at the hour of six the drawing of bolts and the turning of keys had ended the British Ramadan, that weekly interlude of drought our law imposes. The youth of the place were scattered on the beach or playing in backyards, under threat if their clothes were dirtied, and the adolescent were disposed in pairs among the more secluded corners to be found upon the outskirts of the place. Several godless youths, seasick but fishing steadily, were tossing upon the sea in old Tarbold the infidel's boat, and the Clamps were entertaining cousins from Port Burdock. Such few visitors as Fishbourne could boast in the spring were at church or on the beach. To all these that column of smoke did in a manner address itself. 'Look here!' it said, 'this, within limits, is your affair; what are you going to do?'

The three hobbledehoys, had it been a weekday and they in working clothes, might have felt free to act, but the stiffness of black was upon them and they simply moved to the corner by Rusper's to take a better view of Mr Polly beating at the door. The policeman was a young, inexpert constable with far too lively a sense of the public house. He put his head inside the Private Bar to the horror of everyone there. But there was no breach of the law, thank heaven! 'Polly's and Rumbold's on fire!' he said, and vanished again. A window in the top storey over Boomer's shop opened, and Boomer, captain of the fire brigade, appeared, staring out with a blank expression. Still staring, he began to fumble with his collar and tie; manifestly he had to put on his uniform. Hinks's dog, which had been lying on the pavement outside Wintershed's, woke up, and having regarded Mr Polly suspiciously for some time, growled nervously and went round the corner into Granville Alley. Mr Polly continued to beat and kick at Rumbold's door.

Then the public houses began to vomit forth the less desirable elements of Fishbourne society; boys and men were moved to run and shout, and more windows went up as the stir increased. Tashingford, the chemist, appeared at his door in shirtsleeves and an apron, with his photographic plate holders in his hand. And then, like a vision of purpose, came Mr Gambell, the greengrocer, running out of Clayford's Alley and buttoning on his jacket as he ran. His great brass fireman's helmet was on his head, hiding it all but the sharp nose, the firm mouth, the intrepid chin. He ran straight to the fire station and tried the door, and turned about and met the eye of Boomer still at his upper window. 'The key!' cried Mr Gambell, 'the key!'

Mr Boomer made some inaudible explanation about his trousers and half a minute.

'Seen old Rumbold?' cried Mr Polly, approaching Mr Gambell.

'Gone over Downford for a walk,' said Mr Gambell. 'He told me! But look 'ere! We 'aven't got the key!'

'Lord!' said Mr Polly, and regarded the china shop with open eyes. He knew the old woman must be there alone. He went back to the shop front and stood surveying it in infinite perplexity. The other activities in the street did not interest him. A deaf old lady somewhere upstairs there! Precious moments passing! Suddenly he was struck by an idea and vanished from public vision into the open door of the Royal Fishbourne Tap.

And now the street was getting crowded and people were laying their hands to this and that.

Mr Rusper had been at home reading a number of tracts upon Tariff Reform, during the quiet of his wife's absence in church, and trying to work out the application of the whole question to ironmongery. He heard a clattering in the street and for a time disregarded it, until a cry of 'Fire!' drew him to the window. He pencil-marked the tract of Chiozza Money's[70] that he was reading side by side with one by Mr Holt Schooling,[71] made a hasty note: 'Bal. of Trade say 12,000,000', and went to look out. Instantly he opened the window and ceased to believe the Fiscal Question the most urgent of human affairs.

'Good (kik) Gud!' said Mr Rusper.

For now the rapidly spreading blaze had forced the partition into Mr Rumbold's premises, swept across his cellar, clambered his garden wall by means of his well-tarred mushroom shed, and assailed the engine house. It stayed not to consume, but ran as a thing that seeks a quarry. Polly's shop and upper parts were already a furnace, and black smoke was coming out of Rumbold's cellar gratings. The fire in the engine house showed only as a sudden rush of smoke from the back, like something suddenly blown up. The fire brigade, still much under strength, were now hard at work in the front of the latter building; they had got the door open all too late, they had rescued the fire escape and some buckets, and were now lugging out their manual, with the hose already a dripping mass of molten, flaring, stinking rubber. Boomer was dancing about and swearing and shouting; this direct attack upon his apparatus outraged his sense of chivalry. The rest of the brigade hovered in a disheartened state about the rescued fire escape, and tried to piece Boomer's comments into some tangible instructions.

'Hi!' said Rusper from the window. '(kik)! What's up?'

Gambell answered him out of his helmet. 'Hose!' he cried. 'Hose gone!'

'I (kik) got hose!' cried Rusper.

He had. He had a stock of several thousand feet of garden hose, of various qualities and calibres, and now he felt was the time to use it. In another moment his shop door was open and he was hurling pails, garden syringes and rolls of garden hose out upon the pavement. '(kik) Undo it,' he cried, to the gathering crowd in the roadway.

They did. Presently a hundred ready hands were unrolling and spreading and tangling up and twisting and hopelessly involving Mr Rusper's stock of hose, sustained by an unquenchable assurance that presently it would in some manner contain and convey water, and Mr Rusper, on his knees, (kiking) violently, became incredibly busy with wire and brass junctions and all sorts of mysteries.

'Fix it to the (kik) bathroom tap!' said Mr Rusper.

Next door to the fire station was Mantell and Throbson's, the little Fishbourne branch of that celebrated firm, and Mr Boomer, seeking in a teeming mind for a plan of action, had determined to save this building. 'Someone telephone to the Port Burdock and Hampstead-on-Sea fire brigades,' he cried to the crowd and then to his fellows: 'Cut away the woodwork of the fire station!' and so led the way into the blaze with a whirling hatchet that effected wonders in ventilation in no time.

But it was not, after all, such a bad idea of his. Mantell and Throbson's was separated from the fire station in front by a glass-covered passage, and at the back the roof of a big outhouse sloped down to the fire station leads. The sturdy longshoremen, who made up the bulk of the fire brigade, assailed the glass roof of the passage with extraordinary gusto, and made a smashing of glass that drowned for a time the rising uproar of the flames.

A number of willing volunteers started off to the new telephone office in obedience to Mr Boomer's request, only to be told with cold official politeness by the young lady at the exchange that all that had been done on her own initiative ten minutes ago. She parleyed with these heated enthusiasts for a space, and then returned to the window.

And indeed the spectacle was well worth looking at. The dusk was falling, and the flames were showing brilliantly at half a dozen points. The Royal Fishbourne Hotel Tap, which adjoined Mr Polly to the west, was being kept wet by the enthusiastic efforts of a string of volunteers with buckets of water, and above at a bathroom window the little German waiter was busy with the garden hose. But Mr Polly's establishment looked more like a house afire than most houses on fire contrive to look from start to finish. Every window showed eager flickering flames, and flames like serpents' tongues were licking out of three large holes in the roof, which was already beginning to fall in. Behind, larger and abundantly spark-shot gusts of fire rose from the fodder that was now getting alight in the Royal Fishbourne Hotel stables. Next door to Mr Polly, Mr Rumbold's house was disgorging black smoke from the gratings that protected its underground windows, and smoke and occasional shivers of flame were also coming out of its first-floor windows. The fire station was better alight at the back than in front, and its woodwork burnt pretty briskly with peculiar greenish flickerings and a pungent flavour. In the street an inaggressively disorderly crowd clambered over the rescued fire escape and resisted the attempts of the three local constables to get it away from the danger of Mr Polly's tottering facade; a cluster of busy forms danced and shouted and advised on the noisy and smashing attempt to cut off Mantell and Throbson's from the fire station that was still in ineffectual progress. Further a number of people appeared to be destroying interminable red and grey snakes under the heated direction of Mr Rusper; it was as if the High Street had a plague of worms; and beyond again the more timid and less active crowded in front of an accumulation of arrested traffic. Most of the men were in sabbatical black, and this and the white and starched quality of the women and children in their best clothes gave a note of ceremony to the whole affair.

For a moment the attention of the telephone clerk was held by the activities of Mr Tashingford, the chemist, who, regardless of everyone else, was rushing across the road hurling fire grenades into the fire station and running back for more, and then her eyes lifted to the slanting outhouse roof that went up to a ridge behind the parapet of Mantell and Throbson's. An expression of incredulity came into the telephone operator's eyes and gave place to hard activity. She flung up the window and screamed out: 'Two people on the roof up there! Two people on the roof!'

4

Her eyes had not deceived her. Two figures which had emerged from the upper staircase window of Mr Rumbold's and had got, after a perilous paddle in his cistern, on to the fire station, were now slowly but resolutely clambering up the outhouse roof towards the back of the main premises of Messrs Mantell and Throbson. They clambered slowly and one urged and helped the other, slipping and pausing ever and again, amidst a constant trickle of fragments of broken tile.

One was Mr Polly, with his hair wildly disordered, his face covered with black smudges and streaked with perspiration, and his trouser legs scorched and blackened; the other was an elderly lady, quietly but becomingly dressed in black, with small white frills at her neck and wrists and a Sunday cap of ecru lace enlivened with a black velvet bow. Her hair was brushed back from her wrinkled brow and plastered down tightly, meeting in a small knob behind; her wrinkled mouth bore that expression of supreme resolution common with the toothless aged. She was shaky, not with fear, but with the vibrations natural to her years, and she spoke with the slow quavering firmness of the very aged.

'I don't mind scrambling,' she said with piping inflexibility, 'but I can't jump and I *wunt* jump.'

'Scramble, old lady, then – scramble!' said Mr Polly, pulling her arm. 'It's one up and two down on these blessed tiles.'

'It's not what I'm used to,' she said.

'Stick to it!' said Mr Polly, 'live and learn,' and got to the ridge and grasped at her arm to pull her after him.

'I can't jump, mind ye,' she repeated, pressing her lips together. 'And old ladies like me mustn't be hurried.'

'Well, let's get as high as possible anyhow!' said Mr Polly, urging her gently upward. 'Shinning up a waterspout in your line? Near as you'll get to heaven.'

'I *can't* jump,' she said. 'I can do anything but jump.'

'Hold on!' said Mr Polly, 'while I give you a boost. That's – wonderful.'

'So long as it isn't jumping . . . '

The old lady grasped the parapet above, and there was a moment of intense struggle.

'Urup!' said Mr Polly. 'Hold on! Gollys! where's she gone to . . . ?'

Then an ill-mended, wavering, yet very reassuring spring-sided boot appeared for an instant.

'Thought perhaps there wasn't any roof there!' he explained, scrambling up over the parapet beside her.

'I've never been out on a roof before,' said the old lady. 'I'm all disconnected. It's very bumpy. Especially that last bit. Can't we sit here for a bit and rest? I'm not the girl I use to be.'

'You sit here ten minutes,' shouted Mr Polly, 'and you'll pop like a roast chestnut. Don't understand me? *Roast chestnut!* ROAST CHEST-NUT! POP! There ought to be a limit to deafness. Come on round to the front and see if we can find an attic window. Look at this smoke!'

'Nasty!' said the old lady, her eyes following his gesture, puckering her face into an expression of great distaste.

'Come on!'

'Can't hear a word you say.'

He pulled her arm. 'Come on!'

She paused for a moment to relieve herself of a series of entirely unexpected chuckles. '*Sich* goings on!' she said, 'I never did! Where's he going now?' and came along behind the parapet to the front of the drapery establishment.

Below, the street was now fully alive to their presence, and encouraged the appearance of their heads by shouts and cheers. A sort of free fight was going on round the fire escape, order represented by Mr Boomer and the very young policeman, and disorder by some partially intoxicated volunteers with views of their own about the manipulation of the apparatus. Two or three lengths of Mr Rusper's garden hose appeared to have twined themselves round the ladder. Mr Polly watched the struggle with a certain impatience, and glanced ever and again over his shoulder at the increasing volume of smoke and steam that was pouring up from the burning fire station. He decided to break an attic window and get in, and so try and get down through the shop. He found himself in a little bedroom, and returned to fetch his charge. For some time he could not make her understand his purpose.

'Got to come at once!' he shouted.

'I hain't 'ad sich a time for years!' said the old lady.

'We'll have to get down through the house!'

'Can't do no jumpin',' said the old lady. 'No!'

She yielded reluctantly to his grasp.

She stared over the parapet. 'Runnin' and scurryin' about like black beetles in a kitchin,' she said.

'We've got to hurry.'

'Mr Rumbold 'e's a very Quiet man. 'E likes everything Quiet. He'll be surprised to see me 'ere! Why! – there 'e is!' She fumbled in her garments mysteriously and at last produced a wrinkled pocket handkerchief and began to wave it.

'Oh, come ON!' cried Mr Polly, and seized her.

He got her into the attic, but the staircase, he found, was full of suffocating smoke, and he dared not venture below the next floor. He took her into a long dormitory, shut the door on those pungent and pervasive fumes, and opened the window – to discover the fire escape was now against the house, and all Fishbourne boiling with excitement as an immensely helmeted and active and resolute little figure ascended.

In another moment the rescuer stared over the windowsill, heroic, but just a trifle self-conscious and grotesque.

'Lawks a mussy!' said the old lady. 'Wonders and Wonders! Why! it's Mr Gambell! 'Iding 'is 'ed in that thing! I *never* did!'

'Can we get her out?' said Mr Gambell. 'There's not much time.'

'He might git stuck in it.'

'*You*'ll get stuck in it,' said Mr Polly, 'come along!'

'Not for jumpin' I don't,' said the old lady, understanding his gestures rather than his words. 'Not a bit of it. I bain't no good at jumping and I *wunt*.'

They urged her gently but firmly towards the window.

'You lemme do it my own way,' said the old lady at the sill . . .

'I could do it better if e'd take it off.'

'Oh! *carm* on!'

'It's wuss than Carter's stile,' she said, 'before they mended it. With a cow a-looking at you.'

Mr Gambell hovered protectingly below. Mr Polly steered her aged limbs from above. An anxious crowd below babbled advice and did its best to upset the fire escape. Within, streamers of black smoke were pouring up through the cracks in the floor. For some seconds the world waited while the old lady gave herself up to reckless mirth again. '*Sich* times!' she said, and, '*Poor* Rumbold!'

Slowly they descended, and Mr Polly remained at the post of danger steadying the long ladder until the old lady was in safety below and sheltered by Mr Rumbold (who was in tears) and the young policeman from the urgent congratulations of the crowd. The crowd was full of an impotent passion to participate. Those nearest wanted to shake her hand, those remoter cheered.

'The fust fire I was ever in and likely to be my last. It's a scurryin', 'urryin' business, but I'm real glad I haven't missed it,' said the old lady as she was borne rather than led towards the refuge of the Temperance Hotel.

Also she was heard to remark: ' 'E was saying something about 'ot chestnuts. *I* 'aven't 'ad no 'ot chestnuts.'

Then the crowd became aware of Mr Polly awkwardly negotiating the top rungs of the fire escape. ' 'Ere 'e comes!' cried a voice, and Mr Polly descended into the world again out of the conflagration he had lit to be his funeral pyre, moist, excited, and tremendously alive, amidst a tempest of applause. As he got lower and lower the crowd howled like a pack of dogs at him. Impatient men, unable to wait for him, seized and shook his descending boots, and so brought him to earth with a run. He was rescued with difficulty from an enthusiast who wished to slake at his own expense and to his own accompaniment a thirst altogether heroic. He was hauled into the Temperance Hotel and flung like a sack, breathless and helpless, into the tear-wet embrace of Miriam.

5

With the dusk and the arrival of some county constabulary, and first one and presently two other fire engines from Port Burdock and Hampstead-on-Sea, the local talent of Fishbourne found itself forced back into a secondary, less responsible and more observant role. I will not pursue the story of the fire to its ashes, nor will I do more than glance at the unfortunate Mr Rusper, a modern Laocoön, vainly trying to retrieve his scattered hose amidst the tramplings and rushings of the Port Burdock experts.

In a small sitting-room of the Fishbourne Temperance Hotel a little group of Fishbourne tradesmen sat and conversed in fragments and anon went to the window and looked out upon the smoking desolation of their homes across the way, and anon sat down again. They and their families were the guests of old Lady Bargrave, who had displayed the utmost sympathy and interest in their misfortunes. She had taken several people into her own house at Everdean, had engaged the Temperance Hotel as a temporary refuge, and personally superintended the housing of Mantell and Throbson's homeless assistants. The Temperance Hotel became and remained extremely noisy and congested, with people sitting about anywhere, conversing in fragments and totally unable to get themselves to bed. The manager was an old soldier, and following the best traditions of the service saw that everyone had hot cocoa. Hot cocoa seemed to be about everywhere, and it was no doubt very heartening and sustaining to everyone. When the manager detected anyone disposed to be drooping or pensive, he exhorted that person at once to drink further hot cocoa and maintain a stout heart.

The hero of the occasion, the centre of interest, was Mr Polly. For he had not only caused the fire by upsetting a lighted lamp, scorching his trousers and narrowly escaping death, as indeed he had now explained in detail about twenty times, but he had further thought at once of that amiable but helpless old lady next door, had shown the utmost decision in making his way to her over the yard wall of the Royal Fishbourne Hotel, and had rescued her with persistence and vigour in spite of the levity natural to her years. Everyone thought well of him and was anxious to show it, more especially by shaking his hand painfully and repeatedly. Mr Rumbold, breaking a silence of nearly fifteen years, thanked him profusely, said he had never understood him properly and declared he ought to have a medal. There seemed to be a widely diffused idea that Mr Polly ought to have a medal. Hinks thought so. He declared, moreover, and with the utmost emphasis, that Mr Polly had a crowded and richly decorated interior – or words to that effect. There was something apologetic in this persistence; it was as if he regretted past intimations that Mr Polly was internally defective and hollow. He also said that Mr Polly was a 'white man', albeit, as he developed it, with a liver of the deepest chromatic satisfactions.

Mr Polly wandered centrally through it all, with his face washed and his hair carefully brushed and parted, looking modest and more than a little absent-minded, and wearing a pair of black dress trousers belonging to the manager of the Temperance Hotel – a larger man than himself in every way.

He drifted upstairs to his fellow-tradesmen, and stood for a time staring into the littered street, with its pools of water and extinguished gas lamps. His companions in misfortune resumed a fragmentary disconnected conversation. They touched now on one aspect of the disaster and now on another, and there were intervals of silence. More or less empty cocoa cups were distributed over the table, mantelshelf and piano, and in the middle of the table was a tin of biscuits, into which Mr Rumbold, sitting round-shoulderedly, dipped ever and again in an absent-minded way, and munched like a distant shooting of coals. It added to the solemnity of the affair that nearly all of them were in their black Sunday clothes; little Clamp was particularly impressive and dignified in a wide open frock coat, a Gladstone-shaped paper collar, and a large white and blue tie. They felt that they were in the presence of a great disaster, the sort of disaster that gets into the papers, and is even illustrated by blurred photographs of the crumbling ruins. In the presence of that sort of disaster all honourable men are lugubrious and sententious.

And yet it is impossible to deny a certain element of elation. Not one of those excellent men but was already realising that a great door had opened, as it were, in the opaque fabric of destiny, that they were to get their money again that had seemed sunk for ever beyond any hope in the deeps of retail trade. Life was already in their imagination rising like a Phoenix from the flames.

'I suppose there'll be a public subscription,' said Mr Clamp.

'Not for those who're insured,' said Mr Wintershed.

'I was thinking of them assistants from Mantell and Throbson's. They must have lost nearly everything.'

'They'll be looked after all right,' said Mr Rumbold. 'Never fear.'

Pause.

'*I'm* insured,' said Mr Clamp, with unconcealed satisfaction. 'Royal Salamander.'

'Same here,' said Mr Wintershed.

'Mine's the Glasgow Sun,' Mr Hinks remarked. 'Very good company.'

'You insured, Mr Polly?'

'He deserves to be,' said Rumbold.

'Ra-ther,' said Hinks. 'Blowed if he don't. Hard lines it *would* be – if there wasn't something for him.'

'Commercial and General,' answered Mr Polly over his shoulder, still staring out of the window. 'Oh! I'm all right.'

The topic dropped for a time, though manifestly it continued to exercise their minds.

'It's cleared me out of a lot of old stock,' said Mr Wintershed; 'that's one good thing.'

The remark was felt to be in rather questionable taste, and still more so was his next comment.

'Rusper's a bit sick it didn't reach '*im*.'

Everyone looked uncomfortable, and no one was willing to point the reason why Rusper should be a bit sick.

'Rusper's been playing a game of his own,' said Hinks. 'Wonder what he thought he was up to! Sittin' in the middle of the road with a pair of tweezers he was, and about a yard of wire – mending somethin'. Wonder he warn't run over by the Port Burdock engine.'

Presently a little chat sprang up upon the causes of fires, and Mr Polly was moved to tell how it had happened for the one and twentieth time. His story had now become as circumstantial and exact as the evidence of a police witness. 'Upset the lamp,' he said. 'I'd just lighted it, I was going upstairs, and my foot slipped against where one of the treads was a bit rotten, and down I went. Thing was aflare in a moment! . . . '

He yawned at the end of the discussion, and moved doorward.

'So long,' said Mr Polly.

'Good-night,' said Mr Rumbold. 'You played a brave man's part! If you don't get a medal – '

He left an eloquent pause.

' 'Ear, 'ear!' said Mr Wintershed and Mr Clamp. 'Goo'night, o' man,' said Mr Hinks.

'Goo'night all,' said Mr Polly . . .

He went slowly upstairs. The vague perplexity common to popular heroes pervaded his mind. He entered the bedroom and turned up the electric light. It was quite a pleasant room, one of the best in the Temperance Hotel, with a nice clean flowered wallpaper, and a very large looking-glass. Miriam appeared to be asleep, and her shoulders were humped up under the clothes in a shapeless, forbidding lump that Mr Polly had found utterly loathsome for fifteen years. He went softly over to the dressing-table and surveyed himself thoughtfully. Presently he hitched up the trousers. 'Miles too big for me,' he remarked. 'Funny not to have a pair of breeches of one's own . . . Like being born again. Naked came I into the world . . . '

Miriam stirred and rolled over, and stared at him.

'Hello!' she said.

'Hello.'

'Come to bed?'

'It's three.'

Pause, while Mr Polly disrobed slowly.

'I been thinking,' said Miriam, 'It isn't going to be so bad after all. We shall get your insurance. We can easy begin all over again.'

'H'm,' said Mr Polly.

She turned her face away from him and reflected.

'Get a better house,' said Miriam, regarding the wallpaper pattern. 'I've always 'ated them stairs.'

Mr Polly removed a boot.

'Choose a better position where there's more doing,' murmured Miriam . . .

'Not half so bad,' she whispered . . .

'You *wanted* stirring up,' she said, half asleep –

It dawned upon Mr Polly for the first time that he had forgotten something.

He ought to have cut his throat!

The fact struck him as remarkable, but as now no longer of any particular urgency. It seemed a thing far off in the past, and he wondered why he had not thought of it before. Odd thing life is! If he had done it he would never have seen this clean and agreeable apartment with the electric light . . . His thoughts wandered into a question of detail. Where could he have put the razor down? Somewhere in the little room behind the shop, he supposed, but he could not think where more precisely. Anyhow it didn't matter now.

He undressed himself calmly, got into bed, and fell asleep almost immediately.

CHAPTER NINE

The Potwell Inn

But when a man has once broken through the paper walls of everyday circumstance, those unsubstantial walls that hold so many of us securely prisoned from the cradle to the grave, he has made a discovery. If the world does not please you *you can change it*. Determine to alter it at any price, and you can change it altogether. You may change it to something sinister and angry, to something appalling, but it may be you will change it to something brighter, something more agreeable, and at the worst something much more interesting. There is only one sort of man who is absolutely to blame for his own misery, and that is the man who finds life dull and dreary. There are no circumstances in the world that determined action cannot alter, unless perhaps they are the walls of a prison cell, and even those will dissolve and change, I am told, into the infirmary compartment at any rate, for the man who can fast with resolution. I give these things as facts and information, and with no moral intimations. And Mr Polly, lying awake at nights, with a renewed indigestion, with Miriam sleeping sonorously beside him and a general air of inevitableness about his situation, saw through it, understood there was no inevitable any more, and escaped his former despair.

He could, for example, 'clear out'.

It became a wonderful and alluring phrase to him: 'Clear out!'

Why had he never thought of clearing out before?

He was amazed and a little shocked at the unimaginative and super-fluous criminality in him that had turned old cramped and stagnant Fishbourne into a blaze and new beginnings. (I wish from the bottom of my heart I could add that he was properly sorry.) But something constricting and restrained seemed to have been destroyed by that flare. *Fishbourne wasn't the world*. That was the new, the essential fact of which he had lived so lamentably in ignorance. Fishbourne as he had known it and hated it, so that he wanted to kill himself to get out of it, *wasn't the world*.

The insurance money he was to receive made everything humane and kindly and practicable. He would 'clear out', with justice and humanity. He would take exactly twenty-one pounds, and all the rest he would leave to Miriam. That seemed to him absolutely fair. Without him, she could do all sorts of things – all the sorts of things she was constantly urging him to do ...

And he would go off along the white road that led to Garchester, and on to Crogate and so to Tunbridge Wells, where there was a Toad Rock he had heard of, but never seen. (It seemed to him this must needs be a marvel.) And so to other towns and cities. He would walk and loiter by the way, and sleep in inns at night, and get an odd job here and there and talk to strange people. Perhaps he would get quite a lot of work and prosper, and if he did not do so he would lie down in front of a train, or wait for a warm night and then fall into some smooth, broad river. Not so bad as sitting down to a dentist, not nearly so bad. And he would never open a shop any more. Never!

So the possibilities of the future presented themselves to Mr Polly as he lay awake at nights.

It was springtime, and in the woods so soon as one got out of reach of the sea wind, there would be anemones and primroses.

2

A month later a leisurely and dusty tramp, plump equatorially and slightly bald, with his hands in his pockets and his lips puckered to a contemplative whistle, strolled along the river bank between Uppingdon and Potwell. It was a profusely budding spring day and greens such as God had never permitted in the world before in human memory (though indeed they come every year and we forgot), were mirrored vividly in a mirror of equally unprecedented brown. For a time the wanderer stopped and stood still, and even the thin whistle died away from his lips as he watched a water vole run to and fro upon a little headland across the stream. The vole plopped into the water and swam and dived and only when the last ring of its disturbance had vanished did Mr Polly resume his thoughtful course to nowhere in particular.

For the first time in many years he had been leading a healthy human life, living constantly in the open air, walking every day for eight or nine hours, eating sparingly, accepting every conversational opportunity, not even disdaining the discussion of possible work. And beyond mending a hole in his coat that he had made while negotiating barbed wire, with a borrowed needle and thread in a lodging house, he had done no work at all. Neither had he worried about business nor about time and seasons. And for the first time in his life he had seen the Aurora Borealis.

So far the holiday had cost him very little. He had arranged it on a plan that was entirely his own. He had started with four five-pound notes and a pound divided into silver, and he had gone by train from Fishbourne to Ashington. At Ashington he had gone to the post office, obtained a registered letter, and sent his four five-pound notes with a short brotherly note addressed to himself at Gilhampton post office. He sent this letter to Gilhampton for no other reason in the world than that he liked the name of Gilhampton and the rural suggestion of its containing county, which was Sussex; and having so despatched it, he set himself to discover, mark down and walk to Gilhampton, and so recover his resources. And having got to Gilhampton at last, he changed one five-pound note, bought four pound postal orders, and repeated his manoeuvre with nineteen pounds.

After a lapse of fifteen years he rediscovered this interesting world, about which so many people go incredibly blind and bored. He went along country roads while all the birds were piping and chirruping and cheeping and singing, and looked at fresh new things, and felt as happy and irresponsible as a boy with an unexpected half-holiday. And if ever the thought of Miriam returned to him he controlled his mind. He came to country inns and sat for unmeasured hours talking of this and that to those sage carters who rest for ever in the taps of country inns, while the big sleek brass jingling horses wait patiently outside with their waggons; he got a job with some van people who were wandering about the country with swings and a steam roundabout and remained with them for three days, until one of their dogs took a violent dislike to him and made his duties unpleasant; he talked to tramps and wayside labourers, he snoozed under hedges by day and in outhouses and hayricks at night, and once, but only once, he slept in a casual ward. He felt as the etiolated grass and daisies must do when you move the garden roller away to a new place.

He gathered a quantity of strange and interesting memories.

He crossed some misty meadows by moonlight and the mist lay low on the grass, so low that it scarcely reached above his waist, and houses and clumps of trees stood out like islands in a milky sea, so sharply defined was the upper surface of the mist bank. He came nearer and nearer to a strange thing that floated like a boat upon this magic lake, and behold! something moved at the stern and a rope was whisked at the prow, and it had changed into a pensive cow, drowsy-eyed, regarding him . . .

He saw a remarkable sunset in a new valley near Maidstone, a very red and clear sunset, a wide redness under a pale cloudless heaven, and with the hills all round the edge of the sky a deep purple blue and clear and flat, looking exactly as he had seen mountains painted in pictures. He seemed transported to some strange country, and would have felt no surprise if the old labourer he came upon leaning silently over a gate had addressed him in an unfamiliar tongue . . .

Then one night, just towards dawn, his sleep upon a pile of brushwood was broken by the distant rattle of a racing motor car breaking all the speed regulations, and as he could not sleep again, he got up and walked into Maidstone as the day came. He had never been abroad in a town at half-past two in his life before, and the stillness of everything in the bright sunrise impressed him profoundly. At one corner was a startling policeman, standing in a doorway quite motionless, like a waxen image. Mr Polly wished him 'good-morning' unanswered, and went down to the bridge over the Medway and sat on the parapet very still and thoughtful, watching the town awaken, and wondering what he should do if it didn't, if the world of men never woke again . . .

One day he found himself going along a road with a wide space of sprouting bracken and occasional trees on either side, and suddenly this road became strangely, perplexingly familiar. 'Lord!' he said, and turned about and stood. 'It can't be.'

He was incredulous, then left the road and walked along a scarcely perceptible track to the left, and came in half a minute to an old lichenous stone wall. It seemed exactly the bit of wall he had known so well. It might have been but yesterday he was in that place; there remained even a little pile of wood. It became absurdly the same wood. The bracken perhaps was not so high, and most of its fronds still uncoiled; that was all. Here he had stood, it seemed, and there she had sat and looked down upon him. Where was she now, and what had become of her? He counted the years back and marvelled that beauty should have called to him with so imperious a voice – and signified nothing.

He hoisted himself with some little difficulty to the top of the wall, and saw off under the beech trees two schoolgirls – small, insignificant, pig-tailed creatures, with heads of blond and black, with their arms twined about each other's necks, no doubt telling each other the silliest secrets.

But that girl with the red hair – was she a countess? was she a queen? Children perhaps? Had sorrow dared to touch her?

Had she forgotten altogether? . . .

A tramp sat by the roadside thinking, and it seemed to the man in the passing motor car he must needs be plotting for another pot of beer. But as a matter of fact what the tramp was saying to himself over and over again was a variant upon a well-known Hebrew word.

'Itchabod,' the tramp was saying in the voice of one who reasons on the side of the inevitable. 'It's Fair Itchabod, o' man. There's no going back to it.'

3

It was about two o'clock in the afternoon one hot day in high May when Mr Polly, unhurrying and serene, came to that broad bend of the river to which the little lawn and garden of the Potwell Inn run down. He stopped at the sight of the place with its deep tiled roof, nestling under big trees – you never get a decently big, decently shaped tree by the seaside – its sign towards the roadway, its sun-blistered green bench and tables, its shapely white windows and its row of upshooting holly-hock plants in the garden. A hedge separated it from a buttercup-yellow meadow, and beyond stood three poplars in a group against the sky, three exceptionally tall, graceful and harmonious poplars. It is hard to say what there was about them that made them so beautiful to Mr Polly; but they seemed to him to touch a pleasant scene with a distinction almost divine. He remained admiring them for a long time. At last the need for coarser aesthetic satisfactions arose in him.

'Provinder,' he whispered, drawing near to the inn. 'Cold sirloin for choice. And nut-brown brew and wheaten bread.'

The nearer he came to the place the more he liked it. The windows on the ground floor were long and low, and they had pleasing red blinds. The green tables outside were agreeably ringed with memories of former drinks, and an extensive grape vine spread level branches across the whole front of the place. Against the wall was a broken oar, two boat-hooks and the stained and faded red cushions of a pleasure boat. One went up three steps to the glass-panelled door and peeped into a broad, low room with a bar and beer engine, behind which were many bright and helpful-looking bottles against mirrors, and great and little pewter measures, and bottles fastened in brass wire upside down with their corks replaced by taps, and a white china cask labelled 'Shrub', and cigar boxes, and boxes of cigarettes, and a couple of toby jugs and a beautifully coloured hunting scene framed and glazed, showing the most elegant and beautiful people taking Piper's Cherry Brandy, and cards such as the law requires about the dilution of spirits and the illegality of bringing children into bars, and satirical verses about swearing and asking for credit, and three very bright red-cheeked wax apples and a round-shaped clock.

But these were the mere background to the really pleasant thing in the spectacle, which was quite the plumpest woman Mr Polly had ever seen, seated in an armchair in the midst of all these bottles and glasses and glittering things, peacefully and tranquilly, and without the slightest loss of dignity, asleep. Many people would have called her a fat woman, but Mr Polly's innate sense of epithet told him from the outset that plump was the word. She had shapely brows and a straight, well-shaped nose, kind lines and contentment about her mouth, and beneath it the jolly chins clustered like chubby little cherubim about the feet of an Assumptioning Madonna. Her plumpness was firm and pink and whole-some, and her hands, dimpled at every joint, were clasped in front of her; she seemed as it were to embrace herself with infinite confidence and kindliness as one who knew herself good in substance, good in essence, and would show her gratitude to God by that ready acceptance of all that He had given her. Her head was a little on one side, not much, but just enough to speak of trustfulness and rob her of the stiff effect of self-reliance. And she slept.

'*My* sort,' said Mr Polly, and opened the door very softly, divided between the desire to enter and come nearer and an instinctive in-disposition to break slumbers so manifestly sweet and satisfying.

She awoke with a start, and it amazed Mr Polly to see swift terror flash into her eyes. Instantly it had gone again.

'Law!' she said, her face softening with relief. 'I thought you were Jim.'

'I'm never Jim,' said Mr Polly.

'You've got his sort of hat.'

'Ah!' said Mr Polly, and leant over the bar.

'It just came into my head you was Jim,' said the plump lady, dismissed the topic and stood up. 'I believe I was having forty winks,' she said, 'if all the truth was told. What can I do for you?'

'Cold meat?' said Mr Polly.

'There *is* cold meat,' the plump woman admitted.

'And room for it.'

The plump woman came and leant over the bar and regarded him judicially, but kindly. 'There's some cold boiled beef,' she said, and added: 'A bit of crisp lettuce?'

'New mustard,' said Mr Polly.

'And a tankard!'

'A tankard.'

They understood each other perfectly.

'Looking for work?' asked the plump woman.

'In a way,' said Mr Polly.

They smiled like old friends.

Whatever the truth may be about love, there is certainly such a thing as friendship at first sight. They liked each other's voices, they liked each other's way of smiling and speaking.

'It's such beautiful weather this spring,' said Mr Polly, explaining everything.

'What sort of work do you want?' she asked.

'I've never properly thought that out,' said Mr Polly. 'I've been looking round – for ideas.'

'Will you have your beef in the tap or outside? That's the tap.'

Mr Polly had a glimpse of an oaken settle. 'In the tap will be handier for you,' he said.

'Hear that?' said the plump lady.

'Hear what?'

'Listen.'

Presently the silence was broken by a distant howl – 'Oooooo*ver*!'

'Eh?' she said.

He nodded.

'That's the ferry. And there isn't a ferryman.'

'Could I?'

'Can you punt?'

'Never tried.'

'Well – pull the pole out before you reach the end of the punt, that's all. Try.'

Mr Polly went out again into the sunshine.

At times one can tell so much so briefly. Here are the facts then – bare. He found a punt and a pole, got across to the steps on the opposite side, picked up an elderly gentleman in an alpaca jacket and a pith helmet, cruised with him vaguely for twenty minutes, conveyed him tortuously into the midst of a thicket of forget-me-not-spangled sedges, splashed some water-weed over him, hit him twice with the punt pole, and finally landed him, alarmed but abusive, in treacherous soil at the edge of a hay meadow about forty yards downstream, where he immediately got into difficulties with a noisy, aggressive little white dog that was guarding a jacket.

Mr Polly returned in a complicated manner, but with perfect dignity, to his moorings.

He found the plump woman rather flushed and tearful, and seated at one of the green tables outside.

'I been laughing at you,' she said.

'What for?' asked Mr Polly.

'I ain't 'ad such a laugh since Jim come 'ome. When you 'it 'is 'ed, it 'urt my side.'

'It didn't hurt his head – not particularly.'

She waved her head. 'Did you charge him anything?'

'Gratis,' said Mr Polly. 'I never thought of it.'

The plump woman pressed her hands to her sides and laughed silently for a space. 'You ought to have charged him sumpthing,' she said. 'You better come and have your cold meat, before you do any more puntin'. You and me'll get on together.'

Presently she came and stood watching him eat. 'You eat better than you punt,' she said; and then, 'I dessay you could learn to punt.'

'Wax to receive and marble to retain,' said Mr Polly. 'This beef is a Bit of All Right, ma'am. I could have done differently if I hadn't been punting on an empty stomach. There's a leer feeling as the pole goes in – '

'I've never held with fasting,' said the plump woman.

'You want a ferryman?'

'I want an odd man about the place.'

'I'm odd, all right. What's your wages?'

'Not much, but you get tips and pickings. I've a sort of feeling it would suit you.'

'I've a sort of feeling it would. What's the duties? Fetch and carry? Ferry? Garden? Wash bottles? *Ceteris paribus?*'

'That's about it,' said the fat woman.

'Give me a trial.'

'I've more than half a mind. Or I wouldn't have said anything about it. I suppose you're all right. You've got a sort of half-respectable look about you. I suppose you 'aven't *done* anything.'

'Bit of Arson,' said Mr Polly, as if he jested.

'So long as you haven't the habit,' said the plump woman.

'My first time, ma'am,' said Mr Polly, munching his way through an excellent big leaf of lettuce. 'And my last.'

'It's all right if you haven't been to prison,' said the plump woman. 'It isn't what a man's happened to do makes 'im bad. We all happen to do things at times. It's bringing it home to him and spoiling his self-respect does the mischief. You don't *look* a wrong 'un. 'Ave you been to prison?'

'Never.'

'Nor a reformatory? Nor any institution?'

'Not me. Do I *look* reformed?'

'Can you paint and carpenter a bit?'

'Well, I'm ripe for it.'

'Have a bit of cheese?'

'If I might.'

And the way she brought the cheese showed Mr Polly that the business was settled in her mind.

He spent the afternoon exploring the premises of the Potwell Inn and learning the duties that might be expected of him, such as Stockholm-tarring fences, digging potatoes, swabbing out boats, helping people land, embarking, landing and time-keeping for the hirers of two rowing boats and one Canadian canoe, baling out the said vessels and concealing their leaks and defects from prospective hirers, persuading inexperienced hirers to start downstream rather than up, repairing rowlocks and taking inventories of returning boats with a view to supplementary charges, cleaning boots, sweeping chimneys, house-painting, cleaning windows, sweeping out and sanding the tap and bar, cleaning pewter, washing glasses, turpentining woodwork, whitewashing generally, plumbing and engineering, repairing locks and clocks, waiting and tapster's work generally, beating carpets and mats, cleaning bottles and saving corks, taking into the cellar, moving, tapping and connecting beer casks with their engines, blocking and destroying wasps' nests, doing forestry with several trees, drowning superfluous kittens, dog-fancying as required, assisting in the rearing of ducklings and the care of various poultry, bee-keeping, stabling, baiting and grooming horses and asses, cleaning and 'garing' motor cars and bicycles, inflating tyres and repairing punctures, recovering the bodies of drowned persons from the river as required, assisting people in trouble in the water, first-aid and sympathy, improvising and superintending a bathing station for visitors, attending inquests and funerals in the interests of the establishment, scrubbing floors and all the ordinary duties of a scullion, the ferry, chasing hens and goats from the adjacent cottages out of the garden, making up paths and superintending drainage, gardening generally, delivering bottled beer and soda-water syphons in the neighbourhood, running miscellaneous errands, removing drunken and offensive persons from the premises by tact or muscle as occasion required, keeping in with the local policemen, defending the premises in general and the orchard in particular from depredators . . .

'Can but try it,' said Mr Polly towards tea time. 'When there's nothing else on hand I suppose I might do a bit of fishing.'

4

Mr Polly was particularly charmed by the ducklings.

They were piping about among the vegetables in the company of their foster mother, and as he and the plump woman came down the garden path the little creatures mobbed them, and ran over their boots and in between Mr Polly's legs, and did their best to be trodden upon and killed after the manner of ducklings all the world over. Mr Polly had never been near young ducklings before, and their extreme blondness and the delicate completeness of their feet and beaks filled him with admiration. It is open to question whether there is anything more friendly in the world than a very young duckling. It was with the utmost difficulty that he tore himself away to practise punting, with the plump woman coaching from the bank. Punting he found was difficult, but not impossible, and towards four o'clock he succeeded in conveying a second passenger across the sundering flood from the inn to the unknown.

As he returned, slowly indeed, but now one might almost say surely, to the peg to which the punt was moored, he became aware of a singularly delightful human being awaiting him on the bank. She stood with her legs very wide apart, her hands behind her back, and her head a little on one side, watching his gestures with an expression of disdainful interest. She had black hair and brown legs and a buff short frock and very intelligent eyes. And when he had reached a sufficient proximity she remarked: 'Hello!'

'Hello,' said Mr Polly, and saved himself in the nick of time from disaster.

'Silly,' said the young lady, and Mr Polly lunged nearer.

'What are you called?'

'Polly.'

'Liar!'

'Why?'

'I'm Polly.'

'Then I'm Alfred. But I meant to be Polly.'

'I was first.'

'All right. I'm going to be the ferryman.'

'I see. You'll have to punt better.'

'You should have seen me early in the afternoon.'

'I can imagine it . . . I've seen the others.'

'What others?' Mr Polly had landed now and was fastening up the punt.

'What Uncle Jim has scooted.'

'Scooted?'

'He comes and scoots them. He'll scoot you too, I expect.'

A mysterious shadow seemed to fall athwart the sunshine and pleasantness of the Potwell Inn.

'I'm not a scooter,' said Mr Polly.

'Uncle Jim is.'

She whistled a little flatly for a moment, and threw small stones at a clump of meadow-sweet that sprang from the bank.

Then she remarked: 'When Uncle Jim comes back he'll cut your insides out . . . P'r'aps, very likely, he'll let me see.'

There was a pause.

'*Who's* Uncle Jim?' Mr Polly asked in a faded voice.

'Don't you know who Uncle Jim is? He'll show you. He's a scorcher, is Uncle Jim. He only came back just a little time ago, and he's scooted three men. He don't like strangers about, don't Uncle Jim. He *can* swear. He's going to teach me, soon as I can whissle properly.'

'Teach you to swear!' cried Mr Polly, horrified.

'*And* spit,' said the little girl proudly. 'He says I'm the gamest little beast he ever came across – ever.'

For the first time in his life it seemed to Mr Polly that he had come across something sheerly dreadful. He stared at the pretty thing of flesh and spirit in front of him, lightly balanced on its stout little legs and looking at him with eyes that had still to learn the expression of either disgust or fear.

'I say,' said Mr Polly, 'how old are you?'

'Nine,' said the little girl.

She turned away and reflected. Truth compelled her to add one other statement.

'He's not what I should call handsome, not Uncle Jim,' she said. 'But he's a Scorcher and no Mistake . . . Gramma don't like him.'

5

Mr Polly found the plump woman in the big bricked kitchen lighting a fire for tea. He went to the root of the matter at once.

'I say,' he asked, 'who's Uncle Jim?'

The plump woman blanched and stood still for a moment. A stick fell out of the bundle in her hand unheeded.

'That little granddaughter of mine been saying things?' she asked faintly.

'Bits of things,' said Mr Polly.

'Well, I suppose I must tell you sooner or later. He's – It's Jim. He's the Drorback to this place, that's what he is. The Drorback. I hoped you mightn't hear so soon . . . Very likely he's gone.'

'*She* don't seem to think so.'

' 'E 'asn't been near the place these two weeks and more,' said the plump woman.

'But who is he?'

'I suppose I got to tell you,' said the plump woman.

'She says he scoots people,' Mr Polly remarked after a pause.

'He's my own sister's son.' The plump woman watched the crackling fire for a space. 'I suppose I got to tell you,' she repeated.

She softened towards tears. 'I try not to think of it, but night and day he's haunting me. I try not to think of it. I've been for easy-going all my life. But I'm that worried and afraid, with death and ruin threatened and evil all about me! I don't know what to do! My own sister's son, and me a widow woman and 'elpless against his doin's!'

She put down the sticks she held upon the fender, and felt for her handkerchief. She began to sob and talk quickly.

'I wouldn't mind nothing else half so much if he'd leave that child alone. But he goes talking to her – if I leave her a moment he's talking to her, teaching her words and giving her ideas!'

'That's a Bit Thick,' said Mr Polly.

'Thick!' cried the plump woman; 'it's 'orrible! And what am I to do? He's been here three times now, six days and a week and a part of a week, and I pray to God night and day he may never come again. Praying! Back he's come sure as fate. He takes my money and he takes my things. He won't let no man stay here to protect me or do the boats or work the ferry. The ferry's getting a scandal. They stand and shout and scream and use language . . . If I complain they'll say I'm helpless to manage here, they'll take away my licence, out I shall go – and it's all the living I can get – and he knows it, and he plays on it, and he don't care. And here I am. I'd send the child away, but I got nowhere to send the child. I buys him off when it comes to that, and back he comes, worse than ever, prowling round and doing evil. And not a soul to help me. Not a soul! I just hoped there might be a day or so – before he comes back again. I was just hoping – I'm the sort that hopes.'

Mr Polly was reflecting on the flaws and drawbacks that seem to be inseparable from all the more agreeable things in life.

'Biggish sort of man, I expect?' asked Mr Polly, trying to get the situation in all its bearings.

But the plump woman did not heed him. She was going on with her fire-making, and retailing in disconnected fragments the fearfulness of Uncle Jim.

'There was always something a bit wrong with him,' she said, 'but nothing you mightn't have hoped for, not till they took him and carried him off and reformed him . . .

'He was cruel to the hens and chickings, it's true, and stuck a knife into another boy; but then I've seen him that nice to a cat, nobody could have been kinder. I'm sure he didn't do no 'arm to that cat whatever anyone tries to make out of it. I'd never listen to that . . . It was that Reformatory ruined him. They put him along of a lot of London boys full of ideas of wickedness, and because he didn't mind pain – and he don't, I *will* admit, try as I would – they made him think himself a hero. Them boys laughed at the teachers they set over them, laughed and mocked at them – and I don't suppose they *was* the best teachers in the world; I don't suppose, and I don't suppose anyone sensible does suppose, that everyone who goes to be a teacher or a chapl'in or a warder in a Reformatory Home goes and changes right away into an Angel of Grace from Heaven – and oh, Lord! where was I?'

'What did they send him to the Reformatory for?'

'Playing truant and stealing. He stole right enough – stole the money from an old woman, and what was I to do when it came to the trial but say what I knew. And him like a viper a-looking at me – more like a viper than a human boy. He leans on the bar and looks at me. "All right, Aunt Flo," he says, just that and nothing more. Time after time, I've dreamt of it, and now he's come. "They've Reformed me," he says, "and made me a devil, and a devil I mean to be to you. So out with it," he says.'

'What did you give him last time?' asked Mr Polly.

'Three golden pounds,' said the plump woman.

' "That won't last very long," he says. "But there ain't no hurry. I'll be back in a week about." If I wasn't one of the hoping sort – '

She left the sentence unfinished.

Mr Polly reflected. 'What sort of a size is he?' he asked. 'I'm not one of your Herculaceous sort, if you mean that. Nothing very wonderful bicepitally.'

'You'll scoot,' said the plump woman with conviction rather than bitterness. 'You'd better scoot now, and I'll try and find some money for him to go away again when he comes. It ain't reasonable to expect you to do anything but scoot. But I suppose it's the way of a woman in trouble to try and get help from a man, and hope and hope. I'm the hoping sort.'

'How long's he been about?' asked Mr Polly, ignoring his own outlook.

'Three months it is come the seventh since he come in by that very back door – and I hadn't set eyes on him for seven long years. He stood in the door watchin' me, and suddenly he let off a yelp – like a dog, and there he was grinning at the fright he'd given me. "Good old Aunty Flo," he says, "ain't you dee–lighted to see me?" he says, "now I'm Reformed." '

The plump lady went to the sink and filled the kettle.

'I never did like 'im,' she said, standing at the sink. 'And seeing him there, with his teeth all black and broken – P'r'aps I didn't give him much of a welcome at first. Not what would have been kind to him. "Lord!" I said, "it's Jim." '

' "It's Jim," he said. "Like a bad shillin' – like a damned bad shillin'. Jim and trouble. You all of you wanted me Reformed and now you got me Reformed. I'm a Reformatory Reformed Character,[72] warranted all right and turned out as such. Ain't you going to ask me in, aunty dear?"

' "Come in," I said, "I won't have it said I wasn't ready to be kind to you!"

'He comes in and shuts the door. Down he sits in that chair. "I come to torment you!" he says, "you old Sumpthing!" and begins at me . . . No human being could ever have been called such things before. It made me cry out. "And now," he says, "just to show I ain't afraid of 'urting you," he says, and ups and twists my wrist.'

Mr Polly gasped.

'I could stand even his vi'lence,' said the plump woman, 'if it wasn't for the child.'

Mr Polly went to the kitchen window and surveyed his namesake, who was away up the garden path with her hands behind her back, and whisps of black hair in disorder about her little face, thinking, thinking profoundly, about ducklings.

'You two oughtn't to be left,' he said.

The plump woman stared at his back with hard hope in her eyes.

'I don't see that it's *my* affair,' said Mr Polly.

The plump woman resumed her business with the kettle.

'I'd like to have a look at him before I go,' said Mr Polly, thinking aloud, and added, 'somehow. Not my business, of course.

'Lord!' he cried with a start at a noise in the bar, 'who's that?'

'Only a customer,' said the plump woman.

Mr Polly made no rash promises, and thought a great deal.

'It seems a good sort of crib,' he said, and added, 'for a chap who's looking for Trouble.'

But he stayed on and did various things out of the list I have already given, and worked the ferry, and it was four days before he saw anything of Uncle Jim. And so resistent is the human mind to things not yet experienced, that he could easily have believed in that time that there was no such person in the world as Uncle Jim. The plump woman, after her one outbreak of confidence, ignored the subject, and little Polly seemed to have exhausted her impressions in her first communication, and engaged her mind now with a simple directness in the study and subjugation of the new human being heaven had sent into her world. The first unfavourable impression of his punting was soon effaced; he could nickname ducklings very amusingly, create boats out of wooden splinters, and stalk and fly from imaginary tigers in the orchard with a convincing earnestness that was surely beyond the power of any other human being. She conceded at last that he should be called Mr Polly, in honour of her, Miss Polly, even as he desired.

Uncle Jim turned up in the twilight.

Uncle Jim appeared with none of the disruptive violence Mr Polly had dreaded. He came quite softly. Mr Polly was going down the lane behind the church that led to the Potwell Inn after posting a letter to the lime-juice people at the post office. He was walking slowly, after his habit, and thinking discursively. With a sudden tightening of the muscles he became aware of a figure walking noiselessly beside him. His first impression was of a face singularly broad above and with a wide empty grin as its chief feature below, of a slouching body and dragging feet.

'Arf a mo',' said the figure, as if in response to his start, and speaking in a hoarse whisper. 'Arf a mo', mister. You the noo bloke at the Potwell Inn?'

Mr Polly felt evasive. 'S'pose I am,' he replied hoarsely, and quickened his pace.

'Arf a mo',' said Uncle Jim, taking his arm. 'We ain't doing a (sanguinary) Marathon. It ain't a (decorated) cinder track. I want a word with you, mister. See?'

Mr Polly wriggled his arm free and stopped. 'What is it?' he asked, and faced the terror.

'I jest want a (decorated) word wiv you. See? – just a friendly word or two. Just to clear up any blooming errors. That's all I want. No need to be so (richly decorated) proud, if you *are* the noo bloke at Potwell Inn. Not a bit of it. See?'

Uncle Jim was certainly not a handsome person. He was short, shorter than Mr Polly, with long arms and lean big hands; a thin and wiry neck stuck out of his grey flannel shirt and supported a big head that had something of the snake in the convergent lines of its broad knotty brow, meanly proportioned face and pointed chin. His almost toothless mouth seemed a cavern in the twilight. Some accident had left him with one small and active and one large and expressionless reddish eye, and wisps of straight hair strayed from under the blue cricket cap he wore pulled down obliquely over the latter. He spat between his teeth and wiped his mouth untidily with the soft side of his fist.

'You got to blurry well shift,' he said. 'See?'

'Shift!' said Mr Polly. 'How?'

' 'Cos the Potwell Inn's *my* beat. See?'

Mr Polly had never felt less witty. 'How's it your beat?' he asked.

Uncle Jim thrust his face forward and shook his open hand, bent like a claw, under Mr Polly's nose. 'Not your blooming business,' he said. 'You got to shift.'

'S'pose I don't,' said Mr Polly.

'You got to shift.'

The tone of Uncle Jim's voice became urgent and confidential.

'You don't know who you're up against,' he said. 'It's a kindness I'm doing to warn you. See? I'm just one of those blokes who don't stick at things, see? I don't stick at nuffin'.'

Mr Polly's manner became detached and confidential – as though the matter and the speaker interested him greatly, but didn't concern him over-much. 'What do you think you'll do?' he asked.

'If you don't clear out?'

'Yes.'

'*Gaw!*' said Uncle Jim. 'You'd better. '*Ere!*'

He gripped Mr Polly's wrist with a grip of steel, and in an instant Mr Polly understood the relative quality of their muscles. He breathed, an uninspiring breath, into Mr Polly's face.

'What *won't* I do?' he said, 'once I start in on you.'

He paused, and the night about them seemed to be listening. 'I'll make a mess of you,' he said in his hoarse whisper. 'I'll do you – injuries. I'll 'urt you. I'll kick you ugly, see? I'll 'urt you in 'orrible ways – 'orrible, ugly ways . . . '

He scrutinised Mr Polly's face.

'You'll cry,' he said, 'to see yourself. See? Cry you will.'

'You got no right,' began Mr Polly.

'Right!' His note was fierce. 'Ain't the old woman me aunt?'

He spoke still closer. 'I'll make a gory mess of you. I'll cut bits orf you – '

He receded a little. 'I got no quarrel with *you*,' he said.

'It's too late to go tonight,' said Mr Polly.

'I'll be round tomorrer – 'bout eleven. See? And if I finds you – '

He produced a blood-curdling oath.

'H'm,' said Mr Polly, trying to keep things light. 'We'll consider your suggestions.'

'You better,' said Uncle Jim, and suddenly, noiselessly, was going.

His whispering voice sank until Mr Polly could hear only the dim fragments of sentences. ' 'Orrible things to you – 'orrible things . . . Kick yer ugly . . . Cut yer – liver out . . . spread it all about, I will . . . See? I don't care a dead rat one way or the uvver.'

And with a curious twisting gesture of the arm, Uncle Jim receded until his face was a still, dim thing that watched, and the black shadows of the hedge seemed to have swallowed up his body altogether.

7

Next morning about half-past ten Mr Polly found himself seated under a clump of fir trees by the roadside and about three miles and a half from the Potwell Inn. He was by no means sure whether he was taking a walk to clear his mind or leaving that threat-marred paradise for good and all. His reason pointed a lean, unhesitating finger along the latter course.

For after all, the thing was not *his* quarrel.

That agreeable plump woman, agreeable, motherly, comfortable as she might be, wasn't his affair; that child with the mop of black hair who combined so magically the charm of mouse and butterfly and flitting bird, who was daintier than a flower and softer than a peach, was no concern of his. Good heavens! what were they to him? Nothing . . . !

Uncle Jim, of course, *had* a claim, a sort of claim.

If it came to duty and chucking up this attractive, indolent, observant, humorous, tramping life, there were those who had a right to him, a legitimate right, a prior claim on his protection and chivalry.

Why not listen to the call of duty and go back to Miriam now . . . ?

He had had a very agreeable holiday –

And while Mr Polly sat thinking these things as well as he could, he knew that, if only he dared to look up, the heavens had opened and the clear judgement on his case was written across the sky.

He knew – he knew now as much as a man can know of life. He knew he had to fight or perish.

Life had never been so clear to him before. It had always been a confused, entertaining spectacle; he had responded to this impulse and that, seeking agreeable and entertaining things, evading difficult and painful things. Such is the way of those who grow up to a life that has neither danger nor honour in its texture. He had been muddled and wrapped about and entangled, like a creature born in the jungle who has never seen sea or sky. Now he had come out of it suddenly into a great exposed place. It was as if God and heaven waited over him, and all the earth was expectation.

'Not my business,' said Mr Polly, speaking aloud. 'Where the devil do *I* come in?'

And again, with something between a whine and a snarl in his voice, 'Not my blasted business!'

His mind seemed to have divided itself into several compartments, each with its own particular discussion busily in progress, and quite regardless of the others. One was busy with the detailed interpretation of the phrase 'kick you ugly'. There's a sort of French wrestling in which you use and guard against feet. Watch the man's eye, and as his foot comes up, grip and over he goes – at your mercy, if you use the advantage rightly. But how do you use the advantage rightly?

When he thought of Uncle Jim, the inside feeling of his body faded away rapidly to a blank discomfort –

'Old cadger! She hadn't no business to drag me into her quarrels. Ought to go to the police and ask for help! Dragging me into a quarrel that don't concern me.

'Wish I'd never set eyes on the rotten inn!'

The reality of the case arched over him like the vault of the sky, as plain as the sweet blue heavens above and the wide spread of hill and valley about him. Man comes into life to seek and find his sufficient beauty, to serve it, to win and increase it, to fight for it, to face anything and dare anything for it, counting death as nothing so long as the dying eyes still turn to it. And fear, and dullness and indolence and appetite, which indeed are no more than fear's three crippled brothers, who make ambushes and creep by night, are against him, to delay him, to hold him off, to hamper and beguile and kill him in that quest. He had but to lift his eyes to see all that, as much a part of his world as the driving clouds and the bending grass, but he kept himself downcast, a grumbling, inglorious, fattish little tramp, full of dreads and quivering excuses.

'Why the hell was I ever born?' he said, with the truth almost winning him.

What do you do when a dirty man, who smells, gets you down and under, in the dirt and dust, with a knee below your diaphragm and a large hairy hand squeezing your windpipe tighter and tighter in a quarrel that isn't, properly speaking, yours?

'If I had a chance against him – ' protested Mr Polly.

'It's no Good, you see,' said Mr Polly.

He stood up as though his decision was made, and was for an instant struck still by doubt.

There lay the road before him, going this way to the east and that to the west.

Westward, one hour away now, was the Potwell Inn. Already things might be happening there –

Eastward was the wise man's course, a road dipping between hedges to a hop garden and a wood and presently no doubt reaching an inn, a picturesque church, perhaps, a village and fresh company. The wise man's course. Mr Polly saw himself going along it, and tried to see himself going along it with all the self-applause a wise man feels. But somehow it wouldn't come like that. The wise man fell short of happiness for all his wisdom. The wise man had a paunch and round shoulders and red ears and excuses. It was a pleasant road, and why the wise man should not go along it merry and singing, full of summer happiness, was a miracle to Mr Polly's mind; but, confound it! the fact remained, the figure went slinking – slinking was the only word for it – and would not go otherwise than slinking. He turned his eyes westward as if for an explanation, and if the figure was no longer ignoble, the prospect was appalling.

'One kick in the stummick would settle a chap like me,' said Mr Polly.

'Oh, God!' cried Mr Polly, and lifted his eyes to heaven, and said for the last time in that struggle, 'It–isn't–my–affair!'

And so saying he turned his face towards the Potwell Inn.

He went back neither halting nor hastening in his pace after this last decision, but with a mind feverishly busy.

'If I get killed, I get killed, and if he gets killed I get hung. Don't seem just somehow.

'Don't suppose I shall *frighten* him off.'

The private war between Mr Polly and Uncle Jim for the possession of the Potwell Inn fell naturally into three chief campaigns. There was first of all the great campaign which ended in the triumphant eviction of Uncle Jim from the inn premises; there came next after a brief interval the futile invasions of the premises by Uncle Jim that culminated in the Battle of the Dead Eel; and, after some months of involuntary truce, there was the last supreme conflict of the Night Surprise. Each of these campaigns merits a section to itself.

Mr Polly re-entered the inn discreetly. He found the plump woman seated in her bar, her eyes a-stare, her face white and wet with tears. 'O God!' she was saying over and over again. 'O God!' The air was full of a spirituous reek, and on the sanded boards in front of the bar were the fragments of a broken bottle and an overturned glass.

She turned her despair at the sound of his entry, and despair gave place to astonishment.

'You come back!' she said.

'Ra-ther,' said Mr Polly.

'He's – he's mad drunk and looking for her.'

'Where is she?'

'Locked upstairs.'

'Haven't you sent to the police?'

'No one to send.'

'I'll see to it,' said Mr Polly. 'Out this way?'

She nodded.

He went to the crinkly paned window and peered out. Uncle Jim was coming down the garden path towards the house, his hands in his pockets and singing hoarsely. Mr Polly remembered afterwards with pride and amazement that he felt neither faint nor rigid. He glanced round him, seized a bottle of beer by the neck as an improvised club, and went out by the garden door. Uncle Jim stopped amazed. His brain did not instantly rise to the new posture of things.

'You!' he cried, and stopped for a moment. 'You – *scoot!*'

'*Your* job,' said Mr Polly, and advanced some paces.

Uncle Jim stood swaying with wrathful astonishment and then darted forward with clutching hands. Mr Polly felt that if his antagonist closed he was lost, and smote with all his force at the ugly head before him. Smash went the bottle, and Uncle Jim staggered, half-stunned by the blow and blinded with beer.

The lapses and leaps of the human mind are for ever mysterious. Mr Polly had never expected that bottle to break. In the instant he felt disarmed and helpless. Before him was Uncle Jim, infuriated and evidently still coming on, and for defence was nothing but the neck of a bottle.

For a time our Mr Polly has figured heroic. Now comes the fall again; he sounded abject terror; he dropped that ineffectual scrap of glass and turned and fled round the corner of the house.

'Bolls!' came the thick voice of the enemy behind him as one who accepts a challenge, and bleeding, but indomitable, Uncle Jim entered the house.

'Bolls!' he said, surveying the bar. 'Fightin' with bolls! I'll show 'im fightin' with bolls!'

Uncle Jim had learnt all about fighting with bottles in the Reformatory Home. Regardless of his terror-stricken aunt he ranged among the bottled beer and succeeded after one or two failures in preparing two bottles to his satisfaction by knocking off the bottoms, and gripping them dagger-wise by the necks. So prepared, he went forth again to destroy Mr Polly.

Mr Polly, freed from the sense of urgent pursuit, had halted beyond the raspberry canes and rallied his courage. The sense of Uncle Jim victorious in the house restored his manhood. He went round by the outhouses to the riverside, seeking a weapon, and found an old paddle boat-hook. With this he smote Uncle Jim as he emerged by the door of the tap. Uncle Jim, blaspheming dreadfully and with dire stabbing intimations in either hand, came through the splintering paddle like a circus rider through a paper hoop, and once more Mr Polly dropped his weapon and fled.

A careless observer watching him sprint round and round the inn in front of the lumbering and reproachful pursuit of Uncle Jim might have formed an altogether erroneous estimate of the issue of the campaign. Certain compensating qualities of the very greatest military value were appearing in Mr Polly even as he ran; if Uncle Jim had strength and brute courage and the rich toughening experience a Reformatory Home affords, Mr Polly was nevertheless sober, more mobile and with a mind now stimulated to an almost incredible nimbleness. So that he not only gained on Uncle Jim, but thought what use he might make of this advantage. The word 'strategious' flamed red across the tumult of his mind. As he came round the house for the third time, he darted suddenly into the yard, swung the door to behind himself and bolted it, seized the zinc pig's pail that stood by the entrance to the kitchen and had it neatly and resonantly over Uncle Jim's head as he came belatedly in round the outhouse on the other side. One of the splintered bottles jabbed Mr Polly's ear – at the time it seemed of no importance – and then Uncle Jim was down and writhing dangerously and noisily upon the yard tiles, with his head still in the pig pail and his bottles gone to splinters, and Mr Polly was fastening the kitchen door against him.

'Can't go on like this for ever,' said Mr Polly, whooping for breath, and selecting a weapon from among the brooms that stood behind the kitchen door.

Uncle Jim was losing his head. He was up and kicking the door and bellowing unamiable proposals and invitations, so that a strategist emerging silently by the tap door could locate him without difficulty, steal upon him unawares and – !

But before that felling blow could be delivered Uncle Jim's ear had caught a footfall, and he turned. Mr Polly quailed and lowered his broom – a fatal hesitation.

'*Now* I got you!' cried Uncle Jim, dancing forward in a disconcerting zigzag.

He rushed to close, and Mr Polly stopped him neatly, as it were by a miracle, with the head of the broom across his chest. Uncle Jim seized the broom with both hands. 'Lea' go!' he said, and tugged. Mr Polly shook his head, tugged and showed pale, compressed lips. Both tugged. Then Uncle Jim tried to get round the end of the broom; Mr Polly circled away. They began to circle about one another, both tugging hard, both intensely watchful of the slightest initiative on the part of the other. Mr Polly wished brooms were longer, twelve or thirteen feet, for example; Uncle Jim was clearly for shortness in brooms. He wasted breath in saying what was to happen shortly – sanguinary, oriental soul-blenching things – when the broom no longer separated them. Mr Polly thought he had never seen an uglier person. Suddenly Uncle Jim flashed into violent activity, but alcohol slows movement, and Mr Polly was equal to him. Then Uncle Jim tried jerks, and for a terrible instant seemed to have the broom out of Mr Polly's hands. But Mr Polly recovered it with the clutch of a drowning man. Then Uncle Jim drove suddenly at Mr Polly's midriff, but again Mr Polly was ready and swept him round in a circle. Then suddenly a wild hope filled Mr Polly. He saw the river was very near, the post to which the punt was tied not three yards away. With a wild yell, he sent the broom home into his antagonist's ribs.

'Woosh!' he cried, as the resistance gave.

'Oh! *Gaw!*' said Uncle Jim, going backward helplessly, and Mr Polly thrust hard and abandoned the broom to the enemy's despairing clutch.

Splash! Uncle Jim was in the water and Mr Polly had leapt like a cat aboard the ferry punt and grasped the pole.

Up came Uncle Jim spluttering and dripping. 'You (unprofitable matter, and printing it would lead to a censorship of novels)! You know I got a weak *chess*!'

The pole took him in the throat and drove him backwards and downwards.

'Lea' go!' cried Uncle Jim, staggering and with real terror in his once awful eyes.

Splash! Down he fell backwards into a frothing mass of water with Mr Polly jabbing at him. Under water he turned round and came up again as if in flight towards the middle of the river. Directly his head reappeared Mr Polly had him between the shoulders and under again, bubbling thickly. A hand clutched and disappeared.

It was stupendous! Mr Polly had discovered the heel of Achilles. Uncle Jim had no stomach for cold water. The broom floated away, pitching gently on the swell. Mr Polly, infuriated with victory, thrust Uncle Jim under again, and drove the punt round on its chain in such a manner that when Uncle Jim came up for the fourth time – and now he was nearly out of his depth, too buoyed up to walk and apparently nearly helpless – Mr Polly, fortunately for them both, could not reach him. Uncle Jim made the clumsy gestures of those who struggle insecurely in the water. 'Keep out,' said Mr Polly. Uncle Jim with a great effort got a footing, emerged until his armpits were out of the water, until his waistcoat buttons showed, one by one, till scarcely two remained, and made for the camp sheeting.

'Keep out!' cried Mr Polly, and leapt off the punt and followed the movements of his victim along the shore.

'I tell you I got a weak chess,' said Uncle Jim, moistly. 'This ain't fair fightin'.'

'Keep out!' said Mr Polly.

'This ain't fair fightin',' said Uncle Jim, almost weeping, and all his terrors had gone.

'Keep out!' said Mr Polly, with an accurately poised pole.

'I tell you I got to land, you fool,' said Uncle Jim, with a sort of despairing wrathfulness, and began moving downstream.

'You keep out,' said Mr Polly in parallel movement. 'Don't you ever land on this place again . . . !'

Slowly, argumentatively and reluctantly, Uncle Jim waded down-stream. He tried threats, he tried persuasion, he even tried a belated note of pathos; Mr Polly remained inexorable, if in secret a little perplexed as to the outcome of the situation. 'This cold's getting to my *marrer*!' said Uncle Jim.

'You want cooling. You keep out in it,' said Mr Polly.

They came round the bend into sight of Nicholson's ait, where the backwater runs down to the Potwell Mill. And there, after much parley and several feints, Uncle Jim made a desperate effort and struggled into clutch of the overhanging osiers on the island, and so got out of the water with the millstream between them. He emerged dripping and muddy and vindictive. 'By *Gaw*!' he said. 'I'll skin you for this!'

'You keep off or I'll do worse to you,' said Mr Polly.

The spirit was out of Uncle Jim for the time, and he turned away to struggle through the osiers towards the mill, leaving a shining trail of water among the green-grey stems.

Mr Polly returned slowly and thoughtfully to the inn, and suddenly his mind began to bubble with phrases. The plump woman stood at the top of the steps that led up to the inn door to greet him.

'Law!' she cried as he drew near, ' 'asn't 'e killed you?'

'Do I look like it?' said Mr Polly.

'But where's Jim?'

'Gone off.'

' 'E was mad drunk and dangerous!'

'I put him in the river,' said Mr Polly. 'That toned down his alco-laceous frenzy! I gave him a bit of a doing altogether.'

'Hain't he 'urt you?'

'Not a bit of it!'

'Then what's all that blood beside your ear?'

Mr Polly felt. 'Quite a cut! Funny how one overlooks things! Heated moments! He must have done that when he jabbed about with those bottles. Hello, kiddy! You venturing downstairs again?'

'Ain't he killed you?' asked the little girl.

'Well!'

'I wish I'd seen more of the fighting.'

'Didn't you?'

'All I saw was you running round the house and Uncle Jim after you.' There was a little pause. 'I was leading him on,' said Mr Polly.

'Someone's shouting at the ferry,' she said.

'Right-o. But you won't see any more of Uncle Jim for a bit. We've been having a *conversazione* about that.'

'I believe it *is* Uncle Jim,' said the little girl.

'Then he can wait,' said Mr Polly shortly.

He turned round and listened for the words that drifted across from the little figure on the opposite bank. So far as he could judge, Uncle Jim was making an appointment for the morrow. He replied with a defiant movement of the punt pole. The little figure was convulsed for a moment and then went on its way upstream – fiercely.

So it was the first campaign ended in an insecure victory.

9

The next day was Wednesday and a slack day for the Potwell Inn. It was a hot, close day, full of the murmuring of bees. One or two people crossed by the ferry, an elaborately equipped fisherman stopped for cold meat and dry ginger ale in the bar parlour, some haymakers came and drank beer for an hour, and afterwards sent jars and jugs by a boy to be replenished; that was all. Mr Polly had risen early and was busy about the place meditating upon the probable tactics of Uncle Jim. He was no longer strung up to the desperate pitch of the first encounter. But he was grave and anxious. Uncle Jim had shrunken, as all antagonists that are boldly faced shrink, after the first battle, to the negotiable, the vulnerable. Formidable he was no doubt, but not invincible. He had, under Providence, been defeated once, and he might be defeated altogether.

Mr Polly went about the place considering the militant possibilities of pacific things – pokers, copper sticks, garden implements, kitchen knives, garden nets, barbed wire, oars, clothes lines, blankets, pewter pots, stockings and broken bottles. He prepared a club with a stocking and a bottle inside, upon the best East End model. He swung it round his head once, broke an outhouse window with a flying fragment of glass, and ruined the stocking beyond all darning. He developed a subtle scheme with the cellar flap as a sort of pitfall, but he rejected it finally because (a) it might entrap the plump woman, and (b) he had no use whatever for Uncle Jim in the cellar. He determined to wire the garden that evening, burglar fashion, against the possibilities of a night attack.

Towards two o'clock in the afternoon three young men arrived in a capacious boat from the direction of Lammam, and asked permission to camp in the paddock. It was given all the more readily by Mr Polly because he perceived in their proximity a possible check upon the self-expression of Uncle Jim. But he did not foresee and no one could have foreseen that Uncle Jim, stealing unawares upon the Potwell Inn in the late afternoon, armed with a large rough-hewn stake, should have mistaken the bending form of one of those campers – who was pulling a few onions by permission in the garden – for Mr Polly's, and crept upon it swiftly and silently and smitten its wide invitation unforgettably and unforgiveably. It was an error impossible to explain; the resounding whack went up to heaven, as did the cry of amazement, and Mr Polly emerged from the inn, armed with the frying-pan he was cleaning, to take this reckless assailant in the rear. Uncle Jim, realising his error, fled blaspheming into the arms of the other two campers, who were returning from the village with butcher's meat and groceries. They caught him, they smacked his face with steak and punched him with a bursting parcel of lump sugar, they held him though he bit them, and their idea of punishment was to duck him. They were hilarious, strong young stockbrokers' clerks, Territorials and seasoned boating men; they ducked him as though it was romping, and all that Mr Polly had to do was to pick up lumps of sugar for them and wipe them on his sleeve and put them on a plate, and explain that Uncle Jim was a notorious bad character and not quite right in his head.

'Got a regular obsession that the missis is his aunt,' said Mr Polly, expanding it. 'Perfect noosance he is.'

But he caught a glance of Uncle Jim's eye as he receded before the campers' urgency that boded ill for him, and in the night he had a dis-agreeable idea that perhaps his luck might not hold for the third occasion.

That came soon enough. So soon, indeed, as the campers had gone.

Thursday was the early-closing day at Lammam, and next to Sunday the busiest part of the week at the Potwell Inn. Sometimes as many as six boats all at once would be moored against the ferry punt and hiring rowboats. People could either have a complete but unadorned tea, a complete tea with jam, cake and eggs, a kettle of boiling water and find the rest, or refreshments *à la carte*, as they chose. They sat about, but usually the boiling water–ers had a delicacy about using the tables and grouped themselves humbly on the ground. The complete tea–ers with jam and eggs got the best tablecloth on the table nearest the steps that led up to the glass-panelled door.

The groups about the lawn were very satisfying to Mr Polly's sense of amenity. To the right were the complete tea-ers with everything heart could desire; then a small group of three young men in remarkable green and violet and pale-blue shirts, and two girls in mauve and yellow blouses, with complete but unadorned teas and gooseberry jam at the green clothless table; then, on the grass down by the pollard willow, a small family of hot water-ers with a hamper, a little troubled by wasps in their jam from the nest in the tree, and all in mourning, but happy otherwise; and on the lawn to the right a ginger-beer lot of 'prentices without their collars and very jocular and happy. The young people in the rainbow shirts and blouses formed the centre of interest; they were under the leadership of a gold-spectacled senior with a fluting voice and an air of mystery; he ordered everything, and showed a peculiar knowledge of the qualities of the Potwell jams, preferring gooseberry with much insistence. Mr Polly watched him, christened him the 'benifluous influence', glanced at the 'prentices and went inside and down into the cellar in order to replenish the stock of stone ginger beer which the plump woman had allowed to run low during the preoccupations of the campaign.

It was in the cellar that he first became aware of the return of Uncle Jim. He became aware of him as a voice, a voice not only hoarse, but thick, as voices thicken under the influence of alcohol.

'Where's that muddy-faced mongrel?' cried Uncle Jim. 'Let 'im come out to me! Where's that blighted whisp with the punt pole – I got a word to say to 'im. Come out of it, you pot-bellied chunk of dirtiness, you! Come out and 'ave your ugly face wiped. I got a Thing for you . . . '*Ear* me?

' 'E's 'iding, that's what 'e's doing,' said the voice of Uncle Jim, dropping for a moment to sorrow, and then with a great increment of wrathfulness: 'Come out of my nest, you blinking cuckoo, you, or I'll cut your silly insides out! Come out of it – you pockmarked Rat! Stealing another man's 'ome away from 'im! Come out and look me in the face, you squinting son of a Skunk! . . . '

Mr Polly took the ginger beer and went thoughtfully upstairs to the bar.

' 'E's back,' said the plump woman as he appeared. 'I knew 'e'd come back.'

'I heard him,' said Mr Polly, and looked about. 'Just gimme the old poker handle that's under the beer engine.'

The door opened softly and Mr Polly turned quickly. But it was only the pointed nose and intelligent face of the young man with the gilt spectacles and discreet manner. He coughed and the spectacles fixed Mr Polly.

'I say,' he said with quiet earnestness. 'There's a chap out here seems to want someone.'

'Why don't he come in?' said Mr Polly.

'He seems to want you out there.'

'What's he want?'

'I *think*,' said the spectacled young man after a thoughtful moment, 'he appears to have brought you a present of fish.'

'Isn't he shouting?'

'He *is* a little boisterous.'

'He'd better come in.'

The manner of the spectacled young man intensified. 'I wish you'd come out and persuade him to go away,' he said. 'His language – isn't quite the thing – ladies.'

'It never was,' said the plump woman, her voice charged with sorrow.

Mr Polly moved towards the door and stood with his hand on the handle. The gold-spectacled face disappeared.

'Now, my man,' came his voice from outside, 'be careful what you're saying – '

'Oo in all the World and Hereafter are you to call me, me man?' cried Uncle Jim, in the voice of one astonished and pained beyond endurance, and added scornfully: 'You gold-eyed Geezer, you!'

'Tut, tut!' said the gentleman in gilt glasses. 'Restrain yourself!'

Mr Polly emerged, poker in hand, just in time to see what followed. Uncle Jim in his shirtsleeves and a state of ferocious décolletage, was holding something – yes! – a dead eel by means of a piece of newspaper about its tail, holding it down and back and a little sideways in such a way as to smite with it upwards and hard. It struck the spectacled gentleman under the jaw with a peculiar dead thud, and a cry of horror came from the two seated parties at the sight. One of the girls shrieked piercingly, 'Horace!' and everyone sprang up. The sense of helping numbers came to Mr Polly's aid.

'Drop it!' he cried, and came down the steps waving his poker and thrusting the spectacled gentleman before him as once heroes were wont to wield the ox-hide shield.

Uncle Jim gave ground suddenly, and trod upon the foot of a young man in a blue shirt, who immediately thrust at him violently with both hands.

'Lea' go!' howled Uncle Jim. 'That's the chap I'm looking for!' and pressing the head of the spectacled gentleman aside, smote hard at Mr Polly.

But at the sight of this indignity inflicted upon the spectacled gentleman a woman's heart was stirred, and a pink parasol drove hard and true at Uncle Jim's wiry neck, and at the same moment the young man in the blue shirt sought to collar him and lost his grip again.

'Suffragettes,' gasped Uncle Jim with the ferule at his throat. 'Everywhere!' and aimed a second, more successful, blow at Mr Polly.

'Wup!' said Mr Polly.

But now the jam and egg party was joining in the fray. A stout yet still fairly able-bodied gentleman in white and black checks enquired: 'What's the fellow up to? Ain't there no police here?' and it was evident that once more public opinion was rallying to the support of Mr Polly.

'Oh, come on then all the LOT of you!' cried Uncle Jim and, backing dexterously, whirled the eel round in a destructive circle. The pink sunshade was torn from the hand that gripped it and whirled athwart the complete but unadorned tea things on the green table.

'Collar him! Someone get hold of his collar!' cried the gold-spectacled gentleman, coming out of the scrimmage and retreating up the steps to the inn door as if to rally his forces.

'Stand clear, you blessed mantel ornaments!' cried Uncle Jim, 'stand clear!' and retired backing, staving off attack by means of the whirling eel.

Mr Polly, undeterred by a sense of grave damage done to his nose, pressed the attack in front, the two young men in violet and blue skirmished on Uncle Jim's flanks, the man in white and black checks sought still further outflanking possibilities, and two of the apprentice boys ran for oars. The gold-spectacled gentleman, as if inspired, came down the wooden steps again, seized the tablecloth of the jam and egg party, lugged it from under the crockery with inadequate precautions against breakage, and advanced with compressed lips, curious lateral crouching movements, swift flashings of his glasses, and a general suggestion of bullfighting in his pose and gestures. Uncle Jim was kept busy, and unable to plan his retreat with any strategic soundness. He was moreover manifestly a little nervous about the river in his rear. He gave ground in a curve, and so came right across the rapidly abandoned camp of the family in mourning, crunching a teacup under his heel, oversetting the teapot, and finally tripping backwards over the hamper. The eel flew out at a tangent from his hand and became a mere looping relic on the sward.

'Hold him!' cried the gentleman in spectacles. 'Collar him!' and moving forward with extraordinary promptitude wrapped the best table-cloth about Uncle Jim's arms and head. Mr Polly grasped his purpose instantly, the man in checks was scarcely slower, and in another moment Uncle Jim was no more than a bundle of smothered blasphemy and a pair of wildly active legs.

'Duck him!' panted Mr Polly, holding on to the earthquake. 'Bes' thing – duck him.'

The bundle was convulsed by paroxysms of anger and protest. One boot got the hamper and sent it ten yards.

'Go in the house for a clothes-line someone!' said the gentleman in gold spectacles. 'He'll get out of this in a moment.'

One of the apprentices ran.

'Bird nets in the garden,' shouted Mr Polly. 'In the garden!'

The apprentice was divided in his purpose. And then suddenly Uncle Jim collapsed and became a limp, dead-seeming thing under their hands. His arms were drawn inward, his legs bent up under his person, and so he lay.

'Fainted!' said the man in checks, relaxing his grip.

'A fit, perhaps,' said the man in spectacles.

'Keep hold!' said Mr Polly, too late.

For suddenly Uncle Jim's arms and legs flew out like springs released. Mr Polly was tumbled backwards and fell over the broken teapot and into the arms of the father in mourning. Something struck his head – dazzlingly. In another second Uncle Jim was on his feet and the table-cloth enshrouded the head of the man in checks. Uncle Jim manifestly considered he had done all that honour required of him, and against overwhelming numbers and the possibility of reiterated duckings, flight is no disgrace.

Uncle Jim fled.

Mr Polly sat up after an interval of an indeterminate length among the ruins of an idyllic afternoon. Quite a lot of things seemed scattered and broken, but it was difficult to grasp it all at once. He stared between the legs of people. He became aware of a voice, speaking slowly and complainingly.

'Someone ought to pay for those tea things,' said the father in mourning. 'We didn't bring them 'ere to be danced on, not by no manner of means.'

10

There followed an anxious peace for three days, and then a rough man in a blue jersey, in the intervals of trying to choke himself with bread and cheese and pickled onions, broke out abruptly into information.

'Jim's lagged again, missus,' he said.

'What!' said the landlady. 'Our Jim?'

'Your Jim,' said the man, and after an absolutely necessary pause for swallowing, added: 'Stealin' a 'atchet.'

He did not speak for some moments, and then he replied to Mr Polly's enquiries: 'Yes, a 'atchet. Down Lammam way – night before last.'

'What'd 'e steal a 'atchet for?' asked the plump woman.

' 'E said 'e wanted a 'atchet.'

'I wonder what he wanted a hatchet for?' said Mr Polly, thoughtfully.

'I dessay 'e 'ad a use for it,' said the gentleman in the blue jersey, and he took a mouthful that amounted to conversational suicide. There was a prolonged pause in the little bar, and Mr Polly did some rapid thinking.

He went to the window and whistled. 'I shall stick it,' he whispered at last. ' 'Atchets or no 'atchets.'

He turned to the man with the blue jersey when he thought him clear for speech again. 'How much did you say they'd given him?' he asked.

'Three munce,' said the man in the blue jersey, and refilled anxiously, as if alarmed at the momentary clearness of his voice.

11

Those three months passed all too quickly; months of sunshine and warmth, of varied novel exertion in the open air, of congenial experiences, of interest and wholesome food and successful digestion, months that browned Mr Polly and hardened him and saw the beginnings of his beard, months marred only by one anxiety, an anxiety Mr Polly did his utmost to suppress. The day of reckoning was never mentioned, it is true, by either the plump woman or himself, but the name of Uncle Jim was written in letters of glaring silence across their intercourse. As the term of that respite drew to an end his anxiety increased, until at last it even trenched upon his well-earned sleep. He had some idea of buying a revolver. At last he compromised upon a small and very foul and dirty rook rifle, which he purchased in Lammam under a pretext of bird scaring, and loaded carefully and concealed under his bed from the plump woman's eye.

September passed away, October came.

And at last came that night in October whose happenings it is so difficult for a sympathetic historian to drag out of their proper nocturnal indistinctness into the clear, hard light of positive statement. A novelist should present characters, not vivisect them publicly.

The best, the kindliest, if not the justest, course is surely to leave untold such things as Mr Polly would manifestly have preferred untold.

Mr Polly had declared that when the cyclist discovered him he was seeking a weapon that should make a conclusive end to Uncle Jim. That declaration is placed before the reader without comment.

The gun was certainly in possession of Uncle Jim at that time and no human being but Mr Polly knows how he got hold of it.

The cyclist was a literary man named Warspite, who suffered from insomnia; he had risen and come out of his house near Lammam just before the dawn, and he discovered Mr Polly partially concealed in the ditch by the Potwell churchyard wall. It is an ordinary dry ditch, full of nettles and overgrown with elder and dog rose, and in no way suggestive of an arsenal. It is the last place in which you would look for a gun. And he says that when he dismounted to see why Mr Polly was allowing only the latter part of his person to show (and that it would seem by inadvertency), Mr Polly merely raised his head and advised him to, 'Look out!' and added: 'He's let fly at me twice already.' He came out under persuasion and with gestures of extreme caution. He was wearing a white cotton nightgown of the type that has now been so extensively superseded by pyjama sleeping-suits, and his legs and feet were bare and much scratched and torn and very muddy.

Mr Warspite takes that exceptionally lively interest in his fellow-creatures which constitutes so much of the distinctive and complex charm of your novelist all the world over, and he at once involved himself generously in the case. The two men returned at Mr Polly's initiative across the churchyard to the Potwell Inn, and came upon the burst and damaged rook rifle near the new monument to Sir Samuel Harpon at the corner by the yew.

'That must have been his third go,' said Mr Polly. 'It sounded a bit funny.'

The sight inspirited him greatly, and he explained further that he had fled to the churchyard on account of the cover afforded by tombstones from the flight of small shot. He expressed anxiety for the fate of the landlady of the Potwell Inn and her grandchild, and led the way with enhanced alacrity along the lane to that establishment.

They found the doors of the house standing open, the bar in some disorder – several bottles of whisky were afterwards found to be missing – and Blake, the village policeman, rapping patiently at the open door. He entered with them. The glass in the bar had suffered severely, and one of the mirrors was starred from a blow from a pewter pot. The till had been forced and ransacked, and so had the bureau in the minute room behind the bar. An upper window was opened and the voice of the landlady became audible making enquiries. They went out and parleyed with her. She had locked herself upstairs with the little girl, she said, and refused to descend until she was assured that neither Uncle Jim nor Mr Polly's gun were anywhere on the premises. Mr Blake and Mr Warspite proceeded to satisfy themselves with regard to the former condition, and Mr Polly went to his room in search of garments more suited to the brightening dawn. He returned immediately with a request that Mr Blake and Mr Warspite would 'just come and look'. They found the apartment in a state of extraordinary confusion, the bedclothes in a ball in the corner, the drawers all open and ransacked, the chair broken, the lock of the door forced and broken, one door panel slightly scorched and perforated by shot, and the window wide open. None of Mr Polly's clothes were to be seen, but some garments which had apparently once formed part of a stoker's workaday outfit, two brownish-yellow halves of a shirt, and an unsound pair of boots were scattered on the floor. A faint smell of gunpowder still hung in the air, and two or three books Mr Polly had recently acquired had been shied with some violence under the bed.

Mr Warspite looked at Mr Blake, and then both men looked at Mr Polly.

'That's *his* boots,' said Mr Polly.

Blake turned his eye to the window. 'Some of these tiles 'ave just got broken,' he observed.

'I got out of the window and slid down the scullery tiles,' Mr Polly answered, omitting much, they both felt, from his explanation . . .

'Well, we better find 'im and 'ave a word with 'im,' said Blake. 'That's about my business now.'

12

But Uncle Jim had gone altogether . . .

He did not return for some days. That perhaps was not very wonderful. But the days lengthened to weeks and the weeks to months and still Uncle Jim did not recur. A year passed, and the anxiety of him became less acute; a second healing year followed the first. One afternoon about thirty months after the Night Surprise the plump woman spoke of him.

'I wonder what's become of Jim,' she said.

'*I* wonder sometimes,' said Mr Polly.

CHAPTER TEN

Miriam Revisited

One summer afternoon about five years after his first coming to the Potwell Inn Mr Polly found himself sitting under the pollard willow fishing for dace. It was a plumper, browner and healthier Mr Polly altogether than the miserable bankrupt with whose dyspeptic portrait our novel opened. He was fat, but with a fatness more generally diffused, and the lower part of his face was touched to gravity by a small square beard. Also he was balder.

It was the first time he had found leisure to fish, though from the very outset of his Potwell career he had promised himself abundant indulgence in the pleasures of fishing. Fishing, as the golden page of English literature testifies, is a meditative and retrospective pursuit, and the varied page of memory, disregarded so long for sake of the teeming duties I have already enumerated, began to unfold itself to Mr Polly's consideration. A speculation about Uncle Jim died for want of material, and gave place to a reckoning of the years and months that had passed since his coming to Potwell, and that to a philosophical review of his life. He began to think about Miriam, remotely and impersonally. He remembered many things that had been neglected by his conscience during the busier times, as, for example, that he had committed arson and deserted a wife. For the first time he looked these long neglected facts in the face.

It is disagreeable to think one has committed arson, because it is an action that leads to jail. Otherwise I do not think there was a grain of regret for that in Mr Polly's composition. But deserting Miriam was in a different category. Deserting Miriam was mean.

This is a history and not a glorification of Mr Polly, and I tell of things as they were with him. Apart from the disagreeable twinge arising from the thought of what might happen if he was found out, he had not the slightest remorse about that fire. Arson, after all, is an artificial crime. Some crimes are crimes in themselves, would be crimes without any law, the cruelties, mockery, the breaches of faith that astonish and wound, but the burning of things is in itself neither good nor bad. A large number of houses deserve to be burnt, most modern furniture, an overwhelming majority of pictures and books – one might go on for some time with the list. If our community was collectively anything more than a feeble idiot, it would burn most of London and Chicago, for example, and build sane and beautiful cities in the place of these pestilential heaps of rotten private property. I have failed in presenting Mr Polly altogether if I have not made you see that he was in many respects an artless child of Nature, far more untrained, undisciplined and spontaneous than an ordinary savage. And he was really glad, for all that little drawback of fear, that he had the courage to set fire to his house and fly and come to the Potwell Inn.

But he was not glad he had left Miriam. He had seen Miriam cry once or twice in his life, and it had always reduced him to abject commiseration. He now imagined her crying. He perceived in a per-plexed way that he had made himself responsible for her life. He forgot how she had spoilt his own. He had hitherto rested in the faith that she had over a hundred pounds of insurance money, but now, with his eye meditatively upon his float, he realised a hundred pounds does not last for ever. His conviction of her incompetence was un-flinching; she was bound to have fooled it away somehow by this time. And then!

He saw her humping her shoulders and sniffing in a manner he had always regarded as detestable at close quarters, but which now became harrowingly pitiful.

'Damn!' said Mr Polly, and down went his float and he flicked up a victim to destruction and took it off the hook.

He compared his own comfort and health with Miriam's imagined distress.

'Ought to have done something for herself,' said Mr Polly, rebaiting his hook. 'She was always talking of doing things. Why couldn't she?'

He watched the float oscillating gently towards quiescence.

'Silly to begin thinking about her,' he said. 'Damn silly!'

But once he had begun thinking about her he had to go on.

'Oh blow!' cried Mr Polly presently, and pulled up his hook to find another fish had just snatched at it in the last instant. His handling must have made the poor thing feel itself unwelcome.

He gathered his things together and turned towards the house.

All the Potwell Inn betrayed his influence now, for here indeed he had found his place in the world. It looked brighter, so bright indeed as to be almost skittish, with the white and green paint he had lavished upon it. Even the garden palings were striped white and green, and so were the boats, for Mr Polly was one of those who find a positive sensuous pleasure in the laying on of paint. Left and right were two large boards which had done much to enhance the inn's popularity with the lighter-minded variety of pleasure-seekers. Both marked innovations. One bore in large letters the single word 'Museum', the other was as plain and laconic with 'Omlets'. The spelling of the latter word was Mr Polly's own, but when he had seen a whole boatload of men, intent on Lammam for lunch, stop open-mouthed, and stare and grin and come in and ask in a marked sarcastic manner for 'omlets', he perceived that his inaccuracy had done more for the place than his utmost cunning could have contrived. In a year or so the inn was known both up and down the river by its new name of 'Omlets', and Mr Polly, after some secret irritation, smiled and was content. And the fat woman's omelettes were things to remember.

(You will note I have changed her epithet. Time works upon us all.)

She stood upon the steps as he came towards the house, and smiled at him richly.

'Caught many?' she asked.

'Got an idea,' said Mr Polly. 'Would it put you out very much if I went off for a day or two for a bit of a holiday? There won't be much doing now until Thursday.'

2

Feeling recklessly secure behind his beard Mr Polly surveyed the Fishbourne High Street once again. The north side was much as he had known it except that Rusper had vanished. A row of new shops replaced the destruction of the great fire. Mantell and Throbson's had risen again upon a more flamboyant pattern, and the new fire station was in the Swiss-Teutonic style and with much red paint. Next door in the place of Rumbold's was a branch of the Colonial Tea Company, and then a Salmon and Gluckstein Tobacco Shop, and then a little shop that displayed sweets and professed a 'Tea Room Upstairs'. He considered this as a possible place in which to prosecute enquiries about his lost wife, wavering a little between it and the God's Providence Inn down the street. Then his eye caught a name over the window, 'Polly,' he read, '& Larkins! Well, I'm – astonished!'

A momentary faintness came upon him. He walked past and down the street, returned and surveyed the shop again.

He saw a middle-aged, rather untidy woman standing behind the counter, who for an instant he thought might be Miriam terribly changed, and then recognised as his sister-in-law Annie, filled out and no longer hilarious. She stared at him without a sign of recognition as he entered the shop.

'Can I have tea?' said Mr Polly.

'Well,' said Annie, 'you *can*. But our Tea Room's upstairs . . . My sister's been cleaning it out – and it's a bit upset.'

'It *would* be,' said Mr Polly softly.

'I beg your pardon?' said Annie.

'I said *I* didn't mind. Up here?'

'I dare say there'll be a table,' said Annie, and followed him up to a room whose conscientious disorder was intensely reminiscent of Miriam.

'Nothing like turning everything upside down when you're cleaning,' said Mr Polly cheerfully.

'It's my sister's way,' said Annie impartially. 'She's gone out for a bit of air, but I dare say she'll be back soon to finish. It's a nice light room when it's tidy. Can I put you a table over there?'

'Let *me*,' said Mr Polly, and assisted. He sat down by the open window and drummed on the table and meditated on his next step while Annie vanished to get his tea. After all, things didn't seem so bad with Miriam. He tried over several gambits in imagination.

'Unusual name,' he said, as Annie laid a cloth before him. Annie looked interrogation.

'Polly. Polly & Larkins. Real, I suppose?'

'Polly's my sister's name. She married a Mr Polly.'

'Widow I presume?' said Mr Polly.

'Yes. This five years – come October.'

'Lord!' said Mr Polly in unfeigned surprise.

'Found drowned he was. There was a lot of talk in the place.'

'Never heard of it,' said Mr Polly. 'I'm a stranger – rather.'

'In the Medway near Maidstone. He must have been in the water for days. Wouldn't have known him, my sister wouldn't, if it hadn't been for the name sewn in his clothes. All whitey and eat away he was.'

'Bless my heart! Must have been rather a shock for her!'

'It *was* a shock,' said Annie, and added darkly: 'But sometimes a shock's better than a long agony.'

'No doubt,' said Mr Polly.

He gazed with a rapt expression at the preparations before him. 'So I'm drowned,' something was saying inside him. 'Life insured?' he asked.

'We started the tea rooms with it,' said Annie.

Why, if things were like this, had remorse and anxiety for Miriam been implanted in his soul? No shadow of an answer appeared.

'Marriage is a lottery,' said Mr Polly.

'*She* found it so,' said Annie. 'Would you like some jam?'

'I'd like an egg,' said Mr Polly. 'I'll have two. I've got a sort of feeling – As though I wanted keeping up . . . Wasn't particularly good sort, this Mr Polly?'

'He was a *wearing* husband,' said Annie. 'I've often pitied my sister. He was one of that sort – '

'Dissolute?' suggested Mr Polly faintly.

'No,' said Annie judiciously; 'not exactly dissolute. Feeble's more the word. Weak, 'e was. Weak as water. 'Ow long do you like your eggs boiled?'

'Four minutes exactly,' said Mr Polly.

'One gets talking,' said Annie.

'One does,' said Mr-Polly, and she left him to his thoughts.

What perplexed him was his recent remorse and tenderness for Miriam. Now he was back in her atmosphere all that had vanished, and the old feeling of helpless antagonism returned. He surveyed the piled furniture, the economically managed carpet, the unpleasing pictures on the wall. Why had he felt remorse? Why had he entertained this illusion of a helpless woman crying aloud in the pitiless darkness for him? He peered into the unfathomable mysteries of the heart, and ducked back to a smaller issue. *Was* he feeble?

The eggs came up. Nothing in Annie's manner invited a resumption of the discussion.

'Business brisk?' he ventured to ask.

Annie reflected. 'It is,' she said, 'and it isn't. It's like that.'

'Ah!' said Mr Polly, and squared himself to his egg. 'Was there an inquest on that chap?'

'What chap?'

'What was his name? – Polly!'

'Of course.'

'You're sure it was him?'

'What you mean?'

Annie looked at him hard, and suddenly his soul was black with terror.

'Who else could it have been – in the very clo'es 'e wore?'

'Of course,' said Mr Polly, and began his egg. He was so agitated that he only realised its condition when he was halfway through it and Annie safely downstairs.

'Lord!' he said, reaching out hastily for the pepper. 'One of Miriam's! Management! I haven't tasted such an egg for five years . . . Wonder where she gets them! Picks them out, I suppose!'

He abandoned it for its fellow.

Except for a slight mustiness the second egg was very palatable indeed. He was getting to the bottom of it as Miriam came in. He looked up. 'Nice afternoon,' he said at her stare, and perceived she knew him at once by the gesture and the voice. She went white and shut the door behind her. She looked as though she was going to faint. Mr Polly sprang up quickly and handed her a chair. 'My God!' she whispered, and crumpled up rather than sat down.

'It's *you*' she said.

'No,' said Mr Polly very earnestly. 'It isn't. It just looks like me. That's all.'

'I *knew* that man wasn't you – all along. I tried to think it was. I tried to think perhaps the water had altered your wrists and feet and the colour of your hair.'

'Ah!'

'I'd always feared you'd come back.'

Mr Polly sat down by his egg. 'I haven't come back,' he said very earnestly. 'Don't you think it.'

' 'Ow we'll pay back the insurance now I *don't* know.'

She was weeping. She produced a handkerchief and covered her face.

'Look here, Miriam,' said Mr Polly. 'I haven't come back and I'm not coming back. I'm – I'm a Visitant from Another World. You shut up about me and I'll shut up about myself. I came back because I thought you might be hard up or in trouble or some silly thing like that. Now I see you again – I'm satisfied. I'm satisfied completely. See? I'm going to absquatulate, see? Hey Presto, right away.'

He turned to his tea for a moment, finished his cup noisily, stood up.

'Don't you think you're going to see me again,' he said, 'for you ain't.'

He moved to the door.

'That *was* a tasty egg,' he said, hovered for a second and vanished . . .

Annie was in the shop.

'The missus has had a bit of a shock,' he remarked. 'Got some sort of fancy about a ghost. Can't make it out quite. So long!'

And he had gone.

3

Mr Polly sat beside the fat woman at one of the little green tables at the back of the Potwell Inn, and struggled with the mystery of life. It was one of those evenings, serenely luminous, amply and atmospherically still, when the river bend was at its best. A swan floated against the dark green masses of the farther bank, the stream flowed broad and shining to its destiny, with scarce a ripple – except where the reeds came out from the headland – the three poplars rose clear and harmonious against a sky of green and yellow. And it was as if it was all securely within a great warm friendly globe of crystal sky. It was as safe and enclosed and fearless as a child that has still to be born. It was an evening full of the quality of tranquil, unqualified assurance. Mr Polly's mind was filled with the persuasion that indeed all things whatsoever must needs be satisfying and complete. It was incredible that life had ever done more than seemed to jar, that there could be any shadow in life save such velvet softnesses as made the setting for that silent swan, or any murmur but the ripple of the water as it swirled round the chained and gently swaying punt. And the mind of Mr Polly, exalted and made tender by this atmosphere, sought gently, but sought, to draw together the varied memories that came drifting, half submerged, across the circle of his mind.

He spoke in words that seemed like a bent and broken stick thrust suddenly into water, destroying the mirror of the shapes they sought. 'Jim's not coming back again ever,' he said. 'He got drowned five years ago.'

'Where?' asked the fat woman, surprised.

'Miles from here. In the Medway. Away in Kent.'

'Lor!' said the fat woman.

'It's right enough,' said Mr Polly.

'How d'you know?'

'I went to my home.'

'Where?'

'Don't matter. I went and found out. He'd been in the water some days. He'd got my clothes and they'd said it was me.'

'They?'

'It don't matter. I'm not going back to them.'

The fat woman regarded him silently for some time. Her expression of scrutiny gave way to a quiet satisfaction. Then her brown eyes went to the river.

'Poor Jim,' she said. ' 'E 'adn't much Tact – ever.'

She added mildly: 'I can't 'ardly say I'm sorry.'

'Nor me,' said Mr Polly, and got a step nearer the thought in him. 'But it don't seem much good his having been alive, does it?'

' 'E wasn't much good,' the fat woman admitted. 'Ever.'

'I suppose there were things that were good to him,' Mr Polly speculated. 'They weren't *our* things.'

His hold slipped again. 'I often wonder about life,' he said weakly.

He tried again. 'One seems to start in life,' he said, 'expecting something. And it doesn't happen. And it doesn't matter. One starts with ideas that things are good and things are bad – and it hasn't much relation to what *is* good and what *is* bad. I've always been the skeptaceous sort, and it's always seemed rot to me to pretend we know good from evil. It's just what I've *never* done. No Adam's apple stuck in *my* throat, ma'am. I don't own to it.'

He reflected. 'I set fire to a house – once.'

The fat woman started.

'I don't feel sorry for it. I don't believe it was a bad thing to do – any more than burning a toy like I did once when I was a baby. I nearly killed myself with a razor. Who hasn't? – anyhow gone as far as thinking of it? Most of my time I've been half dreaming. I married like a dream almost. I've never really planned my life or set out to live. I happened; things happened to me. It's so with everyone. Jim couldn't help himself. I shot at him and tried to kill him. I dropped the gun and he got it. He very nearly had me. I wasn't a second too soon – ducking . . . Awkward – that night was . . . M'mm . . . But I don't blame him – come to that. Only I don't see what it's all up to . . .

'Like children playing about in a nursery. Hurt themselves at times . . .

'There's something that doesn't mind us,' he resumed presently. 'It isn't what we try to get that we get, it isn't the good we think we do is good. What makes us happy isn't our trying, what makes others happy isn't our trying. There's a sort of character people like and stand up for and a sort they won't. You got to work it out and take the consequences . . . Miriam was always trying.'

'Who was Miriam?' asked the fat woman.

'No one you know. But she used to go about with her brows knit trying not to do whatever she wanted to do – if ever she did want to do anything – '

He lost himself.

'You can't help being fat,' said the fat woman after a pause, trying to get up to his thoughts.

'*You* can't,' said Mr Polly.

'It helps and it hinders.'

'Like my upside down way of talking.'

'The magistrates wouldn't 'ave kept on the licence to me if I 'adn't been fat . . . '

'Then what have we done,' said Mr Polly, 'to get an evening like this? Lord! look at it!' He sent his arm round the great curve of the sky.

'If I was a darkie or an Italian I should come out here and sing. I whistle sometimes, but, bless you, it's singing I've got in my mind. Sometimes I think I live for sunsets.'

'I don't see that it does you any good always looking at sunsets like you do,' said the fat woman.

'Nor me. But I do. Sunsets and things I was made to like.'

'They don't 'elp you,' said the fat woman thoughtfully.

'Who cares?' said Mr Polly.

A deeper strain had come to the fat woman. 'You got to die someday,' she said.

'Some things I can't believe,' said Mr Polly suddenly, 'and one is your being a skeleton . . . ' He pointed his hand towards the neighbour's hedge. 'Look at 'em – against the yellow – and they're just stingin' nettles. Nasty weeds – if you count things by their uses. And no help in the life hereafter. But just look at the look of them!'

'It isn't only looks,' said the fat woman.

'Whenever there's signs of a good sunset and I'm not too busy,' said Mr Polly, 'I'll come and sit out here.'

The fat woman looked at him with eyes in which contentment struggled with some obscure reluctant protest, and at last turned them slowly to the black nettle pagodas against the golden sky.

'I wish we could,' she said.

'I will.'

The fat woman's voice sank nearly to the inaudible.

'Not always,' she said.

Mr Polly was some time before he replied. 'Come here always when I'm a ghost,' he replied.

'Spoil the place for others,' said the fat woman, abandoning her moral solicitudes for a more congenial point of view.

'Not my sort of ghost wouldn't,' said Mr Polly, emerging from another long pause. 'I'd be a sort of diaphalous feeling – just mellowish and warmish like . . . '

They said no more, but sat on in the warm twilight until at last they could scarcely distinguish each other's faces. They were not so much thinking as lost in a smooth still quiet of the mind. A bat flitted by.

'Time we was going in, o' party,' said Mr Polly, standing up. 'Supper to get. It's as you say, we can't sit here for ever.'

ENDNOTES

KIPPS: THE STORY OF A SIMPLE SOUL

1 (p. 33) *Dolly Varden hat*   large brimmed hat with flowers named after a character in Dickens's *Barnaby Rudge* (1841)

2 (p. 35) *Colic for the Day*   a short prayer ('Collect for the Day') which appears in the Anglican Prayer Book

3 (p. 35) *Quodling*   small fish

4 (p. 39) *Ahn's First French Course or, France and the French* popular primer, correctly titled *Dr Ahn's Easy and Practical Method of Learning the French Language, adapted to the Use of English Learners* (1851)

5 (p. 41) *Huron*   Native American Indian tribe from central Ontario

6 (p. 47) *Tit Bits*   popular magazine founded by Alfred Harmsworth in 1881

7 (p. 53) *Manchester goods*   Manchester was the centre of the cotton industry at this time.

8 (p. 63) *Early Closing Association*   group formed to lobby shopkeepers to close for one half-day during the week to compensate employees for working on Saturday morning

9 (p. 64) *masher*   a dandy

10 (p. 68) *Home Educator*   generic term for a magazine correspondence course

11 (p. 69) '*Self-Help*'   *Self-Help* (1859) by Samuel Smiles (1812–1904) was a popular Victorian guide to self-improvement.

12 (p. 75) *Over-human*   Friedrich Nietzsche's concept of the superman (or overman), expressed in *Thus Spake Zarathustra* (1883–5), considers the potential for man to overcome conventional forms of morality (often Christian morality) and to dictate his own value systems.

13 (p. 82) *Fun*   popular comic paper established in 1861

14 (p. 91) *William Archer*   (1856–1924) influential theatre critic and early translator of Ibsen into English

15 (p. 93) *Clement Scott*   (1841–1904) *Daily Telegraph* theatre critic

16 (p. 98) *swapped*   dismissed

17 (p. 109) *Inquire Within About Everything*   reference work first published in monthly parts in 1856; later editions appeared throughout the Victorian period

18 (p. 117) *Marie Corelli*   (1855–1924) bestselling novelist of late-Victorian and Edwardian eras

19 (p. 141) *The Scottish Chiefs*   historical novel by Jane Porter (first published in 1810) focusing on the life of William Wallace

20 (p. 147) *Band of Hope*   temperance organisation founded in 1847

21 (p. 148) *Bookman*   literary magazine first published in 1891

22 (p. 148) *Ten Thousand a Year*   novel by Samuel Warren (1807–77), first published in 1841

23 (p. 149) *Sartor Resartus*   philosophical novel by Thomas Carlyle (1795–1881), first published 1833–4

24 (p. 150) *Paderewski*   Jan Paderewski (1860–1941), classical pianist

25 (p. 150) *Sesame and Lilies*   collection of lectures by John Ruskin (1819–1900), first published in 1865

26 (p. 150) *Sir George Tressady*   novel by Mrs Humphry Ward (1851–1920), first published in 1896

27 (p. 151) *Manners and Rules of Good Society, by a Member of the Aristocracy*   popular book of etiquette which had reached its forty-fifth edition in 1924. *The Art of Conversing* was also written by 'a Member of the Aristocracy'.

28 (p. 173) *After Morland*   painting influenced by the style of the British landscape painter George Morland (1763–1804)

29 (p. 178) *Owenite profit-sharing factory*   inspired by the ideas of the social reformer Robert Owen (1771–1858)

30 (p. 187) *Extension Literature course*   These courses covered a wide variety of subjects and were typically organised in urban areas by university graduates.

31 (p. 199) *Mr Kipling's best-known songs*   taken from Rudyard Kipling's poem 'The Ladies' (1892)

32 (p. 212) *Commonweal*   British socialist newspaper founded in 1885

33 (p. 214) *Walter Crane*   artist and socialist (1845–1915)

34 (p. 249) *Labyrinthodon*   class of amphibious dinosaur from the Palaeozoic and Mesozoic eras

35 (p. 251) *Iguanodons*   large plant-eating dinosaur from the Jurassic period

36 (p. 251) *deinotheria and mastodons*   prehistoric relatives of the modern-day elephant

37 (p. 275) *chromo-lithographs*   technique for producing multi-coloured prints

38 (p. 284) *Dunciad*   Alexander Pope's long satirical poem, originally published in 1728

39 (p. 298) *Nisbet*   John Ferguson Nisbet (1851–99), dramatic critic for *The Times* and author of *The Insanity of Genius and the General Inequality of Human Faculty Physiologically Considered* (1891)

40 (p. 298) *Lombroso*   Cesare Lombroso (1835–1909), Italian crimi-nologist and physician

41 (p. 300) *Daily News*   British daily newspaper founded in 1846 by Charles Dickens

42 (p. 300) *Watts's picture*   painting by George Frederic Watts (1817–1904) entitled *After the Deluge – The Forty-First Day* (1885–6)

THE HISTORY OF MR POLLY

43 (p. 315) *Laocoön struggle*   Laocoön was a Trojan priest who, with his sons, was attacked by giant serpents commanded by the gods.

44 (p. 319) *'penny dreadfuls'*   popular and often sensational Victorian fiction produced in serial form

45 (p. 322) *'Bocashieu'*   Giovanni Boccaccio (1313–75), author of the *Decameron*

46 (p. 323) *'Rabooloose'*   François Rabelais (1490–1533), author of *Gargantua and Pantagruel*

47 (p. 324) *ironclads*   warships

48 (p. 329) *Manchester department*   department of the shop selling cotton goods produced in Manchester

49 (p. 329) *'Rockcockyo'*   Rococo is a highly decorated style of art that emerged during the eighteenth century.

50 (p. 339) *Longfellow*   Henry Wadsworth Longfellow (1807–82), American poet

51 (p. 347) *British Weekly* Christian magazine which first appeared in 1886

52 (p. 362) '*The Quest of the Golden Girl*' novel by Richard Le Gallienne (1866–1947), first published in 1896

53 (p. 364) *safety bicycle* form of bicycle introduced in the 1880s as an alternative to the penny farthing and earlier models

54 (p. 364) *Path to Rome* spiritual travel book by Hilaire Belloc (1870–1953), first published in 1902

55 (p. 364) *Purchas his Pilgrimes* collection of travel writings by Samuel Purchas (1577–1626), first published in 1625

56 (p. 364) *The Life and Death of Jason* poem by William Morris (1834–96), first published in 1867

57 (p. 404) *Obi* African witchcraft

58 (p. 405) *La Perouse* Jean-François de Galoup (1741–88), known as La Perouse, was a French naval officer and explorer.

59 (p. 405) *The Island Nights' Entertainments* collection of stories by Robert Louis Stevenson (1850–94), first published in 1893

60 (p. 406) *Abbés Huc and Gabet* French missionary priests who travelled to China in the 1840s

61 (p. 406) *Fenimore Cooper* James Fenimore Cooper (1789–1851), American novelist

62 (p. 406) *Tom Cringle's Log* novel by Michael Scott (1789–1835), first published in 1834

63 (p. 406) *A Sailor Tramp* volume of travel writing by Bart Kennedy (1861–1930), first published in 1902

64 (p. 406) *Vicomte de Bragelonne* long historical musketeer romance by Alexander Dumas (1802–70), first published 1847–50

65 (p. 406) *Wanderings in South America* volume of natural history, published by Samuel Waterton (1782–1865) in 1825

66 (p. 406) *Bates* Henry Walter Bates (1825–92), naturalist and explorer

67 (p. 406) *Tales of Old Japan* tales of Japanese life by Algernon Bertram Mitford (1837–1916), first published in 1871

68 (p. 414) *Review of Reviews* monthly journal founded by W. T. Stead in 1890

69 (p. 415) *German peril*   fear of invasion from Germany, exacerbated by British failings during the Anglo-Boer War

70 (p. 428) *Chiozza Money*   Leo Chiozza Money (1870–1944), economic theorist and journalist

71 (p. 428) *Holt Schooling*   J. Holt Schooling (1859–1927), statistician

72 (p. 452) *Reformatory Reformed Character*   Reformatory schools for young offenders were first established in Britain in 1852.